*Also by Lisa Alther*

═══

KINFLICKS

THIS IS A BORZOI BOOK
PUBLISHED IN NEW YORK
BY ALFRED A. KNOPF

# Original Sins

# Part One

---

# The
# Castle
# Tree

# Original Sins

## Lisa Alther

Alfred A. Knopf, New York

1 9  8 1

This is a Borzoi Book
Published by Alfred A. Knopf, Inc.

*Because this page cannot legibly accommodate
the permissions acknowledgments, they will be
found on page 595.*

LIBRARY OF CONGRESS CATALOGING IN
PUBLICATION DATA
ALTHER, LISA.
ORIGINAL SINS.
I.   TITLE.
PS3551.L78074   1981      813'.54      80–22823
ISBN 0–394–51685–0

MANUFACTURED
IN THE UNITED STATES OF AMERICA
FIRST EDITION

The Five had always known they were special. During the summers of the polio scare, when their mothers insisted their legs would shrivel if they didn't take afternoon naps, they complied only to humor the poor women. They themselves had good reason to believe they were invulnerable.

The plan was that the Prince sisters, Emily and Sally, would marry the Tatro brothers, Jed and Raymond, so that their children would be double-first cousins—more than double-first cousins since their families were distant cousins to start with. (This arrangement excluded Donny, of course, but he understood the charmed status of double-first cousinhood.) Emily and Raymond, Sally and Jed had signed in blood a lifetime pact to this effect; it lay in a hollow in the Castle Tree. The remainder of the plan involved Emily's going to the top plateau on "The $64,000 Question." With her prize money they would build a treehouse in the Castle Tree, with an elevator. Maybe they would buy a penthouse in New York City as well—so as to live the lives of glamour and achievement they were destined for. They had decided on New York City because the Statue of Liberty was there. (Also in the hollow of the Castle Tree lay a rolled-up picture of the Statue of Liberty with the inscription "I lift my lamp beside the golden door.") Although they didn't know exactly what jobs they'd do in New York City, they knew that whatever they decided on— baseball star or ballet dancer or waitress—they'd have no difficulty doing it, since, number one, they were special. And number two, they lived in the Land of the Free. Every now and then they saw Senator McCarthy on the evening news. He looked mean, but their parents assured them that because he was getting rid of all the Reds up North, Miss Liberty would be able to forever hold her torch on high.

Yes, they would be like the daughter of Dr. Bradley down the street, who played Elvira on the afternoon soap opera "Love for Life." Occasionally she would come down from New York City. The Five would crouch behind the boxwoods next door and watch her sweep down the sidewalk to her parents' white Impala, wrapping her fur coat around herself and impatiently shaking her long blonde hair out from under the collar. Her real name was Mary Lou Bradley, but the screen magazines listed her as Marya Bradford.

Sometimes The Five sat in the Castle Tree and discussed what they would change their names to when they got to New York City. Donny favored Lorenzo. Emily was thinking about Amelia, or Emeline. Jed insisted he liked his name fine just like it was.

The Castle Tree was a weeping beech that grew in the side yard of Mr. Fulton, the Southern history teacher at the high school. It was maybe sixty feet tall, and its branches drooped like a willow's to form a tent. Within, the branches twisted and curled into fantastic sitting places. They sat in them according to a revolving pecking order. The Tire, for instance, was far more desirable than the Couch. And the Throne was preferable to both. Here they'd perch, day after day, a treeful of Cheshire cats, as the Southern sun burned down outside. They would run their hands up and down the smooth grey bark, studying the initials and cryptic symbols carved by generations of climbing children. Mr. Fulton had carved his name on the arm rest of the Couch fifty years earlier. They couldn't believe that the grey stooped old man, whose primary interest in life now seemed to be whether or not Raymond was over-collecting from him on his paper route, could ever have hoisted himself way up here. But there was his name—Arthur F., '05. It was swollen up like scar tissue.

From a distance the tree looked like the mountaintop castles belonging to wicked giants in fairy tales. It was cone-shaped, but with turrets thrusting up like the humps of hunchbacks. Its grey-green leaves would shimmy in even the faintest breeze, making it look as if the tree might vaporize at any instant. With the shimmying went a rustling sound, as though a crowd of faceless strangers were whispering secrets. The tree had to be two hundred years old. Maybe three hundred. But where had it come from? Weeping beeches didn't just spring up in fields like wild raspberry canes. Someone, they suspected, had planted this tree, placing it on purpose in the exact middle of Mr. Fulton's yard. It was intended to convey a message across the years: The Five who now climbed it were meant to know that they were special, had a unique destiny, were being watched over and protected.

Once in the Anderson's Drugstore parking lot, when they emerged with grape snowcones, they saw a coral Cadillac with orange and dark blue New York license plates that read "The Empire State." A fitting destination for denizens of a Castle Tree. The Five peered inside, to see what a car from such a place would look like. They were not disappointed: The seats were covered with white leather, and on a small white satin pillow slept a miniature white poodle with a scarlet bow on its head and a rhinestone collar. They sat on the curb crunching ice for as long as they could without missing "Superman" on television. The owner never appeared, but The Five got the message.

They would ponder these messages as they sat in the Castle Tree and parted the branches and gazed down, down, down into the smoky valley at the mills and factories. Along the Cherokee River was the paper mill—a boxy grey structure surrounded by railroad tracks and flatcars. A yellow crane towered over mountains of logs and tossed the huge tree trunks as though they were toothpicks in the tartared teeth of a giant.

Upriver was the shopping area, the simple townhouses of the original market settlement transformed by plate glass and molded plastic into furniture stores and finance companies. And downriver, often obscured by smog, was Pine Woods, the Negro development of low, red-brick apartments, where Donny lived with his mother Kathryn and his grandmother Ruby, who had worked for Emily and Sally's family as cook for many years.

Next to Pine Woods was the brickyard, filled with acres of stacked bricks in every shade of red and grey, made from the clay of the surrounding countryside. Lining the river below the brickyard were tobacco warehouses, semicircles of corrugated aluminum.

Back from the river, at the base of the hill that was crowned by the Castle Tree, was the red-brick cotton mill, windowless for humidity control, with round towers at each corner. The mill village of nearly identical one-story cottages, where Jed and Raymond lived, surrounded the mill like vassals' huts in the shadow of a medieval fortress. The village crept up the hill almost to the street of rambling, neo-Georgian and late Victorian houses owned by the town professionals and factory managers, among them Emily and Sally's father, who ran the cotton mill. The Five felt great pride in this mill—the largest under one roof in the whole entire South! Jed and Raymond's father would bring home bundles of small cloth squares, samples of the plaids and checks and ginghams woven at the mill. The mill ends of these fabrics, sewn by housewives into shirts and dresses, appeared on people all over town.

In the middle of the river, across from Pine Woods, was a long narrow island called Cherokee Shoals, which had been a sacred site to the Cherokees. With the arrival of white men, the Cherokees hid out there and attacked the flatboats as they wove through the shallows. In a savage battle the white men disposed of these pirates. The treaty between the United States Government and the Overhill Cherokees was signed on Cherokee Shoals, opening the territory to white settlement. Now the island was covered with shacks and gardens belonging to poor white people and to a few half-breed Cherokees whose forebears had evaded the Removal.

Across the river on a bluff stood the ruins of the lead mine that had supplied the entire Confederacy with bullets—some rusted equipment, stone foundations. In school they studied how Union troops marched north from Knoxville to destroy it. They gathered near Pine Woods, only to discover that the ferry had been sunk by Confederate sympathizers. The Yankees offered area residents huge sums for conveyance across the river. The offers were refused. Finally a few soldiers swam their horses across, burned the sheds and ripped up some equipment. Then they marched off, taking as prisoners the locals who had refused help. Two days later the mine was again turning out Confederate bullets.

Beyond the mines and factories were the mountains, stretching range upon range eastward into North Carolina, northwest into Kentucky, north into Virginia. The valley floor on which the town sat was the dried-up bed of an inland sea. Once upon a time waves had lapped and pounded against the mountain walls. Strange sea creatures had bred and fought and struggled and died under fathoms of salt water in the very spot where The Five now sat. Parts of the valley had been reflooded by the TVA and blocked with dams that housed the turbines that produced electricity for the factories. Each of their families had crossed back and forth over these mountains before coming to rest on this valley floor.

Corliss Rainey was removed from a debtors' prison in England and put on a ship. He was working as an indentured servant to a farmer in tidewater Virginia when he met Buck Tatreaux, the son of a Cherokee woman and a French trader. Tatreaux did odd jobs for Rainey's master. One day the farmer sent them both to Williamsburg for supplies. They headed toward Richmond instead. On the way they further darkened Tatreaux's skin with berry juice and charcoal, cut off his braids, and scorched his remaining hair into kinks. They rubbed lard over his muscled body until he gleamed with apparent good health. Rainey put on a stolen set of his master's clothes. In Richmond they found the slave market, and Rainey put Tatreaux up for sale. Rainey soon drove away with more money than he had ever before seen. He supplied the wagon and headed down a dusty road through well-tended farmland toward the hazy mountains. At the foot of the mountains he hid.

Tatreaux meanwhile had run away from his new master. He scrubbed with sand in a stream until his skin was its usual copper color. With a sharp stone he hacked off his kinked hair. Then he ran for the mountains.

Rainey gave him his clothes, and a hat with the braids attached, and the two set off up the mountain. At times the slopes were so steep that they had to hitch ropes to trees and haul on them, to help the mules drag the wagon up the narrow rutted path to the pass. Upon reaching the pass, they saw below them the valley, heavily forested but dotted here and there with cleared land and cabins and sheds. And on the far side, the rugged walls of the neighboring plateau.

Rainey and Tatreaux found their spot, up against the gullied plateau wall. They built cabins, cleared land, raised crops, bred animals, went courting, and married daughters of the Scotch-Irish and German farmers, who had flowed into the valley along the more conventional route southward from Pennsylvania. Their children married and cut down more forest and spread out down the valley with their backs against the plateau wall. By the time the bodies of Rainey and Tatreaux had been turned into topsoil, the forested valley had become rolling green fields, grazed by cattle and enclosed by fences. A Tatreaux son married a Rainey daughter, and they had two sons. When the time came for these two to find wives and build cabins and start their own farms and families, one balked. Maybe the genes from his wayward grandfathers rebelled. From the pastures up against the plateau wall he could see the dusty road down the valley, jammed with people heading south—wagons piled high with household goods and drawn by mules or oxen. These people drove livestock and talked when he ambled down about a new Eden just beyond the foothills at the end of the valley.

He announced that the valley was too crowded, that he couldn't stand knowing exactly what he'd be doing and seeing the rest of his life. He tied his belongings into a pack and hoisted it on his back. His mother cried and loaded him down with beef jerky and corn pones. His father stared at him with glum outrage. The boy assured them he would return and report on what he found. They all knew he wouldn't.

What he found: mountains. Peak after towering peak, separated by narrow valleys, most of which already contained cabins and corn patches. Through the Blue Ridge Mountains of what was to become North Carolina he walked; into the Holston Valley; across the Clinch River; up through Cumberland Gap, following the network of narrow hollows until, like an eddy against a cliff, he couldn't go any farther, and so came to rest. Jed and Raymond were his descendants. Emily and Sally were descended from the brother who stayed behind. Donny's ancestors had been brought to the valley farm from coastal Virginia along approximately the same route taken by Rainey and Tatreaux.

Rainey and Tatreaux's great-great-grandson (Emily and Sally's great-grandfather) left his farm one day wearing a grey uniform with gold braid and a hat with a plume, and riding a prancing black stallion. He returned three years later on a half-starved nag, missing his plume, several gold buttons, his left eye, and his right hand. He found his house half burned, his cattle butchered, his fence posts ripped out, and his fields lying fallow. Calling Donny's forebears around him, he announced, "Yall are as free as I am now. Which ain't saying much. You can leave if you want to, or you can stay here and try to keep from starving with the missus and me."

Donny's great-grandmother left, joined the stream—of rejoicing freed slaves, of defeated soldiers in tattered grey with missing limbs, of victorious soldiers in tattered blue with missing limbs, of brisk scavengers from the North—that flowed through the ravaged country-side. She joined other celebrating Negroes, parted from them, stopped and harvested crops, stood in lines at federal relief kitchens in roiling towns. She meandered through Tennessee and down into Alabama, then turned around and came back to the valley farm where she gave birth to Ruby. Mr. Tatro never rebuilt his farm; he eked with his remaining hand. His son, Emily and Sally's grandfather, moved down valley into Newland, where a cotton mill was being built, and took a job as superintendent. Young Ruby and her mother went along as house servants. Ruby still bore the Tatro family name.

In addition to the Castle Tree, the coral Cadillac from New York, and their failure to succumb to polio, The Five had been given other signs, for as far back as they could remember. For instance, they had built a hut, like the first little pig's, in the woods behind Emily and Sally's house, sinking large sticks into the ground and lashing them together with vines and covering this frame with leafy branches. They would fashion loincloths from dish towels and leather belts, then paint each other's faces with the juice from squished mulberries and stick fallen crow feathers in their hair. Then they would dig with sticks into a small hill they had decided was an Indian burial mound, despite amused denials from parents.

But The Five *knew* it was a burial mound. The main highway through town had been part of the major north/south Indian war-path. Honest Injun's was a shack on this highway that sold country hams and jugs of molasses and chenille bedspreads and silver reflecting balls that people put on pedestals in their front yards. Also for the front yard, flamingoes on one foot, miniature Bambis, smiling plaster darkies in livery. Towering over all these objects of wonder (which their unimaginative parents would never let them buy) was a statue of a huge red Indian in a loincloth, with dark braids. Standing at his feet and looking up, The Five decided he was almost as tall as the Castle Tree. Between his massive moccasined feet was a pond, at the bottom of which were several green iron frogs with bowl backs— ashtrays, they looked like. Customers dropped pennies into the water and won a prize if one landed in a frog. Most people missed, as evidenced by a thick layer of pennies in the bottom. The Five were sure at least twenty-five dollars in pennies would accumulate before Injun Al got around to cleaning them out. But Jed and Raymond's father had once gotten a penny in a frog, before Jed and Raymond were born. His prize still sat on their window sill. It was a small grey teepee of plastic birch bark, laced with plastic cord and stamped with the words "See Rock City." On its bottom was stamped "Made in Japan."

Injun Al French, squatting in his fringed buckskins and feathered war bonnet, with The Five and his daughter Betty squatting in a circle around him, often told them about the days when his ancestors had hunted the surrounding hills and valleys and had stalked on the packed earth underneath the very highway outside his shop—to make war or to find game, in search of a warmer or cooler climate. He explained why Cherokee country was so mountainous: After the Flood, the Great Buzzard flew low over the earth while it was still soft. Where its wings dipped down, valleys formed. Where its wings swept up, mountains appeared. He told about the first people on earth, a brother and a sister. He slapped her with a dead fish, and she had a baby seven days later. (That day at lunch Raymond sneaked up and slapped Emily with his tuna sandwich, but nothing happened. They decided it was because Raymond wasn't her brother.)

It was also Injun Al who taught them the old Cherokee trick of notching their middle fingernails at the base with penknives the day school got out. When the notch had grown out to the tip, it would be time to return to school. They had only to consult their fingernails to know how much vacation was left.

"I didn't know Indians had to go to school," one remarked.

"Oh yeah. Uh, well, I reckon they didn't," Injun Al replied.

"They'd use it—you know—to tell when the Moon of Roasting Ears was starting, and all like that. When the heap big frost was due."

He often assured them the area was filled with burial mounds, that their hill was most likely one. Then he would urge them to try their luck some more at the frog pond.

The fact was that each time they dug in their mound, they found an arrowhead or a pottery shard. Once Jed even found a jagged piece of flint they were sure was a tomahawk head. The message was clear: They were not alone. Clues had been planted. The afternoon would end with whosever turn it was, branches tied on his or her arms, doing a dying eagle dance—swooping and dipping, limping and faltering, while the others sat in a circle and drummed on Quaker Oats boxes.

Then there was the cave. Its mouth was about a yard high. You squatted and crept down a narrow chute for a dozen yards, emerging in a black cavern. It had served as a powder magazine for Confederate troops. The Five kept down there a huge stack of comic books, wrapped in a chain from a swing and locked with a padlock. Shining flashlights over the walls, they found initials and dates scratched in the limestone—one read July 6, 1864. July sixth was Raymond's birthday. There had to be a connection. And on the floor Donny found a button with CSA embossed on it. When they cleaned it with brass polish and Q-tips, it turned out to be gold—pure gold, Raymond announced as he bit it.

Riding in a car across the Cherokee River bridge, they always held their breath—to ensure that the bridge wouldn't collapse underneath them. And in the underpass with railroad cars overhead, they always pressed their palms against the car roof to keep the underpass standing. The only thing they hadn't yet been able to master was flying. One autumn they went every day after school to the hill behind Emily and Sally's house. Arms outspread, they'd run down the hill, throwing themselves into the air when they picked up maximum speed and flapping their arms frantically. They had been sure it was merely a question of time until they would soar off into the sky. They tried tying leafy branches to their arms. Then cardboard wings.

But apparently there was some message in their *not* being allowed to fly. They lay on their backs in the dead grass with their hands under their heads and watched with envy the vast swarms of birds on their way south. "Look! The sky has chicken pox!" one would exclaim. They watched and they wondered—where were the birds going, how did they know how to get there, what if you got separated from your mother and father and from the trees you were used to? Their envy would fade into relief. They'd roll down the hill, leap up, and race toward warm fires, hot suppers, and mothers whose embraces and kisses they could impatiently shrug off.

When The Five had been small, Donny's mother Kathryn had babysat them through the sweltering summer afternoons. They went on hikes, darting across the fields like a school of minnows, with grasshoppers whirring up all around and with the tall grass tickling their bare legs. Against Kathryn's protests, they overturned each stone they came to and squashed every nest of black widow spiders. In the woods, they found forked sticks and crept through the leaves searching for lurking copperheads. The most they ever found were occasional blacksnake skins, bumpy and thinner than onion skins. They would study these, and the crisp brown shells of locusts gathered from tree trunks, and try to understand how creatures could shed their familiar coverings and still exist. They grew new skins, new shells, maybe even nicer than the old ones—but what happened in the meantime? There they were, helpless larvae, cold, naked, and unprotected. It would be better, they concluded, to stick with the skin you already had.

They would race to a nearby hedgerow and pick hundreds of honeysuckle blossoms, pinching off the ends and pulling out the stamens until droplets of sweet nectar popped up, which they would lift away with their tongues, gorging themselves like insatiable bees. They would end up in the pond behind Emily and Sally's house, drifting around and crashing into each other in tractor-tire inner tubes. Then they would sprawl on the red clay shore and mold from clay a replica of Newland—the mills and factories, the river and Cherokee Shoals, the train tracks, Pine Woods, the mill village, the hill, and the Castle Tree—and the mountains all around.

Kathryn had beautiful hands—dark brown on the backs, light pinky-purple on the palms. The white children studied them with wonder. With her long fingers she molded delicate figures—people, animals, bowls. The Five would watch her handsome dark face with its high cheekbones as she bent in concentration. With their clumsy fingers they would try to copy her deft twists and pinches at the balls of clay, gentle smoothing motions with the fingertips, careful indentations with the nails. They made doll-sized dishes for their hut and left them to bake in the sun.

Once Kathryn had each of them build a model of the house he or she wanted to live in later on. Donny built a castle with turrets and crenellated walls and placed it on the hill overlooking town. Kathryn looked at it critically and said gently, "Donny, honey, you can't build up on that hill."

"Why not?"

"Sure he can," said Raymond, frowning as he built a heliport on the roof of his mansion.

Kathryn smiled sourly and shrugged.

Sometimes they would hear the whistle of a train whooping around the bend on the far side of town. They'd race away, trampling their models, heading for the low stone wall that overlooked the valley. Usually the engine would arrive just as they did. The Five would count the cars and insist on Kathryn's yelling over the clacking wheels and the roaring engine the exotic names painted on the sides— Atchison, Topeka, and Santa Fe; Delaware and Hudson; Duluth, Winnipeg, and Pacific; Spokane, Portland, and Seattle; Canadian Pacific; Soo Line; Illinois Central; Frisco Line. . . . Heading north, open cars carrying mounds of coal from Appalachia, iron ore from Alabama; cattle cars; flatcars loaded with huge hardwood trunks, or cotton bales; refrigerator cars filled with produce, meat (corpses, Raymond insisted). Heading south, car after car of new automobiles. You could walk along these very tracks in one direction and end up at the Atlantic Ocean. Follow them in the other direction and you'd reach the Pacific. From sea to shining sea they stretched. Probably all trains eventually ended up in New York City, they decided. As the caboose passed, The Five would wave tentatively: "Wait? Take us with you?"

The men sitting on the back platform with their feet propped on the rail would smile and wave back: "Maybe someday. Just be patient."

The Five would race back through the familiar fields and woods to the pond, in whose red clay banks they knew every muskrat hole. Almost every bluegill who leapt from the water, and twisted and flashed silver in the sun they had caught at one time—and had thrown back after introducing themselves. They would pile into the boat and row around the pond rescuing drowning insects. They called this mission the Bug Patrol.

The Five agreed that Kathryn was as close to being special as any adult could be. As each was shooed out of his or her house by the arrival of a new baby or a new job, Kathryn was there to bandage cuts, wipe noses, and tie shoes. Once when Emily and Sally's mother was in the hospital getting them a new brother, Kathryn took The Five to the lawn below her third-floor window. Mrs. Prince appeared at the window in a filmy white robe with her black hair flowing, looking like a fairy princess. While The Five gazed in amazed silence, she threw down chocolate-covered cherries wrapped in gold and silver foil. For days they hoarded the candies, looking at them and remembering this vision. But it was Kathryn who took the children home that day and fixed lunch and read a story with a different one cuddled in her lap every few pages.

Then one day Kathryn was no longer there. Their parents said she had gone to New York City to learn to be a nurse; she had said to tell them good-bye and that she would see them sometime one of these days. Emily reported to the others having been awakened the previous night by voices in the driveway below her window.

"But I'm scared, Mr. Prince," Kathryn had said.

"Don't be scared, Kathryn," Emily's father had replied. "Everything's going to be all right."

"What do you reckon she was scared of?" Emily demanded. The Five searched their brains and couldn't come up with an answer. They themselves were scared of nothing—not Commies, not Yankees, not Indians, not nothing. They had a pact that if they were ever captured and tortured by the enemy, they would never reveal each other's names, not even to the death. They had drills to prove their courage. On summer nights under the streetlight in front of Jed and Raymond's house, large fluttery shadows swooped through the circle of light on the pavement. Raymond said they were the shadows of vampire bats. The Five took turns standing directly under the street-light as at least twelve vampire bats passed overhead.

Another drill involved the old boarded-up Hardin house down the street. It was crumbling red-brick with vines all over it. The story went that old Mr. Hardin beat his wife. One night as he was beating her nearly to death, their son Carl came in and shot him dead. Mrs. Hardin died of her injuries; Carl was still in the pen. The house was supposed to be haunted by both Mr. and Mrs. Hardin, who continued to carry on even in death. Jed and Raymond insisted they regularly heard screams coming from the broken upstairs windows late at night.

"Why did she let him?" Emily would demand. "Any man who tried that on me would be sorry!" The others nodded in agreement.

The Hardin drill required each to crawl through the wrought-iron fence after sunset, sneak across the overgrown lawn, and dash seven times across the gravel driveway. In bare feet. Then they would reassemble in Emily and Sally's yard to catch lightning bugs and put them on their fingers and pretend they were diamond rings.

Once Raymond led them down by the river in search of a trestle for a defunct railway spur. He had studied in school how the Yankees set fire to it to cut off supplies to Lee in Virginia. An eight-year-old girl from a nearby house dumped a bucket of water on the fire. The Yankees, retreating in their torn blue, their faces black with gunpowder and sagging with exhaustion, saw this and set another fire, which the little girl dowsed. The Yankees squatted down and lied patiently to her in their harsh accents, thinking of their own little daughters, about how the trestle had to be destroyed so that no more Yankees could come south and bother her people. She smiled shyly. As they left, she dumped water on the new fire. They rode back shooting rifles in the air. She ran and hid. And once the Yankees were certain the blaze was going and were riding away, she emerged to drown it.

The Five knew they would have done the same. And if the Yankees wanted to fight about it, they'd have a *real* fight on their hands. In Emily and Sally's dining room was a mahogany table from their mother's family farm. The table top was scarred from when Yankees butchered the farm's steers on it. Their great-grandmother had watched in silence, as her table was hacked up and as blood dripped onto her carpets and splattered the walls. Well, Emily and Sally were certain they would not have just stood there. And all the children cheered at the part of the story when the Yankee officer slashed open the feather bed in search of silver, inhaled a feather, and suffocated to death.

One Christmas The Five received further confirmation that they were special. With Raymond's battered .22 rifle, they trudged through the fields behind Emily and Sally's house. The mustard-colored stubble, stiff with frost, snapped under their boots. Up the high hill they had tried to fly off when they were dumb little kids. In the distance were blue mountains, fronted by row upon row of frosty mustard-colored fields. And immediately below was the woods, the bare limbs of oak and poplar and walnut etching intricate dark designs like wrought-ironwork on the overcast sky.

Enveloped in their own steamy breath, they inspected the oak trees for dark clumps of mistletoe. Each took one bullet. The idea was to shoot through the branch and bring an entire basketball-sized clump floating like a parachute to the forest floor. If you shot through the clump instead, tiny sprigs would shower down. Often even Mr. Tatro failed to bring down more than sprigs. But that year, and for the next three, one of The Five shot down an entire clump. They would race through the tangled dead timothy into the forest and search until they found the clump on its shattered branch. The one who had shot it would inspect it as the others watched in silence. The mistletoe lived on dusty green through the winter when everything else in the forest appeared dead. Like them, the mistletoe was special, chosen to keep watch. Yet the waxy white berries were poisonous. You didn't mess with mistletoe, and you didn't mess with The Five either.

They would carry their totem home—where someone's mother would hang it in a doorway by a silly red ribbon and kiss other adults under it—while The Five watched with disdain.

The Five felt these signs should be acknowledged, so one blustery March morning they pooled their allowances and bought a yellow paper kite and four dozen balls of string. On the kite they wrote, "Messages received. Call Newland 761, collect, day or night." Then they climbed the hill and sent up the kite, which tugged and tossed in the gusts. They let out more and more string until the kite was less than a speck in the distance, with fluffy clouds scudding and colliding all around it. Then they cut the string, certain the kite would be found in New York City. They hung around by the phone, but it never rang for them.

Doubt didn't really set in until the fall Raymond entered junior high school. In the first place, Emily didn't go to Washington, D.C., for the National Spelling Bee. In fact, she hadn't even made it out the door of Jefferson Davis Elementary School. She misspelled "abscess" and had to sit down in the second round in tears. If she couldn't even get herself to Washington, D.C., the others whispered, how could she get to New York City for "The $64,000 Question"? Was it possible that, even with her oversized brain, she might not make it to the top plateau?

The Five were lolling in the Castle Tree one Saturday afternoon. "Boy, I just wish some Commies would try to take over this town," Jed said, his brown eyes gleaming. "It'd be the last place they'd invade, I'm telling you." The Five settled back on their branches and pictured themselves disposing of dozens of attackers—Commies, Yankees, Indians, bandits, pirates, atheists. Judo throws, bayonet thrusts, left hooks to the jaw. . . .

"Yeah," Donny agreed, rolling languidly off the Tire and falling through the air, looking to even the initiated as though he would certainly crash through branches thirty feet to his death. Just in time he grabbed the knotted rope that hung from the Throne and, with a thrust of his skinny black legs, swung up and landed on the Couch. It was his favorite commando stunt. The others watched from the corners of their eyes, pretending to be unimpressed. Jed was too puny for that stunt, Raymond was too clumsy, Sally had recently become concerned with keeping her knees together at all times, and Emily was scared of breaking her neck.

Emily, who was carving "abscess" into the footrest of the Couch, said, "I'm sure we're adopted."

"How do you know?" her younger sister asked.

"Well, I mean, it's obvious, isn't it? *They* couldn't be our real parents, could they? We don't even look like them. They're dark." She gestured to Sally's light brown braids and her own auburn boy cut. "Probably our real parents live in New York City in a penthouse."

"Shit," said Raymond, learning to swear now that he was a seventh-grader. "Your parents screwed like everybody else's, and that's where you came from."

The others looked at him. "Whadaya mean?" Jed asked.

Raymond described the animated cartoon called "The Mystery of New Life" that he had just seen in Physical Education class.

"Naw, you're lying," Jed insisted. "The man puts a seed in the woman and it grows into a baby. That's what Dad said that time."

"Yeah, but where does it come from? How does he put it there?"

"It's true. I seen it myself," Donny muttered. "My neighbor done that to his girl. I sneaked up and watched them in his car."

There was a silence.

"Six inches?" Sally gasped, pressing her knees together. "And how big around?"

"Oh, I don't know." Raymond yawned. "Two maybe? Like a cardboard toilet paper roll sort of."

"Barf!" Sally and Emily said, pretending to vomit over the side.

"Don't knock it if you ain't tried it," Raymond suggested.

"And I suppose you have?" Emily sneered.

"Wouldn't you like to know?"

"Well, I'll tell you one thing, Raymond Tatro: When we get married, I'm not doing that with you."

"Me neither," Sally agreed, fingering the end of one braid.

"According to this movie, we have to if we want children."

"Not me. I'm adopting," Emily insisted. "It's disgusting."

"Then our children can't be *real* double-first cousins," Sally wailed.

"They wouldn't be anyway, since you and I aren't real sisters," Emily pointed out. "Now I'm sure we're adopted. Mom and Dad would never do that."

"Let's not talk about it anymore," Jed requested, looking green.

As the leaves on the Castle Tree that year faded to pale yellow and fell to the ground, The Five met in its branches less often. When they did, they sometimes avoided each other's eyes. Silences seemed awkward. Sally would chatter mindlessly to fill them.

The Five ambled into the newsstand one afternoon the following spring to watch the high school boys play pinball. As the machines bonged and lit up in carnival colors and shuddered to blows from cursing players' hands, Raymond sneaked off. The others saw him by the magazine rack, and with a smirk he gestured to Donny and Jed. Soon all three were pointing and giggling. Emily and Sally wandered over. Raymond flipped the magazine shut in their faces. But not before Emily and Sally caught a glimpse of some naked ladies.

They walked out of the newsstand and across the green in front of the red-brick courthouse. On the wall of the courthouse were bronze plaques bearing the names of all the men from Cherokee County who had died in the two world wars. And outside the doorway was a statue of a Confederate soldier holding a bayoneted rifle, which had been sold to the county right after Reconstruction by a salesman from a Vermont granite company. Traditionally, The Five saluted as they passed. This day Donny kept his hands in his shorts pockets.

"You forgot to salute," Jed told him.

"Don't feel like it."

"How come?"

"Just don't."

The Five had worked all morning collecting soft drink bottles in the mill village and hauling them to the store in a wagon. They gave a penny of the refund per bottle to the person who donated it and kept a penny for themselves, trying to amass entrance fees to the Majestic Theatre matinee *Thing from Another Planet*. At one house, a peeling wooden box on cinder blocks, a woman in a torn housedress came to the door with a squalling baby on her hip. She asked Raymond, "Is these here the Prince gals?" He nodded. She yelled at them, "No, I ain't got no bottles for you! You go tell that daddy of yours to give his gals some of the money he stole from Mrs. Harmon's husband! You tell him that!"

The Five ran down her sidewalk, dragging their red wagon.

"What's she talking about?" Emily demanded. "Our father would never steal."

"Ah, old lady Harmon, she just crazy," Jed assured her.

As they hauled the wagon to the store, Jed picked up a Coke bottle and said, amazed, "Look, this here bottle's from over at Egypt." He pointed to the "Cairo" embossed on the bottom.

Raymond snatched it, looked at it, and tossed it into the wagon. "Cairo, Illinois, dummy."

"It is not," Jed insisted. "How do you know? You think you're so smart just because you're in the seventh grade."

"I sure know more than a dumb fifth-grader. Egypt! Boy, are you dumb!"

Leaving behind the Confederate soldier, Donny began balancing along the curb, Yo-Yoing. The others balanced and Yo-Yoed along behind him.

"I ain't never been to no downtown theater," Donny remarked over his shoulder.

"You ain't?" Jed asked. "How come?"

"Grandmaw, she say stay where the white folks wants you at. Anyhow, most ever movie here comes out to Pine Woods."

They ducked into Woolworth's, packed themselves into the photo booth, closed the curtain, and inserted a quarter. The pictures that emerged showed five faces in snarls and grimaces, some with tongues sticking out, or thumbs in ears and fingers waggling. In one, Raymond was holding up his middle finger. They cut the strip apart, each taking one picture.

The posters outside the Majestic announced that the Thing in person would be sneaking through the downstairs handing out rewards to anyone brave enough to sit through the movie. They studied the titillating pictures in the glass cases—of terrified men throwing themselves against slowly opening doors, while buxom blonde women shrieked in the background.

When The Five bought tickets and started for the doors, the bouffanted, gum-chewing woman in the booth yelled, "Hey, colored boy! Yes, you. You know you can't go in that there door. Get up them steps to the balcony, hear? Don't you go getting smart on me."

"He's with us," Raymond assured her.

"Honey, I wouldn't care if he was with Jesus Christ, he ain't setting downstairs."

Donny was looking down and poking the toe of one high-topped black tennis shoe into a crack in the fake marble flooring. The other four exchanged glances. They'd never noticed the side staircase.

Finally Donny mumbled, "Yawl gwan. I meet you down here after."

"We'll all sit in the balcony," announced Emily.

"You'll miss the reward," Donny said in a whisper.

"That's right," said Jed. "Listen, Donny, we'll get you one too, hear?"

Donny nodded and headed for the back stairs. After the newsreel, a film of the Stars and Stripes rippling in a breeze came on the screen. A band played "The Star-Spangled Banner." Everyone stood, hands over hearts.

Back in the Castle Tree as they chewed Turkish Taffy and discussed what *they* would have done to the hideous green thing from Mars, no one could look at Donny.

"Well, shoot," Jed said finally. "I love the balcony. It's neat sitting up high like that."

Donny shrugged.

"When I reach the top plateau," announced Emily, "I'm gonna buy that theater and give you and your grandmaw a lifetime free pass for up front."

They heard leaves crunching below as someone approached the base of the tree. Looking down, they saw Mr. Fulton, grey and stooped. He called up through cupped hands, "Yall come on down out of my tree now, hear? Yall too old to be climbing around in trees. Those branches can't hold you. I'm sick of worrying about you. Gwan home now and do your lessons."

The boys began spending time crawling around vacant fields on knees and elbows, cradling imaginary rifles. When Emily and Sally would try to join them, they'd lob pretend hand grenades at them, pulling the pins with their teeth. The only day they let the girls play, they tied them down and dripped water on their foreheads until they confessed irritably to sabotage. The boys got army patches out of cereal boxes and nagged their mothers into sewing them on their windbreakers.

That summer at the carnival Raymond and Donny and Jed spent a lot of time looking at the posters of nearly naked women outside the show tent. Emily and Sally tried to persuade them to come look at the hot dog machine: A live dog was fed into one end; after much barking and howling, strings of wieners came out the other end. But the boys chased them off. Emily and Sally ended up at a nearby booth pretending to be interested in tossing pennies into milk bottles. Occasionally laughter would drift over. "Look," Jed said, "it says she shoots Ping-Pong balls into the audience." The three boys collapsed in giggles.

"What's so funny about that?" Emily demanded of Sally. "What's so funny about Ping-Pong balls? I don't get it."

Sally shook her head. "I think they've gone plumb crazy."

The following winter no one shot down mistletoe. Each got only a shower of dead leaves and twigs. The hut in the woods fell in on its treasures, and no one came to prop it up. Raspberry canes grew up around the mouth of the powder magazine. Younger children perched in the Castle Tree and chattered like monkeys. Emily and Raymond, as they strolled home along the sidewalk from the white junior high school, separately, with new friends, pretended not to hear the eager voices from the top of the tree.

# Part

# Two

# Chapter One

## A Team That's on the Beam

At the pep rally for the game against the Bledsoe Station Bulldogs, Sally and another cheerleader dragged the Newland Pioneers' Terrorizing Machine into center court, while the band played "Hot Time in the Old Town." It was a large, elaborately painted cardboard crate. Into one end they put a bulldog wearing a cloth saddle in Bledsoe High's colors, navy blue and white.

The band's song ended abruptly. Emily lowered her flute and watched the box. From it came barks and growls. It pitched, heaved, and shuddered. A cheerleader opened the door at the far end and out walked a Chihuahua in a minute blue-and-white vest. The audience howled and cheered.

As the Terrorizing Machine exited, the captain of the football team lumbered up to a microphone. "Uh, the members of the ball team and me, we really wanna thank all yall for coming out here this afternoon. Uh, it really means a whole lot to us out there on that ball field to know that we got the whole school behind us one hundred percent of the way. Uh, this here game tomorrow night, I reckon yall know it's real important that we win it if we going to have us a chance at the State Championship . . ."

He was shifting from foot to foot and chewing frantically on his gum. While the teacher on duty was strolling to the other side of the gym, Raymond slipped from his seat and ducked down the steps to the exit.

". . . uh, but we can't win it all by ourselves. Uh, we need all yall out there tomorrow night yelling just as loud as yall can yell. So, uh, on behalf of all us on the team, and the coaches and all, we just wanna thank all yall for your alls support this season, and ask yall to keep it coming tomorrow evening in this game against the Bulldogs."

The cheerleaders bounded onto the court, pumping their arms and screaming, "We got a T-E-A-M, that's on the B-E-A-M . . ."

Sally caught Jed's eye where he sat on the bench with the team, and they smiled.

Sally lay on the couch watching "American Bandstand." Kenny and Arlene were back together again, and doing the Mashed Potato. She was glad for them. Yesterday they'd been fighting and had seemed unhappy dancing with other people. She didn't look up as Emily came in and stood over her exuding disapproval.

"I mean, if this is how you want to spend your life—fine."

Sally nodded her head to the music.

"You'd sit in front of this thing all afternoon if only there were a conveyor belt to bring you food. Why don't you do something constructive for a change—come play basketball with me, or read a book, or something?"

Sally sighed heavily. Emily was always picking on her, had ever since she was first born, she supposed. Jealousy. She wished Emily would learn how to relax. She already had frown lines, and she was only sixteen years old. If she didn't frown so much, maybe she'd make cheerleader or Ingenue or something and wouldn't have so much to frown *about*. She wasn't that bad looking, it was mostly her personality. And the way she dressed—her sweaters didn't quite match her skirts, her skirts were baggy because she had no hips. She looked like she belonged with the crowd that came into school every day from the farms. Ina Sue Bascombe, say, who wore her hair in long braids, and who still didn't shave her legs because her daddy was a Holiness preacher and wouldn't let her. And the way Em slouched, like she was ashamed of her chest and trying to hide it. Sally just couldn't understand it. She was proud of her body, loved the ways she could make it move as she led cheers, loved having the boys watch her. Frankly, it wasn't easy having someone so out-of-it for a sister. People were always saying, "I just can't believe you and Emily are sisters! Why, you aren't a bit alike!"

"I practice cheerleading twice a week," Sally replied. "I go to Devout and Ingenue meetings. To movies and dances and ball games. I'd worry about myself if I was you. And why no one ever asked me out except that creepy Raymond Tatro. And why no girls asked me to join their clubs—so that I had no choice but to stay home playing basketball and reading dumb books."

Emily winced. "Do you think I care about your idiot clubs? I would no more join Ingenue than I would . . . watch 'American Bandstand.' "

"Good, since no one's asking you to."

Ruby, her head wrapped in a kerchief, was sitting on a stool watching television and ironing at the rate of one article per program. She wore a pair of Donny's cast-off high-topped black tennis shoes, and her stockings were rolled down to her scrawny ankles. She shifted her tobacco to one cheek and opened her mouth, lips curling in over toothless gums. "Law, you two girls is at each other all the time. How your mama stands it I don't know. But I ain't gonna put up with it. Hush now, hear? Miss Emily, you go upstairs and get me some more coat hangers. And Miss Sally, you fix me a ham salad samich." She couldn't understand how two girls who'd always had ever advantage in the world could be so everlastingly mean to each other. She could of understood it if her Donny was like this with his mama running off, and with hard times all around. But Donny was nothing but sweet. She just didn't understand what this world was coming to. Emily and Sally's parents weren't the people their parents were, and she didn't know what to make of these two girls.

Emily reflected, as she rummaged through closets for empty coat hangers, that everyone in her family always did exactly as Ruby instructed. Wasn't Ruby supposed to be the maid? Even though they fought over who had to have his or her clothes ironed by Ruby on ironing day, since the items came out creased in the wrong places and splashed with tobacco juice; even though her meals were outstanding throughout the country for their indigestibility, each morsel having been marinated in bacon grease; even though it appeared she brought cobwebs from home to strew around on the days she cleaned; in spite of all this, their mother had spent years trying without success to fire her.

"Shoot, missus," she'd say. "You wouldn't hardly know what to do without old Ruby."

Apparently Ruby was their familial cross to bear. The only time they had been emancipated from her was when Sally was an infant just back from the hospital. Ruby had announced she hated babies and small children, especially several at once, and had gone to work elsewhere until they were in school.

Emily thrust the hangers at the skinny old woman, scooped up the basketball, and dribbled toward the back door. In passing, she studied the marks all over it. Each summer The Five used to stand against the door and mark their new heights. There were five rows of marks, each stretching from three feet off the floor to around five and a half feet.

"We really made a mess of this door," she announced to Sally. "We should clean it off sometime."

Sally, absorbed in the Stroll, made no reply.

Outside Emily did hook shots and layups against the backboard on the garage. She rarely missed. Then she stood at the free-throw line and grimly swished in shot after shot. She didn't understand her compulsion to nag Sally. Why couldn't she be aloof and dignified? What was it to her if Sally spent most of her life in front of either a mirror or the TV?

She saw her mother out back weeding in her flower garden, wearing a straw hat and work gloves. Her mother spent most of her time out there. When Emily went to her friend June's house, June's mother always offered snacks and cracked jokes. But Emily's mother never had. Emily wondered if this might be why the Ingenues had never given her a bid. Her mother's lack of interest made them uncomfortable? But of course Sally was an Ingenue, and she had the same mother . . .

A turquoise and white Chevy, with blocks so low that the dual exhausts nearly scraped the concrete, pulled into the driveway. Emily tried to ignore it. A young man in chinos and a plaid Gant sports shirt got out. "Hey, Em," he called. He ran his hand up the front of his flattop, to be sure it was standing up as straight as a fakir's bed of nails.

"Hi, Jed."

He held out his hands. Reluctantly she tossed the ball. He did a one-handed jump shot that fell short. "Shit!" he drawled, pantomiming the shot so that he could flex his biceps. Emily frowned. It was revolting the way he worshipped his wretched body. Working out all the time and standing around preening. When she thought about what a puny little runt he used to be . . . she used to mash him into the dirt when they were kids. She could still outshoot him at basketball, but there was no girls' team. Instead she was expected to stand here and swoon over these obscene bulges, sit in the stands at the Friday night football games and follow Sally's instructions for cheering him on. He made her sick. His lazy good humor made her want to strangle him. What Sally saw in him was beyond her. But what could you expect from someone like Sally?

Jed watched her frown, then shrugged and smiled. What else could you do with a girl who acted all the time like she had the rag on? She'd been bossy as a kid, but not grouchy the way she was now. Well, it couldn't be easy having someone as great-looking and as popular as Sally for a sister, if you yourself was nothing but a brain. Most of the kids over at school resented her because she always raised the grading curve of any class she was in.

He appraised her tall body with sympathy. She stood with her hands on her hips, her weight on one leg. Like a guy, for God's sake. No waist, no hips, frown lines . . . Nice tits, though, you had to say that. Not that she'd be likely to let you near them. Any more than Sally would. Virtue ran in the Prince family, from the old guy on down. He remembered once as a little kid going to the mill with his daddy. Old man Prince, Sally's grandfather, had invited them into his office, sat Jed on his desk, handed him a nickel, and lectured him on the need to save that nickel and turn it into other nickels. "The way to make money, son," Jed remembered he'd said, "is to spend less than you take in." As soon as he got home, Jed rushed to the drugstore and bought and devoured a Baby Ruth. The way he saw it, you spent money when you got it—or else somebody would win it or steal it off you. Probably the old man had had spies in that drugstore. He noticed how Sally's father eyed him now when he picked her up for a date. Here is an unthrifty young man, his glance suggested. At least that was the only reason he could think of as to why

Mr. Prince would look at him like that. There was no way in the world he could know that Jed had his daughter on the five-yard line. The truth was, it bothered Jed a lot. He wasn't used to people looking at him with displeasure. He was his mother's favorite son. And if you played a good game of ball, you had girls chasing after you wherever you went, especially if you had a nice car like his. He couldn't understand parents not being delighted that he, Jed Tatro, had picked their daughter from all the dozens of fathers' daughters that were his for the taking. Not that he had "taken" Sally yet, but her reluctance was part of what made him want her so bad.

He glanced at Emily's tits again and wondered if old Raymond had ever tried to feel them up. He grinned. Most likely Raymond was a queer. No sports. No girls, except Sour Pussy over there. Alone all the time in a darkroom down at the newspaper office jerking off.

Emily seethed with resentment. Jed didn't have a brain in his head. Why he bothered to wear a helmet when he played football was a mystery. Yet he had the right to look her up and down as though she were a side of beef. Her big breasts were embarrassing enough without his making an issue of them.

She recalled as a child telling her father about a new friend at school. "She's a lint-head," she'd explained, parroting the term she'd picked up from the other children. Her father slapped her hard. "I don't ever want to hear you use that word again. Those people work for me and keep food on our table. They're our friends and relatives. They're no different from you or me." Emily was doubly startled, not having even realized the term was cruel. With the slap and the lecture came the awareness that her family was in fact different. How, she wasn't sure. For one thing, they weren't "lint-heads," whatever that was. When she went places with her father, people would stop them in the streets and exclaim, "Is this here your little gal, Mr. Prince?" And new teachers every autumn as they called the roll would pause at her name and inquire with respect whether she was the daughter of Mr. Prince at the mill.

But even being Mr. Prince's daughter couldn't shield her from appraising looks from whatever boy chose to run his eyes up and down her body. She clenched her teeth and shot Jed a defiant look. He grinned.

Emily saw Sally pausing behind the screen door to pat her hair and arrange her brightest smile, before bouncing out and squealing like the imbecile she was, "Why, Jed, honey! I didn't expect to see you this afternoon." She picked up the rolling ball and gave a helpless toss toward the goal, then giggled. Jed lumbered over to the ball, picked it up, and dropped it through the net. Sally sighed with petulant admiration and said, "Jed, you're just a wonder, the way you do that without even trying."

"So you finally hauled yourself up off the couch?" Emily inquired.

Sally and Jed glanced at each other with patient smiles. Jed walked over to the door, stuck his head inside, and called, "Hey there, Ruby! Yall right this afternoon?"

"Why, I be just fine, Mr. Jed. Law, ain't you the good-lookingest thing?"

"Why, thank you, Ruby. You're pretty good-looking yourself, now."

Ruby cackled.

Jed and Sally climbed into the Chevy. Sally snuggled up against him, and they roared off.

Emily hurled the ball at the goal. She didn't like playing Wicked Witch to Sally's Dorothy. But those two irritated her. They were so infernally pleased with themselves, with their friends and their school. Not that she didn't envy them. Yes, she wanted to be asked to join Ingenue. It had been painful the night the Ingenues arrived en masse at her house. She thought they had come to invite her to join and was quickly combing her hair before going downstairs. But as she began her descent, she saw them laughing and exclaiming and embracing Sally in the hall. She watched from the upstairs window as they trooped down the sidewalk to their cars, and she tried to figure out why they had never invited her to join, what she lacked that Sally had. Pep, she had concluded. Sally was invariably enthusiastic and cheerful. Emily often studied her as she walked down the hall at school. She sauntered, her face paralyzed into a wide smile, turning in a dozen directions at once, so as to make eye contact with every student and grace them with a "Hey there, how you?"

In contrast to herself, who usually slouched along the edge of the hall, staring at the floor and clutching her books so as to hide her chest. She didn't know how to be like Sally. She probably would be if she could. But Sally was petite and graceful, not lanky and gawky. Peppy, not moody. Emily had tried out for cheerleader two years in a row. She'd been eliminated in the first round of voting by the student body both times. She knew the cheers perfectly, had practiced in the shower and in the back yard and in the den for years, as had almost every other girl in town. "Who's gonna win, win? Who's gonna win, win now?" But she lacked . . . pep. Which Sally had in abundance. For which Emily hated and admired and envied her.

Ruby sat in the car looking straight ahead, with a jar of bacon grease in her lap. Her bony brown arms and legs were folded up like fried chicken wings. Driving through the underpass toward Pine Woods with freight cars clattering overhead, Emily asked, "How's Donny these days?"

"He be just fine. He play basketball over at the colored school this fall." Her jaws resumed their slow gumming of tobacco.

"I know. I see his name in the paper sometimes. He's a star, isn't he?"

"That what he tell me."

"I haven't seen him in a long time. How come he never stops by the house anymore?"

"Well, honey, Donny, he be a big boy now. He got him his own plans and his own friends."

"Well, tell him hi for me. I wish our schools played each other in basketball so I could watch him."

Ruby's toothless jaw sagged with disapproval. "Whites and coloreds don't play ball together, Miss Emily."

"They do in the NBA."

"Well, honey, they don't in Newland, Tennessee."

"Well, they should."

"That ain't for you and me to say, now is it? And don't you go round talking like that. Else your mama fix you good."

"I bet my mother would agree."

"Mrs. Prince? Law, honey, I knowed your mama before she was borned. I reckon I know what she thinks about most things."

Ruby always took this stance of knowing far more about each

member of the Prince family than anyone else—and in most cases, more than the individuals themselves. She'd worked for Emily's grandparents, had raised Emily's mother. Maybe she really did know what they thought?

Emily pulled up in front of Ruby's red-brick apartment building. Her doorway opened onto a narrow porch that overlooked the street. Other apartments faced inward on a series of interlocking courtyards, landscaped with bare earth and straggly clumps of weeds. Beyond the apartments were fields that stretched down to the willows bordering the river. Ruby was always marveling over the changes she'd seen in her lifetime—from shacks and sticky clay roads, to brick apartments and paved streets and sidewalks.

She glanced at Emily. "Sure do wish I had me something to fry in this here grease."

Emily cleared her throat and looked away.

"A little old chicken neck or something."

Emily stared straight ahead.

"Sure do gets sick of rice and beans all the time. Law, some days I doesn't even have the strength to pick myself up outen the bed." She sighed.

Still not looking at her, Emily emptied the contents of her change purse into Ruby's outstretched hand. She was always shocked when Ruby pulled this.

"Why, I declare! We thank you, Miss Emily! What a lovely thoughtful thing to do!"

Ruby nodded as she unfolded her limbs and slowly pulled herself out of the car. She figured she deserved it. She couldn't hardly get by on what the Princes paid her—wouldn't have got by at all without the money Kathryn sent down from New York City for Donny. Yet Mrs. Prince was a Tatro, and Ruby was a quarter Tatro herself, which maybe nobody but her knew about. According to her mama, back on the Virginia farm during slavery times one of the Tatro boys took a fancy to Ruby's grandmaw, who was a young girl then herself. This white boy would ride out to the field where the niggers was hoeing corn and nod at this girl. Just a nod was all. Then he'd ride off and wait there in the woods. When Ruby's mother was borned high yaller, seemed like that nobody noticed. Ruby herself was almost as light as her mother, though Kathryn and Donny was a good bit darker. When Ruby was little, everyone used to say all the time, "Law, ain't she the purtiest color?" And all her life people in Pine Woods had treated her extra special.

But respect didn't put pork on the table. That you had to get ahold of however you could.

As Emily drove away, she saw a young man in maroon pants and a matching Banlon sports shirt sauntering along the sidewalk. Although this tall loose body scarcely resembled Donny's short skinny one, she knew from the jaunty walk, with the head thrown back and the hands stuffed in the pockets, that it was he. She slowed down and yelled through the open window, "Hey, Donny."

He looked startled, glanced over at her, and said nervously, "Hey there."

"It's me—Emily."

"Yeah, I see you there." He grinned quickly, then stopped grinning and looked down at the sidewalk.

"I haven't seen you in a long time."

"No, ma'am, I reckon not."

"How you been?"

"Just fine, thank you, ma'am."

"You've grown."

"Yes, ma'am."

"Your grandmaw says you're playing basketball."

"Yes, ma'am." He poked a crack in the sidewalk with the toe of his tennis shoe, then looked off across the dusty school playground where some boys were playing football.

Emily had been around Ruby and Kathryn and him enough to know that their not looking at you as you talked didn't mean they weren't listening or weren't interested. Still, he did look uneasy. Emily couldn't think of anything else to say. She continued to smile too brightly.

The hell with him. Boys. Who understood them anyway? One minute they'd be snickering at some dirty joke. And the next minute they'd be opening the door for you, or pulling out your chair. Then before you knew what was happening, they'd have their tongues half-way down your throat and their hands all over you. People could say what they liked about Raymond Tatro, but at least he left her alone that way. From watching her mother and Sally, she knew the way to enthrall a male was to ask him questions about himself, and then listen with feigned fascination to his lengthy answers. That was how you got a reputation for being a brilliant conversationalist. But it wasn't working with Donny. She couldn't think how else to behave with him. That "ma'am" stuff was so creepy, made her feel like his mother. Fortunately, at the rate they were going, they'd only be seeing each other once every decade or so, so it didn't really matter.

"Well, nice to see you. See you around, hear?"

"Yes, ma'am."

As she drove off, Donny looked up, wanting to motion for her to come back. But he still couldn't think of what to say. You didn't talk to white girls the way you did to colored girls. But how you did talk to them was a mystery. Yes, ma'am. No, ma'am. That was the most he'd ever said to a white woman in recent years. His only contact had been to mow their grass, or to buy things from them at store counters. You smiled, no matter what crazy thing they asked you to do. You smiled and you smiled and you smiled.

But Emily . . . she was OK.

He started thinking about her pond and about floating around on inner tubes. He looked way up the hill, past the mill village, to the Castle Tree. He smiled remembering his commando stunt, which none of the others had ever confessed to not being able to do.

His eyes shifted to the huge half-dead oak in the schoolyard—the Lynching Tree, it was called. Years ago, when Pine Woods had been a collection of shacks, white men had come from town on horses and dragged out a man called Nigger Joe. They made him stand on his head, then strip naked except for a bowler hat he always wore. They strung him up by the neck on a branch of that oak, cut off his rod, and left him hanging there—for refusing to move off the sidewalk in town as a white woman passed. Or so the story went, as told by old Granny Tatro in her head cloth and long skirt: "Lord, they kluxed that man something turrible." Sometimes in the schoolyard Donny and his friends would glance up uneasily at the old tree in whose shade they were playing mumbly-peg with their jackknives.

As Emily's car disappeared, Donny waved. Then he shrugged

and took his mother's letter from his pocket and reread it. She was driving down from New York City for another visit. She wished he would go back up there with her to live.

He crumpled the letter and flung it at the sidewalk and stomped on it, his face contorted. She'd left him, damn it! He'd been a little boy, and she'd just up and left him in the middle of the night without saying good-bye or nothing. She'd been writing and phoning and sending money ever since. She'd come home last Christmas and spent the whole time peeping out the window behind the curtains. But the truth was that she had left him. He remembered smothering his sobs in his pillow every night for weeks. Sometimes walking down the street he used to close his eyes and pretend that when he opened them, she'd be walking toward him.

She was so beautiful. He had his own private picture in his head, unrelated to the various photographs his grandmaw had scattered around. He always thought of her sitting on the red clay shore of the Princes' pond making models, her head bent and the sun glancing off her high cheekbones. He leaned down and picked up her letter and smoothed it. She was coming back for him, wanted him to go to New York City. How many times had he prayed to the Lord for this very thing to happen?

But he had his own life now. If he did well for the next two years, maybe he'd get a basketball scholarship and go to college, the way the guidance counselor at school was always saying. And things was just getting going with Rochelle. He'd kissed her for the first time last night. Under a willow tree by the river. And she'd liked it. He grinned. She'd been scared she was going to like it. She had her six brothers and sisters, and spent most of her time babysitting while her mama worked at maiding. She said she wasn't about to go doing nothing that might stick her with kids of her own. But she had liked those kisses, and he was optimistic she might like some other stuff before long. Besides, how could he leave his grandmaw? She was practically his mother now, and she didn't have nobody else.

How was he supposed to pick up and leave everything? Just because *she* wanted him to, just because it was convenient now to have him around, like a cat or a dog or something. It was too late. She wanted him in New York City. What about what *he* wanted? Had she ever considered that in her whole entire life? He crumpled the letter and hurled it to the sidewalk again and place-kicked it into the gutter, then whirled around and stalked home.

He switched on the evening news and collapsed into an old brown armchair in the dark living room. Grease was crackling and flying in the kitchen where his grandmaw was concocting supper. On the television screen some colored people in their Sunday clothes sat at a lunch counter having ketchup dumped on them by a bunch of white people who was angry about something or other. His grandmaw emerged and switched off the set. "What you doing, Grandmaw? I'm watching that."

"Donny, honey, I don't like you watching that stuff. I don't want you getting no smart ideas."

"I got to watch it for Civics. It's our assignment."

"Humph."

"What ideas you afraid I'll be getting?"

"Donny, you growing up to be a fine proud colored man. You do like the white folks says and you be all right. They treat you just fine. All this yelling and carrying on—it ain't right. The Lord don't like it. You got to learn to be a clever nigger. You clever enough, you gets what you wants without you cut nobody up." She spat a wad of tobacco juice across the room into a coal scuttle. Donny had learned to take this feat for granted.

"Aw, Grandmaw, I ain't gonna cut nobody. Turn that thing back on."

"Honey, you don't know what you likely to do when you gets growed." And finds out what you up against, she added to herself as she returned to her hot plate and started turning over chicken wings. She munched her tobacco thoughtfully. She'd never known the best way to raise up children—to tell them right from the start how mean-spirited some folks was, or to protect them for long as you could. You had to teach them to mind their manners, or else they'd get smart and get into trouble. But it was downright pitiful to watch them frown and try to understand things even their parents had a hard time understanding. Kathryn's Buddy was raised to think he could do pretty much anything he pleased. He came home from that war over at France in a big fancy yellow car with a lot of flashy clothes. He had a photo of hisself setting in a bar with his arms around some French girls, white girls they was. He used to pull it out all the time. "That nigger's gon get hisself killed," she used to mutter to Kathryn. To him she'd say, "Buddy, honey, you in Newland, Tennessee, now, not Paris, France." Kathryn thought he was just about the most wonderfulest thing she'd ever laid eyes on, and she up and married him fast as she could.

Then they all had to sit there on their porches and watch as he tried time after time to find and keep a job. His car and clothes got more and more shabby. One day he got all dressed up in his best sharkskin suit and went downtown to apply for a janitor job over at the Parkway Department Store. As he strutted across the street, this white man who was painting the lines of the crosswalk with two other men stood up and painted a yellow line down the back of Buddy's suit. Buddy stood there trembling, clenching and unclenching his fists. He said he knowed if he used his fists, he was as good as dead. So he burst into tears. The white men laughed. A couple of weeks later he robbed a store, got caught and sent to prison. One day he was found in his cell with his throat slashed. In one hand he clutched a weapon —a sock with the toe tied to a padlock. He left Kathryn pregnant with Donny.

Ruby sighed. But if the good Lord had meant for life to be easy, He wouldn't of made people all different colors to start out with.

Through her almost closed eyelashes, by the flickering candles on the coffee table, Sally could see the other Devouts sitting on the couch and the chartreuse carpet of Diane's living room. Judy, the Devotions Deputy, her eyes tightly shut and one hand fingering the gold cross hanging from a chain around her neck, was asking the Lord to bless the football team in the upcoming game against the Bledsoe Station Bulldogs. Diane added the Student Council officers and the principal to the blessing list.

Not to be outdone, Judy intoned, "We ask you, Lord, to bless our Mayor, Mr. Prevost, and to bless our congressmen and senators from the State of Tennessee. And most especially we ask you to bless President Kennedy, even if he is a Catholic." Judy closed with the special Devout Prayer: "*Help us, Lord, in every way / To do Thy will day by day. / Pure in body, mind, and soul, / Working toward our heavenly goal.*"

"Amen," agreed the eleven Devouts. Normally there were twelve Devouts, the number set to correspond to the number of disciples. But one Devout, now an ex-Devout, had just been bundled off to an aunt's in Richmond to await the birth of her illegitimate baby. They joined hands for a silent prayer, as the Devout handsqueeze was passed lingeringly from member to member.

Sally tried to think about the Lord, but her thoughts kept straying to Jed and their fight at the quarry that afternoon. She had told him to keep his hands above her waist and outside her madras dress.

"Now, I think that's fair, Jed honey. That means we can do whatever we want above the waist and outside the clothes."

"Fair? You call that fair?" He folded his muscled arms and leaned against his door. "All right, it's a deal if we say above the waist but inside the clothes."

"No. Absolutely not." Sally studied the gold-plated megaphone on her charm bracelet.

"All right, Sally. We'll try it your way. No hands below the waist, or inside the clothes. No hands anywhere. No nothing." He ran his hand up the front of his flat-top.

"All right. That suits me just fine." She leaned against her door and stared out at the walls of limestone all around them.

Jed started the car. "Where are we going?" she asked nervously.

"I'm taking you home."

"Home? Why?"

"Ain't no point in us setting out here in a gully if you don't want to do nothing."

"But I do, Jed. I want to hold you and kiss you. I want us to talk about what we did today. I just don't want all that other stuff."

"Well, holding and kissing may be what you want, but it ain't enough for me." He gunned the Chevy onto the dirt road, the tires throwing up clouds of dust and gravel. "You get me all worked up, and then you get offended if I try to do anything about it."

"Are we breaking up then, or what?" she inquired.

"I'll go with you to the Sadie Hawkins Dance like we agreed. But I ain't touching you no more, Sally. That should make you real happy. I'll find me some girl who'd like to be touched by Jed Tatro. Lots would, you know."

Tears welled up in Sally's eyes. Jed threw her a look of hatred and pleasure.

Just thinking about it, Sally felt the tears massing again. It was so hard to know what to do. She liked to kiss and hug, but that was never enough for Jed. He wasn't even very interested in kissing, it seemed to her, did it just to get her to relax so that he could slip his hands under her shirt or up her skirt. She had developed the ability to kiss him with one eye open, keeping track of his hands and directing them to the agreed-upon areas. She had also developed the ability to shut down any creeping sensations of enjoyment that might interfere with these powers of surveillance.

She loved Jed. At least that was what she heard herself telling him one night in his car at the Wilderness Trail Drive-In as the fog swirled around and obscured the screen. She wasn't sure what that word meant. It had a lot to do with not wanting to be alone on Saturday nights. But she didn't see why telling him that meant that suddenly he could do whatever he wanted with her body. She had thought nice girls didn't do what he wanted her to do. But he insisted that the difference between nice girls and not-nice girls was that not-nice girls talked about what they did, whereas nice girls just did it.

She knew that women were supposed to do whatever they could to please men. When her daddy came in from the mill, she jumped up so he could have his favorite overstuffed brown leather chair. She brought him the newspaper, switched the television to the news. In contrast Emily sat where she was, nodded, and went on with whatever she was doing. But Sally loved doing these things. Her daddy worked hard all day for them. He deserved to be catered to when he came home tired and hungry. Her mother often brought him supper on a tray, so that he wouldn't even have to move. He said that Southern women treated their men like kings; that if word got out, the South would be flooded with men from every other part of the country.

Here was Jed asking her for something that would please him very much. How could she deny it to him? But how could she grant it either, knowing how her daddy would feel about it? And she certainly didn't want to get into the business of deceiving her daddy. Whenever Jed came to pick her up, he'd try to be polite and pleasant. But her daddy, usually so well-mannered, would either ignore Jed, or grunt a reply, or get up and walk out. Sally couldn't figure it out. Several times when she and Jed had broken up, she'd dated other boys. Her father had always asked, "What does his father do?" But he *knew* what Jed's daddy did, had known the whole family for years. So what could he have against Jed?

In any case, there was no way to please both Jed and her daddy at once on this issue. But she couldn't bear the thought of losing Jed to some girl from Cherokee Shoals who would give him everything. Why, the idea of seeing him with another girl was too repulsive. She'd kill herself first. Why couldn't he be content just to hold her and kiss her and talk? She felt no compulsion to do more than this, and she couldn't understand this urgent neediness he was always referring to. Was it true that boys had savage lusts they couldn't control?

Diane turned on the lights, blew out the candles and passed around butterscotch brownies. Sally dried her eyes as the others discussed whom to invite as their twelfth member.

"I think Louise is real devout."

"But she smokes."

"That's right. She does. We don't want any smokers in Devouts."

"How about Laura?"

"*Laura?* Laura Owens?"

"Sure. Why not? Laura loves the Lord."

"That's not all Laura Owens loves. So I hear."

"What are you trying to say?"

"Just that she's got a bad rep. She's not really Devout material."

"And you are, I suppose?"

"Well, I'm here, aren't I?"

"Just barely. You just barely made it, Clara, and if I was you, I'd watch my step."

"Watch my step! Who do you think you are? You can't kick me out of this club!"

"You may be a member, but you're not an officer. And you never will be, at the rate you're going. . . ."

Jed sauntered into the house. Raymond looked up from his study of the chart on the living room wall. Next to it hung an embroidered sampler that read: "Do nothing you wouldn't want to be doing when Jesus comes." Jed's chinos bulged at the crotch. "And how *is* our Sally?" Raymond asked.

Jed looked confused, then blushed, smirked, and sat down on the sofa, covering his lap with a pillow and running his hand against the front of his flat-top. "She's all right."

"Well, I'm just delighted," Raymond drawled. "It does my little old heart good to know that Newland's own Miss Sally Prince is all right."

"Whadaya got against Sally?"

"Nothing. Absolutely nothing. She's just not my type."

"Well, you're not her type either."

"What a convenient arrangement. The Lord does look out for His own, doesn't He?"

"But she still likes you. I can't imagine why."

"Well, I like Sally, too," Raymond said wearily, returning to his study of the family tree. "Well, Mother!" he yelled. "I see you've finally done it!"

"Done what, Junior honey?"

Raymond scowled. He'd finally gotten everyone to call him Raymond except his parents and his relatives in Tatro Cove. "I see you finally traced our line back to Jesus." He laughed silently.

"You hadn't oughta talk like that, Junior," she called in a hurt voice from the kitchen where she was cutting out biscuit dough. That Junior worried her to death with his lack of respect. Always arguing with his father and taking the Lord's name in vain. She didn't know what would become of him when he left school at the end of the year. With that smart mouth of his, he'd never be able to hold a job. Her own parents had moved into Newland from a mountain farm when she was ten. Her father was a drunkard and her mother supported them all by turning their home into a boarding house for newly arrived mill workers. She'd been working all her life—first on the farm, then helping her mother with the boarders, then shift work at the mill, and now as secretary to Mr. Sutton at Sutton Insurance. He was the best agent in the office, and all the other girls looked up to her. She wore a hat and white gloves to work now instead of coveralls, and sat at a desk with a fresh flower in a bud vase. All this effort to get where they were, with a house and a car and all the food they wanted, and Junior took it for granted. Seemed like that he thought it all fell from the sky. It scared the wits out of her to think he'd take after her own father and look to the rest of them to carry him.

"Shut up, Raymond," Jed muttered from the couch. "Don't joke about Mama's tree thing. You know it means a lot to her."

"But not to me," Raymond replied as he headed for his room. "Why she wants to keep track of a bunch of scruffy crackers and horse thieves and half-breeds, who sat rotting in a cove in Kentucky for centuries, is more than I'll ever understand." He slammed his door.

"They wasn't thieves," Jed called. "They was pioneers. They was better men than you'll ever be, prissing around with your camera like some kind of goddam Yankee newspaper reporter!"

"Jed honey, watch your language," his mother called.

Jed walked over to the chart. It was two halves of a circle, joined in the center by his and Raymond's names. Radiating out from their names were hundreds of names of ancestors. Whenever he was feeling lousy—like right now when he'd been fighting with Sally, or when he brought home straight C's on his report card, or when they'd lost a ball game—he'd come look at this thing and feel better. He was the hub of his entire family. Its whole purpose appeared to be to bring Jed Tatro into existence. It had taken a dozen generations to get from prison in England to Newland, Tennessee. All these dead people was expecting big things from him, and he intended not to disappoint them. Already he was varsity tackle on a state championship team. And at the end of every year his class had voted him "Best Personality." He sometimes thought he hated Raymond for his scorn for this chart and his people, and for the way he used this scorn to hurt their mama. Raymond was always penciling in names that no one but him thought was funny—Alger Hiss and Martin Luther King and Stalin and Mae West. Raymond thought he was a regular scream. But it pretty much proved that nobody else did when his class never voted him "Best Sense of Humor." They never voted old Raymond nothing. In the first place he looked about thirty years old, with his big thick glasses and thin hair. Most Likely to Recede, they ought to vote him. (Now *that* was funny.) He had no friends. You saw him around school with that Audio-Visual Club bunch—those fairies that put together ham radios from kits. Hundreds of dollars those creeps spent, trying to talk about the weather to a bunch of foreigners. They all dressed like models for a rummage sale—rayon shirts, white socks, sweater vests with reindeers on them, pleated trousers. A bunch of brains. Hell, they played chess on Friday nights when everyone else in town was at the ball games. Yankees mostly. Didn't know no better. Their fathers was chemists and stuff over at the paper plant. One of them's fathers was that new man at the mill—Mackay or something. Jed's daddy had come home the other night grumbling about Mackay bringing down this faggot from some Yankee university who sat around with a stopwatch timing how long everyone sat in the can.

Jed didn't like to think about his childhood. He'd been scrawny and weak. Raymond and Emily and Donny had been older and had bossed him around. Teachers always mentioned how smart Raymond was, how well he'd done on the tests Jed had just flunked. But he was showing them now. Raymond maybe had the brains, but Jed felt like that he had everything else. He lifted weights every day and probably had the best body in town. Sally said so. He dated Sally, who was the prettiest girl at school in a lot of people's opinions. Their class always voted her "Most Popular Girl." True, she wasn't putting out for him much. But it was just a question of time. She made him angry sometimes, though—she could be such a prissy little hypocrite. She'd get out there on the gym floor during a pep rally, like this afternoon, and wiggle her ass at the whole entire student body. She'd leap up and try to touch the soles of her saddle shoes to the back of her bouffant hairdo. She'd flash her panties all over town. But get her alone in a car, and she became Miss Goody-Two-Shoes. She'd dribble her tits all up and down the basketball court, but just try to get ahold of one. Either she should put out, or she should make it clear she wouldn't. As things was, about half the time when she said no, she meant yes. But you never knew which was which. Sometimes he suspected she'd like him just to go ahead and do it to her, so she wouldn't have to take responsibility. Girls was like that. They wanted it, but they knew they wasn't supposed to want it, so they tried to get you to force them into it. It got confusing. Sometimes he wished he was a girl and didn't have to be the one to make everything happen. If you was a man, you wasn't supposed to get confused. You was supposed to know all the time what you wanted and how to get it. That was partly why he loved football. Never any question what your goal was. Like Coach Clancy was always saying, "Winning ball games isn't the most important thing, it's the *only* thing. Why, I wouldn't give the steam off of my shit for a man who don't go out there to win." But win or lose, you knew you could count on every man on that team if you was in trouble. You loved those men like they was your own . . . *brother*, he started to say, but he hated Raymond.

Raymond locked his door. Sometimes he thought he'd go crazy in this madhouse if he weren't able to lock himself in here. That chart— either it or he had to go one day soon. It made his insane family and their random matings and birthings and wanderings look like the whole point to the universe. There was his name in the center of that demented bunch, with the implication that he was not only accountable to them but inseparable from them. They'd pass some drunken hillbilly on the street when he was little and his mother would say, "Say howdy to Bill Flanders, your fifth cousin twice removed on your daddy's side." Everybody in this town was related; it was why they were all maniacs. His family were distant cousins to Emily's, as his mother insisted on showing everyone who set foot in the house. One big happy family. One big happy, crazy-as-treed-coons family.

Against one wall was a table holding his stamp albums. Over the table hung a map of the world. Better than anything he loved sorting through the packets of stamps he ordered from New York City and finding one from Mauritania or Sumatra or Afghanistan. In the beginning he'd had to check the map almost constantly. Now he knew where every country was and had a few stamps from most. There were people out there he was not related to. That knowledge was an incredible relief.

People looked at him strangely and asked why he wanted to collect stamps from foreigners. He was never able to answer. He remembered seeing an English stamp on a Christmas card his father received from an army buddy. He'd salvaged it from the garbage and studied it for weeks. One day an acned older boy named Wayne who lived in a house on his paper route invited him inside to see his stamp albums. Raymond had been so enchanted by the huge books filled with colorful stamps from dozens of countries that he scarcely noticed Wayne's hand moving gently but firmly in his pants. He went back often, at first for the stamps Wayne gave him, but soon for the pleasure of his touch and his talk—about other parts of the country his family had lived in. His father, a car salesman, was always on the road in search of a better job. When Wayne moved away, they kissed with tears running down their faces. Wayne presented Raymond with his best album. Raymond hadn't realized until a couple of years later when boys at school began giggling and whispering about homos and queers and faggots that what he and Wayne had done was something to be ashamed of.

Along another wall were shelves filled with his camera equipment —lenses, portable lights, tins of film. He worked for the newspaper. He'd also placed a few pictures with magazines and newspapers in New York City. He had always taken the family photos—endlessly rearranging people and backdrops until everyone lost patience and dispersed. The money from his paper route he used to buy sophisticated cameras and lenses.

He suspected his stamp collection, his photography, had a lot to do with his not making junior varsity football his freshman year. Too small, Coach Clancy said. Try again when he reached his growth. Three years later he was still short and skinny, with that ox of a younger brother to rub it in all the time. Coach Clancy had a huge chest and narrow hips. Destined for lower back pain in late middle age. Veins stood out on his red face. "Yall seniors is good students, but that's about it. It's all most of you'uns can do to stand up on two feet. Tatro over there, he slouches around here all doubled over like a dog trying to hump a football." Everybody cracked up. They'd been calling him the Ball Banger ever since. That was their idea of a good joke. Ha ha. Coach Clancy was wrong, though: Raymond wasn't a good student. An "underachiever," the guidance counselor called him. Did well on tests but had lousy grades.

Well, it figured. Jed got cheered for smashing heads. Him, he got called names for trying to stay out of the way and mind his own business. He sometimes thought he and Jed, by unspoken agreement, had laid claims to noncompeting areas. In any physical confrontation, Jed could beat him to a pulp, so he learned to fight with his tongue, mocking people, usually without their knowing it. Sometimes he felt like a gnat buzzing around a lion, just out of reach of its paws, driving it to distraction. But Jed had certainly claimed the more prestigious area in terms of living in Newland. Raymond couldn't help but be aware of the pride in his parents' eyes when their neighbors came over and said, "Some boy, your Jed. Did you see that tackle on the two-yard line against Chattanooga?" His parents had fifty-yard-line seats at the stadium for home games and drove all over the state to away games. They were outraged when Raymond began playing chess on Friday nights. "Your own brother, and you won't even go see him!" his mother shrieked.

"I see him all the time," Raymond pointed out. "Much more than I want to." Recently they'd given up, gazing at him glumly as they left the house with their cushions, blanket, and thermos.

Raymond sometimes imagined the town gathered in the football stadium while he stood on the fifty-yard line and flipped through *Natural History* magazine showing his full-color spread on Appalachian wild flowers. Sally Prince would bound out and lead the crowd in spelling out "Trillium." Everyone would roar with admiration . . .

Alongside his bed hung several of his favorite pictures—the weathered faces and hands of some people in the area of Kentucky his father came from. One picture, taken from the files of the newspaper office, was of an elephant hanging by its neck from a crane. In 1922 an elephant came to town with the circus. During the parade she trampled to death a boy who was pelting her with watermelon rind. The town tried the elephant, found her guilty, and lynched her. Raymond lay on his bed studying this picture. A crowd of townspeople howled in the foreground. Their faces were distorted with—what? Cruelty?

Righteousness? Whatever it was, it made him uneasy. A contact at one of the New York City magazines had offered him a job in a print shop upon graduation from high school. Every time he thought about moving to New York, he got homesick. How could he possibly leave everything and everyone familiar to him? He couldn't. It was out of the question. But at odd moments, he found himself gazing at that dangling elephant.

# Chapter Two

## The Sadie Hawkins Day Dance

The gym was decorated with posters of Li'l Abner and Daisy Mae, of hound dogs and stills and outhouses with half-moon holes in the doors. The boys were wearing bib overalls with no shirts, straw hats. Their feet were bare, and some carried jugs and chewed on pieces of straw. The girls wore tight short shorts with straw sticking out of the pockets, halter tops, no shoes. They'd rouged their cheeks and drawn freckles with eyebrow pencil. It was hard to tell one person from another. Except that Emily had no difficulty picking out Sally. She sat, smiling, on Jed's back as he did pushups. A crowd of admirers counted: "... thirty-four, thirty-five ..."

"Do you see what your gorgeous brother is up to?" she asked Raymond, who sat beside her on the bleachers gazing down at the gym floor.

"Yeah. Isn't he wonderful? I just can't figure out how he's become such an exhibitionist. He used to be a shy little punk. Remember? He could hardly open his mouth without blushing and ducking his head." Raymond demonstrated. Emily laughed.

They sat in silence. The athletes and the girls in the social clubs were monopolizing the area in front of the bandstand. They barn-danced to the country music being played by men in white Western suits, string ties, and rhinestone-studded shirts, cowboy hats and boots.

Sally looked into the bleachers and saw Emily and Raymond. She sighed. Poor Emily. She just didn't know how to have fun. And Raymond ... well, Raymond was hopeless, was all. He didn't even try. There he sat in his long-sleeved rayon shirt. You'd never know one of the best dressers in the whole school was his brother.

She looked around the gym. She loved organizing parties and watching her friends enjoy them. Maybe that was why Emily and Raymond bothered her. They reminded her of the little match girl in the fairy tale who stood in the snow, dressed in rags, and watched the people in the restaurant laughing and eating. But they didn't have to stay out in the cold. They chose to. Stubborn.

"Don't look now, but we're being watched," Sally murmured in Jed's ear as he crushed her to his chest and swung her around.

Jed looked up and moaned, "Lord, they look like chaperones." He whirled her again and yelped like a beaten dog. He felt good! He loved the way his body moved—dancing, doing pushups, playing ball. He knew that Raymond had contempt for these things, but to hell with Raymond.

"Shoot, boys, this is living, ain't it?" he yelled in an exaggerated hillbilly accent to Bobby.

"Lord, you'd better know it!" Bobby called back. "Hell, I ain't had this much fun since my hound dog treed a skunk!"

"God, I'm freezing," Emily muttered.

"You ought to be, in that handkerchief," Raymond replied, gesturing to her bandanna halter. He put his arm around her—under the pretense of warming her, but actually because he found her touching. She tried hard to participate in this crap. He found it difficult to believe she could want to. She was dressed like the other girls, but she couldn't carry it off. She looked white and cold and self-conscious.

He had already accepted that he would never be "one of the boys," with a case of Bud in his trunk and a pack of Trojan Enz in his glove compartment. He was beginning to take pride in it. Last fall he'd gone hunting with Jed and two of his dumb football friends, Hank and Bobby. Raymond wanted to do a photo-series on hunting. Hank's family had a hunting shack on the side of Buck Mountain. Their Jeep lurched along a rutted dirt track for miles. The shack consisted of a ten-by-ten room, lean-to kitchen, and attached latrine. Bunks along the wall, chairs and table, wood stove.

The first night they sat around the table drinking Bud and playing stud poker and discussing who had done what to which of their female classmates.

"Sure Betty will blow you," Jed assured Hank. "She loves it. Just give her a call."

"She loves to blow you maybe. That don't mean she'd blow me."

"Betty don't love to blow me. She loves to blow, period. You call her and see if that ain't so."

Once they were drunk, they rolled outside with their pistols and conducted target practice by the full moon, howling with laughter as bullets ricocheted through the forest.

When they stumbled back in, Raymond was feigning sleep in his bunk. After more beer and more poker, Hank took off his belt, and they used it to measure their erections.

"Christ," Bobby muttered, "you could use that damn thing for a crutch, Tatro." They collapsed on the table with laughter.

"Jesus, you're a goddam homo, Bobby!" Hank yelled.

Raymond fell authentically asleep. Sometime later he woke up and saw the three still at the table. Hank and Bobby were smoking Pall Malls, holding them between thumb and forefinger. They were looking at each other, smiling and nodding, as they slowly lowered the cigarettes, burning tips first, toward their forearms. Repeatedly they glanced back and forth from the burning tips to each other's eyes. Raymond watched, fascinated, as the tips got closer and closer to flesh, each waiting for the other to back out.

Hairs on each forearm flared and shriveled. Raymond felt his stomach turn as both tips burned into both forearms. Neither Hank nor Bobby made a sound or ceased to smile as he ground out his cigarette in his arm. The odor of seared flesh filled the cabin. Hank and Bobby laughed and shook hands.

Raymond had been here before—out at the lake once with some boys from school. They dove from a cliff into an impossibly small pool with submerged boulders around its edges. As more and more beer was consumed, they climbed higher and higher up the cliff. Raymond squatted to one side, watching as one boy after another made his dive and surfaced in one piece. He couldn't remember what had finally stopped them.

Throughout junior high and high school he was witness to dozens of fights in response to real or fabricated insults, which were preceded by an elaborate round of challenge and rebuttal, conducted by friends of the combatants, culminating in the setting of a time and a place for the fight. Once he himself had been swept into this ritual. He'd been standing outside the junior high doorway chatting with friends. Louanne Little slunk by in a full skirt with many crinolines, a cinch belt, and a tight short-sleeved angora sweater that revealed massive tits at a time when most girls still wore slips. Raymond had been impressed, and a little bit awed; also somewhat frightened. A friend muttered something about how "trashy" she was. Her boyfriend Clyde stalked up in his black leather motorcycle cap and jacket and stomping boots and asked, "Hey, you guys seen Louanne?"

They pointed in the direction of her departure. As Clyde stomped off, Raymond opened the lid to the trash can, peered into it, and called, "Louanne honey, you down there?" His friends killed themselves laughing. But Clyde heard too. He turned around glaring. Raymond released the lid and gave him a sickly smile. All day he received messages via Clyde's minions that he was to meet him at the bus stop after school. All day he sent messages back that he had a dentist appointment, was sorry about the misunderstanding, etc. As he sneaked out the side door after school, Clyde was waiting for him. A circle of heckling bystanders rapidly closed around them.

"Look, Clyde, I'm sorry. I was just trying to be funny. But I can see it wasn't funny. It was just mean. And untrue." Clyde had his fists up and was circling him. "Let's shake," Raymond suggested with a weak smile, holding out his hand.

"Get your hands up, fairy punk."

Raymond felt as though he were in a madhouse. A switch had been thrown, and the charge of electricity had to complete its circuit. There was no way out. The crowd was howling words of encouragement, taunts, and jeers. He lifted his fists.

"Oh come on, Clyde, let's forget it," he pleaded, as Clyde's fist buried itself in his stomach. He doubled over.

As he straightened up and tried to catch his breath, he gasped, "OK, I give up. You win, Clyde." A blow to the side of his head felled him. But it also made him really angry. He leaped up and hurled himself at Clyde, his fists flailing, David confronting Goliath.

A couple of minutes later someone yelled that the principal was on his way. The crowd fled in all directions. Clyde and Raymond snarled, then shook hands hastily. Raymond dragged himself home with bloodied mouth, swelling eyes, and aching knuckles.

Jed, Bobby, Hank, and Raymond stalked through the autumn leaves. Raymond toted his camera and attachments. He shot pictures while the others shot birds and rabbits and looked for deer. They emerged into a field, tromped across it, and came to a small house. Nearby was a pen. A man in overalls sat on the fence looking down into the pen. It contained two huge pigs. They were grunting furiously and circling each other.

"Howdy," Jed said.

"Howdy," the farmer replied. They leaned on the fence, watching the boar trying to mount the sow.

After a while Jed said with a grin, "Hell, I'd a been on her and off again three times by now." Everyone but the farmer chuckled.

He looked Jed up and down and drawled, "I reckon I oughta hire you to breed her instead."

They hit a dirt road and followed it, leaving the forest behind. At a crossroads was a general store. Out front, on scales, hung a deer carcass. Blood dripped onto the dirt, languid flies buzzed. Half a dozen pickup trucks were parked nearby, a couple with does tied to their roofs. A dozen unshaven men in overalls and undershirts and work shoes stood by the scales drinking clear liquid from Mason jars. A poster on the side of the store was entitled Doe Pool, and underneath were names and numbers. In a cage next to the scale was a moth-eaten black bear. One man kept poking his rifle barrel through the wire mesh. The bear swatted at it and shrank up against the far side. The man would move around to the bear's new location and poke her again, grinning and looking to the others for approval.

Jed, Hank, and Bobby were soon passing the jars back and forth, talking and laughing. Raymond stood to one side, trying to be unobtrusive about snapping pictures. He was aware he was using his camera as an excuse not to join in. Because he couldn't. He got drunk on one beer. He always lost at poker. He choked when he tried to smoke. He hadn't shot a gun since he used to go mistletoe shooting at Christmas. Once his father had taken him and Jed hunting. They very carefully flushed a big buck in his direction. He raised his rifle, trained it on the buck. He was a pretty good shot from years of target practice on beer cans in the fields behind the Princes' house. There was no way he could miss. But when the moment came to squeeze the trigger, he didn't.

"What's the point?" he asked as his father and Jed came yelling toward him. "If we were starving, I could see it, but we're not." They stared.

"I tell you the truth," Jed was saying, "when I get a buck in my sights and am getting ready to pull that trigger, I just love that animal. I really do. It's like I'm a part of it, and it's a part of me." What is wrong with me? Raymond wondered as he glanced at the rifle barrels glinting in the sun, and at the patches of gore drying in the dust.

As Raymond and Emily stood up to dance, the music stopped. The president of the Girls' Union, which was sponsoring the dance, appeared before the microphone. "Well, I guess this is the moment we've all been waiting for!" she shouted. "Now, I want all the boys over on my right, and all the girls on my left." Chaos, as the room rearranged itself. She shrieked over the din, "Now, the boys will get them a thirty-second head start . . . and the last boy to get caught and brought back here wins a prize! So put on your track shoes, boys. And get set. And—go!" Boys raced into the halls, up into the bleachers, into the dressing rooms, searching for hiding places like ants under an overturned stone.

"See you," Emily called to Raymond as he sauntered away, torn between wanting to participate for Emily's sake and thinking it was dumb.

"All right, girls!" screamed the president. "Go get 'em!"

The gym floor erupted into squeals and giggles as girls charged off in all directions. Sally flew up the bleacher steps two at a time, grabbed a post with one hand and swung around it, raced down the aisle, jumped and grabbed Jed around the neck and shoulders from behind. He staggered and fell, and they lay on the floor giggling and panting.

Emily spotted Raymond in the hall, standing with one hand on his hip, looking into the trophy case. Short and skinny and acned, the only boy not in overalls. She sauntered over, tapped him on the shoulder, and said, "Gotcha." They gazed into the trophy case at the dozens of gold-plated men bearing aloft balls of different sizes, bats, javelins. There were real balls, autographed and dated. Photos of championship teams.

After the dance they sat in his father's car in Emily's driveway, positioned so that a magnolia tree shielded them from the house, though this precaution was hardly necessary since they sat on opposite sides of the seat. Raymond knew what was expected of him: He should slide across, wrap Emily in his arms, cover her face with wet kisses, rummage around with his hands until she called him off. It was insulting not to at least try. But he wasn't interested. Emily was like a sister. Maybe it was the incest taboo? The ritual of courtship. He just couldn't see it. All the maneuvering, knowing that in the end you'd still have to jerk yourself off when you got home. The girl would be scared of wrecking her reputation, or of getting pregnant. Wayne had maybe ruined him for this game. That had been so straightforward. Each had needs the other could fulfill—for talk, tenderness, and ejaculation, in approximately that order. The idea of backseat struggles with some confused girl left him cold.

Emily regarded him from the corner of her eye, hoping he wasn't about to pounce, as he did every now and then. They'd spent some time in the past kissing, without fervor. What was the point? They were friends. Why not leave it at that? But boys seemed to feel they had to prove something or other. Emily pretended to respond so as not to hurt their feelings.

Raymond drew a deep breath and scooted dutifully across the seat. Gingerly he took Emily in his arms. He pressed his mouth to hers.

Emily trembled all over trying to conceal revulsion. Probably she was frigid. Poor Raymond. She remembered their first kiss—during Spin the Bottle in seventh grade, behind the furnace in someone's basement. She had been a wreck trying to decide whether to moisten her lips with her tongue as they walked back there. Where did the noses go? Where did people put their hands? Should she close her eyes? Now she knew none of this made much difference—it was still awkward and pointless.

Raymond felt Emily trembling. He felt terrible. She was all worked up, and he was about to throw up. He surfaced for air, stroking her hair, and trying to figure out how to put an end to this without hurting her feelings.

"I have to go in," she announced. Her mother was flashing the front porch light, to break up their clinch, as she imagined. Emily was startled when her mother did this because it indicated she was aware of and concerned about Emily's activities. Emily found this notion difficult to accept because her mother was so unobtrusive a presence, running the household and working in her gardens with no interest in dispensing advice, as other girls' mothers did so insistently. On her good days Emily was flattered. Her mother credited her with enough sense to run her own life. But on her bad days she wished there were some adult guidance, if only so that she could reject it. The atmosphere in her house seemed to be that of restrained uncertainty. And the message emanating from her parents was that since this world was too much for them, she was on her own.

"So soon?" asked Raymond, scooting across to his door.

At her doorstep he kissed her forehead. They exchanged smiles and thank-yous. As she shut the door, Emily wondered if she should make more effort to date other boys. People thought of Raymond and her as a couple, though, so that no one else asked her out. On the rare occasions when someone had, it had been awful. She would think up topics for discussion as she bathed, then memorize a word incorporating the first letter of each topic. Most recently her word for the evening had been "scab." S was for snow: What did he think of those four inches they had had? Didn't the winters seem to be getting colder? C was for cheerleader: Which of the sophomores did he think would make it next year? How did he like the new cheer at the last pep rally, in which the cheerleaders linked themselves to form a train and chugged around the gym? A was for Athlete-of-the-Year award: Doug Bennett or Hank Osborne? B was for basketball: The upcoming game—did they have a chance against the Snake Hollow Rattlers? How did this year's team compare to last year's? Would they make it to the championship play-offs in Nashville? Did he plan to go?

Raymond, though, didn't need to be coaxed; and when he talked, it was about things no one else even thought about, like tonight he had been telling her about famous men in Czechoslovak history, based on a set of stamps he had just received from New York. But the fact remained that she didn't enjoy kissing him. Whereas the others she didn't enjoy talking to, but could sometimes manage to kiss without revulsion.

As he walked across the damp lawn toward his house, Raymond decided he should date other girls. He liked Emily better than anyone else, but he didn't love her, if loving her meant wanting to kiss her and all. Maybe he was a fairy. He looked up and saw his house—a squat white box that needed painting. Open porch across the front with a sloping roof and lounge chairs. He contrasted it to the house he had just come from, Emily's three-storey yellow wood thing with pointy roofs and fancy woodwork. It came to him that her family was rich, and his was poor—not hungry or anything, but there were no extras. He and Jed had always worked for their clothes and spending money. Emily and Sally never had. But of course they were girls. Yet they lived in the same town, shared ancestors, their fathers worked at the same mill. . . .

He plopped down in his desk chair and sorted through a pile of stamps. He picked up one from Madagascar and studied it under the light. The background was scarlet, the lettering gold leaf. A smiling Negro woman in a headscarf carried a basket on her head. He ran his fingertips gently across the stamp and felt the thrill that a new stamp from an unfamiliar country gave him. He glanced at his map, located the island. Tomorrow he would look it up in the encyclopedia at school. Who lived there? What did they do? What was the weather like?

Why do I care? he asked himself. He removed his glasses and rubbed his eyes.

As Jed drove out of the parking lot after the dance and headed for Sally's house, she asked, "Are you taking me home now?"

He gave her a look. "Isn't that what you want?"

"No," she said in a small voice.

"What *do* you want?"

"You."

"Yeah, I've heard that one before."

"Can't we go to the quarry and talk about it?"

"I'm tired of talking about it."

He glanced at her cleavage, left exposed by her blouse, the tails of which were tied under her tits to form a halter. He wanted his hand in there.

"Please, Jed."

The moon, a fat orange globe, had just cleared the quarry wall. Darkened cars were all around. "OK. Talk. I'm listening," Jed said, a sulky expression on his shadowy face.

"I've thought it over. I think we should compromise."

"What do you think I been doing?"

"Well, so have I."

"Hasn't looked that way to me."

Her turn to sulk. Her lower lip protruded.

"OK. What?" Jed asked.

"Never mind."

"OK." He started the engine. She grabbed his hand and made his fingers turn it off. Then she ran her fingertips over his palm.

"I think we should keep our hands above the waist," she announced.

He pushed her hand away irritably and sank back in the seat with a long-suffering sigh. "Some compromise. That's the same thing you've been saying."

"Not exactly it isn't," she whispered.

The moonlight shone on the tops of her white breasts. He felt himself getting hard.

"But inside the clothes?" he asked, his voice quavering.

She said nothing.

"Well?"

"Yes, all right."

He scooted over and put his arms around her. They kissed. Then he slid his hand down into her cleavage, until he clasped a breast. He lifted it out of the bra cup and took the nipple in his mouth. Sally looked down at his flat-top and giggled, embarrassed. Babies sucked their mothers' nipples, but she hadn't known grown boys did.

"What?" he asked, looking up.

"Nothing," she murmured. She felt like his mother. She kept reminding herself to keep track of his other hand.

Emily's Girl Scout troop was training for a one-week trek along the Appalachian Trail that summer by going on day-hikes with thirty-five-pound packs. They wore jeans, hiking boots, and flannel shirts. The trees had a chartreuse tinge. The redbuds and pink and white dogwoods put the other trees to shame. The earthworms had barely begun their spring clean-up so that the cushion of dead leaves on the trail was still thick. Occasionally they sang as they marched in single file: "*Valderee, valderah, valderee, valderah, ha, ha, ha, ha, ha . . .*"

Mostly they walked in silence, glancing around dazzled by the spring light, like movie patrons emerging into midday sun. Emily ran her hands under her pack straps where they cut into her shoulders. Leaves rustled as chipmunks, snakes, toads, and squirrels scooted out of their way. Emily loved the weight on her back and the power in her legs as she covered mile after mile in a steady stride. She wore an olive army cap, and the sun through the swelling branches danced on and under the visor. The sense of failure with which she had gone to bed the previous night fell away. She knew each bird song, could name each tree and wild flower. Some people were good at partying, others were good at other things. She made good grades without trying. Sports were easy. She was a Curved Bar Girl Scout. She had played flute in the All-State Band. Admittedly, these things weren't important in Newland, but that wasn't her fault.

They'd been hiking along an almost treeless ascending spine of rock. Scrubby blueberry bushes were all around them. At the end of the ridge they came to a bald—a mountaintop above the tree line covered with coarse grass. Dumping their packs, they lay in the sun in the tall grass and ate sandwiches, chatting lazily about the dance.

After lunch they headed down the mountainside through a hardwood forest. Partway down, they entered a hollow formed by a rushing, boulder-strewn creek. Eventually the woods thinned to a clearing. Several dogs began howling. In the clearing sat a shack, covered with tar paper and roofed with tin soft-drink signs and black and white Tennessee license plates. Perched on stilts against the hillside, it had an open porch across the front. Five blue-tick hounds threw themselves against their chains, which were attached to the stilts. It looked as though they might pull the shack down at any moment. The creek out front was littered with cans and bottles, an old refrigerator, three gutted auto carcasses. Wash hung on a network of lines strung among the trees and the stilts. Six or eight little children played in a scrambled heap near a pile of coal. When they saw the Girl Scouts marching down the hollow, they jumped up, froze and gazed through pale blue eyes. Matted blonde hair obscured smudged faces, soiled shorts hung just below dirty potbellies.

As the others marched on, Emily took off her pack and pulled out some apples and brownies and held them toward the children. They seized each other's hands and edged more closely together.

Emily heard a door slam. Looking up to the porch, she saw a gaunt woman in a long dress, an apron, and high-topped work shoes.

"I was just . . ."

"Thanky just the same, ma'am, but we don't want nothing from nobody," the woman intoned as though it were a recorded message.

"Oh. Sure. I'm sorry." Emily grabbed her pack by the frame and dragged it after her down the path.

When she told her family about the incident that night at supper, her father murmured, "Well, life is difficult, Emily."

Emily frowned. "How come?"

Her father smiled grimly. "It's not a very nice world."

"Now Robert . . ." Mrs. Prince began.

"I think it's a neat world!" insisted Sally.

Mr. Prince shrugged.

As Raymond drove the twisting road into the mountains, he recalled the trips with his family back to the cove his father had left to come to Newland. He and Jed always insisted on being let out of the car the minute they turned off the main road. They raced up the washed-out dirt road to find their cousins, with whom they took off into the woods, scarcely to be seen until it was time to go home. He and Jed basked in prestige because they could instruct their cousins on town ways—what went on in the factories, how to shop in supermarkets, what it was like to ride a bicycle on a sidewalk. Streetlights, movies, drugstores, escalators, boxes that X-rayed your feet for shoe size, pinball machines, carnivals, beauty pageants, bowling alleys.

But of course their cousins knew where to hide to see which animal. They could look at the sky and sniff the air and tell what kind of weather it would be. They knew which berries and leaves you could eat. They could carve anything from a piece of wood. They got to drink whiskey when they were sick. They could shoot knots off pine trees from a hundred yards. They never had to wear shoes, and they could miss school whenever they wanted. And they were all right there—dozens of cousins, aunts, uncles, grandparents. All Tatros, and all in one county.

Raymond remembered thinking it was neat. He hadn't been able to understand why his father had left. He was having the same difficulty today. It seemed like such an uncomplicated life. If his father had never left, Raymond wouldn't be facing this decision about what to do when he graduated. He'd have married and gone to work in a mine a couple of years ago. As things were, he had no idea what to do. The guidance counselor had given up on him. His grades were too lousy for a scholarship to college, and his father couldn't afford to send him. Besides, he couldn't see spending four more years failing to do work he wasn't interested in. His father kept offering him a tour of the mill. His mother was predicting that Jed would grow up to be vice president over there. What he'd grow up to be she'd never speculated on, which bothered him. As though his future wasn't worth thinking about, and Raymond was a foundling or something who had never really belonged in her family. Of course there was the job in New York City. But that would involve leaving everything. Whenever he thought about it, he got furious with Emily. She'd go straight from high school into college. She had good grades and a father with dough. She'd spend four years doing whatever she wanted and would graduate to marry some guy who'd support her for the rest of her life. Girls had it easy. Of course his own mother had always worked, but Emily would never have to if she married some college guy.

He stopped at Tatro Cove. His grandparents lived in a simple, well-tended white frame house at the end of the cove. It was two-storey but only one room wide, with stone fireplaces on either end and porches with railings top and bottom. His grandparents sat on the downstairs porch rocking and looking across the creek to the steep ridge on the other side. Raymond remembered that when their family would arrive here, his father would be tense and would stand on the porch shifting from leg to leg, talking gruffly. By the time they had to leave, he'd be lying barefooted on the porch with his feet propped on the railing, chatting languidly or dreaming in silence. And on the trip home, they could watch the tension start seeping back into his body, as though starch were being injected into his bloodstream.

"Well, sir, who do we have here?" exclaimed his grandfather, standing slowly with the aid of a cane. His other arm was missing below the elbow. The sleeve of his green workshirt was folded up and pinned to the shoulder. "I reckon it's young Junior, Mother."

"Well, I declare," she said, accepting his peck on her weathered cheek.

Raymond sat on the step, wishing he hadn't stopped because now he couldn't think of anything to say. "I'm going over near Clayton to take me some pictures and just thought I'd stop and say hi."

"Law, what you want pictures of Clayton for?" his grandfather asked.

"Well, sometimes newspapers and magazines call me up and want pictures of coal mines and stuff."

"That a fact? Shoot, if I'd a known that, I'd a bought me a camera and made my fortune!"

"What's new?" Raymond asked, amused, since nothing was new over here, which was the whole appeal.

"Oh, nothing much. Lyle and his wife had them a new baby last week. A girl, was it, Mother?" She smiled and nodded and rocked.

"Is that his second?" Lyle, Raymond's cousin, was only two years older. All the cousins with whom he had roamed the surrounding hills were married now with small children. Raymond felt like a kid.

"The creek started in to rising a couple of days ago, but I don't think it's gonna amount to much. Do you, Mother?" She smiled, shook her head no, and rocked.

"Killed me a big old copperhead in the garden patch yesterday.

Musta been two feet long. Don't you guess, Mother?" She smiled, nodded, and rocked.

"Lem's blue-tick was lost for a week last month. He come in all tore up. Looked like he'd been wrassling with a bar, didn't he, Mother?" She smiled, nodded, and rocked.

The hot sun and his grandfather's drone and the rumble of rockers on wood were putting Raymond to sleep. Birds called back and forth, the creek bubbled, the new foliage was blinding bright green. He breathed deeply.

"What your folks up to?" his grandfather asked.

"Oh, nothing much. Same as usual. Dad's busy at the mill."

"He works too hard, don't he?"

"Well, I guess he likes to."

"That's what happens to these fellers who go off to the city. They get all caught up in it. Now they's some that like that pace, but hit didn't never appeal to me."

"I know what you mean."

"But your daddy, he always was an itchy one. 'Now just set down and relax, son,' I used to tell him. But did you ever try telling a tornado to relax?" They chuckled. "Couldn't find him no work. Sometimes he'd cut down a tree or two for a furniture factory. The mines was always shutting down and laying people off. All you could count on was hunting, and your garden patch. And if the creek flooded, or a frost came late, even your garden failed you. Hit was a turrible time." The sun flickered across Raymond's face as a breeze swayed the tree branches.

"Well, what about that good-looking brother of yours?"

Raymond winced. He knew Jed was handsome and that he himself was pretty ordinary, but why did everyone have to emphasize it? "He's just fine. As gorgeous as ever. He lifts weights every day and is bulging with muscles. He spends a lot of time with Sally Prince. Her father runs Dad's mill."

"That a fact? Well, how about you, son? Your tennis shoes wearing thin running from all the girls?"

Raymond blushed. "I've got a girl. It's nothing too serious, though."

"Now, I'll tell you one thing, son. You'd better pick real careful-like. That's what I told all my boys. The love of a good woman is the

most important possession a man can own. Ain't that so, Mother?"
He slapped her thigh. She smiled and rocked.

"We've had us a real good life together, Grandpa and I," she
confirmed.

"We can all see that you have." Raymond was relaxed to the point
of immobility. He looked out to the garden and remembered his
father telling how after each baby was born, Grandpa had carried
it outside. "He'd hold it up, Junior, so it could see the ridges all
around, and he'd say, 'We ain't got much here, but ever speck of land
you can see belongs to Tatros, and we real proud and happy to share
it with you.' Then he'd lay the baby in a patch of sun in the garden,
and he'd say, 'The Lord give us this soil, and you got to learn how to
take care of it, so's it can take care of you.' "

Raymond had missed out on this ritual, and felt cut off. "Well,
guess I'd better move on," he announced, trying to stand up.

"Won't you stay and eat some dinner with us, Junior honey?" his
grandmother inquired.

"I'd love to, Granny. But I got to go take my pictures." The truth
was that he thought his feet would take root in the front steps if he
stayed longer. How his father escaped—and why—he would never
understand. The peace, the calm acceptance. So different from the
noisy factory, the bustling town. An owl hooted on the ridge.

"You'd better stop off and say hidy to Lyle and them."

"I can't this trip, Grandpa. I'm in a rush. But tell them I say hi."

"Come back when you can stay awhile," his grandfather called as
Raymond walked toward the car.

Raymond could hear his father's voice telling (as he had time after
tedious time) about leaving Tatro Cove: "Somebody was going to
drive me to the bus. As I walked down to the car toting my stuff in a
paper sack, I saw Pa coming down the holler driving the cow. It was
dusk, and lightning bugs was blinking all around him. On his hip sat
my sister Inez, who was a little one-year-old baby then. She was
dressed in one of them white knit gowns. She was smiling up at him
and cooing, and he was just chattering away to her. The tears in my
eyes was so thick I couldn't hardly see to get in that car."

Maybe Raymond could reverse the process? Build a cabin, work in
a mine?

He parked near a tipple with Consolidated Coal painted on it. He photographed it, and the train cars being filled one by one with gleaming black chunks, and the huge trucks with names painted on their cabs that brought in loads from the small mines for cleaning and sorting. The men, in hard hats and work clothes, slapped each other on the back and yelled jokes over the din. It was hard work, honest work. Raymond found it appealing. His uncles and cousins were coal miners. His father and grandfather had been. He'd return to the family profession. This is where he would work! He would go down into the belly of the whale, and he would emerge changed. He would emerge a man!

As he ran out of pictures to snap up above, he began to confront the fact that he would be spending the afternoon in the middle of a mountain. The previous year he had photographed some weeping widows after an explosion and cave-in in Southwest Virginia. He hoped no one would have to weep for him this afternoon.

You get used to this, he assured himself as the electric car descended into the tunnel. But until you did, it sure did feel claustrophobic. This was probably how a baby felt being propelled through its mother's birth canal: Until this moment, he hadn't realized how good he'd had it where he'd been before. He became conscious of each limb, of how much he liked and used each hand and foot and arm and leg. What if a roof bolt came loose, and several tons of slate crashed down? His grandfather had lost his arm that way.

He pulled himself together and asked the man driving the car to stop while he lit flares and snapped shots of the passageway and the tracks. On they went, deeper and deeper into the mountain, with only the long narrow tunnel connecting them to daylight.

He snapped—men running the huge continuous miner machines, loading and riding the conveyor belts, mending pumps in water to their knees, eating lunch as water dripped from the ceiling onto their sandwiches, placing roof supports. They ate away at the innards of this mountain like ravenous termites. And like a lacy termite-riddled log, was it possible the remains could collapse into powder?

He rode to the surface, feeling vomited from the maw of a hideous beast. He photographed the men, blinking in daylight, their faces except for their eyes and teeth black as the coal seam they'd been working.

In the showers, water the color of ink flowed down drains. The bodies under the showerheads were bent, twisted, scarred, and bruised. Fingernails were cracked and caked with black. The men coughed up, spit, and snorted out globs of black mucus.

Raymond grasped the fact that he was a frail and cowardly kid. He wouldn't be able to do this work even if he wanted to.

His father, with his slicked-down hair and long sideburns, was lying in green work clothes on the living room couch watching "The Beverly Hillbillies" on television. His mother, sitting in a chair, said, "You missed supper, Junior. Where you been?"

"Sorry. I was up to Clayton shooting some pictures of mining and stuff."

"That don't sound like any kind of a way to spend an afternoon," said his father.

"It was kind of interesting. But scary."

"Oh, them mines up at Clayton is downright modren. You should of seen them dog mines we used to work before all this fancy federal regulation stuff. Why, they wasn't no more than holes in the sides of hills. You put on these knee pads, kind of like basketball players wear, and you crawled in there and started hacking and shoveling. Hit's a miracle we wasn't all killed."

"I stopped off and saw Granny and Grandpa."

"Oh, that's nice. How are they?"

"They seemed fine. Same as always."

"We ought to get ourselves up there, Mrs. Tatro."

"Dad, did you come down here mostly for the work?"

"You're dang right I did. That's what life's all about once you leave school, son. You might as well start facing up to it."

"Do you ever wish you were back there?"

He lay with his eyes closed. "Oh, heck yeah, I used to miss it something fierce. Used to know ever square inch of that holler."

"The only time he used to seem halfway cheerful," Raymond's mother added, "was when the weekend came around and he could load us in the car and go back up there. But it used to take us half a day to get there, the roads was so bad."

Jethro on the television had decided to use his share of the royalties from the oil field discovered under his family's shack in the Appalachians to set himself up as a movie agent.

"Something you got to understand about that cove, Junior," his father said. "The Lord had a long hard time carving it out of them mountains. Our ancestors was the first people to ever settle there, and they had them a long hard time getting there."

"Yes sir."

Jethro was ordering himself a Cadillac and several silk suits.

"The season my daddy loved best was midwinter," Mr. Tatro resumed. "He was happy as a clam when there was a storm, and we'd all be snowed in together there in the house for a week or more. We'd whittle and play cards and listen to the Grand Ole Opry on the battery radio and mess around on the banjo. He'd almost cry when the snow melted and us kids had to go off to school and he had to go back to the mine. Course around about February we'd start running out of the stuff Ma had canned and stored from the garden. Then we'd have us biscuits with flour gravy twice a day, and wonder when the flour would give out. That wasn't no fun."

"Do you think Grandpa minds that you left?" This question seemed crucial to Raymond.

"I remember it was real hard to decide to go. I was just a wreck. I didn't really want to go at all, but it was almost like I was possessed or somethin—just couldn't set still. I heard the mill down here was hiring. Finally I went and said I was leaving. He looked at me real glum-like for a long time. Then he smiled and said, 'Well, boy, I wish you well. I always meant to leave, but I just never did get around to it.'"

He had a faraway look in his eyes. He shook himself. "But I do believe, Junior, that it's better to be able to eat regular until you're full. And to stay warm in winter, and buy your family shoes and clothes. And medicine and doctoring when they're sick. Hell fire, I know it's better. Now I know it is. But there I was that night in the Newland bus station with a brown paper sack and no money. The only thing I wanted was to get on the next bus home. Shoot, I'd never been farther away than the next county. And ever person I'd ever seen I'd been related to one way or another."

"You never saw such a hick as walked into my mama's boarding house that night," Mrs. Tatro exclaimed.

"Your mother used to wear hats all the time," his father confided. "These jobs with feathers and veils. I'd never seen anything like it in my life. White gloves too. Yeah, this old city sophisticate here took advantage of an ignorant country boy. What do you think of that, Junior?" They laughed.

His father added, "Hit ain't easy leaving what's safe and familiar, but some folks just got to. I reckon hit's in their blood to wander or something. And once you go, you can't never go back. You don't fit in no more."

Raymond studied his father, as his parents chuckled over Jethro's attempt to fake knowledge to a real movie agent of a contract he had been incapable of reading. It was strange to think of his father having been through such a drama. His life was so humdrum now. He got up and went to the mill, came home, ate supper, watched television, and went to bed. For twenty-five years. It gave Raymond the creeps.

About twice a year he'd drink too much and throw a piece of furniture at anyone who was dumb enough to stick around. And some Saturdays when he was trying to get Raymond and Jed to wash the storm windows or something, he'd start shouting about what lazy ignorant punks they were, who'd never amount to anything in this world; all his hard work had been for nothing, and why hadn't he just stayed in Tatro Cove and been happy. Once when the phone kept ringing for Raymond, he ripped the wires out of the wall. Another time, when Jed spent too long in the bathroom primping, their father kicked the door down.

Sally spent the morning helping the Girls' Union clean up from the dance. That afternoon she worked downtown at the Ingenue bake sale with Marlene Webb. They were raising money for the annual Plantation Ball. She had baked Toll House brownies, Jed's favorite, which she always baked when it was her turn as a member of the

Young Hostess Club to provide refreshments for the football team and coaches at their "Chalk Talks."

She sat at a card table in front of Anderson's Drugstore as the Saturday shoppers strolled by. As Betty French passed, in white pedal pushers and a tight black sweater, Sally whispered to Marlene, "There goes Betty French. Did you know the boys call her Betty Boobs?"

Marlene laughed. "Now, that's just awful. They ought to be ashamed."

"But you can see why, can't you? I mean she doesn't have to wear her sweaters that tight."

"She sure doesn't. And if you do, you should expect to have exactly the kind of rep she does. Ronny says she French kisses."

"No. If she knew what French kissing means, I bet she wouldn't do it."

"What does it mean?"

"Well, you can just imagine, can't you? If a boy pushes his tongue into your mouth?"

"Screwing, you mean?"

"Well, sure."

"Ronny says she does that too."

Sally sat in shocked silence. "Who with?"

"Anyone who wants it."

Sally gasped. "Just like that?"

"That's what Ronny says."

"I just can't believe it. When I think that someone even nominated her for Ingenue last year."

"I know. Wasn't that *incredible*? Next thing you know somebody will be trying to get Ina Sue Bascombe in!"

They collapsed laughing. "She doesn't even shave her legs yet!" Sally gasped between giggles.

Almost everything had sold but a few date bars and some fudge divinity. Jed sauntered up, his hands in his chino pockets. "I'll buy everything you got left, little lady," he said with his lazy grin, "if you'll drive out to the lake with me."

"You got yourself a deal, mister," Sally said with a smile, wrapping up the food and taking his money. He folded the table and chairs and carried them to his car.

"What you been up to, Good-looking?" Sally asked as they drove out of town.

"Nothing much. Worked out. Played me some basketball. Washed the car. Stuff like that. Slocombe was over at the gym when I was working out. That guy, I swear. He's so bad."

"What do you mean?"

"Aw, I don't know. It's like Coach Clancy says: 'He was standing on the wrong side of the door when the brains was being passed out, and now he don't even have enough sense to pee downwind.' You know what I mean?"

"What did he do?"

"Aw, shoot, I don't know, he just stood around with his mouth hanging open, grinning and watching me work up a sweat. I thought I'd puke after a while. It's like during a game when Coach calls you in off the field, Slocombe comes waddling up to you with a towel, and he's just so damn eager for you to like him or something. Makes you want to squash him."

"Jed, that's terrible."

"Yeah, I guess you're right." It was just too bad Jed wasn't a faggot, was all he could say. He had the feeling if he was, old Slocombe would turn around and touch his toes so you could shove it right up him.

He took a cigarette out of the pack in his shirt pocket and lit it.

"I don't know why you do that, Jed. It's just not good for you."

He grinned. "You sound more like my mama every day."

"Mama was never like this," she murmured, scooting over and putting the tip of her tongue in his ear.

He shuddered with delight. "You're right, darlin." He shrugged and threw the cigarette out the window. She took his hand and caressed his knuckles. He smiled, thinking of the surprise he'd set up for that afternoon.

The lake was flashing by off to the right. They turned down a dirt road, drove past a marina and several cottages, stopped above a field that sloped down to the water, and walked hand in hand through the high grass almost to the water. Jed spread a blanket and turned on his portable radio to the local rock and roll station. They sat and watched some distant water skiing. The lake had been formed by flooding several thousand acres of farmland. Waterlogged tree limbs still protruded close to the red clay shore. Jed lay down and pulled Sally on top of him. They nibbled each other's lips and necks. Sally rolled over on her back, and Jed sat up and chewed a piece of grass.

"Doesn't the sun feel good?" Sally sighed.

"Sure does," Jed agreed, throwing off his shirt. Sally traced his muscles with her finger.

"Goodness but you're a gorgeous man," she said in a low voice.

He lowered his chest onto hers and kissed her, his tongue moving insistently in her mouth.

She turned her head aside. "Oh Jed, stop that. That's disgusting."

He ran his hands under her blouse and unfastened her bra. He massaged her breasts and toyed with her nipples, then removed her shirt and rubbed his chest against hers. They wrapped their arms around each other. "Oh, Jed, I love you so much."

"I love *you*," he murmured, running one hand slowly up her thigh.

She pushed him off and sat up.

"What's wrong?"

"Jed, you promised."

"What did I promise?"

"We agreed last night: no hands below the waist."

"Aw, shit, Sally. What's this 'I love you so much' crap."

"It's not crap. And what does that have to do with it anyway?"

"If you really loved me, you'd want me as much as I want you."

"If *you* really loved *me*, you wouldn't want me to do things I don't want to do."

"You do want it, but you don't know that you want it."

"And I need you to show me?"

"Right."

She threw on her bra and shirt, jumped up and stomped toward the car. "Take me home."

"All right, I will! And for the last time, too!"

"Good!"

"Who're you saving it for, Sally? The worms?"

"You're *disgusting*."

On the trip home she had to bite her lower lip to keep from crying. She knew what Jed wanted. She knew what her daddy wanted. She knew what the Lord wanted. What she herself wanted was to do what they wanted. But they all wanted different things.

"I hope you have a good life," he growled as she got out. Women! Jesus Christ almighty! Coach Clancy was right: You only needed them for two things, and one was to get your meals on the table.

He bought a case of beer and picked up Bobby and Hank at the basketball court. On the way to the lake, Hank reached into the glove compartment for a church key and pulled out an unopened box of condoms. "Not going so great, huh, Jed?"

"Shut up."

They rode in Bobby's family's motorboat to a ski jump and climbed out on the sloping canvas surface. Hank turned on Jed's radio. They lay on the jump drinking and smoking, throwing empty cans and butts into the water. The D.J. said, "And now we have a special request for the Dixie Cups singing 'Chapel of Love.' We're sending it out this afternoon to Sally. Sally, Jed says he loves you, gal, and thank you . . . just for being you . . ."

Jed grabbed the radio and hurled it into the lake.

"Who needs em, huh?" Bobby muttered.

"You ain't kidding."

After taking them home, Jed went to a phone booth. "Hey, Betty. It's me, Jed. You want to tip a few tonight?"

"Well, well. Isn't Blondie putting out for our Jeddy?"

"Never mind. Forget I asked."

"Just teasing," she said. "Sure. I'd like to go drinking with you. Pick me up in half an hour."

He went to a drive-in and ate a pork barbecue and drank a milk shake, which sobered him up enough to realize he should be going home to bed. Instead he drove across the bridge from the paper mill to Cherokee Shoals, then wove through the network of dirt roads which were lined with sagging cottages with cluttered yards. He stopped and hopped out, dodging a bunch of planters that Betty had once made by cutting up and painting old tires to make them look like open flower blossoms. Her father had tried without success to sell them at his shack on the highway. As Jed entered the messy house, he saw Injun Al himself, sprawled on the sofa in his buckskins. His war bonnet lay on a table, and a jar of clear liquid stood on the floor beside his outflung hand. He was snoring loudly. Betty came out in white pedal pushers, black flats, and a tight black pullover sweater. Her hair was teased into a beehive, and she wore bright red lipstick and mascara.

"Hey, Betty. Looking good," Jed said.

"Thanks, doll. You look pretty terrible yourself."

"I was out at the lake drinking beer all afternoon."

"You sure you want to keep going?"

"Yeah."

They roared across the bridge, up the hill, down Sally's street, and down a dirt road through the field behind her house. The Chevy pitched and bobbed, and Betty held on to the dashboard. The full moon coming up over the North Carolina mountains bathed the pasture in an orange glow. The Chevy hurtled to a stop in the woods. Jed jumped out and grabbed some beers, a flashlight, and blanket. Betty followed him as he crouched down and duckwalked into the powder magazine.

Inside the hollow chamber, he spread the blanket and attached the flashlight to the wall like a sconce. He threw himself down, opened two beers, and handed one to Betty.

They drank and he complained about Sally, while Betty patted him, sympathizing. "Why do you bother?"

"Oh, I don't know. She's so pretty and all like that. Her daddy running the mill. I guess it makes me feel important or something. You know what I mean?"

"That's the truest thing you ever said," she remarked.

Eventually he rolled over and buried his head in her lap.

"Hey, I thought we was just drinking beer tonight."

"When have we ever just drunk beer?"

"There's a first time for everything."

"You mean you're not gonna screw me?"

"Oh, all right. Why the hell not?"

"That's the spirit," he said, unzipping her pedal pushers.

He was finished in a matter of seconds, whimpering and burying his face in her neck as he came. He pulled away, sat up, guzzled half a beer, and lit a cigarette, all of a sudden in a terrible mood. She had seen him weak, needing her.

"Maybe someday, if we keep this up," she murmured, "you'll even learn how to screw."

"You don't like how I do it?"

"What's there to like? Or to dislike?"

"What do you mean?" He was always the first to come during the circle jerks in junior high. He had the biggest dick in the whole school. What did she want anyhow—a telephone pole?

"You're too fast. A girl likes it slow, with a lot of hugging and kissing."

"Shit, I been hugging and kissing all week."

"But not with me, darlin. Come on now, I ain't through with you yet." She began stroking him.

"I'm too tired." Actually he was terrified of how much she enjoyed screwing. She couldn't seem to get enough. She acted like a man that way, and he didn't like it. She mounted him and moved up and down on him. He looked down his chest to where her tits swung back and forth over him and was flooded with contempt. Her need was so great. It disgusted him. Sally, whatever their difficulties, was a lady. She would never behave like this. Let's face it: Betty Boobs was a whore.

Afterward she murmured, "You're such a bastard, Jed."

"I ain't no bastard," he said with his lazy grin. "I can be real sweet."

"You *can* be, but you ain't never."

He lunged for her left nipple with his teeth, snapping them shut a fraction of an inch away. "See? I coulda bit your tit off and I didn't. Ain't that sweet?"

"If that's sweet, honey, then we're all in bad trouble." She cradled his handsome head in her arms as though he were a big baby and tousled his light brown flat-top until he fell asleep.

# Chapter Three

## The Minstrel Show

The gym was packed for the Civic Club's annual minstrel show. Many of the prominent business and professional men in town sat in chairs in tiered rows on a stage. They wore orange satin tuxedos with exaggerated lapels, battered top hats, and white gloves. Their faces were blackened, and they held tambourines.

Dr. Pridemore, the town orthodontist, was doing a soft shoe routine to the tune "When Nighttime Comes to Ole Nigger Town." A banker and an insurance salesman were behind him, ineptly parodying. Every time he turned around, they'd be resting on their canes, looking off into the distance and whistling through thickened red lips. The audience was screaming with laughter.

Emily was sitting in the bleachers beside her friend June. Raymond crouched below the stage snapping pictures. Jed and Sally sat a couple of rows below Emily. Jed was trying to slide his hand up Sally's thigh. Sally slapped the hand and said something petulant. Neither took their eyes from the stage. Mr. and Mrs. Prince, Mr. Prince Sr., with his bushy white hair and eyebrows, and Mrs. Tatro Sr. sat in folding chairs on the gym floor. Raymond and Jed's mother, on the far side of the room, was tugging at her skirt trying to cover her slip. Her husband, his long legs crossed at the knees and his chin resting on his fist, was chuckling.

A minstrel named Rastus, who owned a lumber yard in real life, was asking the interlocutor, whose face wasn't blackened, if he'd heard about his cousin LeRoy.

"No, I don't believe I have, Rastus," said the interlocutor. "Tell me about your cousin LeRoy."

"Law, Cap'n, dat man de dumbest thing you ever did see!"

"You say your cousin LeRoy is dumb, Rastus? That's a pretty serious accusation. Why do you say your cousin LeRoy is dumb?"

"Boss, dat man so dumb he went and robbed him a clothing store."

The interlocutor looked blank. "Well, I don't know that robbing a store is a very good idea, Rastus, but I still don't see why that makes your cousin LeRoy the dumbest thing that ever lived."

"My cousin LeRoy, he so dumb, Cap'n, dat when he rob dis clothing store, he put on de new clothes and leave his old ones in de store!"

The audience howled, and the minstrels high-stepped around the stage, shaking tambourines and wiping tears of laughter from their blackened faces.

Mr. Prince Jr. was feeling guilty for not being up on that stage. The Civic Club used to invite him to join every few years. Sometimes he'd try by attending their luncheons in the club room at the Howard Johnson Motel while they planned the Junior Miss Pageant, or this minstrel show. But for some reason, he felt awkward, and so did they. The other men were self-conscious in his presence, and meetings never got off the ground. It seemed as though the biggest help he could give them was to stay away. Even though he'd lived in Newland his whole life, he couldn't do the accent required for this show. And apart from earning money for the Civic Club, he didn't actually understand the appeal of ridiculing Negroes. He'd been raised by Negro women, his mother, a Newland native, being at club meetings a lot. His parents had always treated those women kindly. It upset him to see them made fun of. But he'd learned as a boy to keep such upset to himself, because people around you didn't necessarily share it. And if you wanted to get along with them, you couldn't be accusatory and self-righteous. You were responsible only for your own attitudes and behavior, not for those of your neighbors as well. So you performed a variety of moral self-violation. Which explained how he was able to sit through this minstrel show every year, smiling at the right places. A few weeks before, at church, a young man from Baltimore who was trying out for old Mr. Shell's job had delivered a sermon in which he urged the executives in the congregation to hire more Negroes and to exert their influence to integrate the schools.

Several men stomped out, but Robert Prince stayed seated and was secretly delighted. Times were changing. A new order was coming. His only regret was that he himself was part of the debris that would have to be swept away to make room for it.

Even in high school Robert had felt a gap between himself and his peers. He was the son of a Yankee, the son of their fathers' boss. They were mostly sons of dirt farmers and coal miners down from the hills. They talked different and carried themselves different from Robert, who was a town-born North-South hybrid. They were silent, proud, elaborately polite, and treated him with respectful banter. But among themselves they drank and fought and courted. He longed to participate, but didn't know how to make it happen—and the initiative in relations with them was always up to him. He'd been a loner, had hung around with the few other offspring of professional and managerial families who hadn't been sent North to boarding schools. And toward the end of high school he began dating Melanie Tatro, now Mrs. Prince. Her father was a vice president at the mill under Robert's own father, and they'd known each other forever. It was a match so obvious that, after it happened, everyone wondered why it hadn't happened sooner.

He had gone off to Princeton, where he first came in contact with novels about the British in India and Africa and began to get some perspective on why he felt so out of place in Newland, why his parents' friends looked to the North for standards of sophistication and civilization. He also discovered that to the golden Yankee youth at Princeton he was just another dumb hillbilly, something he'd yearned to be back home. He studied hybridization in biology class and understood that he was doomed to this stance of never quite fitting in with members of either parent species. He might as well stop trying because it just wasn't going to happen.

The following year Melanie went to Randolph-Macon. They traveled to each other's schools for dances and party weekends, and were married in Newland in a big ceremony at the Episcopal church right after her graduation. He'd begun at the mill the previous year and was being groomed to take over when his father decided to retire, which everyone was convinced would be never. It was like being the Prince of Wales to his father's Queen Victoria.

He glanced at his father, who sat next to him with liver spots all over his hands and face. What had confounded Robert's Princeton theorizing was the knowledge that his father, who was from Philadelphia, was able to carry it all off. He'd never been a minstrel up on that stage, but he used to roll up his shirt-sleeves and stroll through the mill all the time, chatting with the workers. He knew most on a first-name basis, as well as their spouses and children, from many years of company barbecues. He could inquire about their latest surgery, their new houses, their softball league. In many cases, their fathers and mothers had also worked at the mill; their cousins and aunts and uncles worked there; their children would eventually work there. They would sometimes ask him, as a favor, to take on a brother or a daughter, and he would do his best. Ever since he'd been able to walk, Robert had been taken on these journeys through the mill by his father, as training.

Heads were craning throughout the minstrel show audience to catch a glimpse of old Mr. Prince. The older people in the well-fed, well-dressed crowd that night felt they owed their current prosperity to his prudent stewardship of the mill. Old Mr. Prince felt so too. Robert knew there was no question of this in the old man's mind: He'd taken a poor muddy little market town and put it on the industrial map, through his own personal foresight and hard work and optimism. At one time Robert had tried to discuss his problems running the mill with his father. The world economic climate was shifting. Just as contracts had been switched from Lawrence, Massachusetts, to Newland, Tennessee, due to cheaper labor, so were they now being switched to Taiwan and the Philippines, where workers were paid thirty-five cents an hour. Just as harness makers had been doomed by the arrival of the auto, so was cotton manufacture doomed by the arrival of synthetic fibers.

"Poppycock!" his father shouted, bushy white eyebrows twitching. "Don't hand me any of your Princeton bullshit, son! I want *action*, not excuses!" His father, who hadn't been to college, delighted in ridiculing Princeton, even though he'd pushed Robert to go there, in a seizure of keeping up with the other professional families in town. So Robert was a class hybrid as well as a regional one. And the result of all this hybridization was uncertainty. He had difficulty ever giving himself wholly to any course of action. He agonized, and delayed decisions, hoping someone else would make them for him, hoping the necessity for making them would evaporate if he ignored them. He felt loyalty to no one group. And whenever he tried to exercise blind allegiance, he was wracked with guilt over all the alternatives he was dismissing.

This unfortunate personality structure almost cost him his life during World War II. He was on a plane from England to Belgium when the instruments went screwy. They wandered around in a thick fog until the fuel was running out, and then had to crash land behind German lines. As captain he knew he was supposed to lead the crew back to no-man's-land. In the dark, with bursts of shell fire on the horizon, he studied the maps and compasses and terrain for a long time, then set out toward a woods. At the woods he turned around and led them back in the direction of the wreckage. This went on until his sergeant grasped the fact that Robert didn't have a clue what he was doing, and took over. It was all written off to shock from the crash, and battle fatigue. The crew joked with him about it for the rest of the war. He'd never let on to anyone that it hadn't been shock or fatigue, but indecision and terror. He'd been in full control of his faculties, but hadn't been able to make up his mind and had been overcome with anxiety. He'd smiled wryly as his father told about leading his platoon over the ridge in the Argonne Forest as showers of shells exploded all around them like a fireworks display.

All his life he'd been thrust into leadership positions because he was his father's son, or a Princeton graduate. But he didn't like leading, or have a gift for it. He hated it—with his soldiers during the war, and now with his workers—when they came up to him with those cringing grins to ask what to do about their personal lives, or work problems, or anything. How the hell should he know? Some mornings he couldn't even decide whether to wear green or brown socks. His father talked about "captaining his ship" and "commanding his troops," and everybody loved it, most of all his father. But Robert, alas, knew that there were economic forces at work that nobody, not even his father, could control. He wondered if it was precisely because individual choices seemed to make so little difference that he had such a hard time making them.

A minstrel named Abraham Lincoln Jones, the town's leading pharmacist, jumped up. "Hey, boss," he called to the interlocutor.

"Yes, Abraham? What can I do for you?"

Raymond held his camera in readiness and studied the men. They looked like the coal miners he'd photographed in Clayton, after they'd emerged from the mine, when the only white on their faces was that of their eyes and teeth. The men who mined coal and these minstrels who in real life wore coats and ties and worked in clean offices—how were they different? Was it just a question of chance—whether you were born on Tsali Street or in a Kentucky hollow? He inspected this new thought.

". . . you say your wife finally figured out how not to have babies, Abraham?"

"Yassuh. Now she keeps her legs crossed instead of her fingers!"

Shrieks of laughter. Tambourines shaking. Businessmen cakewalking across the stage. Raymond started snapping.

From the corner of his eye, Jed could see Sally's cleavage. He wanted his face buried there, a hand molding either breast, while Sally stroked his hair and murmured how much she loved him. That would happen as soon as this infernal show got over with. He glanced at his watch. Oh God, another half hour. He was getting an erection. He crossed his legs, trying to weight the damn thing down. Talk about wearing your heart on your sleeve. Coach Clancy sometimes made jokes about the trouble older men had getting it up. Well, he had trouble keeping it down. It was embarrassing having the damn thing spring up like an eager puppy at the least excuse, or even without one. In junior high the boys had worn jockstraps to the dances to keep them down—diving board dicks, they used to call them. It made it tough to play it cool with girls. They always knew exactly where you were at. But them, with their secret little holes—you never had a clue what they were up to. So you were always barging ahead and horrifying them.

". . . so de Doc says to her, says, 'Maybelle, has you ever been through de menopause?' And Maybelle, she say, 'Law, no, Doc, I ain't even been through de Smokies yet!' " Laughter. Tambourines. Mrs. Prince tried to smile, but she disliked this show. Did jokes really have to be so crude to be funny? Everywhere she looked these days—crudity. She hung etched prisms in the living room windows so that when the sun poured in just right, the room filled with all the colors of the rainbow, and the mellow wood of the antiques gleamed. She played Bach fugues on her piano. Sometimes Emily played along on her flute, when Mrs. Prince could tear her away from her Sousa marches. In the summer she raised gardens full of flowers, and in the winter she filled the house with arrangements of dried weeds. The girls were scarcely aware of this. But she hoped that surrounding them with nice things could develop in them an instinctive feel for harmony and balance and proportion, though in doing so she knew she was preparing them for a world that was ceasing to exist. The radios and record players in the girls' rooms were always blaring with the maudlin self-pity of country music, or the throbbing sexuality of rock and roll. How could Bach and dried weeds compete? It was like trying to wave back a hurricane with a feather duster. She sometimes felt, as she walked her Oriental carpets, like a refugee from a Chekhov play. She preferred to think of herself that way, as opposed to Robert's description of themselves as flying reptiles nearing extinction. He always said that the real problem was that historical time differed so drastically from one's own lifetime. That people wanted the two to coincide so as to feel that what they were doing had significance. But that historical time was so vast that you might very well be a member of a transitional generation without being able to see what had preceded you, or what would take your place.

She often thought about this as she stood at her living room window with rainbows from the prisms dancing across her arms, looking down into the valley where the mill sat. She'd been a history major at Randolph-Macon and knew that the valley had been inhabited by wave after wave of prehistoric peoples—the Adenans, the Hopewells, the Copena, the Mississippians. They came out of the west from "The Place Where the Sun Falls into the Water," they came from Mexico and Central America, they came from the eastern end of Lake Ontario. Then the Cherokees were driven into this valley from the Ohio River Valley by the Iroquois and the Delaware. They had to fight constantly to stay here—the Creeks to the south, the Tuscarora and Yamasee to the east, the Chickasaw and Shawnees to the west. Bands continuously dissolved, or split off from their tribes with ambitious leaders to form new tribes, like a crowded beehive throwing off a swarm. Then De Soto's men marched through the valley and dug gold mining shafts into the hills. Then came the Europeans—the Scotch-Irish and German and Dutch down from Pennsylvania. Scotsmen from the Clearances crossed the mountains from the North Carolina coast. Englishmen arrived from the Virginia settlements, signing treaties guaranteeing the Cherokees their land for "as long as the green grass grows and the water flows." Then they massacred them, using their skin for boots and reins.

Some town father with a morbid sense of humor named the street outside the house Tsali Street. Tsali was a chief who refused to be marched to Oklahoma during the Removal. A soldier prodded Tsali's wife with a bayonet, and Tsali killed him, fleeing to the North Carolina mountains. The troops promised to leave the other cave dwellers alone if Tsali would turn himself in. He did, and was shot.

Like the layers of a compost pile, each culture that had inhabited this valley rested on the decaying remains of previous ones. The ashes from their fires, the graves of their forebears littered the valley. Humanity had existed for 20,000 generations, the most recent consisting of her friends and family. And what culture would replace the Newlanders? She could speculate, but it irritated her that she would never know. She recalled her outrage at Randolph-Macon when she first saw in a textbook a chart illustrating that most species failed to adapt to new conditions and went to extinction.

Having Robert around triggered bleak musings like this. He was like a live-in Hamlet. Getting to know him had been a shock. The men around her—her father and brothers and their friends—had been so flamboyant, forceful, and gallant that she'd just assumed that that was what men were like. Her father owned a large tobacco farm and raised horses, in addition to being vice president at the mill. He wore silk shirts and a diamond ring on his little finger. And when he rode, the horse's hooves scarcely touched the ground, seemed to dance deftly in the air. He merely flicked his wrist and the horse reversed directions or changed gaits.

Robert had been so unflamboyant that she was scarcely aware of his existence until he asked her out in high school. Even then, he had stooped badly. Their parents were great friends, his father being president at the mill. Her father admired his father's blustery optimism. He used to say, "We need us a few Yankees around this town who know there's still such a thing as progress. You take a Southerner: He's positively wedded to the status quo because, however pathetic, it's an advance on the War and Reconstruction." Robert's and her mothers were heads of rival garden clubs that engaged in friendly but fierce competition when members opened their gardens to the public in early summer. All four parents were thrilled with the match, and it seemed a shame to disappoint them, so she kept dating him. And gradually she learned to appreciate his anguished seriousness. There was nothing he could take for granted and enjoy. But if these qualities made him interesting to talk with, they sometimes made him frightful to live with. Some mornings she'd go into their bedroom to see why he was late to breakfast and find him staring bleakly into his sock drawer. "Wear the green ones, dear," she'd say. "They're nice with that tie."

They'd both long acknowledged that he was in the wrong job. But there seemed nothing to be done about it now. She'd been in the wrong job too for a while, but had been able to quit, since no income and very little civic responsibility were involved. When she was a bride, all the various clubs had vied for her membership, and she'd joined half a dozen—her mother's garden club, a bridge club, a book club, the Junior League. After several years of marshaling maids to take care of her house and children so she could be at luncheons and on committees and at fund-raising events, she decided that where she really wanted to be was home. She dismissed the gardener and began doing her gardens herself. Her mother and mother-in-law were horrified. You planned your garden, you supervised your gardener, you cut and arranged the flowers. You did not do the actual spading and weeding yourself. But Melanie liked it. She'd grown up riding horses and building mud dams on the farm with her brothers, and was baffled by the life of a clubwoman, which involved such crises as who had refused to give which recipe to whom. Plants, on the other hand, stayed where you put them and did as they were told. But the gardens taught her more than that: When she and her friends and family were gone, whether or not others replaced them, the sun would still shine, birds would continue to sing, and weeds would grow. Oblivious to the absence of humans. Almost nothing was as important as people tried to make things.

She'd have done her own housework too, except that she didn't know how to get rid of Ruby. Whenever she tried, Ruby informed her that Melanie wouldn't be able to get along without her. Since Ruby had raised her, taught her how to tie her shoes, and made her stop sucking her thumb, Melanie was incapable of disputing anything she said. Which was why her own mother was always marching into her house and telling Melanie that she didn't know how to "handle her servants." As though Ruby were a mule in a field. According to her mother, the way to "handle" Ruby was to tie a cloth around your head and start cleaning with her and gossiping about the other families Ruby worked for. Eventually Ruby would insist on taking over. The one time Melanie tried this, Ruby sat down with a Coke and gave Melanie pointers on her cleaning techniques. But this world in which one "handled one's servants" was passing, so this wasn't a skill she'd felt obliged to figure out so that she could pass it on to her daughters. Unfortunately, she hadn't been able to figure out any other skills to pass on to them either, since she didn't understand what kind of a world she was supposed to be preparing them for.

She glanced at her mother next to her, elegantly coiffed and dressed. Robert's and her parents had spent a lifetime playing bridge together. Not long ago Robert's mother and her father had died. Their surviving spouses now played double solitaire. Her mother had been talking for the past twenty years about getting her house and possessions "in dying order," but Melanie was sure she'd outlast them all. She even said about herself, "Honey, when they plant me in that ground, I'll still be sending up shoots, like an old rotten potato!"

Rastus stood up slowly and hobbled forward. Everyone laughed. "Mr. Interlocutor, suh," he said carefully.

"Yes, Rastus?" the interlocutor asked with a bright smile.

"Mr. Interlocutor, suh, I wants to tell you about my cousin LeRoy."

"Rastus, I believe you've already told us about your cousin LeRoy."

"Yassah, but I ain't tole you everything bout my cousin LeRoy."

He raised his eyes to the ceiling and sighed. "No, Rastus, I expect you haven't."

"I tell you, boss, dat LeRoy, he so dumb. You know how dumb dat LeRoy is, boss?"

"No, Rastus, tell me what your cousin LeRoy did this time," he replied with restrained impatience.

"Dat LeRoy, he went to de doctor and de doctor, he tell him to get undressed. LeRoy, he say, 'Huhun, doc. You got to take me out a couple of times fust!' "

Sally was surveying the gym. This was where the Plantation Ball would be held in a few weeks. They would buy bolts of cotton gauze from the mill, dye it, and transform the room into a billowing tent. The Ingenues had been raising money for this all year. The entire school was invited. It would take days to set up. She could squint and picture it as it would look that night. . . . Jed's hand was caressing the small of her back. She nestled into his side.

". . . so de teacher finally buys de little colored chile some deodorant and says to him, says, 'Honey, you put this under your arms before you come to school in the morning so you'll smell good.' So de next morning dat little kid, he shows up holding dat deodorant can under one armpit!"

Emily smiled faintly. She gazed down at the sea of faces, red and contorted with laughter. She felt the bleachers trembling as their occupants howled. This show had been the high point of every year of her life. The Civic Club worked on it all year. The town looked forward to it all year, and discussed the previous show until they had the new one to talk about. But this year she wasn't laughing.

"Hey," she whispered to June. "I'm not sure this is really funny."

"Shhh!" said those around her.

Kathryn drove her black Ford Galaxy along the highway past the service club plaques welcoming motorists to Newland, "Progress City, U.S.A."

The marquee outside the gym of the white high school announced the Civic Club's annual minstrel show. The parking lot was jammed. Her face registered distaste. This was what she had to rescue Donny from. A minstrel show, for God's sake. In 1961.

She recalled that night four years earlier. Mr. Blanton had been after her for a long time. He worked at the brick factory and she knew him by sight. Every time she walked to the market, she would see him hanging over the fence in front of the huge stacks of red and orange and grey bricks and blocks. He always wore green work pants and a soiled T-shirt, his belly bulging over his belt. He would watch her, grinning. She would smile back, to be pleasant, and say something like "Pretty day we're having?"

"Sure is," he'd reply. Just like a dozen similar exchanges every day.

The next thing she knew, he offered Donny a job sweeping up around his office. Donny was thrilled to have the spending money. One afternoon as she strolled past, Mr. Blanton called, "Some boy you got there."

"Yeah, old Donny is really something," she called back with a laugh.

A few weeks later he called, "Hey, come over here a minute. I want to tell you something."

Assuming it had to do with Donny, she went over. Mr. Blanton grinned, studying her with his pale blue eyes. "You know something? You just about the purtiest thing I ever did see," he said in a low voice. "How's about you and me getting together tonight?"

This was a situation she'd heard about from her friends, but she'd never encountered it directly. She decided to joke him out of it.

"Why, Mr. Blanton! I couldn't hardly do that. You see, I don't believe in this here social equality."

He blushed. "Well, I can see you ain't no ordinary nee-grow. You is an exception."

"I ain't no exception, Mr. Blanton. I'm just an ordinary nigger. And proud to be one."

The next time, he cruised beside her in his green Pontiac as she walked home early one evening.

"They's ten dollars in it for you if you'll come to my office for half an hour," he said gruffly.

"No, thank you, sir."

"All right, twenty-five."

She whirled toward him. "I'm sorry, but I ain't interested, Mr. Blanton. I don't go with no white men."

"I can't help it if I'm white."

"Well sir, I can't help it neither," she said with a pleasant laugh.

She ran up her sidewalk, pleased she'd kept it friendly, so that Donny could keep his job.

Two weeks later she was looking out the window for Donny, who was late for supper. The phone rang. It was Mr. Blanton. "Your boy's been hurt. I think you'd better come have a look."

She ran down the block to the brick company. Mr. Blanton led her in the gate and through the neat squares of bricks. "A pile of bricks toppled on him," Mr. Blanton muttered. "He's out cold."

In a corner of a darkened shed they stopped. "Where's he at?" Kathryn demanded.

Mr. Blanton laughed. "I'm just kidding you, Kathryn. Donny's OK. He's gone across town to do me a favor." He took hold of her wrists. "Now how's about *you* doing me a favor?" He put his hands on her buttocks and pulled her against him. She could feel his erection against her leg.

"Come on, Kathryn. Love me a little," he whispered, burying his mouth in her neck.

She pushed at his chest. "I done told you I don't want none of this action with you, Mr. Blanton."

"I like a woman with spunk." He ground his hips against her. They struggled, the only sounds being scuffling feet and grunts and gasps.

"Uppity nigger!" he snarled, hitting her face. "Stinking black cunt!"

He had her on her back on the ground, one hand on her throat, and was undoing his pants, pushing open her legs with his knees, then lowering himself onto her. She reached out, grabbed a brick and smashed it down on his head. He slumped across her. She shoved him aside and ran.

Back in the apartment she told her mother what had happened. Ruby buried her face in her hands and began praying. Kathryn hitched a ride to the Princes'. Mr. Prince felt she should leave at once—go to her brother's in New York City.

"I'm scared, Mr. Prince."

"Don't be scared, Kathryn. Everything's going to be all right."

She watched the sun rise scarlet over the mountains, as the bus roared up the valley past rolling pastures and grazing cattle. The hazy blue mountains rushed past—those mountains her ancestors had climbed prior to descending into this valley. She was leaving behind this valley, these mountains. She alternated between elation and terror as her body swayed with the hurtling bus.

Shortly after the lunch stop at a crowded rest area off the huge highway, she looked out her window and gasped. All around were lanes of highway, packed with more cars and buses and diesel trucks than she had ever before seen at one time. Across some murky grey water was the skyline of New York City, buildings sticking up like broken teeth on a discarded comb. Around endless curves, under overpasses, over underpasses, through a long tunnel. Her brother had told her he was a guard in a big tunnel under the river. Was this it?

They emerged onto the streets of New York City. Never before had she seen a place where there was no green. At home, even downtown or around the factories, there were empty lots, trees, and bushes. Fields and forested foothills could be seen from anywhere. She looked out the opposite window, out the driver's window, up at the sky through her own window. All she could see was grey concrete—filled with honking cars and rushing bodies. She shrank back in her seat, closed her eyes, and tried to breathe slowly. She thought of her mother's apartment in Pine Woods, with its trampled courtyards. The schoolyard. The fields that stretched down to the willows along the river.

When she opened her eyes, the bus was dark and empty. Except for the driver, who was standing over her saying, "Excuse me, Miss, we're here."

"Miss," he was calling her. And he was white. As she climbed down, he held out his hand. She gave him a sharp look, then took it. Dozens of buses parked diagonally. The air stank of exhaust. Through some windows she could see a huge well-lighted room filled with people of all ages and colors, embracing, crying, laughing, running, dragging luggage, sitting disconsolately.

Suddenly her brother loomed before her, exclaiming and hugging her and grabbing her bags. She allowed herself to be pushed here and there, through doors, down moving steps, through tiled tunnels papered with posters, through crowds, through turnstiles. Into a silver train, with words painted all over it in spray paint. It roared and screeched, and lurched and clattered, stopped and started. Doors opened with a hiss. People—black and white and yellow, well-dressed and shabby, smiling and scowling—got on and off. Her brother kept laughing and talking. She nodded and said, "Uh-huh."

They got off the train, went through some gates, and climbed some steps, emerging into daylight and a street packed with faces all shades of black and brown. More concrete and cars and buildings, honking horns, music blaring from record shops, flashing signs. Past a carry-out shop, laundromat, pool hall, tavern, liquor store, grocery store, secondhand store, loan company, pawn shop, store-front church. Her brother called to people. She smiled and nodded and wanted her mother. Into a dark red-brick building. Up flights of garbage-strewn stairs with missing risers. Into a living room crammed with tattered sofas and armchairs. Her brother's wife enfolded her in her arms. They led her to a darkened bedroom, where she undressed, collapsed, and pulled the covers over her head. What had she done? How could she have been foolish enough to leave Newland? How could Donny manage without her? How could she manage without him? She cried, burying her face in the pillow.

She lay in her brother's bedroom for almost two weeks, weeping, scared to get up, terrified to go out into that roiling sea of black bodies and unfamiliar noises. But one day she didn't pull the covers over her head. The next day she got up, dressed, and ate a meal with the family. She went for a slow walk with her sister-in-law, digesting new sights a few at a time.

Eventually she realized that with five children and four rooms, they needed her to find herself a place soon. This meant a job. So she went downtown and cleaned offices in a tall glass and steel building from 11 p.m. to 7 a.m. She drank coffee, then went to classes at nursing school, for which Mr. Prince had given her tuition. She came home to her room in a residential hotel and studied and slept until time to go downtown again.

For the first few months, as she lay on the single bed in her stuffy room, trying to sleep in the early evening light, Pine Woods would materialize. Old people shuffled out to their porches to watch the night descend and the lights go on in white folks' houses on the hill. Children, Donny among them, tussled under the streetlight and chased each other through the courtyards, bouncing on cast-off bedsprings. Young people gathered for an evening of wisecracks and flirting in front of the laundromat. Couples strolled and petted among the willows by the river.

Abruptly she would recall Mr. Blanton's contorted red face and would know there was no going back. But her heart would ache, and she would wrap her arms around her pillow and bite it to keep from shrieking.

She had gone from a place in which she knew everyone and everyone knew her, to one in which she knew no one except her brother, and not him very well anymore—if she defined "knowing someone" in the Newland sense of knowing their parents and grandparents and children and brothers and sisters and cousins, knowing everything they had ever done or were likely to do. Whenever she passed someone in the street up here, she prepared to smile and say hi and comment on the weather. With alarm she discovered that people looked resolutely ahead or at the sidewalk. And almost everyone had his or her robbery or mugging story. She learned to glance over her shoulder as she walked to the subway late at night.

Her list of complaints mounted: Everything was locked, and she was always losing keys. She'd never climbed so many stairs in her life. Everywhere, you went up, rather than just in. Her calf muscles ached. Some days she craved to kick off her shoes and run outside and bury her toes in topsoil. She was constantly swathed in sweaters and coats, she longed to feel sunlight on her bare arms. All the rushing around. People's most prized possessions seemed to be their wristwatches, and being late was practically grounds for a lawsuit. She got icy stares from teachers as she slipped into her seat after a lecture had begun.

One afternoon as she walked to the hospital where she was training in the emergency room, she passed an asphalt playground surrounded by a tall chain-link fence. Within were some basketball courts occupied by boys about Donny's size. They leapt, dodged, and feinted with breathtaking grace. She almost convinced herself that one was Donny. She began toying with the idea of having him up here. She could send bus fare. Find an apartment. The thought of his cheerful presence was overwhelming. It wouldn't be such a bad life. He could go to the local school, play his basketball here. He'd make new friends in no time, sweet as he was.

As she planned, she walked—past a group of men who were always lounging by the takeout shop on her corner. They took whatever work came along in construction, on loading platforms. They looked burnt-out, as they punched each other, and talked and laughed too loudly. One wore glasses' frames with the lenses missing. Another wore a T-shirt with "Superstud" printed on it. Each time she passed, one would call out something smart.

"Say, mama, can I ride that swing on your back porch?" one called today. The group grinned and made noises with their lips. She hurried by, staring at the sidewalk. Maybe Donny was better off where he was.

In the emergency room she assisted at the treatment of the usual procession of rat bites, knife wounds, drug overdoses, botched abortions. And she dismantled plans to bring Donny to New York City. Besides, he was too young to ride the bus all that way by himself. She couldn't even see bringing him up for a visit. Who'd keep an eye on him while she was working, as she was most of the time? He was so sweet and trusting. A sitting duck up here. Christmas a year later she went home for a long weekend, but spent the whole time peeping through curtains onto the street. Ruby said she'd seen Blanton cruising the apartment in his Buick several times since Kathryn had been gone. If he found out she was home, he'd probably fix her good.

Her savings started accumulating. She received twice the wages for half as many hours as in Pine Woods. It cost more to live, and she sent money home, but even so, for the first time she could afford some clothes, began saving for a used car, ate out now and then.

She met Arthur, an orderly at the hospital. He was proud and ambitious, very much like Buddy. Unlike Buddy, he would never end up in prison, and he might even end up where he wanted to go, which was to medical school. He took her to restaurants, and to shows at the Apollo. Once they went to a musical on Broadway, and she started thinking again about bringing Donny to New York. He was a bright boy, had always done well at school. Outside Pine Woods there were alternatives to yard work and janitorial jobs. She couldn't bear the idea of his jaunty strut becoming a shuffle. She'd watched it happen to the boys who took her to dances at the Masonic Hall and made love to her under the willows by the river. She asked Arthur to go with her to Pine Woods to persuade Donny to return to New York. Arthur laughed and replied, "Oh yeah, they'd just love me down there, baby."

As she entered Pine Woods, as she drove past the school and the shopping street, as she watched the old people on their porches and the children in the courtyard, she was swept with nostalgia. She stopped the car and picked up a photo of Arthur from the seat. She studied it under the streetlight—bushy greying hair, sardonic smile, fierce eyes.

She drove up to the curb in front of her mother's apartment. Through the dusk she saw a tall thin young man in a grey sweatsuit stand up from the porch rocker and look at her. She jumped out, ran to him, and threw her arms around him. He inclined his cheek so she could peck it, then backed off.

"All right," Sally was saying. "Hands below the waist, but outside the clothes. And that's final."

Jed, who was lying on her in the cave, with a hand under each buttock pulling her hips toward his, nodded.

"Do you promise?" she demanded, pushing him off and sitting up. Her bare breasts glowed in the light from the flashlight.

"I promise," he panted.

"You promised the last time, too."

"This time I mean it. I swear to God I do." He ran his hand up her thigh and stroked her slacks where the legs joined.

She ignored him. "I got so excited tonight thinking about the Plantation Ball. You are gonna go with me, aren't you, darling?"

"Is that the thing where you got to rent a tux?"

"Yes, you look so gorgeous in a dinner jacket, Jed. I drool just thinking about it."

"Aw, shit, I don't wanna wear no tux." He lay with his hands behind his head, looking with satisfaction at his chest muscles.

"Please, Jed."

"Naw, I ain't going. I don't like dances where you got to wear a tux. If I was to go, we'd have to do those waltz lessons and everything."

"All right. I'll just ask somebody else." She reached for her bra.

"You do that," he said with a lazy grin. "And I'll ask me somebody else down here to do what I like."

"You do that," she said, standing up and pulling on her shirt.

"In fact I already have."

"Have what?" she asked with indifference, combing her hair.

"Asked me somebody down here to do what I like."

"And what is it you like?"

"You know what I like, baby."

"Lifting weights?"

"Yeah. Lifting weights. That's what Betty Boobs and me done down here last Saturday after you and me had us our fight."

She looked at him. "You're lying."

"I ain't lying." He grinned.

She laughed. Then she screamed, "You brought that . . . whore down here and . . . ?"

He smiled. "Honey, a man's got to have him some action. If you don't want it, fine. But don't expect me to wait around for you, jerking off."

"I don't expect *anything* from you, Jed Tatro! Ohh, I *hate* you!" She stamped her feet and shook her fists. Then she started sobbing. Jed grinned and jumped up and held her, while she pounded his chest. "I hate you! I hate you! I hate you!"

". . . Oh, Jed, I love, you," she wailed, holding her mouth up to receive his. They kissed and she clung to him. He pulled her hips against his, and she could feel his erection throbbing.

"Jed, can't you see I'm scared?"

"They ain't nothing to be scared of."

"Nothing for *you*. I'm the one who'll get pregnant."

"You won't get pregnant, Sally. That's why I've got these things." He held up a box of Trojan Enz.

She looked at him, outraged. "Why do you have those dreadful things down here? We had a deal, Jed. No activity below the waist. And here you went right ahead and brought those horrible things. I can't trust you at all—or ever again."

"I *brought* them so you won't get yourself pregnant some night, you fucking l'il cock tease!"

"Cock tease? *Cock* tease? I don't want anything to do with your stupid cock! I wish you didn't even have it! It's caused nothing but trouble ever since I found out you had one!"

"All right. Fine. You're not interested in my cock. Well, Betty Boobs is. She's crazy about it. Can't get enough. So you go find someone else for your stupid Plantation Ball, some fairy who likes wearing a tux and who won't try to do all these nasty filthy dirty things to you. And I'll screw Betty till my balls turn inside out. And we'll all be happy!"

"I think you're repulsive." She studied her fingernails.

"And I think you're an ice maiden."

"Who cares what you think anyway?"

"You used to." His shoulders sagged.

Sally rushed to him and lifted the tears from his cheeks with her tongue.

"Do you really think I'm cold?" she asked, rubbing her thigh against his erection.

"I think you the hottest ticket I've ever seen," he murmured, nibbling her neck. "You're scared. But I think you going to get over it. Cause they ain't nothing to be scared about."

Kathryn walked up the Princes' sidewalk between the rows of boxwood to the front porch. She hesitated. She could go around to the kitchen door, as she always had when she worked here. Or she could knock on the front door. She veered off the sidewalk. She was back in Newland now, and all her old patterns were taking over. But she wasn't the same woman she'd been when she used to go around back. She returned to the sidewalk, marched up it, and knocked with the huge brass knocker.

A tall young woman with an attractive anxious face opened the door. Could it be Emily? She was standing there, staring. Kathryn realized she'd made the wrong decision. If this lanky teenager was Emily, she was probably claimed by Newland now, and was appalled to find her former maid demanding entrance through the front door. But it was too late, so she stuck out her hand. "Hello, Emily."

"Kathryn?" Emily took the hand. She'd been sitting in the den, practicing Sousa marches on her flute and trying to decide why the minstrel show wasn't funny last night. There had been knocking on the front door. Standing there was a handsome Negro woman in an expensive-looking suit, stockings, and high heels. It had taken intense scrutiny of the high cheekbones to understand that this was Kathryn —whom she had never before seen in anything but grey uniform dresses with white collars.

As they shook hands and smiled awkwardly, Emily found herself reaching with her other arm for an embrace. As she did so, she was seized with anxiety. Kathryn hadn't called her "Miss Emily." Was a hug now inappropriate? But her body had its own notions, and it recognized this body that had cuddled it in infancy and comforted it in childhood.

Kathryn responded with reluctance. She was no longer to be regarded as a mammy. And yet they'd been such lively little creatures. They'd had no notion of what went on in the adult world. Did they now? She and Emily hugged.

"Come in." Emily stepped back. She hesitated in the hall. Guests were normally ushered into the living room. Kathryn, however, had never been in the living room except to clean it. She'd always relaxed in the kitchen and the den.

Resolutely Emily led her toward the living room and waited for her to sit on one of the Empire sofas, while Kathryn waited for Emily to sit. Finally, perching on a sofa, Emily said, "Please sit."

They studied each other, smiling. Kathryn was remembering a serious little girl, earnest about everything. Tall for her age, and worried for her age, just as she looked now. She'd shrunk from caresses. Unlike Sally, who had been a dancing sunbeam, always climbing up on your lap for kisses, hugs, and silly songs. It had been hard to believe they were sisters.

"What's old Sal up to?"

"Well, she's a cheerleader at school and belongs to a lot of clubs and stuff. She spends a lot of time with Jed. Guess they're going steady."

"Jed? Little Jed Tatro?"

"Yes, but he's not so little anymore." Emily laughed. "In fact he's practically Charles Atlas. He lifts weights every day and plays tackle on the football team."

"Well, I declare," giggled Kathryn. "That child was so puny I never thought he'd survive childhood. Just goes to show you. What about Raymond? He still smarting off?"

"Yeah, I guess so."

"That child used to be so clever. Remember how he used to insist that the refrigerator cars on trains were full of corpses?"

Emily looked blank, then struggled to reclaim the memory. It was an expression Kathryn had often seen on the faces of whites in Newland. They had no way to reconcile the warmth they shared with Negroes as children with the attitudes that set in as the world claimed them. So they simply cut themselves off from their childhoods.

Emily realized she should offer Kathryn something to eat or drink. Tea? Or was that too fancy, something her mother would serve the Altar Guild? "Would you like something to drink, a Coke or something?"

"Sure. That would taste good. But I'll get it." Each stood, poised to get the other a Coke.

"Sit down. I'll get them. It's my house," Emily finally said, laughing nervously.

Kathryn laughed. "That's right. I almost forgot." Anxiety showed on both faces.

As Emily opened Cokes, she tried to figure out what relationship those men in blackened faces last night bore to the woman sitting in her living room.

Sally burst through the back door.

"Kathryn's here," Emily informed her.

"Kathryn! You're kidding? Where?"

"In the living room."

"The *living* room?"

"Oh, shut up."

"What did I say?"

She shrugged and bounced through the hall and into the living room, where she hurled herself into Kathryn's arms and wept, while Kathryn laughed.

As Emily walked in, Sally was saying, ". . . and he's just the cutest thing, Kathryn. All these muscles and things. I just wish you could see him!"

"How's Donny these days?" Emily asked, hoping to turn off her sister's mouth.

"Oh, he's all right. But I don't think he approves of me right now."

"Why not?"

"Well, I guess he wants me to be the same mama I was when I left. But I've changed. In ways he doesn't care for. I keep trying to point out that he's changed too."

"That's silly," Sally announced.

"Well, I think he's just never forgiven me for leaving in the first place."

"None of us have," Sally assured her. "That was just terrible, Kathryn. Running off to New York City without even saying good-bye."

Kathryn frowned. "Well, I had my reasons." Emily blushed at the put-down Sally failed to notice.

"I got to be going," Kathryn announced. "Donny's waiting in the car."

"You should have brought him in," Sally said.

"Well, he thought you should have a chance to see me alone. And anyway, he said he had him some thinking to do."

As she walked down the sidewalk, she thought about what different futures were in store for the Prince girls versus her Donny. Their daddy had money. They could go wherever they wanted, do whatever they pleased. She didn't have Mr. Prince's money. And even if she had, Donny didn't have much choice. Because she'd been realizing since she'd been home that New York City wasn't that much of an improvement on Pine Woods. She and Arthur still took their orders from white people—the doctors and head nurses. The only difference was that white people in Newland were more relaxed and pleasant about issuing their orders. Downtown this morning she'd run into Mrs. Tatro Sr. on the street.

"Why, Kathryn honey, I just don't know how I get from one day to the next without you! I could have just killed that horrible man for taking you away from me." They were so charming, these people. They'd have you cleaning their toilet bowls in minutes, and thanking them for the privilege.

"That's real nice of you, Mrs. Tatro. But I been doing just fine up in New York City. It's worked out real good."

Mrs. Tatro looked at her with surprise. She was breaking the rules by not grinning and exclaiming, "Well, Miz Tatro, I misses my white folks something terrible, I surely does."

"You'd better come on back home now, hear? Where folks care whether you live or die or not. What you want to stay up at New York City for, without you have to?" This came out as a gentle command rather than a question. Ignore it at your peril. If charm failed, coercion followed. Besides, it was true: A Negro could go to a lot more places in New York City, but nobody cared if you lay dying in the street. Another thing, she'd been watching Donny since her arrival. He had a grave self-confidence from knowing his surroundings, from being known as Ruby's grandson, from making good grades and having lots of friends and being a basketball star. She wasn't sure anymore that New York City was a good idea.

She shook herself. Pine Woods was tightening its grip. She'd better get back to New York right quick.

She sighed and said to Donny as he started up her car, "Well, they sure have grown up."

"Yeah, I saw Emily the other day. I like to not recognized her."

"I dee-clare! All my chilluns is growed up on me!" She laughed and scrubbed her knuckles on Donny's head. He ducked irritably.

"I been thinking, Mama. I believe I bout decided to go back up at New York City with you, like you say." He wasn't really sure this was what he wanted, with his whole life down here. But he wanted to call her bluff.

She frowned. "Well, I don't know, Donny . . ."

"Well, I wouldn't want to interfere with your life none."

"It's not that. It's a question of what would be best for you."

"Ha! When has it ever been a question of what was best for me?"

She gave him a pained look.

"You feel like running off to New York City, so you just up and run off to New York City."

She sighed. "Donny, honey, you know I didn't have no choice about that."

"I don't know no such thing." He glared at her. "You could have gone, or you could have stayed until you figured out how to take me with you."

She looked at him, surprised. "Donny, I had to clear out of this town from one minute to the next. You know that."

"What you talking bout—one minute to the next?"

She stared at him. "You don't know why I left, do you? Mama didn't tell you like I told her to."

"Tell me what?"

"Why, that old witch! Donny, honey, I hit a white man over the head with a brick."

He glanced at her. "Who?"

"Mr. Blanton over at the brick company."

"How come?"

"He wanted me to . . . be his girlfriend." She smiled at her uncharacteristic delicacy.

"So why didn't you just say no?" They were carefully avoiding each other's eyes.

"I did."

"And then he . . ."

"Tried to."

Donny gripped the steering wheel. After a minute he announced, "I'm gon cut that man all to pieces."

Kathryn laughed. "Sorry, but you've missed your chance. He had him a heart attack early this year. That's why I'm down here now."

Donny trembled.

"I thought you understood this. Grandmaw was supposed to tell you. You must have been hating me all this time." The significance of this gap in Donny's information was dawning on her. She slid over and put her arm around his shoulders. "Aw Donny, baby, I'm so sorry. I didn't just up and leave you. Hasn't a night gone by I didn't think about you, and wonder how you was doing, and want to send for you. I just couldn't see any other way to manage things."

"Grandmaw said you'd gone to New York City to learn to be a nurse. She made me quit my job over at the brick plant. I couldn't never figure it out. Said you was gon earn money for us, but here she was making me give up what I was earning." He beat the steering wheel with a fist. "That white son of a bitch! That pink pig of a bastard!"

After supper Donny went off in the Galaxy, leaving Kathryn and Ruby facing each other in the armchairs in the living room. Kathryn cleared her throat. "Mama, how come you never told Donny about Blanton like I asked you to?"

Ruby spat tobacco juice across the room into the coal scuttle. Tightening her head cloth, she crossed her legs at the knees and swung one tennis-shoed foot. "I told that child what I thought he was old enough to hear."

"But Mama, I asked you to tell him the whole thing."

"Honey, you was out of your head that night. You said a lot of things no one woulda held you to."

"Mama," Kathryn said, struggling to remain calm. "Donny thought until this afternoon that I went up to New York just for fun, or to earn us more money or something."

"I told that child how it like to killed you to leave him, but that you'd be writing letters and would be back afore long. I told him how we didn't have much money, and how things would go easier once you was a nurse."

"That may be what you told him, but what he heard was that I'd run out on him."

Ruby stretched her neck and munched her tobacco. "You told that child the en-tire story this afternoon?"

"He's not a child and he should have been told four years ago!"

"Well, honey, I was in charge here, and I felt like that he shouldn't of been."

"Damn it, Mama! You been trying to steal my son! Making him hate me!" She jumped up and pointed an accusing finger.

"I was trying," Ruby said with a glint in her eye, "to keep your precious boy *alive*, woman. Now shut your mouth and sit down." Kathryn collapsed in her chair. "Losing his mama was bad enough. Now what you think that child woulda done if I'd of told him the white man who'd been so nice to him tried to rape his mama?"

Kathryn buried her face in her hands. When she looked up, her face was wet. "Mama, you got to tell them from the day they're born."

"You just plain *wrong*, Kathryn. You got to raise them up to be strong and unafraid and full of love. Then you tell them. Then they find out for themselves."

Kathryn shook her head no, slumped in exhaustion.

Donny walked across the yard to Rochelle's house, the last of the wooden cabins that had made up Pine Woods before the development. In the two-room house lived Rochelle, her mother, and six more children.

Donny and Rochelle sat in the Galaxy at the Wilderness Trail Drive-In playing bingo. They'd been given cards as they entered, and now the attendant was calling numbers over the speaker. ". . . N-6, N-6 . . . G-4, G-4 . . ." Winners brought their cards to the concession stand.

As the movie began, Donny scooted next to Rochelle and put his arm around her. They sat back to watch *That Touch of Mink*. After a few minutes Donny leaned over her. They kissed for a long time. He began running his hand up and down her neck.

"OK. That's enough," she announced. "I don't want no fancy stuff."

"All right," Donny said. After his mother's story, he wasn't feeling too great.

Cary Grant pulled into the driveway of his ranch house in a new Buick Riviera. He stood smiling and waving at Doris Day, who came running down the sidewalk. Donny trembled. He wanted to grab that guy by his polka-dotted necktie and tighten the knot until that ugly white face turned red and then purple, and those eyes bugged out with terror.

The seizure passed as quickly as it arrived, leaving Donny alarmed and exhausted.

Rochelle glanced at him. She took his hand in both hers. "It's like this, Donny. I done spent my whole life rocking my mama's babies. I don't wanna do nothing that might give me one of my own. Cause I got things to do first."

"Like what?"

"First I want to finish high school. Next I want to get me a scholarship to college. I expect I'll be a teacher, or a librarian." She wanted a house like the one Cary Grant and Doris Day had just walked into. Carpeting, appliances. She wanted a husband coming home in a suit and tie. She'd had enough of sharing a bed with her little brothers and sisters and waking up damp from their pee. She was tired of roaches in the cereal boxes and rags stuffed into broken windowpanes.

"Well, yeah, I can dig that, Rochelle. You told me this before. Don't worry bout it none." He returned his eyes to the screen. She studied him.

"But I am worrying, Donny."

"What about?"

"About what it means if I don't let you do nothing but kiss me."

"I don't care right now. If I start to care, I'll let you know."

"That's what I mean. I never went out before with a boy who didn't care about that stuff."

"Well, now you have. You see, right at this particular moment, I don't feel so hot."

"Are you sick?"

"Not with anything you could treat."

"You been fighting with your mama?"

"Something like that."

"I fought with mine today. She's having her another baby. I said, 'This one I ain't having nothing to do with, Mama. You have them, you take care of them.' She started crying and said it made her feel like she was accomplishing something when her belly was full. And when she was nursing them. Then they started growing up and getting mean, like I was being. And it hurt her so much that she had to go right out and start another one, hoping she'd do better next time."

"That's the craziest thing I ever heard."

"That's what I told her. That's when I knew that's what she is—crazy."

"I figure we all crazy," said Donny. "It's just a question of figuring out how, not whether."

# Chapter Four

## Hollowed Be Thy Name

The sun, nearly overhead, was white-hot in a deep blue sky. The cacophony of competing church bells filled the valley as the citizens of Newland, dressed in their best clothes, strolled out of almost every house over to freshly polished cars. The streets filled with snarls of traffic.

In the pasture bordering the grey river were gathered several dozen members of the Mount Zion Baptist Church. Men and boys wore suits and ties, starched white shirts and suspenders. Women and girls wore dresses and suits, heels and flowered hats with veils and white gloves. Several held umbrellas to fend off the sun. The preacher, Mr. Stump, stood before them on a hillock in a black robe and tam-o'-shanter. Next to him in a midnight-blue robe stood the deacon, Mr. Husk. In front of them were assembled half a dozen frightened adolescents in white robes with knotted white handkerchiefs on their heads.

". . . and I have brothers and sisters come up to me in the street and say, 'Mr. Stump suh, when is the bottom rail going to be the top rail?' Now I knows what these people means, friends. You knows, and I knows, bout ever kind of sorriness on the face of this earth. We knows, friends, what it is to be mocked and scorned and despised ever way in the world!"

"Yeah, tell it, preacher!" a man moaned.

"Our people been raised up to believe we'll never mount to much. We been hongry, friends, and the high and the mighty, sitting at their sagging boards, wouldn't toss us a bone! We been ridiculed, we been called beggars and crooks and scoundrels. But I'm here to tell you, friends, that they was another who was hated and despised, amen! Another who was born in a stable cause the innkeeper turned his mama away from the door!"

"Preach good this morning, Reverend!" a woman called.

"Do you *know* what happened to this man, brothers and sisters? Do you know what the big shots done to him? They tried him in a court of law, friends, and they found him guilty. Called him a traitor! Called him a blasphemer! Beat our Lord Jesus! Shoved a crown of sharp thorns on his forehead! Nailed him to a cross! They *crucified* our Lord! Murdered the Son of God!"

"Oh, yeah, He be my man!" a woman wailed.

"Some people in this church, they says to me, 'Mr. Stump, me and my old lady, we thinking bout going up to Washington, D.C. Or to New York City.' They talk like the streets up there is paved with gold. Like they gon be waved in with palm fronds."

"I'm Born to Die and Lay This Body Down" rose and fell softly among the congregation.

"Then they come back, these people. Yeah, I see them strutting down our streets wearing brand-new silk suits and driving big expensive Cadillac cars. They come up to me and say, 'Stump, why don't you go up at that courthouse and get your people what's due them? Get them the vote. Get them the welfare. Get them hired out at the mill. Get them this. Get them that.' All the time reproaching me with the Reverend Mr. Hyatt over at Donley, who marched up to the school board last month and demanded that colored children go to the white high school next fall. Huh!" He snorted.

Ruby snorted, too. The idea of whites and coloreds going to the same school! Just no telling what they'd come up with next. If you was truly smart, you stayed out of the way of white folks. And when you couldn't, you acted clever and got what you wanted. And if you couldn't manage that neither, you got by, and you thanked the Lord for the strength to do it.

Kathryn narrowed her eyes at Mr. Stump, who was referring to her. She'd asked him the other day what plans Pine Woods was making to integrate the Newland schools. She'd about decided, given the chance to go to white schools, Donny was better off here. The school near her in Harlem would be all Negro. Whites had the power and money on this earth—by associating with them you could learn how to cop yourself a piece of that action. But Stump was hopeless. All this reveling in suffering, every nigger a persecuted Jesus who'd be resurrected into Glory. It made her sick. There was no question: She had to get out of this place soon, Donny with her—before he turned into one of these black masochists, consoled by the promise of an afterlife that didn't exist.

Donny, by shifting his eyes, could encompass his entire world. Everyone important to him—his mama, his grandmaw, his neighbors, his classmates—was all right here. His best friend, Tad, whom he'd known forever. He'd always been a little biddy guy, which was why they called him Tad. But this year he'd shot up to six feet, so everybody'd started calling him Tadpole. School was off to one side, his grandmaw's apartment off to the other, with the field next to it where revivals were held in big tents. The sounds of preaching and testifying and praying had drifted through his open window, to mix with his dreams on summer nights. The river straight ahead, where he'd floated on homemade rafts. And all around, the mountains. He must have been out of his mind the day he asked about going up to New York City. He liked things fine the way they were. Now that he'd been around his mama some, he realized that New York City hadn't done her much good. The woman he remembered as warm and smiling was often cool and scowling now—at that very moment, for instance.

He spotted Rochelle. Usually she sang with the choir, wearing a long white robe. He enjoyed seeing her long legs encased in nylons, and the arches of her feet peeking over the sides of her spike heels. Looked like she was having to work at it not to sink backwards into the dirt. He smiled at her, and she smiled back. Her brothers and sisters, scrubbed and dressed in poor-fitting suits and starched white dresses, stood in a row on either side of her. How she managed to keep them so tidy-looking was a mystery. One of the boys grinned and stuck out his tongue at Donny. Donny tried to look stern, but the corners of his mouth twitched. As he looked at the row of little children, he became aware that some were much lighter than others. Their fathers might have been white men. Fury swept through him. His hands clenched into fists.

The fury drained away quickly, like air out of a bicycle tire. He looked down at his clenched fists.

"... so the king, he picked this Esther to be his queen. The king's counselor, he'd arranged for her people the Jews to be murdered. Well now, this Esther was real beautiful, and this old king, he couldn't deny her nothing. But did she march right in there and demand that he save her people?"

"Huhun!" people murmured.

"Well sir, what did she do then, this clever and beautiful woman? She prepared a big old feast. The king, he says, 'Esther, what is thy petition and it shall be granted thee?' But did she ask the king to spare her people? No sir, she did not. She asked him to a second banquet. And a second time, the king, he says, 'Esther, what do you want from me, honey?' Well, Esther, she was decked out in these flowing robes bordered with gold. Her table was weighted down with food—bowls of fruit, platters of chitterlings, goblets of wine. This time she says, real sweet and quiet-like, 'If I have found favor in thy sight, O king, let my life be given me at my petition and my people at my request.' And the king, he says, 'Now hold on here a minute. What's this all about, Esther?' And she told him about his wicked counselor, and the king, he set the Jews free and hanged the counselor."

"You preach it, Reverend!"

Kathryn felt a sneer on her face. She was a lapsed Esther. When she'd been baptized in this river by Reverend Stump twenty-three years earlier, she'd been devoted to the concept that the world was shaped in accordance with the Lord's wishes—that her assignment was to make white people's lives more comfortable, that by doing so she'd assure herself of a place in the glorious hereafter. She didn't go to church in New York City. If this world was what the Lord had in mind, she didn't want nothing to do with Him. She glanced around. Her friends and neighbors spent their days following white people's orders and smiling as they did so. They spent their evenings and weekends unleashing on the Lord and on each other the stormy emotions that accumulated. But what if there was no Lord to turn to, and your resentment was allowed to pile up day after day ...

She studied Donny, buttoned up in his dark suit. Serious and polite and obedient and well-meaning, just as she had been at his age. What incident would finally turn him sour? Nothing maybe. Look at his grandmaw. She'd be shuffling to her dying days.

Stump had paused and the crowd was silent. Suddenly he stabbed the air with an index finger and shouted, "You there with that big diamond ring a-glittering on your finger! You there in your city-bought finery! You there with that blonde wig hat on your head! You is lost! Lost! Cadillac cars rust! Sharkskin suits shred! Diamonds fall out of their settings and into the gutter—and then where is you? You is *nowhere*, friend—unless you has accepted Christ Jesus your savior."

"So glad this morning, bless our God!" called Ruby.

"We is slaves. Bound by fetters to the prison of our earthly bodies. And I'm here to tell you this morning, brothers and sisters, that the only thing that can set you free is giving your life over to the Lord Jesus Christ. He frees us from our sins just as surely as the masters freed their slaves from bondage. Hallelujah! The new Jerusalem, the Holy City where the streets is paved with gold, where the gates is inlaid with pearls, it ain't no New York City. Ain't no Washington, D.C., or Cincinnati, Ohio. It commences at death for the faithful who in this life accept Christ Jesus as Lord and savior!"

"That's right!"

"Yeah, tell it, brother. Tell it!"

"That's why we here this morning, friends, to welcome into the fold these young people who have seen the error of their ways and days and have made the decision to commit their lives to Christ Jesus. Who wish to prepare theirselves for their triumphal entry into the Holy City of God. But even Christ hisself had to get purified, at the hands of John the Baptist in the water of the River Jordan . . ."

He waded into the murky foam-flecked river, reciting, " 'And he showed me a pure river of water of life, clear as crystal, proceeding out of the throne of God and of the lamb.' " His robes floated around his waist. Mr. Husk and the young people in white formed a circle in the water. The crowd wailed in complicated harmony, "I was a back-slider once, but praise God I'm on the Glory Road now."

Donny watched as the young people were dunked like doughnuts. He recalled his own baptism. He'd been sitting for many years on the mourners' bench in church, with the women on one side and the men on the other exhorting him to call on the Lord to bring him across. It had become downright embarrassing, both for himself and for his grandmaw, who was the most important lady in the church. Sunday after Sunday, revival after revival, he had waited to be struck between the eyes by a thousand bolts of celestial power, as his playmates seemed to be. Finally Reverend Stump had taken him aside and assured him it was enough just to believe in his heart in the one true God. When his time came to testify, he said just this—no voices in the night, no visions or trances, nothing. But everyone seemed pleased, and sang and wailed. His grandmaw thrust out her arms and shrieked with joy and collapsed into the arms of three ladies, while they fanned her with Sunday School bulletins. Her veiled hat sat askew. Since then he'd gone on to become a junior usher. Straightened up the church after services and swept it once a week.

Ruby glanced at Kathryn reproachfully for not joining in the singing. Others had sung for her. It was the least she could do. Instead she stood in silence and stared across the river. She'd been behaving peculiar ever since she'd been home. Harsh and shrill now, just like a Yankee. She didn't do nothing but badmouth Newland and tell everybody how they ought to act. Happened ever time someone from Pine Woods went up North. Came back know-it-alls, in fancy cars with fine clothes and jewelry and all like that, talking about nightclubs. From the looks of it, her own daughter had turned into one of these godless people, concerned only with the tawdry comforts of this wicked world. Ruby was determined not to let this happen to little Donny. She looked at the grim set to Kathryn's jaw and was afraid for her. Buddy had had that same set to his jaw when he came home from Paris, France, and a few months later he got his throat cut. Ruby agreed with every word Reverend Stump had just said about tact and guile. The Lord meant for people to treat each other good. Just because some folks didn't always abide by this was no reason for the godly to waver.

The Tatro family sat in a pew in the red-brick Methodist church in the mill village. Mr. Tatro, his perpetually grease-stained hands clasped between his knees, was next to Mrs. Tatro in her white gloves and aqua linen suit. Then Jed, arm extended along the pew back.

Then Raymond, hunched in the corner trying to pretend he wasn't
there. Each Sunday he'd announce he wasn't going. His father would
reason with him about the state of his soul. Raymond would reply
that he didn't believe in God. His mother would burst into tears. Jed
would threaten to squash him like the insect that he was. His father
would command him to put on his suit. Raymond would throw himself onto the sofa and stare at them. Eventually he would stomp into
his room and get dressed.

The deacon Mr. Boggs was intoning the lesson from Luke in a
pious nasal whine: "'But which of you, having a servant plowing or
feeding cattle, will say unto him by and by, when he is come from the
field, "Go and sit down to meat?" And will not rather say unto him,
"Make ready wherewith I may sup, and gird thyself, and serve me, till
I have eaten and drunken." So likewise ye, when ye shall have done
all those things which are commanded you, say, . . . "we have done
that which was our duty to do." ' "

Mr. Marsh ascended to the pulpit and leveled a stare fraught with
significance at his flock. He asked quietly, "How many of us here in
this church this morning can look our neighbor in the eye and truth-
fully say, 'I have done that which was my duty to do?' How many of
us? Let ever person in this church who feels he has a right to say
these words turn to his neighbor right now and do it."

There were uneasy rustlings as everyone tried to figure out what
behavior Mr. Marsh wanted from them. All finally concluded cor-
rectly and remained silent.

Mr. Marsh crowed, "Not one person in this church, friends! Not
one! 'I have done that which was my duty to do.' That one little
phrase and not a one of us can claim to have fulfilled it. Now, what
are our duties, friends? Before we can fulfill them, we got to know
what they are. In general our duties pertain to what we owe other
people—what we owe our ancestors, what we owe parents, what we
owe our children, our spouses, our bosses, our town, our state, our
nation. And most especially they pertain to what we owe our God . . ."

Raymond watched Mr. Marsh closely, mentally framing each pose
for his photo series on religion in the South. He smiled with delight as
Mr. Marsh twisted his pudgy frame so his head blocked out a can-
delabra on the altar. The candlelight cast an aura around his bushy

grey hair. The brass cross seemed to grow out of his head like an antler. He stretched out his arm in a Nazi salute.

Tiring, Raymond watched a wayward honey bee explore the vivid reds of Jesus's blood in the stained-glass window next to him. It buzzed around, alighted briefly, then flew on to the next droplet. Mr. Marsh was ranting about duty. Do-wah-ditty ditty dum ditty do. Do-wah duty duty dumb duty do. Raymond considered the topic. What was his duty, and was he going to do it? School would be out in a few weeks, and he still had no clue about what to do for the rest of his life. Last week he'd taken a tour of the mill. Room after barnlike room full of deafening machines doing things to cotton fibers. Warm moist air, hazy with lint, which coated the machinery like thick frost. His father was a foreman in the roving room, which was filled with rows of frames, each supporting a couple of hundred spindles. He demonstrated how to balance the tension so that the rovings, as they wound on to the bobbins, neither broke nor snarled. Raymond was amazed at the enthusiasm his father could summon after twenty-five years for the topic of the constantly fluctuating number of rpms required to keep the winding speed equal to the front delivery speed. He watched as his father scrawled calculations in a small notebook.

His father pointed out the small clocks on each frame. "You divide the hanks by the size of the roving to determine the pounds per spindle. Then you multiply that by spindles per frame to get your total production per frame. Multiply by the number of frames per operative . . ."

Raymond nodded. Bobbins were whirling and whirring as fluffy white bundles of fiber were twisted, stretched, and wound. Watching them was making him dizzy. Men and women in work clothes or coveralls tended the frames. Some spindles had halted, and people were removing full bobbins, packing them in boxes on wheels and replacing them with empty bobbins. The place was a giant sewing machine.

Raymond had always loved figuring out how things, anything, worked. But now that he had the picture, could he spend his life at it? He glanced at his father's face and read enthusiasm. His father kept glancing anxiously at him—eager for approval? This thought unnerved Raymond. He'd spent his whole life wanting, and failing to earn, his father's approval. And now here his father was wanting approval from him? Did his duty require that he follow in his father's footsteps?

On the other hand, his father had left Tatro Cove, hadn't gone into the mines like his own father. Leaving places was practically a family tradition. Maybe his duty lay in upholding this folkway?

After visiting the mill, he'd gone to the newspaper office to ask about a job. The photo editor praised his work but said they couldn't use more staff. "I'm afraid you'll just have to wait for me to die, Raymond," Mr. Monroe quipped.

While he was standing there, word came of a murder on Cherokee Shoals. A mother had shot her son for putting a lighted cherry bomb in her roast chicken. As Raymond snapped pictures of the corpse, he wondered what a lifetime of this would do to him. Was there some way to make a living from playing chess or sorting stamps? A job in the post office? He could steam off exotic stamps. But who in Newland got letters from exotic places?

If he went to New York, took the job at the print shop, left behind everything and everyone familiar—he might fail, and be stuck in a strange city all alone. It seemed like a non-choice. Newland or New York City. Suffocation or terror.

Mr. Tatro was also pondering Duty. To do his duty to his parents, he maybe should have stayed in Tatro Cove. They were old and feeble now, and his brothers and sisters had to tend them without his help. But his duty to his unborn children had required that he leave. He glanced at his handsome healthy family, contrasted them to his gaunt brothers and sisters, nieces and nephews still in Tatro Cove. His glance lingered on Junior. He just didn't know what to make of that boy. Never had. He used to whip him black and blue with a belt almost every week trying to make him mind—say "yes sir," instead of "uh huh." Now he was talking about going off to New York City. "What you wanna go up there with a bunch of Yankees for? You're never gonna mount to nothing without you find you a steady job and work your way up." Junior had seemed interested in the mill at first, but he got bored real quick.

It all began to come back—what he'd gone through getting used to mill work. He'd always done exactly as he pleased in the cove. Mostly he was around the house tending the garden. But even when he was working at the mine, he took off to go hunting when he felt like it. And all of a sudden, he was having to wait until a whistle blew to eat his dinner, having to watch those hundreds of spinning bobbins. He remembered thinking he'd go crazy the first few weeks, between being homesick and turning cross-eyed. But then those checks started coming in—one ever week, as regular as that noontime whistle. And they rented him his house at fifty cents a room; it seemed like a palace. And the current Mrs. Tatro started making eyes at him. The war came, and off he went to Guam. When he got back, all he wanted was to settle down someplace safe and comfortable.

Gratitude. That's what he felt toward the Princes. Something Raymond Tatro Junior had never felt in his whole entire life, cause he'd never known what it was to wonder where his next meal was coming from. He remembered up in the cove going to the Presbyterian mission school ever day he could just because they served a hot lunch. Once a year the sponsors would come down from Philadelphia on a train. The students would line the tracks on the night of their arrival, holding lighted candles. They would go to the mission and do folk dances for the sponsors, watching them shyly and feeling—gratitude for those hot lunches.

Shoot, it would be easy for that boy just to walk into the mill and do the job. He was town raised, used to schedules and being indoors. But he didn't have a coal mine dogging his heels. Mr. Tatro felt a rush of affection. The boy was earnest and restless and ambitious— that way he sat, like a coiled spring. Mr. Tatro had been like that at eighteen himself. His own father had helped him leave without more than a normal helping of guilt, and he'd do the same. That was his duty to his oldest son.

Mr. Marsh had folded his hands atop his ample stomach. Mr. Tatro tried to pay attention. Marsh usually had some pretty important messages.

"Our boys in grey came home to find their houses burnt, their crops destroyed, and their animals run off. It was a turrible, turrible time, friends. The little towns like ours was just jammed with starving farmers down from their gullied patches of mountain soil. Jammed with freed slaves who didn't know what to do with theirselves. We poor vanquished Southerners milled around like latter-day Jobs, in sackcloth and ashes, bewailing our woes and invoking heaven for assistance."

Jed was trying to decide whether to take Sally water skiing or to play miniature golf that afternoon. Miniature golf was over quicker. A couple of fast games and they'd be out at the quarry. But if they was to go water skiing, she'd already be wearing a bathing suit. And if it was hot enough, she might take a few sips of beer. . . . Or should he play hard to get, not even kiss her until she was begging for it? But would Sally be likely to beg? Probably not. And would he still want her if she did? Also probably not. Betty Boobs would sometimes beg, and it disgusted him. The fun was getting them to go along even though they didn't really want to.

Yesterday after working out at the gym, he'd taken a whirlpool bath. It had felt so good just to lie there as the swirling water made him hard. He lay on his back, with his knees open and his eyes closed, until he came. That was probably what it was like to be a girl. They really had it easy. Sometimes he thought he should use the money he spent taking Sally out, hoping she'd repay him with a lousy little peck on the mouth, to buy his own whirlpool bath.

He glanced around. He knew almost everyone in the place, had been coming here all his life. He'd been baptized in the pool on the stage behind Mr. Marsh, would probably settle down back here himself and go to this church with his own kids. But first he figured he'd go to some college—Alabama or Tennessee—on a football scholarship. Then what he'd really like to do was play pro ball. He saw no reason why not. He'd always done everything he set out to do. Turned himself from a skinny little kid into a varsity left tackle. He could press two hundred pounds easy. It ran in his family. His father got hisself out of Tatro Cove and was now a foreman at the mill. Tatros did what they set out to do. Except maybe his faggot older brother over there, who'd been moaning around the house for months over what to do with hisself. Jed couldn't have no sympathy for somebody like that, all wishy-washy, like some damn girl. Balls on him like a Boy Scout. You picked something, and you did it, and you shut up about it. Like Coach Clancy always said, "Either shit or get off the pot."

". . . well, the Lord looks after his own, friends. Yes, he does. Hit is writ in Isaiah 41:17, 'When the poor and needy seek water and there is none, and their tongue faileth for thirst, I the Lord will hear them, I the God of Israel will not forsake them.' And in our day of travail, friends, he sent to the people of this town the means for their salvation. He sent them a group of concerned citizens—names we all recognize today, like Barnes, Johnston, Benson, Prince, Tatro. These fine socially concerned gentlemen decided to open them up a cotton mill. People flocked down out of the hills for jobs—the parents and grandparents of you folks setting here today. The Lord sent them the means for their salvation. They had only to do their duty to the fine men who hired them, and they need never go hungry again. Our Lord came through! Like it says in Psalm 107, 'He turneth the wilderness into a standing water, and dry ground into water springs.' Them that does their duty, they don't have to worry about nothing, friends, cause their Lord God He . . ."

Mrs. Tatro was wondering about the duty other people owed her. If it wouldn't of looked like bragging, she'd of turned to her husband and exclaimed, "I have done that which was my duty to do!" Goodness knows she hadn't enjoyed much of what she'd done in her life, so it must have been duty that kept her at it—washing and ironing, cooking and cleaning, on top of full-time work—first at the mill, now at Sutton Insurance. She remembered the night Raymond Tatro walked into her mother's house wearing faded overalls and a suit jacket, and holding everything he owned in a brown paper sack. She had stifled a giggle. But as the days went by and she chatted with him walking to work and at suppertime, she realized he wasn't no ordinary dumb lazy hick like most of the mountain boys who turned up at her mother's. He had plans and energy. Seemed like that nothing could stop him. They both expected he'd be a foreman before long, then a superintendent. Who knew—maybe even vice president? Seemed like that when he came back from the war, though, some of that drive had left him. He was content just setting around the house.

Mr. Marsh married them in this very church. His family came down from Tatro Cove for the ceremony and embarrassed them both to death, looking like something out of ancient history.

Tatro had been on the hoot-owl shift, and she'd worked days, and they hardly saw each other, except long enough to conceive two sons. She'd get up and get the boys off to babysitters or to school. As she went out the door, he'd come in. When she got home, she'd wash and iron and cook. She'd wake Tatro up for supper, then he'd rush out to work. For a long time she didn't mind. She'd done mill work for a couple of years before her marriage. Her friends were there. You could chat as you wove. But seemed like that the machines, the new models as they come in, just got louder and louder till, before you knew it, you was reading lips rather than hearing. And your quotas kept getting put up until you didn't hardly have time to catch a breath.

They used to lie in bed and dream about moving to a new ranch house in a development—with a brick patio out back and an electric barbecue grill. He'd be earning enough money so she could stop working and raise their sons up proper. But he'd bogged down at foreman, and they were still here in the mill village. He was always exclaiming about how far he'd come since Tatro Cove. She tried to point out how far he had yet to go. She met Melanie Prince in the street the other day. Looked like a million dollars—silk dress, high heels, a hairdo straight out of a beauty parlor. She could of passed for thirty. But in high school she'd been homely, nothing but a brain. No one wanted to date her. Rose Tatro had been a sponsor for the marching band, and every boy in that school had wanted to go out with her, including Melanie Prince's current husband. And she had to go pick Tatro here. . . . She exchanged a wry smile with him.

Each spring he turned up the soil in the back yard and planted huge crops of vegetables, which she canned come harvest. Each spring she suggested he grow just enough for fresh eating, with canned and frozen so cheap in the supermarket. He explained he wanted to be sure his family wouldn't never have to go hungry like up in Tatro Cove. She'd point out he was in the Benson Mill village now, earning regular wages, and not in Tatro Cove with no job. Each spring he'd reply that if you'd grown up hungry, you didn't never get over it.

Junior heaved himself around. That boy had never been anything but difficult, ever since his first month home from the hospital when he drove his daddy out of the house with his screaming.

"Chew your food, Junior."

"Why?"

"Look both ways when you cross the street, Junior."

"I don't have to."

Restless. Whenever he was home, it was like there was a turbine throbbing in his room. Now he was talking about going off to New York City. Every time he brought it up, she left the room without speaking.

She glanced at Jed. Her baby. Big and strong, but so gentle and affectionate. He loved his mama, loved his home. No problems with Jed. He'd done her proud. He'd take up where his daddy gave out, go to college, come back to the mill, start off in management . . . She pictured him, dressed in a suit and tie as he was now, seated behind a big desk in a carpeted office, instructing his secretary to send his mother some flowers, as she sometimes did for Mr. Sutton.

". . . so we have these reds from up North coming in here ever oncet in a while—telling us how to run our jobs. Say what we need is to start us up one of these here unions like they got em up North.

"Now I say to you, friends, if things is so great up there, why is these Commie agitators all the time coming down *here*? I'll tell you why, friends. We got us a good thing going. And them folks, they know it! We do our duty here, friends. Do better work for less cost, and we're stealing away all their bidness. They stay in the plushest rooms the Howard Johnson Motel has to offer. They eat big old steak dinners down at the Corral Restaurant. We sit home and we eat hot dogs. And they want *us* to pay *them* dues? Why, we'd have to demand higher wages just to get the same take-home as before! Mr. Prince would have to raise prices, and we wouldn't be able to win so many jobs away from the Northern mills. Which is exactly what our Yankee organizing friends want!"

A handful of people near the back got up and stomped out, grumbling.

"Don't be deceived, friends, by these smooth-talking Communist radicals with their tinted glasses and their miniature cigars. I'm sure yall know who I mean."

The congregation whispered.

"All the time talking about the 'downtrodden oppressed workers.'

You poor, poor things, they moan, you is earning fourteen percent less than your working brothers in Lowell, Massachusetts. I guess fourteen percent would just about cover their phone bills home to Boston, don't yall?"

Mr. Tatro nodded agreement, thinking how the Princes took all the risks, bore all the responsibilities. It was a relief when he got home to stretch out on the couch and forget about the mill until the next morning. Whereas the Princes had to live with it day in and day out. It was their place, and they could offer whatever wages they pleased, which a man could either accept or reject. The notion of a union was humiliating. Damn, he could look out for hisself, always had, always would. On the day when he made the last payment on his house, he invited Mr. Prince Sr. over to celebrate. And he came! The president of the mill, but he took time out to sit on the back porch with one of his foremen and sip iced tea and talk about the garden and termite-proofing and asphalt shingles. As Mr. Prince walked down the front sidewalk in his shirt-sleeves, trying to smooth down his scrambled white hair, Mr. Tatro had stammered his gratitude. Mr. Prince Sr. said, "You don't need to say it, son. There's gratitude flowing in both directions." Shoot, he didn't need him no middlemen with the Princes.

During slow periods, Mr. Prince Sr. would keep production as close to normal as he could, stockpiling goods in warehouses all over town until demand picked up again. You had to be a dead loss for him to ever let you go. But unions was one thing he wouldn't tolerate. His face would go all scarlet when the topic came up, and his bushy white eyebrows would start in to twitching. In the old days when the organizers would arrive, the mill men would usher them to the town limits singing "Praise God from Whom All Blessings Flow." And tell them not to come back cause they wasn't wanted. But these days they was more sneaky. They hired Southerners as front men. Them you could sometimes pick out even easier, because they was all the time exaggerating their accents and talking about the dirt farms they was raised on. One question they'd never answered to his satisfaction: If they was such avid Southerners, how could they allow theirselves to be used as mouthpieces by a bunch of Yankee Communists?

The loyalty the old-timers felt for Mr. Prince Sr. extended to his

son, though he was tough to figure. Seemed like he didn't hardly have
no personality at all. Especially compared to that daddy of his. You
couldn't say he was stuck up or nothing, even though he went up
North to college. He chose to come back here, married a local girl.
His daughters went out with Jed and Junior. But he didn't seem to
have no backbone. Why, he stooped when he walked, and he wasn't
no older than Mr. Tatro hisself.

"... now John, he says in the fourth chapter, thirty-sixth verse,
says: 'He that reapeth receiveth wages, and gathereth fruit unto life
eternal: that both he that soweth and he that reapeth may rejoice
together.' Well, I know it's difficult for our good union friends to
understand how we see things down here, since workers and management up there is at each other's throats ever minute of ever day. But
just cause we got us a mill in this here town, hit don't mean we're in
no hurry to give up our Southern way of life.

"It is writ in the 126th Psalm, 'They that sow in tears shall reap in
joy.' And I say to you, friends, that we has known tears. But we
sowed, and now we're reaping. And hit is joyful! Yes, hit is, friends.
And I say to these Communist agitators coming in here all the time
trying to stir up trouble—thank you all the same, you with your dues
check-offs and your health plans and your binding arbitration, but the
Lord is our negotiator. And when that last spindle's been wound,
brothers and sisters, heaven is the only closed shop we're hankering
after. The only collective bargaining we gonna do is right here in
this church on our knees with our Lord God!"

He launched into prayer with his arms upraised.

Raymond wasn't sure he agreed with this message he'd been hearing all his life. One big happy family, was how his father portrayed
the mill. They'd gone once a week to the company ball field to watch
their father play in the mill league. When they were little, he and Jed
spent the game climbing on the jungle gym, sliding, and swinging. As
they got older, they watched the game and cheered at the right spots.
Every summer there were company barbecues at a park on the lake.
The Princes were there in Bermuda shorts, laughing and talking just
like everyone else. But recently he was understanding that the Princes
*weren't* "just like everyone else." Something was fishy in this here
happy family. He couldn't say exactly what. Maybe there was a limit

on how many generations a family could be expected to show gratitude. There was a job waiting for him at the mill that dozens of men would kill to get, but he didn't feel grateful. He could see his life laid out before him. In twenty-five years he'd be just like his father, content in a dumpy house with a boring job.

But there was an appeal to it. Safe and comfortable. He wouldn't have to prove anything to anyone—couldn't prove anything, since he'd been pegged since birth, like an etherized moth.

In the grey stone Episcopal church at the top of the hill, the congregation was confessing, ". . . we do earnestly repent and are heartily sorry for these our misdoings. The remembrance of them is grievous unto us . . ."

Sally was trying to decide whether or not she had sinned. The previous night at the quarry, Jed had handed her the stubs from all the movies he'd taken her to since they first started dating. She counted them up—over two hundred. At a dollar and a quarter each, he'd spent over two hundred and fifty dollars on movies alone. Reeling, she allowed Jed to put his hand in her panties. Before she knew it, he had his finger inside her. She shrieked and leaped out of the car. When she got back in, she absolutely laid down the law: Jed was never to do this again. But did this mean she was no longer a virgin? Had that membrane, or whatever it was, been broken? And was it for sure a sin to be unmarried but not a virgin? Was there any way this could have made her pregnant? She opened one eye and glanced at her father, who knelt next to her with his head bowed and his eyes closed. At breakfast she kept wondering if he could see in her eyes that Jed had done this.

". . . spare Thou those, Oh God, who confess their faults . . ."

Yes, Lord, it was wrong, Sally prayed. And I'm sorry. (It didn't even feel good. At least it could have felt good if she was going to have to feel this guilty. If a finger had felt so unpleasant, what must a . . .)

She decided to think about something else. Punch cups! The Plantation Ball was in two weeks. Each Ingenue was chairman of something, and this year she was Punch Cup chairman and had to borrow cups from all over town, and label them, and keep them washed and filled at the dance, and replace broken ones, and return them afterward. It was a big job. What if she didn't plan for enough cups? What if people ended up drinking out of Dixie cups, as they had at the prom two years ago? It would be so embarrassing. Someone had suggested disposable plastic cups, which just grossed everyone out. She'd better get plenty of extras.

Robert Prince, his elbows on the pew back in front of him, was pondering the collect from the first Psalm: "Blessed is the man that walketh not in the counsel of the ungodly, nor standeth in the way of sinners, nor sitteth in the seat of the scornful . . . And he shall be like a tree planted by the rivers of water, that bringeth forth his fruit in his season; his leaf also shall not wither; and whatsoever he doeth shall prosper." Profits were up nine percent this year. Was this a sign that he was doing all right? "To him that soweth righteousness shall be a sure reward." He had just authorized construction of a new employee recreation area with four tennis courts, a playground, and a baseball diamond. He was trying to run the mill as his father had. The well-being of his employees was his responsibility. It weighed on him. He wasn't doing enough, or not the right things.

Some of the younger men at the mill he didn't even know. On his walks in his shirt-sleeves through the rooms, the older men would introduce them. Some were sullen and would glance around impatiently as he and the older men tried to chat about hernias and Charolais—Angus crosses and the Dodgers. From among these younger men sprang those who were listening to the union organizers. A small local had been formed. Under total secrecy, but he usually heard about whatever went on. He wished he could reassure them: If they felt he'd engineered some plot by which to exploit them, they were overestimating his efficiency and competence.

His father's ways didn't work anymore. No one *wanted* a union in the old days. They were thrilled to have a steady salary, a house in the village with services nearby. And his father heaped on softball leagues and picnics and paid vacations, knowing that benevolence was good business, that every dollar spent on employee benefits saved a couple in terms of the demands of a union of unhappy employees. Besides, his father had liked his workers and really did want to see them happy. But nowadays good will and barbecues weren't enough.

The young men were talking health benefits and pension plans and grievance procedures and cost-of-living raises. Things were changing. When his father had been brought down from Lawrence, Massachusetts, after the strike there, to run this mill using "native-born Anglo-Saxon workers," he'd been received like Christ entering Jerusalem. The mill was a community undertaking, and many of the workers were from outside the community. They were offered wages and housing, which they could take or leave, since there were hundreds more who would gladly take them. Now the attitude among the younger workers seemed to be that it was *their* mill.

He smiled bitterly. As far as he was concerned, they could have it. Unfortunately, it wasn't his to give anymore. He had stockpiled extensively during the recession following the Korean War. The entire bottom floor had been packed to the rafters with bales of cloth. He was on the verge of bankruptcy and didn't see how he could hold out until the next war came along. Finally he had to close down or sell out, so he'd sold to Arnold Corporation—which had forty-five mills, 35,000 employees, fourteen million dollars in profits last year. They'd kept him on as a figurehead, but he had little real authority now. He was sure the home office would cancel the recreation area.

The minister, Mr. Shell, was talking along the same lines: ". . . it is doubtful whether Anglo-Saxon people at any time since the Norman Conquest had lived in such abject poverty. I was a young man then, fresh out of seminary. I found a region devastated by war, humiliated by Reconstruction, inhabited by hungry and hopeless people. I remember standing in this very pulpit trying to fire up my congregation about a textile mill as a means of escape from this dreadful idleness and despondency.

"People told me I was an outsider, meddling in a way of life I didn't understand. I sustained myself with the knowledge that Joseph, a foreigner in Egypt, nevertheless inspired and assisted the Egyptians. The South was a civilization founded on agriculture, some argued. I was proposing to graft a shoot from another species onto the Southern rootstock. The North had defeated the South on the fields of battle, but it had not defeated it as a cultural entity. But should the South embrace industry, cultural defeat would follow.

"The North was materialistic, they insisted. A person's worth was determined by how many goods he had amassed. Decisions were based on maximizing profits. These were not traits my parishioners admired or wished to emulate. I maintained then, and I maintain now, that there need not be this dichotomy between the spiritual and the material. In the words of our collect, 'Blessed is the man that walketh not in the counsel of the ungodly, nor standeth in the way of sinners . . . Whatsoever he doeth shall prosper.' The righteousness of a righteous man permeates all his activities and causes them to flourish and to benefit those involved. Only to the superficially spiritual do the industrial successes of Newland appear materialistic. To those with eyes to see, they are evidence that our undertakings have been regarded with favor by our Lord . . ."

Mr. Prince lowered his head and shielded his face with his hand, under the guise of prayer, but in fact to hide the bitter smile stamped permanently across his features these days. A team of efficiency experts—or management consultants, or some damn thing—had arrived from Arnold headquarters in New York City. They'd followed him around for days taking notes, then sat him down and presented their findings. It was not cost-efficient for him to spend so much time strolling around chatting with employees. He was paying subordinates good money to represent him to the workers. He needed to increase the number of machines supervised by each man. The workers spent too much time in the bathrooms. For once, he felt something unequivocally: He requested in a wavering voice that they leave. They marched off in their pinstriped suits and horn-rimmed glasses, informing him he'd be hearing from the home office. And he did—via a memo ordering him to increase quotas and monitor bathroom time. Since then, rumors had been flying about organizing in the village. Some days he even wished them well. But what scared him was the suspicion that the union leaders were just using them. If expenses rose at this mill, contracts would have a better chance of going to unionized mills in the North, where the bulk of the union membership worked. His workers were such naive people that they'd never be able to see this, or to believe it if someone told them.

He felt as flying reptiles must have when rodents began their climb to ascendancy. He was a man cast in an old mold. A flattering way of looking at his indecisiveness was to regard it as judiciousness: There was validity to each person's point of view, and the challenge was to reconcile them, not to prevail over them with your own point of view. He tried to keep his dealings polite and pleasant and voluntary. He felt how people treated each other was more important than any consensus they might reach. People who didn't abide by this code— the management consultants and the younger workers and the Arnold executives—he didn't know how to deal with. And didn't want to know. When it came right down to it, he couldn't bear being disliked. He wished he were out of it altogether. Too young to retire, too old to start off in a new line of work, children to send through college, a family name to uphold, workers with families who depended on the mill for their livelihood.

But at least he *knew* he was a flying reptile, something his own father couldn't grasp. He was always saying, "Now you take good care of my workers, son. They need us." Sometimes he thought the old guy was schizophrenic. He'd talk about "his workers" and the "Benson Mill family," and you'd almost forget that he'd been scooping off hundreds of thousands of dollars of profit for decades. Yet there was nothing cynical about him. He really did care about "his workers," and really did see the profits as rightfully his. Unlike the ranks of executives from Arnold who'd flowed through Newland. You couldn't hate these men. There was nothing there to hate. They were too bland. They weren't even Yankees. They had no regional loyalty at all, no religious compunctions. Their loyalty was to the Arnold Fiber Corporation profit-and-loss statements, which determined their own personal fortunes and their ascent up the corporate ladder. You couldn't expect them to care about Newland or the workers because they never stayed around long enough to get involved.

Not that Robert himself was one to talk. He knew the setup wasn't just, but he didn't know what to do about it, so he passed most of his profits on to the children in trust funds. To be the beneficiary of a system you knew was askew put you at cross-purposes to yourself. Sometimes he wondered if, apart from uncontrollable economic forces, he hadn't actually engineered his own failure when he had to sell the mill after the Korean War, in a half-hearted attempt to extract himself from an iniquitous system.

He glanced down the pew at his family. Melanie was still a gorgeous woman. From time to time he thought wistfully of the excitement of their courtship—when her hair swinging against his cheek as they danced to Tommy Dorsey sent stabs of passion through him. Then the high drama when he went off to war, not knowing if they'd ever see each other again. The excitement had faded over the years, but he still felt a quiet peace when he was with her. Sometimes he looked at her as she read in the lamplight and felt a stab of poignancy. When the house was full of little children, it seemed as though the chores would never end, but with middle age came the knowledge that they would end all too soon. Their love wasn't forever. Each new day was a gift, and one day not too far off, one of them wouldn't be there any longer to enjoy it. It was similar to how he'd felt leaving to fight Hitler, only more painful because more drawn out, less heroic, and more inevitable.

Bouncy little Sally took after Robert's father, had the "common touch." Too common, he sometimes feared as he watched that oaf Jed Tatro pick her up for dates and recognized that glazed gleam in his eye. He understood what drove men to lock their daughters in towers, or clamp them into chastity belts. But here, as everywhere else, he realized that forces beyond his control were at work— hormones and God knew what all. It was horrible. As for Emily, poor child, she was stuck with his own grim determination to fit in and inability to do so. She also had his capacity for outrage, but without the indecisiveness that kept it under wraps. She stalked around the house these days like a hand grenade whose pin has just been pulled.

It was too soon to tell about little Robby. At Robby's age Robert was being dragged by his own father on walks through the mill. There had never been any question what Robert's career would be. He sometimes wondered what he would have done otherwise. Taught history maybe. Been a dog catcher. As far as he was concerned, Robby was on his own. The atmosphere in the mill office now was all intrigue and jockeying for position, as Arnold executives marched in and out. He wouldn't wish it on his worst enemy, to say nothing of his own son. Sometimes he even wished the kid would be a crazed revolutionary and blow the place sky high. But maybe Emily would instead.

Mr. Shell, his father's crony, also was not aware of his whooping crane status. A sweet old man in a long black robe, who had once been farsighted and flexible, and who was now sounding like a broken record: ". . . right from the start, and no doubt down to this very day, there were those who clung to the old ways and the ancient gods, those who repudiated every attempt to lead our people out of their wilderness of despair and desolation. But no doubt there were some with Joshua, too, who refused to enter the Promised Land, and returned to the grave of Moses to await their deaths. But for the rest of us, our sufferings in the desert have given us an immense delight in and gratitude for our brave new land of milk and honey. The Gospel counsels us to care for the weak as though they were our children, to practice generosity to the less fortunate, to aid all mankind as though each and every unfortunate were Jesus Christ himself. We have lifted our workers out of their mire of ignorance and disease and filth. We are instruments in the hand of a merciful God. Truly we can say of the mills and factories that stretch proudly along the banks of the Cherokee River, that they are 'like trees planted by the rivers of water, that bringeth forth their fruit in their season.' "

Emily inspected the congregation as she walked back from the communion railing. The kids her age were sons and daughters of factory managers, doctors, lawyers. "Brains" at school. Emily felt put upon having to attend this church when most of the Ingenues went to the Methodist or Baptist churches. Both had active Sunday night youth groups—arranged hay rides and suppers. How could she be expected to get a bid from Ingenue when she was forced to go to this weird church where you had to wear a hat? She glanced at her parents resentfully, plopped down on her knees and pretended to pray, then slumped into the pew corner with her arms folded. Her parents were weird compared to everybody else's, who joked and shouted at their kids and really *cared* about them. Their drafty barn of a house was like a morgue. Everybody else had family rooms with pine paneling and dart boards, linoleum floors for dancing, Ping-Pong tables and pin-ball machines. Instead of junky old antiques you couldn't touch. No wonder Ingenue didn't want her.

She wanted to be an Ingenue, not a Junior Servicette. She wanted to spend her time collecting punch cups, rather than serenading at the Poor Farm. To join the Junior Service Club, you had to have good grades, good marks in citizenship, and be a good Christian. In other words, you had to be a fink. A bunch of finks got together and did finky things. Like going to the Poor Farm, as they'd done yesterday. (Their adviser kept reminding them to call it the County Home.) It consisted of a white residential building, out-buildings, and surrounding fields, which the more able inmates tilled and planted in nice weather. But most inmates were too senile and fragile for farmwork. They were there because their families wouldn't or couldn't care for them, or because they had no families.

The party was held in a dreary ground-floor room. Bare wood floors, wooden benches around the walls, flaking paint on the walls. On the benches sat a dozen inmates, scrubbed, combed, and dressed in fresh overalls and housedresses. They grinned toothlessly and murmured shy words of welcome.

The boys hung crepe paper, while the girls arranged flowers and put out piles of gifts and organized cake and punch on a table they covered with a paper cloth. The old people watched, even though most had already endured several identical Junior Service Welcome-to-Spring parties.

Roger, a slight young man who played organ at the First Baptist Church, sat at an out-of-tune piano and played "I'm Looking over a Four-Leafed Clover." Marge, a Madrigal, said with a big smile, as though addressing two-year-olds, "Everybody let's sing now!" Mostly Marge sang, with some help from the Junior Servicettes. The inmates droned an uninspired basso continuo. A man in freshly pressed overalls with a watch chain across the bib pounded time with his cane and grinned toothlessly. Several others clapped faintly, out of rhythm. A gusty April wind rattled the windows in their frames like chattering false teeth.

The Junior Servicettes passed out gifts—lacy handkerchiefs for the women and billfolds for the men. They grinned and exclaimed, and Emily began to feel irritated that so little could excite them to such gratitude.

As the old people ate cake and sipped punch, the Junior Servicettes chatted with them. Or rather, listened, as each old person told his or her life story, delighted to find a fresh audience. Emily sat with the old man who had pounded his cane. He told her about his childhood, hired out to a farmer by his stepfather from sunrise to sunset for twenty-five cents a day. His youth, in lumber camps and saw mills. His forty years in the card room at Benson Mill. His old age here at the County Home due to a complicated story of broken promises and abandonment, illness and death. He talked with a toothless smile. Occasionally he paused to wheeze and cough. "Hit's my lungs," he explained. "Done gone plumb punky. The Doc, he says hit's the empheeseemee done got me. Too much smoking. Funny thang is, I ain't never smoked." He heaved with soundless laughter.

Above the smiling mouth, in his eyes, Emily read misery, loneliness, lovelessness, bitterness, resignation, fear, humiliation—and contempt for young people who understood nothing. She got up and moved away, muttering an excuse.

In closing, Emily on her flute accompanied Marge, who sang, "*Shine glorious sun. / Banish all our cares and sorrow. / Set thy radiance in heaven / To greet the morrow.*" The old man pounded his cane loudly and off the beat, smiling, until an attendant led him away.

"Well!" said their adviser as they drove away. "That went very well. You all did a real nice job."

"I don't think we should go again," Emily murmured.

"How come?" everyone asked with surprise.

"I don't know."

Mrs. Prince noted Emily's sour look in her direction and was swept with guilt. What had she done now? Emily was at an age at which she seemed to need to expend energy making her parents feel bad for having brought her into this imperfect world.

Next, right on schedule, arrived sympathy. (The two alternated, like flashing neon signs.) Sally was everything Emily wanted to be, and there was no way to tell Emily that the cheerleading set, force-bloomed, shriveled early and spent the rest of their lives consumed by a disembodied sense of injustice that they were no longer the focus for the entire community. Mrs. Prince had watched this happen to her own high school class. The athletes, the "fast" set had had their years. But now the classmates she'd envied so much were tired middle-aged householders like herself. Rose Tatro, for instance. She'd been a sponsor for the band, had marched in front at football games carrying an armload of carnations dyed orange and purple, the Newland High colors. Several boys had fought almost to the death over her. Melanie had seen her downtown the other day. Her hair was frizzy, she was too heavy, was wearing too much makeup in a attempt to conceal wrinkles.

But Emily took after Robert and was almost impossible to console. She specialized in varieties of frowns and grimaces, and had ever since birth really. That was the astonishing thing—to realize that Emily had been Emily right from the womb. And Sally, Sally. As a baby, Sally gurgled and giggled and climbed all over anyone who was around, touching their eyelashes with fascination as they blinked. Emily had spent most of her early years sitting absolutely still in a playpen, looking as though she were carrying on a dialogue with unseen beings. Several times Melanie had looked out the kitchen window into the back yard and seen chipmunks down from the trees sitting quietly beside her in the playpen. Sometimes it felt as though the two girls were living out two aspects of Melanie's own personality. Sally was the clubwoman, though she was successful at it. And Emily brooded about time and space and the meaning of life, while feeling bad about not being able to do what seemed to satisfy everyone around her.

Melanie looked at the altar with an expert eye. She'd set up this communion. She liked draping the embroidered cloths over the chalice, straightening the corners. Changing the hangings for the different seasons and holy days. Changing the numbers in the overhead racks. Keeping the vestments clean and pressed for the choir and the acolytes and the deacon.

Mr. Shell was about to retire, and they were having to pick someone new. Various young men were giving guest sermons. Recently an earnest young man from Baltimore chastised them for their non-involvement in the Negro struggle. He'd not gotten the job. But the points he'd raised had remained with her. Was church the place to raise such issues? She'd always thought of it as a place of refuge from the problems of this wretched world, like her garden.

". . . May the Lord bless you and keep you. May the Lord make His face to shine upon you and give you peace, this day and ever-more. Amen."

# Chapter Five

## The Plantation Ball

The spotlight was on Jed and Sally as they strolled down the ramp, her arm through his. "Miss Sally Prince, escorted by Mr. Jed Tatro."

Sally was wearing a strapless white gown with a full ballerina-length skirt. Atop her dark blonde hair was a rhinestone tiara. The carnations she had shamed Jed into sending were tied on her wrist. She was overcome with pride and had to blink back tears. This was the moment each Ingenue had been working for all year. This was the whole glorious reason for the bake sales, the car washes, the raffles. She glanced with a proprietary smile at Jed in his rented white dinner jacket. He wore a ruffled shirt, and a plaid cumberbund and bow tie. Across his chest was the purple sash that identified him as an Ingenue Escort. He was grinning at their friends, who were applauding as she and he descended the steps to "Moon River," played by the dance band on the stage. She and Jed took their position in the formation on the dance floor, just to the right of the free-throw line, and watched and applauded as the other club members were presented.

Sally glanced around the gym, which had been transformed by coral gauze draperies into a voluptuous harem. The rest of the student body stood in the shadows and sat at tables around the circumference of the dance floor. She loved being able to provide everyone with such a lovely dance. Things would get so humdrum without special occasions to work for and look forward to.

Behind the band was a mural the club used each year—of a plantation house with white pillars. Jed studied it. This was the kind of house he'd always imagined he'd live in when he returned to Newland after his pro ball career to live off his endorsements and raise his fam-

ily. Never mind that there wasn't no such house in town. He'd build
him one. Pulling up in front of the mansion was a horse-drawn coach,
driven by a nigger in a satin uniform. On the verandah stood women
in long dresses and men in white suits. A fat black mammy chuckled
in the doorway and shielded pink-cheeked children in her long home-
spun skirts. Fancy writing said, "Our Southern Way of Life."

Jed glanced around the room. It looked good. The girls had done a
nice job. The coral walls of the tent swelled and billowed. It reminded
him of Betty Boob's cunt when she was coming. This notion of being
a midget trapped inside a giant cunt made him feel suffocated. He
stretched his neck to loosen his collar.

All twenty-eight Ingenues and their dates had assembled. The band
began "The Champagne Waltz," and the couples waltzed around
each other in intricate patterns while the audience applauded. Bill
Rogers, president of the boys' social club, the Rebels, climbed up on
the ramp with the president of Ingenue. He held up a cut-glass cup
of fruit punch and gave the ritual toast: "To the young women of
the South, exceeded by none in beauty and virtue. We pledge ourselves to your service and protection."

Sally blinked back tears as all the young men in the room raised
their cups, then tossed down their punch. She glanced down to be
sure her bodice wasn't slipping.

Emily, standing in a corner, glanced at Raymond, uncomfortable
in his rented dinner jacket. He grinned and tossed off his punch. Then
he put his arm around her and said in a deep voice, "Don't worry,
little one. You've got me to take care of you." She removed herself
from his grasp and gave him a disapproving look. "Virtue, my ass,"
Raymond whispered. "Do you think there's a virgin in this room?"

"Besides me?" As she gazed at the assembled Ingenues, she felt
gangly, unattractive, and envious. What could she do to become one
of them?

Raymond studied the mural of "Our Southern Way of Life" and
thought of his kinfolks in Tatro Cove. Who were they trying to kid?
He didn't know anybody who lived like that. Of course, his great-
grandfather had died defending "Our Southern Way of Life." And
Raymond himself on the junior high playground had participated in
elaborate campaigns against the horrified sons of Newland's Yankee

industrialists. Occasionally he fought on the Yankee side because he played chess with them. But usually he'd devoted himself to restoring the lost honor of the South.

"Let's dance," he suggested, steering Emily onto the floor as the band swung into "Sweet Little Sixteen."

As she and Raymond did their best to simulate chickens scratching after grain, Emily saw a Negro boy in a white waiter's jacket by the refreshment table gathering up used cups. He looked up, as though feeling her stare, and glanced around.

"Look, Raymond. It's Donny."

They stopped dancing and stared. Donny, long and lanky, was grinning and serving someone punch. "Christ," Raymond muttered.

"Maybe we should go say hello?"

"Let's get out of here," Raymond said, dragging her toward the door.

"But why? We just got here." Raymond was a drag, always wanting to leave parties early and refusing to join in while he was there. No wonder Ingenue hadn't given her a bid. Maybe she needed to break up with him and find another boyfriend who wasn't so determined to be a creep.

"Why is he grinning like that?"

"Maybe he's having a good time. Some people do at dances, you know."

"It's bad enough that he's doing it at all. But it's terrible if he's enjoying it."

"But why?"

"They're trying to fit him into his slot, same as they're trying to do to me. I know a slot when I see one." That week at school classmates had begun squealing through the halls waving college acceptances. Raymond was starting to feel frantic over the topic of what to do with himself for the rest of his life.

Donny sloshed punch into cups, grinning grimly. His grandmaw had taken to telling him lately, "Good manners is the best life insurance a colored person can have." Besides, a grin set you free. As long as you grinned, you could think whatever you wanted. And at this particular moment, he was wondering if these white boys was knocking off their girlfriends or what. So many of them looked so awkward out there, jerking around like they was half paralyzed or something. Even if they got it in, they'd never be able to keep it in, lurching around like that. No wonder Blanton was out after his mama. He felt the rage begin to rise in his throat. He squelched it, listened to a few bars of "Long Tall Sally," did a couple of loose-limbed dance steps, and flashed his teeth at the white boy whose cup he was filling.

"What you so happy about?" the boy asked, smiling back. "You having you a good time?"

"Yes sir, I sure is!"

As far as his mama knew, he wasn't here tonight. His grandmaw had come home with Sally's message offering him this job. His mama yelled, "Why, that little slut! Who she think she's talking to?"

"Ten bucks, Mama, for one evening."

"I don't care if it's ten thousand bucks. You write back and tell her to go douche with her fruit punch!"

"Kathryn! You watch that mouth of yours in front of your little boy!" Ruby snarled.

Donny was laughing. "I ain't so little, Grandmaw."

"That's twice what I make in a day," Ruby pointed out. "You put on a white jacket, and you dump punch in cups, and they pay you ten dollars. Law, I don't see a thing wrong with that."

"I don't neither," Donny said.

"If you don't see, I can't tell you. But I'm still your mama, Donny, and I forbid you to take that job."

Their eyes locked, Donny's amazed. "Mama, I'm sixteen years old. You ain't been around here for four years. I decide what I gon do."

"If you take that job, I don't want to know about it."

If this was what New York City did to people, made them too picky to earn a living, then he thought he'd better stay put. As far as he could see, his mama had turned plumb hysterical up there.

It was early morning, too early for other boats to be out, but not too early for the sun to be scorching. The inlet was surrounded by wooded cliffs. Buzzards wheeled around nests high overhead. Jed cut the motor and drifted alongside the ski jump. He tied the boat to a leg of the jump and hopped out, then helped Sally onto the sloping canvas surface.

They lay side by side, half-dozing, the hot sun burning into their tired bodies. In keeping with tradition they'd been out all night at post-ball parties that eventually became breakfasts. They were well fed on scrambled eggs and sweet rolls.

Jed took Sally's hand. She squeezed his. "Wasn't it wonderful?" she sighed. "Everything went so beautifully. I can't believe it's all over."

Jed rolled over, nibbled at her neck and ears, and pushed the damp blonde hair back from her forehead. "You're so beautiful."

"Of course, it isn't really over, is it? We have to go clean up this afternoon. How will we stay awake?"

Jed lowered his mouth onto hers. They kissed for a long time, their tongues playing hide-and-seek. "I want you so much, Sally."

"The band was OK, but I liked the Dukes last year better."

Jed worked a knee between her legs. He slid his hand down her bathing suit top and stroked a nipple.

"You won't forget to borrow that truck for the clean-up this afternoon, will you, Jeddie?"

"No," he murmured, rubbing his erection against her thigh.

The sun beat down. Through half-closed eyelashes Sally could see the surrounding cliffs, sun-struck and shimmering in the heat. The ski jump rocked gently in the swells. The deep green water was penetrated by shafts of sunlight.

She dozed, and awoke to discover that her own and Jed's bathing suits had been removed. Jed was kneeling between her legs, lowering himself.

"No, Jed," she murmured faintly.

"Please, Sally," he whispered.

"Please don't, Jed."

"Please."

"Please. No," she whispered, as he pushed himself slowly into her.

"Please," he gasped as he moved ever less tentatively in and out.

Sally lay absolutely still. If she didn't participate, if she didn't enjoy this in any way whatsoever, it would be OK. It would be as though it hadn't even happened. Jed jerked and shuddered and gasped and sighed and lay silent.

And in fact, it was exactly as though it hadn't happened. She felt nothing. Except terror. But this wasn't how she'd always imagined it. That song last night: *"When you hold me so tight, / I just know this is right . . ."* This conviction was lacking. What had gone wrong?

"Will you always love me, Jed?" she whispered in a fearful voice.

He was lying on her, absently stroking her hair and trying to fathom the enormity of what he'd just done. Mr. Prince's daughter. It hadn't been as good as with Betty Boobs. It hadn't even been as good as jerking off. She just lay there, like a corpse. The Chuck Berry song last night that all the boys had hooted at, and all the girls had blushed at: *"I looked at the clock / it read ten to four. / She said, 'Come on, daddy, do it some more.' / I looked at the clock / it read ten to nine. / She said, 'O yeah, daddy, that sure feels fine!' / . . . ten to ten. / She turned to me, made me do it again."*

"Yeah, Sally, I will. You know I will." God, he had no choice now. He'd taken her virginity. She was his for life. They looked at each other uneasily.

Raymond and Emily drove in the golden light of early evening down a valley of well-tended farms toward Donley to a meeting Raymond was covering for the newspaper. A lazy river wound through the valley. Forested hills rose up on either side. Tiny figures in the distance threw hay bales onto wagons.

They drove into the sleepy little town, a shopping community for coal miners and farmers. It consisted of a shopping street, an old brick courthouse, a street of dignified frame houses, and lots of drooping elms. Abruptly they found themselves in a traffic jam, unheard of for Donley.

Hearing the roar of a crowd on the courthouse green, they found it packed with several hundred white people—men in khakis and short-sleeved white sports shirts with the sleeves rolled up, white socks, black pointy shoes, long sideburns, and slicked-down hair. Women in housedresses and white socks and flats. Babies in diapers. Signs waved: "We won't go to school with no niggers!" "Get rid of the Supreme Court." Men were yelling, "Yeah, he's right!"

Raymond snapped pictures hurriedly while daylight lasted. Emily worked her way through the crowd, across the grass, toward the courthouse steps, where a man identical to the others stood shouting. A woman handed her a pamphlet headlined "Beware of the Unholy Three." It was a harangue against fluoridated water and polio serum and mental hygiene—all Yankee Communist plots to undermine the health and will of a free people.

"They's three of us Anglo-Saxons to every seven niggers on this earth! But we pure-blooded Anglo-Saxons is the only ones who run free guvmints for free men!"

"Tell it, buddy!"

"These here nigger-loving Reds on our Donley school board, they tell us we gonna have *coons* in our schools next year. Setting up against the fair white bodies of our defenseless little daughters. Well, I say we ain't!"

The crowd roared.

"When Ham gazed on Noah in his nakedness, friends, and mocked and reviled him, Noah put a curse on the sons of Ham. In Genesis he said, 'Cursed be Canaan; a servant of servants shall he be unto his brethren.' Now, I ask you, does that sound like the Lord meant for us to send our sweet little children to *school* with them black devils?"

"*No!*" roared the crowd.

"No, naturally not!" roared back the man. "Hit's a plot by them Jews up at Washington, D.C., to weaken Caucasian manhood by mixing up our blood with a bunch of lazy savages! The Lord meant for em to keep to theirselves. Why, he says rat cheer in Joshua, 'Let em be hewers of wood and drawers of water.' He don't say *nothing* bout letting em go to school with our children and letting em mongrelize the white race!"

"No, He don't!"

"We got to let them Reds running our schools and running our federal guvmint know what we think down here! We been pushed around just about long enough! We done had Yankees ordering us around long as anyone in these parts can remember—set your slaves free and elect em to public office! Move your family offen your farm cause we gon flood it to make these here TVA lakes for rich people to water ski on! We gon turn your farms into that there Smoky Mountain National Park—so's we can come down from Washington and take pictures of bars! We gon turn you off your land and put up big ole fences and build us an atom bomb—so's if it blows up, yall is the ones that gits killed! We gon chop up your stills and put you in jail! We gon run a turnpike through your cornfield! We gon put niggers in your schools! We gon destroy the South altogether! Friends, they ain't no stopping em—these Yankee radical Communists. I don't know bout yall, but my family is been moved around four times in the last hunnert years to make room for all these fancy projects. We don't want no trouble. We never has. We just want to be left alone. We just want to live out our lives. We just trying to run a farm and raise our kids up to be decent God-fearing Amuricans . . ."

A cavalcade of cars crawled by the green, horns blowing. From their radio antennas fluttered banners reading "Whites for Whiter Schools." The blaring was too much for the crowd. They surged in all directions, like a cell about to divide. A loud angry hum filled the square.

". . . They trying to *destroy* our Southern way of life! They won't be content till they've wiped us off the face of this earth!" screamed the speaker.

A young boy sitting on an older man's shoulders threw a rope over an elm branch. He fitted the noose around the neck of a dummy wearing a sign reading " 'Justice' Earl Warren." The crowd fell silent, watching. The dummy dangled and twisted in the dusk. The boy dumped kerosene on it and held a match to it. As it was enveloped in leaping flames, the crowd howled.

Emily, standing on the steps looking around frantically for Raymond, saw a car containing three Negroes—man, woman, and child —drive along the edge of the square. They looked terrified and were trying to turn around to go back in the direction they'd come from. The crowd saw them first. They surged over and surrounded the car and began rocking it. The driver gunned the engine and roared straight ahead, narrowly missing several people, further enraging the crowd, which pursued the car. A rock came hurtling through the twilight and shattered the rear window. With screeching tires the car shot down a side street, pursued by several men.

Emily was in a state of near-collapse. She had not known this was possible. In Newland Negroes and white people were unfailingly polite and kind to each other, liked and respected each other. In many cases, they helped each other out. Who were all these people, their faces contorted with hatred? What swamp had they crawled out of? She located Raymond in the middle of the mob, snapping pictures. How could he? Why didn't he *do* something? Why didn't *somebody* do something?

Raymond noted that he was functioning like a machine. He waited for his shots, like a basketball player, his finger clicking of its own accord. His personal reactions—disgust with the crowd, pleasure to be getting a good story—were in abeyance.

As the crowd broke up, he found Emily sitting with her back against the courthouse wall, her eyes tightly shut.

"Let's get out of here," he suggested.

"Who are all these horrible people?"

"Our neighbors. Our cousins."

"Not mine, they aren't."

"Are you sure about that?"

"Of course I'm sure. Nobody I know would behave like this."

The next day, at lunch after church, Emily told her parents what had happened at Donley. Her father said grimly, "Charming."

"But I don't understand why they'd do that," said Emily.

"Because they hate Negroes."

"But why?"

He shrugged. "Human nature."

"But I'm human, and I don't hate anybody."

"You're not trying to earn a living yet either."

"Huh?"

"Sally darling, are you all right?" Mrs. Prince asked.

Sally had said nothing all morning and was now toying with her peas with her fork. She looked up, smiled her famous smile and said,

"Yes ma'am, I'm just fine, thank you!"

Her parents and Emily looked at her and said nothing.

"Hell, I ain't going to school with no jigs," Jed announced, concerning the rumors that had been sweeping through school all day. They were walking along the sidewalk to Sally's house.

"Who says they even want to in Newland?" pointed out Sally. She clung to his hand, seeking from his fingertips assurance that he still respected her, would protect her reputation, would eventually marry her, and would love her forever. That didn't seem like too much to ask. She had dark circles under her eyes. She'd been awake all night. Was what they had done a sin? She was pretty sure it was. What if he wanted to do it again? Should she say no? If she didn't, what would happen as punishment? He was wearing one of those rubber things. Would that for sure keep her from getting pregnant? How could she find out? Did he really enjoy it? She liked kissing and petting a lot better herself.

"Our niggers got more sense than that bunch over at Donley. They better *not* go getting any smart ideas. They go to school with us, next thing you know they'll be dating our girls and taking up all the spots on our ball teams. Before you know it, they'll be wanting to work in the mill and live next door to us." He laughed incredulously. He used to stop by their ball field and watch them scrimmage when he was doing Raymond's paper route. They had some top-notch ball players. No question about it. He didn't know how he'd fare in competition with them for a spot on the line. He hoped it'd never come to that. As for the girls, everybody knew about niggers—they humped like rabbits. But any nigger who dared so much as look at Sally was one nigger looking for an early grave. He slipped his arm around her shoulders. She snuggled up against him.

They were walking past the Castle Tree. "Remember how we used to spend all day up in that tree, Jeddy—you and me and Raymond and Em and Donny?"

"Yeah, we used to do a lot of dumb things." He just couldn't believe he'd spent his first ten years hanging around with a jig, two girls, and a fairy. It was a wonder he still had a pair.

Donny and Kathryn sat in the armchairs as Ruby cooked. The local news included clips of the burning dummy at Donley. They watched in silence. Afterward Kathryn said, "I was talking with Mr. Dupree over at the luncheonette today. He says he's getting a committee together to go talk to the school board about enrolling some of our students in the white high school next fall."

Donny raised his eyebrows to indicate boredom.

"He asked if you'd be interested. If you're really not going back to New York with me."

"Why is it always me going back up at New York City, Mama? What's to stop you staying here?"

"Won't nobody give a Negro nurse no job down here."

"You try?"

"Are you crazy? I don't go out of my way to get humiliated. But you're changing the subject. What about going to the white high school?"

"Me? What I want to go over there for, Mama? I like it just fine right here."

"Somebody's got to."

"How come 'Somebody's got to'?"

"It's coming, Donny. It's gon happen. Whether anybody likes it or not. So you might as well decide to like it and help it along." The Pine Woods part of Kathryn hated every word she was saying and longed to be the Kathryn of five years ago who had felt no responsibility except to keep food on the table. It was enough then to feel the sun on her back as she molded clay on the pond shore with the little children.

"Humph," said Donny. "I ain't studying to get myself cut up. You see those pictures on the TV?"

"But Donny, honey, they're people, just like us."

"Then how come you got to go out convincing people to go to school with them?"

"Their schools are better than ours. They spend more on them. You're my son. I want you to have the best education possible."

"Since when you worrying bout what's best for me, Mama?"

"Let's not get into that again, Donny. I explained myself as well as

I could. You can accept it or not, but don't let's keep beating each other over the head with it."

"All right. Yeah. I'm sorry. But anyhow, the answer is no. I don't wanna go to no white high school."

"But there's nothing they can do to us they haven't already done. You might even be pleasantly surprised."

"I ain't scared, Mama. It's just that I like it here. My friends are here. The basketball team and all like that."

"You can't play basketball all your life, Donny. What you gon *do* with your life?"

"What you mean what I gon *do* with it? I gon *live* it, what you think, woman?"

"To live you need money. How you gon get it?"

"Well, shoot, Mama, I gon get me a job. What else?"

"What kind of job you gon get in this town?"

"Hell, I don't know. A job job. I gon be a U.S. senator. What you *think* I'm gon do, Mama?"

"You a real smart boy. You thinking bout college?"

"Shit, no! I ain't thinking, period! Leave me *alone*, Mama."

"If you ain't thinking, somebody's got to." She shrugged. "You just hopeless, Donny."

"Well, why don't you just go on back up North where niggers is men?"

Donny and Rochelle walked hand in hand that night through the streets of Pine Woods, past the ranch houses of the undertaker, some of the teachers, Reverend Stump, Mr. Dupree.

"I want me a house like that someday," sighed Rochelle. "When I'm out of college and running me my library."

"Well, I'll come visit you when I'm passing through your town with the Harlem Globetrotters." Donny laughed.

"You do that. Maybe I'll even invite you to spend the night."

He stopped and turned to look at her. "That'd be real nice," he said, pulling her to him and kissing her as he ran his hand up and down the small of her back. On the basketball bus to out-of-town games one of the cheerleaders was always wanting him to sit with her and make out, but he always sat with Tadpole and fell asleep in the seat thinking about Rochelle home taking care of all those children.

He left her off and sauntered back to his grandmaw's apartment. People sat on porches in the hot dark night, as little children tumbled in the courtyard. Couples strolled on the sidewalks. A cluster of men laughed and talked by Dupree's Luncheonette. Women lounged around the door of the laundromat and exchanged insults with the men. Donny liked it here. He didn't want to go to no white school. He didn't want to go up at New York City. He didn't want to go no-where. Now that he thought about it, he didn't even much want to go on the road with the Harlem Globetrotters. He'd just said that because he didn't want Rochelle to give up on him. He was trying to trick her into thinking he was some kind of go-getter or something. It probably wasn't fair. Maybe he'd become a go-getter, since that's what she seemed to want. But what could he go and get?

A car raced down the street from the highway. White arms reached out and heaved beer bottles at the curbs in front of the clusters of people. Shattered glass flew up. Most everyone ducked into doorways and alleys.

Donny stood frozen. A laughing red face appeared at a back window; a hand holding a bottle by its neck extended from the car. The arm bent at the elbow, preparing to hurl the bottle at Donny's feet. Donny's eyes met those of the laughing face. It was Jed. The brief seconds seemed to stretch into several minutes.

The arm, still holding the bottle, drooped and fell against the side of the car.

# Chapter Six

## Booklearning

Jed and Sally, the other Devouts and their dates, the Student Council officers, and members of the Citizenship Corps sat around the mahogany table in Sally's dining room at the monthly Devout Prayer Breakfast.

Jed had a double reason for being there. He was Sally's date and also president of the Citizenship Corps. He carried a tape measure in his pocket, and it was his responsibility to measure how far off the floor the girls' hemlines were, and to issue passes for first offenders to go home and change if the distance was greater than eighteen inches. Repeat offenders got detention slips. Emily had maintained that this meant the shorter girls could wear shorter skirts than the taller girls. But he told her the Citizenship Corps couldn't play no favorites. Short or tall, you had to follow the rules, or they was no telling what outfits some of them girls from Cherokee Shoals might turn up in.

As Judy led them in a prayer for divine assistance in running Newland High, Jed opened his eyes just enough to see Sally, her eyes closed tight and her head bent. She was so pretty with her bouncy blonde hair, and she was all his now. She had given him her virginity, would open her legs whenever he wanted. His years of jerking off over *Playboy*, sneaking around with Betty Boobs, lusting and burning and not finding release was over. He reached under the table for her hand. She frowned. This was just not the place. He smiled at her with all the gratitude he was feeling. She smiled back with reproof.

He would protect her. No other boy would dare come near her with impure thoughts. Not if they valued having their teeth fixed in their gums. He would also protect her rep. No one would ever know they were doing it. Not even Bobby and Hank. Yesterday playing basketball, Hank had said, "What you grinning like a panting dog for, Tatro?"

"Nothing much."

"Don't nobody grin like that without he got him some tail last night," Bobby insisted, as he broke for a crip shot. "Ain't that so, Tatro?" he demanded as he returned to the ground.

"Ain't nobody's bidness."

"That means yes," Bobby explained to Hank.

They were doing a rotating prayer now. Each person in turn added a sentence.

". . . we want to thank you so much, Lord," Sally was saying, "for making the Ingenue Plantation Ball such a success this past weekend . . ."

The next boy said, ". . . uh, look down, Lord, on our graduating seniors with Thy favor, and hep em all to get good jobs, or to do good work at college, or whatsoever things they may want to pursue with their lives . . ."

Sally was feeling let down with no Plantation Ball to work for. She'd returned the last of the punch cups yesterday. They had had enough, hadn't had to fall back on plastic or Styrofoam. It had been such a relief. At least they could move right on into fund raising for next year's dance.

She wished Jed would stop looking at her like that. Someone would see. And during the prayer! Honestly, he was like a little boy with a new toy. Couldn't keep his hands off her. She sort of liked knowing she could make Jed do whatever she wanted by simply giving or withholding her body. On the other hand, she couldn't withhold too seriously because her rep was at stake. If she got him angry, he might spread it around school, and she'd be done for. Devouts would demand her resignation. She only hoped Jed knew how to be discreet. The least tell-tale sign, and you'd had it. Like the night Eddie Tabor had seen Buzz Backer and Ellen Borgard at the Busy Bee Drive-In. She was combing her hair in the rearview mirror. He got out of the car and dropped a used rubber in the garbage can. It was all over school the next day.

———

Mr. Fulton, grey and stooped, was sketching the battle plan of Antietam on the blackboard. He stabbed with his pointer at a rolled-down map, and the map fell on his head. The class giggled as he struggled to disentangle himself. Raymond was the only one who'd been listening to how a few hundred Georgia sharpshooters stalled General Burnside and four divisions of Yankees for several hours. Two students were sitting sideways in their desks playing Hangman on a piece of paper. A boy in ducktails was carving his girl's initials in his arm with a switchblade, a small boy with big glasses was rolling cherry Life Savers down the aisle to a friend in the back row.

In the preceding weeks they had been lectured about the Boys in Grey wading through falling peach blossoms at Shiloh; about Jeb Stuart and his cavalry riding a circle around Yankee troops in the valley of Virginia; about Cold Harbor where Confederate troops charged twenty deep with their addresses pinned on their backs so survivors would know where to send their corpses; about General Armistead, his hat on his sabre, falling dead while reaching for the barrel of a Union cannon that terrible day at Gettysburg.

They had learned that slavery provided its beneficiaries with a better standard of living than that endured by free white factory workers in the North. That most slaves had been sold to slave traders by rival tribesmen. That many of the large houses on the Northern coasts were built by sea captains who made fortunes off the slave-rum-sugar triangle. That a couple of prominent abolitionists were descended from such captains. That many plantation owners had freed their slaves by the time of the war, and that many more wanted to if they could figure out how to keep them fed and clothed and housed. That eighty-five percent of Southern whites owned no slaves at all.

Raymond sat up straight and raised his hand. Mr. Fulton looked at him through watery blue eyes and nodded.

"Mr. Fulton, if we won all these battles, how come we lost the war?"

Mr. Fulton gazed at him with distaste. "Don't get smart with me, son."

"No sir, I wasn't, sir. I was just . . ."

"Maybe if you stay after class and wash my blackboards, young man, you'll learn you some manners."

Mrs. Dingus was giving an English test. Her husband was a highway patrolman. She was noted for hating students whose fathers earned more money than her husband. Mr. Dingus patrolled the roads, Mrs. Dingus patrolled the corridors.

It upset Sally to be disliked. It was a novel experience. Yesterday she'd gone out of her way to bring Mrs. Dingus a brownie from the Ingenue lunchtime bake sale. Mrs. Dingus took it as though picking up a turd, squinting her eyes in what was supposed to pass for a smile. Then she asked, "Now Sally, do you have you a pass to be in this hall during lunch hour?" Sally did not, so Mrs. Dingus issued her a detention slip.

"Question number seven: spell shag-rin," said Mrs. Dingus.

Hands shot up. "Would you please repeat that, Mrs. Dingus?"

"Shagrin."

Puzzled looks. "Could you define it for us, please, ma'am?"

"Shagrin. Embarrassment."

"Would you repeat it again please?"

"Shagrin!" she shouted. "Shagrin! Can't you people hear?"

"Could you spell it please?"

"C-H-A-G-R-I-N."

Everyone copied it down.

"Question number eight: define 'caricature.' "

A hand went up. "What is the choices, Mrs. Dingus?"

"What do you mean, Cyril?"

"Ain't this multiple choice?"

"Cyril, ain't isn't a word."

"Huh? Ain't ain't no word?"

"No. The proper word for ain't is isn't."

"If ain't ain't no word, how come everbody I know uses hit and unnerstands what hit means?"

"And hit isn't a word either. The word is it."

"What's his name—ole Shakespeare there uses hit."

"Don't get smart with me, Cyril."

"No, ma'am. I ain't looking for no trouble. I mean, I isn't looking for no trouble, ma'am."

A girl in back removed her stretchy straw belt. She and a boy in the next row used it as a giant slingshot to bombard classmates with paper wads.

"Question number nine, true or false: Silas Marner was an old sailor in a poem written by Samuel Coleridge."

A paper wad landed in Mrs. Dingus's lap. She glared at the back of the room, wrote out hall passes for six students in the vicinity of the catapult, and sent them all to the office. "And don't you come back without you have detention slips," she called as they shuffled out. "Question number ten, multi-pull choice: an albatross is (a) a ship, (b) a sailor, (c) a bird, (d) none of the above."

A boy raised his hand. "How many of them choices is correct, Mrs. Dingus?"

"Just one this time."

Jed was standing at a window in the rear of Mr. Boyd's second-floor room, holding a sharpened pencil, point down, waiting to drop it on the school superintendent who was walking up the sidewalk. Jed was supposed to be dissecting a frog, but Mr. Boyd was involved in sending Hobart Sharpe to the office. Jed knew he shouldn't be doing this, being president of the Citizenship Corps and all. But sometimes it just all built up, and he had to cut loose.

". . . and I don't want you to set foot in this classroom again, Hobart, until you have a note from the office okaying your absences this week." He handed Hobart a hall pass.

Hobart grinned, shrugged, and ambled out, waving good-bye. Someone was watering the houseplants with formaldehyde. Jed had just inserted his pencil in the fan, and tiny pieces were flying around the room. Emily felt sorry for Mr. Boyd as she read the marked passages in *Peyton Place*, which she had hidden underneath her notebook. He was new this year and had been enthusiastic at first, calling them "Class" and offering to lend them books. Lately he had begun merely sitting at his desk and babbling, while brains from the Audio-Visual Club made chlorine gas in back. Emily tried to look as though she were listening to his monologues.

"Once upon a time, class, four and a half billion years ago, a swirling cloud of gases began to cool and condense into a molten sphere. In the hot seas that eventually covered our cooling earth, carbon, nitrogen, oxygen, hydrogen, and sulphur combined under the influence of lightning, or ultraviolet rays, or ionizing radiation to form amino acids, which in turn combined to form nucleic acids. For some unknown reason, bundles of a quarter of a million of these protein products began to band together inside protective membranes. They could reproduce, mutate, and get the supplies they needed from their surroundings. This is called Life. The seas became jammed with it—in the form of bacteria.

"While most bacteria were fighting over diminishing energy supplies, some discovered how to make their own energy from the sun. Algae—from which the whole plant world springs. The bacteria that weren't so clever died off. Except for those that developed the ability to prey off their brothers. These predators gave rise to the animal kingdom, starting with worms and going through snails and sponges and corals and exotic creatures with no modern equivalent—trilobites, crinoids, nautiloids, cephalopods, ostracods, graptolites, brachiopods . . ."

As he wrote "ostracods" on the blackboard, the chalk broke and his fingernails skidded. Everyone shrieked and groaned and threw hands to ears. It was about the only way he could get their attention.

"Outside the seas, the cooling crust was colored black and grey and brown. Storms of dust and sand howled across the rocky surface. The sun was a smeared red glow. Green fingers began pushing out from the seas and lakes and swamps six hundred million years ago . . ."

Hobart was climbing through the transom above the door. "Hobart, what are you doing? Get down here right now!"

Hobart climbed down and grinned. "Well sir, there wasn't nobody in the office to give me no excuse. So I was just trying to get back in the room without setting foot in it, like you said." The class howled.

Mr. Boyd looked at him, then resumed his monologue.

Emily pulled out the student newspaper. She'd done a report for English class on a book by William Faulkner and had tried to imitate his style for an article commemorating the death of Nathan Hale. When it appeared, it was rewritten. She complained to the sponsor, Mrs. Dingus.

Mrs. Dingus replied, "I bet you thought that was a pretty good piece?"

Emily thought over this trick question. "I didn't think it was bad enough to need rewriting."

With a look of triumph, Mrs. Dingus crowed, "Why, that piece wasn't even written in complete sentences!"

Emily stared at her. Finally gesturing at the paper, she said, "This isn't the piece I wrote. It shouldn't have my name on it. It should have your name on it, Mrs. Dingus."

"Don't you get smart with me, young lady."

Emily knew she was making a big mistake, but she thrust out her chin and replied, "I'm not. I'm just stating facts."

By the end of the afternoon, it was all over school that Emily Prince had gotten smart with Mrs. Dingus. That night at supper Sally asked, "Why do you want to go and be rude to Mrs. Dingus for, Emily? That's just dumb."

Emily looked up. "Because she wrecked my article."

"Who cares about a silly old article?"

"I do," growled Emily.

Mrs. Prince nodded approval as she chewed, and Mr. Prince murmured, "Good going." Emily was flooded with gratitude.

Sally looked at them all. "But what's good about being rude to an adult?"

"Sometimes you have to stand up for what you think is right," said her father. "Even if nobody else does."

Today Emily had been summoned to the office by Mrs. Musk, the guidance counselor. (Mrs. Musk's paper boy claimed that one day when he'd been collecting at her house, he'd seen a padded bra hanging from her bedroom doorknob.) Emily studied her chest with interest.

"Mrs. Dingus tells me she thinks you may be disturbed emotionally, Emily."

Emily looked up. "Well, yeah, I mean, yes ma'am. If she means that I was annoyed that she rewrote my article without asking me."

"She says you were rude to her. Is this correct?"

Emily said nothing. She kept reminding herself that her parents thought she'd done right. It was the only thing that prevented her from begging for forgiveness.

"Well, I've spoken to Mr. Horde about it, Emily. He'd like to see you in his office."

Mr. Horde was the principal. Emily always remembered how to spell "principal" from a jingle she'd been taught in the fourth grade: "The principal / is our pal." This wasn't strictly correct in Mr. Horde's case. He had two rules. One was that students should be seen and not heard. The other was that principals should be heard and not seen. He spent most of his time locked in his office communicating over the public address system. He did have his reasons for refusing to court overexposure. When you saw him in person—short, fat, balding, and hunched over his desk like a toad—his credibility diminished.

Mrs. Musk ushered Emily into Mr. Horde's office.

"Sit down, young lady. Now what's this Mrs. Dingus tells me about you being smart-alecky?"

"I wasn't, sir. I was just upset that she rewrote my article without my permission."

He raised his eyebrows. "Your permission? Who do you think you are to give permission to Mrs. Dingus? She's a teacher and sponsor of the paper. You're just a student."

"But it was my article!"

He gazed at her, his jowls puffing out like a bullfrog about to croak. "Yes, I do see Mrs. Dingus's point. You have a choice, Emily: you can be suspended for the rest of the year. Or you can apologize— first to me, then to Mrs. Dingus."

Emily sat trembling, her eyes on the floor. "I'm sorry I was rude, Mr. Horde," she murmured.

"All right, Emily. Now go apologize to Mrs. Dingus, and we'll all try to get on with our work."

Her face bathed in tears, Emily got a bathroom pass from Mrs. Musk. The bathroom was packed with girls from third-period study hall, who were smoking and drawing on the mirrors with lipstick and discussing where to send a note claiming there was a bomb in someone's locker . . .

Mr. Boyd's drone penetrated her reverie: ". . . about three hundred million years ago, in tidal basins and drying-up swamps, a creature appeared called the crossopterygian. It possessed three features new in the history of life—bony fins like muscular paddles, an internal air sac in addition to gills, and tiny cerebral hemispheres. Some survived on land when the swamps dried up, while the fish who'd regarded them as oddballs starved or suffocated." Emily wrote this down.

"Twenty-five million years later its descendants, the ichthyostega, discovered they could do without water altogether, except for being born there and taking an occasional drink, since they contained the sea within their bodies. Then came the reptiles, who laid eggs with hard shells on dry land. Some developed feathers and took to the skies as birds. The world of the reptiles was one of giants—dinosaurs with tiny instinct-driven brains, flying reptiles with a twenty-eight-foot wing span, towering Sequoia trees. And hiding out among these massive creatures were tiny mammals, warm-blooded and able to survive severe weather reversals. Flowers appeared in an explosion, relatively speaking, one hundred million years ago, a funerary offering to the dinosaurs, who died off for reasons unknown, precipitating a ferocious struggle for dominance among the remaining species. Some giant ground birds almost took over. One species after another, arising, developing, going to extinction. This has happened thousands of times, class. It's called evolution. . . ."

Hobart was lobbing frog parts on to squealing girls' desks. Mr. Boyd raced to the back of the room. Hobart ducked into the supply closet. Mr. Boyd followed him. Hobart slipped back out and slammed and locked the door. The class cheered, jumped up, and streamed from the room.

Emily watched them go. Then she got up and let Mr. Boyd out.

"Thank you, Emily," he said.

"Oh, you're welcome. I was wondering if you could tell me about any books on what you were just talking about . . ."

Delighted, he wrote down some titles and gave her a library pass. "But please, don't tell anyone where you heard about evolution," he whispered. "It could get me fired."

The littered parking lot of the quick-service hamburger stand was filled with cars, most with open doors. Radios were blaring, ". . . I want to be Bobby's girl. / That's the most important thing to me . . ."

Emily and June sat eating their fries and watching Hobart sneak a Bud from the case in his trunk.

"Mr. Boyd said some interesting stuff today."

"Yeah?"

"About this animal that grew in swamps and was able to crawl out on dry land."

"Sort of like the Creature from the Black Lagoon?"

"Yeah, I guess so. Only it was three hundred million years ago."

"How come something that long ago is interesting to you?"

"I don't know. But it sure makes you think."

"You maybe. Not me. Oh God, look!" June tittered. "Those football guys are making poor old Slocombe do his Elvis imitation."

Slocombe was pasty and puffy with a brown flat top and an idiotic grin. He was slicking back imaginary hair with one hand, and thrusting an imaginary guitar with the other. He kept lurching forward on rubbery legs and wailing with what was supposed to be a sexy sneer. He was surrounded by the hulking football players, whom he served as waterboy.

Emily watched. "God, I can't stand it. I wish they wouldn't do that."

"Why not? It's a scream."

"He doesn't even know they're making fun of him. He thinks he's being cool."

"Oh Em, honestly. You're such a softy."

"Come on, Slocombe! More hip action there!" Jed yelled.

"Yeah, grind it right into her, Slocombe!" Hank yelled.

Slocombe grinned, and twisted and thrust his hips with awkwardness.

"That's it, Slocombe! Do it, baby!" Bobby called, glancing at Jed and Hank. They all shook with laughter.

"Jed, honey, your fries are getting cold," Sally called from the Chevy. Jed sauntered over.

"Jesus," he muttered. "That old boy. If you told him to eat shit, I believe he'd ask, 'With salt or without, sir?' "

"He just wants yall to like him."

"How can you like a turd?"

"Now be nice, honey."

Slocombe went up to the order window and patted Louanne Little on the ass, looking around for Jed and Bobby and Hank with his cringing grin. Louanne turned around with an angry look and said something. He grinned, shrugged, and scuttled away.

Jed sat in Health and Hygiene class with his feet in the aisle and his arms folded. He couldn't see why ball players had to take Health and Hygiene. They was about the healthiest and cleanest-living boys around. They should of been teaching the class theirselves. At least it was with Coach Clancy, who didn't like it any better than they did.

Coach Clancy was reading out of a book called *The Kinsey Report*, about "oral sex." "A fancy name for cock-sucking and cunt-licking," he explained. "Now how many yall has done this with your girlfriends?"

Everyone glanced at each other with nervous grins. Jed wondered if he should try this on Sally pretty soon. It sounded kind of fun.

"I just want to remind yall that I'm grading partly on classroom participation here."

Still no one responded.

"Now Mrs. Clancy, she don't like none of this fancy stuff personally. She likes what you call your missionary position. Now, who knows why they call it that?"

Alan Vernon raised his hand. "When they got over there at Africa, they found them natives doing all kinds of weird stuff, so they told them how the Lord wanted it done. Face to face and all like that."

Jed was mortified at having thought about "oral sex" with Sally. He hadn't realized it was preverse. And how about when Betty Boobs climbed on top of him like that? He'd always felt it was disgusting, but now he knew it was preverse as well. It made you wonder about old Betty all right. He sure was glad to be finished with her.

"Yeah, that's right. Now how many yall has heard the one about the nigger woman at the revival?"

Sally was watching Mrs. Courtwright demonstrate how to set a table. "Now I know most yall is been setting tables your en-tire life. But, girls, I tell you, hit's different when you're a-doin it for your husband in a happy home of your very own. You want to provide all the little touches that let him know how ex-try special he is to you. Now, who's got some ideas on extry little things you can do to show your love?"

Sally was trying to decide on her flatware pattern. If you picked an elaborate silver like La Scala, then you just better choose you a fairly plain china. But if you picked a plain silver like Fairfax, then you could have fancy china, like Doulton English Renaissance or something. Now your crystal, that was hard to know about . . .

"Yes, Anna Lou, fresh flowers is a very lovely touch for your table. Now they's some that would disagree with this, but I happen to feel like that in winter when you can't get you no fresh ones, they's some plastic ones that would almost fool you into thinking they was real . . ."

Sally decided to take Jed down to Parkway Department Store on Saturday and let him help her decide. After all, he was going to be eating off them for a lifetime too.

". . . yes, candles. Certainly candles. Candles that match your day-core or your flowers. Now you can light them or not, like you choose. How many yall like to light your candles?"

Sally raised her hand. Her mother also had a crystal chandelier with a dimmer switch, which was real elegant for dinner parties. She started to suggest this. Suddenly it occurred to her only a few houses on Tsali Street had chandeliers. Why, she wondered. They were a real nice thing to have. She just hoped Jed liked them.

Emily couldn't figure out why Miss Melrose always made her chase the balls when they played softball outside and made her collect the sweaty team halters after basketball. In Hygiene class if Miss Melrose caught them passing notes, it was always Emily she made stay after class and scrub desk tops—even when half a dozen others had been involved. Today, in a burst of energy, Emily had raced out the dressing room door in her shorts and tennis shoes, sprinted as fast as she could down the gym, and run six feet up the tile wall at the far end. As she dropped to her feet, she saw Miss Melrose stalking toward her. Miss Melrose, in her late forties, was unmarried and unhappy-looking. There was a story of a fiancé who'd died in a car wreck/war/of a wasting disease with her at his bedside.

"Just look at how your tennis shoes have marked up this wall, Emily Prince!"

Emily studied the wall but could find no marks.

"Now I think you'd just better plan to come back here after school and wash this wall."

"Yes ma'am." Miss Melrose's dark unhappy eyes seemed to impale her.

They did calisthenics. One exercise involved lying on the back and lowering the small of the back to the floor, so as to elevate the hips. Emily felt Miss Melrose's eyes on her as she diligently performed this.

In the dressing room afterward, Miss Melrose marched through as she always did, wrenching open stall doors to ascertain that everyone had showered. Emily was bending over shaking her breasts into her bra cups as her door flew open. Miss Melrose glared.

"Emily, you know you're supposed to shower unless you have you a doctor's excuse!"

"Yes ma'am. But I did."

"Don't lie to me, young lady. You're not even wet!"

"But I already dried off, Miss Melrose."

She reached out and touched Emily's shoulder with her fingertips. A shiver ran down Emily's back.

"I'll take your word for it this time," she said in a trembling voice.

June whispered as the door banged shut, "Somebody said the other day maybe Miss Melrose is a lesbian!"

"What's that?"

June laughed. "God, you're so naive, Emily. A lesbian is a woman who does it with other women."

Emily looked perplexed. "But that's not even possible. I mean how would they? What would be the point?"

June shrugged.

Last-period classes were called off. The boys were sent to study hall, and the girls to the auditorium, where the doors were locked. Miss Melrose got up on stage and announced that Louanne Little's lace slip had been stolen during fifth-period gymn class. "Now one of you ladies right here in this very room took that slip. One way or another we're going to catch you. You can confess now and save us all a lot of trouble."

The room buzzed.

"All right," said Miss Melrose. "If this is how you want it, fine. Now Louanne and I are going to stand at the bottom of these steps. One row at a time I want you girls to climb these steps, stop while Louanne examines your slip, then file across the stage and down the other steps and back to your seats."

Emily watched the procession. Sally was blushing and giggling and lifting her skirt high enough for Louanne's inspection. Louanne was looking embarrassed. Miss Melrose was overseeing like a guard dog. Emily went forward. As Louanne okayed her slip, Emily saw Miss Melrose examining her calves.

Louanne found her slip on Marsha Turner, a girl from Cherokee Shoals who wore ducktails and too much makeup and carried a switchblade in her pocketbook.

"I could have a slip just like hers, couldn't I?" she protested, as Miss Melrose ushered her out.

Some boys from the Audio-Visual Club lowered the movie screen. The lights went out. Miss Melrose's voice called out, "Thank you so much, boys. Would yall now go on back to study hall please? This here is strictly for girls only."

The film was made by the U.S. Army. It featured babies born blind; babbling men in straitjackets; people with hideously swollen arthritic joints, paralysis, deformed noses. The room filled with gasps.

Sally began running her tongue around the inside of her mouth, searching for sores. She knew it! This was what happened when you had sex. Jed had done it at least once with that horrible Betty French. Everybody knew what those girls from Cherokee Shoals were like. It was awful. Their babies would be born blind with squashed noses. She would tell him this afternoon that they must never do this horrible thing again. Someone was vomiting in back.

"Miss Melrose!" someone yelled. "Wisteria has just fainted!"

In study hall almost every boy stood up in unison and ambled into the library, until it was packed. Notes had been passed earlier instructing everyone to do this at exactly 2:57. Coach Clancy pushed up from his desk and rolled across the study hall like a Nazi tank through the heart of Paris. He planted himself in the library doorway and barked, "Now, what the hell do you shitfaces think you're doing? I want everbody back in their goddam seats in sixty seconds!"

Hobart, meanwhile, was greasing the podium underneath Coach Clancy's chair with Crisco.

The study hall quiet once again, Coach Clancy sat down and leaned his chair back on two legs. It went shooting out from under him. The room rocked with silent laughter. Coach Clancy stood up and looked around defiantly, trying to pretend he'd done a back flip off the podium on purpose, just to show them who was boss.

Raymond watched with indifference. These stunts had been going on his entire high school career. He used to dream them up and execute them to fight the boredom. Now he no longer participated. Sometimes the others called him a "scab," but what did he care what a bunch of cretins thought of him?

Marbles began rolling from one end of the huge room to the other. Coach Clancy was pretending not to notice.

Raymond gazed across the room. In a few weeks most of the senior boys would be working at the mill, or in the paper plant, or in stores downtown. And where would he be? At the mill, twisting cotton strands and kissing Mr. Prince's ass as he walked by, having been trained for this all his life. And to make the boredom tolerable, he might throw a cup of water on the man next to him every now and then. He felt like a heel resting on a shoehorn.

The boy behind him passed a note: "At exactly 3:16, everyone drop your books on the floor."

Donny was in the library helping Rochelle set up a display for Negro History Week. They had just taken one down entitled "Our Pilgrim Fathers." Now they were pinning up pictures of Booker T. Washington and Al Jolson and Joe Louis on the bulletin board. On the shelf underneath were biographies of them.

Donny toyed with the notion of a biography on himself someday. At games he'd race out onto the court in his lemon yellow satin warmup suit—long trousers and windbreaker. Someone would shoot him the ball as he loped in toward the goal. He'd leap up and flip it through the hoop, the fingertips of both hands curling over the rim. The stands would holler. The team would go through its routines— elaborate patterns of running men and bouncing balls, breaks toward the goal and passes, feints and handoffs—while the band played and the cheerleaders led the crowd in rhythmic clapping. He'd pretend he was playing in New York City for the Knicks. New York. His mother had gone back up there. Without him. He reckoned he missed her, but, man, was he glad not to be in no New York City.

"I just love working here," Rochelle murmured. "I almost hate it when the afternoon ends, and I got to go back home. It's so quiet. And clean. And once you get the books in order, they stay that way for a while."

"Yeah, there's usually a lot happening over at your place, all right."

"If they'd let me, I think I'd move in here!"

"You wouldn't never do that, Rochelle. I know you. You'd miss all them little kids too much."

"Try me," she laughed.

"I'd like to, but you won't let me, mama." He shot her a sly grin. She raised her eyebrows.

# Chapter Seven

===

# Independence Day

The Fourth of July was the hundredth birthday of Newland, and a huge parade was staged along the highway through town. All the civic groups and high school clubs had floats. Raymond stood on the street edge of a crowd ten feet deep with his camera poised. The Industrial Development League float was a flatbed truck with a papier-mâché model of the town's industrial district—smoke stacks and railroad yards and warehouses. At one end stood Mr. Prince in a shirt and tie, smiling and shaking hands interminably with Raymond's father in dark green work clothes.

On the County Historical Society float, men in fringed buckskins with long rifles fought a battle behind a log stockade with attacking Indians in warpaint and loincloths. Behind them, in full uniform, with scuffed white bucks and faces scarlet from the heat, staggered the high school band. Their plumes drooped like melting cotton candy, and the braid across their jackets looked like the ribs on Halloween skeleton costumes. From time to time they blared through "Dixie," or a march medley of "Swanee River"/"Old Black Joe"/"My Old Kentucky Home." Emily was in the last row with her flute. She kept hopping, trying to get back in step. When the drum major signaled with his whistle and baton an intricate reversal and interweaving of the ranks, Emily didn't notice and marched straight ahead, screwing everything up. Raymond snapped a picture of her consternation, and doubled over laughing.

The Civic Club's float featured half a dozen dentists and insurance salesmen in blackface and orange satin tuxedos. They grinned and cakewalked and shook their tambourines to the noise from the band.

Sally rode by with the seven other cheerleaders. They wore their letter sweaters, full corduroy skirts, and saddle shoes, and led the crowd in familiar cheers: *"Dixie Cup, Seven-Up, pecan pie! / We are the gang from Newland High! / We don't smoke, and we don't chew, / And we don't go with boys who do . . ."* Four young men, one each dressed in football, basketball, baseball, and track attire and carrying appropriate equipment, stood smiling shoulder to shoulder against the truck cab.

Then came the Brownie and Cub Scout troops in full regalia, then some prancing horses in elaborate Western tack, ridden by men in either fancy cowboy outfits or Indian buckskins and headdresses.

The Ingenue float, on a haywagon pulled by a tractor, commemorated the annual Plantation Ball. Several girls in long white dresses lurched around with young men in white sport coats to a scratchy version of "Moon River," from a hidden record player. Donny stood smiling in a white jacket behind a cut-glass punch bowl.

Next came the Miss Newland float, featuring last year's winner and her two runners-up, all in bathing suits. Also Miss Congeniality, less curvy but with a wider smile and a more determined wave.

The Rod and Gun Club float consisted of two men, one dressed in hunting gear, the other in fishing gear. One held a string of birds, the other a string of fish. They were handing these to two women in aprons who clasped their hands with delight.

Next came the National Guard, marching in formation with weapons, followed by the most enormous tank Raymond had ever seen. Its gun swiveled, pointing playfully into the crowd as bystanders squealed.

Raymond dropped his camera. It hung from his neck twisting slowly, its elaborate long-distance lenses projecting like a muzzle. He had spent the morning lying on his bed, studying his photo of the elephant hanging from the crane, surrounded by cheering townspeople. He had just realized he was going to leave this crazy place.

He and Emily sat in his father's car at the drive-in that night watching Rock Hudson slogging through the Everglades, trampling wild orchids, evading rattlesnakes and alligators and panthers, and succumbing to yellow fever, while hunting Seminoles. Emily waited with dread for Raymond to pounce and perform the obligatory necking. Instead he started up the car.

"What are you doing?" Emily protested.

"Leaving."

"But we don't even know what's going to happen."

"*I* know. Rock Hudson is going to capture Anthony Quinn, I mean Osceola, marry Perry Mason's secretary, and make Florida safe for tourism."

Emily laughed.

"What really happened is that Osceola was captured when he honored the cavalry's white flag. They put him in prison. And when he died, the attending physician cut off his head and would hang it in his children's bedroom when they misbehaved."

Emily laughed.

"It's true. I read it in a book."

"I didn't know you read books."

"There's lots about me you don't know."

"Like what?"

"Like that I've decided to take that job in New York City."

"You're kidding?"

"I don't think I belong here. I don't think you do either."

"Leave me out of this. You go if you want, but I'm doing just fine right here." She couldn't imagine wanting to go someplace where you didn't know a soul. But what would it be like here without Raymond's complaints all the time? She felt a stab of loss. But maybe with him gone someone else would want to date her, someone more acceptable to the Ingenues.

After the parade, the Ingenues went to a rented cottage at Myrtle Beach, South Carolina, for their annual week-long Beach Bash. Jed and several other Ingenue dates rented a cottage nearby. The Ingenues spent their days basting themselves with Coppertone, and rolling and unrolling spit curls. The boys threw a football, galloped in the surf, or raced their cars on the hard sand. Sometimes they lay on beach towels beside corpselike girlfriends, peeking at greasy pinkening flesh. At night they tried to bluff their way into nightclubs, rode the Tilt-a-Whirl at the amusement park, or retreated to an oceanside pavilion to dance to a jukebox and drink Coke laced with rum from a bottle in a brown paper bag. Couples would drift off to the dunes.

Every time they made love, Sally demanded, "Are you sure there's no way I can get pregnant, Jed?"

"Sally darlin, just trust me. These rubbers is foolproof. They blow them up on this machine to test for holes before they even send them out." He'd read this in the folder inside the packets. They were the most expensive brand Anderson's sold—sheep gut, or some damn thing. Whenever he had to buy some, he'd hang around outside until Mr. Anderson, a golf companion of Mr. Prince, was in back filling a prescription. Then he'd race in, snatch some up, and hurl the money at the assistant.

On the day Sally's period was scheduled to arrive, it didn't.

"God, Jed, what are we going to do?" They sat in the cottage living room. The others were on the beach. She'd told the Ingenues she wasn't feeling well. They smiled knowingly and said maybe Jed could make her feel better. Actually she needed quick access to the bathroom, where she went every half hour to search her panties for a bloodstain.

"Girls' periods are sometimes late for other reasons," Jed assured her. He'd heard different boys say this. But back in his cottage he read and reread the folder about the testing machine.

The next day Sally inquired, "What will Daddy say?"

"He won't say nothing. He won't know. You're just late is all. Happens all the time. Don't get all hysterical now." He was trying to decide if he dared ask Bobby or Hank about this. But it would be bad for Sally's rep. And it would make him look like a stupid jerk-off.

On the third day Sally said, "Jed, we've sinned. I know it. This is our punishment." It wasn't fair. If she'd enjoyed it, then she could see how she deserved to be punished. But she only did it to make Jed happy.

"That ain't nothing but nonsense, Sally. It ain't no sin to love somebody." But actually he was wondering. It didn't hardly seem fair. If Betty Boobs got in the family way, he could see it might be punishment. Betty was just for fun. But Sally he loved. If Betty Boobs did get in the family way, you'd be home free anyhow because the whole school knew it could of been any of a dozen boys.

Sally went into the bathroom and sat on the toilet and pressed toilet paper against herself. It came away bloodless. She buried her face in her hands and promised the Lord she would never screw again if only He'd restore her period.

Her period arrived that afternoon. She fell to her knees by the toilet, her hands clasped, and thanked the Lord.

That night at the pavilion Sally and Jed danced every dance, in shorts and bare feet on the sandy floor.

"What's got into you, Tatro?" Bobby asked. "Or should I say, what have you got into?"

"Glad to see you feeling better, Sally," smirked Mo, next year's Ingenue president and head cheerleader.

Lying on a blanket in the dunes under the full moon, Sally explained they could do everything else, but had to stop screwing. Jed saw her point and agreed to make do with a hand job.

This arrangement lasted for several days. One night at the pavilion, though, Jed and Sandy Ellis danced together twice. Jed lit three cigarettes for her, and the last time she rested her cigarette hand against his match hand to steady it. Then she raised her eyes to his, over the flame. He was gazing back so intently that the flame burned down to his fingers. He plunged his scorched fingers into her rum and Coke, and she sucked them clean, saying, "We don't want to waste this good rum, do we?"

Later, in the dunes, Jed lay on his back with his hands behind his head, waiting for Sally to do something about his erection. He kind of liked this business of just lying back and being taken care of. To his alarm, Sally squatted over him, his prick entering her.

Everybody in Ingenue knew about Sandy. She majored in other girls' boyfriends. Sally was damned if Sandy was going to move in on her.

"I don't have no rubber," Jed gasped, putting his hands on her waist and trying to lift her off.

"Don't worry. I've just finished my period," she said, moving efficiently.

Jed shrugged. You couldn't refuse a lady. But could you call a girl who behaved like this a lady?

# Chapter Eight

## Miss Newland

Beth Crawley was dressed in an Alpine climber's outfit—lederhosen embroidered with edelweiss, a felt hat with a feather. A coiled rope hung from her shoulder, and she held a pickaxe. She was singing "Climb Every Mountain." Emily had to admit she had a pretty good voice. But in fifth grade her nickname had been Creepy Crawley. She'd looked like a praying mantis, tall and gawky and hunched, predatory and pious at the same time. A metamorphosis had occurred in junior high. Now she was gorgeous, and looked like a shoo-in for this year's Miss Newland. Emily felt alternately sorry for Sally and delighted that she had just dropped the microphone at the most poignant moment of her rendition of "Since I Don't Have You." She remembered Sally as a little girl singing into her jump rope handle, and lashing the rope as though it were a microphone cord.

She thought about Raymond's letter that had arrived that afternoon: "Dear Emily: Well, so here I am. Do you remember how we used to sit in the Castle Tree and discuss our New York City penthouse? My new place is no penthouse, but it *is* on the roof—of an old building on the Upper West Side. I sweep the halls and stuff in place of paying rent. It's one room, with a sink and tiny refrigerator against one wall, which I hide with a folded screen when I'm entertaining the mayor. A small bathroom. The view's pretty neat—the Hudson River with the New Jersey Palisades on the other side.

"All day long I do layouts for people's brochures. I got my first paycheck—sixty-three dollars a week, once everything is deducted. Sounds like a lot, but it's barely enough to get by on up here.

"The night I arrived Gus (the guy who got me the job) met me, thank God, because I had no idea what to do next. I probably would have been in that exact same spot two weeks later. He's a nice fellow, young, single. It was fun to meet him after so many notes and phone calls. He said he wanted to take me to dinner, what kind of food did I like. I said I liked everything. He said, 'I'll give you a choice of what's close by—Indian, Japanese, or Finnish.' Well, I felt like the original hick. I tried to play it cool and said I was too tired, he'd have to order for me. I ended up eating raw squid or something. It's amazing how little I've seen of the world, Emily. But I'm trying to make up for it. Please write when you can. Love, Raymond. I miss you, but nothing else about Newland."

He sounded happy, for maybe the first time in his life. But imagine not even missing your own family. Well, he always was a weirdo. But a weirdo whom she found herself missing at times. Like right now. He'd be whispering sarcastic remarks about each contestant out of the corner of his mouth. With him sitting next to her it would hurt less not to be up on stage herself.

The girls were coming out in bathing suits and spike heels, as the announcer read their measurements: ". . . thirty-four, twenty-two, thirty-four . . ."

Why had the JayCees invited Sally to be in this pageant but not her? What about seniority? She couldn't even blame it on her father for not being a JayCee, as some girls did, because there was Sally.

". . . Miss Emily Prince . . . thirty-eight, twenty-nine, thirty-six . . ." She just hadn't been poured in the right mold. She wrapped her arms tightly across her chest and slouched down.

". . . Miss Sally Prince, thirty-four, twenty-four, thirty-four . . ." Sally heard this with pride. She'd worked hard to get her waist exactly ten inches smaller than her breasts and hips. She'd been measuring weekly for years. If her waist began to thicken, she'd do one set of exercises. Another set if her bust began to diminish. It seemed like her breasts had begun swelling since she and Jed had been making love. Could everyone out there see that she was no longer a virgin? Would she get all coarse like Betty French and Sandy Ellis?

She loved being under the spotlight with the entire town admiring her. She smiled for all she was worth, trying to project pep. If only she hadn't dropped the mike. But maybe no one noticed. Or maybe they thought it was part of the act.

Jed watched Sally pause and turn from side to side. God, she was gorgeous. The whole town could look at her and want her and speculate, but he was the only one who got to touch what was underneath that bathing suit. Thank the Lord she'd got over her notion that sex was a sin. Now he blew up every rubber like a balloon to be sure there was no leaks. Hank and Bobby, sitting on either side of him, poked him with their elbows, and he grinned. Everybody knew she was his girl, and he felt proud. She lived on Tsali Street, her daddy ran the town, she could have picked any boy in the whole place, and she'd picked him. Of course he'd picked her too. And he could have had any girl—except maybe Sister Sourpussy, whom he spotted hunched over several rows below. But who'd want her now that Old Ugly had gone up at New York City? It sure was nice around the house with him gone. No more arguments at dinner.

Donny and Leon lay under the hemlocks by the stadium wall, looking down at the spotlit stage through binoculars Leon had found. After the football games, when the floodlights were cut, as the Rebels were cleaning out the popcorn poppers, Leon would climb the stadium wall and creep through the bleachers searching for forgotten blankets and thermoses, fallen change. Rats would be scurrying up and down the concrete steps, carrying popcorn, peanuts, and heels of hot dogs. Leon's parents had sent him down from New York City, where he'd been getting in trouble with the laws, to live with an aunt. He had all kinds of daring ideas, and Donny thought he was wonderful.

Donny watched the girls strut across the stage, remembering last winter when he and Tadpole had been at the newsstand in town playing pinball. As they were leaving, they took a *Playboy* off the rack. Miss March had long blonde hair and huge jugs. Donny was imagining what it would be like to have that silky blonde mane swirling around your face as those white tits lowered themselves onto your chest, when Tadpole whistled and said, "Look at that hair, man. Charlene, now, she's a hot number. But her hair, man, you could scrub the kitchen floor with it."

The owner of the newsstand called from behind the counter with a leer, "White tail turn you boys on?"

"Naw sir," they said in unison, replacing the magazine and racing out.

Sally Prince was swaying onto the stage, and Leon wouldn't give him his turn. Donny punched him and grabbed the binoculars, saying, "Goddam, Leon, it's my turn, motherfucker!" They scuffled in the dirt. A flashlight beam swept the bushes. "Hey, who's that up there?" a deep voice called. They crawled frantically to the wall, as the flashlight came rapidly up the hill. They dragged themselves up and over the wall, then ran like hell down the highway toward Pine Woods. Donny was terrified. He'd never been in no trouble. His grandmaw would kill him. She'd been complaining about him hanging around with Leon. Maybe she was right about Leon being destined for a life of crime.

Hundreds of cheerleaders from all over the South gathered at the cheerleading clinic on the college campus near Birmingham to stay in the dormitories and learn each other's cheers. In the mornings the huge football field was packed with girls in uniforms practicing. Several instructors, in outfits like tennis dresses, sauntered around, watching and critiquing.

"The little blonde in the middle . . . Yes, you. More pep to your jump, honey! Bounce when you come down!"

In the afternoon were workshops on poster painting, float construction, pom-pom making. Sally was inseparable from her notebook, in which she wrote down new cheers and project ideas.

And in the evenings the clinic head, a short pudgy gym teacher from Mobile, lectured on school spirit: "In order for our teams to play their very best, girls—be the game football, basketball, baseball, or track—our boys need to know that the en-tire school is behind them one hundred percent all the way! They aren't just playing for themselves, or for the coach, or for the team—they're playing for your whole student body. And in fact, they're playing for your whole town. Their victories reflect credit and glory on the entire community of which they and us are a part of. And it's up to us, girls, as the chosen representatives of that community, to let our boys out there on that field know that, whatever happens, we're behind them one hundred percent all the way!"

Everyone cheered. Sally wrote in her notebook: "Team represents entire community." She chewed the tip of her pencil. As the youngest member of the Newland squad, she felt she should try hardest. Mo was always telling everyone she was "a real good little worker," and it made her proud. Sally was hoping Mo might nominate her as her successor as president of Ingenue the following year. She had finally decided she was satisfied with being only second runner-up in the Miss Newland contest. She got to ride on the JayCee float in the Fourth of July parade next summer. And besides, it gave her something to work toward.

"Now some of you girls are old timers at all this. And you know as well as I do that being a good cheerleader requires exactly the identical qualities as being a good wife does. You have to know your man—only in this case, you have to know a couple of dozen of them!"

Everyone laughed.

"Now I'm not joking, girls. When your team comes out of that locker room after a defeat, you have to be there to let them know they're still winners in your book. Now some boys you have to hug. Others, you should stay away from and let them recover alone. Some like to explain to you what went wrong. Others like to make it into a big joke. And your job, girls, is to know which player to treat which way. And this quality, girls, is what makes the difference between a good cheerleader and a really great cheerleader!"

Everyone cheered, and Sally wrote, "Great cheerleader = knowing how to treat each player after a defeat." She nodded her head forcefully. That was really true, too. Now, Jed you had to baby, while he grumbled. Hank would bite your head off if you got near him. She vowed to try harder to be more attentive to the individual needs of each of her players. It was good practice, too, for when she had her a family of her own. This was what her own mother always did—anticipated her husband's moods and needs. She did it with her children, too, knowing when to hug them and when to stay out of the way.

Sally guessed her own mother was just about the perfect woman, taking pleasure in making her family comfortable and happy.

Jed got up late, lifted weights, worked on the Chevy, practiced with the football team. Some afternoons he and Sally would go water skiing with Bobby and Hank. With beers on the dashboard, they'd haul her around the lake as, time after time, she failed to stand up on the skis. She would toss her head, frown, and purse her lips, as she bobbed in the water, holding the handle between her two skis. He would take off with a roar; and she would be dragged under the water, arms first, her skis tangling and shooting off in all directions, and her bathing suit top billowing out to reveal breasts, and sometimes nipples. As hard as it was to understand how she could fail to stand up, he just had to glance at her pouty little face to roar with laughter and then circle around to try again, chugging his beer. Hank and Bobby would yell over the roar of the motor, "You're one lucky man, Tatro. Jesus, would I like a piece of her action!"

Jed, pleased, would try to look annoyed. "Yeah? And how'd you like this beer can up your ass, Osborne?"

After eighteen or twenty tries, Hank would drive the boat while Jed swooped around on a single ski, enveloped in a fine spray. He would leap across the wake and shoot out to the side, almost even with the boat, where he would raise the handle high over his head to keep from sinking while the boat caught up.

As Hank steered the hurtling boat between submerged logs and rocks, Sally would squint into the sun at Jed. He could feel her eyes moving all over his brown muscled body as it rippled and glistened in the spray. He would tuck one knee behind the other, and lean over to form a forty-five-degree angle with the lake surface. Sometimes, if there wasn't much activity on the lake, Bobby and Hank would leave them off at a ski jump and go for a long long drive, while Jed's white buttocks drove insistently up and down on top of her.

At night he would pick her up, wearing his Benson Mill cap and T-shirt. Her father would either question him minutely about when they'd be home, or would eye him with distaste and stalk from the room. Jed would just smile. Sally was his now, he could afford to be generous to her grouchy old man.

She would sit on the bleachers and watch him play third base. He loved to have her there. He'd chatter more to the pitcher: "Pitcherrightintherebabyattaboyhumbabyhum." He'd jump higher than he thought he could. He'd throw straighter and faster to first. He'd hit home runs. Her presence gave him powers. He felt larger than life—this must be what it meant to be in love. He would never leave her.

Afterward they would go to the quarry and make love in the back seat, him streaked with dust, sweat, and grass stains.

You drove several hours up narrow twisting dirt roads to reach the bowl that contained a small lake, a log dining hall, and several groupings of four-person tents with cots and wooden floors. Camp Tuscarora, where Emily was a junior counselor.

The director, a hearty woman in a green gym suit and yellow Girl Scout tie, instructed the staff on orientation day as they sat around the tables in the dining hall: "The parents of our campers have entrusted us with their most precious possessions, girls—their daughters. And it's up to us to see that these little children are kept safe here at Camp Tuscarora. But I don't need to tell yall that your job involves much more. Parents are sending their daughters here to give them experiences they couldn't have at home—good Christian fellowship with clean-living, God-fearing young women. Now yall must set a good example, girls. No smoking except in the counselors' hut. It goes without saying that you don't drink—at camp or anywhere else.

"Now, when campers come to yall with their little problems, girls, it's up to yall to give them love and comfort. This will be good practice for when yall have husbands and children of your very own in a few years. This is a woman's rightful responsibility in this life, and it's never too early to learn how to do it right. And of course yall wouldn't be here tonight if we didn't feel you'd already exhibited this ability. A good counselor will attune herself to the unspoken needs of her campers."

Emily was nervous. Could she be a good counselor? Sometimes she thought she didn't even like children much. But when she heard herself think like this, she was appalled. What kind of a woman didn't like children? A monster. She expected to have at least five or six of her own. But sometimes she watched her own mother around the house and garden, and thought that the poor woman didn't much like any of it, had gotten stuck with it and was trying to make the best of things. There didn't appear to be much pleasure in it for her.

She was assigned to help the early teens, who were doing primitive camping, digging latrine holes in the forest and lashing limbs between tree trunks for toilet seats, cooking over open fires with black pots and reflector ovens. Their pup tents were pitched in a circle on a soft floor of pine needles. Often they hiked down to the lake for swimming and canoeing, sometimes for a meal in the dining hall with the other campers. Each morning they attended the flag ceremony in the field above the dining hall, and at night they sat around the fire, sang songs, told stories, and acted out skits.

Emily wrote Raymond in the light from a kerosene lantern. His latest letters to her conveyed the same elation as his first: "When I'm not working, I walk around the city taking pictures. The wharves where the ocean liners dock. The streets off Seventh Avenue crammed with boys pushing racks of suits and dresses. Messengers on Wall Street with attaché cases chained to their wrists. The fancy stores on Fifth Avenue. Mulberry Street and the Italian delicatessens, their windows crammed with sausages and salamis, strings of peppers, bunches of herbs. Chinatown. The weirdos around the fountain in Washington Square. (That's in Greenwich Village.) The wholesale flower market. Yorkville, the townhouses in the East Sixties. One night I walked by chance out into Times Square. A huge cigarette billboard was blowing smoke rings. Neon signs glittered like a vault of precious gems.

"I went with Gus to his parents' in New Jersey for Sunday lunch last week. We came back across the George Washington Bridge, and there was the skyline stretching below us. We drove down the Henry Hudson Parkway past huge brick apartment buildings with all this fancy molding and with thousands of windows reflecting the sunset. I felt a great surge of pride that I was part of this now. Sometimes I stand for half an hour or more on Park Avenue in the Forties and stare at these huge glass and steel skyscrapers. They take my breath away, Emily. This city is like a turbine. It throbs with energy . . ."

Emily blew out the lantern and stretched out in her sleeping bag, listening to the frogs and crickets and an occasional mournful owl.

Babs, her tentmate, a sophomore Phys. Ed. major from the University of Georgia, taught canoeing. The first time she saw Babs, Emily was standing on the porch of the counselors' hut on orientation day, looking down to the lake. A tanned girl in a red tank suit was gripping the edge of the diving board and slowly pressing herself into a handstand. After coming down, she jumped into a canoe and glided across the lake, executing complicated maneuvers. She landed at the dock accurately, then hoisted the aluminum canoe out of the water and carried it to the rack. Emily sat by her at dinner that night and studied her burnt nose, coated with greasy white ointment.

The campers arrived a couple of days later—mostly from Newland and other towns in the valley. One girl named Rowena was from a farm on the road up to camp. Her eyes were crossed, her hair was stringy and greasy, she was overweight, acned, and mildly retarded. She wore someone's cast-off gabardine maternity slacks and a coral Orlon sweater. Her tongue hung from a corner of her mouth when she laughed. The other campers avoided her. They wore blouses with Peter Pan collars and circle pins, Bermuda shorts, new tennis shoes called Grasshoppers, which had only two holes per side for laces, and college sweatshirts from older brothers and sisters. They made Emily nervous. She was sure they'd be voted into Ingenue when they got to high school. They always knew the right thing to wear, the right thing to say.

There was an uneven number, and Rowena ended up tenting by herself. Emily paired herself with Rowena in jobs requiring partners, and talked with Georgia and Sissy, the most popular campers, trying to persuade them to include Rowena. They were just at the age to start thinking that Girl Scout ideals like kindness were finky.

Rowena began following Emily around like a dog, trying to sit beside her at meals and to stand beside her at flag ceremony. Emily in turn was devoting effort to standing and sitting beside Babs. Emily's skin crawled as Rowena tried to hold her hand. But she wouldn't have minded holding Babs's. Babs was pinned to a Sigma Nu named Rob. She wore a tiny gold crown studded with pearls on her breast. After supper, they sometimes played keepaway. Emily and Babs passed the ball under their legs and behind their backs as they ran— while the campers squealed with delight and frustration. Rowena galumphed up and down the field with very little idea what was going on, screaming with laughter, her tongue protruding over the corner of her lower lip. Emily tried to toss her the ball every so often, but she always threw it straight up in the air, howling with delight.

One night the campers hid Rob's photo. He was a handsome chunky-looking young man with dark curly hair, a sneaky grin, and a beer mug tie tack. Emily and Babs searched the woods. Finally Rowena led them to it behind a boulder, and stood looking at them with her crossed eyes, hungry for praise.

Back in the tent Babs murmured, "It's really gross not seeing him all summer."

"I know what you mean."

"Do you have a boyfriend?"

"Sort of. He's in New York City now, though. Has a job up there."

"For good?"

"Looks like it."

"Gee, that's tough."

"Well, I don't know. We're more like friends, I guess. We grew up together."

"Oh, that's nice."

"It's nice, but it's not very romantic."

"Yeah, I see what you mean. Why don't you get somebody else?"

"Nobody else asks me out. I guess they figure Raymond and I are going steady or something. I guess we are really. Or were."

"Well, now's your chance."

"Yeah, but there's nobody I'm much interested in."

"That's what you always think right after you break up. But someone else always comes along."

"But we didn't actually break up."

"But you weren't actually going steady?"

A couple of days later they went in two trucks to a TVA lake for a canoe trip, in preparation for a three-day trip. Babs and Emily rode in the cab of one truck, which was being driven by Earl, the camp caretaker. Earl was a junior at the state university. He was tall with messy shocks of light brown hair, piercing green eyes, and a good-natured smile. He wore riding boots, tight jeans, and a wide leather thong around his wrist.

"Cigarette?" he asked, holding out a pack of Marlboros. Babs grinned. They weren't supposed to smoke in front of campers. Babs removed her big straw hat and put it over the back window. Then she took a cigarette and lit it, cupping her hand around the match.

Emily had never smoked. It was one more failing—she made good grades, she didn't smoke, she didn't drink, she didn't pet. She didn't particularly *want* to make good grades. It was something that had been thrust upon her, like menstruation. Each year her class elected her Most Studious or Most Likely to Succeed. The point was that she didn't *want* to succeed, she wanted to be popular. Sally of course always got Most Popular or Best Smile for her class. Sometimes Emily would try to make a bad grade, but it was almost impossible on true-false quizzes and multiple choice. As for the drinking, smoking, and petting, these were things she was prepared to try, but opportunities didn't present themselves. In junior high she had concluded that if only her mother would allow her to wear a bra, shave her legs and armpits, use deodorant, and wear lipstick, she would be a social success. Eventually she achieved these goals, but nothing changed. Ingenue still hadn't given her a bid, and she was still voted Most Likely to Succeed.

She took a Marlboro and sucked the match flame into its tip, as Babs had. The cab filled with billowing smoke, and Emily choked. Earl and Babs looked at her with concern. Her face purple, she gasped, "Oh, it's nothing. Just went down the wrong way." She crossed her legs and positioned the cigarette between extended fingertips as Babs had done. She looked casually out the truck window where trees were flying past, then glanced at the cigarette, adjusting it slightly.

Babs flicked her ash into the tray with her thumb nail. Emily did likewise, flipping the cigarette into Earl's lap. The truck skidded as Emily dived across Babs and between Earl's legs. She smiled, recrossed her legs, and repositioned her cigarette.

"Either of you girls ride horses?" Earl inquired.

"I used to, but I haven't in a long time," replied Babs.

"Me neither," said Emily.

"You should come down to my cottage sometime after supper. I'm training a mare to jump. You could ride her if you wanted."

"Thanks. Might do it," Babs said, squashing out her cigarette.

On their first evening off Babs and Emily went to the clearing behind Earl's cabin. Earl had set up two uprights joined by a bar of adjustable height. They sat on the leaf mold on the hill smoking Marlboros in the twilight and listening to whippoorwills. Time after time Earl headed the mare toward the jump. Sometimes she snorted and tossed her head and balked, her eyes rolling back. He'd whip her and whirl her back to the starting position, kicking her flanks with his boot heels. Other times she'd clear the jump, knocking down the bar. Occasionally she'd clear it altogether. Then he'd stroke her sweaty neck and murmur endearments.

Afterward the three sat on the hillside smoking. As the sky went black, Earl brought out beers. Emily took sips until she felt a weakness creeping up her legs to her knees. Earl and Babs progressed to a giggling stage. They began wrestling in the leaf mold, insulting each other. Emily felt like a chaperone, but Babs insisted on her going the next time.

They returned to the lake for their trip—six canoes, three people to each. Emily paddled stern in one, with Rowena riding in the middle; Babs paddled stern in another. Through the long hot afternoon they paddled. Emily watched Babs's long steady strokes, watched the sun burn down on her bronzed back and flash off her wet paddle. At one point Sissy threw some marshmallows at Rowena when Rowena wasn't looking. Then she convinced her it was raining marshmallows. The other campers laughed as Rowena gazed trustingly at the sky.

When the canoes were side by side, Emily proposed a race to Babs. Each brought up one knee and dug in her paddle. The canoes shot forward. They and their bow paddlers searched for a steady rhythm. Emily watched Babs's back and arm muscles tighten as she slid the paddle into the water and pulled on it. It made a sucking sound and left behind tiny whirlpools. Water dribbled off the paddle as she swept it in a half circle, parallel to the water. Emily timed her strokes to Babs's, and both canoes surged through the water toward the dam, leaving wakes.

They beached at the base of the dam and climbed up the gravel bank to the snack bar that overlooked the concrete face. Far below, water gushed out after its journey through the turbines. They bought

Cokes and candy bars. Emily stared at the families in their camper-trailers, feeling out of touch with this world after many weeks in a tent in the mountains.

Babs said, "Rob wants us to buy one of those things and go cross-country after we get married."

"Married? Are you getting married?"

Babs laughed. "Well, sure, after I graduate. We'll get engaged a year from next Christmas, and the wedding will be the following June. Rob says we'd better take this trip before we start to have us our kids."

"How many are you going to have?"

"Four."

They spread sleeping bags on a deserted gravel beach at the far end of the lake that night. Behind them towered wooded, cave-pocked cliffs. They sang grace and cooked stew from dehydrated meat and vegetables. The sun, a huge copper gong, inched behind the mountain across the lake. As far as they could see in all directions, there was no sign of human existence except their own. After supper the campers began teasing Rowena, calling her names until she cried. Roweener. Ro the Weener. Weener.

Later they drank hot chocolate and lay around the fire listening to wild boars rooting in the underbrush. Buzzards settled in nests at the clifftops. Babs sat behind Sissy, brushing and braiding her long hair, as the group sang about anthropomorphic frogs and pigeons, with whippoorwills whistling a refrain from the forest. Emily watched Babs's strong brown hands smoothing and patting Sissy's hair and wished that her own weren't chopped off in a curly cap. But she was a junior counselor now, supposed to pamper, not be pampered. But it wasn't coming easily to her. Rowena was clinging to her hand, and it disgusted her. Why do I always end up with the freaks, she asked herself.

After the girls crawled into their sleeping bags and began to doze off, Babs grabbed Marlboros from her knapsack and nodded down beach. They walked across gravel and climbed over driftwood. Waves lapping at their feet, they lit cigarettes and puffed in silence. The sky was so clear that even the clustered Pleiades looked almost separate. Emily recalled Injun Al's telling The Five how Cherokees tested braves' eyesight by asking them to count the stars in the Pleiades. She thought about the difficulties of being a nearsighted brave—perhaps equivalent to the difficulties of being a brainy, athletic girl at Newland High.

The moon had not risen, but the millions of distant stars seemed to light up the black. Except for waves licking the shore, rustlings in the forest, their own sighs as they exhaled, and the distant crackling of their campfire, all was quiet.

"God, I'm missing Rob tonight," Babs murmured.

"Yeah, I know what you mean."

Babs looked at her. "Do you?"

"I don't know. Maybe not."

"A summer without sex. What a rotten idea."

Emily sat in rigid silence, not daring to pursue this topic. Was Babs actually saying she'd had sex? If so, she was the only self-proclaimed nonvirgin Emily had ever met.

Babs smiled and patted her leg. "You're a good kid, Emily."

Emily felt the bottom drop out of her stomach. Her leg tingled where Babs had just touched her. She grabbed another cigarette and lit it with trembling hands. What in the world was that?

A letter from Raymond was waiting when she got back to the main camp. She read it lying on her back in a stand of poplars, whose rustling leaves sprinkled drops of sunlight back and forth across her body. "I spend a lot of time riding the subways. I sit and watch the people getting on and off—every skin color and style of dress in the world. Or I go to a newsstand and look through newspapers from almost every country—the Irish *Advocate* and *Staats-Zeitung*, *Novy Świat*, and *La Prensa*. Or I stand on Madison Avenue during rush hour and watch ad men and editors bustling past. The most talented people in the world are here. This is where everything is happening. Sometimes I go out to the airport and watch passengers getting off planes from Osaka and Dubai, Bangkok and Melbourne. I never before realized how boring Newland is—everyone looks and thinks exactly alike. You wear the wrong color socks one day and you're an outcast for life. For the first time, I feel like a real person, an individual. Anything seems possible here. Can you understand this, Emily?"

On the whole, she thought not. She was dwarfed by trees. The nearest person was a mile away. Raymond was dwarfed by glass and steel skyscrapers, surrounded by crowds. How did he expect her to understand?

Emily wandered alone over to Earl's. As usual he and the mare were struggling out back. Insects, birds, and frogs provided a continuum for the mare's snorts, Earl's curses and cooings, the whack of his whip, the pounding of hooves, the thud of the bar hitting the ground. The bar was up to three feet. Afterward he sprawled on the hillside with his beer and cigarette, attired in his usual brown leather riding boots, tight jeans, and T-shirt.

"I'm getting there."

"I can see the improvement."

"Yeah, she's a good horse. Learns fast. Did you have a good canoe trip?"

"Yeah, it was nice. No rain. No accidents. Perfect."

"Where's Babs at tonight?"

"She's on duty. Do you mind just me being here?"

"Do I mind? Are you kidding?"

"Well, I didn't know. I mean I thought . . ."

"What? Me and Babs?" He threw his head back and laughed. "She's pinned."

"Yeah, I know. So what?"

"That's the next thing to being engaged, you dope. You're just a dumb little high school punk, ain't you?" he teased in the tone he used with Babs when they wrestled. "Ain't you?"

She smiled. "Yeah, I guess so." She didn't know how to play this game.

"Em's a little high school jerk!"

She decided to try. "Not so little!" she announced, punching him in his hard stomach as she had seen Babs do.

"Aha! She fights!" Grinning, he twisted her arm into a hammerlock. She threw her other arm around his neck and got him in a head hold. "Take it back!" she demanded, tightening her arm.

"Em's a little high school creep!" He tightened his hammerlock. With one foot she kicked his chest, forcing him to release her arm. He flung himself on top of her, sitting on her stomach and forcing her arms to the ground over her head.

"All right now!" he said triumphantly. "Tell me I'm wonderful."

"You're a worm!" She brought one leg over his head and thrust it hard against his chest so that he toppled backward and rolled down the hill. He leaped up and ran back up in exaggerated, slow-motion strides. She was laughing, crouched. He tackled her. She fell back on her elbows. He grabbed her hair with both hands and pulled her head backward, until her mouth opened.

Suddenly she wasn't having fun. She had often seen his mare's mouth drop open similarly as he sawed on her reins. She tossed her head trying to free her hair. His mouth lowered onto hers, and his tongue stabbed her compressed lips. She shoved him off.

He lay looking at the sky. "I'm sorry, Emily. I thought you wanted that."

Emily understood she'd been playing out of her league. From her days with The Five she was accustomed to tussling with boys. But she was no longer a child. "I'm too young for that stuff, Earl."

He laughed. "Too young? Look at you! I hate to break it to you, kid, but you're a big girl."

"Not that big. I'm just a high school punk. Remember?"

"OK. You're a punk. I'm sorry. I lost my head. But I'll wait." His jaw muscles clenched and unclenched, like Gary Cooper's in *High Noon.*

"What are you talking about?"

"I like you, Emily. A lot."

"What? Who? Me?"

He laughed. "Never mind."

By the flashlight beam Emily brushed her teeth in the water from the spigot. She looked down and saw a frog. On closer inspection it looked deformed. She crouched. It was Siamese twin frogs, one on the other's back. She raced to her tent and summoned Babs. Babs looked and began laughing.

"Emily, those frogs are screwing."

"I . . . I didn't know frogs . . . did that."

"As far as I know, every creature alive does it."

Emily walked back to the tent, mortified.

The last night of camp all the campers and counselors gathered around the lake and shoved pieces of bark with candles fixed to them out into the lake. They sang the camp song, *"Oh Camp Tuscarora / It's you we adore—A / long life's hard trail / We'll think of you dail / lee and recall just how much we love you."*

After the ceremony Emily said to Earl, "What did you wish for?"

Babs said with a laugh, "We know *what* you wished for. But who with?"

Earl grinned. "Not telling."

Walking back to their campsite, Babs admitted she had wished for Rob to come early tomorrow to pick her up. Emily had wished to be asked to join Ingenue, although she didn't confess this. They came across Rowena, walking alone.

"What did you wish for, Rowena?" asked Emily.

Rowena grinned. "For my eyes to be straight so that Sissy will like me."

Donny stopped in the luncheonette to buy some gum, shouldering his way apologetically through the circle of men outside.

"How you making it, Donny?" Mr. Dupree asked.

"I be just fine, thank you, sir." He pointed to a new picture on the wall above the cash register. "Who you got there, Mr. Dupree? That your daddy?"

Mr. Dupree looked at him incredulously. "Son, that's the Reverend Mr. Martin Luther King Junior. Ain't you watched no TV in the last five years?"

"Oh yeah, I thought I recognized him."

"Now how bout it, son? You gon go with us over to the white high school this autumn?"

"Who, me? Naw, I don't reckon so, Mr. Dupree. My grandmaw, she don't want me mixed up in no trouble."

"Trouble? Donny, you already in trouble, right up to your brown ears."

"What you talking bout, Mr. Dupree? I ain't never been in no trouble."

"You born a Negro in this country, you in trouble from your first breath."

"Well, I don't aim to go heaping trouble on trouble, sir."

"Son, you think life is gon be one big happy fish fry. But you better wake up right quick, or you'll find yourself in the skillet." Waving his hand as though shooing a fly, he turned away.

Donny cut lawns and hedges on Tsali Street, saving up for a car. Leon had him an old beat-up maroon Dodge, and all the girls were falling all over themselves trying to get him to take them out. Not that Donny had any interest in any girl but Rochelle. But he wouldn't a bit have minded *her* falling all over him a time or two. Leon said a car was what it took. And he hadn't known Leon to be wrong yet.

Some days he walked to the country club and carted bags around. The white caddies from Cherokee Shoals had them a clubhouse. Once when Donny tried to go in during a rainstorm, they said, "Get the hell out of here, you motherfucking coon." Now he sat under a tree by the putting green, watching above the hedges as white kids sprang off the diving board. Sometimes he saw Sally Prince strolling in her suit from the pool to her car. Or he watched the women on the putting green in Bermuda shorts and straw hats, hunched over putters, shifting from one cleated shoe to another. Rochelle cleaned the houses of some of these same women while they knocked little white balls all over the place. Seemed like a crazy way to spend your time. But you didn't question the behavior of white folks.

The white caddies were chosen first, but Donny usually got a nod at some point. Mr. Prince, for instance, always picked him, even if there were white boys waiting. They would eye him as he heaved Mr. Prince's huge zippered bag onto his back. Occasionally, one would warn him not to come back, but he always ignored them and stayed within view of the pro shop while he was waiting. Once walking home along the highway, he was nearly run over by a caddy on a motorcycle. He jumped the ditch as the cycle threw up a shower of dirt and pebbles.

Although Donny had never played golf, he had learned enough from watching to know when to free which club from its leather mitt. He enjoyed hiking with a couple of bags on his back around the bright green course, listening to the birds and watching the little white balls and scrubbing the grass stains off them in the ball washers. The white men liked him and sometimes chatted.

"Hot enough for you, son?"

"Yes sir, it sure is."

"A real scorcher, all right."

"Yes sir, it sure is."

"Hit me a pretty good ball off that last tee."

"Yes sir, you sure did."

"Boy, wouldn't a beer taste good right now?"

"Yes sir, it sure would."

They always tipped him good. He'd walk home picking up soft drink bottles along the highway. With his refund, he'd buy candy for Rochelle's brothers and sisters. Each time he walked back into the familiar streets of Pine Woods, he felt like a secret agent returning from enemy territory. All those pale faces. Starting to look sick to him.

Rochelle's brothers and sisters would squeal when they saw him coming across the yard. They'd climb his long legs and search his pockets for treats. "Whoa there! Hang on here now!" he'd laugh. Rochelle minded them when her mother was maiding. When her mother was home, Rochelle maided on Tsali Street or in the development across the river. Donny would horse around with the kids, throwing them over his shoulders and whirling them by the arms. He'd get into a crawling position, and they'd hurl themselves on his back and tickle him. Rochelle, her mother, and every woman in Pine Woods discussed what a marvel he was with those children.

The town decided to integrate the first grade city-wide that fall, so the children could grow up together in mixed classrooms. Most people in Pine Woods thought it made good sense. But Mr. Dupree snarled one afternoon when Donny stopped in for candy, "What the hell are eleven grades of our children in an inferior school supposed to do?"

"Aw, Booker T. ain't such a bad place, Mr. Dupree," Donny insisted.

"Not unless you want to learn something."

Donny went over to Rochelle's and sat under a tree while she brought him a Nehi and sandwiches. He ate, and they watched the children tussle in the dusty yard. Their skin color was of every hue, from dark brown to café au lait, but Rochelle was the lightest. He remembered even in third grade thinking she was the prettiest thing he'd ever seen. She'd been the teacher's pet all through school.

Seemed like he was getting obsessed with the color of people's skins lately. He often caught himself gazing at his dark nose from the corner of his eye. He remembered being unaware of skin color when he was a kid. Until one afternoon when he couldn't sit with the rest of The Five in a movie. This had set off weeks of worrying, in which he'd begun to grasp that he was colored and they were white, and there was a difference. That awareness had gone away for years, but here it was back again.

One of Rochelle's brothers would be starting in a white school in the fall. Others would follow. Donny couldn't imagine what that would be like. Seemed like that the white students would win all the offices and run the school. At least over at Booker T. his classmates edited their own paper, ran the student council. He was glad he wouldn't be around to see it. Although Rochelle's bunch would. Even kids of his own might be.

Donny liked to pretend he and Rochelle was married and these was their kids. He knew his own father only from a photo his grandmaw had hid in a drawer at the apartment. A dark grinning man in an upside-down vee of a soldier's cap, a white woman on his knee. His grandmaw always told him his father was a fine strong man who'd been killed by the war. His mother mentioned something about stealing and prison. He never really got it straight. But he missed knowing him. He decided to be around for these kids the way he wished his father had been around for him.

Although he never acknowledged this to his friends at the swimming pool. Later that day they sat in the painted metal chairs in their bathing suits, watching the girls and commenting.

Lorraine slunk by, and Leon called out in a falsetto, "Where you going at, Lorraine baby?"

"Walking," she growled.

"Man, if I could get me a piece of that pussy," Leon sighed, "I'd be stone living."

"Don't give me none of that action, man. You said the same thing last month about Charlene. Now you got her, you want to cut out on her. Can't no woman keep you happy for long, Leon."

"Ah, I can't take no more of Charlene's shit, man. She all the time saying, 'What you gon *do* with yourself, Leon? You ain't never gon mount to nothing.' I says to her, 'Mouth, now you just listen here to me. You ain't my ole lady yet, so you just hush up that flapping hole in your face.' "

"Well, when you get done with her, man, you just let me know," said Sidney.

They got up and sauntered to the snack bar. On the rear wall was a soft drink poster with a busty blonde white woman in a tight sweater and pedal pushers, standing beside a red Sting Ray which was parked next to a split-level ranch house. As they ordered hot dogs, their eyes studied her. Leon announced, "Man, I really laid me some hot pipe last night after the revival." Everyone listened when Leon talked about girls. He claimed he'd been screwing since he was eleven. Donny kept hoping maybe he'd pick up some pointers that would work with Rochelle.

"Naw, you never did."

"I swear it. I swear I did."

"You got that little chick from North Carolina to put out for you?"

"Sure did."

"Naw, you're lying."

"I ain't lying, man. Who you calling a liar?" They scuffled and slugged each other, until Donny dragged Leon over and dropped him in the pool to cool off.

Sally and Jed had moved their trysts to the powder magazine. They kept pillows and blankets down there, and a battery lantern. Sometimes Sally brought down a vase of flowers. One night Jed lay propping his head on one hand and gazing at Sally's pubic area. Now that he had easy access to every area of her body, he wasn't really that interested. Or rather, he wanted her available when he wanted her. But he didn't want all this other stuff—comforting her when she was getting the curse, having to account for every minute of his day, listening to criticisms of Bobby and Hank. It was like being a kid again and having to ask Mommy's permission. He hadn't known it would be like this. With Betty Boobs you was in and out, and that was that. You didn't have to spend your whole life keeping her happy. Of course while you was in Betty, she expected a hell of a lot. Her cunt had been like some big dark warm slimy sink hole that he would get mired down in and never escape from. It was like the mouth of one of them hairy tarantula spiders. God only knew what germs festered in there. It seemed like that he couldn't win. Why couldn't he find him a nice normal girl who took what he gave her and was grateful?

Sally watched Jed watch her. He was so good-looking. She guessed this was worth it to keep him. If you sinned but knew it was sin, did that make it less sinful? But it took her breath away to think of him down here with that Betty French. He'd promised he'd never do that again. What he saw in screwing, though, she'd never know. He'd heave himself on top of her and push that big thing in. It was over before it ever started. All in all, it was one big disappointment. And now that she'd given him everything, he didn't seem to love her as much.

"Do you love me?" she demanded.

"Yeah. Sure."

"No, I mean do you really love me?"

"Yeah."

"Really really?"

"Yeah."

"You sure don't sound like it."

"How would I sound if I did?"

"Not like that."

He shrugged.

"You don't, do you?"

"I love you," he said, with a hunted look.

"If you really did, you'd tell me so without me asking."

He glowered. She inched closer. He inched away.

She burst into tears. "You despise me!" she wailed. "I've given you everything, and now I'm nothing but trash to you!"

"Goddam it to hell, I love you!"

"You don't!" she shrieked, pounding his chest. "You're just using me! You've ruined my rep, and now you hate me!"

"I don't hate you," he snarled, glaring with hatred.

"Then why are you looking at me like that?" she moaned, burying her tear-drenched face in her hands.

He grabbed his hair with both hands, as though about to rip it out. He smashed his fist repeatedly into the dirt floor, growling. Sally sneaked an awed look through her fingers.

"OK. What do I have to do to prove that I love you?"

"Hold me," she pleaded. "Love me a little bit."

Gingerly he pulled her to him, wanting only to be far away. She melted into him and murmured endearments, her hand stroking his erection.

# Chapter Nine

## Homecoming Queen

At half-time the band marched onto the football field to a martial version of "A Pretty Girl Is Like a Melody." They formed a five-pointed crown. The homecoming queen and her attendants rode out, each perched atop the back seat of a white Cadillac convertible. Sally, the junior attendant, wore a strapless yellow net ballerina-length gown and a rhinestone tiara and held an armful of yellow roses. Slowly the cars circled the field, as the stands applauded. Sally smiled until her cheeks ached and waved a white-gloved hand until she thought her arm would fall off.

The floodlights were cut, and a bonfire was lit in center field. The Cadillacs pulled up around it like Conestoga wagons. Band members switched on lights on their hats, so that the outline of the crown remained. Majorettes in white boots with flaming fire batons stationed themselves at each point and performed a complicated routine, as the band played "The Sabre Dance."

Sally reflected, as she gazed into the snapping fire, that she had had a hard time zipping her dress this evening. Of course, she hadn't worn it since the Rebel Christmas Formal last year. She wondered, still, if she really might be pregnant.

One night in the cave when Jed withdrew, he whispered, "Oh Christ!"

"What, Jed honey?" Sally murmured, her eyes closed.

"The goddam rubber came off!" He grabbed a bottle of ginger ale, wrenched off the top, put his thumb over its mouth and shook it up, then inserted it in Sally's vagina. She screamed and tried to sit up, as ginger ale shot into her. Jed shoved her down, shook the bottle and repeated the process.

He jumped up and stalked back and forth. "When's your period due?"

She was sobbing.

"When's your goddam period due?"

"I don't know," she wailed.

"What do you mean you don't know?"

"I've got it marked on the calendar, but I can't remember."

He dragged her to her feet. "Come on."

They raced to the library where they sweated over anatomy and physiology texts. The librarian, an old lady with a grey bun who had read to them both at Story Time when they were five, smiled benignly. High school sweethearts at work on term papers.

"It looks like it's fourteen days after the first day of your last period," Jed concluded.

He waited in the driveway as she sneaked into her house and consulted her calendar. "This is the eighteenth day," she said, climbing back in.

"Thank God for that. I think we're safe." They fell into each other's arms and kissed fervently. "From now on I wear two rubbers."

A couple of weeks later Sally threw up in the girls' room. She decided her breakfast ham had been spoiled. When she began falling asleep before supper, she decided to go to bed earlier. The aching and burning in her nipples she explained by the enthusiasm with which Jed sucked them.

When her period was several days late, she decided she'd miscounted and went back over the calendar half a dozen times. But her period had been late before, so she refused to worry. The timing had been wrong, and Jed had been wearing two rubbers ever since.

When she missed her second period, she began to get nervous. She made an appointment with a gynecologist in a neighboring town. After the exam he sighed and said, "Well, young lady, I can't say for sure whether or not you're pregnant. I'll give you a prescription. If you don't begin your period five days after finishing the pills, you'll know you're pregnant."

Each morning she took a small peach-colored pill. A dozen times a day she retired to a bathroom, where she prayed for bloodstains. Even a hemorrhage would do. Her prayers remained unanswered. She'd sit on the toilet long enough to regain composure, before returning to the classroom or dinner table with her pep-squad smile intact.

One night Jed delivered her home from a Devout meeting where they had prayed for success against Chattanooga Central. Darlene, the new Devotions Deputy, shut her eyes in the flickering candlelight and said, "We thank Thee, Lord, for last week's victory over Roaring Fork. But we would have been even more grateful if Thou hadst not let their JayVees defeat ours by such a wide margin. But Lord, we really need this next one against the Purple Pounders if we're going to have us a go at the state championship . . ."

Parked in the driveway, Jed slid his hand up Sally's thigh. She shoved him away, wrenched open the door, and ran toward the house. He ran after her. "What's wrong? What did I do?"

"Nothing," she gasped. "I have to be in early." She twisted away and ran into the house.

"Those pills didn't work," she told the doctor over the phone.

There was a long silence. "Well, I'm sorry, young lady."

"Can't you give me something else?"

No reply.

"I mean, my period's late is all, doctor. It's been late before. I'm out of whack. Maybe something's wrong with my ovaries." She'd been reading in the library about the diseases and deficiencies that could interrupt menstruation. She'd stood in front of mirrors inspecting her coloring for signs of anemia.

"I'm sorry, young lady. I've done all I can."

"But what should I do?"

"I don't know, young lady. I'm sorry. Good luck." He hung up.

She stared at the phone. After a while she walked into the bathroom and threw up. Then she picked up her calendar and counted off her periods. It was just humanly impossible for her to be pregnant.

"Come on!" whispered Leon, pushing aside hemlock branches and dashing across the open space between the wall and the band bleachers. The boys from Cherokee Shoals who hung out there during the game and the highway patrolmen who broke up their fights were all up by the fence watching the fire batons.

Donny got halfway to the bleachers before he froze. This wasn't right. "Thou shalt not covet thy neighbor's goods," the Bible said. Leon kept calling him Mr. Junior Church Usher and saying that white people had been stealing from niggers for three hundred years. So you was just getting some of your own back.

Rochelle's mother had gone into the hospital with a ruptured tubal pregnancy last month. She was in bed at home now, and it didn't look like that she was getting her strength back. The county was paying the hospital. Neighbors brought over groceries. Rochelle's mother's employer brought down boxes of old clothes and canned goods. Donny had given Rochelle his car money from this summer. Even so, she'd had to quit her library job to work at maiding every afternoon and on Saturdays. The neighbors took turns minding the kids. Mr. Dupree was giving them credit. But things couldn't go on like this. Rochelle was up at six every morning to get the kids dressed and fed and off to school and to babysitters, then off to school herself, maiding in the afternoon, home to fix supper and clean up the house and tend her mother and wash the kids and put them to bed and wash and iron their clothes; then she sat down to her homework. Every time she and Donny went out, she fell asleep on him. Her clothes were often unironed. She hadn't smiled in weeks.

"What about their daddies?" Donny asked one night.

"Law honey, you know what men is like. They long gone," replied Rochelle's mother with a bitter laugh, as he and Rochelle sat by her bed. She was wrapped in an old quilt and looked haggard.

"How bout farming the kids out? Your sister could take a couple. Grandmaw might take one or two."

"If they's one thing I'd hate to see happen, it's to break us up. Cause we all each other's got."

"Yeah, but then you and Rochelle could both have you a good rest. And once you was back to work again, they could come on back home."

Damn, he had to help them. He ran under the bleachers. Leon was reaching up and slipping his hand into musical instrument cases to remove pocketbooks.

Through the planks Donny saw a patrolman gazing out toward the bonfire. Wide-brimmed hat, gun on his hip, legs planted, hands behind his back. The fire batons twirled twenty feet into the night sky. The crowd whistled and cheered and hollered.

The floodlights would come on. The cop would whirl around, spot him, grab him, drag him out to the bonfire. The crowd would screech, and the band would play as they barbecued him . . .

On the national news that evening was a shot of a cross burning in the front yard of the school superintendent in Donley, Tennessee. A stone had been thrown through his window with a note wrapped around it that read "Stone this time—dynamite next." White folks didn't mess around. This white kid was interviewed saying, "I jes can't set next to em. They dirty, and they stink. Hit like to make me sick. They just animals, is all. Yall want em in our schools, *you* set next to em!"

"Grandmaw, you know I never realized before how much they hate us," he'd said.

"Hush, honey. They mostly just plain working people like your mama and me. They be a few nuts in ever town. And sometimes they be colored."

Donny opened a case lid and felt around inside. Leon was racing for the hemlocks, pocketbooks hanging all over him.

Donny was choked for a moment with anger, at all the men who'd been through Rochelle's mother's bed, having a good time and then running off without a second thought. Was that what being a man meant? But was this? No, there was plenty of men around Pine Woods who went to work every morning at whatever jobs they could find. They came home in the evenings and played with their children and made love to their wives. They paid their bills and went to church on Sunday. Mr. Junior Church Usher. All right, that's what he was then. He flew toward the hemlocks empty-handed.

In between trilling her flute to "The Sabre Dance" and marching in place to the drums, Emily sneaked glances at the queen and her court around the campfire. It was a big relief not to feel resentment any longer at being in Sally's backup band.

Earl had come over from State several times to take her to movies. Her classmates saw them, and word got around that Emily Prince was dating a college man, a frat man, a KT yet! He began holding her hand in the theater. And one night when he left her at her door, he kissed her tentatively. Missing was the revulsion she felt when Raymond kissed her. In fact, she felt mild enthusiasm.

They were lavaliered the weekend before the KT Fall Formal. As they watched *Gone With the Wind* at the Wilderness Trail Drive-In, Earl fastened a chain around her neck on which dangled a tiny gold-plated sabre. They kissed as Atlanta was consumed in a holocaust.

Emily wore her long white gown from the Plantation Ball to the Fall Formal. Earl wore a Confederate uniform and sabre. They strolled up the sidewalk between rows of boxwood to the white-columned KT house. To one side of the porch steps was a boulder painted green. Inside, the double living room was packed with brothers in grey uniforms and gold braid, and their dates. Several girls in long dresses struck decorous poses on the spiral staircase. Fires burned in fireplaces at either end of the room.

Partway through the evening Emily found herself surrounded by brothers. They sang the KT anthem, about Honor and Virtue and Fidelity. The president presented her with long-stemmed white roses, in honor of her lavalierhood.

Emily spent the night in a dorm. She and Earl walked up to the KT house the next morning, past a purple boulder.

"Wasn't that rock green last night?"

"Uh, gee, I didn't notice."

Emily stared at the boulder.

One day at school Mo sauntered up to her. She and Mo had been grade school chums. Mo had gone on to become head cheerleader and president of Ingenue. And Emily, fink and brain.

"Hey, Em. How's it going?"

"Fine, thank you," said Emily with suspicion.

Mo reached out and touched the tiny sabre at her throat. "KT, huh?"

"Yes."

"Not bad. He's nice-looking, too. I saw you and him at the Majestic last weekend. You're the talk of the school."

"No kidding?"

"No kidding."

The next week the Ingenues, in their cream blazers with royal purple crests on the pockets, arrived at Emily's front door.

"Oh, hi," said Emily. "I think Sally's in her room. I'll get her."

"But it's you we want!" exclaimed Mo.

"Me?"

"We've brought you your bid!"

Emily knew you were supposed to act like the honoree on "This Is Your Life," and squeal and cry. She'd seen Sally do this. The most she could manage was a wary smile.

The initiation was held at Mo's, a small ranch house in the mill village. Her parents had moved out for the night. The Ingenues, clad in shortie pajamas, their spit curls pinned with crossed silver hair clips, sat in a big circle on the living room rug conducting a Lemon Squeeze. Each member was featured in turn, with the other members going around the circle saying one nice thing and one criticism of her. The initiates sat on the sofa and chairs taking notes on correct Ingenue conduct. Emily was trying to French inhale her Marlboro, as she had observed several old members doing. You let the smoke drift out your mouth and inhaled it in a steady stream through your nostrils. Emily's head was obscured by clouds of swirling smoke.

"That's really true, Dawn. You smile so much that nobody can tell when you mean it."

"Insincere, that's what it seems like, Dawn."

"But it's not," Dawn insisted, picking her lacquered big toenail. "I just smile when I'm happy. I can't help it if I'm usually happy. I mean, I'm not smiling now, am I?" She burst into tears and buried her face in her hands.

The group sat in disapproving silence. Finally the vice president said, "Dawn honey, we're just trying to help you be the best Ingenue possible. And besides, you know the person being discussed isn't supposed to say nothing." Dawn wailed and buried her face more deeply.

They moved on to Sandy, who was accused of flirting with other members' boyfriends. "But you have very nice teeth, Sandy," her accuser added.

Emily watched through her clouds of smoke.

"You don't smile enough, Connie. Everyone thinks you're a sourpuss. We don't want Ingenues known as a bunch of sourpusses, do we?"

By the end, most Ingenues were in tears, mopping at eyes and cheeks with the hems of pajama tops. Sandy was passing around a piece of paper. She had a way of sauntering up to boys at school, and bumping them with her hip, and asking them in her lazy smiling drawl if they'd had their mileage that day. As members read the paper, they either gasped or blushed or tittered. Emily read: "Math problem: A cock is six inches long. At sixty strokes per minute for five minutes per day, how many days does it take to cover a mile?" The answer was upside down: "Depends on whether or not you have a blow-out. Smile if you've had your mileage today."

Emily quickly exhaled another smoke screen and passed on the paper to the girl beside her. The old members began discussing boyfriends like a harem its sheiks. The new members were led into a bedroom. Earlier that week each had turned in a set of underwear. These were returned, dyed royal purple, the club color. Holes were cut in the bras for the nipples, and in the panties for the crotches. Everyone was shrieking with embarrassed delight. Emily lit another cigarette and inspected her mutilated underthings. She could put them on and become an Ingenue. Or she could walk out and resume being a fink. She took a big drag. The others had put on spiked heels and were inspecting each other, screaming with laughter.

Emily squashed out her cigarette, stood up and undressed. She wanted to be an Ingenue. Why, she didn't know. It had a lot to do with all those years of not being one.

The girls marched into the living room, where the old members sat ogling and commenting and French inhaling and guzzling Nehis. The models posed and preened, while the old members cheered and applauded and leered like Lions at a smoker. Several whistled through their fingers.

The initiates pranced and strutted. Emily slouched out blushing, her head hanging. There was a brief silence. Then the room erupted in cheers.

"Pose for us, Em!" someone shouted. As Emily dutifully turned sideways and backward, she glanced at Mo, who sat cross-legged on the couch, her eyes gravely inspecting Emily's nipples. Emily felt a rush of—what? Her nipples began to stiffen. She raced toward the bedroom. The old members began stamping on the floor. "We want Emily! We want Emily!" She was pushed toward the living room. She stumbled into the smoky room and stood before the smirking Ingenues, one of them at last.

In the locker room Coach Clancy was critiquing the first half. "Yall run like your shoes is cast in concrete. Why, I believe yall is slower than the Second Coming. Yall bout as much use as tits on a jaybird. Lord God, I ain't never seed such a sorry bunch of ball players in my whole entire career!"

Jed sat with his elbows on his knees, his hands and head hanging. He knew scouts from some Southeastern Conference teams were in the stands tonight, and he'd played miserable so far.

"That fumble on the twenty-five, Tatro, that was the most pathetic feat of ball handling I've ever witnessed. Why, you looked like a one-armed paper-hanger with crabs. I do believe a girl could of did better! And you, Osborne, you just stood there like a spare prick on a honeymoon. I declare, if yall keep this up second half, we got less chance than a fart in a windstorm. And Miller, the line's opening up them holes. How come you can't get yourself into them? You want me to put some hair around them for you?"

Jed tossed down half a Coke in one swallow.

"Coach," Hank asked, "how come you to punt there on their thirty-eight with one to go? We coulda made that easy."

"You so full of shit your eyes are brown! Yall ain't making *nothing* easy tonight."

Jed ran back out on the field through the gauntlet of cheerleaders, feeling confident they'd pull this game out of the bag. They'd been in tighter spots before. Like Coach Clancy always said, when the going got tough, the tough got going. He could count on these guys for anything. Every man had their particular job. You opened up that hole, you faked that handoff. From old Slocombe, through the Jay-Vees, to the varsity starters, to Coach Clancy himself. No doubt as to where you stood, or what you was supposed to be doing. And when you all done it right, the team moved down that field like a Continental Mark IV car. They were a team and they functioned best under fire. Wasn't no way they weren't going to stage a comeback this evening. You *had* to win the homecoming game.

After the game, as the dejected crowd poured from the bleachers and headed for the parking lot, the driver of Sally's Cadillac, an embalmer at Creech's Funeral Home, stopped the car outside the stadium for her to move to the front seat for the drive to the homecoming dance at the gym.

Sally sat in front waving and smiling at the throngs on the sidewalks. They waved back and called congratulations.

Sally discovered the driver's free hand working its way up her skirt. Continuing to smile and wave, she used her free hand to push his away. Their hands waged a grim and silent struggle, as he looked intently at the road and she waved resolutely to her fans.

"Stop it!"

"Love me a little, baby," he said without moving his lips.

"No!" she growled, smiling at the crowd.

"You like it. You know you do," he ventriloquized, stroking her thigh.

She began feeling the familiar nausea. "Stop the car. I'm going to throw up," she ordered, bending back one of his fingers.

"Not a chance."

"I mean it!"

The car turned on to the highway and picked up speed. His hand fought its way to her crotch. She grabbed it with both hers, the adoring crowds falling away behind them.

"I said stop it!" She threw up all over him.

"Jesus Christ!"

She was too busy heaving to point out that she'd warned him.

"Oh Christ," he muttered, inspecting the mess she'd made of his white dinner jacket.

When she emerged from the Cadillac at the gym, her tiara hung over one eye and her hooped skirt was bent into a figure eight. She stumbled up the sidewalk.

She sat on the stage in a throne to the right of the queen, surveying her boogalooing classmates. Jed hadn't arrived yet, probably wouldn't since he hated losing so much. Between records the gym buzzed. From time to time people glanced up at the stage. She saw Marsha Roller laughing. Last year Marsha had swelled up to weather-balloon size. One week she was absent. She returned restored to her original shape. Her best friend announced she'd had malnutrition, which caused her to swell up. She'd gone to the hospital to get cured. Dede Black whispered that she bet Marsha had been pregnant. Soon it was all over school that Marsha Roller had had twins and had put them in an orphanage. Marsha Roller was a whore. The boys had flocked around her ever since.

Sally imagined the room falling silent. Heads would swivel in her direction. Everyone would know: Sally Prince was pregnant. Sally Prince was not a virgin. Just like Betty French and Marsha Roller and Sandy Willis, Sally Prince was a whore.

She stood up and ran from the stage.

Outside she took deep gulps of cool air. Her hands shook as she blotted her tears. She walked aimlessly. Then she ran. She ran through the night down unfamiliar sidewalks until her breathing was staccato gasps. She fell to her knees. Clasping her hands, she bowed her head and prayed to God to make the baby growing inside her give up its grip. She had sinned and known she was sinning, and this was punishment. But she begged her Creator to be merciful.

For the next week she took scalding baths. Her skin became the color of cooked lobster. Alone in the house, she ran time after time up and down the three flights of stairs from cellar to attic, like a squirrel on an exercise wheel. She jumped off high tables. Then she sat on the toilet and waited for the embryo to come out. By raising her arms she could make thousands of people leap to their feet and yell. By granting or withholding her smile, she could make teachers raise her grades. By giving or denying parts of her anatomy, she had Jed wrapped around her little finger. But this growth in her womb was unimpressed.

She searched her mind for someone to talk to. Her parents would be so disappointed. She couldn't face telling them. There would be no scene, no yelling or weeping, only stunned silence as their good opinion of her crumbled. Probably lots of girls at school were going all the way, but no one talked about it. It was like a lottery, and if your number came up, you endured the consequences alone.

If only she had never heard of Jed Tatro. She promised God that if He would get her out of this, she would never go all the way again ever.

Failing that, she wanted to be dead. She would kill herself. She straightened out a coat hanger and poked around inside herself, drawing blood. She sat with her legs spread, holding the vacuum cleaner hose to her vagina. Nothing happened.

"All right," Jed said one night when she wouldn't let him touch her because she was trying to figure out how to tell him he was going to be a father, "if you ain't interested, they is plenty of girls who is."

"Fine. Good. Go ahead," she snarled. "Only you don't need a girl. You just need a mud bank to shove that thing in."

# Chapter Ten

## Touch Your Woman

"Whew, boys, hit's cold in here, ain't it?" purred Honey Sweet into the microphone, wrapping her arms around herself and shivering so that her enormous, half-bare bosom shook.

Her lead guitarist, in a lime-green Western-cut suit, strode forward, put his arm around her and said in a low voice, leering, "Darlin, you'd be awright if you didn't go running around half dressed."

The audience in the gym howled.

Feigning indignation and shoving him away, Honey pouted, "You stick to your gui-tar playing, Slim, and you'll do just fine. You ain't got no sense of fashion. In fact, I reckon you ain't got no sense at all."

Slim leaned over and announced into his mike, "Any yall pretty women out there who's cold, yall come on over at the Howard Johnson Mo-tel after the show, and ole Slim'll warm you up real good!"

The women in the audience giggled, while Honey Sweet pushed cascades of blonde hair out of her face, cocked a hip, and rested a fist on it. "Anytime you feel like playing some music for the folks, Slim, we'll do it."

"Room 153," he added into his mike.

Honey gave a long-suffering sigh. "Hit's a shame he plays such a mean guitar," she confided. "Otherwise we could just do without him altogether." She laughed and signaled to the band to introduce her next song.

Sally's one regret was that now she'd never be Miss Newland. She'd never have her a singing career like Honey Sweet's. But never mind. She had the man she loved, and they'd have them a beautiful baby soon.

As the steel guitar whined, Honey Sweet threw back her head and closed her eyes and wailed, "*A woman needs a man to hold, / Who'll protect her from the cold, / Who'll keep her safe from harm her whole life long . . .*"

Jed glanced at Sally, who smiled up at him. He slipped his arm around her. He had to admit he was glad now at how things had turned out. He'd spent a couple of weeks driving around smoking pack after pack of cigarettes, had missed several practices, and was benched during the Cold Gap game. Other than in the halls and from a distance at pep rallies, he saw Sally only once. They went to the Wilderness Trail one Saturday night.

"Isn't there something you can do?" Jed asked.

"I've tried everything I can think of," she replied sullenly. "Except eating rat poison. Maybe I'll try that."

It seemed like a real good idea. "Don't talk like that, darlin. We going to figure something out."

"Oh Jed, what are we going to do?"

He started to say, "What you mean 'we'?" His fists clenched, and he knew he was close to burying them in her stomach time after time. He wanted to murder that little bastard in there. He threw open his door and stalked to the refreshment stand.

After he let her off at her house, he tried to figure out what she would do if he didn't do nothing. Probably go to her old man, and he'd send her away. The whole town would know anyway. Girls didn't just leave in the middle of the school year unless they was that way. It was so embarrassing, like being caught in a spotlight with your pants down.

He could cut and run. Hop in the Chevy and go . . . where? Do what? Never come back to Newland? Never see his parents again?

Besides, he loved Sally. He couldn't just abandon her. He wished there was someone to talk to. His parents would be horrified. The guidance counselor at school was a seventy-year-old old maid with a lobster claw for a cunt. Bobby and Hank . . . they claimed they was humping the honeys all across town. But he doubted it. And even if they was, they probably managed to keep their rubbers on.

Finally Jed dragged himself to the minister's house in the mill village. Mr. Marsh took him into the living room and shut out his wife and kids. As Jed explained, Mr. Marsh pressed the fingertips of both hands together like starfish screwing.

"Son, you've committed the sin of fornication."

"Yes sir, I know that. I'm sorry I ever did. But now that I have, I don't know what to do."

"You're being punished for your sins, you and your girl."

"Yes sir."

"Well son, I don't see that you have no choice. You can't continue to heap sin upon sin. You must marry the girl and raise the child up to be a clean-living Christian."

"Yes sir, but see, I ain't through school yet. She ain't neither."

"Well, she won't be able to go to school no more once hit's known she's pregnant."

"No sir."

"And you won't be able to neither, cause you'd most likely want to leave town if you wasn't to marry her."

"Yes sir."

"So you'd best marry her."

"Yes sir, but I had me some plans . . . college . . . pro ball . . . all like that."

"No doubt the young lady had her some plans, too. But I reckon you'll both have to change em. Cause the Lord has his own plans, and they override whatever piddling little notions we get into our heads. You should of thought about your plans before you went and give in to the indulgence of your fleshly lusts."

"Yes sir."

"Good luck to you, son," he called as Jed stumbled down the sidewalk, his cheeks wet with tears. "And God bless you and forgive you of your sins."

They were married by a Justice of the Peace in Virginia. The town rocked with the news that they'd been secretly married since summer and were dropping out of school to have a baby. Mr. Prince, polite and grim, offered Jed a job on the loading platform at the mill. Jed, standing at attention in front of his desk, stammered out that he would love Sally forever, and take good care of her and their children.

Mr. Prince said nothing, just looked at him. Finally he said in a low voice, "You'd better."

Jed was covered with a cold sweat as he walked out. Never had any words sounded so ominous.

A few days later Mr. Prince called him in again and offered to give them the down payment on a house so that they could move out of Jed's parents' house.

As Jed expressed gratitude, Mr. Prince said, "Get this straight, Jed: I'm not doing this for you."

Sally was a good little wife, just like he knew she'd be. She kept their house spotless, tried to cook everything he liked. She'd make a good little mother, too. Now that things had settled down, Jed was starting to look forward to being a father.

"You're just a hero, Jed," she'd whisper in bed at night. "What would I have done without you, sweetheart? You saved me. I aim to spend the rest of my life making you glad you did."

"I already am, darlin," he'd murmur . . .

Honey was moaning, "*When I'm blue or down or weak, / When tears of pain roll down my cheek, / A woman needs a man to hold, / Who'll protect her from the cold, / Who'll keep her safe from harm her whole life long . . .*"

Earl took Emily's hand and stroked her palm with his fingertips. A shiver shot up her arm. She contrasted it to the shiver of revulsion she used to feel when Raymond took her hand. It was so strange actually to want a boy to kiss you.

There were other contrasts. Earl's father was president of a chemical plant down the valley, and they lived on a six-hundred-acre cattle farm. One day she and Earl rode out on horses to see the calves— café au lait, nursing from jet-black mothers, as a placid beige bull looked on.

"Do you want to be a farmer when you grow up?" Emily asked.

He smiled. "Emily sweetheart, I am grown up. I'm going to work for my father when I graduate. But I'd like to live on a place like this. Hire some tenants. Raise cattle. Keep horses."

She looked at him. He knew exactly what he wanted. It was a refreshing switch from Raymond's anguish and vacillation. She also liked the way Earl fixed drinks at the KT house, put new people at ease; the way he rushed to light her cigarettes and took her elbow when they crossed the street, ordered for her in restaurants. He was vice president of KT. Everyone liked him. It was a relief after Raymond's determination to be disagreeable. Even her parents seemed to like Earl. Her mother was almost flirtatious around him, something Emily had never seen before and was appalled by. Earl made a point of complimenting some aspect of her mother's appearance or the decor or the menu—unlike Raymond, who had always replied to her attempts to be conversational with grunts. If Raymond was in a bad mood, he'd sometimes sit in her driveway and blast the car horn for her to come out. But Earl always came to the door and chatted with her parents about where they were going and when they'd be home —even if they were actually only going to the hill overlooking town to neck in the back seat.

Emily had never questioned that she would go to college. The only question was where. Raymond in his letters kept making different suggestions, based on which college graduates he'd met recently. So far he'd installed her at Sarah Lawrence, Swarthmore, and NYU. She wrote back each time thanking him but informing him she was going to State. He'd write back: "State? Are you out of your mind? You've got to get away from there. Haven't you been reading about Meredith and Ole Miss?"

"What does Meredith and Ole Miss have to do with me?" she wrote back. If this was what the North did to people, she certainly didn't want to spend four years there.

She and Earl went to football games in the big stadium and sipped bourbon from his silver flask. Emily studied the coeds in their blazers and pleated skirts and loafers, talked with them at the KT house. They liked State a lot. It was near home. Friends from high school would be there. Because of Earl, she'd probably get bids from both Kappa and Tri Delt. She'd work on car washes and bake sales. Freshmen teas and Christmas formals. Football in the fall. Basketball in the winter. Baseball and track in the spring. Movies on Friday nights.

Beer in the KT bar. And Earl. Lots of Earl. He stroked her hand, sending more shivers up her arm.

She realized her eyes were fixed on Honey's cleavage. She looked away quickly.

On the night before their Career Week projects were due, Donny and Rochelle sat under a bare bulb at the table in her kitchen. The kids were asleep. Her mother was back in the hospital having a hysterectomy. They copied their final drafts—Rochelle's on library science, Donny's on pro basketball.

When Donny arrived the next afternoon to find out why she hadn't been at school, he found the yard littered with paper airplanes made from the first several pages of her final draft.

Cereal bowls and boxes from breakfast were still on the kitchen table, covered with flies. Soaked in spilled orange juice were her last ten pages. Rochelle was lying in one of the chipped white iron bedsteads in the kids' room. The kids were climbing over and around her and bouncing on the other mattress.

"Hey, mama, you sick?" he called.

She didn't open her eyes or reply.

"What's happening, baby? You OK?"

She opened her eyes and stared at him.

"Hey, you look like you in bad shape." He led the children, Pied Piper-like, into the front yard, where he busied them with sour balls.

Rochelle whispered, "I can't take it no more, Donny."

"Can't take what, honey?"

"I ain't never gon be no librarian."

"Sure you are, baby."

"Huh-uh." She rolled over on her side, away from him.

"You be feeling better tomorrow, sugar. You got you a case of the flu or something is all."

Rochelle didn't feel better the next day, or the next week. She took a full-time maiding job and didn't go back to school.

# Chapter Eleven

## Black-Eyed Peas

On New Year's Day the Tatro table was loaded down with ham hocks, black-eyed peas, collard greens, and corn bread. Missing were the family silver, china, and damask tablecloth that adorned the Prince table on holidays. But the food looked every bit as good to Emily.

Having hitched from New York, Raymond had appeared on her doorstep the previous day in a full beard and a man's hat with the brim turned down. Emily giggled. "What are you supposed to be—a beatnik or something?"

"You don't like my beard?"

"I love your beard. I especially love the hat."

"Thank you," he said.

"And I'll bet your father is crazy about both."

Raymond grinned.

Emily explained to Earl that Raymond was only home for a day and a half, and that she'd like to spend New Year's Eve with him. He'd never been a boyfriend really. More like a brother. Earl consented. But just to be sure, he asked her to wear his KT pin in addition to his lavalier. It was a miniature Confederate flag with pearls for stars. He pinned it on her crew-neck sweater, over her left breast, with the pledge pin (the Greek letters kappa and tau in gold, attached to the Confederate flag by a small gold chain) atop her nipple. She felt like a general decorated for valor. It required no valor, though: She liked his hands moving across her body, his tongue in her mouth. He had finally told her why the boulder in front of the KT house was constantly changing color: A brother painted it the color of the sorority of any girl he scored with. Earl had been embarrassed, and she'd been shocked out of her mind. Now, though, she knew that if that was what this pin was leading up to, she was nearly ready. Earl, a gentleman through and through, stopped whatever he was doing whenever she objected. But the next time he would proceed to the stopping point and go just a little farther. In this fashion they had come quite a way.

"What is all this hardware?" Raymond had demanded as he helped her on with her coat on New Year's Eve.

"You remember I told you Earl and I were lavaliered in September? Well, now we're pinned."

Raymond grinned. "What's next? A ball and chain?"

"Oh Raymond, honestly. A ring comes next."

"Through your nose or what?"

"Are you jealous or something?"

He laughed. "Jealous? Of servitude? Are you crazy?"

"It's not servitude. It's love. And I'm sorry for you if you've never felt it."

"I suppose you call what's going on between my brother and your sister down in the mill village 'love'?"

"I think you call that a mistake."

"Yeah. It tore me up this afternoon watching them. Him staring at the ball game, and drinking too much beer. Her sewing up these tent things to wear, and writing up recipes on index cards. God, it was depressing."

"Well, I don't know. I mean I'm sorry they got rushed into it. But I think they're managing real well."

"Well, if it doesn't depress you, I guess there's no way I can explain."

"Who's this Maria you're all the time writing about?"

"A girl."

"I gathered."

"We aren't going together or anything."

"But you're thinking about it?"

"I'm not interested in going with anybody. But I wouldn't mind sleeping with her."

Emily's mouth fell open. "Why Raymond Tatro Junior! What a terrible thing to say!"

"Is it? Why?"

He honestly didn't seem to understand. Was this how people behaved in New York City? Emily narrowed her eyes at him.

The party was at the house of a gaunt bearded man named Albert, who looked like a short Abe Lincoln. He was an officer in an area civil rights group. Raymond, who had met him in New York, said in a tone of respect that he had had several ribs broken in Anniston, Alabama, on a Freedom Ride. To Emily this sounded dumb rather than admirable. Why would you deliberately antagonize people into busting your ribs? At the party were various white people Emily had never met—and Mr. and Mrs. Dupree from Pine Woods in their Sunday best. Everyone was standing around spearing shrimp on toothpicks with trembling hands, and carefully dipping the shrimp in horseradish sauce.

"Well. Look like we might get us some snow this evening," said Mr. Dupree.

"What did he say?"

"Snow."

"Oh, snow."

"You're right there, Mr. Dupree."

"Yeah, sure does."

"It does indeed."

"Maybe we can have us a white New Year's Day, even if we didn't get no white Christmas," suggested Mrs. Dupree. She was a large, powerful woman, who dwarfed her skinny husband.

Everyone laughed like canned laughter on TV.

Raymond walked over. "Say, Mr. Dupree. How you making it?" He offered to shake wrists. Mr. Dupree cooperated, looking at Raymond oddly.

Albert put on some records, and people began dancing. Albert's wife dragged him aside, and they whispered intently, then asked Mrs. Dupree and Mr. Dupree to dance. A hush fell over the room, similar to the hush that falls over shopping crowds when an untended package is found. The other dancers watched from the corners of their eyes as the two couples moved onto the floor, laughing nervously.

Emily was speechless. She'd never been to a party where Negroes were guests, only where they'd served drinks in white uniforms.

Raymond was glaring at the white people, ashamed of their shocked silence. He went all the time to racially mixed meetings and benefits in New York. Why was everyone in Newland determined to show what bigoted hicks they were? Gradually the decibel level in the room began to rise again. At midnight everyone gathered around the TV and watched as the ball at Times Square descended. When the crowd in New York City began hurling themselves into each other's arms, the crowd in Newland gingerly pecked and embraced biracially, eyes wide open inspecting each other.

"Junior, take your hat off in the house," Mr. Tatro muttered. "Now, you know bettern that. Done forgot your manners up there with all them Yankees."

Their eyes locked. Eventually Raymond shrugged and sailed the hat into the living room. Everyone around the table joined hands, while Mr. Tatro chatted with God about the evening meal: "We just so thankful, Lord, to have our boy Junior with us, down from New York City."

Jed didn't know about the rest of them, but he sure as hell wasn't thankful. The more miles between Raymond and him the better. Raymond had turned up yesterday looking like the garbage man and had sat there looking at him with . . . pity, it must have been. Pity, for the Lord's sake! When Raymond himself was the pitiful one! He, Jed, was doing just great. He liked this business of being an adult. The mill was kind of like school. You went there, worked as little as you could get away with, told jokes, and played tricks. What he did on the loading platform was run a forklift and maneuver five-hundred-pound bales of cotton. It was man's work, and he came home to back rubs and hot meals and TV and sex whenever he wanted it. Sally was fixing their new home up real nice, sewing curtains and all.

She wasn't such a hot cook, true. Her beaten biscuits tasted like lumps of plaster. But she'd get better the more she did it. He was proud to be able to give her the time to get better. His mother had always had to work. But Jed was earning enough right now so that Sally wouldn't have to take no job. Mr. Prince had called him into the office and told him he'd be switching him from room to room so he'd get a picture of the whole operation. This meant Mr. Prince was already thinking of him as a possible foreman. Eventually he'd even be able to get Sally a maid like she was used to.

He glanced at her, her hands folded across her swelling belly. She'd started wearing these smock things, even though nobody but him could tell the difference yet in her body. Their son was growing in there. Jed smiled. Quarterback at the Orange Bowl in a few years.

Mrs. Tatro was refilling the serving dishes and glaring at Sally. Sally realized she should be helping. She struggled up from her chair and went into the kitchen.

"Can I help?"

"No. No, it's all right. I think I can manage."

"Please let me help . . . Mother Tatro. I'd love to."

Sally resumed her seat. Mrs. Tatro stationed herself behind Mr. Tatro. She'd stand like that until all the men had finished, replenishing as necessary. It was the mountain way. The first meal Sally had served Jed in their new house, she'd sat down. He'd looked at her with surprise.

"What, Jed honey?"

"You're sitting down."

She laughed. "You don't expect me to eat standing up, do you?" Then she remembered meals at his house, and his mother's imitation of a guard dog. "Jed, do you want me to stand behind you while you eat?"

He raised his eyebrows. "Well, the women in my family always do."

"The women in my family don't. We have maids," she muttered, standing up.

He considered this. "Never mind. Let's skip it, Sally."

Sally bit into Mrs. Tatro's corn bread. She didn't care what Jed said: Her mother's was better. At first he wouldn't even eat any when she used her mother's recipe.

"My Lord, whoever heard of sugar in corn bread?"

"She makes it that way for Daddy. That's how his mama made it. Yankees like their corn bread with a little sugar." He thought it over and decided if it was good enough for Mr. Prince, it was good enough for him.

But if Prince corn bread was good enough for Jed, Tatro corn bread didn't seem to be good enough for her own parents. They'd been invited today and had declined. Sally wasn't sure why, but it upset her. When she told them about her secret marriage and pregnancy, they sat in silence.

Finally her father sighed. "Well, Sally, what can we say? What's done is done. Now we all have to figure out how to live with it."

Her mother shook her head. "A baby? Sally, you're only a girl yourself."

"I thought you'd be pleased," Sally lied. "I'm having your grandchild."

"You thought we'd be pleased? My daughter pregnant by a numbskull from the mill village and I'm supposed to be pleased?" her father replied.

Sally was shocked. She'd never heard her mild father talk like that before.

Raymond glanced around the table. His family. What a strange notion. By some accident of birth he was tied to these strangers for life. But it was mostly a charade. His real life was in New York City. His real family, a family he'd chosen voluntarily, was there. Justin, Maria, Morris. These were the people he was really kin to, not this bunch of backwoods bigots. Before dinner, sitting in the living room, he'd mentioned the integration of Donley High School—the reports on the evening news and in national news magazines of Negro students being chased by a white mob; having scalding soup dumped on them in the lunchroom; being attacked with hat pins; having eggs broken on their books.

They looked at him.

"But Donley's only thirty miles away. How can you not know about these things?"

He told them about the dynamiting of the school and the mobilization of schoolchildren across the country, each donating the price of a brick to the rebuilding fund.

"Goddam Yankee do-gooders," Jed muttered. "Why don't they mind their own business?"

"It *is* their fucking business," Raymond snapped. "If we're not going to see that all the citizens of the South are treated justly, someone's got to."

"Now look here, son: we treat our niggers fair," Mr. Tatro informed him. "If they don't want to work, that's their bidness. But they shouldn't expect the rest of us to carry them. You just drive through Pine Woods in the middle of the day. You'll see there in front of Dupree's Luncheonette a whole gang of perfectly healthy men just standing around."

"Where are they going to find work?"

"Why, just look in the want ads! Hundreds of vacant jobs!"

"Yeah. Yard work at a dollar twenty-five an hour."

"Son, when I started in over at the mill, you know what I earned?"

Raymond stifled a yawn. His father was off and running on his self-made saga.

"Twelve cents an hour?"

"That's right. Twelve cents an hour, boy! And I was grateful. Do you hear me? Grateful! Now some people is too proud or too lazy . . ."

Emily looked at Raymond with sympathy. But later on even she said, "But Raymond, that Donley stuff, it's got nothing to do with us. Just some maniac is all."

He was trying to figure out how to liberate Emily from Newland. It was like trying to get Aunt Jemima onto the Underground Railroad.

"So where have you applied to college?" he had asked her in the car on the way to the party the night before.

"State. I mean, if I already know I want to go there, why bother with other applications?"

"What's-his-name who's been sticking pins in you—he's over there?"

"Earl. Yes, Earl goes to State."

"He putting it to you, or what?"

"Raymond! That's just not any of your business."

"I'm trying to figure out why it's so important to go to some second-rate diploma mill fifteen miles from home, when you could go anywhere in the world."

"Well, maybe I'm just not very adventurous. I mean, what's it to you?"

"I hate to see potential wasted."

"God, Raymond, you're so arrogant. What makes you assume Sarah Lawrence is better than State?"

"Better or worse doesn't matter. The whole point is to get away from where you've grown up, so you can see what's really you and what's just a product of your upbringing."

"Then girls up there should come down to State?"

"Definitely. Listen, do me a favor, will you? Apply to a couple of other places. You won't hear if you're accepted until spring, and you may have changed your mind."

"Raymond, I'm not going to change my mind."

"Please."

"Oh, all right."

But Jesus Christ, she'd turned into a goddam coed since he'd been away. She said things like, "Why, Raymond Tatro Junior! I never!" Most of her attention was directed to the shine on her Bass Weejuns and the press of her Villager shirtwaist. Yesterday after his arrival she shrugged on this cream-colored blazer with the royal purple crest of that dumb club of hers on the pocket, and ran off to a bake sale with a batch of sea foam divinity, saying, "Gracious me, Raymond honey, I'm late! I just got to *fly*."

As impatient as he felt with her, though, he recalled how scared he'd been to leave Newland last summer. Now his timidity seemed laughable, but at different points during the fall it had seemed justified.

One morning after his initial elation had receded, the elevator stopped at his floor, and two paramedics in starched white rushed out pushing a stretcher and a large green oxygen tank. They asked Raymond to hold the elevator door. Soon they re-emerged with a woman on the stretcher, his neighbor, whose name he didn't know, gasping through the oxygen mask. She never returned. He had no idea what happened to her. On the one hand, after eighteen years of knowing everyone's business—their loves and fears and hemorrhoids and favorite recipes—it was a big relief to have no interest in or responsibility for this woman. On the other hand, he realized his corpse could rot in his room, and no one would know the difference. Or care.

He became obsessed with the notion of dying alone, among strangers. A man with a Pancho Villa mustache, who was always wearing a dirty trench coat with the collar turned up, often came into the print shop with posters or handbills. He and Raymond chatted, though he had a habit of turning his head sideways as you talked to him so that you had to gaze at his profile instead of into his eyes. One day he tossed a pamphlet down on the counter and asked, "What do you think of this layout?"

Raymond made a couple of suggestions, which the man adopted, murmuring, "That's great."

"Who is that guy?" Raymond asked Gus after he'd left.

"His name is Justin Lawson. He's a prick, but he gives us a lot of business."

"What's wrong with him?"

"Aw, he works for this civil rights group called FORWARD. Thinks he's Jesus Christ or something."

"What's wrong with working for a civil rights group?"

"Nothing. It's just his attitude or something. Hell, I don't know. The guy really bugs me. Doesn't give a shit about Negroes, he's just using them to try to solve his own psychological problems."

"That's a pretty harsh accusation."

"Well, he's all the time trying to talk me into donating press time to his projects. And here he's got him this trust fund. His family lives in one of those mansions in Newport. Have a penthouse on Central Park West, too. Sea captains, they were. Made their fortune off the slave trade. So this guilt-plagued son of a bitch comes in here trying to manipulate *me* into feeling guilty."

"You seem to know an awful lot about him, to dislike him so much."

"Well, it worked. I *felt* guilty. So before turning my shop over to him, I checked him out. Smooth bastard, isn't he?"

Justin asked Raymond for more and more "input" about layouts. And one day he invited him to a meeting of FORWARD, which he explained stood for Friends of Rural Workers Against Racial Discrimination. They'd picketed Woolworth's in support of the sit-ins in North Carolina. They were raising money for voter registration drives in the South and needed photographs of their activities as documentation, and as evidence if there was trouble. They needed picture research and layout skills for brochures. Justin explained that over the weeks he'd concluded that Raymond had real potential.

Raymond asked if Justin was president of FORWARD. Justin smiled tolerantly and explained that FORWARD had no president, no officers, no hierarchy of any kind. It was true that FORWARD had been his idea, but he saw himself as a catalyst rather than a leader. He had no wish to be followed, simply wanted to establish an atmosphere in which members would pool their differing skills and equipment with the goal of training each other in their specialties so as to become interchangeable. Where individuality was unimportant, rank also became unimportant.

It sounded wonderful to Raymond. In any ordinary ranking system, he knew he'd end up almost at the bottom every time. He accepted the invitation, flattered that Justin felt he had potential. And he was lonely.

His first meeting was in a cluttered loft on the Lower East Side. Eight or ten people sat or lay in a circle on cushions. A Negro man in overalls walked in, and another Negro in a cap made from a knitted stocking jumped up and locked palms with him in arm-wrestling position, saying, "How you making it, baby?"

A white man in overalls and purple-tinted glasses stood up and shook wrists with the newcomer.

A white woman in wheat jeans, black jersey, and sandals gave him a kiss.

Justin said, "Maybe we ought to get started."

The man in the stocking cap said, "Yeah, well, first off, I'd like to hear a few words from this new cat in the back there."

That meant Raymond.

"I invited him," Justin said.

"Beautiful, Justin. Like we ain't got enough problems as it is. You got to go dragging strangers in off the street."

"He's got access to a print shop. He owns a camera, lenses, the whole trip."

"Yeah, but the point is, you didn't consult nobody before asking him here."

"We consulted last week. We agreed we need photography skills."

"We agreed on needing the skills. We didn't agree on no particular person."

"I didn't notice you consulting anybody, Ralph, when they filmed you for Huntley-Brinkley saying 'We' this and 'We' that."

"Shall ah leave, Justin?" Raymond offered. The room fell silent.

The man in the tinted glasses said, "Fantastic. Now we're complete. We've got us our own resident cracker."

Raymond gave him an injured look and stood up.

"The cat's OK," Justin insisted. "I checked him out."

The woman, Maria, said, "This beats all. Using this poor guy as a weapon in your power struggles. Sit down," she said to Raymond. "I apologize for my rude co-workers."

Raymond sat down, staring at her.

"Well hell, I ain't got all night," muttered Ralph. "I'm leaving for Nashville in two hours. Can we get on with this meeting?"

Raymond was unable to sleep that night he was so excited at the idea of being part of this group. He was now trying to divest himself of all the reactionary racist rubbish Newland had crammed into his head so that he could be worthy of them. He was reading Marx and Engels and Fanon, listening to records by Thelonius Monk, Bessie Smith, and Bob Dylan. Attending lectures and movies recommended by Justin.

"Honey, you ain't had you no black-eyed peas," his mother pointed out.

"I don't want any," Raymond announced, as his mother tried to load his plate.

"Why, Junior honey, you got to have you some peas. It's good luck, honey. Lord, you got to eat you some black-eyed peas on New Year's Day!"

"Forget it. I don't *have* to do anything."

Everyone sat still.

"No, that's true," his mother agreed.

"Black-eyed peas on New Year's Day for good luck!" He threw back his head and laughed. "Southern superstition. Hocus-pocus. I don't want anything to do with it."

"It's just a custom," Emily murmured, "not a superstition."

"You always et em before and never said nothing," his father said. "Now you come back from up North with all your goddam Yankee beatnik ways. Scorning the rest of us. But I ain't having it in my house!" His voice had risen. "Now you eat some of them goddam peas, or you get the hell out of this house!"

Raymond stood up, looked around, then stalked out.

Donny had the feeling it was going to take more than a mess of peas to help this bunch. They needed to meet up with someone with a pocketful of cash. Rochelle and him and the kids sat on the floor at his grandmaw's eating black-eyed peas and chitterlings. His grandmaw and Rochelle's mother, wrapped in a quilt and looking puny, sat in the armchairs. Donny felt like a failure. For all his big ideas, he hadn't been able to keep Rochelle in school so she could be a librarian. And now the kids was having to be farmed out, and he couldn't do nothing about it. Big man.

He glanced at Rochelle, who was daydreaming. He'd stop by her house in the evenings, and she'd fall asleep at the kitchen table as he tried to talk to her. She refused to listen to anything to do with school. Since that was where he was spending most of his time, they didn't have a lot to say to each other. He wanted to tell her about his basketball games, about the coach and the guidance counselor telling him he'd almost certainly get some scholarship offers from colleges next year if he kept it up. But she only wanted to talk about their friends who'd left school. Tadpole was doing basic training now at Fort Campbell. He came home some weekends in his uniform with a wallet full of bills. Leon was back in New York City and came to Pine Woods sometimes in a burnt-orange suit and slouch hat, driving a bright yellow Buick. Sidney and Charlene worked in the paper mill. They had them their own apartment and a baby on the way. Everybody was moving on, and here he was racing around the gym in satin shorts. No wonder she looked at him with a mocking grin sometimes and called him "our little Donny."

Leon had been at the dance at the Masonic Hall last night, strutting around in his orange suit and shades. He'd brought with him a new dance step that involved collapsing to one side and hopping sideways. Rochelle picked it up right away, but Donny couldn't seem to get it, so Rochelle danced with Leon. She gazed at him, her lips parted and smiling. The band played a slow song, and he watched Rochelle's hips move against Leon's. She'd changed since she'd quit school. Now he was the one who had to hold back. He'd explain about not wanting to mess up his chances for a scholarship. She'd nod, but when they walked down by the river, she'd rub her hips against his the way she was doing right then with Leon, and she'd laugh when he got hard. Sometimes she'd lie down and pull him down on top of her and thrust her hips until he came.

Leon whispered something in her ear, and she shrieked with laughter.

When she came back to the table, she said, not looking at Donny, "Woo, honey! That Leon, he *bad!*"

From the way she said it, he knew that "bad" here meant "good."

Leon came over. "And how's Mr. Junior Church Usher this evening?"

After Rochelle and her mother and the kids left, Donny sat watching "Ramar of the Jungle" on television. A white man and woman in shorts and helmets had their hands tied behind their backs, and anxious frowns on their faces. A row of natives in these grass skirt jobs, with bones and junk through their lips and noses, were chanting and pounding their spears on the ground. The white woman's eyes was all wide and terrified. This fat black cat in shorts and a helmet was hiding behind a grass hut whispering reassuring things to the man with the tied-up hands. Everybody in shorts was good guys. Everybody in grass skirts was bad guys. But what was in it for that chubby nigger there in his shorts, except getting to be thought of as a good guy by bwana and pussy? Donny shrugged and bit into an apple.

# Chapter Twelve

## Graduation

After receiving her medal for Most Studious, Emily climbed back up to the stage and stood behind the podium in her rented black gown. Her classmates sat on the gym floor in folding chairs, having processed to "Pomp and Circumstance," repeated by the band twenty-three tedious times. Families sat in the bleachers looking bored.

"Percy Bysshe Shelley said in a poem, 'Nought may endure but mutability,'" began Emily. "We can never be sure how things will change. We can only be sure that change will occur. Five billion years ago our sun was born from a cloud of hydrogen. Ever since, two competing forces have been at work—the tendency toward change and the tendency toward stagnation. Charles Darwin in the 1800s proposed a mechanical process of adaptation: Creatures best adjusted to altered physical conditions survived. Today some scientists prefer the notion that life as a whole reaches out, not just to survive but to develop any new potentiality. Otherwise, they ask, how can we explain snow crystals, or the staggering variety of flowers, or the instinct to make music?"

Sally sat with her legs spread and her hands holding up her enormous belly, which looked as though it would burst open like a seed pod at any moment. Emily's mother had a faint smile on her face. Her father, with his legs crossed, seemed to be listening. Earl was gazing at her with a bemused frown. When she had told him last month that she'd sent in her acceptance to a college in New York, he'd stared at her just as he was doing now.

"But you're going to State."

"I changed my mind."

"But Emily . . . I mean, what do they have in New York City that we don't have down here?"

"I have no idea. Nothing maybe."

"Why, I bet they don't even have Chi O in New York City."

"I know."

"Well, if you changed your mind once, you can change it back again."

"I'm not changing it back, Earl."

"But Emily . . . Christ, I *love* you, Emily."

"I love you, Earl."

"Then why? I mean, I had it all mapped out. We'll have next year together at State. Then I'll go to work at Dad's plant. When you're a junior, I'll give you your diamond. Then when you graduate, we'll get married."

"I can't, Earl."

"But why not?"

"I don't know."

"You keep saying that. Don't you think you'd better know before you go wrecking our lives?"

"For God's sake, don't be so melodramatic, Earl. I'll be home for holidays and during the summers. You can come to New York. We can write letters and talk on the phone. It doesn't mean it's all over."

He laughed. "Jesus, you're still just a dumb little high school punk. You don't even know that that's not how things work."

"They can if we want them to."

"Bullshit."

"Oh come on, Earl. You could make this much easier."

"Goddam, I don't *want* to make it easy! It's not easy. I love you. I want you to go to State. I want you to be my wife. I want you to have my babies and share my life."

"I can't, Earl."

"Why not? What are you going to do instead?"

"I don't know."

Earlier that spring she and Earl had gone riding one afternoon at his farm. Earl rode the mare he'd trained at camp. Emily rode a retired show horse, a gelded Tennessee Walker who, even without the weights in his hooves, pointed them during his running walk as though he were an aging ballerina. Earl trotted beside her, posting.

They crossed the valley and went up into the hills. The farm buildings and tobacco beds fell away beneath them. They passed through a strip of woods and into a field. Stopping under a tree, Earl unloaded the knapsack that held their picnic. Then he uncinched his saddle and laid it under the tree. His mare snorted and twitched with pleasure, like a woman shedding a girdle. Emily unbuckled her saddle and dumped it. Earl jumped up and hooked his elbows over his horse's backbone, then threw a leg over the rump and wiggled into sitting position. He looked at Emily. She smiled, then duplicated the procedure. "Thought I couldn't do it, didn't you?"

"You can do anything you set your mind to."

"Damn right."

Without a word both horses and riders gathered themselves up, then sprang forward into canters. They raced across the field, hooves thudding, grass swishing, breeze whipping manes and tails and human hair into flying tumbleweed.

At first Emily was afraid: If a horse stepped in a woodchuck hole, its leg would break; its rider would catapult onto his or her head. But after a while, she felt as though her horse's hooves were scarcely grazing the ground. No chance to become lodged in a hole. It was one of the rare times when she felt she wasn't a burden to a long-suffering horse. The horses, saddleless under a bright blue sky and hot sun, were enjoying the race.

She hugged her horse's sides with her knees; her calves and feet hung loosely, swaying with the rocking motion of the horse as it plunged through the sea of high grass. She and Earl rode side by side, each trying unsuccessfully to pull ahead.

For a moment Emily felt as though the four of them had become a unit, a rocking, floating, gasping creature, plunging in place under a white-hot sky as the earth turned beneath.

Abruptly the horses shied and reared and danced to a halt. A barbed wire fence stretched across their path. The horses stood heaving and drooling foam, their bodies black with sweat. Earl and Emily slid down and lay on their backs in the high grass, breathing heavily.

"You ride pretty good for a girl," Earl finally murmured.

"Pretty good for anybody."

"Yeah."

"You wish I didn't, don't you?"

"Who, me? Why would I wish that?"

"I don't know."

He rolled over and kissed her. She drew his tongue into her mouth greedily and pressed her hips against his. Was this what people meant when they said they were "in love"? This craving for Earl's flesh, was it love? His hands moved over her body, removing clothing. He was whispering things she couldn't catch. Their horses had moved away, grazing quietly. The sun screamed overhead.

His chest pressed against her breasts. His lips and tongue moved across her face and down her neck.

What happens if I go ahead, she asked herself. I could get pregnant. What else?

And just as abruptly as the woodchuck holes had ceased to matter, so did these questions. The race was the only thing that mattered— the straining and the rocking, the plunging.

The exhausted slide from the horse's sweaty back.

The smile on Earl's face as he lay beside her she had seen last summer when he maneuvered the mare into taking a higher jump than ever before.

She stood up and began pulling on clothes. Earl grinned lazily from their hollow in the grass. "What's the rush?"

Grimly she zipped her jeans and fastened her belt. "What color are you going to paint that rock—black?"

He sat up. "What's wrong? Are you OK? Didn't you like it?"

He looked so crestfallen that she muttered, "I loved it. That's the trouble."

"Why's that trouble?"

"What if I started wanting it, needing it? Having to have it?"

"So much the better for me," he said, smiling.

"What's good for you doesn't necessarily coincide with what's good for me."

"What are you talking about?" he asked, jumping up and taking her in his arms.

"I don't know," she replied. As his tongue gently prodded open her reluctant mouth, she realized that it was exactly how you put a bit into a horse's mouth—just prior to quietly slipping the leather straps over its ears. Bridle. Bridal.

As Earl tried to drag her back down into their nest of grass, she was seized by a shortness of breath and gasped for air.

Shortly after, she went to visit Sally. As she walked in, she was greeted by an aroma from the stove. In the living room she found Sally on her knees in a maternity jumper, cleaning the molding with a Q-tip.

"What you cooking? Smells good."

"Oh, hi. Nothing. I just keep an onion simmering on the stove so it will smell to Jed like I'm taking as good care of him as his mama." Sally stood up slowly, her hands holding up her swelling belly. She pushed her blonde hair off her face and smiled her pep-squad smile.

"How you feeling?"

"Oh fine. Great. Never better. You know, I really love being pregnant."

"Good. It must be fun to have your own house, and do what you want when you want."

"Yeah, it is. Jed and I are just loving it. We're like a couple of honeymooners. Can't keep away from each other."

"No kidding? That's really nice." Probably the last thing in the world she wanted to know about was her sister's sex life. She looked into the bedroom at Jed and Sally's bed, though. She'd begun craving sex, and imagined what it was like being able to have it whenever you wanted in a bed all your own. By now Earl and she were devoting most of their energy and intelligence to finding places where they could be alone. Once when she was a guest at his parents', he let himself into the bathroom while she was brushing her teeth. She gasped at his daring. He closed the toilet cover, sat down, and pulled her down on his erection. Right in the middle his father knocked on the door. "Be out in a minute, Dad," Earl called.

One afternoon when Earl's parents were out, they drove toward the farm past his father's plant. A high chain-link fence with barbed wire on top surrounded it. There were warning signs. Tinker-toy towers that supported hundreds of power lines, rows of colored glass insulators, turned the scene into a giant abacus. Towers like silos.

Long low grey concrete bunkers with no windows. Uniformed guards at gatehouses.

"Gosh, this place is creepy," murmured Emily.

Earl laughed. "Only if you don't understand what's going on in there." He explained how to construct a uranium core.

"Yeah, that sounds OK. It's what happens next that's creepy."

"What? Installing them in nuclear reactors so people can have lights and heat and things?"

"No, installing them in bombs."

"That doesn't happen here. They're shipped to New Mexico and Washington State."

"What difference does that make?"

Earl and Emily sat in the breakfast room the following morning. Hot spring sunlight poured through the sparkling-clean multipaned windows onto place mats and napkins. Fresh flowers were everywhere. Hanging baskets of houseplants. Freshly polished antique flatware with script initials. An entire shelf of matching china dishes for each person. Gleaming antique chest and corner cupboard.

Lottie, the fat Negro maid in a starched white uniform, carried in heaps of cut-up fresh fruit, platters of country ham and biscuits. Earl gazed at Emily as he ate, smiling. He often said, in Mrs. Prince's presence, that if you wanted to know what a girl would be like as a woman, look at her mother. He'd add to Mrs. Prince that this was why he'd picked Emily. Emily extended this procedure: If you wanted to know what a boy was looking for in a girl, look at his mother.

Through the doorway Emily could see her, in a wide-brimmed straw hat and silk dress, pulling on white gloves and looking out the window across the flower-bordered brick terrace. On a far hill the tenant and his hired man in faded blue overalls and limp felt hats hoed in the tobacco seedling bed.

"Missus, you want me to stuff some chicken salad in them pastry shells?" Lottie asked.

"*Those* pastry shells. Yes please, Lottie, if you don't mind. And would you take a roast out of the freezer for supper, please?"

"Yessum."

"It's nice here," Emily said.

"Thank you," said Earl. "Dad's finally got him his plantation."

"What do you mean?"

"He's a city boy. From New York. Came down during the war. Top-secret stuff at the plant for the Pentagon. Afterward he stayed on. Started buying up land. Says all he wants is all the land that borders his."

"Sounds like Alexander the Great."

They walked into the living room with its mellow antiques and oriental carpets, flowers and bowls of fruit, paintings on the walls. Earl's mother was on the terrace instructing the gardener. In the bright sunlight Emily could see the makeup she'd applied skillfully. Her bouffant hairdo was perfect, hemline straight, stockings un-run, shoes polished, nails polished. Emily felt a tightening in her chest. She wheezed.

This time she fought it. There was nothing wrong with this scene. There was order here, beauty and peace. Careful perfection. The wheezing subsided. If this was what she had to do to have Earl whenever she wanted him, she'd do it.

On the morning news on television, uniformed men were flailing with night sticks at some people, white and Negro, who knelt in postures of prayer. Snarling police dogs were lunging at them. Blasts of water shot out from fire hoses. Earl switched off the set.

At the Wilderness Trail that night they watched a short about a Northwoods trapper who staked a tame female wolverine near a trap. She made mating sounds that lured a male. As he circled her with lustful intent, the iron teeth of the trap snapped shut on his leg. Eventually he gnawed his leg off to escape.

The following afternoon Emily discussed with Earl whether she should pledge Tri Delt or Chi O at State next year. And that evening she mailed off her acceptance to college in New York.

". . . Three hundred and seventy-five million years ago, in lakes and swamps, creatures developed which we call crossopterygians. They were like fish, but with bony fins and air sacs. The regular fishes probably thought they were freaks. But eventually some crossopterygians left their ponds. Maybe they were chased out by the other fish. Maybe the food supply gave out. Maybe the swamp dried up. Maybe they were just curious. Nobody will ever know. But for some reason a few dragged themselves on their fins across dry land, gasping air into their sacs. They didn't know until then what dry land *was*, much less whether it would suit them. Some probably flung themselves as fast as possible into new swamps. Maybe they were terrified. Maybe they were excited. Maybe they were just responding numbly to instinct. The fish in the swamps died out, while the descendants of the crossopterygians took over the earth for several million years . . ."

A graduate farted loudly. Students tittered.

". . . So as we leave behind these friendly faces and familiar halls to go out into the world, we can fight change every step of the way. Or we can pledge ourselves to accept and assist the inevitable. The choice is ours. Thank you very much."

The band broke into "Pomp and Circumstance" for the twenty-fourth time, as the audience applauded politely and the graduates cheered to be getting it over with so they could take off their hot robes.

Mr. Horde shook her hand and gave her her diploma. As she put her tassle on the other side of her mortar board, she surveyed the restless crush of classmates moving forward on the gym floor. In their identical robes they resembled black bass minnows in a fish hatchery. Most of the boys would soon be working in the factories and stores and warehouses. Most of the girls would marry them and keep their houses and raise their children. Some would go to State. A few would leave the region. "The choice is ours." She smiled. Who among them was choosing? Certainly not herself. If she could have chosen, she'd have stayed here with the scenes of her childhood and the graves of her forebears. It sure didn't feel like choice.

# Part
# Three

# Chapter One

## Emily

Emily passed through a wrought-iron gate, emerging in a huge paved courtyard surrounded by neoclassical buildings of grey stone. Up a flight of steps, in front of a building with an elaborate frieze of cavorting gods and goddesses, was a landing on which sat a stone statue of a Greek goddess who held tablets. At her feet were fold-up tables and chairs, around which milled students, most dressed in faded denim. The tables held petitions, pamphlets, donation boxes, stacks of tickets. Signs read: "SUPPORT VOTER REGISTRATION IN THE SOUTH" and "SHARECROPPER BENEFIT TICKETS HERE." Voices exhorted and disputed. The words "redneck" and "cracker" jumped out at Emily like pop-up pictures in storybooks.

Emily's dorm was one of several massive brick buildings dwarfing a tiny courtyard. A high iron fence separated the courtyard from the crowded sidewalks of Broadway. She had met her roommate an hour earlier. Joan had smiled in a way that indicated a smile was not her most compatible expression: The corners of her mouth turned up at sharp right angles, but her eyes continued a process of cold assessment. Emily unpacked while Joan lay on her bed and read a newspaper and sighed and muttered, "Oy, the things that go on in this world. They should rot, these people."

"Who should?"

"These crackers in Alabama. These schmendricks who blow up churches. Four little girls those cretins murdered."

"I didn't hear about it."

"What, they don't tell you what your neighbors are doing down there?"

"I'm from Tennessee."

"Tennessee. Alabama. Mississippi. Georgia. What's the difference?"

Emily paused in her unpacking and studied Joan, perplexed. "But my neighbors don't blow up churches."

"Are you sure?"

"Of course. We have other things to do."

"Like what?"

"I don't know. Lots of things."

"For instance, what were you and your neighbors doing last spring when I was getting chewed by a German shepherd in Birmingham?" She smiled her rectilinear smile.

"Uh, getting laid, I guess."

Joan didn't hear her. "What were you doing last summer when Medgar was shot?"

"Who's Medgar?"

Joan looked up, amazed. She had crumpled her paper into a ball.

"Most Popular" Emily had never won at Newland High, but she'd gotten along all right. The Ingenues had eventually given her a bid. She went down to the Residence Office and inquired about the single room she'd requested on her application.

A young woman in sandals, whose thongs, patterned like cats' cradles, bound her calves to the knees, was asking another, "Did you hear about Edward?"

"No, what?"

"He's taking next semester off to go to Tennessee."

"He isn't?"

Sandals smiled faintly and nodded, shuffling her benefit tickets like a deck of cards.

"He's an example to us all."

"I know."

"Is he scared?"

"Oh, I'm sure he must be. Wouldn't you be? It's unbelievable what goes on down there. They're psychopaths, those people."

Emily frowned and blinked. She'd ridden to New York on one of the trains she'd watched sweep through the valley all her life. The fields, washed in early evening sunlight, flashed past her roomette window. She propped her feet on the padded toilet seat. Yellowing pastures, peppered with grazing Angus; harvested cornfields, bristling with a five o'clock shadow of stubble. The train veered through foothills, then climbed toward the pass in the mountains. Emily saw way below a weathered wooden corn crib, in a field framed by oaks whose foliage showed a faint rusty hint of autumn. The sun, about to set, shed a soft golden glow. She knew what she was leaving. But what was she heading toward, she wondered.

As she wandered back toward Broadway, she saw Joan sitting on the protruding cornerstone of a building, holding the hand of a young Negro man. He kissed her lingeringly on the mouth. Emily walked on, her personality structure tottering.

Raymond appeared that evening in his hat and beard to take her to a small Chinese restaurant on Broadway. He ordered with proficiency. Emily picked suspiciously with a chopstick at bamboo shoots and water chestnuts. Weren't the Chinese supposed to be Communists or something?

Raymond talked nonstop about a documentary film on Negroes in the South he was working on for his group. He was taking a leave of absence from the print shop to go to Tennessee as a volunteer photographer on a voter registration project.

Emily poked at her peanuts and chicken in silence as he talked about upcoming rallies and benefits. Most of his face was hidden by his beard, but his eyes gleamed.

"Raymond, what is it everyone up here has against the South?"

He raised his eyebrows. "I forgot: You're just off the boat. It must be kind of overwhelming."

"Well, it's just that I wasn't around when the Crusaders were going off to Constantinople."

"Is that supposed to be funny?"

"At one time I think you'd have found it funny."

"At one time I was a bigot."

"I see. Well, then, do I disgust you now? The way I seem to my exroommate?"

"You don't disgust me, Emily. But you've got a lot to learn."

Emily speared an evasive slice of water chestnut with her chopstick.

"But there's no reason why you should. After all, your family has nowhere to go but down when the South topples."

"What are you talking about?"

"That blasted hierarchical town we come from: a place for everyone, and everyone in his place. With Daddy Prince on his throne."

"I always thought you liked my father."

"That has nothing to do with it."

"It doesn't?" She envied him his new air of certainty.

"No, it doesn't. We're talking ideology now, not personality."

"I don't understand."

"Look, if I hadn't left, I'd be working for your daddy right now. And I'd be at his mill the rest of my life."

"But you could have worked your way up, like your father. Or you could have switched to the paper mill. You could have done whatever you wanted down there, Raymond."

"But that's not the point. Why would I want what I wanted? Because I'd been raised to believe that was all I was good for. I'd be grateful for what Big Daddy paid me. And meanwhile, he'd be living it up on Tsali Street."

"Living it up? His idea of a big time is supper at the Barbecue Pit. Raymond, what you're saying has no bearing on real people."

"You can't see it because you're the crown princess. There's no percentage in your seeing it."

"Raymond, it's me: Emily. Your old childhood buddy."

"You're not cute, Emily."

"I'm just trying to figure out how come you put up with me?"

"It ain't easy," he drawled.

"By the way, what have you done with your accent? You sound like a Yankee."

He shrugged. "You'll find it's not very fashionable to be a white Southerner up here right now."

"I've noticed. I've never even thought of myself as a Southerner, and here I am, hated for being one. Southerner. What does that mean?"

"You'll find out fast, and lots you won't like."

"Oh, thanks a lot, Raymond. When I think I could be going to State . . ."

"So go to State. Never leave the goddam place."

"I've already left," she pointed out.

Brakes screeched, horns blared, drivers cursed and gestured obscenely. Huge glass and steel buildings ringed the crowd, most dressed as though ready to call home the hogs. The young man in overalls addressing them had spent forty days in Parchman State Prison following a Freedom Ride. Although white and a Yankee, he for some reason was speaking like an Alabama sharecropper: "They's several hunnert of us gathered here this afternoon. We can be real proud since we competing with a football game."

Derisive laughter.

"But we ain't got much else to be proud of, friends. Thousands of the brothers and sisters can't be with us today because they got them no long green to get here on. Never mind that. They got no money to *eat* on. They working as maids and yard 'boys' for ten dollars a week, for families who got theirselves a hunnert thousand dollars a year. They working in fields from sunup to sundown for fifteen dollars a week. Not only ain't they got no money, they ain't even got the *right*, friends, to demonstrate about not having nothing. Old women is being tore into by po-lice dogs. Little girls in their own Sunday school room is being blown to bits. Negro students is being throwed in jail for ordering greasy old hamburgers at dumps they wouldn't get caught dead in otherwise. And thousands of Negro citizens can't do nothing to change this because they ain't allowed a vote. So it's up to us, brothers and sisters—all of us here this afternoon, and the thousands who couldn't be—to change all this."

Emily didn't know what to make of it all. Jed would have jumped up there and punched the guy out, but Emily's responses were more confused. On one side of her was Joan; on the other, Corinne. They had taken her political education in hand. Intent on being polite when a guest in other people's countries, Emily was attending each benefit, rally, concert, and coffee house they suggested. They appeared to regard her with the same delight Victorian missionaries lavished on a naked savage whom they'd persuaded to wear a loincloth. They assured her that her moral inadequacies were not her own personal fault, but the result of an upbringing in an iniquitous social system. (One of the South's inadequacies, Emily had decided, was to instill in its children the ability to listen politely while people dumped on their homeland.)

Joan's parents owned a furniture store on 125th Street, which made her an expert on race relations. Several times a week she'd perch on Emily's bed and compare the South to a large Nazi concentration camp.

The first time Emily replied, "Yes, but it's not like that."

Joan looked at her. "Listen, Emily, you don't know from nothing."

"But Joan, I lived there eighteen years."

Statistics, broken down by race, showered down like balloons at a convention rally—infant mortality rates, per capita income, expenditures on education, welfare payments, violent death rate. There was nothing Emily could say. Joan would never discuss if she could argue or lecture. You had to become sly, go to rallies like this one when you really wanted to be at the football game, appear to be convinced; then you could think as you liked in the privacy of your own brain. She liked Joan and Corinne. She just couldn't understand what they were so upset about all the time. And she felt a little bit guilty pretending to understand in order to have friends to drink coffee with after supper.

"People here in the North, they all the time saying, 'Hey, man, what you wanna go sit in some rat-trap Southern bus station for anyhow?' And Southerners, they sez to me, sez, 'Son, you just keep quiet about it, and you can sit wherever you want with whoever you want. But don't you go stirring up no trouble now, hear?' Well, I sez to them, 'Baby, I *want* to stir up trouble.' Hell, I don't give a shit bout no bus station, man. I'm talking serious revo-loo-shun.

"We can't wait no more on the courts. The brothers and sisters in the South *been* waiting on the courts for a hunnert years. We got to grassroots it, baby! We want Freedom! We want Justice! We want Brotherhood! We want them for all the people! And we want them *now!*

"We going out in the streets—of the Mississippi Delta, of south-west Georgia, of the en-tire state of Alabama! Wallace, Eastland, Thurmond, they ain't stopping us! We gon march through Dixie like Sherman through Georgia, and we gon burn ole Jim Crow down!"

The crowd went crazy. Bearded young men, holding bed sheets taut, moved through the crowd yelling, "Support the brothers and sisters in the South!" People threw coins and wadded bills. The young men shook the sheets so the change jingled like a camel caravan. Emily held Joan's and Corinne's hands and swayed and sang "We Shall Overcome." As they hummed, tears streamed down everyone's face. Back home, Emily reflected, people who intended to lead a new life in Christ would now have been called down front by the preacher.

Corinne, who lived in the room next door to Emily, was the daughter of an investment banker. She had stringy blonde hair, baleful blue eyes, and a way of cringing that made Emily want to slug her. She was constantly hocking her ancestral jewelry and turning over the proceeds to startled blind Negro amputees who sold pencils on the corner of Forty-second Street. A trip downtown with her was like a tour through a leper colony with a Sister of Mercy.

Corinne dated Negro musicians whom she met at coffee houses in the Village. She usually sported a few stitches or a chipped tooth because they didn't hesitate, as Emily did, to slug her when she cringed. Emily had gone to listen to Corinne's latest boyfriend play the drums. The marble-topped tables were filled with white students disguised as field hands who sat with closed eyes, nodding their heads to the music.

"Have you ever had a Negro boyfriend?" Corinne asked. Emily nodded no.

"They're wonderful. So . . . oh, I don't know. So forceful. So sure of themselves compared to white boys. They're men, not boys. They've coped with adversity all their lives. Maybe I can get Fishbait to fix you up." Fishbait, who had a black patch over one eye, came over, saving Emily from trying to shoehorn Donny into this description of Negro Male.

"Well, well. Look here what the cat's dragged in." Corinne cringed. "How come you to always look like shit, mama? I swear, don't white girls know how to dress. Or do much of anything else." He laughed. "Ain't that so, mama?" Corinne nodded obediently. "Shit, woman, you so ugly tonight I can't hardly look at you."

"I *try*, Fishbait."

"Look to me like you don't hardly try enough." He took a handful of her stringy blonde hair and pulled it until tears came to her eyes. "You call this hair, mama? Look like dirty spaghetti to me. Can't you put no curl in it?"

"I'm sorry, Fishbait. I thought you liked it straight."

"Well, guess I'd better be going." Emily stood up, feeling as if she were sitting in on someone's lovemaking.

"What did you think of Fishbait?" Corinne asked Emily the next day as she powdered a black eye in the bathroom mirror.

"He's really something."

Corinne laughed. "Yes, isn't he wonderful?"

After supper in the cafeteria, Emily, Joan, Corinne, and Lou would gather in Joan's room to drink instant coffee, smoke, listen to records—Joan Baez; Peter, Paul, and Mary; Ma Rainey; Billie Holiday; Bessie Smith—and to discuss their classes and their autobiographies. Corinne and Joan also discussed the news, which usually concerned the racial situation in the South.

"Those bastards! Those redneck bastards! They should rot!" Joan raged.

"Those poor *people*. And all because of the color of their skin," Corinne moaned.

"I'm ashamed to be a citizen of the same nation," announced Joan one night.

"We did try to pull out," Emily pointed out. "You wouldn't let us."

"Me? Listen, I had nothing to do with that. My family came from Russia in 1903."

"And after all," Corinne said, "that was a hundred years ago."

"That's right. Only a hundred years ago."

Lou was sitting in silence sipping coffee. At this, she closed her eyes and threw her head back, smiled faintly, and made a noise that sounded like "huh." Lou, who lived across the hall, was up from Charlotte on an exchange program designed to rescue promising

Negro students from unpromising Southern colleges. Though it wasn't strictly an "exchange," since no students from up here went down to Lou's college. Emily and Lou nodded to each other warily from time to time. Emily, having discovered she was the Oppressor, no longer knew how to behave around her victims. But she was very aware of Lou's "huh," which was halfway between a mirthless laugh and a snort of disdain. The first time Emily noticed it, she had just made a response Joan and Corinne found politically acceptable. Corinne said, "It's so nice, Emily, to hear you say something intelligent in that accent of yours."

Lou closed her eyes, threw back her head, smiled wearily, and said, "Huh." Emily wasn't sure what it meant.

After the rally, Joan and Corinne were heading for the Village. Emily declined Corinne's offer to fix her up with a friend of Fishbait's. "I have to work on a paper," she mumbled. She received from Joan and Corinne gazes accusing her of racism. "I *do*," Emily pleaded.

She walked west toward the Hudson. As she crossed West End Avenue, she saw a white woman in a nanny uniform holding the hands of two well-dressed young Negro children. Emily stared at them until they turned a corner.

The sidewalks were sprinkled with tattered yellow and rust leaves. As her feet crunched them, their acrid scent rose to her nostrils. She recalled The Five's raking leaves into great piles; then jumping off branches into the soft centers yelling "Geronimo!" Burrowing through the piles like earthworms through topsoil. Leaping out to terrify passing first-graders. Prancing around huge bonfires, pretending they were burning cavalry officers.

If she wasn't incarcerated in Freedom City right now, she'd be at a football game with Earl, wearing a Chi O blazer and plaid pleated skirt, instead of wheat jeans. He'd have his arm around her, and they'd be sipping bourbon from his silver flask. The cheerleaders, the marching band, the teams in bright jerseys working out their intricate square dance on the green field with its pattern of white lines. Afterward she and Earl would drink more bourbon at the KT bar, and sing fight songs, and upstairs in his room . . . Why had this seemed so unappealing a few months earlier?

She climbed the tower of Riverside Church and looked out, turning around time after time like a dog unable to find its spot. Across the Hudson, the high-rises of New Jersey lurked behind a veil of smog. Southward stretched the apartment buildings of Riverside Drive, in their decaying, multi-windowed elegance. Inland lay brick row houses and redevelopment projects. But even if she could have looked in every direction at once, the city was too vast to take in. She'd gone on a boat tour up the East River to the Harlem River and into the Hudson. The rivers intermingled. The boat cut through the exact same mix of waterlogged crates, candy wrappers, and rat corpses. The city sat on a small island. But it was composed of hundreds of self-contained worlds. Getting a fix on it was like trying to do a jigsaw puzzle with pieces from many different puzzles. From the Castle Tree you could take in all Newland at once. Most everyone you ever saw, you already knew. You knew what church they went to and which dentist cleaned their teeth. You knew which shop the clothes they were wearing came from and how much they cost. You knew which movie they'd seen last weekend and with whom. You knew whose third cousin once removed they were, and which three houses in town their family had previously occupied. And they knew all those things about you. You could sit on the beach at a TVA lake with the ageless cliffs and perennial forests behind you, and the billions of receding stars overhead—and know exactly where you fit. Here in New York she didn't have a clue.

At home at this time of day the sun would have been at a forty-five-degree angle with the horizon. Here it was almost setting. At this time of year The Five used to pluck persimmons from the trees behind her house. If they'd been frost-struck enough, they'd be transformed from hard sour opaque balls into sweet juicy translucent orange delicacies. When they'd eaten their fill, they'd gather handfuls and hurl them at each other in roiling battles through the woods and fields . . .

She put her face in her hands and cried.

The cafeteria was almost empty that evening as she and Lou ate in silence. It was the first time they'd been alone together. Emily couldn't think of things to say.

"Uh, how was the football game?"

"Oh, fine," Lou said. "Didn't realize how much I'd been missing them."

"You watch a lot of football in Charlotte?"

"Oh, yeah. Every weekend. Nothing else to do. How bout you?"

"Same."

"How come you to miss the game today?"

"Went to that rally at Columbus Circle."

"Huh," said Lou. "And how was it?"

"Fine." They glanced at each other. Emily wanted to ask how come Lou hadn't gone to the rally, what she thought of it. But she didn't.

Emily asked Lou back to her room for coffee. She surveyed her record collection, wishing she had some Bob Dylan or something that might indicate to Lou her racial good will. But all she had was rock and roll and Honey Sweet. She settled for Chuck Berry. She handed a mug of coffee to Lou and sat down, then she jumped up and opened her window. In the middle of Broadway right outside her second-floor room was a pothole. Each car that hit it clattered like a skeleton falling off a tin roof.

Emily sat back down and sipped her coffee. She looked at Lou, who smiled and sipped her coffee. Emily felt an anxious need to convey to Lou that she liked her, a need to elicit from Lou that same reassurance. Then she was seized with irritation and wished Lou would leave.

"What would you be doing in Tennessee right now?" Lou asked.

"Dancing. Drinking. Making out."

"Huh."

"You?"

"Same."

"Did you go to that mixer the other night?"

"No. How was it?"

"I got stuck with this guy from the Business School who spent a half hour explaining pork belly futures to me."

Lou laughed. Emily wanted to ask whether she was dating. If Corinne and Joan wanted to fix Emily up with Fishbait's friends, were they trying to fix Lou up with white men? She couldn't think how to phrase it, so she asked about Charlotte instead. Lou said her father was an undertaker, and they lived in a big house on a street that formed a border of the Negro section. Growing up, she played with Negro children in one direction and poor white children in the other.

"My mother used to make me take ballet lessons and piano lessons. Filled our house up with all this china and silver and linen and junk. Huh."

Emily was stunned. Nobody in Pine Woods had owned china or taken ballet lessons. She felt a twinge of indignation. Then guilt over the indignation.

"I always thought I was just about the hottest thing on two legs. We were rich, and all my playmates were poor. They were dirty. I was sparkling clean. I could do an arabesque, and they couldn't. Huh. It was the shock of my life one day when I was playing house with these trashy white kids and they made me be the maid. *The maid?* Hell, my mama had a maid, and none of theirs did. I wasn't about to be no maid, so I stopped going over there." Her accent was getting thicker.

Emily relaxed listening to the emerging accent but was uneasy about the content. But hell, what did a bunch of rude little children in North Carolina have to do with *her*? Emily announced brusquely that she had to work.

"Yeah, me too," said Lou, standing up. "You going to the library?"

"Guess I'll work here." She was swept with relief as Lou left.

The showing of Raymond's new documentary took place in a loft on the Lower East Side. Emily brought Joan and Corinne, who were impressed. "You actually *know* someone in FORWARD?" Joan interrogated.

"Sure."

"Who?"

"A friend from home."

"From *Tennessee*?"

"Yeah. I guess he's been rehabilitated."

The room was packed with people in sharecropper disguises. The background to the film was songs by Pete Seeger and Joan Baez. The film itself consisted of news clips: the Montgomery bus boycott, the National Guard barring students from Little Rock High, Negroes being beaten in North Carolina during a lunch counter sit-in, Freedom Riders being spat on in Montgomery, the corpse of Herbert Lee, Meredith entering Ole Miss while whites rioted outside, King arrested in Birmingham, Wallace in the University of Alabama doorway, the corpse of Medgar Evers, the bombed-out Birmingham church, the ruins of Donley High. Flailing nightsticks, snarling police dogs, sharecroppers' shacks, Negro faces looking through prison bars, chain gangs. Greensboro, Clinton, Selma, Montgomery, Birmingham, Little Rock, were read off in the background like a litany. Black faces gaunt with hunger, eyes wide with fear, mouths screaming with pain. Fat pale faces in white helmets and reflecting sunglasses.

The lights came on, and the audience buzzed. Raymond was soon surrounded, having his wrists shaken, his fists pounded, and his back slapped. Joan and Corinne demanded that Emily introduce them. Raymond in turn introduced her to Maria, a woman in a tight black turtleneck and African trading beads; to Justin, a tall thin man with a Pancho Villa mustache; to Ralph, a Negro in overalls and a cap made from a lady's stocking.

Emily got off the IRT and walked up Broadway past the junkies in the center island, then down the blocks lined with welfare hotels. A letter from Earl talked about the tobacco harvest, the last cut of hay, the woods turning gold and rust. The KT Fall Formal, the UT game, the Hot Nuts concert, serenading the Tri Delts.

Emily peered into windows, watching people embrace or argue, laugh or weep, eat or snore in front of TVs. They sat in their apartments encircled by lamplight, while she wandered dark dirty dangerous streets alone, with no one to talk to and nowhere to go. What was she doing in this weird place among strangers who'd abhor her if she let them really get to know her? Those people surrounding Raymond seemed to include him and care about him like a family almost. Like the Ingenues. To fit in here as he now did, though, meant agreeing that her homeland was inhabited by psychopaths. It seemed like a lot to ask. After all, some among them had washed her cuts, told her stories, hugged her when she was sad, provided her with the love and support that gave her the self-confidence now to be able even to consider rejecting them. If those people were psychopaths, then everyone was . . .

As she paced, she thought about the valley, how The Five used to sit through a sultry summer afternoon by the river, with the current barely moving. Dark clouds would roll in fast. The tall grasses would bow down under a suddenly black sky, as rushing winds announced the arrival of lightning. Like the wand of a crazed conductor, the stabs of lightning cued kettle-drum rolls of thunder, then the full orchestra tuning up at top volume. Raindrops the size of bird droppings would splatter. Then cascades, a waterfall from heaven. The Five would throw off their clothes, screaming gleefully into the thunder and dodging lightning bolts. Afterward, the setting sun would turn the swollen storm clouds to royal purple, making the sky a giant bruise.

All right, maybe a few of the people there imitated nature. Like lightning rods they picked up violence in the atmosphere and brought it down to earth. Raymond used to keep a file of atrocities from the Newland paper. A woman who knifed her husband for refusing to take out the garbage. A man who shot a hole through his wife's bouffant hairdo as she rode by in a pickup truck with her lover. But this you could understand. You knew who was doing you in and why. Here in Freedom City she could be raped, robbed, murdered at any moment by someone she'd never seen before, whose cousins she didn't even know. A land where people were still involved enough with each other to want to kill their loved ones was almost touching by comparison.

She was on a block of gutted tenements. Several streetlights were out. She was lost. A drunk sprawled in a doorway. She walked fast to a brightly lit avenue and flagged a taxi driven by a large Negro in a felt slouch hat. Her feet began to hurt, and she propped them up on the seat. In front of her dorm she discovered she had only enough money for the fare plus ten percent. She dumped the change into the driver's hand. He counted it, then turned and said, "Shit, lady, I can't make no living on this."

"I'm really sorry. It's all I've got."

"Hell, what you doing in a cab then? Should have taken you the subway."

She stared at him. No Negro had ever spoken to her in this tone. "I didn't know where the subway was. I was lost."

"Listen, lady, that ain't my problem, is it? Shit, I'm trying to make my goddam living. Just my luck to get stuck hauling some hick halfway across Harlem for twenty-nine cents."

"It *is* a ten percent tip."

"Ten percent of nothing is nothing, lady. Now get out."

He roared away before she could close the door. It flew open. He screeched to a stop and banged it shut. "Goddam cracker!" he yelled, careening off, hitting the pothole beneath Emily's window and almost fishtailing into an oncoming cab.

She staggered into the dorm. A Negro who was not prepared to put her problems before his own? It was a startling concept.

In her room as she removed her shoes, she discovered her socks were caked with blood. Her shoes had rubbed; blisters had formed, popped, turned into open sores. All without her being aware of it.

"To the Puritans there was good and there was evil, the elect and the non-elect. As the elect, they considered it their mission to carry the word of God into the wilderness. The Massachusetts Bay Colony regarded the Algonquin as heathen, in dire need of conversion . . ."

Emily scrawled this in her notebook. She'd gotten up late, wore a nightgown under her London Fog raincoat. Hands shot up. Young women expressed opinions, and disagreed with each other and with the professor, a small man with a dark flat top and an acid sense of humor. Emily observed this, as always, with groggy amazement. Most of her efforts at Newland High had been directed at not having opinions, and certainly not ones that disagreed with those of a man. The Ingenues didn't give bids to girls who raised their hands in class.

"Jamestown, by contrast," continued the professor, "was founded as an economic venture by broken-down cavaliers and inmates of debtors' prisons. The Pilgrims found a cold climate and rocky soil. Virginia settlers found a warm climate, rich soil, plentiful game. The two settlements attracted and formed different types of people."

Emily wrote "Earl" in her margin several times. A stab of desire shot through her. She recalled the last time they'd made love—in her roomette on the train that brought her to New York, before it pulled out of the station. "You better not go and fall for some goddam Yankee, you hear?" he called as he jumped down to the platform.

"Don't worry, I won't," she called through her tears. And she was keeping that promise. Though it required very little effort. She'd been attending fraternity Freshmen Teas. But the brothers were all clods compared to Earl. She pictured him in his Confederate uniform, boots and sabre, recalled the way his erection would strain against his tight jeans. Raymond had fixed her up a couple of times with friends of his, but sharecropper costumes didn't excite her the way they did Corinne and Joan. Real farmers in overalls and rusted pickup trucks were a fixture around Newland, and overalls reminded her of rural poverty rather than heroic toil.

Emily's professor for Introductory Sociology was a tall thin Negro woman who peered out over Ben Franklin glasses. She was lecturing that morning on the characteristics of a cult—its saints and martyrs, totems and shrines, its missionaries and its devil. "Of course a group doesn't have to have a religious basis to qualify. It can have a political or social basis. The essence is that there is an out-group by which the in-group can define itself."

As she copied this, Emily realized she'd never seen a Negro woman in any job except maid, cook, or babysitter. Joan informed her that her background hadn't prepared her for many of the situations she was having to deal with, and Emily had to admit that this was so. Maybe this explained why she was so tired all the time, always oversleeping and having to race to class in her nightgown. She could never just react, because all her reactions were geared to a different reality; she had to examine each of her responses all the time. But Joan seemed to be treating her with more respect since the showing of Raymond's documentary. "It's really admirable, Emily," she'd say, "that you were able to drag yourself out of that swamp." Emily was grateful.

That afternoon on her way to the Hall of Man at the Museum of Natural History for her anthropology course, Emily passed some tableaux in glass cases. One case contained models of two apelike creatures. One with black skin was loping naked across a savannah. The other, with white skin, was dressed in animal furs and was hunched over a fire in a cave. The card read,

By a million years ago homo erectus had spread across Asia, Africa and Europe. He made huts of branches and stone, clothes of animal skin. Seven hundred and fifty thousand years ago he discovered how to make fire. With his movement into cooler regions came physical changes. His skin, originally dark from the pigment necessary to block ultra-violet rays in the tropics, bleached out as he inched northward over many generations; fair skin that allowed synthesis of vitamin D had survival value in regions of sparse sunlight.

Emily found herself reading this card over and over again with irritation.

At dinner Joan walked past Emily's table with a woman named Leslie whom Emily had seen at rallies. She always wore a red ban-danna around her head like a pirate, and large hoop earrings. Emily felt a rush of gratitude as they surveyed all the tables and came over to sit at hers.

"This is Emily," said Joan. "She's from Tennessee."

Leslie looked her over: a Regenerate Southerner. She nodded firmly, as though approving her. Emily sat back, relieved. "They say the situation is pretty grim down there," said Leslie with narrowed eyes, like Cotton Mather contemplating Salem.

Out of the blue Emily was swept with anger. For a few moments she was speechless. Then she said, in what was meant to be a blasé voice, "Oh, it's all right. We let our niggers roam the streets until eight o'clock at night now."

As Emily raced out, not looking back, she noticed Lou at the next table. Emily blushed and her stomach contorted. Lou, fork poised, threw her head back, smiled faintly, and said, "Huh."

Returning from the library that night, Emily crept toward her room, dreading to meet any hallmates. A Bach cello suite floated out of the transom over Joan's door. Joan pronounced Bach with a growl at the end, as though clearing her throat to spit. "Bach-ch-ch," Emily mimicked to herself. The full horror of what she'd done was beginning to dawn on her: She'd have no one to eat supper with, to drink coffee with, to bum cigarettes off, to borrow lecture notes from. She'd been lonely before, but now she was a pariah. Panic gripped her. She was used to a big family, a close neighborhood, a tight community, church, classmates. Her future as an electron with no nucleus, no network of fellow electrons, darting through the void alone, was hideous to contemplate.

She heard a thick Southern accent: "Hey, gal, how you making it?" Lou was leaning against her door jamb, observing Emily as she crept down the hall.

Emily froze: Lou had heard her at supper. How could she explain what had come over her, her need to thwart any party line, a need she'd kept under wraps in Newland for long enough to get a bid from Ingenue. Tonight it had been stupid, and pointless, self-indulgent.

"Come on in here a minute. Got something I want to show you." Lou walked into her closet. She picked up her laundry bag and fished around and pulled out a bottle of Southern Comfort.

Emily stared at it. They sat in the closet on Lou's laundry and shoes, with her dresses hanging in their faces, and passed it back and forth.

"Look, I'm sorry about what I said at supper," Emily ventured. "I just got fed up."

"Huh. I was tickled."

"You were?"

"I get fed up too, child. This New York City is one weird place."

They reminisced about Charlotte and Newland, their accents getting thicker the more Southern Comfort they consumed. The *way* Lou expressed herself was familiar—stringing together little stories, describing people by where they came from and whom they were kin to. As opposed to the statistics and theories that Joan and Corinne specialized in. But the content of Lou's stories was so different from that of Emily's that they might have been talking about two separate countries: "So I was standing by the door of my daddy's funeral home. They was carting out flowers and putting them in a hearse with a coffin that held an old man from our neighborhood, who always used to carry hard candies in his pocket for us kids. He'd paid burial insurance his entire life preparing for this day. These two little white kids was watching these wreaths and bouquets come out, and one whispered, 'All them flowers just for that dirty old nigger man?' I beat the shit out of them. Then my daddy beat the shit out of me."

"How come you to tell me this?" asked Emily. "Looks like you'd stay away from white people."

Lou exhaled slowly. "I guess I been so goddam churchified I think I got to hate the sin but not the sinner."

"Is that possible?"

"Maybe not. But if you Negro and you go round hating everybody that does you dirt, you got time for nothing else. You see what I'm saying?"

As Emily stumbled out the door, Lou called, "Don't you be no stranger now, hear?" The familiar phrase, the familiar accent, and the excess of Southern Comfort combined to send a searing stab of homesickness through Emily.

On their way to class Emily and Lou joined a long line for coffee at a takeout shop on Broadway. Judging from their accents, the Negro women behind the counter were fresh off the boat from Louisiana. As they took orders and poured coffee and snapped on lids, they moved as though suspended in a vat of molasses. The shoppers and businessmen and students in the line, which stretched to the door, shifted, twitched, consulted watches, and heaved irritated sighs. The waitresses continued their languid pace.

The woman in front of Emily and Lou was trembling. She muttered under her breath, "Hurry up, hurry up, hurry up." Her plastic shopping bag rustled steadily in her shaking hands.

Finally she stepped out of line, pointed to the waitresses, and announced in a loud voice, "I marched on Washington for these people, but I'll never make *that* mistake again!" She stomped out, leaving the room in dead silence. The customers looked annoyed or embarrassed. Emily fought to suppress a grin. Finally Lou gave a throaty chuckle. She glanced at Emily. "It's OK. You're allowed to smile."

By the time they reached the counter, Lou and Emily were giggling sporadically—whenever Lou whispered with piety, "I marched on Washington for these people!" The waitress looked at them and smiled and drawled, "Boy, some folks sure is in a hurry."

Joan and Corinne were no longer speaking to Emily. They took Lou aside and informed her that Emily was racist. Lou said, "Thank yall so much. I do preciate yall telling me this."

"You're welcome," said Joan, turning up the corners of her mouth at right angles.

During supper that night Emily put on a white terry-cloth beach robe with a hood. Lou wrapped her head in a rag. Emily, hefting a meat cleaver from the kitchen, chased Lou through the cafeteria while Lou shrieked, "Naw! Don't do it to me, missus! I be a good nigger!"

The student body watched, appalled.

Her first night home for Christmas vacation Emily sank into Earl's embrace like a solitary marathon runner breaking the tape and collapsing into the arms of the crowd. "God, I've missed you, Earl."

He held her stiffly. "Have you?"

"You know I have," she said, her lips seeking his. From the car radio came the wail of a steel guitar and the fevered voice of Honey Sweet: "*A woman needs a man to hold, / Who'll protect her from the cold . . .*"

Emily pictured the cascades of blonde hair and the astonishing masses of breast tissue. God, the appeal of it all—to be taken care of, to be relieved of the burden of her own personality. She'd given this up, and for what? To hang out with a bunch of hypocritical self-righteous do-gooders. She was finished with New York. There was no way she could go back there anyhow after her and Lou's stunt. She'd return just long enough to pick up her stuff. She'd pledge Chi O at State during spring rush. . . .

"There's something I have to tell you, Emily." She looked at Earl. "It's not easy for me to tell you this, but I have another girl. We're lavaliered."

"I see." Emily felt remorse, then nothing.

"She wants me, Emily. And I guess you don't, or you would have gone to State."

"It's not that, Earl. It was just . . ." What *was* it? She could no longer remember why she'd had to get away.

"What?"

"Shit, I don't know." All she knew for sure was that she wanted to make love. But Earl had moved away, was clutching the steering wheel and resting his forehead against it. Emily rubbed his thigh. "Well, let's not worry about it."

"About what?" He was watching her hand with alarm.

"About who's wearing your lavalier." She began unbuttoning her blouse.

He stared at her. "It's not just the lavalier, Emily. I love Dawn. I want her to be my wife."

"Fine," said Emily, removing her blouse.

"But Emily, I can't just . . . I can't be unfaithful to Dawn."

"You can't?" She'd moved away from his world without even realizing it.

In bed that night she wept for several hours. What a fool she'd been! She'd turned her back on the love of the best man she'd ever meet. A once-in-a-lifetime guy. And now what? She couldn't turn back, but she didn't want to move forward. Apparently she had to stay put.

The usual cooking smells greeted her as she walked in Sally's door the next day. Joey sat on the floor intently tearing a newspaper into ever tinier pieces with damp chubby fingers. Sally sat watching "Mr. Rogers" and copying recipes from *Family Circle*. She was very pregnant. Her breasts sagged and her belly protruded. Tied through a buttonhole was a teething ring, and a clean Pamper stuck out of her skirt pocket. Around her waist was a belt of large wooden beads in bright colors.

"Still cooking onions?" Emily inquired. "Jed hasn't figured it out yet?"

Sally laughed. "All these poached onions, and he's still complaining that I don't take care of him like his mama."

Abruptly Emily recalled part of her reason for going to New York. She juxtaposed the emotion of domestic suffocation to her grief over losing Earl, and they short-circuited each other. As Emily sat down feeling neutrality, Sally said with a coy smile, "So how's that sweet Earl?"

"Sweet as ever. But he's lavaliered to someone named Dawn."

Sally gasped. "He's *not*, Emily?"

Emily nodded.

"You must feel just awful."

"I've been feeling pretty bad, but I'm all right now."

"Do you have someone in New York?"

"No."

"Well, aren't you lonely?"

Emily was damned if she'd admit to her baby sister that she might have made a mistake. "Oh, I keep busy."

Jed sauntered in in green work clothes, smiling. "Whadaya say, Em? The Yankees won you over yet, like poor old Raymond?"

"Hell, no. Not hardly."

They laughed. "Well, they will," Jed assured her.

Emily went to Ruby's apartment, as she had every Christmas of her life, with a small cedar tree and several presents. Usually Sally came too, but she said she wasn't up to it this year. Ruby was ill, with what nobody was sure. She sat in a worn armchair, her head swathed in a rag and her body wrapped in a tattered quilted housecoat that had been Emily's in high school. She was bonier than ever, and her face had a flaky ashen look.

"Why, I declare!" She smiled, revealing her toothless gums. "Miss Emily home for Christmas!"

Emily patted her knobby shoulder, then turned down the television, on which a young couple was winning a chaperoned trip to Rio on "The Dating Game."

"How you doing, Ruby?"

"Why, I be just fine, Miss Emily." She spat tobacco juice across the room into the coal scuttle. "How you making it up North, Miss Emily?"

"Just fine, thank you." Were a broken heart and a blighted future worth commenting on? Probably not.

Emily saw Ruby's apartment as though for the first time. The seat covers and rug were worn and torn. The kerosene heater gave barely enough heat to keep them from seeing their breath. Emily stared at the wasted, toothless old woman. Her parents had been slaves. Emily's great-grandparents had *owned* Ruby's parents. Was this possible? Ruby had cooked and cleaned and ironed for Emily's family most of her life. Her wages allowed her to live at about the same level, comparatively speaking, as her mother. The only difference was that, if she had had the money and time, she could have come and gone at will. On a plantation she'd have been put out to pasture by now, like a faithful horse. "Freedom" meant she was alone now with her social security checks and Christmas presents from the Princes.

"Sorry to hear you're sick," Emily mumbled.

"Oh, I just under the weather. I be all right soon."

"Kathryn coming home for the holidays?"

"Naw, she can't get her no time off this year. Donny, he gon cart me over at his place."

"How is Donny?"

"He be just fine. He got him a little baby daughter now. Plus two of Rochelle's mother's childrens. They just the cutest things."

"Where's he working at?"

"Over to the mill. Your daddy got him a job sweeping up and all. He like it real good over there."

"Well, guess I better be going. I got to do my Christmas shopping."

"Well, yall have you a real nice Christmas, hear?"

"Thanks, Ruby. You too."

As Emily was walking out, Ruby said petulantly, "Your mama didn't send me no cash this Christmas?"

"She said you mentioned needing some stuff, so she decided to buy you that instead of just sending money."

Ruby stopped munching her tobacco, clamped her jaws shut, and turned her head away.

"Well, see you," Emily called. "Say hi to Donny for me."

"Yeah. See you."

Emily was limp. She could hardly grip the steering wheel. She was literally seeing things differently. Driving through Pine Woods for years bringing Ruby home, she'd look for Donny in the gangs of

children, and that was about it. Sometimes she felt vague fear or
embarrassment, which made her look straight ahead and drive away
fast.

But today she was noticing how the December rains had turned the
courtyards into seas of mud, in which swam rusted auto carcasses,
construction rubble, and torn mattresses bursting with sodden stuffing
like milkweed pods in an autumn drizzle. A child toting a bucket
trudged alongside the train tracks gathering chunks of coal.

She drove up her driveway. A yellow Victorian structure that could
easily house twenty people. Borders weeded and cut back, hedges
trimmed, probably by Donny. Why had she grown up here, and
Donny in that dark cramped room by the river?

As she walked in, her mother informed her that Ruby had phoned
to report that Emily had failed to deliver the Christmas cash. Emily
laughed, then fell silent so abruptly that her mother looked at her.

Later in the loft above the garage Emily was poking through barrels, boxes, discarded furniture, and stacks of magazines. It had occurred to her that she was giving up Earl too easily. If she enrolled at
State, pledged Chi O, bought some cashmere sweater sets to replace
her turtlenecks, it was entirely possible he'd give this Dawn creature
the shove and return his lavalier to its rightful place at Emily's throat.
But if she was going to leave New York, she'd need an extra trunk
or large suitcase to carry home the stuff she'd acquired while there.
She decided to base her decision on whether or not to leave New
York on whether or not she could find an empty suitcase of sufficient
size. If so, it would be an omen to proceed.

She overturned a barrel and spilled some photo albums and bundles of papers on the floor. As she crammed them back in, she paused
over a small book with a faded green cover. The pages were eaten
into lacy doilies by silverfish. The name of a dead great-uncle was
written on the inner cover. The title page read *Manual of the United
Klans of America.*

> . . . We do not choose to be common men. It is our right to be uncom-
> mon if we can. We seek opportunity—not security. We do not wish
> to be kept citizens, humbled, dulled, by having the State look after
> us. We want to take the calculated risk; to dream and to build; to fail
> or succeed . . .

Emily stared at the book for a long time, as though it were a dead rat.

Weak afternoon sunlight shone through the prisms in the windows of the Prince living room. All the colors of the spectrum spread across the pale wall-to-wall carpeting.

"Those prisms is a real nice idea," said Mrs. Tatro, her huge breasts straining the seams of her red wool dress.

"Yes, it's lovely, isn't it?" agreed Mrs. Prince. Rainbows also darted around the ceiling from the diamonds that swung from her ear lobes.

Joey crawled across the rug, grabbing at the shifting shafts of color. "What do you think of this grandson of ours, Raymond?" Mr. Prince asked Mr. Tatro, who perched in his dark suit on a Victorian side chair, his long legs crossed at the knee.

"Pretty good-looking little fellow," observed Mr. Tatro, taking a sip of sherry from a small cut-glass goblet.

"I guess it must run in both families," said Sally with a laugh, her forearms resting on her large belly.

"Not real bright, though," observed Jed. "Just watch him chasing them rainbows all around the room." Everybody laughed.

Except Emily, who was in the dining room pouring water into the crystal goblets. She was just realizing what it meant that Ruby had done this chore almost every Christmas she could recall: Ruby had waited on the Prince family at Christmas dinner. And what about her own family dinner?

The Mormon Tabernacle Choir singing "Joy to the World" wafted out of the living room. Her mother had decided the Tatros would prefer carols to the "Hallelujah Chorus," which the Princes traditionally played before Christmas dinner. Emily looked out the window and down the hill to the brick apartment buildings in Pine Woods. Yesterday afternoon she'd phoned Earl to go with her to the midnight Christmas Eve service, as they had the two previous years. She intended to tell him afterward of her decision to enroll at State.

"Uh, I'd like to, Emily," he'd said. "But I'm going already, with Dawn. I'm afraid I really can't see you anymore. I've just given Dawn her diamond, as a Christmas present."

"What do you reckon Junior is doing at this very moment?" Mrs. Tatro was demanding in the living room. "Wonder what church he went to." Emily smiled sourly. Raymond had told her he didn't give a shit about Christ, so why would he want to celebrate His birthday? Raymond was probably still in bed, or working at the FORWARD office.

She studied the table—the damask cloth and napkins, the place settings each with many pieces of silver and china. Wonderful smells came from the kitchen. The mahogany sideboard was loaded down with silver bowls and platters. Polite gentle laughter drifted in from the living room.

It was all a fraud—a scum of civility over a swamp of injustice, exploitation, misery, and hypocrisy. This house perched over that swamp like an elevated hut whose stilts were planted in termite nests.

She called her mother in from the living room and explained that she was getting sick and had better go to bed, please to apologize to everyone for her. Her mother studied her face, but Emily turned away and headed for the stairs. She simply couldn't participate in this charade any longer.

In the morning she drove to Ruby's. "Well, I declare. Miss Emily again. Now, what you doing back here, child?"

Emily handed her an envelope containing some of her own Christmas money. "Mama asked me to bring you this. It got lost in the Christmas rush." Money wouldn't make up for it all, but Emily couldn't think of anything else.

"Why, I declare. That's real sweet. You thank her for me now, you hear?"

"How was your Christmas?"

"Just fine."

"How's Donny?"

"He be just fine."

Emily studied Ruby's face and saw it as a mask of deceit. Goddam it, you've just sat there all these years, gumming your tobacco and grinning and saying, "We be just fine." When you've actually been cold and sick and hungry and scared and resentful and contemptuous. For God's sake, why didn't you say so? She glared at Ruby.

"And Rochelle and the kids?" Emily asked weakly.

"They be just fine." Ruby smiled and shot a wad of tobacco juice across the room. She looked at Emily strangely. "Yall right, Miss Emily?"

"Yeah, I'm fine, thank you."

On the train back to New York Emily felt relief: At least she'd had the sense to get away from that terrible place. Was the setup she'd been born into her fault? No, of course not. But it became her fault if, seeing what she now saw, she did nothing.

Her parents had been perplexed by her decision to return to New York several days early. She didn't see any point in telling them how much they disgusted her. They must have seen all along the things she was now seeing. They weren't stupid. And yet they hadn't raised her to be aware of the injustice, hadn't encouraged her to fight against it, had lived with it and profited from it all their lives. She wanted as little to do with them in the future as possible.

The porter knocked, bowed, grinned, and asked her to sit across the corridor while he fixed her bed.

"I can do it myself, thank you."

He looked startled, then grinned and drawled, "Yes, ma'am, I reckon you can. But it be my job."

"Well, it shouldn't be."

He looked puzzled. "I feel real lucky to have it."

"You shouldn't have to."

He grinned and backed down the aisle. "Yes, ma'am. You just suit yourself now."

As he helped her down at Grand Central the next morning, she handed him a huge tip. He stared at it, then at her, then grinned the Grin. "Why, I surely does thank you, miss."

"Don't," Emily rasped. "Please."

When she got to the dorm, Lou leaned out her door and called, "Hey girl, how you making it?"

Emily was unable to reply or look her in the eye, as Lou held her face in both hands and kissed her on both cheeks. "Hey, baby, what's happening?"

"I'm so sorry, Lou," she whispered, squinting and at last understanding the origin of Corinne's cringe.

"Sorry for what, child?"

"I didn't understand."

"Understand what?"

"What my people have done to yours."

"Shit. You starting to sound like some kinda Yankee. I ain't no 'people.' It's me—Lou."

Emily began avoiding her. She wouldn't accept Emily's apologies. "Now listen here," she'd insist. "What you say is true, but it ain't got nothing to do with me and you. I don't need none of this Lady Bountiful action from you. Anyone lets you crawl, I *know* you gon take it out on them later. You see what I'm saying?"

Emily began thinking of Lou as a house nigger. More middle class than the white middle class. And when Joan said privately that Lou was an Oreo, black outside but white inside, Emily agreed.

In American History class they were reading the slave narratives—about Negroes being beaten and tormented, worked like mules, bred like cattle. Emily began saving her allowance and sending checks to NAACP and SNCC, CORE and SCLC and the Urban League. To Save the Children and the Sharecropper Relief Fund. She was promptly put on every mailing list in the nation and was swamped with appeals. Every few days she'd lie on her bed and look through them—droughts in Africa, starvation in Pakistan, slums in Manila. Epidemics here, floods there, little children with hollow eyes and swollen bellies. She studied the mailings and suffered and parceled out her allowance: $7.50 for illiteracy in Alabama, $4 for pellagra in Mississippi, $8 for Negro men on death row in Georgia. She bought by mail boxes of notepaper, decorated with a sketch of flower blossoms and bees. A Negro woman in Florida, with no arms from a birth injury in a backwoods cabin, had done the sketch by holding the pencil in her teeth. As penance, Emily held a pencil in her teeth and tried for hours to sketch bees. She couldn't. All these brave resourceful people facing insurmountable odds imposed by *her* forebears.

One night she spent several hours staring at her arm. This pinkish, yellowish skin, pocked with hair follicles, designed merely to allow synthesis of vitamin D—this was the sign of her privilege. It was hideous. She wanted to peel the ugly stuff off, strip by strip, like a plum skin. She got a knife from the kitchen. It didn't hurt. She felt nothing. But it just wouldn't peel. She turned her forearm into a pulpy red mess.

# Chapter Two

===

# Raymond

The members of FORWARD sprawled on cushions in a corner of the huge loft, which was otherwise crammed with stacks of printed matter, a mimeo machine, a couple of projectors, film tins, cartons from carry-out food. As Raymond walked in, he saw Emily, her left arm wrapped in gauze to the elbow.

"Jesus, Em," he said, squatting. "What have you done?"

"I cut myself shaving my legs."

"How can you cut your arm while shaving your legs?"

"With difficulty."

She'd phoned as soon as she got back from Newland to see if she could join FORWARD. He was taken aback because he knew she'd been faking it all fall—wearing the right clothes and attending functions, but not really understanding what it was all about. The rallies and concerts must have been the exposure, but the fixative was apparently applied in Newland. She wouldn't talk about it. But one night at a coffee house in the Village she began crying when the guitar-player sang, "Yes, and how many times can a man turn his head / And pretend that he just doesn't see?"

She had no skills FORWARD needed, but they agreed to let her sit in on meetings because she could clearly profit from the exposure. With a humility Raymond had never before witnessed in her, she was busy finding and absorbing the books and films and records they all recommended. He had to admit to some satisfaction at having her value his opinions again, after what she'd put him through over that fraternity creep last year. He hadn't even grasped that it was all over between them until he went home to Newland at New Year's and found her decked out in some dumb blazer with that guy's pins all over her boobs. Back in New York he'd felt pretty betrayed. He'd picture her in that long Plantation Ball gown, though, and feel glad to be rid of her. But the relief never lasted long because he knew her so well, knew that there was more to her than that. Over the months the hurt had healed. Still, it was nice now having her phone him to ask what "power elite" or "psychic guerrilla warfare" meant. Even when he gave answers that Justin and Maria would have laughed at, she seemed impressed and grateful.

Last week, walking to supper, they came upon a derelict lying across the sidewalk, newspapers lining his overcoat. Everyone else, rushing home from work, was stepping over him. Emily insisted they prop him up on some garbage cans. She also insisted he stuff a ten-dollar bill in the man's pocket. The old man raised his mangy head, looked at Raymond through bloodshot eyes, and snarled, "Fuck you, buddy."

Emily turned away with tears streaming down her cheeks. He wished he knew what was going on with her.

Justin was talking to her, so Raymond turned to Maria, who lay on her side on a pillow, wearing a flared skirt, black tights, a black turtleneck, and African trading beads. Her long dark hair concealed half her face. "For God's sake, sit down, Raymond," she ordered. "You look as though you're about to run the mile."

He looked down at himself—one knee raised, forearms resting on thighs. His father and uncles and cousins squatted this way on the porches and in the yards of Tatro Cove. The men in the mill village squatted like this at ball games and picnics. Blushing, he sat down. He'd worked on his drawl, his rayon shirts and reindeer sweater vests, his bigoted attitudes, but reminders of his origins were always taking him by surprise. Fortunately, no one here but Emily and himself would have recognized the Country Store Squat.

And Emily was too wrapped up in what Justin was saying, "Justice . . . crackers . . . brotherhood of man . . . struggle . . . equality . . . rednecks . . ."

Raymond wondered if he should shave off his beard, leaving a Pancho Villa mustache like Justin's. It made him look fierce. Raymond felt he could use some fierceness. Combing his beard with his fingers, he watched Justin turn his profile to Emily and gaze with steely eyes into the farthest reaches of the loft, as though at the future he was pledged to usher in. A cigarette hung from his lips. Emily craned her neck trying to meet Justin's eyes. Maria had once told Justin that he had a heroic profile. And he did—with his narrowed eyes, hollow cheeks, and straight nose. Now he took every opportunity to display it.

Emily was murmuring, "Oh-really-you-don't-say-how-very-interesting-aren't-you-wonderful." Raymond caught her eye and received a faint wry smile that gave him the creeps. She'd done this with him for years—nursed his ego, a skill from her mother and from his own sister-in-law, the lovely Lady Sally of the cotton-candy hair. Like bicycle pumps, they'd inflate their men to weather-balloon size and then roll them out the door to face the world. But Emily would have to eradicate this slavish Southern Belle in herself if she was going to make it with FORWARD. Straightforwardness and utter equality were the qualities FORWARD valued and nurtured. He frowned at Emily, hoping to convey this.

Maria yelled, "Aw, bullshit, Justin! You're full of crap!" Now there was a woman for you—a woman who said what she meant and meant what she said. An intelligent woman, a politicized woman, a strong, courageous, independent woman. He hadn't known such women existed, after a lifetime of watching his mother stand behind his father's chair at meals. Maria terrified him, but she also excited him as no woman ever had. He hoped Emily would get to know her, spend some time with her, shed some of the attitudes Newland had burdened her with—just as being around Justin had helped him shed his own crippling attitudes.

Justin and Maria were arguing about Democratic Centralism. Raymond wasn't exactly sure what that meant. He read the books everyone had recommended. Last night he'd stared interminably at the sentence, "Each thing is a combination of contraries because it is made up of elements which, although linked together, at the same time eliminate one another." And he'd come close to going crazy trying to understand it. Yet the others could argue for hours about its ramifications. Either something was wrong with his brain, or the others were on a higher mental plane because of having been to college.

On the other hand, he did understand some things. For instance, he knew that Maria and Justin had been lovers and were splitting up. He knew the former by the glances they used to exchange, the latter by the ferocity of their current ideological disputes. Raymond reflected that if you grew up among hypocrites, you learned to ignore the stated content of a conversation, and instead to study facial expressions and gestures and the feeling tone of words.

Morris sauntered in wearing overalls and a wool undershirt and drawled to the group at large, "Hey, baby how you making it?" He had bushy black hair and glasses with tinted lenses. Raymond was surprised to realize how little he knew about Morris—only that he was a graduate assistant in political science at NYU. Presumably every member of FORWARD had a complicated life beyond the confines of this room, but Raymond knew only what they all looked like here and what they said during meetings and project work. He liked this situation just fine. In his experience, the more he knew about a person, the less he wished to know. The closer he got to people, the more they resembled the people he'd grown up among in Newland.

Morris slapped Ralph's palm. "Ralph! My man!" Then he squatted behind Maria, blew in her ear, and kissed her cheek. Gazing at Justin defiantly, he put his arm around her, his hand molding a breast. Justin glared back, then focused resolutely on Emily.

Maria, jabbing Morris in the stomach with her elbow, snarled, "Get stuffed, creep."

Morris, laughing, sat down next to Bud, a short squat man in army fatigues and an olive Eisenhower jacket. He had no neck and a red face, looked like an olive stuffed with a pimento. He kept passing around an agenda which no one would read. Some nights meetings never happened because anyone who tried to call them to order was accused of perpetrating a "cult of personality." Raymond really admired FORWARD's determination to do away with hierarchy.

Morris yelled to Maria and Justin, "OK, you two, shut up. Now what about this fund-raising statement?"

Justin looked up. "Do you mind, Morris? I was in the middle of a sentence."

"Mind? Hell no, Justin. I should mind if we're here all night while you finish your sentence?" He folded his arms.

Five minutes later Justin concluded his sentence and asked, "All right. What is it we need, guys?"

The room fell silent. Morris's face colored. Raymond wasn't sure why.

"We need a statement of purpose," explained Bud, "for a grant application that's due tomorrow."

Raymond studied the breast that Morris had fondled. Maria raised her eyes and caught him. Rather than look away, he forced himself to let his eyes linger, then slowly raised them to hers. A faint smile played around the corners of her mouth.

Raymond realized he was letting personal preoccupations interfere with his politics. He tried to concentrate on Morris: ". . . our role should be primarily that of a channel of support and communication among groups that have arisen from the direct action of the people themselves, working to alter the status quo in the South, that could serve to solidify evolving societal patterns, and simultaneously . . ."

"I'm not following you, Morris," Raymond muttered.

"That's because you weren't listening," Maria announced. "You were staring at my tit."

Everyone laughed. Raymond blushed. Justin looked at him, then turned his profile to Maria. Raymond hadn't suspected until that moment that Justin could feel threatened by him. What a bizarre thought. Justin was everything Raymond hoped to be, once he'd re-educated himself.

"Shit, Southerners can't grasp anything that isn't couched in a Br'er Rabbit tale. They got cornmeal mush for brains," snarled Morris.

Raymond realized this was probably true. You asked Justin or Morris a question, and you got back statistics, or a quote. You asked Emily or him a question, and you got an interminable anecdote involving several generations, like an Old Testament chapter. He only hoped his condition was curable. He vowed to memorize some of the statistics he'd been reading.

Bud was challenging Morris's term "channel": "The time has come for the current phase of disorganized protest to be replaced by a dedicated cadre of revolutionary visionaries. Lenin says, 'A vanguard which fears that consciousness will outstrip spontaneity, which fears to put forth . . .' "

"Yeah, yeah, we've all read *Toward the Seizure of Power*, Bud," growled Morris.

"It's not Lenin," Justin informed him. "It's Guevara. *Guerrilla Warfare*."

"Fuck it man! I know where I read it! It's Lenin."

"Wanna make a bet? Five bucks?"

"You're on, buddy." They shook hands, glaring.

"That vanguard stuff always sounds so elitist to me," mused Maria.

This triggered a discussion of Democracy, Fascism, State Socialism, and Communism. Raymond reclined on his pillow, feeling stupid. He'd give anything to be able to join in. He glanced at Emily, who was gazing at Justin's profile. Did she wonder why Raymond wasn't participating? Did she realize he wasn't able to? He sat up straight and assumed a severe expression. He sneaked a glance at Maria. Dating had never been easy for him. He'd held himself aloof in Newland. Now that this was no longer necessary for self-preservation, he didn't know how to behave any different. Whenever he tried to get romantic up here, girls always said, "Oh Raymond, let's just be friends."

But goddam, he didn't *want* to just be friends, he wanted to get laid. Everybody's favorite kid brother. How had he gotten stuck with this image? Maybe he did need him a Pancho Villa mustache. He'd worked hard to get rid of the attitudes Newland had saddled him with, but he couldn't seem to overcome his courtliness in favor of a quick screw. Newland insisted that the sex act Matter. (Pleasure didn't matter.) In Newland it mattered because everyone eventually knew about it. The town offered no entertainment except sex, no birth control except the Ten Commandments. They used sex as a carrot over a donkey, to get people into marriage, babies, jobs in the factories. Witness Jed.

But this wasn't Newland. He'd watched the other guys in FOR-

WARD for pointers. The glances, gestures, remarks that indicated they wanted a screw, but not babies, mortgage payments, and dinner parties. He had to get laid soon. It was getting ridiculous. It was interfering with his political work. FORWARD members had a responsibility to take care of their personal needs as efficiently as possible, to free up their energies and concentration for what was *really* important—the building of a just society.

Maybe Maria would be open to helping him out, now that she and Justin were on the rocks. He'd admired her right from the start, especially her sharp intelligence. Emily was bright, but in Newland she'd devoted herself to concealing it. Over the months he studied Maria closely, the way she drew so deeply on her cigarettes, the way she swung her head to get her hair out of her eyes. Ever since his documentary, she seemed interested in him too, jokingly calling him "our resident redneck." She was a couple of years older, a junior in college, but seemed to respect him, often made comments about his "guts" and "backbone" for being able to extract himself from Newland. Possibly, he reflected, she could be persuaded to take an interest in other portions of his anatomy as well. He liked the notion of an experienced older woman who'd initiate him sexually, like the South Sea islanders. Of course Raymond, Maria, the actual individuals made little difference. The point was to take care of one's petty personal needs in a fashion that would be most beneficial to the group as a whole, and enable one to funnel one's personal energies back into the collective.

"Without vision there can be no strategy," Justin was saying. "And without strategy, actions are meaningless flounderings."

"We're not getting anywhere on this statement," Maria interrupted.

"Christ, we're going to be here all night," Morris grumbled.

"I need this thing for tomorrow morning," Bud reminded them.

"Well, tell me how we can write a position paper when we don't agree on what we're doing?" Justin demanded.

"Obviously a couple of our theoreticians have to give in," said Maria.

"We could vote," Raymond suggested.

"Vote?" Morris sneered. "What do you think this is? A student council election? There's an ideologically correct position. It's just a question of allowing the consensus to emerge."

Raymond felt humiliated. He thought he understood about Democratic Centralism. Clearly he understood nothing. He'd made a fool of himself. When would he learn to keep his stupid hillbilly mouth shut? Emily smiled at him with sympathy. Fuck her sympathy! She knew even less than he did. Where did she get off, giving him that Southern Belle smile?

"How about if Morris and Bud have an arm-wrestling tournament?" Maria suggested.

"Get off us, Maria," Morris growled.

Maria, Emily, Ralph, and Raymond sat and listened to the debate as though watching a tennis match, with Justin as the linesman who corrected quotes and statistics.

". . . democratic participation in the decision-making process and . . ." insisted Morris.

"No revolution is 'spontaneous,' " replied Bud. "They're staged, manufactured by the few people with vision and courage."

"Debray says, 'It is always the movement which precedes the organization and the political strategy which follows, or which takes shape at the same time as the involvement in the action.' "

". . . catalyzing energy among the most deprived . . ."

". . . encouraging potential local leadership to adopt participatory methods . . ."

Raymond was impressed. He and the others, about all they could do was get out mailings and clean the loft. Here among Morris, Justin, and Bud was where the real action was. God, if only he'd read and understood enough to be able to quote Lenin and Marx like that. He vowed to study harder.

"Debray says," Morris concluded with a smug nod, " 'There is no separation between masses and intellectuals, movement and party, those who theorize and those who act, between "leaders" and "followers." ' "

Justin looked at his watch. "I'm sorry, guys, but I've got an appointment in fifteen minutes."

"Who is she?" asked Morris.

Justin smiled. "That's none of your business, is it?" Maria twitched. Justin caught her eye, then turned his profile to her.

"How about this statement? I need it in the morning," Bud reminded them.

"Well, I hate to pull rank," said Justin, "but . . ."

"Like hell you do," murmured Maria.

". . . I have been at this longest. FORWARD was my conception."

"Yes, and you just happen to be paying the rent," muttered Maria.

"I've listened to what everyone has to say. And I have to insist on this one point: FORWARD has no hierarchy and no inflexible ideology. You dig?"

Raymond listened with awe as Justin summed up the two hours of discussion in a handful of eloquent sentences: ". . . liberating ourselves from the assumptions of a racist society, formulating new identities based on a fresh analysis, changing that society's network of organization and control so as to include the dispossessed . . ."

He paused. "Are you getting this down, Maria?"

There was a long silence while Maria studied her fingernails. Finally she looked at Justin. "Why don't you just take your Brotherhood of Man and shove it, Justin?"

Justin, laughing, turned to Morris. "She's cute when she's angry, isn't she? So who *is* going to write this down?"

"I will," offered Emily.

"Stay out of this, Emily," snarled Maria. "Write it down yourself, you fucker. What was all this big talk about 'training each other in our specialties so that we could become interchangeable and practice an equality lacking in society at large'? I haven't seen you exhibit any interest in learning how to run the mimeo, Justin, or go for Chinese takeout."

"Let's face it: because of my ruling class privilege, I have skills and training it would take years to develop in someone else. We should think of the group more as an organism, each individual being an essential limb."

"So you're the prick, Justin. And what am I? The asshole?"

Raymond stood before the mirror in his bathroom and practiced: "Uh . . . hey, baby, how bout you and me . . .

"Maria, it's come to my attention that, uh . . .

"Maria, I was just wondering if you'd like to . . ."

The strong silent approach: Alone in the loft he'd turn to her, put his hand on her thigh . . .

He'd shaved his beard, leaving the mustache. It definitely made him look less cuddly.

He should court her. Candy, flowers, singing telegrams. He'd ask her to dinner. He knew he was being childish. Certainly Justin never suffered from timidity like this. He marched to the phone, picked it up, and held it to his ear, as the dial tone switched to an angry whine, and then to nothing. She'd laugh at him, turn him down with a pat on the head. She might even mention it to the others.

He slammed down the phone, threw himself on his bed and masturbated. As he lay with his hand full of semen, he took satisfaction in the knowledge that he had no Kleenex to clean up with. He'd made an effort to reduce his life to the essentials. After a lifetime surrounded by his mother's gewgaws—samplers, plastic teepees, family trees, mugs from Ruby Falls and Rock City and Gatlinburg—it was a relief to live in one small room with nothing in it except a bare bulb hanging from the ceiling and a mattress salvaged from the incinerator room. He *chose* to live as Negroes in the South were *forced* to live, so that he would never become softened by creature comforts into settling for the status quo. His one indulgence was a trench coat like Justin's, which he hung with care on a hanger on the back of his door.

Wind off the Hudson was gusting around his windows and fighting its way into his room. He felt grim satisfaction as goose bumps crept up his arms.

He jumped up and stalked to the phone. With his free hand, he dialed Maria's number, clearing his throat. When she answered, he froze. After she'd said hello several times in an increasingly annoyed voice, she whistled through her fingers and nearly broke his eardrum.

He flopped onto his bed again and looked around the bare room. Cold terror began to creep over him. He recognized it from his first days in New York. He would die alone in this room, his corpse unfound and unmourned. He would simply cease to exist, missed by no one, having left no mark on the world. He breathed deeply, but the terror kept coming. He moved his arms, blinked his eyes, touched his tongue to his nose, to prove to himself that he still existed.

"*Who* still exists?" he asked himself.

There was only one cure. He searched among some books on the floor by the bed and found the photo from his room at home of the hanging elephant. He stared at it and felt the terror halt. Maybe he didn't know who he was, but he did know who he *wasn't*: He wasn't part of that howling mob of demented hillbillies.

As the terror slowly receded, Raymond began to remember who he was—FORWARD's resident redneck, a regenerate Southerner who'd had enough brains to leave, a dedicated revolutionary who was devoting his life to the betterment of the lot of those dispossessed by the social system he'd grown up under. Maria, Justin, Morris, Ralph—they'd mourn his death, tend his corpse . . .

He laughed aloud. What a silly thing to be worrying about. He was nineteen years old, for Christ's sake, and in perfect health. He blew a huge sigh of relief, put down the photo, and picked up *Das Kapital*.

Raymond stayed behind after the next meeting to stuff and address a mailing about the availability of his documentary. He folded, licked, and stamped with machine-like precision. Soon irritation was making his movements jerky and causing him to rip stamps in half. He stood up and lit a cigarette. Trying to let it hang from his lips, he paced the loft. The truth was, he was bored. The folding and addressing, frankly it was hard to see what it all had to do with restructuring the social system of the South. He drew deeply on his cigarette as he'd watched Maria do, and exhaled. And how come he was having to do this all alone anyhow? "It's your ego trip, man," snarled Morris when Raymond had asked for volunteers. Well, if it was, then he might just as well trash the whole thing. Ego trips weren't what FORWARD was all about. If Emily or Maria had been there, he'd have taken the prints of the documentary and flung them from the window. As it was, he contented himself with kicking a metal waste can across the loft.

The door opened and in walked Maria. "I got halfway home and felt guilty about you here slaving away in the night all alone," she explained.

"Oh, no problem." Raymond waved his cigarette dismissingly. "But I'm glad to have company."

He worked for a long time with renewed efficiency. Maria addressed as he folded and stamped. He kept glancing at her. She knocked him out. A woman you could work shoulder to shoulder with. Of course they personally counted for nothing, but drop by drop their efforts would eat away the boulder of human misery.

When they'd finished, he took a breath, cleared his throat and croaked, "Maria?"

"Yes?" She looked up.

"Uh. I have to discuss something with you."

"Yes?"

"Uh . . ." Jesus, how could he get out of this? "What's going on with you and Justin and Morris?"

She looked at him with surprise. "Why do you ask?"

"Uh, yes, well . . . Maria, I feel like my political work is suffering."

"You do? How come?"

"Well, because of . . . you know, tension, and all like that."

"Sexual tension?"

"Uh . . . well . . ."

"Between you and me?"

"Uh . . ."

"Well, so do I. But that's easy enough to deal with, isn't it?"

"It is? Yes, it is." He felt almost disappointed that she was so willing to descend from her pedestal. In a way, he'd hoped she might get angry with him for injecting the personal into the collective, for debasing ideology with common physical hunger. He'd hoped he might have to duel ideologically with Justin for her favors, that she might require proof of his worth and suitability.

"Well?" She put down her pen.

"What? You mean here? *Now?*" If she could accept him like this, without hesitation, who was so undereducated and inexperienced politically, maybe she wasn't so neat after all?

"Why not? I mean, we don't want our political work to suffer, do we?"

"No, I guess we don't." With a trembling hand he took her arm and pretended he was leading her to the cushions. He was so terrified he couldn't even joke about his inexperience. Foreplay he could handle; after all, he'd had maybe six years of it. And eventually the rest began to seem remotely possible.

"I'm afraid I'm not very good at this," he murmured.

"That's what you all say," she moaned, her hips rising to meet his.

"We do?" Who was this "all"? Was he merely the most recent in a cast of hundreds? Was she comparing him to all those others? He started feeling like a fool. Then he realized that among those others were Justin and Morris.

They began spending their spare time in his crow's nest apartment, rocking on his moldy mattress while the winter winds whipping in off the Hudson howled around his windows. She lay in his arms as he talked about growing up an oddball in Newland and about his struggle to get away. She talked about being pushed in her stroller in May Day parades down Fifth Avenue by her father, who was a professor at the School for Industrial and Labor Relations at Columbia. She introduced Raymond to the concept that he was working class: "Do you realize how unusual you are, Raymond? You've purged yourself of the traditional prejudices of your class, all on your own, by sheer instinct."

He smiled. "You make me sound so heroic, Maria. But I'm just a plain working man."

She bought him new sheets, and poison for the cockroaches. He watched as she scrubbed his walls, maintaining that he preferred it as it had been.

"God, this place is revolting!" she insisted. He accused her of being middle class. "I bet your mother didn't grow penicillin on her walls," Maria replied.

Raymond laughed. "She sure as hell didn't. Her kitchen was as clean as an operating room."

"What was she like with you? Bossy, I bet."

"Yeah, pretty overwhelming. But what makes you say that?"

"Well, there's something so remote about you, Raymond. As though you're protecting this secret inner chamber from assault. You're not going to let any woman near it."

"Me? Remote?" He slid his hands under her sweatshirt and squeezed her breasts.

She laughed. "Go ahead. Change the subject."

Raymond felt Maria was a softening influence. He became more gentle and kind when he was with her. He whistled when he was alone in his room after she'd been there. He felt she was tempering the steel that formed his core. But he drew the line one afternoon when she brought him a bouquet of tulips. "I don't want to have to sit here and watch them die."

"But Raymond . . ."

"That's final, Maria." She nodded. They went out on the roof and tossed them one by one over the edge. Passers-by on the sidewalk looked startled as tulips fell at their feet.

Raymond and Emily were eating curry in a small Indian restaurant off Times Square.

"Well, I finally did it."

"Did what?"

"It. With a girl."

"Yeah? Well, good for you."

"Guess I'd better not say who with."

"Probably not. It wouldn't be very chivalrous. It isn't Maria, is it?"

He looked at her. "How did you know?"

"How could any of us not know?"

"It's been that obvious, huh?"

"Um."

"I recommend it highly."

"Thanks. I'll remember."

"Or did you make it with that fraternity creep last year?"

"God, Raymond, that's none of your business, is it?"

"It isn't? But I just told you about Maria."

"What is this—the Swap Shop?"

"You and Justin are certainly getting along well. He thinks you're fantastic. He told me so."

"Well, he's right, of course."

"He only thinks so because you listen to him endlessly, pretending to be enthralled."

"But I am enthralled. I can't understand anything he says, but I'm enthralled. I think he's a beautiful person. The way he's devoted his life to the dispossessed."

"Yeah, I agree. Are you sleeping with him?" He felt jealousy and couldn't imagine why. He was besotted with Maria, was convinced she was the most wonderful woman in existence. He just didn't like Emily doing things without first seeking his blessing. In a way it was a good thing, though. A time or two he'd noticed Justin studying him at meetings with scarcely concealed belligerence. But Justin's claiming Emily maybe compensated for Raymond's taking up with Maria. Though as far as Raymond could see there was no contest. But let Justin think what he liked.

"God, Raymond, why do I let you talk to me like this? It's really no concern of yours."

"Yeah, but I need to know."

"You're obsessed, is what you are. Like a kid with a new toy. Hey, you heard about our new niece, didn't you? Laura?"

"Yeah."

"Sally phoned last night. Seven pounds, six ounces. Twenty-one inches long. Sally said the birth was much more difficult than Joey's. Her water broke about 4 a.m., and . . ."

"So the kid got born and has all her fingers and toes. That's all I'm interested in."

"Huh?"

"Christ, Emily, what does any of that garbage have to do with me?"

"But she's my sister, Raymond. Your sister-in-law. Your brother's wife. You've known her all your life."

"My boring bigoted baby brother and his boring brainless bouffanted wife are leading their bland boring blighted lives in Newland, Tennessee. If you know that much, you can fill in the blanks." He stood up and shrugged on his dirty trench coat. "Oh, for Christ's sake, stop looking at me like that. You don't care about that scene any more than I do."

"That's not true."

As he walked into the street, he glanced in both directions for the FBI tail he was sure would one day be there. Maria was waiting for him by a streetlight near the IRT entrance. It was Berlin. During the war. He'd sidle up to her. She'd offer him a cigarette. He'd take it, pocket it; the paper, unrolled and heated over a flame, would reveal information that would save hundreds of lives . . .

Maria, smiling, buttoned his trench coat and fastened the belt. "You'll freeze to death, you silly Southern boy."

He looked at her and didn't respond when she kissed him. "Now what?" she asked with a smile.

"Come on," he said, grabbing her hand and descending into the subway.

Back at his room, he phoned Emily. "Look, I'm sorry about what I said about Sally."

Emily sounded disappointed. "No, after you left, Raymond, I decided you were right. It's ludicrous talking about Sally's labor pains when half the world is going to bed hungry tonight. Sally was lucky not to have to drop her baby in a furrow, get up, and keep picking cotton."

Raymond was irritated. He wanted Emily to be annoyed with him, threaten never to speak to him again. Then he could say to her what she'd just said to him.

Justin and Morris, Maria and Raymond, were going to training sessions in a church basement, for their trip to Tennessee. A Negro in overalls instructed the two dozen volunteers on how to roll into a ball to protect the head and vital organs during a beating. A night stick, a cattle prod, a piece of hose, brass knuckles, were brought out—their uses described and demonstrated. How to behave when attacked by police dogs. Raymond felt pleasure to be preparing to do something real at last. Sending out mailings, sitting in on ideological disputes, weren't what he had in mind. He wanted to be in on making change happen. Frankly, as amusing as it was, he was even getting weary of lying around in bed all weekend with Maria. He was ready for some action.

The man described having been beaten in jail by fellow prisoners, on instructions from the sheriff. He pointed out scars on his face. He warned about cars without license plates, cops without badges. They did role-playing, practicing how to avoid responding to taunts, how to answer state troopers, how to approach potential voters.

As a woman sociology professor lectured on the folkways of the Negro and white communities of his home state, Raymond scarcely recognized the place. He'd been brutalized down there, conditioned not to question the status quo, to accept that status quo as the only possible reality. Well, there were alternatives, and he'd devote his life to bringing them to fruition.

The car hurtled down the valley of Virginia, the vagina of the South. As Raymond watched the greening pastures, he reflected on how many groups had penetrated the South via this route—wave after wave of warring Indian tribes, German and Scotch-Irish settlers from Pennsylvania, Yankee troops. The atmosphere in the car was that of a kamikaze plane. They all knew they might die down here in the struggle for justice for all the people. Until now people spoke about Brotherhood and Equality, and everyone agreed. But there were people out there who would just as soon kill them as look at them. This knowledge permeated them, making them feel deep kinship with each other. Raymond told himself that once you realized that death wasn't something that happened only to strangers, you were an adult.

"So where are the shacks?" asked Morris.

"They'd tear them down along main roads," Justin assured him. "P.R."

Hour by hour the fields got greener. Buds on trees became tiny chartreuse leaves. It was like a Walt Disney time-lapse movie. Maria and he sat in the back seat pressing their thighs together. He had his hands folded over his hard-on, and Maria kept looking down and grinning. As they crossed into Tennessee, small white crosses by the roadside marked traffic deaths. Raymond knew he was home.

Passing through Newland, Raymond didn't mention that it was his hometown. He looked out of the corner of his eye at a stoplight and saw his fifth-grade teacher, Mrs. Moody, stooped and walking with a cane. She'd had a portable organ in her room, and they'd sung

"Heaven Is Closer Cause Mother Is There." He'd loved her as she sat at her organ warbling and pumping the pedals. But no, he wouldn't allow petty personal affections to taint his awareness that the world she inhabited, and had tried to train him to inhabit, had to go.

Wilbur sat in the same valley that contained Newland, but Raymond had never been there. Newlanders, like iron filings in a magnetic field, oriented themselves northward, since their economic survival depended on it. Raymond knew Kentucky, North Carolina, Virginia, Maryland. He did not know Alabama, Mississippi, Georgia, or the southern part of his own state. Yet this was the South of legend, the rural South. His own South, the New South of the industrialists, was too mountainous for large farms. There'd been few slaves, were now few Negroes. In the War between the States, East Tennessee had tried to secede from Tennessee when Tennessee seceded from the Union. Cherokee County in turn planned to secede from East Tennessee. Life wasn't as simple as people imagined. It'd seemed much simpler sitting in that loft on the Lower East Side of New York than now, confronted with actual earth and trees, skin and bones. He was surprised to find himself gazing at the others, his chin jutting out defiantly.

He reprimanded himself. Some things were simple to those objective enough to see them. The Negro population of this region had been systematically starved, exploited, and abused for far too long, and it was time to put a stop to it, which was why he was here. What's complicated about that, Raymond Redneck? he asked himself.

The major place of work in Wilbur was a canning factory. Houses and services for its workers comprised the town. Surrounding it were farms that grew vegetables for the factory. On the outskirts of the farms were rows of two-room cottages on red clay roads in which lived the Negroes who picked the crops. Farther out, scattered through the red clay hills, were the tenant farmers, white and Negro.

Raymond's carload joined another in the basement of a Negro church on the edge of the cottages. They slept all together, boys and girls, Negroes and whites, on the floor in sleeping bags. The project director was a Negro woman from Atlanta named Glenda. At the first staff meeting Justin began quoting Marx.

Glenda dismissed him with a shrug. "Honey, I don't give a shit bout no Marx. I got to get me six crates of baked beans out to Taloosa, Tennessee, by early this evening." They were divided into teams and assigned areas to canvass. Glenda made suggestions on how to approach people, and described the actual mechanics of getting someone registered.

Morris and Justin and a couple of others argued about the "manipulation of community people."

Glenda interrupted. "All right, white boys, who's gon drive the Ford into Newland for groceries tomorrow?" Raymond was aghast. People screamed at Justin, struggled to outquote him. But no one had ever shrugged him off like an annoying puppy. And certainly not a woman, not a Negro woman, not a Southern Negro woman.

Maria suppressed a smile as Justin's face turned grey. Glenda glanced at him. He gave her a tight smile. She continued assigning chores, not smiling. Weakly, Justin turned his profile to her. She looked away.

To Raymond's astonishment Justin began hanging around Glenda all the time. Raymond overheard her say, "Listen, baby, white boys don't want but two things from nigger women: housework and pussy. And Justin honey, I *know* you ain't got you no house." This only seemed to spur Justin on. Raymond couldn't figure it out. He himself stayed as far away from her as possible. He was a mass of anxious confusion around her. Ruby and Kathryn had cuddled him when he was a child, but he was no longer a child, and the role of the white male in Negro women's lives in the South was that of rapist. Yet he found himself wanting to sit on her lap, his head resting on her breast, while she tied his shoes. And he hated himself for seeing her like this.

One night Raymond was propped against the wall on his rolled-up sleeping bag trying to read *Kapital*. Morris and Justin beat a hollow rhythm on the Ping-Pong ball. Reports had drifted in that afternoon of a voter registration team in Chattanooga—a rabbi, a priest, and two students—who'd been knocked down and kicked by angry whites. Raymond had met the priest once at a meeting in Chattanooga. He was from Massachusetts and exclaimed to Raymond over how cute the little pickaninnies were, with their big wide eyes and grins. Frankly, Raymond had also wanted to kick him.

Raymond thought about his documentary—the bombing of the Birmingham church, Medgar Evers's murder—and realized he was terrified. He glanced at the others, who were writing letters, reading, or talking quietly. On the rare occasions when a car would pass on the gravel road outside, all activity would cease. The girls cleaning up in the kitchen would stop talking. The guitar being picked would cease abruptly. Pens would hang over paper. The Ping-Pong ball was held in front of an upraised paddle. As the headlights swept through the windows and across the room, each person listened intently—to the basso continuo of frogs, locusts, and crickets, to the crunch of car over gravel—praying that neither noise would alter or cease.

They heard footsteps, a knock at the door. All activity in the room halted at once. Raymond assured himself that the Klan wouldn't bother to knock. Glenda went to the door. An old Negro man in overalls, carrying a chocolate cake, entered. A couple of people laughed nervously, and Morris served the Ping-Pong ball.

The old man nodded shyly to the group and handed Glenda the cake. "The missus, she say can you use you a fudge layer cake?"

Glenda talked to the old man in a low voice, apparently about the incident in Chattanooga. He chuckled. "Yeah, that's a tough cat to clean up after, ain't it?"

The *courage*, thought Raymond. To have lived with intimidation his entire life and still to be able to chuckle, still be thoughtful enough to bring others fudge layer cakes. It blew Raymond away.

After the old man left, Morris said to Justin, "Did you *hear* that cat? Did you really *hear* him, man?"

Justin nodded. "Dig it."

In his sleeping bag Raymond imagined a casement window pushed open, a fire bomb dropped in. The door opening silently to admit ranks of white-sheeted maniacs. Weapons: knives from the kitchen. The Klan would have guns. Every man in the South had several. Would Negroes from nearby houses help out? Probably not. They were even more terrified than he, had every reason to be. The girls. Would they be raped? It was bad enough being an unarmed man. Imagine being a girl. No, Southern males were too hung up on chivalry. They wouldn't rape defenseless girls. Unless they were Negro girls. . . . There was another besides Glenda—Annabelle. They should be spirited upstairs, hidden under the altar. The Klan wouldn't think to search upstairs. If they did, they wouldn't defile a church. They were mostly Fundamentalists—Baptists, Church of God, Holiness people—took their religion very seriously. But a Negro church? How about that church in Birmingham? True, he was short and skinny, had never won a fight in his life. But the time came for every man when he had to make a stand against Injustice. He lit a cigarette and hung it from his lower lip.

Raymond was so worked up he couldn't sleep. He crawled out of his sleeping bag, stepped over the others, and let himself out the door. It was like stepping into a warm bath—lukewarm air enveloped him, insect chatter filled his ears. He walked to the rear of the church and climbed the ladder onto the flat roof, a spot he came to often when he needed to recover from group living.

They could all climb up here and pull the ladder up. There was a low wall on all sides to crouch behind. What could they throw down? He tried to remember the tactics of beleaguered Christians in Crusader movies. Boiling oil? Rocks? What if the Klan set the church on fire? They'd be roasted alive up here, like pigeons in clay. What did Gregory Peck do in *Pork Chop Hill*?

Then he remembered the sessions in New York. Passive resistance. They weren't supposed to fight back. They were supposed to roll into balls, like those orange and black caterpillars The Five used to collect. By accepting violence without reprisal, the volunteers could illustrate that it was possible not to hate those who reviled and persecuted you. Those performing the violence could see the loathsomeness of their behavior and repent. On the rooftop this strategy violated his instincts, which tended toward defiance. He wanted to go to his death kicking and cursing.

Maybe he should talk the others into taking turns guarding up here at night. He strode back and forth chewing his fingernails. As the black in the east turned to dark grey, he clambered down. Back in the basement he kissed Maria awake and led her, yawning, to the roof, where he spread his sleeping bag. He buried his face between her large breasts. He felt her vagina tighten around him as he thrust into her.

They weren't able to be alone much. Raymond knew that each time they made love might very well be their last. These bodies that gave them so much joy were fragile, infinitely vulnerable. And there were people out there who wanted to maim and destroy them.

An overwhelming greed for life gripped Raymond. He thrust harder and faster, making Maria writhe against him; she moaned so loud that he had to cup his hand over her mouth.

Afterward they lay in each other's arms and watched the long pale fingers of dawn gently stroke the night sky until the grey became engorged with crimson. The fiery ball burst up over the horizon, spurting streams of molten sunlight. The green hillsides were swathed in drifting veils of mist. Dew glittered red in the rising sun, like diamonds in a furnace. The birds began their daily din. Cows cropped tender shoots of new grass. Raymond reflected that he had drunk the milk of those cows, eaten the flesh almost his whole life. He'd eaten fruits and vegetables grown in that sticky red clay. His body—this body that was giving him so much pleasure with Maria—was actually composed of the soil out there on those hillsides. Whereas the elements that made up Maria's luscious body were from all over the country, all over the world. Mangoes from Mexico, she was formed from. Borscht from Kiev.

"Christ, it's so beautiful here," Raymond said in a choked voice.

"Too bad it's filled with such unbeautiful people," Maria murmured.

Raymond looked at her. "They're my people."

"Not anymore. You left, remember?"

"How would you feel, Maria, if I said Jews were unbeautiful people?"

"Lots are."

"But how would you feel if I said it?"

"Annoyed."

"But I'm not supposed to feel annoyed when you all say that about Southerners?"

"Oh come on, Raymond, don't tell me you're trying to defend crackers?" She laughed.

"I'm just trying to point out that you're as racist as they are. As we are."

"But that's ridiculous. Jews have been persecuted. Southerners have been persecutors. You can't compare them."

"But you're treating people as categories rather than as individuals."

"Isn't that what Southerners are doing when they deny someone a job just because his skin is dark?"

"But that's my point. You're doing the same thing."

"Garbage," said Maria.

When they'd first started canvassing, they'd all been unsure of themselves, in spite of their training. But by now they'd established a style. Justin, Maria, and he walked to a tenant's house—three rooms of weathered wood. The name on the mailbox was T. R. Randall. They marched across the dirt yard onto a rickety porch. Justin knocked. Eventually a Negro woman in a tattered maid's dress answered.

"Howdy, Mrs. Randall. Justin Lawson here," he drawled, trying to hide his New York accent. Her eyes grew wide with alarm that he should know her name. "This here's Maria Stoneberg and Raymond Tatro. We're staying over at the church. There's a lot of us working in this area. You may have heard about us?"

"Yes sir, I did. Won't yall come in?"

Raymond could tell she was praying they'd decline.

"Why, thank you, we'd love to." They marched in and perched on her sofa, which was exuding stuffing like popped cotton pods.

She clenched her apron hem and watched them. Two small children hid in her skirts and peeped out. "Yall excuse me just a minute, I'll go fetch Mr. Randall." She went to the back door and sent a child racing across the yard to a listing shed.

"Hot enough for you?" Justin demanded.

"Yes sir, it sure is."

They sat in silence.

"Got your crops in yet?" Justin asked.

"The tabbacky is out. But the corn ain't in. Too wet to plough."

"Wet?" Justin and Maria said simultaneously. "You've had a lot of rain this year?"

"Yeah, Lord, we like to been warshed away."

"That a fact?" They'd already been told this at a dozen different houses.

Mr. Randall appeared in the doorway. He wore overalls, an undershirt, and work shoes. He smiled shyly and said, "Hidy. How yall today?"

Justin thrust out his hand. Mr. Randall stared at it, then shook it gingerly, as though being passed leprosy spores.

"You see, Mr. and Mrs. Randall, we're going from house to house trying to get folks to go down to the courthouse and register to vote."

There was a long pause.

"Are you registered voters?"

Another long pause.

"No sir, we ain't," Mr. Randall finally replied.

"Are you planning to go down there soon?"

Mr. and Mrs. Randall glanced at each other. "We ain't never felt no need to vote."

"But it's so important," Maria interjected. "The way things are right now, the man that gets elected doesn't have to pay any attention to your people. But if you all were helping to put him in office, he'd have to, wouldn't he?"

"Yes ma'am, I reckon so."

Raymond could tell by the set of Mr. Randall's jaw that he was increasingly determined not to vote. Maria interpreted his polite agreement as encouragement. "I mean, for instance, the road commissioner would have to pave your road if you could vote him out of office, wouldn't he?"

"Thas a fact," he said with a shy smile.

Raymond was confused. What Maria was saying was true. But they were violating the Southern code by not heeding the signs that said Mr. Randall wanted them out of his house. Maria and Justin couldn't be expected to recognize those signs, not knowing that Southerners of both races were reared on the aphorism "The true test of good manners is whether or not you can be pleasant to someone with bad manners." Raymond had a responsibility here to take charge.

"Well, guess we'd better be going," Raymond announced, standing up. Mr. and Mrs. Randall looked at him with gratitude. Maria and Justin looked at him with amazement since they'd barely begun their pitch.

"Yeah, the elected officials should be working for you," Justin continued. A glazed look came over Mr. Randall's dark eyes. Similar to the look that comes over a buck's eyes when it's been shot.

"Can I offer yall folks some coffee?" Mrs. Randall asked, her tone indicating this was a formality to be declined.

"No, thank you, m'am," Raymond replied. It would use up a week's supply. He realized with a start that he had more in common with the Randalls than with Maria and Justin. The Randalls kept food on their table with difficulty. They weren't interested in whether their road was paved or not because they and their friends didn't have cars.

"That would be lovely," replied Maria, probably operating out of the Yankee convention of accepting cups of hot something as a social gesture.

"Please." Justin nodded.

"You sure you won't have none now?" she asked Raymond.

"No, thank you, ma'am." His skin crawled with anxiety. Yes, it was important to get them registered, if only to give them the self-respect that the status of Voter was supposed to bring. Yet the Randalls already exuded a quiet self-contained dignity.

As they sipped coffee, Justin took out a registration form and handed it to Mr. Randall. From the way he handled it, Raymond could tell he could barely read. "We've found some folks are a little bit scared to go down to the courthouse because they don't know just what to expect. They don't know what they're getting themselves into. But it's no big deal really."

"Where yall from?" Mr. Randall asked, gazing at the form.

Justin paused. "Well, Maria and I, we're from New York. Raymond there's from Tennessee."

Mr. Randall looked at him as though he were a sparrow in with a flock of buzzards. "Where at?"

"Newland."

"I been there once. Got me a aunt up there. Pearly Randall. You know her?"

"No, I don't. Where does she live?"

"Over by that river. I disremember her street name."

"I know that river pretty well. Some other kids and me had us this club and we used to . . ."

Raymond and Mr. Randall swapped Newland stories, while Maria and Justin glanced at their watches, their forms, and each other.

On the porch Justin asked, "You reckon you and Mrs. Randall will go down there and register soon?"

"Well now, I surely will think on it. Yes sir, I surely will. And I do preciate yall coming by."

As they walked down the road, Raymond said, "You might as well mark them down no." It felt good to Raymond to be able to offer Justin an insight. Justin could help him understand New York City, and he'd help Justin understand Tennessee.

"He said he'd think about it."

"He was just being polite."

"We were doing fine until you launched into your downhome back-woods bullshit."

Raymond was unnerved by Justin's belligerent tone. He'd thought they were finally exercising some reciprocity. "No, we weren't. We were in trouble from the minute we called her Mrs. Randall before letting her introduce herself." He felt he was being generous saying "we" since it was Justin who'd done it.

"Oh Christ, you crackers slay me! Now he's pulling his 'we know our niggers' routine."

Anguish shot through Raymond. The truth was finally out: The man he admired most in the world thought he was a cracker. Only as long as he accepted with wide eyes everything Justin said would Justin tolerate him. Was there some way now to appease him, to regain his patronage? He'd make a joke! He opened his mouth to say, "Yeah, I guess you're right, Justin." But the words stuck in his throat. "I don't know nothing about Negroes. But I do know some-thing about Southerners. Because I am one."

Maria looked at him.

Raymond and Maria lay on his sleeping bag on the roof, which was still warm from the afternoon sun. Raymond had been talking for twenty minutes without pause: ". . . so I get rid of my accent; I grow a beard; I wear jeans and workshirts; I read Marx and Lenin and Fanon; I go to concerts and rallies and benefits, and give money and time and effort. Then I find out that all along he's been thinking of me as a 'cracker.' He goes crazy when a white person calls someone a nigger, but he doesn't hesitate to call Southerners crackers and . . ."

"Raymond, you've been talking on and on, and you don't even realize I haven't been listening. I might as well be a priest in a confessional. At least I'd get paid." He looked at her, stunned. She was smiling sadly. "I guess our sexual problems stem from the same source."

"Sexual problems? I . . ."

"You didn't know we had any? That illustrates my point. You haven't noticed I hardly ever come?"

"I . . . well . . ." He hadn't realized girls came.

"You haven't noticed that lots of times I go into the bathroom and masturbate after we make love?"

"I always thought you were . . . you know, cleaning yourself up." They sat in silence.

"God, this is awful, Maria. I've been having a wonderful time, and thinking you were too . . ."

"Well, it's had its charms, Raymond. But unassisted orgasm hasn't been among them."

"Why didn't you say something?"

"I guess I thought it was my own problem."

"What's changed your mind?"

"Yes, well. That's why I wasn't listening to you on the tribulations of a Southern upbringing. I was trying to figure out how to tell you this."

"What?"

"That I spent all afternoon in bed with Carson, that guy in Newland."

Raymond felt as though he'd been punched in the solar plexus. Carson was a cheery Negro from Birmingham who'd dropped out of Howard to drive people to work during the Montgomery bus boycott. Raymond and Maria had met him one night at a meeting. He was wearing a Howard sweatshirt. He told about being born in the back seat of a car on the way to the hospital, so his father had named him Carson. Raymond was being swept with waves of rage, humiliation, pain, and all kinds of emotions so new that he didn't have names for them.

After a couple of minutes, Maria said, "But it's no big deal, Raymond. When you and I want to make love, we will. And we'll figure out ways to cope with our problems."

He looked at her with amazement. "Aren't you in love with this guy?"

She laughed. "Who's talking love? I'm talking lust."

She kissed him and left. He lay through the night assaulted by unfamiliar emotions. She was screwing a Negro, she wanted to screw him as well. Disease: Carson would give her VD, which he would pick up. She didn't want to live happily ever after with him? It hadn't occurred to him it wouldn't go on forever. Things always had in Newland. This was the woman with whom he'd pledged himself to struggle to build a more decent world. Carson was a better lover. It was true what they said about Negro men. Of course if Raymond had been lying around some sleepy Southern town with loose Negro girls, instead of struggling to get away and slave for the Negro cause, he'd know how to make love too. Was Carson's cock bigger? How long could he last? How long did you have to last to make a girl come?

He watched the string of stereotypes marching through his numb brain.

He would challenge Carson to a duel. The winner would have Maria's devotion forevermore. He would string the bastard up and slice off his goddam balls. How dare he touch a white woman? *His* woman. More than one man at a time? He'd never heard of such a thing. For a man, maybe. But not for women. Not for *decent* women. He'd string *her* up. Sex before marriage was bad enough even if you loved the guy and planned to marry him. But sex for *fun*? Sex to quell lust? It was revolting. *Maria* was revolting. A jig in a college sweat-shirt was like a monkey in a tuxedo. Who did Maria think she was anyhow? *He* was the man, he had the cock, he decided what went on when. She was just a stinking sink hole of a cunt. He pounded his fists rhythmically on the roof. Orgasms for women! These aggressive demanding Yankee bitches! She should spread her legs and be grateful for what she got! He was how he was, and she could take it or leave it! (Stunned, he began to realize that she'd probably leave it.)

By morning, as he descended from the roof with crazed bloodshot eyes, he understood that you didn't stop being a Southerner just by saying "you" instead of "yall." He stopped eating, lay awake on the roof all night, excused himself from canvassing. The project doctor was coming by regularly to hand out Valium, which Raymond popped in great quantities. Though he was almost too far gone to notice, the violence the group was carefully hiding from the outside world they were turning in on each other. Almost every day now some kind of altercation erupted—between those who'd been jailed versus those who hadn't, Yankees versus Southerners, whites versus blacks, men versus women, middle class versus working class, college-educated versus non-college-educated, religious versus atheist.

Raymond began wandering around the countryside with his camera, taking pictures of the farmers, their families and crops. One afternoon he walked past the Randalls', en route to a woods to photograph wild azaleas. The damp green fields were steaming under the hot spring sun. Mrs. Randall was sitting in an armchair on her front porch snapping string beans while her two children tumbled in the dirt in the yard. Raymond raised a hand, and she replied with a shy, "Hidy, how yall today?"

"Just fine, thank you, ma'am. Pretty day?"

"Yes sir. Sure is."

Raymond watched the children, remembering his days with The Five. "You mind if I take some pictures of your children?"

"Shoot, no. But what you want pictures of them rascals for?"

"Just for fun. Yall mind?"

The children put their hands to their mouths and giggled.

Raymond shot, with long waits between pictures, during which he studied their faces and tried to understand their games. He contrasted this to the way he'd made the documentary—splicing together every horrifying sequence he could get his hands on. He bludgeoned the viewer into accepting FORWARD's interpretation. But was it reality? If he instead set up a camera trained for forty years on the Randalls' front porch, recording people occasionally walking in and out or standing and chatting, was *that* reality? Year after year, cotton bolls forming, swelling, popping, getting picked. This boredom I get so impatient with, Raymond mused, is that actually reality? Do I then go and stir up drama where it wouldn't otherwise exist just to escape reality, which is boredom?

The next time he brought some candy, which the children stuffed in their mouths as though afraid it would vanish. Another day he brought Mrs. Randall some macaroni he'd liberated from the project supply. She hesitantly invited him for supper, and during the meal he asked if they'd mind if he did a picture book on their children.

They looked dumbfounded, and Mr. Randall asked, "Who'd want a book like that cepting their mama and me?"

"People up North might want to know how yall live down here."

Mr. Randall thought it over. "Why?"

"Folks everywhere are curious."

"Yeah, ain't it the truth? Well, yeah, I reckon it'd be all right."

Raymond photographed their house, their sheds and fields; Mr. and Mrs. Randall sitting on their porch in their Sunday clothes—a board-stiff gleaming white shirt and black suit for him, a clinging white rayon dress for her, and a hat with a veil. Mr. Randall had ten acres of cotton, a tobacco allotment, and ten acres of green beans. Raymond photographed him among his crops and played long involved games with the children.

One night Maria invited him to the roof. They sat down, and she took his hand. A shudder of revulsion ran up his arm. He retrieved his hand. "I didn't know you'd be so upset, Raymond."

"Who's upset?"

"Well, look at you. Your clothes are hanging on you like a scarecrow's. You've got black circles under your eyes. When you aren't lying up here brooding, you're stumbling around the countryside like a zombie."

"It just never occurred to me it wouldn't last forever, Maria."

She laughed. "It never occurred to me it would last more than a few weeks. I was delighted when it went on for several months. In my life people have always come and gone, so to speak. You don't let yourself get too caught up in it or you get hurt. I didn't realize you were playing by different rules. I'm really sorry. But I didn't mean to say it was all over. I like you a lot, Raymond. I'd still like to spend time with you. And make love with you if we feel like it."

"I don't know if I can handle that, Maria. I want you all to myself."

"You can have me all to yourself, Raymond. But not all the time. That's how I am."

"And this is how I am."

"So who's going to change?"

"Neither probably."

"Probably not."

Raymond, Justin, Maria, and Annabelle were lying on a dam that formed a pond. The afternoon sun was scorching. They had caught some bluegill and cooked them over a fire. Justin, his shirt off, was playing his guitar, and they were singing Dylan and Baez songs. Annabelle was kneeling behind Justin kneading his shoulders. Raymond, buoyed up by Valium, was feeling better than he had in days. Maria and he had begun having pleasant chats on the roof again, though he felt toward her body as he would toward a coiled copperhead. If she touched his forearm for emphasis while she talked, he twitched and moved away. And the vision of Carson's black hips rising and falling over her writhing body almost made him vomit. Carson had come to the Wilbur project once, and Raymond had had to race for the woods to keep from hurling himself at the bastard and gouging his thumbs into his windpipe.

Justin was being very friendly, had invited him along on this picnic, and had praised his fishing and firebuilding skills. Apparently, Raymond thought with resentment, I'm down and out enough now not to threaten him.

A cross had been burned on a hill overlooking the next town two nights earlier. But Raymond had learned by now to live with fear. He doubted that anyone could hurt him as much as Maria had. These Yankees abhorred physical violence so much, clucked their tongues about vicious rednecks, then unleashed such psychological violence on each other that a beating would have been preferable.

He noted that he was thinking of his comrades now as "Yankees."

In the middle of "We Shall Overcome," three crewcuts appeared over the edge of the dam. They stopped singing and watched three sunburnt faces appear, followed by three T-shirted chests, and six chinoed legs. One man held a tire iron, another a length of chain. The four hopped to their feet.

"This here's private property."

"We were just sitting here," Justin said in his belligerent New York accent. "We weren't doing anything."

"What was that there moaning coming out of yer mouth if you wasn't doing nothing?" The man looked at the other two and grinned.

"Well, yes, we were singing, true. But there's no law against singing, is there?"

Christ, Raymond saw that Justin was intent on getting them killed. Martyrs to the cause. For the first time he noticed Justin's hair curling over his collar. Neither of them had shaved today. They looked like bums.

"Naw, they ain't no law against singing. Unless you happen to be singing on private property. But you Reds don't hold with the notion of private property, do you?"

"We're not Communists," Raymond assured him.

"You with that there nigger-loving bunch from up North?"

"Uh, the voter registration project. Yes."

"Well, let's hear can you play 'Dixie' on that thang."

"I don't know 'Dixie,' " Justin said defiantly.

"I'll whistle it, and you see can you pick it up." The man whistled.

"Nope, I can't," said Justin, jutting his chin out.

"Try," the man said, menacingly raising his chain.

Justin eyed the chain and the tire iron, then fumbled with a few chords.

"Yall sing," said the man.

The other three sang "Dixie" in quavering voices.

"That's not real good. See can you sing it louder."

Justin threw down the guitar, dived into the pond and began to swim. The man brought his chain down and smashed the guitar, picked it up and broke its neck over his thigh and tossed the pieces into the pond.

"Run!" Raymond yelled to the girls as he threw a flying block at

290 O R I G I N A L   S I N S

all three men, bringing one down. Christ, what am I doing? he asked
himself.

He rolled into a ball and covered his head. His not fighting back
seemed to enrage them, rather than reform them. The fervor of the
blows increased, and they started snarling "fairy creep" and "Commie faggot." The chain slashed. The tire iron rose and fell. Fists and
shoes connected with bone and flesh. He caught glimpses of khakis
and T-shirts, flat tops and red faces. And he was flooded with sensations of—gratitude.

"Go back where you came from, you mother-fucking nigger-loving
Yankee do-gooder. Why don't you mind your own goddam bidness?"

Raymond sat in the sun on the roof, reading about himself in the
Chattanooga and Newland papers. He was covered with dark bruises.
His nose and several ribs had been broken, and he had stitches in his
scalp. He was a hero. Justin offered to shake wrists with him. Maria
invited him to the roof for a blow job, which he declined. All he
could think about was the gratitude he'd felt toward those guys. It
baffled and appalled him. He stared at his high school graduation
picture on the front page of the paper, his eyes shifting to the date
under the logo—May 2, 1964.

He looked out across the fields, carpeted by bright yellow dandelions. 1964. A hundred years ago these fields had been filled with
marching soldiers and booming artillery.

At this time of year in Tatro Cove he and Jed and their cousins
used to climb the hills filling paper sacks with dandelion blossoms,
which their grandpa would make into wine. In his cellar dandelion
wine from previous years would start fermenting again, as though
somehow aware that the fields were abloom. A few corks would blow,
spewing wine around the cellar.

Those boys had beaten him shitless thinking he was a Yankee. But
he was actually one of them—a redneck, cracker, peckerwood, clay
eater, poor white, white trash, hillbilly, ridge-runner, rebel, stump-
jumper. All labels pinned on Southern working people by the Yankees. He'd grown up surrounded by boys like those who'd beaten him
up. Any of the three could have been Jed. He knew all about their

stubborn pride, their trigger-quick anger, their resentment of outside criticism and coercion, their loathing of men who didn't display these characteristics. He understood what had provoked them into attacking him. They were descendants of the fierce over-mountain men who'd routed the British at King's Mountain. And so, by God, was he.

He climbed down from the roof and walked over to the Randalls', trying to decide what to do now that it was clear to him that his participation in the project was a bad joke. He watched the children playing house and snapped an occasional picture. Looking up, he saw Mr. Randall striding across the yard to say in a low trembling voice, "What you always hanging around here for, son?"

Raymond looked at him with surprise. "I . . ."

"Gwan. Get out of here. We don't want you round no more, hear?"

"But I . . ."

"Can't you hear me, son? I said gwan."

Raymond backed toward the road. As he turned to walk away, Mr. Randall caught up with him and handed him a crumpled piece of paper. The childish scrawl read "THIS CAN HAPPEN TO RED-LOVING NIGGERS TO."

"What can?"

"Killed our cat. Hung her up from a tree in the woods and set her on fire." His face crumpled, then quickly resumed its facade.

"Who did?"

"Whoever writ that note. Probably the same gentlemens who beat you all black and blue like that. So don't come out here no more. Please."

"I won't." He backed away, sweeping the surrounding woods and fields with his eyes. "I . . . shit, I'm sorry."

"Yeah, me too, son. Watch out now, hear?"

This was a result of the project, Raymond concluded. How he wasn't sure, but he meant to figure it out.

The project people concurred with his decision to return early to New York. Back there he spent hours studying the pictures he'd taken of sharecroppers. White or Negro, their houses, their crops, their clothes, their children's games and toys were identical. He put together a book juxtaposing photos of the Randalls and of white tenant families in identical poses in front of similar houses, and a publisher accepted it.

The others were soon back from Tennessee, and FORWARD meetings resumed. Raymond felt confused to be a hero as a result of an undertaking he now repudiated. Because Justin was being sarcastic to him, Raymond saw that he now had sufficient clout to influence the course of FORWARD—if only he understood in what direction to exert that influence. Unfortunately, he lacked Justin's brains and education.

Justin for the time being had them focusing on fund raising. Carson came up to see Maria, and FORWARD had a cocktail party at Justin's parents' penthouse on Central Park West. The large living room was packed with businessmen and college professors, writers and dancers, Louis XIV antiques and Aubusson carpets. Raymond, talking with a woman in a pale green silk suit, became riveted by her brooch—a silver turtle studded with diamonds.

As caviar and toast points were passed and Chivas Regal flowed, Carson in his Howard sweatshirt described his participation in the Montgomery bus boycott, and his experiences in the field registering voters. Raymond told his tired old story about growing up in a racist society and coming to see the light. Justin described the incident next to the pond and somehow emerged sounding like the hero. Maria glanced at Raymond and suppressed a grin. Raymond didn't grin back: She had her arm through Carson's.

Justin's father called the maid, whom he introduced as Mrs. Walters, in from the kitchen. She wore a wool dress instead of a uniform. The idea was that she was a friend who just happened to stop by to fix hors d'oeuvres. Mr. Lawson seated her on the couch and brought her some Scotch. A fat man in a pinstriped suit said as he sat down beside her, "Mrs. Walters, I want you to call me Luther." Justin began playing "Swing Low, Sweet Chariot" on his new guitar.

As people around the room began pulling out checkbooks, things clicked into place for Raymond. He looked at Carson and himself, performing like dancing bears for these Yankees in their jewels and Gucci shoes. In an instant, like a chemical solution crystallizing, he stopped seeing people as Negro or white—and instead saw them as rich or not. The Wilbur canning factory, the Newland mill, the Clayton mines—these Yankees with their pens poised over checkbooks probably owned them! These checks were a minute portion of their profits. As long as Negroes and whites in the South were kept busy hating each other because of skin color, they'd never recognize their shared exploitation. The violence those guys had unleashed on him by the pond—it was nothing compared to the quiet day-by-day draining away of the human and material resources of an entire area.

Raymond spent much of the following week in the Columbia Business School library on a pass Maria's father wrote for him. The Newland mill where his father had sweated blood for thirty-five years was now owned by a New York-based conglomerate. The corporation that owned the Wilbur canning factory was on the New York Stock Exchange. The Clayton mines where his grandfather had lost his arm were owned by a multinational oil corporation whose headquarters at Columbus Circle had towered over several of the rallies last fall.

Raymond drew up wall charts. One showed the board of directors of the corporation that owned the canning factory, and the other corporations on whose boards those directors sat. It looked like the web of a spider on amphetamines. Another illustrated the interlocking directorates of supposedly competing oil companies. A third chart listed social clubs to which directors of competing textile firms belonged: the Weston, Connecticut, Country Club; the Cohasset, Massachusetts, Yacht Club; the New York Yacht Club; the Princeton Club; the Westchester Golf Club; the New York Athletic Club; the New York Racquet and Tennis Club; the Harvard Club. A fourth chart listed the ten largest stockholders for the three corporations; almost all were New York banks, investment firms, and insurance companies.

As he carried his charts up the steps to the loft, Raymond was proud to have done a political analysis at last. Everybody would be impressed. Maria would fall in love with him on the spot and get rid of Carson.

Raymond finished by quoting how many millions of dollars in profits from the Newland mill, the Clayton mines, and the Wilbur canning factory were going to stockholders in the North: "Much of the hostility between races in the South concerns how to divide up a pie that's too small. The reason it's so small is that profits are leaving the region. FORWARD activities have pitted Negroes and poor whites against each other. I recommend we suspend our current operation and formulate new plans, based on a fresh analysis." He waited for hosannahs.

They looked at him as though he were an escapee from maximum security at the Bronx Zoo.

"I think he may have a point," murmured Maria.

"Are you out of your mind, Tatro?" inquired Morris.

"I think your beating has addled your brain," agreed Justin.

Emily gazed at him with uncomprehending sympathy.

Raymond looked back at them. His conclusions were self-evident. How could they fail to be overwhelmed? "But just think about these cats up here sitting on their asses in yacht clubs and getting dividend checks in the mail. While my father, who's worked for that mill for thirty-five years, is living in a wooden box on cinder blocks."

"So what?" asked Morris.

"What about you, Justin?" demanded Raymond. "That mansion in Newport built on money from the slave trade."

Justin looked startled. "That was over a hundred and fifty years ago."

"What was?" asked Maria.

Justin ignored her. "Besides, I'm using the bread the system yields me to try to alter that system."

"But I don't see why Emily and I are responsible for what goes on in the South if yall aren't responsible for what's going on up here."

"Thanks for the analysis, Raymond," said Justin. "OK, now what about this benefit next month, people?"

Raymond's book came out and received modest reviews. At a meeting Justin said, "Saw your book today, Raymond. A very handsome ego trip."

Raymond looked at him with distress. "I was trying to make a political statement."

He chuckled. "What about?"

"About the similarities between Negroes and poor whites in the South."

"Not a bad rationalization for ripping off the project."

"Ripping off the project?"

"All that time you spent wandering around the woods playing Hamlet, while the rest of us had to canvass your territory."

"I was non-functional, Justin. You could see that."

"Yeah, you let your personal emotional dramas destroy your revolutionary potential."

"I guess I did."

"I don't guess, I know."

"Man," said Morris, "you really did a job with that book, Raymond."

"What do you mean?" Raymond asked warily.

"Well, I mean, the way you romanticize poverty, man." He laughed derisively.

During the meeting Raymond thought about his book. He hadn't meant to romanticize his subjects. But he had intended to convey their dignity and decency and generosity, whether in spite of, or because of, their material deprivation. Wasn't that a valid point? Apparently not, to FORWARD. Was there nothing he could do to earn Justin's and Morris's respect?

Maria came up afterward. "You did a nice job with the book, Raymond."

"Thank you." He'd just been thinking about those farm wives—their loyalty, fidelity, forbearance. Maria, he'd finally realized, was nothing more than a camp follower, running from man to man as his stock rose and fell on the power exchange. It was no coincidence that she'd taken up with Carson right after that day when Justin had put Raymond down about registering the Randalls. Even if his penis was about to fall off from disuse, Raymond wouldn't entrust it to Maria again. Let's face it, he reflected, she was just along for the writhe.

"You're such a strange guy, Raymond. So aloof and lonely and determined to be an outsider. Newland's really scarred you."

He stared at her with disdain. "Everything that's best about me is a gift from Newland."

She shrugged. "OK, if you say so."

The next day he stayed home from work to go with his camera to the tip of Manhattan to the cotton exchange, to stand in the balcony looking down at the trading floor. Men formed tiered rings around the

central desk and shouted and gestured frantically with their hands.
They raced back and forth to telephones. The floor was littered with
wadded papers. A hum like a swarm of angry bees filled his ears.
Men like those at the party the other night were making and losing
thousands of dollars gambling on the cotton crops that the farmers in
his book hadn't even planted yet, crops the farmers themselves would
earn several hundred dollars on, after months of tilling, hoeing, spray-
ing, and picking in the hot sun.

He climbed on an uptown bus. When the driver handed him a
transfer, he smiled and said, "Thank you, sir." The driver looked at
him through narrowed eyes: What are you a nut or something,
buddy? The bus passed through the Bowery, where drunks lay sprawled
in doorways and up against mission walls and staggered through the
traffic asking drivers for quarters at stoplights. He got off the bus in
the East Fifties and walked west, past the elaborate townhouses of
the corporate executives. He stood on Park Avenue and stared at the
businessmen walking in and out of the glass and steel office buildings.
On Fifth Avenue he paused in front of Tiffany's. In the display
window was a turtle like that worn by the woman at Justin's party. He
walked inside. The guards eyed him and fondled revolver handles. He
asked a startled clerk how much the turtle brooch cost. The answer
was twelve thousand dollars. He headed for Times Square. A woman
in a tight dress with thick makeup handed him a card. On one side
was a price list. On the other, a photo of her, naked, lying on a
leopard skin, smiling. A Negro man in a flashy suit and slouch hat
sidled up and said from the corner of his mouth, "Hey, white boy, you
want you some brown pussy?"

"No, thanks."

"I can give you a real good price on it."

"No, thanks."

Up Broadway. The benches in its center strip were filled with old
people. He'd been forgetting to take pictures. On the sidewalk at
Eighty-fifth Street stood an aged ex-whore feeding an ice cream cone
to a poodle in a jacket and matching tam. He put on a telescopic lens
and raised the camera to his eye and focused. Before pressing the
button, he lowered the camera and stared at it. He took the strap
from around his neck. If Maria or Emily had been there, he'd have

dumped it in a trash basket or handed it to the nearest junkie. Since they weren't, he took it into a pawn shop and made a vow to send the money to the Randalls.

He could almost hear Mr. Fulton at Newland High, stabbing at the blackboard with his pointer and talking about the War between the States: "The real conflict, boys and girls, was between a bunch of farmers and a bunch of used car dealers who treated each other and everything they touched as raw material for moneymaking schemes. Certain aspects of what we were fighting for were worth fighting for, and the war isn't over."

That New Year, back in Newland, Raymond ate a plateful of black-eyed peas, then stood up and raised his glass: "To the New Year. And to the liberation of our homeland." His family smiled uneasily, not knowing what crazy Raymond was talking about now.

# Chapter Three

═══════════

## Donny

The apartment in Pine Woods where Donny and Rochelle lived was identical to the one Donny had grown up in except that it was crammed with furniture. Whenever people at the mill wanted to get rid of something, they told Donny. He'd pick it up and bring it home, whether he had any use for it or not. He hated to turn them down— seemed like it made them feel good to give him something they didn't want no more. But the apartment was starting to look like a junk shop, however much Rochelle tried to make it look nice, with pot plants in the windows and pictures she cut out of magazines on the walls.

Nicole, a year old, often refused to sleep on the Hide-A-Bed with Sue and Billy, Rochelle's youngest sister and brother. So that Donny, Rochelle, Nicole, and the baby sometimes ended up in one bed together.

"It ain't that I mind sleeping with my babies," Donny explained with a grin. They sat watching the news on television. Nicole climbed all over him while Rochelle suckled Isaac. A good-looking man in glasses was referring in a quiet voice to "white devils." Donny tried to hear what else he was saying, but Nicole was cooing in his ear and bouncing on his lap. His attention became fixed on not allowing her to give him an erection. Sue and Billy sat on the floor playing Go Fish.

"But when does you and me get any time alone together, mama?"

"Look to me like any more time alone together, and this whole place is gon fill up with babies."

"Yeah, you more like your mama every day." They laughed. "You get any more like her, and I'm cutting out," Donny added with a smile.

"Yeah, it's all my doing, ain't it?" She smiled back. "Well, I reckon we do need us some more room."

Donny looked at her and shrugged. "Where we gon get us more room from? Can't hardly pay for what we got." It looked like that colored man on the television had got himself shot. Well, you didn't run around calling white folks devils and expect to live. You could get in plenty of trouble without you called them nothing. Like his grandmaw was always saying, good manners was the best life insurance a colored person could have.

"I'm fixing to go back to maiding soon as I get this one off of my tit."

"You ain't never gon get that one off your tit. Appears he likes it there almost as much as I do." He felt a twinge of jealousy toward this tiny brown usurper, with his greedy little gums and his kneading fingers.

"Your grandmaw's gon mind them."

"Yeah, but I was fixing to save your maiding money for a car."

"A *car?*"

"Yeah, Leon's selling his Dodge."

"Shit, honey, we don't need us no car."

"It'd save me a heap of time not standing around waiting on the bus."

"Honey, that's all you got is time. Why, you don't need you no car when we can't hardly keep food on the table."

"I ain't noticed you starving none," Donny muttered, glancing at her ample figure.

"I just ain't had time to get my figure back is all."

"Get it back? Mama, it got such a headstart you ain't never gon catch up with it."

Rochelle started crying.

"Ah, come on now. I was just teasing. You look fine to me, baby. I sure hate it that I never get a chance no more to show you how fine."

"They gon be asleep soon. Then you can show me all you want to."

By the time the four children were shut in the bedroom, he'd lost interest. "Baby, I'm just too tired," he groaned as she lay on the couch stroking the crotch of his trousers. He remembered when they were first married how they'd sit at the kitchen table splitting a beer, and all of a sudden find themselves going at it on the floor while the pork chops burned in the frying pan. Shit, now, with children all over the place, they had to plan it nearly to death.

The next morning when the alarm went off, Donny stretched and kissed Rochelle awake. They got up quietly, careful to let the sleeping babies in the next room lie. She began frying grits while he pulled on the dark green work clothes a man in the roving room had given him. The trousers were baggy and had to be held up with suspenders. As he walked into the kitchen, he noticed that Rochelle was avoiding looking at him. He knew he looked like a rag doll. She hadn't bargained on this transformation from a basketball star who slithered around the court in yellow satin shorts, and who swaggered around school in trousers and matching Banlon shirts. But he hadn't figured on her bulging out of no maid's uniform neither. A librarian, she'd said. A teacher. He threw back his head in a silent snort.

"Look at me, Rochelle."

She glanced at him, startled by his tone. "What, honey?"

"Ah, nothing."

He sauntered out of Pine Woods toward the bus stop on the highway carrying his black lunch pail. Walking the same route were other men in dark green or khaki or dark blue work clothes, or denim overalls, whom he'd known his entire life. Several were on the board of deacons at Mount Zion with him. They were on their way to yard work on Tsali Street, stockroom or janitorial work downtown, jobs in the yard at the paper mill. Their wives worked as maids, and the families they worked for fetched them and brought them home. Sometimes the Princes sent Ruby home in a Checker cab. She'd emerge from the back seat, toting a jar of bacon grease, pretending not to notice all her neighbors, who'd never been in a taxi, watching her with respect.

Donny straightened his lanky frame and held his head higher. The first colored man on at the mill. His grandmaw had gotten Mr. Prince to hire him. It was steady, which almost none of these men had. Donny hummed, in between exchanging greetings and remarks about the warm sunny early spring morning. Randall Jarvis, who was on at the paper mill, strode past in his royal blue satin windbreaker with "Building Maintenance" stretched in gold across the back, and "Randall" over the front pocket. Donny eyed it and wondered if he could persuade Rochelle to get him one with her maiding money.

He began the day by breaking open bales and feeding them into the mixer. The air swirled with motes like in a snowstorm, and lint frosted the mixer parts. Donny wore a toboggan cap to keep the stuff out of his hair. When he didn't, his head ended up looking like a giant cotton boll. This whole thing was a mystery to him. You fed these clumps of cotton through all the machines in the other rooms, and you ended up with huge bolts of light grey cloth that got loaded in trucks and on boxcars and sent places to be dyed and turned into book jackets and stuff. You could call white men "devils" if you didn't mind getting yourself killed, but you had to confess that they was smart devils. All colored men knew how to do was work till they dropped dead from it. He'd never heard of none who could invent machines to save them from *having* to work.

As he swept up trash in the parking lot and emptied garbage cans, he glanced at the red-brick building with its round towers at each corner. He remembered The Five sitting in the Castle Tree looking down here and feeling proud to have the largest mill in the South under one roof in their very own town. Now that he knew what actually went on in there, the place didn't seem one bit less amazing.

He felt the spring sun on his back and was glad to be outdoors. On any given day he never knew just what he'd be doing, and he liked it like that. Sometimes he'd watch the white people running the machines—the exact same movement time after time, all day long, every day of the week—and wonder why they didn't go crazy. He was pretty lucky. Whistling, he studied the rows of late-model cars. On the other hand, doing those jobs paid them enough to buy these big cars. He stopped whistling.

He mopped the hallways to the locker rooms with disinfectant, making swirls down one side, then interlocking swirls up the other side. As he rested on his mop, he surveyed the pattern of dark maroon swirls on lighter dusty maroon. Hearing voices approaching, he began hurriedly erasing the pattern with his mop.

At the end of the afternoon he got off the bus and joined the straggly line of men walking back to Pine Woods. Their clean, pressed work clothes of that morning were dirty and wrinkled and sweat-stained, the lunch boxes empty. They avoided each other's eyes in a way they didn't at church when they wore dark suits and stiff blue-white shirts and stood at the ends of the pews passing the offering baskets.

The baseball team was practicing in the field next to the high school. He stopped and watched the coach pop flies to the outfielders. Every boy on that team saw himself as a future Jackie Robinson. Donny smiled. He remembered standing at shortstop during practice and watching the line of sweaty men home from work snake past. He'd felt sorry for them. He'd never get caught dead wearing dark green work clothes. He'd be wearing a satin warm-up suit and playing for the Knicks . . .

The cheerleaders were practicing a complicated clapping and shouting routine at the other end of the field. Almost every girl on the squad had been after him, but he'd wanted only Rochelle. He wondered if this crop of cheerleaders would find him as desirable. Or was it just that he was a big star back then? Was that what had made Rochelle want him? The cheerleaders, Rochelle, every girl in sight, used to think everything he did was wonderful. Seemed like now, though, he couldn't hardly do nothing right. Couldn't get it up when Rochelle wanted it, couldn't earn enough to get them a bigger place.

In front of Dupree's lounged men in sports clothes. They'd been hanging around all day, passing a bottle of Four Roses to celebrate spring. All winter they'd clustered around the kerosene heater in the pool room, moving away a couple at a time for games of Eight Ball. As the line of sweaty men filed past, those in front of Dupree's called out greetings, and received tired waves in reply.

Donny got into cream slacks and a matching pullover left over from high school. The slacks were too tight, and Nicole had chewed some snags in the shirt. As he strolled toward Dupree's, he glanced into the laundromat. Rochelle was sitting and talking with Charlene as she nursed the baby and joggled Nicole's stroller with her foot. She looked up and spotted him through the window just as he tried to duck behind the wall. She motioned him to come in. "How you, honey?"

He pecked her forehead.

"Just fine. How you?" He sat down, nodding to Charlene.

"You look real nice, Donny," said Charlene. "Real springlike."

"Thank you. Thought I'd go talk to them boys over to Dupree's."

"Honey, you know I don't like you hanging around them men."

"Mama, I knowed them cats all my life." Leon had come down from New York City not long ago calling everyone a "cat," and now the expression was all over Pine Woods.

"They a bad influence."

"Bad influence? What trouble is they to get into around this place?"

"Now, Donny, listen to me, hon. Them men don't work without they have to. Most has left their families. Half of them'll run off to New York City or Cincinnati, Ohio, by the end of the year. We seen it happen all our lives. Honey, I don't want to lose you."

He put his arm around her. "Baby, you ain't gon lose me." It was true: The men with families sat on their porches when they got home, and played with their children. They strolled up the street to the soft ice cream stand with their wives and kids. Once they joined the men at Dupree's, it was usually just a question of time before they left their families, and eventually left Pine Woods. Or ended up in the alley next to Dupree's drinking liquid shoe polish, after-shave lotion, and paint thinner.

But as they passed Dupree's, him carrying the baby and her pushing the stroller, he noticed her sideways glances at the men out front, the increased thrust of her milk-swollen breasts, the added sway to her hips. The men noticed, too, and watched her pass, not daring to comment with him there. But what about earlier in the afternoon when she'd gone down to the laundromat, while he was pushing his mop for her and these babies? He glanced at her. These cats were rested, and hungry for women because they weren't working. When they did, they spent the money on fancy clothes and let the county take care of their babies. What did she want—a stud, or a husband and father? Looked like she wanted everything.

In front of the Palace Theater some boys and girls from high school were flirting and bad-mouthing each other. The boys kept glancing at the men in front of Dupree's, copying the way they stood, the way they held their cigarettes, the way they examined and commented on each woman who passed, as though judging a dog show. Donny and Rochelle as they strolled past didn't even merit a glance. Although those kids were only three or four years younger than him, Donny felt like their father. He smiled.

"What you grinning about, nigger?" asked Rochelle.

"Those boys, they all think they gon be big heroes." He recalled sitting in the Castle Tree confidently planning to be a commando trooper in a camouflage uniform, a penthouse dweller in New York City. "They gon turn around all of a sudden and find out they ain't nothing but ordinary niggers like all the rest of us."

"What's funny about that?"

"What you want me to do, woman, cry?"

They strolled down the street of ranch houses belonging to Mr. Dupree, to the mortician, to the principal at the high school, to several of the teachers, to Reverend Stump. The houses were freshly painted, with shutters and shiny brass door knockers. Their gleaming windows reflected the spring sun.

"Wouldn't you just love a place like that, Donny? You reckon we'll have us one someday?"

"Don't see a way in the world."

She looked at him. "Mr. Can't never could do nothing."

A bigger apartment wasn't enough. Now she had to have her a house. He couldn't hardly keep up with her. What about the car *he* wanted? She wanted to settle in. Well, maybe he wanted to be all set to cut out. The street ended abruptly in a faintly greening cow pasture. They stood by the fence and watched a Holstein bull mount a heifer.

Rochelle asked, "How come you ain't like that ole bull, honey?"

"If you look real close, you'll see he ain't knocking off the same heifer time after time."

Rochelle glanced at him. "I was just teasing, hon."

"What you on about sex all the time for anyhow? Before we got hitched, it was all I could do to get me a kiss off of you."

"Well, I didn't want to go getting pregnant."

"And now you do?"

"Twice is enough."

"OK, so just shut up about sex then."

She looked at him.

He saw things different from her. He didn't think much beyond this evening. Tomorrow he'd do pretty much what he'd done today, last month, last year. Next year he'd still be doing it. Whereas she seemed to see him rising into jobs that paid more. She hadn't been able to turn herself into no librarian. How did she expect him to turn himself into someone who could buy her a ranch house? She'd been so excited when Mr. Prince phoned and told him to start work. The first colored person taken on at the mill—and even white people poured out of the hills when word got out that the mill was hiring. But here she still wasn't satisfied. He yanked Isaac's fingers out of his mouth. Isaac whimpered. He thrust him into Rochelle's arms and began shoving the stroller so savagely that Nicole began whimpering.

Raymond Tatro in his denim coveralls came up to Donny at work, glanced around, held out a blue card, and said, "Here you go, Donny. You want to sign this?"

Donny took the card. "What is it, Mr. Raymond?"

Raymond grimaced. "Just call me Raymond like everybody else, OK?"

Donny shrugged. "Sure. Whatever you say, Mr. Raymond. Raymond."

"It's a union card. You want to join the union?"

"I don't know nothing bout no union, sir."

"It's sort of like a club. With meetings and things."

Donny looked at him. Since when did whites want coloreds at their club meetings? Not since the Castle Tree.

"We working to get higher wages and health benefits and a pension plan and all like that."

"How you do that?"

"Well, we all join together and ask for them. And if we don't get them, we stop working."

"Mr. Prince, he won't like that, will he?" He felt gratitude toward Mr. Prince and wasn't studying to go doing nothing that might upset the man.

"Mr. Prince won't care. He's got him his big house on the hill. He don't own this company anymore anyhow. A bunch of rich men up North do."

"You sure about that? Mr. Prince, he all the time talking about us being one big happy family."

Raymond laughed. "Yeah, we one big happy family, all right. But Big Daddy, he's up in New York City running around on us. But we gon get us our share."

"Yeah, all right. I'm with you, Raymond." He signed the card and handed it back, feeling proud to be asked to join.

"Don't talk about this to nobody. We just trying to get going. I'll let you know what's happening."

"It ain't dangerous or nothing like that? I don't want no trouble."

"Huh-un. It's just a little bit secret for right now."

He watched Raymond walk away. Didn't know what to make of the man. He turned up at the mill last fall, seeming rushed and tense. Just like Donny's mama. Going off up North did weird things to people. His grandmaw told how Emily had come down to her apartment last Christmas after just a few months up at New York City and had stood around squinting and frowning and shifting from foot to foot like a nutcase. It'd be real interesting to know just what went on up there, to make folks act so strange.

At supper Donny announced, "We might could start looking around for a bigger place, mama. I gon get me a raise."

Rochelle looked at him, delighted, and ushered the four children into the bedroom after finishing up the dishes. They made love on the sofa, like when they were first married.

The next day as Donny was pushing a broom through the card room, he heard Raymond and Al Grimes talking behind some machines.

". . . ain't setting at meetings next to no lazy, stinking, stupid niggers, Tatro. Lots of others feel the same."

". . . motherfucking bigots . . ."

". . . new here, Tatro . . . ain't running this show . . ."

Mr. Al tracked Donny down in the spinning room and handed him his blue card, torn in half. "I'm real sorry, Donny. Mr. Tatro didn't know colored people ain't allowed to join no union."

Raymond walked up later, averted his eyes, and mumbled, "... really disgusted ... won't always be like this ..."

Donny grinned. "Don't you worry none, Mr. Raymond. I be just fine."

Raymond walked away. What *was* the matter with that man? Donny was the one not allowed in the union. What was it to Raymond anyhow? Donny didn't need his sympathy. Sympathy didn't pay the rent on no bigger apartment.

Donny propped open the door to the ladies' room with a trash can and began cleaning the toilets. As he scrubbed, he wondered how come white folks thought niggers was lazy and dirty. Seemed like that him and Rochelle, his grandmaw and mama, most of his neighbors spent their whole lives working at trying to keep things neat and clean. The dirt went from the white folks' homes and factories onto you, and then you toted it home. But where did it come from in the first place? He scrubbed at a toilet bowl ferociously.

Back home Donny studied his face in the bathroom mirror. His mother's almost white features, his father's darker coloring. He used to go for months without being aware of himself as a colored man. But lately, seemed like he was always seeing his dark nose from the inner corner of his eye. What would it be like to look down there and see a pink nose?

He turned away. His skin stretched taut over his cheekbones like a mask of badly tarnished copper, a mask that marked him for life. Ah, shit. All he wanted was to earn enough money to move his family into a bigger goddam apartment. Buy himself a crumbling junkheap of a second-hand Dodge. He stared at Rochelle's jars of vanishing cream and bottles of hair oil and remembered taking a jar of vanishing cream up to the Princes' one day. The Five had slathered themselves with it, then waited to vanish. That dumb Sally had been scared to death she wouldn't reappear. They'd finally had to accept that it was the *cream* that vanished, not the people wearing it. Donny saw his dark face smile in the mirror, felt himself relax a little.

Rochelle was sitting on the sofa in the lamplight watching "Wagon

Train." He plopped down in the armchair and gazed at her. The woman was beautiful. Like his mother and grandmother, she had light skin. Almost like the women in magazines and on television and in movies. Unlike himself. Her father might have been a white man. Maybe one of the cats who didn't want his unknown colored son-in-law to join his motherfucking union. He felt the tension building again.

"What you staring at, nigger?"

He smiled faintly. "You."

"See anything you like?"

He said nothing.

"Well, don't just set there looking. Come on over here and do something about it." She stretched out her arms and he went, but was unable to fulfill the rest of her request. She ran her hand over his rough head and cooed, "Don't matter none, sugar. Don't get all upset now." But he already was.

At Saturday morning breakfast Rochelle asked, "When you reckon that raise is coming through, Donny?"

"Ain't sure it is no more."

A long silence. "Well, I sure do hate to hear that."

"Yeah, I'm sure you do."

"Don't be like that, honey."

"Like what?"

"Mean-mouthed." She burst into tears.

"Ah, hell, don't, mama. Listen, I'm sorry."

She sniffled. "I'm sorry honey. It's just that my monthly's a couple of weeks late. What we gon do?"

"We be all right," he said, touching her hand. A car horn sounded out front. Mr. Prince picking him up for yard work.

"I got to go," he said, kissing her quickly. "Be good now."

In the car he nodded to Mr. Prince. "Mighty fine day, sir?"

"Yes, sir, sure is. Thought I might play some golf."

As they drove under the railroad bridge, Mr. Prince cleared his throat. "Donny, there's something I want to talk to you about."

"Yes sir?"

"This union business."

"Yes sir?"

"Mr. Mackay is thinking about letting some of those people go."

"Yes sir."

"They were doing union business on company time."

"Yes sir."

"It's not that he minds employees considering being represented by a union."

"No sir."

"But he does mind their doing it on company time."

"Yes sir."

"Now Donny, I hear you signed up to join. Is that right?"

"They told me you wouldn't care none."

He sighed. "Not unless it's on company time."

"Yes sir."

"My son-in-law, Jed Tatro, says he doesn't believe you understood what was going on. Is that correct?"

"They say if you join the union, you get you a raise in pay." Goddam that Raymond Tatro anyhow. Promised him he wouldn't get in no trouble.

"Well, it's not quite that simple. But do you really feel you're not being paid enough for the work you do?"

"Well sir, Mr. Prince, sometimes it's hard to make ends meet, with two babies and another on the way."

"Another baby? Congratulations. That's wonderful."

"Thank you, sir."

"Well, if you need more income, I can speak to my neighbors about yard work. I can certainly recommend you."

"Yes sir. Thank you, Mr. Prince. I surely would preciate that."

"But let's not have any more union stuff on company time, all right?"

"Yes sir. But they wouldn't let me join anyhow, sir."

"They *wouldn't*?"

"No sir."

"Ah."

As Mr. Prince turned into his driveway, Donny felt a surge of gratitude. It was the same gratitude he felt when Mr. Prince paused on his tours of the shop floor in his shirt-sleeves to remark to Donny on the weather. The white people at their machines noticed and sometimes made a point of talking to Donny themselves later the same day. With the sleeve of his work shirt he polished a dirty spot on the front fender of Mr. Prince's Mercury as he walked past. Mr. Prince nodded his thanks.

After a day cutting grass, Donny went to the back door of the big yellow house. Mrs. Prince was wearing a flowered dress that kind of clung around her hips. Her long dark hair, curling up on the ends, bounced and swung as she handed him a glass of lemonade, a jar of bacon grease for Ruby, and his eight dollars. He stood far away from her as he drank, feeling his green work shirt with sweat stains the size of cow piles under the arms would be offensive. Rochelle's maid dresses were always stained like this at the end of a day, but did white women sweat? Not that he'd ever seen. Mrs. Prince he always thought of as standing at a third-floor hospital window in a white gown, tossing foil-wrapped chocolate-covered cherries to The Five on the lawn below, after giving birth to Robby. He smiled at her shyly, then ducked his head.

"You look all tired out, Donny."

"Naw, ma'am. I be just fine. Just a little hot is all."

Walking from the bus stop to his apartment, he turned down the street of ranch houses that Rochelle coveted. He wished he could get her one. The Princes' big yellow house, colored people didn't live in places like that. But these here ranch houses had been built, were owned by colored people. How'd they done it? They owned businesses, were teachers, a dentist, preachers. Most had been to college. He could have gone. He had good grades, could have won a basketball scholarship. Instead he dropped out his junior year to marry Rochelle. He remembered being obsessed with not letting Leon steal her away from him. Leon, with his wallet stuffed with bills from pimping in New York. Donny had to find a job, get some cash. But how come nobody warned him what life was really all about?

Then he remembered he had been warned. But since the advice came from his mama, who'd left him and Pine Woods behind, he hadn't been able to hear it. So here he was with a pregnant wife and two babies in a two-room apartment. His mother was disgusted when she found out he'd dropped out of school to get married and had hardly been in touch since. But he was doing it, goddam it. Between the mill job and the yard work, he was supporting this show. Lots of men in Pine Woods just gave up after a while, and hung out in front of Dupree's, or left the area. But he wouldn't never give up.

He stopped off to give Ruby her bacon grease. She was sitting in an armchair in a head cloth, quilted bathrobe, and high-topped tennis shoes, watching "Wild Kingdom" on television. The doctors had decided she had leukemia, but it was OK now. "In transmission," she'd reported.

"Hey, Grandmaw. What you know good?" This was another phrase Leon had brought down from New York. He kissed her.

"Humph. Don't know nothing good," she growled. "How you, baby boy?"

"Well, I ain't no baby no more, that's for sure." He laughed.

"Poor old thing. Got yourself tied down too early, if you want to know what I think."

"Can't afford to hear that, Grandmaw. I in it now up to my neck. Just got to keep on treading water."

"The cross, and the strength to tote it, Donny. Look to your Lord."

There was a dance that night at the Masonic Hall with a live band from Charlotte. Tadpole was home from Fort Campbell and turned up in his uniform with badges and braid and shit all over him. He and Rochelle danced to "Reach Out, I'll Be There," while Donny watched, too worn out from yard work to cut in. Rochelle strutted and batted her false eyelashes, her fat swaying. Tadpole stomped his paratrooper boots in time to the music. Rochelle threw back her red wig and laughed a throaty laugh, her eyes meeting Tadpole's and narrowing suggestively. Donny never saw her like this anymore himself. She was always rinsing diapers in the toilet, hollering at the kids, nagging him for a bigger place, or busting the seams of her maiding outfit. He watched her prancing around in her high heels and stockings and felt himself getting hard for the first time in a couple of weeks. He wondered if he should jump up and drag her out back and stuff it in her, with her leaning up against the wall in the alley, as Leon had been known to do.

Shit, he didn't even have the energy to get up out of his chair. He'd spent all day earning money to pay their bills, trying to figure out how to get her her ranch house—and there she was moving her hips against Tadpole's. He smashed his fist down on the table so that all the glasses jumped, but no one noticed. Goddam, what did that woman want, anyhow? He almost started crying, but Rochelle and Tadpole were on their way back to the table. Instead he smiled and said, "Yall looked real sharp together."

He was still thinking about Rochelle's hips moving against Tadpole's the next morning as he stood with his hand folded at the end of a pew waiting for the offering basket. Rochelle stood up front in a white robe with the rest of the choir singing, "Don't Call the Roll Yet, Jesus, Cause I'm Coming Home." Leon could make money better than him, and Tadpole could make love better. Well, if Rochelle wanted to be married to Donny, she'd just have to find herself some other reason. The Reverend Mr. Stump had just preached on some verses from Ecclesiastes about the need to remember the Lord even when you was young and didn't have the threat of decay and death hanging over you to reveal the vanity of all things of the flesh. "Fear God, and keep His commandments: for this is the whole duty of man." Mr. Stump had pointed out how you couldn't run a church on shouting because the spirit came and went, but the electric bills was always with you. You had to run a church on your sense of duty, fortified at random times by the shouting. Donny figured it was the same with marriage. Hard-ons came and went, but the rent didn't vary. Children had to get fed and washed. But did that mean that sex went out the window once you got hitched? He'd thought being married meant you'd get it regular. It never occurred to him you might not *want* it regular. Did it mean you got it somewhere else, from somebody not all wore out by all that duty? He glanced at Rochelle's familiar face and felt loss. But as far as he knew, she wasn't gone yet. All he had to do to keep her was to get him a raise and get it up. Both of which he aimed to do.

Walking home, he carried Nicole on his hip. She wore small black Mary Janes and white socks and a starched white dress a woman at the mill had given him. Rochelle wore a pink linen suit and straw hat and white gloves. "You look real nice, Rochelle."

"So do you, sugar." She carried Isaac, asleep in his little jacket and bow tie. Donny suspected she didn't really think so. If he'd been wearing a Special Forces uniform like Tadpole, or a flashy suit and slouch hat like Leon, or a satin warm-up suit like he used to wear, then she'd be thinking he looked nice. As things were, in his dark suit and white shirt and tie, the youngest deacon, he knew he looked like her uncle. He just didn't know what to do anymore.

At work that week he had a dizzy spell. The mill nurse checked him over and told him he had high blood pressure and had better find ways to take it easy. He decided the yard work would have to go for a while, so he consolidated his debts into one loan from Harmony Home Finance Company.

The following Saturday morning he found himself watching cartoons with the kids. Nicole sat on his lap bouncing and waving her little arms at Bugs Bunny. A commercial came on for a doll that drank from a bottle and wet its diapers.

"Dat!" Nicole shrieked. "Want dat! Daddy, want dat!"

As the morning rolled on, Billy or Sue or Nicole registered their desire for each toy shown on the screen—things to ride on, a walkie-talkie, a doll's house. They wanted them all.

Abruptly, Donny pushed Nicole off his lap. She landed on the floor and began screaming. Sue and Billy looked at him. It was different from what he'd imagined. When the kids were Rochelle's mother's, everything he'd done for them had made him look good. All the women in Pine Woods had exclaimed over what a marvel he was. His own kids, though, just made him feel like a flop. He couldn't never give them the things they wanted. Couldn't hardly even give them the things they needed.

"What you doing to that child?" Rochelle called from the bathroom, where she was bathing Isaac.

"Ain't doing nothing." He stalked to the door. "Going out."

"You what?"

"Out. I'm going out." He slammed the door on her protests. He meant to take a walk and cool down some, but he found himself heading for Dupree's.

"Hey," he said to the group out front, slapping a shoulder, punching an arm, shaking a hand. He felt real self-conscious, even though he'd known most of these men all his life. He'd generally avoided this scene. But there couldn't be no harm in him chatting with them, maybe cheering himself up.

"Who we got here? Why, I do believe it's Mr. Donny Good Boy Tatro himself!"

He lounged on the curb for the rest of the morning, while different men went into the shop and emerged with soft drinks or candy bars. Occasionally a bottle of Four Roses in a brown paper bag was passed. Cigarettes were shared.

A hefty woman in curlers leaned out an upstairs window in the apartment complex and bellowed, "Paul Morton, you get your ass home this minute!"

"Old lady, you go get stuffed!" he called back.

Donny listened as the group mimicked her savagely. He'd always done his best to keep the women around him happy. It had never occurred to him to mock them.

Donny went into Dupree's to get himself a Moon Pie. On the wall next to Martin Luther King hung a picture of Jack Kennedy, surrounded by a wreath of plastic flowers. Mr. Dupree sat behind the counter slowly fanning himself with the Newland *News*.

"What you know good, Mr. Dupree?"

"Huh?" He looked up from his fanning.

"Yall right this morning?"

"Yeah, I reckon."

That cat looked like he didn't know what hit him ever since the voter registration people cleared out last fall. He'd been a big man for a while there, letting them use the room above his luncheonette for an office. He and Mrs. Dupree and various other members of the African Methodist Episcopal church had put them up at their houses and fed them.

Donny's grandmaw told about some of them, including Charlene, coming to her place to get her to go down to the courthouse and register. She asked them to leave saying, "I ain't voted for seventy-six years, and I ain't studying to start now." Later she said to Donny, "The idea of a bunch of chilrun coming by and telling *me* how to run my life! Why, I remember that Charlene wetting her panties while she was jumping rope on the sidewalk right outside this door!"

But Donny knew his grandmaw had to be against anything the African Methodist Episcopal church body was for. As for himself, he'd tried to stay in good with them all. Hell, he'd be nice to anyone who was nice to him.

". . . Now, a light-skinned woman, she'll turn on you so fast . . ." The talk in front of Dupree's drifted up into the warm spring air like cigarette smoke.

"Hell, she'll turn you *on* so fast too."

"Yeah, that Lorraine, she was something else. I loved that woman, but I just couldn't give up chasing pussy. Not even for her. So she kicked my ass out."

"Well, marrying, shoot. I used to think it was a big deal—responsibilities and all like that. Make a man of you."

"Shit, make a motherfucking mouse of you."

Seemed to Donny like sour grapes. They couldn't make it work, so they dumped on it. A couple of the men glanced at him.

"Where's Willie at?"

"Done been inducted. They sending him off to that war over at Asia."

"What war, man?"

"Some war I seed on the TV."

"Ole Willie over there at Asia?"

"That what his mama say."

"Well, I guess Asia beats the shit out of Pine Woods, Tennessee."

"Why don't you leave?"

"Where I gon go, nigger, with no cash on me?"

"Hitch somewheres. They say Cincinnati, Ohio's, real nice."

Donny couldn't believe the ease with which they talked of leaving. But the more they talked, the less terror the notion aroused in him. For a few days he tried to stay away from Dupree's. But it was hard to resist hearing them turn their failed marriages and inability to support their children into triumphs of manliness and courage. The exact opposite of everything the congregation of Mount Zion had been telling him his whole life. Felt like a real relief, and one that was enabling him to keep his nose to that grindstone. Rochelle had gone back to maiding, but was vomiting and bleeding from her pregnancy and seemed tired all the time. He'd of liked her to be able to stay home, but they needed her salary to cover the payments to Harmony Home Finance.

One afternoon after work she was in the bathroom vomiting. Donny, still in his work clothes, lay in a chair in the living room gazing at Nicole and Isaac as they messed around on the floor. There wasn't nothing in the world he could do to prevent them from turning out exactly like him and Rochelle. Seemed like the biggest favor he could do was to bash their brains in and get it over with.

In between heaves Rochelle called, "Honey, when you reckon we could move into a bigger place?"

Donny leaped up and yelled, "Shit, what do you want from me, woman? I give you every penny I earn!"

She came out, her uniform stained down the front. "I want you to act like a man again, Donny. I want you to spend time with me and your children. I want you to head up this family, instead of sneaking off all the time to that gang over by Dupree's. Honey, I want you to laugh and joke with *me* instead of them. I need you, Donny."

He almost walked over and took her in his arms. Instead he growled, "Shit, woman, I can't head up nothing. I couldn't organize a fuck in a whorehouse."

He stomped out as she shouted, "Honey, please stay here with us this afternoon."

"I can't take much more of her shit, man," he complained to the others.

"Yeah, know what you mean, man."

He looked down at the sidewalk, littered with cigarette butts, candy wrappers, some shards from a broken Four Roses bottle. He knew every square inch of this sidewalk. He'd played hopscotch and jacks and marbles, had jumped rope, roller-skated, and ridden tricycles and bicycles all up and down its grey pocked length. After his mama left, he'd carefully stepped on each of its cracks, hoping to break her back. His bare feet had slapped along it in the summer. In brand-new tennis shoes he'd sprinted up it in the spring. In rubber boots he'd danced in its gleaming puddles during the winter rains. His mother had done all these things before him, Sue and Billy were doing them now. Yet his own mother, these men he was standing with, dozens before them could just pick up and leave it all behind?

Could he? Never mind about Rochelle and his grandmaw and Nicole and Isaac. What about this old grey sidewalk?

The more time Donny spent in front of Dupree's, the more time Rochelle spent at Mrs. Baxter's, leaving the children with Ruby. When they were both home, she talked a lot about which white women had which silver or crystal patterns, which she liked best. She said she loved it when Mrs. Baxter went off to the Garden Guild meetings and she could kick off her shoes and lie on the plush living room carpet she'd just vacuumed, listening to the silence and smelling the lemon and beeswax polish she'd just rubbed on the antiques, knowing the house would stay almost this straight and clean until the next time she came.

"Yeah?" said Donny. "Well, I'm glad you like it over there so good, Rochelle. Cause over here it's like the garbage dump."

"How would you know? You ain't never here."

"I'm here about as much as you are, mama."

They got behind with Harmony Home Finance. Two men came to repossess the TV. Donny sat and watched glumly as they toted it out the door, then he walked over to Ruby's to pick up the children. He plopped down in a chair and told her about the TV as she shook her head in disbelief.

Mrs. Saunders from next door came in all upset, explaining that she'd just had news that her son in Vietnam had lost a leg.

"Law," sighed Ruby, "I hate to hear that. Seem like they's trouble all around. Donny gets him the blood pressure. And now they come and cart away his TV set. Lord, Lord."

One night Leon was visiting, and Donny and Tadpole went riding in his new yellow Pontiac. Tadpole was getting shipped off to Vietnam the next week. As they drove out the highway through town, a reporter on the radio was describing rioting and looting in Watts. Some cat in the background hollered, "This is for Selma, man!"

"Who she?" asked Donny.

Leon and Tadpole laughed. Donny couldn't figure out why. On the far side of town they pulled into the Barbecue Pit.

Donny said, "Hey, man, you hadn't oughta stop here. You cats is been gone too long. They don't serve niggers here."

"You ever try?" asked Leon.

"Well, no, but you know how things is here. You might as well stay where they wants you at."

"Why?" demanded Tadpole.

Leon turned off the engine, and they sat there for a while. Eventually a white girl in short-shorts and cowboy boots and a ten-gallon hat swayed up. She bent over, her order pad poised, looked into the car, then straightened up and walked away.

"See what I done told you," Donny mumbled.

"Well, we'll just set here a spell, see does she change her mind."

"Aw, come on, Leon. Never mind. Let's go over to Hog Heaven."

Leon and Tadpole sat back, grinned, and lit cigarettes.

Suddenly the car was surrounded by half a dozen white men in T-shirts and khakis. One twanged the radio antenna. Another tried to unscrew the hood emblem.

Donny sat very still. Tadpole and Leon squashed out their cigarettes, their eyes nervous. Donny was sure his showed pure terror.

"Something we can do for you fellers?" one said into the window to Leon. He repeatedly flicked open, then closed, a switchblade.

"We waiting to order," Leon said evenly.

"This place, they don't serve niggers."

"I see," said Leon.

"Yall some more of them there civilian rights people?"

"Huh-un," Leon said. "We live over at Pine Woods."

"Sure you do. That's how come you to have New York license tags." They laughed. A white hand grabbed every door handle.

"I live up there, but I grew up down here. I'm home visitin." Leon inched his fingers toward the key in the ignition.

"Where'd you get this car from, nigger?"

"Bet he stole it," one man announced.

"I bought it."

Donny looked out his window and discovered the man about to open his door was Jed Tatro. Their eyes met and locked. Finally Jed said, "Lay off them, boys. They really are from Pine Woods. I recognize this boy in the back here."

"How come you to stop here if you're from Pine Woods? You know bettern that."

Leon looked at him.

"I asked you a question, boy."

"I forgot," Leon mumbled.

"Well, don't forget again, or you might get yourself hurt. They sometimes put fancy ideas into niggers' heads up at New York City."

They drove off in silence.

"Bastards!" Leon finally murmured. "Motherfucking white devils!"

Donny felt rage building. His hands twitched with wanting to be around one of those muscled sunburned necks. He wanted to watch some white face turn pink, then red, then purple. Wanted to see those cold blue eyes bulging.

"Yall better get the hell out of this place," Leon counseled. "While you can still get it up at all."

Tadpole snarled, "Yeah, man, I see how it is. I get to fight their motherfucking war, but I don't even get to eat their goddam barbecues."

The next morning Mr. Stump preached on the verse "Be not hasty in thy spirit: For anger rests in the bosom of fools." Donny thought about it as he took up the offering and was alarmed at his rage last night. They beat up Jesus and shoved a crown of thorns on his head. He didn't fight back. But now two thousand years later, everybody knew about Jesus Christ, and who knew anything about those Roman soldiers?

He was scared of how much he wanted his hands around some white throat. It was being with Tadpole and Leon. They'd always been a bad influence on him. His grandmaw was right. He didn't want no trouble. He didn't want to harm nobody. Besides, he had to take it easy like the nurse at the mill warned or his blood pressure would shoot sky high again.

Walking home, he decided to do anything he could to make things peaceful. He put his arm around Rochelle. "I'm sorry I been messing up lately, mama. I guarantee you I gon do better from now on. That's a promise."

For the next several weeks he stayed away from Dupree's. The men called to him as he walked home from work, "Hey, Donny, where you been at, man? You coming over after you change?"

"Gotta spend some time with the family, man. Know what I mean?"

Hands waved him away, dismissing him once again as Mr. Junior Church Usher, Donny Good Boy Tatro. But so what? This was how he wanted to live his life—fulfilling his responsibilities to the people he loved, staying clear of people he didn't love or who didn't love him. Taking it easy. Rochelle had stopped nagging him and was at home more often. Some afternoons they'd meet in the kitchen before picking up the kids, split a beer, and talk over that day. A time or two they ended up on the floor or the couch or the bed. It was beginning to seem almost like old times again, and he was glad.

He started doing some light yard work on Saturdays, and some afternoons after work. That, plus his salary, plus Rochelle's wages, kept them abreast of the bills from Harmony Home, plus rent and groceries. They even got them another TV. But Isaac's toes turned in too far, and the doctor recommended casts, then a brace during the night. Rochelle's teeth started going bad from the pregnancy. They still hadn't paid the midwife for Isaac and here another was coming. But Donny was determined to make it through and out the other side. His mother sent money from New York, and Ruby cashed in her burial insurance.

One day as he was sweeping around the loading platform, Al Grimes came up and gave him two old pipes.

"Why, I surely do thank you, Mr. Al." He grinned and took them, even though he didn't smoke.

"I think you'll enjoy them, Donny. They draw real good."

"Yes sir, I reckon I will."

After work Donny caught the bus to Tsali Street. He understood he was exhausted when he heard a white man opposite him growl, "What you looking at, boy?" He'd been staring straight through the man.

"Nothing, sir," he mumbled, lowering his eyes.

"You calling me nothing?"

"No sir," Donny said, closing his eyes, silently begging the man not to give him a hard time.

"Watch out who you stare at, boy, or you'll wish you had."

"Yes sir," Donny sighed, burying his face in his hands.

"Did you listen at what I said, boy?"

"Yes sir."

"Cause it's for your own good." The man had decided to lecture him rather than torment him. Hard to say which was worse. "Now, some men, they'd as soon kill you as have you staring at them all insolent like you was doing."

"I'm sorry, sir. I didn't know I was. I'm just so tired."

"Tired? Who ain't tired, young feller?"

"Yes sir. I reckon so."

"You reckon so. Well, I *know* so." The bullying tone returned. "If the good Lord meant us to rest, He wouldn't of given us two hands to do His works with, I always say."

"Yes sir."

"The onliest ones who ain't tired is resting in their graves. Or setting on their cans up on Tsali Street."

Donny smiled faintly and nodded. "Yes sir, ain't it the truth?"

"How would you know, boy? I don't reckon you hang around much with Tsali Street folks."

"I works in their yards. That's where I'm headed now."

The bus had reached his stop, and he stood up.

"Take my advice, son, and keep your eyes to yourself after this."

"I surely will." Donny grinned, wanting to claw the ugly pink cheeks and watch blood well up. He reminded himself to relax or the high blood pressure would come back.

He trimmed hemlock hedges, each opening and closing of the shears feeling like his last movement on this earth. As he mowed the lawn, he reflected on how he knew every square inch of this yard, every hollow in the hedges, every boulder and leaf pit, from playing Kick-the-Can with The Five on summer evenings.

The Princes were out, but a jar of bacon grease and his check sat on the back step. He walked down Tsali to the bus stop on the highway. He'd just missed one bus, and another wasn't due for twenty minutes. Going into Anderson's Drugstore where The Five used to buy grape snowcones, he leaned on the soda fountain counter and wiped his sweaty upper lip and forehead with his shirt-sleeve. The counter was almost full, and a woman in a white dress was busy filling orders. Her hips strained against the tight white cloth of her uniform.

"What can I get you, honey?" she asked as she rushed past.

"Just a glass of water, please ma'am."

She filled a glass and shoved it down the counter. He said, "Thank you, ma'am." And downed it in one long gulp. As he walked toward the door, he could see her reflected in the plate glass window. Looking up, she studied him. She looked toward the druggist behind the prescription counter, looked back at Donny, gazed at the empty glass in her hand, gave a couple of people at the counter a perplexed look, shrugged, and tossed the glass into the garbage can, where it splintered.

He heard Rochelle in the kitchen opening a bottle of beer. Almost whimpering, he took her in his arms and buried his face in her neck, unable to speak.

"Whew, nigger, you stink!" she exclaimed with a laugh, pushing him away. He felt his arm draw back. His fist smashed into her laughing mouth. She screamed. Time after time his fists sank into her flesh. He caught glimpses of her terrified face—her pale face. The face of the mother who left him, the face of the woman at the Majestic Theatre, the face of the woman at the soda fountain, the face of Mrs. Prince handing him bacon grease. Stinking cunts, all of them. He was a nigger, but at least he wasn't no stinking cunt. Blood dribbled down Rochelle's chin. His fist smashed into her pale cheekbone.

She grabbed the beer opener and raked it down his face. He clutched at his left eye, as it filled with blood, and stumbled out of the apartment.

# Chapter Four

═══

# Jed

Jed picked up his black lunch pail. "Be good now," he counseled Sally, pecking her cheek.

She bounced Joey on her hip. "When do I ever get a chance to be anything else?"

"It's a good thing. I'd beat hell out of anyone who touched you." This was true, too. The mere idea of Sally lying in some other man's arms and revealing that Jed had hemorrhoids and sometimes missed the bowl when he pissed could make him frantic.

Sally laughed. "You make me feel like Rapunzel or something."

"That's just how I think of you, darlin. The princess at the top of my tower. Am I right?"

"Yes, hon, you sure are."

They kissed while Joey grunted, trying to push Jed away.

As he got in his Chevy left over from high school, Jed surveyed his home. He'd paid off twenty-five percent already; in sixteen more years it would be all theirs. He glanced at his calendar watch. In 1981, to be exact. He'd been over every square inch, inside and out, with his own hands—scraping and painting, puttying and pasting up the wallpapers Sally had picked out. He was building a third bedroom on the back for Joey. He was making payments on a TV console, and a new Dodge wagon for Sally and the kids. He'd mowed, pruned, weeded, trimmed, and planted throughout the small yard, built a sandbox, set up a swing set. He'd married the prettiest girl in town, had two cute babies—his son first, then a daughter. He'd be a fore-man over at the mill before long. Maybe in a few more years a supervisor. Who knew after that? Maybe production manager, or even operations manager. Anything was possible. After all, his father started out a broke, uneducated hillbilly, and here he was today recently promoted to supervisor. Yes, all right, he'd messed up in high school, with him and Sally cheating the starter and all. But he'd been doing real good ever since. Besides, most everbody believed the story about them being secretly married. Or pretended to.

His plans for the future included joining the Elks, and buying him a motorboat. And maybe a new car—a T-Bird.

Recently Hank said to him, "Yeah, and when Sally's old man dies, I bet you gonna come into a bundle, buddy."

This had never occurred to Jed. He'd been aware that her daddy ran the mill and her family had them a fancy house. But he hadn't figured it had much to do with him, apart from making him feel like a big shot to be Sally's steady. But maybe Hank was right. Maybe Sally would be rich someday—and him too as her husband. They could buy a new house in a development, take trips to Disneyland with the kids, eat out, everything. He grinned.

Jed drove slowly through the streets where he'd spent his whole life, past the house where he'd grown up. He could recite the life histories of most people here. He liked knowing each day exactly who he'd see and what he'd be doing. Hardly ever did he have to face anything he hadn't planned on.

He smiled thinking about making love that morning right after the alarm went off. He'd woke up with a big hard-on, had just rolled over and put it to her. He liked it best in the morning, when he was rested. And since he had to go to work, it had to be over with fast. At night and on the weekends you had to go into all that do-you-really-really-love-me junk that sometimes made jerking off seem preferable. He didn't understand why Sally couldn't just take it for granted that he really really loved her. Why did they have to go over it time after time? It was like the Lord's Prayer at church—after a while it stopped meaning anything. The secret agent in the paperback he was reading said, "I've never told any woman I love her. I don't know if I'll even be alive tomorrow, and it's not fair to let you think you can count on me. But if only my life were like other men's, believe me, Rachel, I would want to spend it with you." Coach Clancy used to say, "A woman gets hooked on love like a junkie on dope. But don't let them pass their habit on to you, men."

He pulled into the parking space next to Raymond's battered army surplus Jeep. It was weird having Raymond back. He'd driven out last week to the crumbling house Raymond had rented on an abandoned farm in the hills on the way to Kentucky. He was rebuilding the house and sheds, had planted a garden, bought a cow. Lived all by himself. What he did for pussy out there in the boonies was a mystery. But that never had been one of old Raymond's major interests. Couldn't have been with a girl like Emily. She was about as sexy as a telephone pole. Raymond had cut his hair off, shaved his mustache, went around in coveralls like everyone else. When he was up in New York City, he used to be some kind of beatnik or something. But now he tried to chat and joke with the folks at the mill. He'd gotten rid of his Yankee accent. Sometimes he sounded more country than real country people. It was almost embarrassing. That boy should of been an actor or something. The whole town had been pretty shocked when his Newland High graduation picture had been all over the newspapers and on the TV right after he got beat up. You knew they was shocked because nobody mentioned it. They pretended like it hadn't happened, like a Newland boy hadn't *really* been working for a bunch of Yankee Communists. Jed felt like Raymond probably got what he deserved. Looked like Raymond felt that way himself now, and was turning over a new leaf.

He talked some junk the other night about "the strength of Southern working people being based on their connection with the soil." If they didn't like how they was being treated on the job, they'd quit—because they could grow food in their gardens and hunt in their woods.

"When's the last time you shot a deer, Raymond?" Raymond had always had all these big theories that didn't have nothing to do with what he actually did.

"Yeah, you're right, baby brother. But I've come home to stay now." Jed tried to act glad. "But anyway, what I'm saying is that we don't have to be lackeys to no Yankee capitalists."

"What's that—lackeys?"

"Servants."

"Shoot," Jed said, spitting into the stone fireplace. "I don't know bout you, buddy, but I ain't nobody's servant."

Raymond glanced up from the stick he was whittling on. "That's what you think."

"All right, whose then?"

"The shareholders of Arnold Fiber Corporation."

"Shit, man, I ain't serving no shareholders. I don't even *know* no shareholders."

"You know Prince, don't you? And that guy from New York. What's his name—Mackay? They put money into the mill and then get back a share of the profits without doing any work."

"Prince and Mackay work damn hard."

"Well, that's debatable. But lots of shareholders don't. They sit on their asses in New York City yacht clubs and get checks in the mail."

"Naw, you're lying." He'd looked up to Raymond when they were kids, but it seemed like Jed had grown up, taken on marriage and a family and responsibilities, and Raymond was still just a jerky snot-nosed kid who told fibs about half the time. But Jed was never sure which half.

"It's the truth, Jed. I swear it."

"Don't hardly seem fair."

"That's what I been trying to tell you."

Jed thought this over on the drive home and decided it was so unlikely Mr. Prince would do his workers that way that it couldn't possibly be true. Though he did wonder if Raymond wasn't maybe connected up with them union people and down here to stir up trouble, just like he'd been doing all his life. He began watching Raymond around the mill, but he was acting so normal-like and eager to fit in that Jed began to feel guilty about being suspicious of his own brother. But rumors was circulating that the union was making another try. Their efforts came in waves, like locusts. The first time was in the thirties. One of his father's stories concerned the mill men dragging the organizers out of their boarding house and carting them to the town line, singing "Praise God from Whom All Blessings Flow."

In the fifties an organizer disguised as an insurance salesman had leafleted the mill and started setting up an organizing committee. His father and some others began driving down to the Howard Johnson Motel every night and shining their high beams through the organizer's window and throwing pebbles, to keep him awake and nervous all night. He didn't take the hint, so they came at him in the mill parking lot one afternoon with tire irons and crowbars. While he jumped in his car and locked the doors and revved his engine, they let the air out of his tires.

"He looked so scared," his father would relate with a grin, "I have to laugh even now. You know, Yankees is scared to death of the South to start with. They get fed so many tales about us savages down here. You kindly hate to disappoint them."

As he got out of the Chevy, Jed straightened his tie. Mackay was requiring all supervisory personnel to wear dress shirts and ties now under their coveralls. At first, his father insisted he'd gotten along just fine for thirty-five years without wearing no goddam tie to get caught in a roller and strangle him to death. But Mr. Prince took him aside, and he'd been wearing one ever since. Jed actually liked wearing one. Seemed like he got more respect from his workers.

Jed nodded and waved to people as he walked from the locker room through the breaking and carding rooms to the spinning room, where he was assisting the foreman Mr. Meaker. He'd been assigned to several months in almost all the rooms by now. It looked likely he'd be foreman of his own room before long. One night a week he went to foreman class, where you learned how to handle your workers. He knew that some who'd been at the mill for a long time resented him. They sometimes made jokes about how they wished they could have married the boss's daughter. That may have been partly why he was given this special treatment. But it was also that his father had been there thirty-five years and was a strong company man. Also, a lot of the workers was women, and of course you couldn't have no woman running a room. Although some of them sure acted like they owned the place—Mabel Pritchard, for one. Now there was a ball-breaker for you. Even if she had taught him Sunday School when he was six. Yesterday she'd disputed a plan he'd come up with for staggering breaks. He'd called her over.

"Seems like you think you run this place, Mrs. Pritchard."

"I don't have no ambitions to run nothing but my own life, Mr.

Tatro. But I do aim to do that." She had real thin frizzy red hair, kind of like Sally's pubic hair.

"I wonder do you realize who's in charge of this here room, Mrs. Pritchard."

"I realize you and Mr. Meaker is running this room. Now you tell me what you want done regarding the spinning of thread, Mr. Tatro, and I'll do hit."

If she'd been a man, he'd of busted her in her smart mouth. (This was what he was learning how not to do in foreman class. The teacher told him he had to learn how to control his "gunslinger mentality." Jed had been flattered. He didn't see it was necessarily something that should be got rid of.) The way she threw her head back and glared at him as she talked. Ranks of bossy women marched through his brain—his mother, Ruby, Kathryn, Emily, Betty Boobs, twelve years of schoolteachers and Sunday School teachers. He felt almost like a helpless little boy again. But no goddam woman was going to tell him what to do now that he was a grown man, and almost a foreman. Women! Like Coach Clancy said: They was good for two things, and one was to get your meals on the table.

He was just glad he'd played ball in high school and learned how to grit his teeth and eat some crow and get the job done. Like Coach Clancy said, you had to direct your anger into constructive channels. "Go out on that ball field and bust some heads. Or take your girl into the woods and fuck the cunt out of her. But I don't want to see no fists flying between my athletes."

Besides, you couldn't hit no woman. "Now you get on back over there, Mrs. Pritchard, and you do your job," he said in a choked voice, his face flaming red.

"Let me tell you something, Mr. Tatro: that was exactly what I was a-doing when you interrupted me."

Their eyes locked. She called herself a woman. Shit, he'd have to see her cunt first to believe it. More and more he saw how lucky he was to have Sally. She never disagreed with him, always tried to please him. Some nights he'd come home growling like a grizzly, and she'd set him down, and rub his neck and shoulders, and turn on the TV, and bring him his supper. She'd bathe the kids and bring them to him, all clean and powdered, to kiss goodnight. And once they was asleep, she'd lead him to their bed, and he'd roll into the warmth of her arms, while she whispered how much she loved him. He sometimes had to act all tough and mean at work so bitches like Mrs. Pritchard didn't think they could take over. But Sally let him be what he really was underneath—firm but fair, and a little bit shy. She gave him the strength to get up the next morning and go back to the mill.

People was all the time saying how easy he had it just watching other people work. The truth was that doing the work was easy. Getting people to do it right was what was hard. All his sympathies was with the foremen and supervisors and managers. Trash like Mrs. Pritchard left it all behind them when they punched the clock and walked out the door. But management took their problems home. He was getting used to this kind of responsibility, had to if he was going to be a foreman.

He waved across the room to Betty Boobs, who'd just arrived. She'd put on some weight since marrying Hank right after high school. Even those green coveralls couldn't conceal her huge tits. She used to be a good time, but he'd reformed since marrying Sally and didn't run around on her anymore, although Sally pretended not to believe it and pouted if he stopped off for a beer after work. Even to go to Raymond's the other night, he'd had to bring Raymond in from the car to verify his story. Raymond had looked at them like they was crazy. But poor old Raymond had probably never been in love himself. It made Jed feel good to have Sally worrying over him, and sometimes he dawdled in the locker room and parking lot to keep her guessing. She got real sexy on such nights and would sometimes even blow him. It was a funny thing: He loved that when it was actually going on. It was damn nice just to lie back and let it happen. But after it was over with, he'd feel terrible and jump up and smoke cigarettes and be mean to her and refuse to hold her. He couldn't stand knowing she'd seen him all helpless on his back and whimpering like that. And he couldn't stand the idea of her performing on him like some kind of high-paid hooker.

Every now and then him and Betty Boobs exchanged a look that indicated neither had forgotten their good times. It was strange having her married to his best friend. Did she talk to Hank about how he screwed? What did she tell him? That he was pretty good at it? Or not? Was he or wasn't he, he often asked himself. As he gazed at Betty, bursting out of her coveralls, he wished he could get Sally to show more enthusiasm, like Betty used to. Screwing Sally was like screwing a corpse. He studied the V where Betty's coverall legs joined. Her cunt had a way of tightening around you so you wondered if you'd ever get out again. Both Hank and him had pushed their dicks time after time into that dark tight slimy hole. His breathing quickened.

He felt ashamed. He was a married man now. Betty was his best friend's wife. What he'd been thinking was sinful. As for wishing Sally would behave as Betty had . . . In high school Betty had been nothing but a whore. That was a horrible thing to think about your own wife—particularly such a sweet girl, who was so good to their children. Sally was a saint. He was a monster to be having such lustful thoughts about her.

In the lunchroom he sat with Hank and Betty. He generally made a point of not getting too chummy with his workers. At first his father scolded him: "You've known these people all your life. You work with them, you live with them, you put your pants on the same way as them ever morning. What you want to go being so snooty for?" But in foreman class they told him to be careful that way, not to let your workers lose sight of who's boss. They hadn't had no foreman class when his father had got into it all, so his father didn't know all the modren ways.

Jed looked at Hank and Betty with sympathy. He could afford to have Sally not work. It had taken his father up until a couple of years ago to be able to let his mother quit. Hank and Betty couldn't even afford one child yet, and here he already had him his two.

His mouth full of bologna sandwich, he said, "Some people are saying them organizers is back in town." Hank didn't reply. "They better have a better disguise than last time." He laughed. Hank smiled. "Some folks you got to kill before they get the idea they're not wanted. You take a Yankee: You have to spell things out for him like he was a little kid or something."

"Maybe some folks around here wants them," Betty said. Hank looked alarmed.

Jed was surprised, both at her sentiment and also at the fact that she expressed it. Sally generally had enough sense to let the men do the talking on topics she didn't know nothing about.

"They wouldn't be hanging around without they think they got a chance. Shoot, I can see why some folks is interested," she added.

"They talk more money and pensions. Sure, they promise you whatever you want. But what do you actually get? You get to buy diamond rings for a bunch of Yankee gangsters." Jed waited for agreement. "Am I right?"

Hank looked at him. "Maybe. Maybe not."

"You calling me a liar?"

"No, I ain't. But there might be more to it than that."

"Listen, I figure if I do my job, I get me my raises. If I don't deserve them, they won't give them to me. And if I don't deserve them, I don't want them. Prince is fair. I don't question his decisions." He'd been to foreman school and understood these things. It was up to him to explain them to Hank, if he could just keep his temper like they taught him.

Hank snorted. "Prince ain't running this show no more, buddy. He done cashed in his chips."

"He's in here every day, ain't he?"

"Yeah, but he ain't calling the shots no more."

"You ain't interested in joining up with no union?"

"Naw, I don't know. I'm just thinking is all."

"Yeah, well, you may just think yourself right out of a job."

"Are you threatening me, Tatro, or what? Cause if you is, you can just take your father-in-law's job and stuff it."

"Now just cool down. I was referring to the strike at that radio factory in Dunmore in the fifties. Shut the whole place down when the union come in."

"Yeah?"

"Shoot, yeah. You talk pension funds and health benefits. What you really talking is unemployment." Jed could tell Hank was impressed, and he was pleased with himself for keeping cool and helping him understand how unions worked. He glanced around the lunchroom and saw Raymond sitting at a corner table talking intently to Mrs. Pritchard.

After lunch a consultant from the home office, whatever that was, appeared with a man who had a stopwatch and wanted to time how long it took to remove full bobbins from spindles. Raymond's were almost full, so Jed and the men went over to his machine. Raymond had already called a cart. When Raymond switched off the machine, the man switched on his watch. Raymond looked at him, then went over and leaned against the wall, his foot propped up. He reached inside his coveralls pocket and pulled out a foil pouch of tobacco and some rolling papers. With great care he rolled himself a tight cigarette. He offered it to Jed, who looked at him. Then he offered it to the men, who stood dumbfounded, watching the second hand sweep around the dial. Raymond lit up and inhaled deeply.

Jed was paralyzed. "It ain't time for your break yet, Raymond," he finally murmured.

Raymond looked at him and smiled. "I feel like a smoke."

Home Office and Expert exchanged looks.

Jed felt his fists tightening. "This man needs you to do your job so's he can time you."

Raymond exhaled. "I know yall'd like me to be a machine, but I'm afraid I ain't. Sometimes I want a smoke. Sometimes I get tired. Sometimes I'm sad or hung over. How do you time that?"

"Look, Raymond, this here man's got him his job to do. And so do you. Now unload them goddam bobbins."

Raymond blew out a steady stream of smoke and gazed at Jed through it. "Baby brother, why don't you just go get yourself stuffed? And then enroll yourself in some kind of industrial museum, like the anachronism that you are."

Jed felt his face go red. He didn't have no idea what Raymond was talking about. This was what Raymond had always done in high school—started using big words nobody could understand. But in high school Jed could just punch him out. They'd trained him in foreman school to handle such situations. Expert was watching him, but he didn't have a clue what to do.

Expert spotted another machine that was about to switch off and walked toward it. Jed followed, glaring over his shoulder at Raymond. He saw Home Office make a note in his book and wondered if it was about his unsuitability to be foreman. Goddam Raymond anyhow. Always trying to make him look bad.

In the locker room he changed from his coveralls and shirt and tie into his softball shirt. Grey with red lettering: Benson Mills I. They had them their own mill league, half a dozen teams. And the best players from each, of whom Jed was one, were on the Benson Mill team that played in the city league. The Princes had always supplied the shirts, and awarded trophies at a banquet at the season's end. He'd like to ask those union people how many companies had presidents that would of did this. Gingerly he touched the roll of fat that was beginning to hang out over his belt. Sally spent her days trying to cook his favorite foods. Even if he wasn't hungry, he ate them, so he wouldn't hurt her feelings. Frankly she couldn't cook as good as his mother. But she was trying hard and improving fast. He better start doing some regular exercises.

The one bad thing about being foreman, Jed reflected as he stood in center field poised for the next pitch, was that then he'd have to play on the supervisors' team. They usually lost 23–1, or something pitiful like that. They was mostly too old and too fat. And what your workers couldn't do on the shop floor, they did on the ball field, so that they was really out to get you. If they was one thing Jed hated, it was losing. Coach Clancy used to say, "I don't hold with none of this 'it's how you play the game' fairy crap. I don't want nobody on this team who ain't going out on that field to *win*. If you lose, you've failed, is how I see it. You're a disgrace to your school, a disgrace to your town, a disgrace to your coach, and a disgrace to yourself."

The carding room foreman popped a fly to left field. Jed caught it on the run and shot it to second for a double play. As he trotted in to bat, he caught sight of Sally sitting on a blanket in the grass, to one side of the bleachers. The kids toddled and tumbled around her, while she smiled at them lovingly. He grinned and waved, and she waved back. She was a good girl. A wonderful mother. A devoted wife. As his teammates got on base, or failed to, he sneaked glances at his family. Joey was walking underneath the bleachers; squatting and playing with candy wrappers; crawling up on the seats from below, startling and charming their occupants. He could remember doing the exact same thing. And here he was a big huge man now, who could no more fit between those bleachers . . . It was a funny thing thinking that one day your little baby son was going to be a big man just like you. And you, you'd be . . .

He hit a line drive past the shortstop and got on first.

Back in left field he took off his cap and put it back on the way he liked it, with the bill just above his eyebrows. He had to jut out his chin to see out from under it, but it kept the sun out of his eyes when he was trying to follow a fly. The sun was setting behind the hill in back of the bleachers, where several players stood in the bushes with their backs to the field taking leaks.

Mr. Meaker hit a low line drive toward left field. Mr. Meaker was his boss this month. Whatever Mr. Meaker wanted was fine. If he wanted to run around those bases, wonderful. As Jed thought and dismissed this, he was automatically running in on the ball. He put down his glove to scoop it up—and it shot past him. He stared at it. He never missed this catch. The crowd roared as Meaker rounded second. Jed retrieved the ball and stopped him at third.

"That was pretty pathetic, Tatro," Hank said, grinning as they trotted in to bat.

"Jesus, I don't know what happened. Must of taken a bad bounce."

Hank laughed. "It didn't take no bounce, Tatro. You just lost your interest in killing the bastards is all."

"What you talking about?"

"Well, you're about to join up with them, ain't you?"

"Yeah, but I don't see what that's got to do with playing ball."

"You don't?"

"No, I don't."

In the bottom of the sixth the score was 27–3. The supervisors couldn't get three outs. Everyone's supper was getting cold. Finally they forfeited good-humoredly, as they usually ended up doing. Jed wasn't sure he'd be able to stand it. Was it worth the extra salary and prestige to forfeit ball games with a smile? He guessed it probably was. Like Coach Clancy used to say, you had to pick your fights careful-like. "You got only so much fight in you, right? You fight with your girl, you got no fight left for the ball field. But which is most important?" Well, this situation here was the opposite. All right, sure, you lost softball games, but you was winning at the really important game.

He flopped down on the blanket and kissed Sally. She was laying out fried chicken. He stuffed half a deviled egg in his mouth and said as he chewed, "Lord, woman, I could eat me a horse. What you got for us here?" He rolled over and knocked over a Coke bottle with a jonquil in it.

"Hey, honey, you're squashing my flower!" He sat up while Sally stuck it back in the bottle and set it off to one side.

Jed was gnawing a chicken thigh. "Hey, Sal! Remember this blanket?"

She studied the olive army blanket with the dark wet splotch in the middle. "Sure. We've always had this blanket. You carry it around in the back of the Chevy."

"Don't you remember? We used to keep it down in the powder magazine. We was lying on it that night when ... uh ..."

"Oh yeah."

"Those were wild times."

"Yeah, they sure were."

They had never talked about it, not even while it was going on. Did she know about his struggle over whether to marry her or leave town? He'd never told her about the talk with Mr. Marsh. What had it been like for her? "Are you sorry it happened?"

She hesitated. "How could I be sorry, silly?" She leaned over and kissed him. "Look at all the nice things that have happened to me because of it." She gestured to Jed and the children, who were scuffling in the grass over the jonquil. "Are you sorry, darling?"

"Oh hell, no. I mean it's too bad we was rushed. But it's what I would of wanted anyway." He was recalling how good it felt that evening to run in on flies and pluck them out of the air and shoot them like bullets to the basemen, to connect with a pitch and send the ball hurtling beyond the outfield. He remembered the thrill of placing a block just right, so that the back could move through the hole for a first down. He remembered feeling and hearing the crowd rise as one to cheer his tackles. He never had this now. He could of had four more years of it at college. Then pro ball? Had he been good enough? He'd never know. Sometimes he'd imagine Joey playing halfback for the Rams or something. You'd have to be tough, though—either not want the girls, or not feel responsible if you knocked them up. Like that cowboy in *Beyond the Rio Grande*, which he'd read last week. Fuck them and then ride off into the sunset, never looking back, while they fell to their knees and wept and pleaded with you to stay. Not care about being away from your parents and family most of the year. Living in hotels, picking up strange girls, eating in restaurants, flying all around the country . . . He sighed.

"Are you sad, honey?" Sally asked, playing with his damp hair.

"I don't know." He sat up, picked up Joey's large inflated ball, and threw it at him. Joey had been stumbling around holding the jonquil in both hands, his nose stuck in it like a giant besotted bee. The ball hit him in the forehead. He looked up, startled.

"Hey, Joey! Don't cry, son. Boys don't cry. Be Daddy's little man."

Unconvinced, Joey began to shudder, preparing to wail.

"Come here, son!"

Joey edged closer, fearfully. Jed took the jonquil. "Flowers are for girls. Let's you and me play ball." He handed the battered jonquil to Sally, who handed it to the baby, who shoved it in her mouth.

Joey and Jed tossed the ball. Joey would gather in both arms when he saw it coming. If he happened to have the ball in them when he did so, it was strictly by coincidence. Eventually Jed took him by the hand and led him to the bushes on the hill behind the bleachers. They stood with their backs to the field and their hands in front of them. Joey's head was nearly hidden by the bushes.

"Daddy and Joey, we the men!" he announced as he swaggered back to Sally.

"That's right, darling," she cooed, gathering him in her arms and planting a kiss on his pink cheek. He pushed her away, struggling to escape.

The next morning was brilliantly sunny. Jed and Hank were putting siding on the new room. Joey was stumbling around hitting things with a hammer.

"I really preciate your help on this, Hank old buddy," Jed said as he drove a nail.

"Hey, would you please stop telling me that? It's getting downright boring."

"But I do."

"Shit, I know you do. And I know you'll do the same for me when I need it."

"You going to be needing you an extra room sometime soon?" Jed looked up with a grin. He took a long drink of beer.

"We're thinking on it."

"Well, you won't never regret it. Children is a real blessing to a marriage."

"Yeah, but we're worried that you can't just pick up and go out to a movie no more when you feel like it."

"Well, yeah, that's true. But pretty soon you stop feeling like it. You get so you'd rather stay around the house with the kids."

"That's what we're afraid of."

Jed looked at him indignantly. "It ain't so bad."

"Not for some people. But we ain't sure we're that type." He put down his hammer and took a gulp of beer and wiped his forehead with his forearm.

"Well, you just do what you do, buddy, and one day they's three of you where there used to be two."

"That's what happened to *you*. After that, I swore it wouldn't never happen like that to me."

"Goddam, I don't know how you can be so cold and calculating about it. Sally and me, we just couldn't help ourselves."

Hank inquired unpleasantly, "You trying to say, Tatro, that you just so much more of a man than me? I do hear tell you're a pretty horny fella."

"You do? Who from?" Jed grinned.

"Who do you think from?"

"What's your old lady been telling you?"

"Just that you never treated her like nothing but shit. Jumped on her and came and took her home."

Jed was stunned. "That ain't so."

"She said you never had no use for her whenever things was going good with Sally. Except to get laid. She said you wouldn't even say hi to her in the hall at school."

"Ah, come on now. That ain't fair. She was putting out for ever boy in town."

"That's what you used to spread around school. But it wasn't true. She loved you, Tatro. You're the only one she was putting out for. And you didn't treat her like nothing but dirt."

"I never did. That's just a lie, pure and simple."

"You calling my woman a liar?"

"Yeah, if it comes to that." They had raised their fists and were slowly circling, stepping over construction rubble.

"She says you all the time leering at her over at the mill, like you and her's got some kind of dark secret or something. But I tell you what, buddy: From now on you keep your eyes offen her, and your filthy thoughts too. Cause she's *my* woman."

Jed laughed. "You don't have to worry, Osborne. Why, I wouldn't screw that woman with a ten-foot pole!" He'd never speak to Betty Boobs again.

Hank laughed. "Dream on, Tatro. Ten-foot pole! Sally's lucky if she can even tell when you've put it in her!"

Jed's fist caught Hank in the stomach. They began exchanging blows. Joey dropped the hammer and watched with wide eyes and mouth. A couple of neighborhood dogs stopped by and began barking.

Locked in a clinch, each tried to push the other away and free up a hand to get in a punch. Sally came out the door in her apron with Laura on her hip. Joey was hopping up and down yelling, "Pow! Pow!" Sally sighed.

Jed heard her yelling, "All right, stop it right now, you two! And I mean it!"

She pushed them apart, them scowling but cooperative. "Now aren't you ashamed? A couple of big men acting like little boys!"

Jed's snarl began to feel ridiculous. He hung his head sheepishly. "Hank started it."

"Oh, stop it!" Sally snapped. "For goodness sake, come and eat some lunch."

They sat at the table in silence as Sally served up pot roast and mashed potatoes and gravy. On the TV David Niven was waltzing around. "What is this shit?" Jed muttered, switching to the Knicks–Celtics game.

"I was watching that, honey," Sally murmured.

"And now you ain't." She glanced at him and went to put the baby down for her nap. Joey wandered in from the bathroom, naked except for a stained T-shirt. His tiny penis was erect—a fact he seemed unaware of and uninterested in. The two men laughed, breaking their strained silence.

"Like father, like son," Hank exclaimed.

"You'll be having you a good time with that in a few years, son!" He instantly erased from his mind the sudden awareness that Hank and he had had erections during the backyard clinch. Joey looked up questioningly, smiled, eager to please, then toddled out.

After lunch they sat drinking beer and smoking and watching the basketball game. Six of the ten players were Negroes.

"What do you reckon them jigs earn in a year?" Jed muttered.

"Fifty, sixty thou, easy."

Jed digested this. Close to ten times what he earned, and he thought he was doing pretty good.

"At least it keeps them off the welfare and out of prison," Hank added.

"Motherfucking coons."

"Yeah, but they're good ball players. Shit, did you see that one-handed jump shot?"

Jed sat in silence, hating them. Their dark bodies, gleaming with sweat, stretched and strained toward the net, muscles rippling. Four of them in pursuit of a rebound rose into the air in unison, their long limbs floating upward and intertwining, their torsos twisting and turning and colliding. His breathing quickened. "Did you hear the one about the nigger and the deodorant bottle?" he asked, jumping up.

Hank nodded no and Jed told it as they walked out the back door and returned to their hammering. Joey came out and picked up his hammer and began hammering the bright yellow jonquils growing next to the house.

"Hey, Joey, what you doing?" Jed yelled. "Stop that!"

Joey looked up, hammer poised. "Naughty flowers! Joey not like flowers!"

Hank and Jed laughed. Jed took away the hammer. "You don't hit them, Jo-jo. You pick them." He handed him a bunch. "Now go give them to Mommy and Laura, and they'll put them in water and make our house pretty."

After church the next day they sat at dinner with his parents and with Raymond, who had refused to go to church.

"Same old Raymond," Jed was saying with a grin.

"I just never will understand, Junior," their mother moaned as she moved from kitchen to table with loaded serving plates, "what you got against the Lord."

Raymond paused, a forkful of rice and gravy almost to his mouth. "You get all wrapped up in the world to come, and it takes your attention away from changing things in this world."

Jed sat back and folded his hands across his starched white shirt front and gave a long-suffering sigh. "Things ain't so terrible like they is."

"They could be better," Raymond muttered, his mouth full.

"Junior, don't talk with your mouth full," his mother said.

"Yeah, and apples could be redder," Jed remarked.

"Apples is red. But apples is also green or yellow. And there's pears and peaches and plums too. The way things is set up ain't the only way they could be."

"How they are is fine with me," said Jed, chewing. Ah hell, Raymond had climbed on his hobby horse again, like he did every goddam time you was with him.

"Jed honey, don't talk with food in your mouth," his mother murmured.

"That's easy for you to say. You ain't running golblamed machines all day every day. Going cross-eyed watching spindles turn. Counting the minutes till the shift's over with."

"If you don't like it, you know where the door's at." Why Raymond stayed at the mill if he hated it so much was what Jed couldn't figure out. Why he came back to Newland in the first place. Nobody had missed him while he'd been gone.

"That ain't the point."

Jed clamped his mouth shut, determined not to ask what the point was. If he did, Raymond would never shut up.

"The point is," said Raymond, needing prompting from no one, "the Yankee capitalists moved in after Reconstruction and took over the plantation system. They turned some of us into overseers and the rest into wage slaves."

"What's your uncle over there talking about, Joey?" Mr. Tatro asked the child at his elbow, who was mashing together rice and butter beans with his fingers. Joey looked up and smiled. "I declare, I never saw such a flirt," announced Mr. Tatro. "I do believe he takes after his mama." Sally and Mr. Tatro exchanged smiles. Mrs. Tatro stood behind her husband, her hands on his chair back. "For the Lord's sake, sit down, Mother. You make me nervous back there."

"I can't help it, Raymond. I just don't feel right setting while my men is eating."

Mr. Tatro gestured behind him with his fork. "Now there's an old-fashioned country woman for you, boys. That's the trouble with you young people. No respect. Time was when the younger men over to the mill would let their supervisors win at softball. You'd get an older man who ran the weave room up to bat, and you'd pitch slower. Maybe you'd let him get on base when you could of throwed him out easy. But showing respect was more important than winning ball games. Seem like everything nowadays is strife and struggle. Lord, boys, I tell you, I hate to see it happen."

"Coach Clancy used to say a good ball team was like a Continental Mark IV car," said Jed. "You had all different kinds of parts, but if any one wasn't doing their job, the car wouldn't run."

Raymond looked at them as though they were the Missing Link. "Yall is playing by the old rules. But they done gone and switched games, and you don't even know it."

"Come on, Sally," Mrs. Tatro said softly. "Let's you and me go set in the living room and let the men folk do their talking." Sally got up and unhitched Laura from her high chair. Joey looked back and forth between the two groups, then scrambled down and followed his mother.

"The way I figure it, Raymond," said Jed, "is that you gon feel real different when you get you a mortgage and a wife and some kids."

Mr. Tatro laughed. "Ain't it the truth?"

"Ah, shit," said Raymond. "I can't get nobody at this table to talk serious."

"Just cause we don't agree with you means we ain't serious?" demanded Jed, jutting out his chin. He clenched his fists under the table. Raymond was like a mosquito. Made you want to swat him.

"It's the *way* yall talk. Darting all over the place like mice in a maze."

"Well, some of us ain't blessed with your exposure to the temples of learning in New York City, Junior," Mr. Tatro replied. "I'm truly sorry we ain't up to your level of discourse, but I reckon you'll just have to babble along with us hillbillies. Or go back up there with your interlechurl Yankee friends."

"I'm sorry," Raymond muttered. "I didn't mean that."

Mrs. Tatro was saying, "Well, Sally, I just don't know why we can't get along any better."

"I don't either, Mother Tatro. Lord knows I've tried. I get along pretty good with everyone else . . ." Mr. Tatro and Jed exchanged glances.

"Now I know for a fact that ain't true, Sally Tatro. Why, just the other day I was talking with Ellen Louise Smithey, and she said you and her quarreled something terrible last June . . ."

Laura crawled up in Jed's lap. "Sally, this baby's wet!" He held her at arm's length with an expression of distaste, until Sally ran in and took her.

". . . now that's just what I mean about respect," Mr. Tatro was saying. "Where is your respect at, you young people today?"

"Sally's trying, Dad, she really is. Why, she called and asked Mother for her spoon bread recipe just last month."

"Yeah, but it shouldn't have to be a special effort. It should come natural-like. I just don't know what this world's coming to. I'm glad I won't be around to see."

Mrs. Tatro was saying, ". . . and you never wear my Christmas presents, Sally!"

"Now that's not true. That's absolutely untrue."

"Remember those swatches you used to bring home, Dad?" asked Raymond.

Jed and Mr. Tatro smiled, remembering the squares of each print made at the mill, hooked together through holes in their corners by a ring.

"Yeah, we'd sort through them and know whose clothes around town were made from mill rejects." Jed chuckled.

"So now they've shut down the dye room. The weave room will be next. They're turning us into gears on machines that spin thread. And as soon as they can, they'll replace us with machines."

"Mr. Prince'll never let that happen," maintained Mr. Tatro.

"It's already happened. They've replaced half the old machines in the roving room and turned those people out. They've upped our quotas and cut down on breaks. They're getting more work from fewer people, so they're making more money. But have wages gone up? Lots of families here have donated three generations to the mill, and they're bleeding us dry!"

"Here, boy, have some more of this red meat," Mr. Tatro said, holding out some roast beef on a serving fork and chuckling. "We don't want you bled dry."

"What you're saying," said Jed, thrusting out his chin, "is that Mr. Prince is out to do you in? Boy, have those Yankees done a job on you! You some kind of Communist or something?" Seemed like Raymond didn't know how to chat. He always had to be arguing or lecturing you. It drove Jed crazy.

"No, I'm a Southerner."

"Well, you ain't like any Southerner I ever saw."

"The only ones you've ever seen are in captivity."

Jed scowled. "Hell, *I* ain't no captive. This here is America, U.S.A., not Russia. The Land of the Free."

"Tell that to Wall Street."

"Who's that?" asked Mr. Tatro.

"The Yankee capitalists who've colonized the South."

Jed and Mr. Tatro stared at Raymond. His eyes looked frantic behind his glasses. Jed thought he really was a little crazy. Maybe getting beat up had damaged his brain.

"Mr. Prince and his father has been real generous to us Tatros," Mr. Tatro pointed out. "Why, I remember the day I paid off the mortgage on this house. I called up old Mr. Prince, and he . . ."

"Dad, we've heard this story a hundred times," Raymond snapped. Jed gave him a nasty look. *Raymond* had no respect, that was for sure.

"You call it generous that he lives in that huge yellow airplane hangar on Tsali Street, and yall live down here?" Raymond demanded.

"What's wrong with down here?" snarled Jed. If he'd had a can of Flit, it'd have given him great pleasure to spray Raymond.

"Listen to me, son. Excepting for Prince and his dad, yall would be up in Tatro Cove right now, eating possum meat instead of roast beef."

"But how long do we have to go on being grateful?"

"For as long as the Lord sees fit to leave a single breath in your body."

Raymond brought his fist down on the table. The silverware clattered. "I ain't talking about Prince, goddam it! I'm talking about an entire economic system that just rolls along, trampling anybody in the way!"

"You look all right to me, Raymond," Jed said, grinning. "Does Raymond look trampled to you, Daddy?"

Mr. Tatro rocked back on his chair legs. "I declare, Junior, I believe you done stayed up North too long. Trampling. What was that Yankee song? 'Trampling out the vintage where the grapes of wrath are stored.' "

Raymond stood up. "Jesus Christ, yall are hopeless."

Mrs. Tatro called from the living room, "Junior, I won't have you using our Lord's name in vain in this house."

He stomped to the door and slammed it behind him.

"Boy, he's a mess, ain't he?" Mr. Tatro asked of Jed.

"Just about like always."

"I was kindly hoping when he come back this time, he'd of settled down some."

"Just wait till he gets hisself a mortgage and a wife and some kids."

"Yeah, ain't it the truth? I expect he needs him the love of a good woman."

Jed woke up mean. He rolled over and screwed Sally before she was
hardly awake. She whimpered when he jabbed her at a bad angle.
As he pulled out, she asked in a sleepy voice, "What's wrong,
honey?"

"Nothing."

"Come on. Tell me, baby."

"Nothing."

"I can see something's wrong, darlin," she said, rubbing his shoulders.

He felt spied on. She always knew what he was feeling and thinking. He had no privacy. Even his moods couldn't be just his own
business.

"What is it, sweetie?"

"Aw, shit, Sally, why can't you just leave me alone? If I'm in a bad
mood, I'll get over it if you just ignore it."

"But I need to know if it's something I've done. So I won't do it
again."

He didn't know anymore whether it was something she'd done or
not. But since she seemed so willing to take the rap, he started
searching for dissatisfactions to lay on her. "Shit, I don't know, Sally.
It's just that when I make love to you, it's like screwing a corpse."

"But I was sound asleep, honey."

"Awake. Asleep. Who can tell the difference?"

He raced into the bathroom so she wouldn't have a chance to bring
the discussion around to whether he really really loved her. Sometimes he wondered if *she* really really loved *him*. If he wasn't paying
the bills, would she have anything to do with him?

She gazed at him throughout breakfast.

He opened his lunch box to see what she'd packed. "Damn it, Sally.
Do the sandwiches always have to be bologna?"

"But Jed honey, you love bologna."

"Not ever day I don't."

She looked at him, perplexed, retrieved the lunch box and refilled it
with egg salad sandwiches.

As he pecked her good-bye, Joey toddled over and tried to push his
way between them. Jed pushed Joey with his foot. The damn kid was

always in the way. Right from his conception. If Sally hadn't gotten pregnant . . .

"Jed honey," Sally said, looking at him with confused hurt. She didn't hardly have time for him anymore, in between what the babies wanted. Him and her, they couldn't just run out to a movie. They was like servants to these tiny tyrants.

"Sorry," he muttered.

As he got out of his car, he saw that the parking lot was blanketed with handbills. He picked one up. It said that Benson Mill was one of forty-five owned by Arnold Fiber Corporation, that Arnold employed thirty-five thousand workers, that their sales the previous year topped eight hundred and seventy-five million dollars, that fourteen million in profits went to shareholders that included fourteen banks, insurance companies, and investment companies in New York City.

". . . you are earning twenty-five to forty percent less than Arnold workers in the North. These same fellow workers also have pension plans, grievance procedures, seniority rights, maternity leave, medical benefits, safety protection, job bidding, arbitration, and dues check-off. People up at Wall Street are getting rich off of your sweat. You are being taken advantage of by those who claim to be your friends. Stand up and be counted. Sign your union card when your local Allied Textile Workers representative contacts you."

Jed wadded up the leaflet and threw it down. As he headed for the door, he passed a Negro sweeping up leaflets with a push broom. Donny had disappeared back in the fall. Gone up to New York City, according to Sally, whose mother had it from Ruby. That was just about what you could expect from a jig. Couldn't hold a job if you put it in a basket for them.

"Good man, there."

"Yes sir, they sure does mess things up, these union peoples."

"Who did it?"

"Seems like that somebody toted them in in their lunch pail. Opened the pail in the shift change when nobody wasn't looking, and the wind just picked them right up."

"Did you read it?"

"Glanced at it."

"Well, don't you believe it. Mr. Prince does right by us."

"Yes sir, I expect he does. He a fine man, Mr. Prince."

"What you think about all this union foolishness?" You couldn't hardly ever tell what a jig thought about something without you asked him. A white man, his face would color, or his mouth would twitch. But a jig had a face like a cat in front of a mouse hole.

"Ain't studying no union."

"Well, that's good, cause they don't let coloreds join anyhow."

Niggers. They was now two in the breaking room. When he'd first started in, there was only one in the whole entire place—Donny, who was the janitor. They was sort of like weevils—they spread. Next thing you knew, the spinning room would be infested, then your lunchroom and your locker room. All this civilian rights shit, it couldn't help but go to their heads.

He never would forget that night at the Barbecue Pit last summer when this big ole Pontiac pulled up, full of jigs thinking they'd get theirselves served. The Pontiac had New York license tags, and this was round about the time when the whole area was full of Yankee Communist agitators. You'd sometimes see them around town—these smart-ass white kids in blue jeans and sweaty T-shirts, who hadn't shaved or had a haircut all year; and these surly nigger bastards in college sweatshirts, who didn't have the manners not to look you right in the eye when you spoke to them.

Anyhow, there was this carload of jive-ass jigs down from New York wanting milk shakes. And setting there in the back, about to get the shit kicked out of him, scared to death, with his eyes all bugged out, was old Donny. Jed had never had a kid brother, but sometimes he felt that way about Donny—all the time having to get him out of scrapes he'd been dumb enough to get hisself into. Why Jed bothered he couldn't of said.

First the civilian rights assholes, and now the union turds—it got plumb exhausting trying to maintain your freedom and democratic rights in the face of all this infiltration from up North. He surveyed the room as the workers found their places. Everyone knew niggers wasn't smart enough to run these machines. Couldn't most white folks run them right. All the calculations and adjustments. Had to have a head on your shoulders, and a brain in that head. All niggers had was cocks—big ones, to hear it.

Toward noon it occurred to him that Mrs. Pritchard had been to the bathroom about five times. Well, maybe she had diarrhea or something. He watched her close on her next trip. She sidled up to Joe Macon at his machine, exchanged greetings, then slipped a folded paper towel into his hand and walked on. Joe glanced around nervously, unfolded the towel, removed a piece of blue paper, wrote something on it, and rewrapped it in the towel. Mrs. Pritchard walked past from the bathroom, not looking at him, and he passed her the towel.

At lunch a note from Sally fell out of his box as he opened it: "When you read this, darling, I'll be at our home minding our cute little babies and thinking of you, and waiting on you to get home to me." He felt a twinge of irritation.

"What you got there?" Hank asked, trying to grab the note.

"None of your bidness," Jed said, forcing a lecherous grin.

"It's dirty, I bet," Betty said with a knowing smile.

Jed realized that if he never spoke to her again for betraying him to Hank, he'd have no one to eat lunch with. So he decided to speak to her, but never to forgive her.

Jed asked Hank, "Did you see them leaflets this morning?"

"Yeah." They sat in silence. "But you know," Hank added, "I don't like being told by nobody what I can and can't do. I got my freedom of speech, just like every other American."

"So who's telling you what to do?"

"Appears to me management is saying they don't want nobody starting up no union."

"Shit, we done all right without no union. I can run my own life. I don't need to pay no union to solve somebody else's problems."

"Yeah, but I got my right to speak up without getting run out the door."

"You don't have to pay nobody dues to be able to speak up."

They ended up arguing over whether Willie Mays or Mickey Mantle was the greatest all-round outfielder of all time.

Mr. Prince called Jed into his office that afternoon. Jed stood at attention in front of his desk. His wife's father, his children's grandfather. Jed respected Mr. Prince, always had. He was thankful for those years on the ball team. Unlike poor old unhappy Raymond, he understood that you had the backs, the line, the reserves, the water-boys. Each had their responsibilities. And over them all you had Coach Clancy, whose word was law if you wanted to win ball games. The same in a family—the children of different ages, then the mother, then the father in charge. If you didn't have no chain of command, if everbody wanted to do ever job and wanted the last word on ever decision, you'd never get no thread spun. Like Coach Clancy used to say, "You couldn't have all chiefs and no Indians." Raymond had never accomplished nothing in his whole life and didn't have no idea how to cooperate. He saw everything in terms of struggle. It was probably why he was so skinny. He wore hisself out struggling all the time.

"Have a seat, Jed," Mr. Prince suggested.

"Thank you, sir. I'd prefer to stand."

Mr. Prince smiled faintly. "As you like. What I wanted to ask you, Jed—you're out on the shop floor. Have you heard any talk about this union organizing?"

Jed hesitated. He was pretty sure Raymond was involved. Loyalty to his family vied with loyalty to his company. And Mrs. Pritchard. She was up to something. But she'd taught him Sunday School when he was six. "Just talk so far, sir. And those handbills in the parking lot this morning."

"Well, it's no secret, Jed, that you're being groomed to become a foreman, and Mr. Mackay feels . . . Mr. Mackay and I feel that a union isn't in the best interests of the company. Will you let us know if you hear anything definite?"

"Yes sir. Of course I will, sir."

They looked at each other.

"How's Sally?"

"Just fine, thank you, sir."

"And the kids?"

"Yes sir, they're fine too."

"We'll have to get you all over for a meal sometime soon."

"Yes sir. That'd be real nice." Jed felt uneasy when Mr. Prince got friendly. It didn't seem quite right to mix up work with family. Boss, father-in-law. You had to keep them separate or it got too confusing.

Back in the spinning room, he summoned Mrs. Pritchard. "Appears to me like you practically haunting that ladies' room today, Mrs. Pritchard."

"I reckon that's my bidness, Mr. Tatro."

"I reckon it's *my* bidness, Mrs. Pritchard, when you start using company time for personal matters. You want to tell me what you're passing around in them paper towels? Invitations to your retirement party?" He studied the bare patches of scalp showing through her thin red hair and tried to forget that it was she who'd made him memorize the Ten Commandments when he was six.

She blushed. "I don't reckon I do, Mr. Tatro."

"All right, Mrs. Pritchard. But I don't want to see you running back and forth to the bathroom all afternoon when you ain't even meeting production."

"That's a lie, Mr. Tatro. I'm the best worker in this room, and everbody knows it. You got no right to complain on grounds of me not getting my work done."

"I'm just thinking, Mrs. Pritchard, if you got so much spare time on your hands, maybe we ought to up your quota."

A machine broke down. Unable to fix it, Jed had to go hunt down a utility man.

During the quiet moments that followed, he stood watching the room full of whirring clattering machines. Threads wrapped round and round hundreds of spinning bobbins, weaving ever tighter and thicker cocoons. His father, his mother, his brother, himself, eventually his son, probably his daughter's husband—how many hundreds of thousands of miles of thread would wrap onto bobbins in their combined lifetimes? "When you read this, darling . . ." Would she love him just for himself and not for anything he could do for her? If he'd never been varsity tackle on the state championship team, if he lost his job, if his prick fell off tomorrow night, would she still love him? Is this what it was all about then? The house, cars, bank loans, a wife and kids and parents, church on Sunday. This bittersweet mix of duty and obligation, possessiveness and mutual comfort and occasional passion. Day after day, until days added up to years, and years became a lifetime. Was this it? In the Castle Tree they'd had such big plans . . .

His fists tightened with his need to smash something.

In the locker room he persuaded Hank to go to the Mill House. He phoned Sally to say he had to work half the next shift.

"But what about supper, honey? I got your favorite meal setting right here on the stove—chicken-fried steak."

"Can't you heat it up when I get home?" Thinking: take your goddam steak and shove it.

"But it'll be all dried out, honey."

This problem stumped him. "Well, eat it yourself then."

"Honey, I can't eat one pound of rump steak!"

"Well, shit, throw it out. I don't care what you do with it."

Silence. Then a sniff.

"Oh, come on, darlin. Don't cry. Be Daddy's big girl."

"It's just that I been cooking your favorite things all afternoon," she wailed. "And waiting on you, and wanting to see you, and now you tell me you won't be coming home after all."

"I am coming, darlin. I'm just gon be a little late." He gripped the receiver as though it was a hand grenade he was about to lob into a schoolroom. "You'll be all right, won't you, sweetheart?"

She sniffed and said miserably, "Yes, I'll be just fine, Jed honey. You come on home when you can, hear?"

"Yeah, but there's something I gotta tell you, honey."

"Who is she?" she asked in a small scared voice.

Jed laughed abruptly. "No, darlin. There's no one else. It's just that chicken-fried steak ain't my favorite no more."

Silence. "But, honey, chicken-fried steak has always been your favorite."

"I know, but it ain't no more."

"Well, how come not, honey?"

"I guess I'm getting tired of it or something. Twice a week for three years is a lot to eat of one dish."

"Well, Jed, I just don't know what to say. First you tell me you don't like bologna sandwiches anymore. And now you tell me you don't like chicken-fried steak."

"I know. I'm sorry, honey. I feel awful having to tell you. But I thought I'd better."

"No. No, I'm glad you did, sweetheart."

He walked up to Betty in the parking lot. "Me and your old man, we gon cut up over at the Mill House. You wanna come?"

"Huh-un," she said. "I got to get on home. But yall have one for me, OK?"

"You one lucky man," he informed Hank as they roared off. " 'Have one for me.' Christ, Sally almost divorced me when I said I'd be late."

"Aw, you love it. Both of you do."

"Naw, I don't. Not this evening I don't. Sometimes I think I can't take it no more. Sometimes I just want to tear something all to pieces."

"You just feeling ugly this evening. You used to get like this at school. You'd go out on the ball field and bust a few heads and feel better real fast."

"I feel like—I don't know—like I'm in some kind of a trap or something."

"You feel back to normal after some beers, buddy."

Afterward they assembled a dummy from some grain sacks and laid it on the railroad track just before the arrival of the night train from Chattanooga. They hid in the bushes and watched the engine's headlights sweep up the valley. And they howled as the lights picked up their dummy and the engineer threw on the steam brakes in a great whoosh. The wheels pulverized the dummy as the train hurtled to a halt.

As they stumbled through the woods back to the car, they clung to each other to keep from falling.

"Shoot, Tatro, if anybody was to see us, they'd think we was a couple of faggots!"

They laughed uproariously. Jed threw his shoulder against Hank and knocked him off-balance, then threw a block that brought him down. They lay giggling in the leaves. The arms around you in the huddle, the slaps on the rear, the horseplay in the showers, the frenzied embraces after touchdowns, the blocks and tackles. He missed them.

He jumped up and stood peeing into the creek. Hank joined him.

"Boy, that Miller really puts lead in your pencil, don't it?" Jed demanded.

Hank laughed. "I reckon it's about time for a fishing trip, don't you?"

"Sure feels like it."

As they rode back to town, Jed started whistling.

"See what I mean? You feeling better now, ain't you?"

Jed pulled the Chevy into the garage, got out and surveyed his little house. It contained the people dearest to him in all the world—Sally and their kids.

He strode into the house. And was greeted by Sally, red-eyed, rocking the baby and glaring at him. He bent to kiss her, and she turned her head away.

"Aw, now, baby, don't do me like that."

"Hush. You'll wake the baby."

" 'Hush, you'll wake the baby,' " he mimicked, jealous of this tiny creature who was in both her good graces and her warm arms. "Well, put it back in bed."

"I will when I feel like it."

"I said put it back to bed! A man works hard all day, he deserves some attention from his wife when he gets home."

"Yeah, you really smell like you been working hard."

He grabbed at the baby. Sally hugged it tightly and swept it out of his grasp. The baby began whimpering. "Now you've gone and woke her up. You're no bettern a great big baby yourself. Why don't you grow up?"

She disappeared into the children's room.

He sank into a chair. She emerged, babyless, and sat down across from him. "Well! Did you have a good time?"

"What do you mean?"

"I know you weren't at work. I phoned the mill."

He glared at her. "Yes, I did have a good time."

"Cheating on me's bad enough. Lying about it makes it that much worse."

"I ain't lying." He knelt on the floor and laid his head in her lap. "I swear to you I ain't running around on you."

She began stroking his hair. "I wish I could believe that."

"You can, darlin. I swear you can." His hands moved inside her housecoat and found her breasts. She moaned as he squeezed her nipples. Jealousy always excited her.

Jed and Mr. Meaker stood before Mr. Mackay's desk. Mr. Mackay sat in a business suit, with Mr. Prince on his right.

"Mr. Meaker, I'd like you to think of good reasons why the following people in your department should be let go: numbers 18045, 63794, and 43572."

Jed and Mr. Meaker looked at each other and at Mr. Prince blankly.

"Mrs. Pritchard, Mrs. Osborne, and Mr. Grimes," Mr. Prince interpreted.

There was a long silence.

"They're all three doing their work, sir," Mr. Meaker mumbled.

"I'm afraid they're all three doing other work, too, Mr. Meaker. Union work, on company time."

Jed opened his mouth to say he knew Betty Osborne would never do nothing like that, but no words came out. Mr. Mackay terrified him. He was like God—a sweep of his hand and Jed's house, his cars, and TV console would vanish into thin air.

"They got families, sir," Jed mumbled.

"Yes, I know, Mr. Tatro. So do you. You notice I'm not asking you to get rid of your brother, although I should."

"Mr. Mackay," Mr. Prince interrupted, "we don't do business like this down here."

"Robert, if you people knew how to do business, you wouldn't have had to sell to Arnold, would you?" He raised his eyebrows.

Mr. Prince flushed. "Mrs. Pritchard has been with us for twenty-seven years. Her father was one of our original employees."

"Robert, I've already told you that this family retainer number doesn't impress me. We're in business to spin thread, not to run a social welfare service. There are government agencies for that. Now, I want those people let go as pleasantly and quietly as possible."

Mr. Meaker gave Mr. Prince a questioning look. Mr. Prince hung his head.

"But, sir, they haven't done anything wrong to fire them for," Mr. Meaker said.

Mr. Mackay stared at him wordlessly, until Mr. Meaker lowered his eyes to the floor.

In bed that night Jed felt a need to force himself on Sally. He turned her over roughly, rolled on top of her, pinned open her legs with his knees, and drove himself into her time after time. To his horror, she began moaning and raising her hips to meet his. Betty Boobs used to do this. He froze in mid-thrust, and his erection wilted.

"What's wrong, honey?" she gasped.

"Nothing," he growled, rolling off and turning his back.

"Did I do something wrong?"

"Where did you learn that?"

"What?"

"The way you was moving."

"I don't know. I made it up."

"Well, don't do it no more."

She said nothing.

"It ain't ladylike."

"I . . . OK, Jed honey."

That weekend Jed and Hank went to Hank's cabin on Buck Mountain. They cast for trout all day in rushing streams and at night sat before a campfire with a cooler of Miller's.

"You hear about Betty gettin laid off?"

"Yeah." Jed felt full of remorse that he hadn't been able to intercede.

"That Mackay's a real fucker."

"He thought she was working for the union. Was she?"

Hank said nothing.

"If she was, I ain't got no sympathy. If she wasn't, I got all the sympathy in the world."

"Sympathy don't pay the mortgage, Tatro. But she ain't taking it lying down."

"She getting her another job?"

"Huh-un. She's filing her an appeal."

"What's that?"

"With the government. To get her job back."

Jed digested this. "But it's Mackay's mill. If he don't want her there, she ain't *got* no job. It ain't 'her' job. It's his job, to give to whoever he wants."

"That ain't how Betty sees it. Or me. Or the government."

Jed stared at him. "Hank, that's Communist, thinking like that, buddy."

"Call it what you want to. We got us bank loans and a mortgage."

Jed sighed. If he lost his job, they'd be in a real fix. At least Hank was still bringing home a paycheck. But Hank didn't have him no babies. Jed's whole entire family depended on him alone. If he got sick or fired or something, they'd go hungry, get kicked out of their house, have their Dodge and TV repossessed. He felt terror. "Shit, life ain't no joke no more, is it?"

"Used to seem like it sometimes in high school."

"You got to be tough."

"Yeah, that's the truth. You weak, you don't make it."

"Thank the Lord I was born tough."

Hank laughed. "Shit, Tatro, you a creampuff if they ever was one."

Jed, unamused, unbuttoned his wool shirt, removed it; then took off his thermal undershirt, exposing his hairy chest to the cold night air. The fire popped and crackled. "I'll show you who's tough," he murmured.

Hank looked at him, then removed his own shirt and undershirt, then his jeans. He hunched on a log by the fire in his long underwear, staring defiantly at Jed.

Jed stood up and removed his trousers and long underwear and sat back down in his jockstrap. A slow shivering began to take over his body.

Hank took the lid off the cooler, removed two ice cubes and put one in each armpit.

Jed did the same, and put one inside his jockstrap as well.

Hank put an ice cube in his jockstrap, then planted his feet in the ice water in the cooler. He gazed at Jed with triumph, his arms tight to his sides, hugging the ice cubes.

Sally reported that Mrs. Pritchard arrived on their doorstep one morning and spent an hour drinking coffee and explaining the benefit program a union could bring in. "Now I want you to work on that man of yours, Mrs. Tatro. I know he's a strong company man, but people do change. And a wife's in a position to point out some of these advantages to her husband."

"Jed honey, don't you think it makes sense?"

"You stay out of this. You don't know nothing about it. Neither does Mrs. Pritchard. You do what you're good at and leave this kind of thing to me."

"What is it I'm good at?" she asked with a coy smile.

"Cooking and cleaning and taking care of the kids."

"And?"

"Yeah, that too, darlin."

One day at lunch Jed read a poster on the employee bulletin board announcing that a majority had signed union cards and that an election would be held over whether or not the ATW would represent employees in negotiating a contract with management. Jed's mouth fell open. A majority of the people he worked with had been taken in by Mrs. Pritchard's Communist bullshit? When he walked into the lunchroom, he saw a banner draped from opposite walls. Everyone was craning their necks to read it. One side was a photo of an Arnold mill in Massachusetts that had shut down because of union demands. Across it was a huge black X. On the other side was a photo of Benson Mill with the caption "It Could Happen Here." Jed nodded. Mr. Prince wouldn't take this sitting down. Even if the election took place, the union wouldn't stand a chance. All those people must have been threatened into signing cards.

As he opened his lunch box, a note fluttered out: "Just remember I'll love you always." He wadded it up impatiently. She was so goddam stuck on herself, always demanding his attention. As though he didn't have more important things to think about. Such as which people in this room had signed those blue cards. If only he knew, he personally would punch them out. Or at least try to talk some sense into their ignorant hillbilly heads, like they'd taught him at foreman school.

In the Chevy on the way home he listened to a radio editorial from the station manager, who pointed out that a vote for the union would be a vote against the Father, and the Son, and the Holy Ghost. Jed couldn't of agreed more. He only hoped the people who'd signed those cards was listening.

As he sat in his Naugahyde La-Z-Boy Lounger waiting for supper, he read the Newland News. "Honey," he yelled into the kitchen, "did you know that that union that's trying to get in over at the mill has made contributions to subversive groups like the NAACP and the Jewish Labor Defense Fund?"

"What's subversive, darlin?"

He hesitated. "It ain't good."

She came in and put on a record. Stopping behind him, she kneaded his shoulders as Honey Sweet wailed, "*My man, understand? / He holds me in the palm of his hand / And I like it . . .*"

"The only thing I can't understand," he said, "is who around here would fall for their Commie line."

She continued kneading.

"Am I right?"

"Well, apparently there's some it makes sense to. Not everbody thinks the same."

"*. . . he's a king, the real thing . . .*"

"Yeah, but they just ain't thinking it through, is how I see it."

She didn't reply.

"Am I right?"

"Well, they could maybe think it through and still come up with a different conclusion."

His shoulders began to twitch under her hands.

"*. . . his arms are warm / And they keep me away from harm . . .*"

"Not if they had all the facts, they couldn't. Am I right?"

"*. . . and I want to keep it like this all the time . . .*"

"Yeah, honey, I guess you're right."

He relaxed into his chair. "Damn right I am."

"Supper's almost ready."

"Good. I'm starved."

"Smothered pork chops. Is that all right?"

"Yeah. Great."

"You don't sound very excited."

"Sure I am. I love pork chops, honey."

"Do you love them smothered?"

"Especially smothered."

"You promise?"

"Yeah, I promise." Why did she need reassurance all the time? It was irritating having to convince her at every meal that Betty Crocker herself couldn't of did better. Why couldn't she just put it on the table and shut up?

The next morning handbills swirled through the parking lot. They featured the Vulture of Communism being overcome by the American Eagle. Jed folded one up to take home to Sally. He signed a petition in the locker room that supported management. It appeared the next day as a full-page newspaper ad, signed by 93 percent of "our happy Benson workers."

"If 93 percent is happy," Jed explained to Sally, "and 51 percent signed union cards, then they's 44 percent is lying. Or else the union's done forged signatures. See what I mean? You can't trust nobody no more."

No reply. "Am I right, Sally?"

"Right, Jed."

The day before the election Mr. Mackay appeared in the lunchroom with Mr. Prince and a couple of men in suits whom no one had ever seen before. The room fell silent. Mr. Mackay spoke: "As you know, tomorrow you vote on the future of your mill. Up to this point, the ATW has done us a big service by prodding us into weeding out the people among us who didn't want to work for their living. Instead, these people sneaked around on company time spreading false rumors about those of us in the front office. They attacked us personally, and they attacked how we run your mill. They intimidated a lot of you into signing their little blue cards, with their crazed Communist rhetoric. But with that scum out in the gutter now where they belong . . ."

Up to this point Jed had been listening in a state of polite boredom. Mackay wasn't blessed with the gift of firing people up with his words. He hadn't even quoted from the Bible yet. But as words like "scum" and "gutter" appeared, as Mackay's face began to turn red, as he began stabbing the air with his index finger, everyone sat up straighter and listened.

". . . and it's up to each of you out there, my friends, to decide whether the interests of our Benson Mill family are best represented by men like Mr. Prince here, who've known you and your kin all your lives, who've helped you through hard times, who've cared for your concerns as though you were his own cousins (as some of you are). Or whether our interests are best represented by a bunch of Communist troublemakers from up North who want to use their destruction of your mill as a stepping-stone in their destruction of the entire Free World."

One of the unknown suited men, looking agitated, stepped forward and whispered something to Mackay. Mackay, face red and hand raised, pushed him away. The suited men each took one of Mackay's arms and ushered him out, Mr. Prince following. People returned to their lunches, disappointed. Jed reflected that it was like high school— necking but not coming. "Who were the guys in the suits?" he asked Hank.

"Don't know. Heard someone say the home office sent them down. Public relations."

"What's that?"

"I don't rightly know."

That evening as Jed walked into the parking lot, what looked like a pep rally was in progress. People from both the outgoing and incoming shifts crowded around a flatbed truck on which stood Mrs. Pritchard, Betty, some men he didn't know—and Raymond, who was shouting into a microphone: "This here place was started up by local Newland people with their own money. The wages was a fortune to people who'd been starving on dirt farms in the hills. Old man Prince really did know and care about our parents and grandparents. But now the place is owned by Arnold Fiber Corporation. They got them forty-five other mills. The profits get divided up by banks on Wall Street. These gin-soaked, jet-lagged capitalists fly in here from New York City and make decisions on the basis of what will make them the most money. Then they fly home to their penthouses on Park Avenue.

"But we run those machines, people. Day in and day out we stand over them and sweat and try to meet quotas that are too high, under conditions people wouldn't keep their coon dogs in. We don't have old man Prince to look out for us anymore. Each of us by ourself, up against a company with 35,000 workers and 875 million dollars in sales, is pretty pathetic. But if we all stand together, they'll have to listen to us. It's hard times, folks. The old ways is dead, and the new ways is yet to come. We got here a corpse giving birth to a half-formed fetus."

Police sirens wailed. Some men ran toward trucks and cars. A couple on the flatbed truck grabbed guitars. Raymond moved away from the microphone, and they began singing "We Shall Not Be Moved." The crowd picked it up.

Jed stood on the loading platform in a state of shock, trying to digest the reality that his own brother, his former Sunday School teacher, and a girl he had slept with in high school, his best friend's wife, were all Commie trash for the ATW. There was no longer any way he could make excuses or ignore evidence. He knew what he had to do now. He squared his shoulders. His blue eyes glinted. He would devote his life to getting rid of the scum that was trying to destroy the mill and the American way of life, whoever they might be.

Highway patrol cruisers raced up the access road. But a chaotic jam of pickups and cars had blocked off the entrance to the parking lot. The flatbed truck pulled away, as the people on it jumped off and were lost in the crowd.

The morning of the election old Mr. Prince arrived on the shop floor in his shirt-sleeves, his son and Mr. Mackay following in his wake like dinghies behind an ocean liner. As they passed through the roving room, Jed and Mr. Meaker fell in line. The older workers smiled and chatted with old Mr. Prince as he came up. The younger ones watched the living legend with curiosity. At one point he rolled up his shirt-sleeves, got down on his knees, and tinkered with a wrench on some gears.

Mr. Meaker said to Jed in a low voice, "Used to be able to fix ever machine in the place himself."

Eventually he stood up, brushed himself off, handed the wrench back to the operator, and muttered, "Infernal newfangled machines."

When they arrived at Raymond's machines, old Mr. Prince said, "Now what's this foolishness I hear, son, about you being mixed up with these Reds from up North."

"You mean the ATW? Yes sir, I'm involved with them."

"Why, I just don't understand that, Raymond. Your daddy ought to take you out back to the woodshed." The others laughed politely. Raymond stared at him. "Why, I remember you in diapers, boy. The day your daddy paid off the mortgage on your house, I came over and sat on the back porch and drank a glass of iced tea with him. And you were crawling around in the grass with your diapers about to fall off." He laughed heartily.

"Yes sir," Raymond said. Old Mr. Prince looked at him, his bushy white eyebrows twitching. After a long silence, Raymond said, "You always treated our family real good, Mr. Prince."

"I'm glad you feel that way, son. I've tried to treat my people good. I think of them almost as family."

"Newland owes you a big debt of gratitude, sir."

A puzzled frown from old Mr. Prince. Another long silence.

"But things has changed, sir."

"They sure have, son. We started out with a little biddy shed in a cow pasture, and twenty-five employees!"

"Yes sir, but it ain't like that no more."

Jed stood listening to the conversation that followed, but couldn't take it in. ". . . movement of capital . . . concentration of corporate power . . ." To him there was Mackay, who was God; Mr. Prince, Junior, who was well-meaning but a little spineless; Raymond and Hank and Betty, who were misled by the Commies; Mrs. Pritchard, who was a ball-breaker and deserved everything bad that could ever happen to her. "Power elite." What did that mean?

All Jed knew for sure was that he resented it when old Mr. Prince said, "You're a bright boy, Raymond. Always have been. You'll go far in this world." He, Jed, was the one loyal to the mill. Raymond was out to destroy it. Probably it was like the prodigal son story. But that story had always bothered him. Just didn't seem fair.

"Where's my jacket at?" asked old Mr. Prince, unrolling his shirt-sleeves and looking around. "I'm getting out of here."

He called to the room at large, "Listen, friends, yall have you your union, hear? Yall gon need it. You're gon need *something*. God help us all." He stalked out.

Jed watched him in disbelief. The old guy had gone off his rocker. That sometimes happened with old people.

# Chapter Five

## Sally

Sally lay in bed propped on pillows, watching on TV as Ingrid Bergman reclined next to Cary Grant in an elegant flat in London, England. It was crammed with flowers he'd just brought her. "My darling," Ingrid murmured, drawing Cary's mouth toward hers, a hand on each side of his head.

Sally sighed. If only Jed would sometimes think to bring her flowers . . . She knew she mustn't cry because her mascara would run. She'd already noticed hints of crow's feet when she smiled and had decided to stop smiling. Also, she'd made up her eyes different tonight—in a way *Glamour* magazine promised would draw attention away from the wrinkles. She didn't know if it was successful because Jed still wasn't home, and here it was eleven o'clock at night. Running through her mind was the Honey Sweet song she'd heard on the radio while fixing the supper that was now ice cold: *"She's out there, too, / And she's a whole lot better looking than you, / And she can do things to a man you never dreamed a woman can do. / If you think you keep your man with a gold wedding band, / You better listen . . ."*

Usually he called if he was working late. Still and all, he'd been running around like a crazy person ever since the strike started. She'd never seen him in such a good mood. Probably he just forgot to call.

What if there was someone else? In high school he'd been mixed up with that horrible Betty French. She worked at the mill, too, or used to. A few times he suggested asking her and Hank to dinner, but she refused to have that girl in her home. Jed was late lots . . .

She glanced down at her white nightgown and peignoir set, bought for their honeymoon trip to Blowing Rock. She hadn't known then that it would be like this—him gone most of the time, and her here alone with no one to talk to except two babies. When Joey was an infant, she started going once a week to a bowling league. She left Joey with a sitter in the bar at the alley. She couldn't bowl worth anything, but it was fun to sit around in her orange Ben's Body Shop and Salvage shirt, eating jelly doughnuts and chatting with girls she knew from high school. But it turned out a girl on her team was married to a man who worked for Jed. He said to Jed, "I hear you don't like liver neither." Jed asked her not to go anymore because it would undermine him on the job to have her gossiping about him with an employee's wife. "A wife should be absolutely loyal to her husband," he told her. Anyhow, he felt like that she ought to be with a better type of girl, with him about to be foreman and all.

All her close friends were gone. Melissa was at State. Kim was in Atlanta taking a business course. It was a real switch from being Most Popular to being nothing. All the things she learned in school and in Ingenue—how to set a nice table and organize successful parties and be a good hostess—she never had a chance to use anymore. Sometimes she asked Jed if he didn't want to invite some friends from work to dinner on the weekend. He said except for Hank and Betty he didn't have friends there, he had workers, and he couldn't socialize with them because it would undermine his authority. Besides, he saw them all week. On weekends he just wanted to be with her and the kids. "A husband and wife don't need no outside friends. They should be each other's best friends." And he *was* her best friend. But still she sometimes felt lonely. And when she did, she felt guilty for being disloyal. She raised her eyes to the Norman Rockwell picture over her dresser of a smiling mother standing over two sleeping children. After all, she did have her babies to keep her company.

What would she do if Jed had him another girl? What *could* she do with two babies, except swallow her pride and put up with it? She couldn't go home. Her daddy had been so unpleasant about the marriage in the first place. She didn't know what his plans for her had been, but she'd messed them up.

"Daddy, what exactly do you have against Jed?" she'd asked once. He blushed and muttered, "Nothing. Jed's a fine boy. But he chews gum with his mouth open."

She'd suggested to Jed to chew with his mouth closed, which he'd been doing ever since, but it didn't seem to help much.

Jed said once, "You know, Sally, I don't think your daddy much likes me."

She'd said, "Jed honey, that's just plain silly. He's training you for foreman, isn't he?" But secretly she thought he was probably right. Not long after they moved into this house, her mother and father came down for Sunday dinner. They looked around the house.

"Well?" demanded Sally with a smile.

"It's very nice, dear," said her mother in a quiet voice that suggested it *wasn't* very nice.

She saw them carefully avoiding looking at Jed as he chewed with his mouth open, his forearms resting on the table edge. Jed was nervous and laughed loudly at anything her father said, whether it was funny or not.

"It's sure been great having you here, Mother and Dad. You're our first guests," Jed said as they were leaving. They looked at him, then smiled politely.

"It's nice having you in the family, Jed," her mother said, her smile strained.

Her father called soon after to tell her he'd given her some mill stock, but that she couldn't sell it or collect the dividends without his permission until he died. He added that she could have his permission if she wanted to spend it on some project of her own, like going back to school.

"How could I go back to school, Daddy? I'm about to have me a baby."

"Hire a babysitter. Or I'm sure your mother and Mrs. Tatro would help out."

"I don't think Jed would like that, Daddy. He thinks a mother should be with her baby."

"Fine. Good-bye." He hung up. Just like that. How could she finish school when Jed hadn't? He'd given up college for her, so she would for him, too.

She went to her dresser and dabbed on some fresh Evening in Paris perfume. Ever since Jed said making love with her was like screwing a corpse, she'd tried to think of ways to make herself more exciting. She tore an article out of *Modern Wife* called "How To Keep That Man Coming Back for More." It suggested hair styles and makeup techniques, a shape-control program.

. . . and once you've rinsed that gray right out of your hair, don't neglect that gray matter inside your head. Check books out of your local library on topics of interest to Him. Read the newspaper every day—all of it now, not just the recipes! Take a night course (if He doesn't object to staying with the children on Mom's Night Out). P.S. Inject your new knowledge into conversations in a modest, low-key way. No one likes a girl who knows it all! . . .

Earlier that week she checked out the *Handbook of Cotton Manufacture in the United States*. Last night at supper she said, "I was reading today about hank clocks, darling."

"Uhn," he said, hunched over his plate, shoveling in soup beans. "What about them?"

"Well, they sound real interesting."

He glanced up. "Well they ain't."

"Do yall use you a Buckley or a vertical opener?"

"What?"

"In the opening room."

"Sally, I got to think about that shit all day long. I just want to relax when I get home."

"Sorry, honey."

She took the book back and was now reading one of his detective paperbacks about a girl who wore high silver boots and had small pistols concealed in her bra so that the barrels poked out her blouse like nipples.

She got back in bed and listened for the car. All she could hear was the pulsing of crickets, and the distant roar of diesel trucks on the highway. Down the block a woman shouted. TV sets of neighbors erupted with canned laughter. Laura whimpered in her sleep and flung out an arm, rattling her crib bars.

Sally went into the bathroom and blotted her eyes and blew her nose. Jed hated her to cry, got all huffy. "Sally, this ain't like you," he'd mutter. As though he knew everything about what she was like. Would he be surprised if he knew some of the things she thought about! A few months ago she'd read a book called *Castle Keep* about a girl on this windswept moor over at England, who was carried off to this stone castle and held prisoner by a tall dark stranger. At first she'd pounded on his big chest with her little fists. But he was kind and patient, brought her presents. Little by little she began to lose her fear, and even to like him . . . There was this tall dark man who worked in the lumberyard where she sometimes bought building supplies for Jed. Whenever she came in, he would look up from his loading to give her a faint smile. Sometimes she imagined he would grab her wrists and force her into his truck and carry her off to his cabin in the mountains. She found herself stopping by the lumberyard as often as possible.

He reminded her a little bit of Earl. Emily must have been crazy to let him get away. And all for what? So that she could end up with that Justin creature she'd brought home last winter. Earl had been so smooth. Justin was about as smooth as a sink coated with Ajax. All the time wearing a dirty old trench coat with the collar turned up, and turning his head sideways when you were trying to talk to him. She and Jed and Emily had driven him on a tour of the area, and it seemed like there wasn't anything he couldn't find something wrong with—the weather, the way the town was laid out, the houses people lived in, the pork barbecues they ate for lunch. Several times Jed looked about ready to relieve him of his teeth. Justin insisted they stop at Injun Al French's house in Cherokee Shoals while he went in and bought for twenty dollars one of those ugly tire planters Betty had made in high school, which had been sitting unsold in the yard ever since. Injun Al in his war bonnet and buckskins, just sober enough to be amazed that he'd finally sold one, carried it over and put it in the trunk. On the way home Justin asked Emily if she'd ever seen the beadwork and silver jewelry and woven rugs in the American Indian Room of some museum in New York. Emily said no.

"Reduced to cutting up tires and painting them with enamel. It's pathetic."

"Why'd you buy it if you don't like it?" demanded Jed.

"As a reminder, a reprimand."

"What of?"

"Of the genocide on which this nation is predicated."

Jed nodded politely, but Sally knew he didn't any more know what "predicated" meant than she did. Looked like Emily did know, though, because she was nodding in agreement.

But then Emily agreed with everything Justin said the whole time. It looked pretty serious. But it had looked serious with Earl, too. They'd even been pinned. Emily and Justin laughed about him sneaking from the guest room into her bed after Emily and Sally's parents were asleep. Both Jed and Sally were shocked but said nothing.

"It just ain't respectful to your parents," Jed said later to Sally.

Justin wasn't big on respect anyway. He tried to argue with Sally's father at supper one night about how the mill was set up, and he didn't even say "sir" as he did so. Her daddy only smiled politely and said, "I'm sure you're right, Justin."

"Then why don't you change it?"

"Things are changing fast enough without my assistance."

Justin shrugged. Emily smiled. She seemed to think that he was wonderful, and that everyone else thought so too. Looked like she didn't notice he was driving the rest of them crazy. At least if Emily brought Justin into the family, it would give her parents someone to be even more displeased with than poor Jed. They hadn't mentioned Justin since.

Sally looked in the mirror and traced her newfound wrinkle with her fingertips.

As she slipped back into bed, the back door slammed. "Hi, honey!" she called, puffing up her bouffant with her fingers.

Jed walked into the bedroom. "Hey, darlin." He unbuttoned his shirt and dropped it on the floor. "What is this crap?" he muttered, turning off Ingrid and Cary.

He sat on the bed and took the jagged rings from poptop beer tabs off each finger and put them on the nightstand.

"What's that for?"

"Kind of like brass knuckles."

"What for?"

"In case of trouble."

When he climbed into bed, she took his face in her hands and murmured, "My darling."

He pushed her hands away.

Regrouping, Sally slipped her hands inside his pajama top and caressed his hairy chest. He turned over impatiently and switched out the light.

Undaunted, she groped for his crotch.

"I don't feel like it tonight, honey."

She retracted her hand. "I fried you some chicken tonight, darlin."

"Yeah? Sorry I missed it."

"It's all right," she said bravely. "I covered the pan and saved it long as I could. I kept thinking you'd surely be home soon. But it got all mushy, and I had to feed it to the cat."

"I'm sorry. I tried to call. The line was busy. Joey must have knocked the phone off the hook again."

"No. No, I don't think so."

"Well, I did try."

"Yes."

"I did, damn it!"

"I believe you."

"You don't sound like you do."

"How would I sound if I did?"

"I don't know. Different."

"You feeling guilty or what?"

"Hell no, I ain't feeling guilty. I spend half the night guarding your old man's house, and I'm supposed to feel guilty?"

"Guarding Daddy's house? What for?"

"Last night they dynamited Mackay's carport. We was afraid they might try yours tonight."

"Dynamited? But why?"

"Who knows? Bunch of trash, led on by that Commie brother of mine."

"Who? Raymond? Is Raymond a Communist?"

"Damn right he is."

"I don't believe it. When I think I used to climb trees with that boy . . ." Raymond had refused to go to dinner at the Princes' when

Justin was in Newland. Nobody could figure it out. Hadn't they been friends in New York? They'd decided he was still stuck on Emily and was jealous of Justin. But Raymond was so strange these days, even stranger than normal. Before the strike he stopped by after work for a beer and an argument about the union with Jed. Sally tried to play peacemaker, and Raymond said, "It's not like this ain't got nothing to do with you, Sally. Marx says, 'The nature of individuals depends on the material conditions determining production.' Look at yourself: You've gone and turned yourself into a product and then marketed it."

Sally smiled uncertainly. Was this a compliment? She glanced at Jed. Looked like he didn't know either.

Jed narrowed his eyes and clenched his fists. "Are you saying my wife sells it? Is that what you're a-saying?"

Raymond started laughing and stood up. "Christ, no! Just relax and forget it, baby brother."

"You poor thing," Sally said, cuddling Jed and stroking his hair. "My poor baby must be all tired out—working all day and guarding all night."

"Yeah, that's a fact," he sighed, resting his head against her breasts.

As she stroked, she thought about how unfair it was. He was tired. Well, she was tired, too—taking care of the kids all day, cooking and cleaning, waiting up for him half the night. But who ever cuddled her and stroked her hair and said, "You poor thing." Nobody, that's who.

And when she was in the mood for love, which wasn't all that often, he never was, so nothing happened. But when he was in the mood, which was usually when supper was getting cold, or the baby was screaming, or the alarm was buzzing, they went right ahead. You couldn't argue with a limp penis, but it still didn't seem fair. The harder she tried, the less interested he seemed. Unless he hadn't really been guarding tonight . . .

She knew she could get him interested if she offered to do it with her mouth. He was always grateful when she would. When they'd be making love, he'd take her head in both hands and try to direct her mouth down there. Sometimes she would and sometimes she wouldn't, depending on how nice he'd been. But really she could hardly stand it. She hated seeing him lying there on his back with that pleading expression. The man was supposed to be on top and in charge. The same way she hated seeing him all curled up against her like a little boy right now. But as long as she was doing these things for him, maybe he wouldn't go looking for another woman who would.

But it never worked out the way she planned anyhow. After she'd blow him, he'd get all mean and nasty. And in the morning, after she'd held him all night, he'd be cold. He'd probably like to shut her in the freezer until the next time he needed her, so he wouldn't have to worry about her revealing to anybody that he was sometimes tired and weak and didn't like liver.

She vowed to reread the *Modern Wife* article first thing after he left in the morning.

Jed kissed her at the door. "Well, wish me luck."

"Something special going on today?"

He sighed. "Yeah, a strike. How many times have I got to tell you?"

"Oh yeah. Well, good luck, hear? Why? It's not dangerous or anything is it?"

"Sure. Can be. When you cross their line, they throw stuff at your car and call you names and all like that."

"Oh honey. I wish you wouldn't go then."

"I got to go, darlin." His blue eyes glinted in the sunshine. "We don't have enough people as it is. I was running half a dozen machines all by myself yesterday. They brung in some coloreds, and some women from Cherokee Shoals. But they don't know how to run nothing. And don't hardly have the sense to learn. But they try real hard. You got to respect them for that. And you never saw such a happy bunch of people in your life. They consider it a privilege to be on at the mill. I say we should keep them and forget about them Commies howling around outside. Am I right?"

"I'm sure you are."

"Damn right I am."

"Well, I'm just so proud of you, honey."

"Well, it's kinda like Coach Clancy used to say: 'When the going gets tough, the tough get going.'"

Sally smiled. She just didn't know what to think about this union business. Mrs. Pritchard had made it sound pretty good that day. But Jed and his father and her father said it was bad, so she guessed it was. Mrs. Pritchard must have gotten misled by the Communists or something.

"Am I right?"

"Yes, honey, you sure are."

He kissed her again.

"Notice anything different about me?"

"Huh un. Uh, I don't know, your lipstick's lighter?"

"Huh un. I made up my eyes different. Do you like it?"

"Honey, you always look gorgeous to me."

"You gonna show me tonight after the kids are asleep?"

"Might do it, if I don't have to guard or something."

As he drove off, Sally went into the bathroom and removed her makeup with cold cream. Then she applied a face masque with a double thickness around the eyes, and put her hair up in rollers. She went around the bedroom and picked up Jed's dirty clothes and the bath towels he'd dropped, mopped up the swamp he'd made of the bathroom floor, made their bed. She fed Joey his cereal. As he watched Captain Kangaroo, she strapped Laura in her highchair with a dish of mashed banana and sat at the table with a cup of coffee reading "How To Keep That Man Coming Back for More."

. . . The bedroom is one arena many wives turn into a battleground. A man needs to draw from his wife at night, like a bee drawing nectar from a bright blossom, the sense of self-worth to send him back to his struggles in the world the next morning. A good wife is the safe harbor in the storm, not the raging sea . . .

Sally saw Joey cradling one of Laura's dolls in his arms and nursing it with an imaginary breast.

"Joey, come here, sweetie." She laid the doll out of reach on a shelf and handed him a cowboy pistol. "Dolls are for girls, honey."

He studied the pistol, perplexed. Finally he pointed it at the doll and yelled, "Pow! Pow!" He galloped around the room.

She looked at the red-patterned café curtains on the dining nook windows and wondered how it would be to have matching place mats. Maybe matching napkins, too. She'd ask Jed tonight.

She strapped Laura in the jump seat that hung in the doorway. Then she got out her S & H Green Stamp catalogue and studied the various place mats and napkins they offered. One nice-looking set was only four books. She put a sponge in a dish of water, got out her box of stamps, and began pasting.

After lunch she removed her face masque and put a scarf over her rollers, then loaded the kids in the Dodge. She drove slowly past the lumberyard and caught a glimpse of the tall dark man out back stacking two-by-fours. Her heart faltered, like someone whose pacemaker batteries were going dead. His smile. It was always so sad. Some woman must have done him wrong. Now he was leery of all women. You'd have to woo him, win him over, teach him to trust again . . .

At Kroger's she put Laura in the shopping cart seat, while Joey trotted alongside. Laura squirmed and grunted and pointed to the floor, wanting to walk too.

"No, darling. Hush now. Be Mommy's good girl and ride quietly."

She kept whimpering, twisting, and turning.

Sally felt rage sweep through her. "No! Be *still* now!" Laura looked at her tearfully and did as instructed.

Joey came stumbling up carrying a can of Niagara spray starch. "Joey want to iron."

"No, put it back please, Joey. Mommy doesn't need starch."

"Joey want to iron." He dumped the can in the cart.

Sally returned it to the shelf and pressed on. Clutching the starch, Joey caught up.

"Joey *going* to iron!"

Sally grabbed the can. "Joey *can't* iron. Joey's a boy. Girls iron."

His face turned dark red. "Me want to iron!" he screamed.

Shoppers turned and stared at Sally, the child abuser.

"*Please*, Mommy! Joey can iron!"

Gritting her teeth, she pushed the cart into the next aisle, leaving him lying on the linoleum kicking his feet. "Teddy Bear's Picnic" was playing over the public address system. A voice broke in: "Ladies, we're having us a special, today only, in aisle four: Nabisco Chips Ahoy! cookies, a big double bag for only fifty-nine cents. One to a customer please!" Housewives hurtled past her in search of aisle four. Sally stopped in front of the margarine. Two cents off Parkay. But she'd cut a coupon from the newspaper for four cents off on Fleischmann's. She took out the coupon and read it. Four cents off on two pounds. Which was the same as two cents off on a pound, wasn't it? And after all, she only wanted a pound. She took the Parkay, pleased with herself for being a good shopper. Jed liked real butter. But an article in *Modern Wife* had cautioned her to watch his cholesterol. What would she do if he dropped dead of a heart attack and left her with two little children? He was getting a roll around his middle. She was thinking about putting him on a diet, had been collecting diet recipes from magazines for several weeks. She might be able to do it so he wouldn't even know he was on a diet.

Joey caught up, red-faced and bedraggled. Laura struggled in her cart seat.

"Can Joey ride?" he whispered.

"Aren't you ashamed? A big boy like you riding?" She took a large roll of Saran Wrap off the shelf. She'd read in *Modern Wife* if you wrapped yourself in it while you exercised, it was good for your pores.

The bag boy loaded her groceries into the Dodge. "I just got one question," he said with a grin, as she thanked him.

"What?"

"When do you girls ever take your rollers out? Or do you keep them on all the time? All day long that's all I ever see, is big old rollers!"

Sally laughed. "It's so we'll look nice when our men get home in the evening."

The boy, tall, thin, and dark, looked enlightened. "Why don't you give the rest of us men a break sometime?" he said with a sweet smile.

Sally was enchanted—and grateful. Was he flirting? No one had flirted with her in years—not since Jed had claimed her when she was fifteen or so.

"I might just do that."

"Hurry back now," he said with a grin.

"Oh, I will."

She drove home, smiling and singing the Honey Sweet song, "*All I want is just to be your girl. / Please come and get me, / And take me to your world.*" She glanced over at the Castle Tree as she drove past. It was covered with tender pale green baby leaves. When she used to climb that tree, she'd planned to be a singer in New York when she grew up. She remembered the fervor with which she wailed into her jump rope handle. That had been her talent for the Miss Newland pageant. If only she hadn't dropped the microphone, she might have won. Her answers during the question session had been pretty good:

"If you were Miss America, Sally, traveling around to other countries as our Ambassadress of Beauty, what would you tell them about our great nation?"

"Well, Stan, I'd tell them first of all about the ideals that have made our country what it is today—our belief that all men are created equal and endowed by the Lord with rights that nobody can ever take away from them. Let's see . . . I'd tell about the beauty of our terrain—the towering mountains, the rushing streams, the vast plains. I'd tell about the people from every end of the globe who have come here and found for the first time in their lives Justice and Brotherhood . . ."

If she'd been crowned Miss Newland, she'd have gone to the Miss Tennessee pageant. From there to Atlantic City for the Miss America pageant. She might have begun a career as a popular singer, like Anita Bryant. She'd have spent the following years traveling around doing personal appearances. She'd have had to leave Jed behind. He'd have found another girl. She wouldn't have gotten pregnant.

She pulled into the driveway and studied their little house. She turned and looked at Joey and Laura in their car seats. But for one ill-timed stumble, none of this would have existed.

For a moment, she willed it all to oblivion.

She shook herself, got out, and began unloading groceries.

She fed the kids, and took them into their room and put Laura into her crib, pulling up the side bar. She wound up her musical angel mobile. She made Joey lie on his bed and look at his mobile of sailboats. She knew once she left, he'd climb down and play with his tank and poke Laura through her bars, but she just ignored the commotion unless Laura began screaming. She couldn't wait for Jed to finish the new room, so she could separate them once and for all.

She put a load in the washer and turned on the TV to "Love for Life." She arranged her entire day so she wouldn't have to miss it. Sometimes Brad and Elvira seemed more real than Jed. Brad was taking his secretary to a motel today. Sally removed her Ever So Ice nail polish and put on some Eat Me Orange. She felt bad for Elvira, at home sneaking gin from a bottle and replacing it with water.

Sally blew on her nails. If they didn't dry before Laura began shrieking to have her diapers changed, she'd ruin them. Would Jed be likely to do that—take a girl to a motel? How would she ever know if he did? Could she ask him? And if she did, would he tell her the truth? If he wasn't seeing another girl already, probably he would eventually. That was how men were. But did her daddy have other women? Surely not. Who? It was too small a town. If that's how men were, how were women? Was she supposed to sneak gin alone in the afternoon?

Immobilized by her nails, she ran through her outfit for supper— mauve silk shirt and matching wool skirt, a paisley scarf around her neck. Yes, Jed liked that outfit. Oh dear, no, not mauve. Not with orange nail polish. Darn. She just hadn't been thinking.

And for supper—steak, baked potato, corn bread, molded Jell-O salad. Which place mats, now? What if he did have another girl? Was that why he hadn't wanted to make love much lately? The gold woven ones. With candles to match.

She waved her nails in the air. Those windows next to the TV were streaky. She'd have to remember to tell Rochelle to wash them tomorrow. A pie! She'd bake a cherry pie this afternoon. Jed's favorite. If only her nails would get hard.

She reached for the phone and dialed carefully with the ball of her finger.

"Hi, Mama . . . nothing much. Just thought I'd say hi. What are you doing? . . . Yeah, I'm sitting here waiting on my nails to dry. Waiting for the kids to wake up . . . Yeah, a little bit lonely. None of my friends are around anymore. Besides, when would I have time to see them? . . . Yeah, I'm going to Happy Homemakers tomorrow with Jed's mother. They're having them a Hawaiian luau. Mercedes Marshall is showing her slides. You ought to come . . . Poor Little Joey, he was bound and determined I was gonna buy him some spray starch at Kroger's this morning. Said he wanted to iron. Can you imagine? . . . Let him? Are you kidding? Jed would croak! . . . Yeah, I know he's just a baby. But like Jed says Coach Clancy always used to say, 'The way you bend the twig is how the branch grows!' . . . Yeah, well, see you soon, Mama."

As she hung up, she was surprised to find tears running down her cheeks. She'd thought she was doing what her mother wanted. After all, it was what her mother herself had done. Sally had started it all too young, yes, but that was in the past. She'd been making a success of it. What did she have to do to make her mother proud? Cheerleader, Ingenue, Devout, Homecoming Attendant, runner-up to Miss Newland—none of these had seemed to impress her. Some days she'd walk the kids over to her mother's house and prop them up in front of her: Here, isn't this what you want from me? Emily had left Newland, came home dressed in jeans, and was losing her accent. But Emily was the one they talked about at Sunday lunches—what courses she was taking, what concerts she'd been to, what witty remarks she'd made in letters. Ha, ha. Sally wondered if there wasn't some way to let them know that Emily had been having sex with that repulsive Justin under their very roof, and had laughed about it later. How could she manage to let this bit of information slip out?

She picked up "How To Keep That Man Coming Back for More": "*. . . every man finds mystery alluring in a woman. Don't let him in on all the tricks of your trade. Shut him out of the bathroom when you're putting on your face . . .*" She put a check in the margin. "*. . . don't run around the house in rollers when he's there . . .*" She checked this off. "*. . . re-dye your hair before the roots grow out . . .*" Check. "*. . . let him suspect he doesn't know everything there is to know about you. Go out from time to time without telling* *him exactly where you're going . . ."* She thought this over. She could hide a photo of some man—an uncle he hadn't met—in a drawer where Jed would be sure to come across it . . .

"Who is this?" he'd demand.

"Oh . . . someone."

Laura started shaking the bars of her crib. Joey toddled out, rubbing his eyes. "Laurie wake Joey up."

"Naughty Laura," she intoned. Laura was jumping on her mattress, holding the bars. Sally felt a wave of irritation that alarmed her. Mothers weren't supposed to dislike their children, but she often did Laura. Joey's energy and determination enchanted her, unless she was in a hurry, like today at Kroger's. Laura's annoyed her. Little girls were supposed to be calm and polite, affectionate and cooperative.

She swept Laura up and smothered her with guilty kisses, strapped her on the changing table, and tickled and nuzzled her. Laura giggled, cooed, and kicked her pudgy legs. Sally plopped Laura in her playpen, then took her rollers out, and combed her hair. Then she put on her face and changed her clothes.

As she dumped a can of cherry filling into a frozen pie shell, she thought about what a lucky girl she was. To make a pie and watch your family enjoy it. To watch them grow healthy and put on flesh from what you fed them. This was an honor. Emily had read a lot of books and knew some fancy words, but had she ever actually done anything *real*? Emily thought she was pretty smart, but had she been smart enough to keep Earl?

Sally turned on the radio loud enough to compete with the Tom and Jerry cartoons Joey had switched on in the living room. Honey Sweet was wailing, *"You get close to what I cherish most: / You make me want to be a mother / And walk around with pride / With your child inside . . ."*

Should she have her another baby? Both times she was pregnant Jed hadn't been that interested in sex, which had been nice. He'd turned into a real gentleman and brought home surprises. Sometimes he'd rub her feet.

At supper Sally said, "How's the strike, honey?"

"Same."

"Any trouble?"

"Eggs on the Chevy when Dad and me crossed the line this morning. Lazy bastards. Standing around waving signs. Do you know, they was having them a pork barbecue down there this evening when I left? Seems like they think it's a party. And that insane brother of mine running around playing hero. He called Dad and me 'traitors to the working class' today."

"What's that mean?"

"Damned if I know. Dad fixed him good, though. Hollered out the window, 'Where was you when I was on Guam, you damned Commie?' " He laughed, so Sally did, too, although she didn't get it. "All I know is we got orders to fill. I figure if you accept a job, you have a responsibility to do what they pay you to do. Otherwise you should clear out. Am I right?"

"I'm sure you are, honey. What do you think about place mats to match the curtains in here?"

"Huh? Oh, sure, fine."

"Yeah, but would you tell me if you *didn't* like the idea?"

"Yeah, sure I would. That'd be real nice, honey."

"Maybe cloth napkins, too."

"Uh huh."

"You don't really care, do you?"

"Not really, darlin."

She sat in silence, her chin quivering. "As far as you're concerned, we could be living in a mobile home, with rented furniture and flour sacks for curtains."

"Now honey, you know that ain't so. I love our home. What you think gets me through work ever day. Come on now. This ain't like you, darlin. Be Daddy's big girl."

She reminded herself she was supposed to be the harbor, not the sea. "I'm sorry, darling. It's getting to be my time of the month."

He nodded. "I got to hurry. Got to go out guarding."

"But I thought maybe we could have us a quiet evening tonight. Go to bed early. Watch some TV. See if we can't find us some mischief to get up to." She smiled coyly.

"I'd like to, darlin. But the strikers threw ball bearings through your daddy's windows last night after I left. Didn't you hear?" She studied his face. Was he telling the truth, or was he going out to meet someone at the Lazy Daze Motel? She could hire a sitter, tour all the motels in the area looking for his Chevy . . .

"No. I talked to Mama, and she didn't even mention it. Why would they do a thing like that?"

"Bunch of Reds. Want to wreck the whole country and take over."

"Poor Daddy. Do you reckon he's upset?"

"Wouldn't you be? After all he's done for this town? I sure am, and it ain't even my windows. Somebody oughta string them up."

"Cherry pie for dessert!"

"Don't have time, darlin. I'll have some when I get in."

"But it'll be all cold, honey."

"I like it better cold."

"I thought you liked your cherry pie warm."

"No, honey. I've always liked it better cold."

She looked at him, her painted face gone haggard. "Jed, don't ever leave me, honey. Your love is all I got."

He coughed, embarrassed. "Now that ain't true, Sally. You got you a washer-dryer ensemble, a Dodge wagon, a TV console, two healthy children . . . Am I right?" He smiled winningly.

He reached in his pocket for the beer tab rings and began putting them on. Then he took his rifle from the rack on the living room wall and filled a pocket with bullets, his mouth set.

After giving the kids their bath, reading them a story and getting them to bed, cleaning up from supper and folding the clothes from the dryer, Sally went into the bedroom. As she picked up Jed's dirty clothes, she wondered if she could ask him to put them in the bathroom hamper himself. Or should a wife be in charge of her husband's dirty clothes?

She lay in a steaming bath, inspecting her body. Nice legs, but not long enough. Jed thought her ankles were too thick. He liked her breasts, though. A lot. So did she, but she liked them better before the nipples got huge from nursing, and before they got streaked with silver stretch marks. Her waist seemed a little too thick these days. She'd better start the exercise for it in the *Modern Wife* article.

She sat up and shaved her legs, her armpits, the edges of her pubic area, then plucked a few dark hairs from around her nipples and below her navel.

After she dried and oiled herself, she plucked her eyebrows, then examined the roots of her hair. She used cleansing cream on her face, reapplied her makeup, and rolled her hair. She sprayed herself with cologne and deodorant. She douched.

She took her eyebrow pencil and put it against her ribs, underneath her right breast. When she removed her hand, the pencil stayed in place, instead of falling to the floor as it always had. She felt the pencil with horror. She had failed the *Glamour* magazine two-piece bathing suit test. Her breasts were starting to sag . . . Those darn children anyhow. Were there exercises to make breasts perky again? She'd have to check the article.

She slipped on a coral silk kimono and climbed into bed with a newspaper and the article and some magazines. She read the article and pressed the heels of her hands together for half an hour.

The front page of the newspaper was all about the ball bearings through her parents' windows. Apparently Jed wasn't lying. At least not this time . . .

She sighed and flipped open *Modern Wife* to a questionnaire to determine the durability of your marriage:

When he leaves the cap off the toothpaste, do you (a) put it back on; (b) ask him nicely to put it on; (c) get angry and make a scene; (d) leave it off and let the toothpaste dry up, so that he can experience the result of his thoughtlessness?

Sally peeped before marking, discovered (a) was the desired answer, and marked it. Probably she shouldn't ask Jed to put his dirty clothes in the hamper. That was a wife's job.

Sally circled her remaining answers without cheating, totaled her score, then realized Jed would have to answer his part before they could say for sure how long their marriage would last. How could she get him to? She discovered the author had anticipated this problem:

If your husband refuses to participate in this questionnaire, will you (a) get angry; (b) cry; (c) try to guess his answers; (d) abandon the questionnaire?

She chewed the eraser. Suddenly she looked at the clock. She dashed to the bathroom like Cinderella at midnight, brushed her teeth, and rinsed with mouthwash. She took out her rollers and teased her hair. Climbing back in bed, she arranged her kimono, straightened the covers, and turned on the radio. Honey Sweet was singing, "... *a woman is just made to be hurt. / Cheated on, lied to, treated like dirt ...*"

Eleven-thirty, and Jed still wasn't home. He took his rifle. What if he was lying dying somewhere, calling for her? What if he was lying in some other woman's arms? She couldn't decide which was worse.

She glanced at the Norman Rockwell picture over her dresser of the smiling mother hovering over two sleeping children and went in to check on Joey and Laura. They always slept with such ferocity, tossing, sighing, slurping on fingers. Funny little creatures that emerged from her body. She felt tenderness for them, the kind available to her only when they were asleep.

She went into the kitchen, illuminated by the light inside the wall oven. She stood in the middle of the linoleum in silence, listening, hoping to hear the roar of the Chevy at the far end of the street. She heard only the hum of appliances. The glass doors on her oven and washer and dryer seemed for a moment like eyeballs watching her, making fun of her. Her job was to put things in them, punch buttons and turn dials. What was it crazy Raymond had said to her that night? "Can't you see, Sally? They've turned you into an appendage of your machines, an appendage made of flesh." She wasn't sure what appendage meant. But Raymond was right for once: There sure was something creepy about these machines ...

She dashed into her bedroom, climbed into bed, and pulled up the covers.

When Jed stomped in a half hour later, he looked radiant.

"Everything OK?" she asked. Why did he look so happy?

"Yeah. We sat up on the roof of that garage next door to yall. A bunch of cars went by, but no one stopped." He let his shirt fall to the floor.

"Honey, would you mind putting your dirty clothes in the bathroom hamper?"

He looked at her.

"It'd be a big help."

He picked up the shirt between two fingers, gazing at her. He marched into the bathroom and dropped it in the hamper, still gazing at her.

"Thank you so much, darling. I feel just terrible asking you."

"Mama always did it at home. Said it was the least she could do when her men worked so hard all day long."

"Never mind. Don't do it anymore," she pleaded.

"No, I'll manage."

"Please don't, Jed. I *like* doing it."

"You want my clothes in the hamper, Sally, you'll get my clothes in the hamper."

"But I don't, Jed. I want them on the floor. I don't know what got into me, sweetie."

He climbed in bed and turned his back. She ran her hands under his pajama top and scratched his back with her Eat Me Orange nails. He lay as still as death.

"Jed, honey, what's wrong?"

"What you mean? Nothing's wrong."

"You haven't held me in weeks, honey. And here I am knocking myself out not to be like a corpse."

He said nothing.

"What am I doing wrong, honey? If I knew what you wanted, I'd do it."

"I'm tired, Sally. I just want to sleep, is all."

Tears began eroding her Revlon pancake makeup. She sniffed loudly.

"Goddam, Sally! For Christ's sake!"

She sniffed again.

"Shit, Sally. All right, look: When I said that about screwing a corpse, I didn't mean for you to go turn yourself into a whore."

"A *whore*? Here I've been trying to be exciting, and now you call me a whore!"

"It ain't exactly exciting to have a woman all over you all the time. In fact it can get downright repulsive."

She wailed.

"Damn it, will you shut up? You said you wanted to know what I want. Why can't you act—you know—hard-to-get sometimes? Turn me down when I want you. Like I can't always have you just because I want you. Or come at me when I'm not expecting it. Surprise me sometimes. That's what I mean by exciting."

Sally digested this. It seemed to conflict with the safe harbor advice. "I'll try, Jed. I really will. If you want me not to want you sometimes, then that's exactly what I want."

"And when I want you, I want you sometimes to act like you want me, not that you're just going along with what I want to please me."

"Whatever you want, Jed, is what I want."

"Fine."

They settled in for sleep.

"Jed," Sally whispered.

"Ummm?"

"I just want you to know that I don't want you now."

"You don't?"

"No."

"Are you sure?"

"Yes."

He rolled over and ran his hands inside her kimono.

"I'd rather you wouldn't," she said.

"Really?"

"Really."

He pushed her knees apart as she moaned, "No, please don't."

Sally was rushing around in a flowered muumuu when Rochelle arrived in her grey maid uniform the next morning. There was a purple stain on the white collar, which made Sally recognize the dress as one of Kathryn's from many years back. The stain was the result of one of Raymond's failed magic tricks involving grape juice.

"Rochelle, would you please wash and wax the kitchen floor, and wash the back windows? And the ironing's already damp." Even though she'd watched her mother with Ruby all her life, Sally felt uncomfortable telling Rochelle what to do. Even if Rochelle was being paid. It didn't seem quite right. She could do these things as well as Rochelle, and after all, it was her own house. But Jed was determined for her to have a maid. Said he didn't want her to break her nails. She pointed out that she could carry a baby in one arm and a load of wash in the other.

"But you can't expect no woman to set up ladders and scrub windows," he insisted.

"Your mother always did. Besides, Rochelle is a woman, isn't she?"

"Neither of them is *my wife*."

True, Sally's own mother had never washed windows. But Sally still felt awkward. After all, Rochelle was Donny's wife, and The Five hadn't believed in bossing each other around. Or rather, they'd taken turns at it. But Ruby insisted Rochelle needed the work.

"What do you hear from Donny?"

"Oh, he just fine, thank you, ma'am. Got him a job parking cars up near the Nunited Nations."

Sally recalled seeing Donny when she drove Rochelle home one afternoon shortly before he left for New York. He stood on his porch in green work clothes with an ugly scar down one cheek.

"Goodness, Donny, what have you done to yourself?" she'd demanded through the Dodge window.

"Car wreck."

"You all right now?"

"Oh yes, ma'am. I just fine." He grinned.

Sally stopped in front of the Tatro house. Mother Tatro came out in a bright orange muumuu. As Sally waved, she tried to figure out why they couldn't get along. At first Jed had complained that Sally's turkey stuffing didn't taste like his mother's, her biscuits weren't as flaky, her shelly beans didn't have enough fatback. She'd started calling his mother for her recipes, but when she used them, she was always disappointed when the results didn't taste like *her* mother's version of the same dish. Sometimes Jed would get his mother to bake him a pecan pie, which he'd bring home to show Sally what a *real* pecan pie should taste like.

Mother Tatro would bring over her discarded furniture. Sally would make Jed put it in the garage. When Mother Tatro babysat,

Sally would return to find her living room rearranged to accommodate the pieces Mother Tatro had carried in from the garage. She also straightened Sally's drawers and shelves. Scorning the electric dryer, she'd string a clothesline through the back yard, iron the sheets, take Jed's rumpled shorts from his dresser and iron them. She'd bake several days' supply of biscuits and corn bread and spoon bread, as though sending her baby son into a culinary wilderness, and she spread it around town that Sally didn't keep Laura's feet covered properly. Sally thought she deserved better. After all, she'd agreed to switch churches.

Mother Tatro heaved herself into the Dodge like a sack of chicken scratch. "Hey, Mother Tatro. You look really nice. How are you?"

"Well, I'm just fine, thank you, Sally. How you, honey?"

As they walked through Myrtle Kendall's front door, Myrtle put crepe paper leis over their heads. "Aloha, Rose! Aloha, Sally!"

The room was filled with large ladies in tentlike dresses of bright fabric, with flowers in their hair and sandals on their feet. "Why, aloha there, yall!" they greeted each other. Sally looked around. No women her age. Mostly Mother Tatro's friends. Their gossip filled the room like bees swarming—whose new car had been repossessed, whose children were turning out a disgrace to their parents. Sally was trying to abide by the saying Mr. Marsh had put on the church marquee last week: "When tempted to gossip, breathe through the nose." Because she knew how it felt to be the target of gossip. For months after her marriage, as her belly got larger and larger, she'd had to hold her head high as people exchanged glances and whispers.

"Hear about Coach Clancy over at the high school?"

Sally strained to hear.

". . . floating in the Whirlpool at the high school."

". . . dead."

"Dead as a doornail."

". . . hands bound behind his back, and a plastic bag tied over his head."

". . . suicide, they say."

Sally listened with horror. Oh dear, poor Jed would be so upset.

Waikiki punch was served. Then open-faced ham and pineapple and cream cheese sandwiches. Dessert was pineapple upside-down coconut pudding cake, which had won a national recipe contest two years earlier.

After the business meeting, two girls from the high school came out in grass skirts and halters. One played "Little Grass Shack" on her ukulele, while the other did a hula. Then Mercedes Marshall showed her slides of the South Pacific. Most featured either Mercedes or Harvey, or Mercedes *and* Harvey, against an exotic backdrop—a grass hut, a listing coconut palm, a distant wall of wave with surfers hanging halfway up it.

". . . but you know, ladies, you couldn't *give* me one of them palm trees," Mercedes was saying. "Why, a palm can't hold a candle to one of our Tennessee poplars. Forty feet of trunk with a little biddy ole clump of leaves at the top—why, it's just pitiful . . ."

On came a slide of the American memorial at Pearl Harbor: ". . . and I want to tell yall, it brought tears to my eyes just thinking about those brave Amurican boys who gave their lives there on that December morning that we might be together here this afternoon in peace and in freedom. Harvey and I looked at each other, and we was just so choked with emotion that . . ." Her voice cracked. "Well, ladies, words just fail me, is all."

"Lord, I tell you, it makes you think," someone said.

"Makes you think about them Reds down at the mill," someone whispered to her neighbor.

"Are you trying to say that union members aren't ever bit as much loyal Amuricans as our boys that died at Pearl Harbor?" Clara Campbell demanded in a loud voice.

The room erupted. Mother Tatro sat silent, with a son on each side.


Sally was sitting in the living room clipping a recipe for Cherry Cheese Delight out of *Modern Wife* when Jed walked in.

"Hey," he said, kissing her.

"What's wrong, honey?"

"What makes you think something's wrong? Can't a man be in a bad mood without always having to explain himself?"

"Sure, honey. Here, have a seat." She went into the kitchen.

She called, "It's Coach Clancy, isn't it?"

No answer.

"You must be real sad."

"Stop telling me what I feel."

"OK, honey." She was seized with anxiety. What if it wasn't Coach Clancy? What if it was something she'd done? Was it that she'd asked him to put his clothes in the hamper? Did he have himself another woman who wouldn't ask him to do this? She went into the bathroom and looked in the mirror, tracing the faint wrinkles at the corners of her eyes with her fingertips. She fluffed up her hair, molded her breasts with her hands and lifted them. Not all that much sag yet. She smiled her pep squad smile.

For breakfast Sally cooked Jed's favorite—fried eggs, grits, fried potatoes, sausage, toast and coffee. He declined to speak while eating. Sally only wished she'd been struck dumb before asking him to put his clothes in the hamper. He'd been doing it ever since—and speaking and making love very little. She thought about strewing dirty clothes around the bedroom, so he'd get the idea it really was OK. If he resumed dropping his clothes on the floor, maybe he'd resume speaking and making love.

During the afternoon Sally was in the kitchen making corn bread for supper, using Mother Tatro's ghastly sugarless recipe. The kids had just gone down for naps. She heard Jed calling from the garage.

He was lying on his back under the Chevy with just his legs, in green work trousers, sticking out. She stooped and called, "What, honey?"

He pulled himself out from under the car. His face and hands were black with grease. "I'm having me a crisis here. I wonder could you run down to Ben's Body Shop and ask him for an oil pan for a '58 Chevy Impala?"

"Will you listen for the kids?"

"Yeah, sure. Take some money out of my wallet on the dresser."

She drove out to the highway, thrilled to have him let her do something for him. Maybe he was going to forgive her. She got the oil pan and crept through heavy traffic back to the mill village.

As she walked over to the Chevy, she had an inspiration. The kids were asleep. The house blocked the garage from the street. Jed wanted her to surprise him . . . She crept up to the car, squatted, put down the oil pan. Then she quickly unzipped his green trousers, and began stroking his penis, fighting repulsion at the pale squishy little thing.

A voice croaked, "What the . . ." He tried to double up. There was a dull thud, and he lay still.

She laughed. "Just relax and enjoy it, darling."

He wasn't getting hard.

"Bad idea, huh?" she called anxiously.

No answer.

"You don't like this, Jed?" What a horrible mistake. He wouldn't even speak to her now.

"Here's the oil thing anyway." She shoved it under the car, feeling frantic. She put his penis back in his trousers and zipped them up. What could she do to win his love again? Who was this other woman she was competing with anyway? Was it someone she saw every week at church, passed every day on the sidewalk, shopped with side by side in Kroger's? Did everyone in town know about it except herself? Were they pitying her behind her back? How could Jed make it so humiliating for her? What had she ever done except love him and try to make his life easier and more pleasant? She walked in the kitchen door, tears streaming from her eyes. Jed walked out of the bathroom. She stared at him.

"Any luck with the oil pan?" he asked pleasantly.

"It's under the car," she whispered.

He started for the back door.

"Jed?"

"Huh?"

"Who's under the car?"

"Oh, Hank come over to help me out."

"I thought it was you."

"Huh-un."

He pushed open the screen door.

"Jed?"

He turned. She blurted out what she'd done. He laughed. Relieved, she joined him through her tears. They could laugh together. He'd forgiven her for whatever it was she'd done. They went out to the garage.

"Hank?" he yelled. "How's that for hospitality, buddy?"

No answer.

"Hank?"

He grabbed Hank's ankles and dragged him out. He was motionless, a gash across his forehead. "Christ, you've killed him!"

She stood with her hands to her mouth, her eyes wide.

"Well, call the Lifesaving Squad or something! But shit, how do I explain this?"

"Just tell what happened."

"What, that my wife was playing with my best friend's dick?"

"But I thought it was you, Jed."

"That my wife can't tell my dick from my best friend's? Shit, Sally, what the hell did you think you was doing?"

"I was just trying to be how you wanted me to be—surprising you and all."

"I never asked for no hand jobs under the Chevy."

Her chin began quivering.

"Well, shit, Sally, don't start crying again. Go call the Lifesaving Squad, and then stay in the house and let me handle it."

She sat in the living room reading in *Modern Wife* "Can This Marriage Be Saved?" It sounded unlikely. The ambulance arrived and departed, Jed with it. Laura began whimpering, and Sally got both kids up and gave them juice and cookies.

Jed walked in. She was scared to look at him. "How is he?"

"He'll be all right. Some stitches in his head and a broken arm."

"Broken arm? I didn't touch his arm."

"Well, at first I wasn't going to tell them lifesavers nothing. But when we got to the hospital, I realized when Hank came to, he might think it was me feeling him up or something."

"You? Why would you do something like that?"

"Well, I wouldn't."

"Why would Hank think you might?"

"Well, he wouldn't."

"So why were you worried?"

"Ah shit, I don't know! I had to tell them something, didn't I?"

"I guess."

"So I told them the truth. They got to laughing so hard, they dropped him and broke his arm in two places."

"Oh poor Hank. I feel awful."

"Some of them lifesavers is on over at the mill. It's probably all over town by now."

Sally began putting sweaters on the kids. "Well, I'm sorry."

"I don't know, Sally. It just ain't right. The mother of my kids and all, acting like some kind of . . . whore or something. And now it's all over town."

Sally clenched her teeth. "I can't figure out what you want, Jed. If I could, I'd do it. But I just can't."

She strapped Laura in the stroller and took Joey's hand. "We're going for a walk. See you later."

If only she could turn this feeling in her guts into tears. She tried to, tried reminding herself of the many ways she'd tried to please Jed, and how consistently she'd failed. Boo hoo. The tears wouldn't start up. She tried quivering her chin. Still no tears. And that awful feeling remained. It was alarmingly close to anger. Except that it wasn't "like her" ever to get angry.

Joey galloped half a block ahead, then looked back and waited with tolerant superiority. They came to a low wall. Joey struggled to climb up on it, then fell onto the sidewalk. Sally tried to lift him up, but he pushed her away and resumed his combat with the wall, saying, "Joey can do it!"

"I'm sure he can," Sally murmured automatically.

Laura threw herself against the straps of her stroller. She pointed frantically to the wall, which Joey was now tottering along. "Uh uh uh!"

"Be still, Laura! Be a good girl."

They reached the sidewalk outside the sports stadium. The doors were open, so Sally pushed the stroller into the hallway beneath the tiered seats. An old Negro man in tattered khaki work clothes was pushing a broom past the shuttered concession stand where the Rebels sold candy and soda pop during the games. Joey's galloping feet echoed through the hallway.

The hallway opened out onto the bleachers. Leaving the kids, Sally walked out among the rows. She looked down to the manicured green field. This was the first time she'd ever seen this place empty. The stands had always been packed. She could raise her arms and make the band play, make the crowds yell. She had ridden around this field on the back of a white Cadillac, while the entire place thundered with applause. She had sung and danced on a stage in the middle of this field. She had stalked across that stage in a bathing suit, while every man in the audience devoured her with his eyes.

But act on it—take a boy in your arms, give him the body dozens had slobbered over in their wet dreams . . .

Cheerleader, Miss Newland, Homecoming Queen, Virgin, Wife, Mother, Daughter, Whore. What about plain old Sally? Everybody was always telling you how to be. The feeling that was alarmingly close to anger was churning in her guts.

She looked back into the hallway. Joey was pushing the stroller. Two pale naked larvae. She could take them in her arms. She could drop them over the wall behind her. They would splatter on the sidewalk below. She could flee with the bag boy from Kroger's, the man at the lumberyard. Or she could find a small dog and kick it very hard. She could pull the wings off butterflies . . .

She walked into the hallway, took Joey's hand, and pushed the stroller. As she passed the Negro janitor, he said, "Hidy, missus. Yall right today?"

"Why, I'm just fine, thank you," she said with a bright smile. "How yall?"

"I be just fine, thank you, ma'am," he replied with a big grin. Their eyes locked.

Out on the sidewalk she unstrapped Laura from the stroller, lifted her down, and let her stumble alongside Joey.

# Part
# Four

# Chapter One

====

# Emily

The line of friends and neighbors viewing Jed in his casket wound through the sanctuary of the Methodist church in the mill village. Directly in front of Emily were her parents and grandfather. They peered into the coffin. At the Episcopal church on the hill, coffins were always closed, as though the corpse inside were a shameful secret that everyone tried politely to pretend didn't exist. But her parents knew the forms: When in the mill village, behave as the villagers. Even so, they couldn't quite bring themselves to wail and moan, as the Webb sisters ahead of them were doing on the way back to their pew.

A gospel quartet from the village was up front singing hymns in tribute to Jed. At that moment, "... *drop kick me, Jesus, through the goal posts of life. / Not to the left and not to the right ...*"

Behind Emily were dozens of Jed's relatives down from Tatro Cove, beginning to sniff, preparatory to weeping. Thoughtful of Jed to arrange his accident at Christmastime so that she didn't have to make a special trip. The fewer trips to this loony bin she called home, the better. She'd spent a lot of time deciding what to wear, whether or not to conform to what Newland considered appropriate funeral attire. She'd have had to go out and buy a black dress and hat, which she'd never wear again. Until the next funeral. So she was wearing her dark brown pants suit and vest, boots, a silk shirt, and loosely knotted tie. As she came downstairs, her parents in their basic black studied her. Finally her mother murmured, "Oh well, I suppose it's your life."

In front of the church waiting to process, she saw Raymond in bib overalls, work shoes, and a suit coat. He grinned, sidled over, and whispered, "So it's come to this, huh, Em? Well, it's just like you to come out at a funeral."

She squelched a smile. People on all sides were glancing at her and whispering to each other. Fuck them. It had taken her her entire life to get here, but she no longer cared what Newland thought. In fact, she felt pleasure at their outrage.

Matt was holding her hand tightly. He'd never seen a corpse before. "Will Uncle Jed be all bloody, Mommy?" he'd asked on the way to the church with a delighted shiver.

"No, honey. They clean them up, and dress them in their best clothes, and put makeup on them."

"Makeup on boys?"

"Yeah, on dead boys anyhow."

She'd scarcely thought about Jed in recent years. Hardly at all since the time she and Justin were doing community organizing in Cincinnati and brought Matt down to Newland. Jed almost punched Justin out half a dozen times over his analysis of the character structure of Southern mountaineers. "They're just so irrational," Justin explained. "The feud mentality lives on. If something doesn't go their way, they get violent."

"Oh yeah?" said Jed, jutting out his chin and clenching his fists.

But as she stood looking down at Jed (or at what was left of him after being totaled by a semi), dressed in his Sunday suit with his head resting on mauve satin, she felt the sorrow she'd been warding off for days start to well up in her. Now that he couldn't swagger around, she realized there had always been something pathetic about her poor brother-in-law. A hero manqué, a pioneer with no wilderness, a cowboy without a horse. He was the type of man who, if he walked past someone trying to parallel park, would stop and direct. At gas stations he used to get out of his car and purposefully kick his tires. Courage, Loyalty, all those tired old virtues pronounced with capital letters—he possessed them in an abundance equal to his brawn. But who needed them to detach bobbins from spindles day after day?

It was strange feeling sympathy for a man again. She thought she'd recovered from her need to do that. All her life she'd been at it. With

Raymond through his high school harangues about the iniquities of Newland. With Earl about her inability to devote her life to his service. Her mother and Sally and Kathryn and Ruby and she had knocked themselves out sympathizing with her father about his hard days at the mill. And then of course there was Justin's unending appetite for sympathy.

She recalled the day she first began to realize she was all sympathized out. She'd woken up before the alarm, rolling out of bed, careful not to disturb the sleeping Justin. She glanced out the window and down the street toward the Hudson. Smog was shrouding the high-rises in New Jersey. She fed and dressed Matt, then herself.

As she walked Matt to the day-care place, he wailed that he didn't see her enough, other kids didn't have to be at the center as much, other kids had really nice mothers. The usual. It always worked. A Real Mother should be: forever at home, eternally available, unquenchably interested. A Real Mother will: bake cookies, stew vats of hot chocolate, make Christmas tree ornaments, play Monopoly on demand. This was the model Emily was stuck with from her own childhood, and from too many years of glancing through *Ladies' Home Journals* in dentists' offices. And she suffered about her inability to conform. Once a month she'd crawl into bed, pull the covers over her head, and weep. Loudly. Boo hoo hoo, yes, you're right, I'm failing you. But she usually managed to deliver *some* sympathy to Matt, knowing that he required lots, in order to grow into an adult male with an insatiable need for it.

As she descended into the subway at Eighty-sixth Street, a man in tattered clothes accosted her and began an elaborate story about his dying mother. She reached in her pocketbook for change. But when she handed it over, he handed it back. "Listen, lady, I don't want your money!"

"Well, what *do* you want?"

"I want you to listen to what I'm telling you!"

"But I'm late for work."

He started yelling, calling her a bitch and a cunt and a whore and a dyke. Emily had begun to catch on: Either you played the Great Ear, or you accepted the label of Festering Hole. One way or another, men were determined to fill your orifices.

As she sat at her typewriter high atop attractive East Forty-third Street and answered her boss's morning mail, he stomped in and delivered a tirade against the Erie-Lackawanna for making him an hour late and forcing him to stand in the aisle in a steamy car all the way from Teaneck when he had a sore throat that might very well turn into pneumonia. He looked at her, waiting for—sympathy. She even opened her mouth. But nothing came out.

Glancing at her uneasily, he discussed the unfortunate character formation of his bratty children, his wife's eagerness to charge unnecessary items at the new Saks near their house, the defects in the transmission of his new Volvo. Again he awaited Sympathy—which seemed to be assuming the proportions of the Holy Grail. He was paying Emily to deliver. If she didn't, she'd lose her job. Her child would starve in the streets. She opened her mouth. Again, nothing came out.

He stormed to his desk, on which lay letters and contracts awaiting his signature.

"I'm sorry," Emily croaked—in terror. Please, don't put me out to graze. See? I can sympathize with the best of them.

After she'd phoned an agent to postpone her boss's lunch, and as she strolled to the coffee wagon to get him his fix, she thought, The fucker! He had her to do his crap here, his wife and a maid to do it at home. Emily was paid fifty-five hundred dollars to his twenty-seven five. Yet he had the gall to come to *her* for sympathy?

She glanced around nervously, to see if anyone had overheard these subversive thoughts.

As she staggered back through the apartment door with her arms full of groceries and laundry and manuscripts, Justin was lying in the middle of the hall floor. Rather than drop her packages to straddle him and give him a back rub, she stepped over him and went into the kitchen. From the corner of her eye, she saw him raise his head and stare at the Great Ear with surprise. She began putting groceries away. He started talking in a dull monotone about his latest failure to get his outdated articles on draft resistance published, about the difficulties of being pure in an impure world.

Ever since the Revolution had failed to arrive, he had been directing his organizing energies inward. Five years on civil rights, and about all that had been accomplished was that he'd been arrested for speeding by a black state trooper the last time he'd driven through Georgia. Three years of organizing among Appalachian migrants in Cincinnati, and slum housing and infant malnutrition still existed. Three years of draft resistance work, and a report had just come out that the United States had finally pulled out of Vietnam because of diminishing oil supplies. Justin had concluded the individual was powerless to control socio-economic situations, but that one *could* control one's personal intake. Since control was what it had always been about with him, he began wearing a surgical mask to filter the air that entered his lungs. He also had Emily and Matt drinking a concoction of brewer's yeast and carrot juice. When Matt would refuse, Justin would tie him to a chair, placed on a square of plastic, and dribble it into his mouth. Matt would let it trickle from the corner of his mouth until his clothes, Justin, the chair, and the plastic were drenched. Eventually one or the other would give in. Emily tried to reason with Justin: "Isn't this what the British do to the IRA?"

"It's for his own good."

"But it tastes like dire-rear, Mom," Matt would shriek.

Once she tried punching Justin, which was a big mistake. He hurled her across the room, and she hit her head on his ionizer, which was replacing the negative ions air pollution had destroyed.

Matt got even more upset and ordered in a brave little squeak, "Stay out of this, Mom. This is between Dad and me."

Emily began using these times to go out shopping for lecithin, mung beans, bottled spring water, and various other staples.

Justin had also chosen this moment in history to "get in touch with his feelings," having concluded the Revolution failed because everyone was "headtripping." Each morning upon awakening he'd deliver a lengthy description of how he felt that day, and why. Like a psychic weather report. The problem was that most of his feelings turned out to be either hostile or helpless. Emily never knew from one day to the next whether she'd be greeted from work by a bully or a baby. Today it was the latter.

She stepped over him on her way to the bathroom. As she sat on the toilet, he came in and continued his lamentation, his voice muffled by his surgical mask. He glanced at her dolefully and waited for— Sympathy.

"Why don't you just go get stuffed then?" she suggested amicably. She was starting to feel like one of those vomit bags on an airplane.

"What?"

Emily was seized with panic: If she didn't give Justin what he needed, he'd get it elsewhere. She'd be reduced to a lifetime of lonely masturbation. She forced a smile.

Deciding he'd misheard, Justin continued his description of the insensitive ranks of publishing executives who had once again failed to recognize his virtue and talent.

If she could just grit her teeth and emit sympathetic sounds, like radar bleeps, if she then rubbed his back or fucked him, and cooked him a nice macrobiotic supper, she could get him to do the dishes and put Matt to bed. He might even be enticed to help clean the apartment. It was potentially a nice place—high ceilings, parquet floors, elaborate molding, rent-controlled in a once-elegant townhouse. She'd already explained to him that by picking up the apartment, one could control one's visual intake. But he remained unimpressed and pointed out that Emily was trying to impose her standards of cleanliness on him, which was a form of domestic imperialism. And besides, he had to go to the Village for his course in Body Language II: From the Neck Up.

At supper Emily said, "I've just understood that it's not fair. Harold goes to martini lunches with authors and agents, while I file and fend off phone calls and answer his mail. And he gets paid five times what I do."

Justin shrugged. "So switch jobs."

"To what? Where would it be any different?"

"Christ, how should I know?"

The Great Ear wasn't supposed to appeal for sympathy herself. "Justin, what I don't understand is why it's politically acceptable for your wife to work within the System and support you, but it's not OK for you to." She was sure there was a rationale that, silly her, she just couldn't see. Justin always had politically correct explanations on tap. If Emily couldn't see his point, he'd inform her that she didn't have a "political analysis." This was partly why she'd married him. As a Southerner in the North during the civil rights era, she'd needed all the help toward political correctness she could get.

Besides, she thought at the time he was the most wonderful man she'd ever met. She remembered sitting across from him at the West End Grill on upper Broadway after a planning session for a fund-raising concert. Their coffee sat untouched. She studied the lines on his face, etched by the acid of human misery, which he was working so valiantly to eradicate. He held both her hands on the scratched wooden tabletop. She gazed into his eyes and sang along with the jukebox: *"Baby, I'm yours, / And I'll be yours till the stars fall from the sky / Yours till the rivers all run dry . . ."* She vowed that evening she'd devote her life to assisting Justin and comforting him in his struggles on behalf of all the downtrodden peoples of the world.

Tears began to fill Emily's eyes as Justin lectured on about the System, which occupations were inside it, and which outside. It was like a cowboy movie—it turned out there was Good Money and Ba-a-a-d Money. Justin's trust fund had been Bad Money because it was based on stocks in defense industries and interest from banks that were slumlords, the capital having originated from the slave trade. But it became transformed into Good Money because he spent it on behalf of those who'd been exploited to earn it. The problem by now had ceased to exist on more than a theoretical level, however. In Cincinnati one night he overheard another organizer: "I'll say this for Justin: He never touches his capital." Defiantly, he gave it all away in upcoming years. In doing so, he became what he'd been working to do away with—jobless and broke.

Matt began talking in tandem. "You know what happened today during nap, Mommy? Andrew took the white mouse out of his cage and put it in with the boa constrictor, and Janie said . . ."

". . . state socialism . . ."

". . . kicked and bit her arm . . ."

". . . let the People decide . . ."

"Damn it, I can't listen to you both at once!" Emily took a deep breath and tried to calm herself, while they looked at her with shock. She regarded herself with shock. The Great Ear was not supposed to talk, particularly in a less than loving tone. "Decide between you who gets the floor," she requested.

"Matthew, don't interrupt!"

"But he . . ." The poor kid hadn't spoken for hours. Besides, Emily was tired of state socialism. She wanted to hear about the boa constrictor. But could she challenge Matt's father in front of Matt. She felt she was a rag doll being ripped in two by competing children.

After Matt was in bed, Emily went to Maria's apartment on Broadway and Ninety-fifth for her women's group. Several members had worked together on a parents' cooperative day-care center, which in most cases meant "mothers' cooperative." The center, held in the church basement that housed workshops on nonviolence during the sixties, included children of every hue, relics of the Revolution: mocha children of black-white unions; Maria's daughter, Cleo, who'd been conceived to keep her father out of Vietnam; adopted American Indian and Vietnamese children. Instead of cowboys and Indians, the children played Capitalists and Workers.

Emily had lost track of Lou after her freshman year when she'd concluded Lou was an Oreo, but one morning at the center they found themselves face to face. Lou's greying hair was cut short and looked like steel wool. She wore a khaki army shirt and sunglasses. Her hands rested on the heads of two small dark children; she explained later they were to have been soldiers for the Black Nation. Her husband apparently spent most of his time stockpiling weapons. She was in law school on a grant and was in love with a white woman law student. They stared at each other for a long time. Finally Lou smiled and drawled, "Hey, gal. How you making it?"

When Emily first started going to the women's group, Justin asked, "What do you girls do—swap recipes?" He chortled.

Emily smiled, pinchedly. "No, we examine the ways in which this society has conditioned us to put up with remarks like that. I mean, really, Justin. Would you say to a Black Panther, 'What do you do, eat watermelon?' "

"The lady talks back! Well, my dear, you're getting there."

"Don't you patronize me, Justin Lawson."

"You're quite right," he said with a grin. "And I'm proud of you for not letting me get away with it."

The first meetings consisted of discussions of why they were meeting. Unable to come to a unanimous conclusion, they decided just to meet and not worry about it. For the next several months they discussed what the format should be, given that they all loathed the hierarchical pattern bequeathed them by the patriarchy. Should they rotate discussion leaders, or do without leaders altogether? Should they pick a topic for each week, read the same book? Or should topics just evolve? They could never make up their collective mind. They finally decided whoever was having the meeting in her apartment would be responsible for the structure of that meeting.

Justin, meanwhile, was less than enchanted. "Next thing you know, you girls will be referring to yourselves as Third World. Colonized by male imperialists!" He crowed from where he lay with his parachutist boots on the couch.

"The analogy's been drawn," said Emily.

He gazed at her with amazement. "Counterrevolutionary," he announced. "A bunch of spoiled middle-class white women coffee-klatching. When millions of nonwhites and workers across the world are being exploited."

"Two of us are black. And we're all working—the housewives for room and board, and the rest of us for half what men are paid."

He gave her a look of such political contempt that she shriveled like a cock facing circumcision, scuttled over and kissed his forehead, a heretic slobbering over the ring of the Grand Inquisitor.

"What I want to know," Emily explained as they drank red wine in Maria's cluttered living room, "is when *I* get sympathized with."

"When are you going to get yourself a good woman?" Maria asked with a grin. She drew on her cigarette, while everyone except Kate and Lou sputtered indignantly. Kate, a lover of Maria's, was a small woman in bib overalls with lots of curly hair, who worked as an electrician's apprentice. She spoke little but gave disdainful looks when anyone said something thoughtlessly heterosexual, referring to the rest of the group as the Het Set.

"Listen, don't hand me any of your lesbian chauvinism," Emily requested.

"I was just answering your question: If you want sympathy, you aren't going to get it from a man. All I've ever had from them are long self-absorbed monologues, followed by short premature ejaculations."

Emily frowned. Justin and Raymond were two of the men she was referring to.

"But isn't that sexist, Maria?" asked Gail in a bewildered voice. Gail and Emily were the only women still living with husbands, and Gail was the only full-time housewife. She pinned labels on everyone's remarks, like name tags on children's camp clothing.

"I'm simply stating a personal truth, derived from extensive experience. I spent my whole life until three years ago listening to little boys disguised as men and murmuring, 'Oh-you-don't-say-how-very-interesting.' But I have flat out had it with that!"

"It annoys you, doesn't it?" asked Gail, looking concerned.

"Yes," said Maria, after a pause.

"But are you getting anything different from women?" asked Sammie. Sammie, a tall thin black dancer, wore clanky jewelry and high boots with sharp heels. "Angela's mom," the other mothers sometimes referred to her. Angela was a café au lait product of the civil rights movement. Emily was "Matt's mom," and Matt was notable for being one of the few unpremeditated mistakes in this world of sexual politics and politicized sex. Justin and she were married one morning in a civil ceremony and had spent that afternoon chartering buses to an anti-draft march in Washington the next week. No one could ever accuse them of putting their personal preoccupations ahead of their political work.

"Sure. Put two people together who've been trained to sympathize —and they spend most of their time fighting over who gets to be the Good Listener," explained Maria.

"You'd like someone who'd listen to you sometimes, wouldn't you?" inquired Gail.

Maria ground her teeth. Then she forced a sisterly smile. "Yes, I would. And I have it." She glanced at Kate.

"Something I've never had the nerve to ask you, Maria," Emily said. "Why did you first get involved with a woman? Was it political?"

Maria grinned. "Hell, no. It was lust."

When Emily got home, Justin's men's group was meeting in the living room. The women's group referred to it as the Men's Auxiliary. "It's like rednecks meeting during civil rights years to discuss White Liberation," Maria announced. "Or American soldiers meeting in Vietnam about Soldiers' Liberation."

It smelled as though they were smoking hash. Emily puttered around hanging up stuff and clearing the table. As his first step toward men's liberation, Justin had broken his promise to do the dishes. Emily could hear them reliving some demonstration at a draft board.

". . . oh man, it was so far fucking out! Don't you remember? When I put on my football helmet with the face guard and grabbed up that lead pipe . . ."

"No, listen, *I* was the one who brought the football helmet . . ."

"Don't hand me none of that shit, man. I still have that fucking helmet. You want to come over to my place and see it?"

Emily sighed. They reminded her of the men her father's age who hung around the Newland Moose Club and argued about which units had gone ashore first at Omaha Beach.

When Justin and she made love that night, she had another hint that something was up. After he came, she lay still as his semen oozed out of her, seething with resentment that once again a man had succeeded in transferring his mess to a place where she would have to clean it up.

One weekend she went to a women's bar in the Village with Maria and Kate. The bouncer was a lady wrestler type. Women in armbands behind the bar mixed the drinks. A woman DJ in a white satin windbreaker picked the records. A stout woman in a green eyeshade and a cream three-piece suit with a red carnation in the buttonhole took on all comers at the pool table. Women were looking each other over with frank sexual intent and sending drinks to each other across the crowded dance floor, asking each other to dance.

Dykes. Apart from her women's group, Emily's only experience with them had involved Miss Melrose in junior high. Yet here she was, trapped with a whole platoon. She was confused. With men she'd often felt like sexual prey. But women had been safe. They had had no ulterior motives. Here in this club with dozens of women whose bed partners were other women, she felt reduced to prey status. It was like being a virgin again, but different, in that she didn't know the signaling system.

A tall woman with long dark hair, who looked part Indian, came up and began a conversation about the attractions of New York City over Des Moines. "I was the town dyke. Motorcycle jacket, boots, the works. But here I can finally concentrate on my painting, rather than spending all my energy being Superdyke."

"I know what you mean," Emily lied.

Emily could see Maria watching and smiling. They danced to a LaBelle song: "*Voulez-Vous Coucher avec Moi Ce Soir?*"

Am I being flirtatious? Emily kept asking herself. Am I promising things I don't intend to deliver? What *do* I intend to deliver? Two women next to her were dancing cheek-to-cheek. Periodically they kissed on the mouth.

As the song crashed to a conclusion, Emily blurted, "Well, it's sure been great talking to you, Althea. But I came with a friend, and I've got to get back to her."

Kate was fighting her way to the bar. Emily demanded of Maria as she sat down, "How do you know what's going on—whether someone's putting the make on you or just being friendly?"

"You know."

"Shit, man, *I* don't know!"

"You learn."

"I don't have time to learn. I've got to know right now. I mean, it's not really fair, my even being here. I don't want to lead anyone on, when I'm straight and all. What's that supposed to mean?"

"What?"

"That smile that didn't happen."

"You've never been attracted to a woman?"

Emily blushed, and Maria aborted another smile. "Well, all right, yes, of course. I mean, some of my best friends are women."

"All your best friends, if you'd just face up to it."

"Jesus Christ, Maria. Gail's right about you. You're so goddam sexist." Sometimes Emily had difficulty thinking in categories—Blacks, Middle Class, Men, Southerners. She herself, she'd learned during her sojourn among Yankee politicos, was a Ruling Class Southern White Woman. These categories explained everything about her.

But Maria was usually Maria for her—rather than a White Intellectual-Elite New York Jewish Lesbian. You couldn't categorize her way of suppressing an ironical smile; the way she dragged with such greedy pleasure on her cigarettes; the belligerent way she sat in trousers, with her knees wide open, both inviting and defying invasion.

"I mean, this club, for example. Not letting men in. Where I come from, it's the blacks who can't come in, and we call it segregation."

"Yeah, but this is different because it's the exploited keeping out the exploiters. We've got to have some place to gather the strength and support to go away and face the fuckers every day. The sound of one male voice, insisting on being agreed with, would wreck the atmosphere. Besides, if it were open to men, they'd pack the place just to get their rocks off imagining what we do in bed."

"I've been wanting to ask you, Maria: What do you do in bed?"

Maria grinned. "Why don't you come to bed and find out?"

"I couldn't handle the crush of competition." Maria was a notorious Doña Juana. In Emily's current mood, she admired Maria's ability to do what she wanted when she wanted, apparently free from that awful need of the Great Ear to fulfill the needs of other people.

"Then you don't deserve to find out why I draw such a crowd, do you?"

Emily was trying to be as inept a secretary as possible. This actually took little special effort. She made so many typos that, by the time she corrected them with white fluid, a letter looked as though it had lined the bottom of a bird cage. She filed using her own whimsical system of free association. If Harold was in the men's room and she answered the phone while distracted, she was likely to reply, "Sorry, he's taking a leak." Her plan was that she'd be kicked upstairs, rather than out on the street. There were women in big jobs in publishing, and they must have come from somewhere. Why not from among the typing pool rejects?

Meanwhile, she was trying to establish an image of competence in matters other than Correcto-Tape dexterity. She asked Harold for extra work. Stunned, he asked her to read a manuscript that concerned the ways in which female roles in movies and books and plays by men counteracted what was going on in society. When women were faring well socially and economically, they were increasingly debased and assaulted in male fiction. Emily was impressed and spent a lot of time on a plan to rearrange the sections to enhance the argument. The author was a lively attractive woman named Maggie Something. Emily sat in while Harold outlined her plan. Maggie liked it.

Pleased, Emily said, "I think it's a wonderful book. But I thought if . . ."

"Emily, could you please get us some coffee." She stared at Harold. "Cream for me. No sugar. Maggie?"

As Emily stomped to the coffee wagon, she reflected that in the Movement (she could never use that word without associating it with Matt's infancy and toilet bowls full of soiled diapers) this situation had become a cliché. Most political women had spent years typing and mimeoing and fixing coffee, while the male heavies led the demos, made the decisions and the speeches. Why, then, was she so surprised? Harold's consciousness wasn't even in the basement, it was in the crypt—but he'd never claimed it was elsewhere. Maybe he was a pig, but he was no hypocrite, unlike certain other pigs, who would go unspecified.

Once in Cincinnati she'd been walking down the street toward the community center with a black man from Chicago, Duane. They passed a woman who sat on the sidewalk in an armchair, holding an infant and weeping. Furniture and boxes of clothes and dishes were piled around her. She'd been evicted for not paying her rent because her welfare check had been stolen. Duane and Emily went to the welfare office. He got nowhere, probably because he was both black and belligerent. Emily took over, and through some complicated maneuvers got the woman an emergency rent check. Duane was impressed since he'd never seen Emily do much except make instant coffee and handle the push broom. Back at the office he said, "Hey, baby, how bout you and me getting something going here?"

Apart from the fact that Emily liked his woman friend Mary and was aware of how insulted many black women were that black men were going after white women, she was uninterested in Duane. She said with a laugh, "Oh come on, Duane. You don't want me any more than I want you."

His back stiffened, and he said, "Oh yeah, I know all about you Southerners." He walked out. Leaving Emily crawling with anxiety.

She'd worked hard trying to uncover her racial prejudices from both a Southern and an American upbringing. It had been like chasing minnows in a stream with bare hands. You thought you had something, then it would slip through your fingers. When you weren't looking, it could turn into the Loch Ness monster. She was uninterested in sleeping with Duane. Should she sleep with him anyway to prove she was unprejudiced? On the other hand, she hadn't slept with any white man she was uninterested in. To single Duane out from all the men she was uninterested in, just because of his skin color, seemed prejudiced. The only solution appeared to be to sleep with several men she was uninterested in, white and black, including Duane.

Then she realized that not only was she uninterested in Duane, she disliked him. But could this be because of his skin color? But there were white men she disliked as much. Also, there were black men she disliked less. She concluded with relief that she wasn't necessarily prejudiced in this instance.

Opening the door, she yelled down the street toward some startled winos, "I wouldn't sleep with you if you were white either!"

Standing in line at the coffee wagon, she understood that what Harold had just pulled was parallel. In both cases, she'd displayed competence. She'd been assertive. She had to be put in her place: She was "just" a cunt, she was "just" a secretary. It was unconscious on their parts, which made it worse.

Emily was trembling with such uncontrollable anger that she splashed coffee all over the hallway.

As she sat typing labels for review copies of the latest novel Harold had edited and listening to the rumble of his and Maggie's voices, Emily concluded she was hanging out with the wrong crowd. Maria and Kate were good company, but what if lesbianism was communicable? Was this irritation toward men a symptom? Christ, what a horrible thought . . .

During the following week she first found Justin's little idiosyncrasies annoying rather than endearing. The way his jaw cracked when he chewed. She began handing him Kleenexes when he sniffed upon waking—which he would eye irritably and drop unused into the waste basket, still sniffing. She studied his drooping crew socks and bought him new ones with the elastic intact—which he shoved into the back of his drawer.

She found herself having consciously to itemize all the things she loved about him. *His courage:* Justin rolled into a ball on her dorm sitting room floor, practicing the nonviolent response to assault. Justin collecting draft cards on the steps to the induction center while policemen yelled into megaphones. Justin in his crash helmet hurling himself at the Pentagon. *His blinding generosity:* He'd become frantic knowing the government was spending one hundred million dollars a day in Vietnam, and here was this woman whose kid couldn't go to school because she didn't have eighteen dollars for a winter coat. Anyone who'd asked him for money for bail, rent, food, got it. He'd known that it occasionally went for liquor or a TV set, and that he had the reputation of being a guilt-ridden sucker, but he hadn't cared. *His intelligence:* The ease with which he'd manipulated words and concepts at FORWARD meetings. Emily had had through him a sense of participation in something she still regarded as important— the building of a just and humane world.

She thought of the afternoons they'd spent at art galleries and concerts and movies. He'd asked her opinions, then corrected them. He'd picked her up out of the dirt and turned her into the clod she was today.

Then she realized that, like all memories, these were in the past perfect tense.

At the next women's meeting everyone tried to drop out. Gail's plan was to have everyone mention something important that happened that week. The mass exodus began when they got to Susannah, a nurse at the Roosevelt, Levi's mom. She announced with great pleasure, "I met a man this week!"

"Oh, no, I don't want to hear it," Kate moaned, burying her head in her arms.

"No, he's fantastic. He really is."

Maria sighed.

"Now come on, yall," murmured Lou, removing her sunglasses to glare at them. "She listened to your crap."

"Tell us all about him, Susannah," urged Gail.

"Well, he's a social worker." Emily reflected that in Newland the response to that request would have taken the form, "Well, he's so and so's cousin/uncle/son. And he lives in such-and-such a place."

". . . and, well, talking to him is almost like talking to a woman. I mean, he actually listens. And he doesn't quote Marx or anything. And he doesn't try to direct the conversation back to himself. Sometimes he has emotional reactions and stuff . . ."

"It sounds as though you think he's pretty special," suggested Gail.

"He sounds very nice," Emily murmured. They could always tell a meeting was in trouble when Lou and Emily reverted to their best Southern manners.

"Shit, I'm sorry, gang," announced Maria, sitting up from where she lay on pillows. "But, like, I just can't handle this group anymore. I think I need a group of lesbians. You straight women still need men—sexually, emotionally, and in some cases financially. But I don't. And I need support for forming alternative structures. I don't want to sit around listening to a bunch of heterosexual soap operas."

"I'm with you," Kate grunted.

Susannah collapsed in tears.

"Aren't you being elitist, Maria?" Gail inquired.

Sammie jumped to her feet and struck a pose so graceful it could have been choreographed for this moment. "Well, that's just fine with me. Cause, honey, I've had it with lying around listening to a bunch of white women moaning. Every black woman I know is earning a living, plus raising her kids, plus trying to prop up a man who's been so fucked over by Whitey he can't hardly get out of bed in the morning. You white women are just spoiled little children, whimpering around about your O-pression. And whenever you get tired, you can go on back home to Daddy or Hubby, and he'll take care of you. But this stuff is *real* to black women, honey, and we got to live with it our whole life through . . ."

"Now wait just a minute . . . ," snarled Maria.

"Aren't you being elitist?" asked Gail.

"I got something to say!" Emily yelled. To her surprise, the room fell silent. She couldn't remember what it was.

Susannah started talking through her tears. "This group isn't meeting my needs. This group has never yet met my needs. I'm sure none of you has a clue what I'm talking about. You've all been through college . . ."

"I ain't been through no college," muttered Sammie.

". . . while you were studying all your fancy theories, I was *working*. Nothing new to me. I've been working since I was fourteen. It was me behind that counter at Woolworth's when you were buying the pens and paper to write your theses. Gail over there whimpering about wanting to go out and work. Shit, go out and work. But I don't see anything wrong, if I can find a man who wants this too, in me staying and raising Levi and keeping house. You people are so out of touch with what life is really like for working people that it's pointless for me even to be here!"

"Ooh, that's not fair," complained Gail. "What we're talking about here is the ways women have been trained to passivity."

Emily remembered what she wanted to say: "Actually, I've been thinking for a long time that I need to find me a group of Southern women. The thing that bothers me most, you all don't even realize how different I am from you. You all go out to work and leave your kids and take lovers and all that—you're just conforming to your conditioning, and imitating the women who've surrounded you all your life. Me, I'm having to fight my conditioning with every move I make . . ."

"Aren't you being elitist?" asked Gail.

"Would you shut up?" Maria snapped.

Kate snarled, "Shit, all this Matt's mom crap. You all know it's not cool to define yourself through your lovers, so you define yourself through your kids, just like society's always done. Instead of being able to stand up and say, 'Hey, I'm me.' Well, I got no kids. Does that mean I'm not a woman?"

Gail began talking about the importance of motherhood, her resentment at its being dumped on. She called the group a bunch of man-haters and complained that they were trying to force all men to conform to the same image, just as men did to women.

"Now listen here, yall!" yelled Lou. "You talk about fucked over, you try being black and a woman and a dyke and Southern and a welfare mother all at once. I ain't got no sympathy for none of you. But what I think is this: You confront a carrot with a potato, and it'll probably insist, 'Hell no, I ain't no potato. Honey, look at me. Hell, I'm orange, and long and thin. And lookee here, I got me this lacy green top.' Stops them seeing they're all in that garden together, and all gonna get dug up come fall."

Everyone fell silent.

"If we stick together, we're something to be reckoned with. If we split up over our precious differences, we ain't nothing. Look what happened during civil rights: You had CORE, NAACP, SCLC, SNCC, Urban League, Panthers, Muslims, Toms and Jemimas, Methodists against Baptists, men against women, Southerners against Yankees, college against non-college, militants against cultural nationalists, black capitalists against Marxists, all fighting among themselves. You even had poor whites saying, 'Maybe I ain't making it so good, but at least I'm better off than them niggers.' "

Everyone began nodding in reluctant agreement. And by the end of the evening they were embracing each other, swept with feelings of solidarity with all the women of the world. But as Maria hugged her, Emily felt a sensation shoot through her body that was much more specific. She pulled away, and Maria glanced at her, surprised.

That weekend Emily went with Maria and Kate to a women's music festival. The college amphitheater, with its elaborate polished oak woodwork, was packed with women of every size and shape and color, dressed mostly in jeans or overalls, flannel shirts or sweat shirts, boots or tennis shoes. A woman in jeans and suspenders and a flannel shirt, with close-cropped hair, played a guitar and sang love songs to a woman in her backup band. From the corner of her eye Emily saw that Maria and Kate were touching fingertips, trying to be unobtrusive so that Emily wouldn't feel left out. But she did anyway. All around her, women had their arms across each other's shoulders, were holding hands or pressing thighs. Emily felt titillated. Women making love to women. It was unheard of in Newland, and Emily had always been drawn to anything Newland forbade. If Newland forbade it, it couldn't be all bad. She decided she adored these tough defiant women lounging all over each other. Her shoulder pressed against

Maria's, and she increased the pressure. Maria smiled and pressed back, and Emily felt a stab of electricity down her arm so intense that her delight transmuted into alarm. She shifted in her seat.

Meanwhile, on stage women plucked dulcimers about strip mining in Appalachia, shook tambourines over torture in Chilean jails. Women in Frye boots and plaid lumberjack shirts twanged Jews' harps for the lettuce harvesters in the Imperial Valley. Castanets clattered on behalf of Cuban (pronounced Coo-ban) sugarcane harvesters. Four women in red flannel shirts and bib overalls stood with raised fists, shouting "Puerto Rico libre!" while a flamenco guitar hemorrhaged offstage.

Emily found herself scowling. She'd just recalled whom she was exiled among: descendants of the Puritans, who arrived in the New World determined to civilize the savages. Their heirs had been pursuing missions ever since. They'd persuaded African tribesmen to cover their loins. They carried the concept of land ownership to the American Indians. They invaded Virginia. They rode Greyhounds through Alabama. They brought Coca-Cola to Cairo, and peace to Pleiku. Like malignant cells from a tumor, they'd colonized the entire world. They couldn't help themselves. It was in their genes. Out the back door of this building was Harlem, which had gone up in flames eight years earlier. Yet these women had the gall to warble on about injustice in Latin America?

Emily clenched her teeth. Maria looked at her questioningly. Emily tried to smile politely, but ended up grimacing. The woman who'd opened the concert was now singing about her surprise at first realizing that she was in love with a woman. On one side of the stage was a woman interpreting the song in sign language for the deaf. On the other side a woman did a karate demonstration. Women were passing cardboard buckets through the audience for donations to a lesbian mothers' legal defense fund. Emily sighed. Civil rights, Appalachia, Vietnam, American Indians, migrant workers, Chile, Puerto Rico. Emily, under Justin's tutelage, had done them all. Now it was Women. And next week the sisters would be stacked in someone's attic like cast-off hula hoops. Political consumerism. Fuck it, she'd been taken in too many times by this Cause-of-the-Month mentality.

Maria put her arm around Emily in the crush moving toward the exit, murmuring, "One of the nicest things about women is that half the babies they give birth to aren't male."

Emily moved irritably out from under her arm, eyeing Maria's Badge-for-the-Day with annoyance: "When God created man, she was only joking."

"What's wrong?"

"Bunch of self-righteous consumers," Emily muttered.

"So what? Why not just relax and enjoy it?"

"Because next week all you career lesbians will have moved on to the next fad."

Maria said curtly, "I doubt it. Many of us have burnt certain bridges. It'd be very difficult for me to go back to men."

"I've seen it happen time after time. People seize on a cause, devote their lives to it, get bored, and cast it off like last summer's Top Ten records. Besides, anything this many Yankees agree on can't be right."

"You see it as a series of fads. But I see it as a progression."

"Yeah, but you Yankees always equate change with progress. You've obviously never lost a war."

Maria laughed. "But in this case I think it really is progress."

"How?"

"Well, during civil rights, women found themselves cleaning the Freedom House while the brothers were off being interviewed for the evening news. And then Stokely Carmichael came out with that bit about the only position for women in the struggle being prone. Then Cleaver described how he raped white women to get even with white men, practicing up first on black women. And then during Vietnam, the women were trying to find ways to pay the phone bills, while the men were out dumping blood on draft records. But some of us began realizing it was *men* who were dropping napalm, *men* who were making fortunes manufacturing war materials. *Men* who lynched blacks, *men* who wouldn't pay them decent wages. Government, business, churches, the military—all run by men. They'd set up this shitty world and were benefiting from it . . . Sorry, I didn't mean to lecture."

"It's OK. I'm used to it."

Maria stuck out her tongue. "But anyway, Emily, even if I agreed with you about it's being nothing but fads, so what?"

"I like serious people." Two women were kissing passionately by the doorway. Emily glared at them. Bunch of goddam fly-by-night Yankees.

"But we *are* serious while we're embracing whatever it is. And we're equally serious about whatever we move on to. You're saying you have to be eternally devoted to the same things? The one true love that lasts a lifetime? Honestly, you poor saps and your Lost Causes. This continuity and stability Raymond used to carry on about—it's all a big joke. People die, houses burn down, rivers dry up, mountains crumble. Why not just accept flux?"

"Accepting it is one thing, seeking it is something else. You people are constantly changing jobs, apartments, lovers, ideologies, cars. As though by changing the surface appearance of your life you've accomplished something. Where I come from nothing changes from one decade to the next."

"Where's it gotten you?"

"Where's there to get?"

"So why are you living here?"

Ignoring Maria's last question, Emily reached home determined to make her marriage and the verities on which it was founded endure. She often felt scorn reading Sally's boring letters about teething and new slipcovers and Bake-off recipes, but Sally had had the right idea all along: She considered it a privilege to make life easier and more pleasant for the people she loved. Emily defrosted the refrigerator, vacuumed under the couch, even paired and rolled the socks in Justin's drawer.

But Justin failed to notice because he'd taken to lying on the hall floor full time. The last straw was when a large paper company accepted his proposal regarding a public service announcement for television on their anti-pollution program. "I mean, I can see it all spread out before me, man," he said. "Like, I'll do it, and they'll love it. They'll hire me to do more. On their recommendation, other firms will hire me. I'll start, like, renting offices, buying equipment, hiring employees. Eventually I'll, you know, go public. Sell shares, get bought up by a conglomerate. Retire to the Bahamas, spend my days fishing and lying in the sun. Man, it's just too awful." He buried his face in the crook of his arm. "I'm so depressed."

Emily was kneeling by his side trying to think how to comfort him. "I know what's bugging you, Justin. It's that party last week at Morris's, isn't it?"

He nodded miserably.

Most of FORWARD had been there. Ralph, a doctor now, had insisted on wearing his green operating clothes all evening, with an electronic pager at his waist. Morris, a lawyer, kept working Latin phrases into his conversation: *Sub rosa, de jure, habeas corpus.* Bud, a stock analyst, would whip out his pocket calculator to prove his points. Morris and his wife Susan served daiquiris made in a Waring blender. They barbecued steaks on a hibachi on the iron landing outside their Brooklyn Heights apartment.

"Emily, Morris *boiled ears of corn.*"

"There, there, it's all right, dear." Emily scratched his back gently.

Dessert had been apple pie and Neapolitan ice cream. Everyone fondled new babies, and discussed vacation homes in Vermont, sailboats, and auto loans. These were the people with whom Justin had once plotted the Revolution.

Justin's major problem, as Emily saw it, was that he had planned on either Utopia or Armageddon. He had made no arrangements for dealing with the same tired old world he'd grown up in. Once you'd been a hero, how did you revert to being an ordinary mortal? Besides, it was in his genes to fight the sabre-toothed tiger.

"I feel used," he moaned. "Devoured. Like an empty cereal box. Like Miss January for Fruit-of-the-Month Club."

"But you achieved important things," Emily insisted, trying on Maria's point of view.

"Like what?"

"Well . . . uh . . . I mean you can't list things just like that. But a lot of learning went on."

"Like what?"

Like about the limitations of collective human endeavor. "Hell, I don't know, Justin. That's your department." Emily was feeling guilty. She for one had used Justin—to gain acceptance in FOR-

WARD. Then she'd called it "love," but recently she'd begun to wonder.

In the old days Justin's spirits would sometimes sag, but Emily was always able to cheer him up by telling him how important his projects were, assuring him how intelligent and competent and irresistibly sexy he was. Her words alone could make him puff up like a bullfrog about to croak. But the Great Ear was losing her touch. His strategy sessions and teach-ins and rallies and marches and committee meetings and phone trees and leaflet writing—they now seemed like designs children make against the night sky with a sparkler. The sparkler goes out, and you're left with only the empty black night. Emily was just beginning to realize how lucky the women had had it. All along they'd been cleaning and getting food on the table and tending the children. The utopian expectations had collapsed, dragging some of the men down into a nighttime of the soul. But the women were just grooving along on the same old survival trip.

Emily wanted to help. Justin had helped her when she was an intimidated Tennessee hick. Besides, it was her role as Wife in this marriage she was determined to make work. She tried and she tried, but none of the Great Ear's old tricks got him up off the floor.

He decided to go for a few weeks to a meditation center upstate, which someone in his Advanced Massage course had recommended, to try to "get my head together." At first Emily panicked and tried to persuade him that she was all he needed. But gradually the Great Ear conceded defeat.

Joe from the art department brought Harold the jacket design for Maggie's book. Harold exclaimed over it, then called Emily in to see it. The title was *Making the Second Sex Suck: Women in Male Fiction*. The illustration was of Marilyn Monroe, her neckline plunging almost to her nipples. Her eyes were closed. Her mouth, pursed, looked remarkably vaginal, and in readiness for the insertion of a large cock.

"What do you think, Emily? Isn't it great?"

"Very nice."

"Fantastic," he assured her, walking back to his desk. "She thinks it's fantastic," he said to Joe.

Suddenly Emily saw herself as Stepin Fetchit: "Yassuh, that noose is mighty fine. Law, it fits so good and snug! Why, boss, you just the smartest thing!"

She crept back into Harold's office. "Actually, Harold, I think it's awful," she whispered.

Harold and Joe stared at her.

"You're doing just what Maggie's book says—degrading a serious achievement."

Harold gave a short laugh. "But I like women," he protested. "Some of my best bunnies are women." He and Joe killed themselves laughing. The corners of Emily's mouth twitched: She had to smile at her bosses' bad jokes. It was her job. By burning at least three hundred calories in her facial muscles alone, she managed not to.

"The trouble with you women's libbers," said Harold, "is that you have no sense of humor."

She looked at him. She hadn't known she came across as a "women's libber." She'd thought she was well-established as the Great Ear, at least here if no longer at home. ". . . apart from exploiting female sexuality to sell your product," she added, amazed at her daring.

"That's what we're all here for—to sell books. I'm sure Maggie wants as many people as possible to read it."

"But the people who buy it on the basis of that jacket will be disappointed by the content. And people who'd be interested in the content won't buy it because of that repulsive jacket."

"So who asked you?"

She decided not to point out that he had.

"The jacket stays as it is," Harold snapped. "Coffee please, Emily. Cream, no sugar. Joe?"

The first Friday Justin was away, Maria had a women's fancy dress party. She greeted guests at her door in a maid's uniform, black with ruffled white apron, carefully helped everyone out of her fur or coat, then hurled each wrap into the hall corner, where it flopped to the floor.

Emily put a cigarette in her long tortoise-shell holder, drew on it, and looked around. Most of the women she knew at least by sight. The women's group was out in full force. Women were wearing flappers' dresses, rayon dresses with padded shoulders from the forties, wedding dresses. Sammie wore only a girdle, a fox boa, and high red boots with spurs. She kept tugging at the girdle and announcing through clenched teeth, "This girdle is *killing* me!" Elaborate hairdos, gobs of makeup. A dozen brands of perfume mingled in the air. Emily was wearing a long pink bridesmaid dress from Corinne's wedding to a Lowell. She stood by herself and watched. There was nothing wrong with this scene. She was determined not to get into a twit and start seeing these nice women as merely missionaries and consumers of political fads. They were her friends and potential friends. Just because she was straight and committed to her marriage was no reason not to enjoy them.

Lou came over and they embraced. A record of sixties' songs was playing, and they began dancing to "Mustang Sally."

"Remember how we used to drive Joan crazy talking about my natural rhythm?" asked Lou.

"Weren't we terrible?"

"Wasn't *she* terrible?" said Lou. "You know, Emily, that hurt me real bad when you turned on me freshman year."

"I'm sorry, Lou. I didn't know what I was doing."

"Shit, none of us did back then."

"Meaning we do now?"

"Getting there."

Getting where, wondered Emily, thrusting her hip sideways.

"... *ride, Sally, ride* ...," wailed the roomful of women.

Maria was by now stripped down to support hose, white nurse shoes, bloomers, and a Merry Widow long-line bra. Emily felt nostalgic looking at the bra. The Ingenues had called them Iron Lungs. She'd worn one to the Plantation Balls and the KT Formals. Maria glided and elbowed her way through the dancers, prancing and joking with women on all sides, several of whom had been or still were her lovers.

Lou and Emily wandered into Maria's bedroom, which she'd turned into a photography studio with a Victorian settee and a vase of feather dusters, backed by a velvet drape. Two women in high-necked Edwardian dresses were being photographed. They struck poses in their prim dresses, most involving shoving hands up each other's skirts or grabbing breasts, while sitting with their backs and necks rigid, their eyes straight ahead and their lips pursed like stern school-teachers.

Emily contrasted this party to the scene she'd return home to. She'd pay the babysitter; look in on Matt and kiss him and tuck him in; climb between cold sheets and lie there, grateful to be alone if poor Justin and his un-together head were the alternative. Meanwhile, these women would be going off to do God knew what to each other.

She was close to thirty now. She had some grey hair, and her breasts and belly were starting to sag. She was about to reach her maximum sexual capacity, according to Justin, who'd read it in *Playboy*. Yet sex for her had become merely another household task, like taking out the garbage. The last time she was in Newland, her mother had said, "The thing about your generation is that you've never grown up. When I was your age, I had three children. I was running this house and Ruby and a yard boy, entertaining for your father." As Emily saw it, they'd grown up too fast. At the age when her parents were dancing to Tommy Dorsey, Emily and Justin were marching on Washington. They hadn't seen how they could bring children into such an inadequate world, so they set out to remake it first. Maybe it was childish to think this was possible. But in any case, lots of people Emily knew were just now entering the adolescence they'd missed out on. And she could see their point, as she watched the raucous dancing to Booker T and the M.G.'s. Women were bumping, grinding, thrusting their arms pistonlike into the air, and shouting with laughter. She wanted to get out there and play, too.

She tried to tell herself that most of these women didn't have children, but there were Lou and Maria bumping with the best of them.

". . . *yeah, yeah, yeah, yeah, yes indeed! All I really need . . . Good loving! . . .*"

Maria grabbed her for a slow song. Embarrassed, Emily said, "What's the politically acceptable way for women to slow dance?"

"No one leads," she said, putting a hand around Emily's waist and one on her shoulder. Emily did the same, and Maria taught her a slow swaying step that involved pushing against each other with upper thighs. She barely caught the words: *". . . after all these years of trying, / self-denying, / and lonely waiting, / and fears and hesitating, / yes, we'll laugh / as we see this thing / finally begin . . ."*

The dancing stopped while two women in wedding dresses, one pregnant, were married by a woman in a blue doctoral gown and cap and hood. Afterward they embraced with mock desperation. One tossed a vibrator to the waiting bridesmaids. As they ran the gauntlet, everyone threw handfuls of Quaker Puffed Rice.

As Emily was leaving, Maria and she kissed on the mouth. Maria studied her, frowning. All the way home Emily could think only of the fact that there had been no beard.

The next morning Emily marched back and forth through the apartment, abandoning cigarettes and cups of coffee. Matt scurried after her, dragging toys. The Great Ear carried on a conversation about the likelihood of there being tadpoles in the Hudson. But the rest of her was locked in a silent dialogue: This is a big mistake. It is the last thing I need. It would be so inconvenient socially. How would I explain a woman lover to my friends and family? They'd feel they'd have to invite her places with me, and then they'd be uncomfortable.

She knew she was in deep trouble when Amy Vanderbilt took over.

Making love to a woman. Bad enough. But making love to anyone besides her husband was shocking. When she was growing up, every adult had been coupled. If someone was unhappy, no one knew it. When Doctor Borgard divorced his wife of twenty years to marry his nurse, the town talked about nothing else for weeks.

Monogamy: If her sex drive were released from it, what would happen? It was possible it would prove uncontainable. Maybe she'd lust after everything in sight. Broomsticks and doorknobs and gear shifts. No energy for her work or her child. No time to eat properly, or get enough sleep. Her health would begin to fail . . .

She looked in the bathroom mirror. Her face was wrinkled like an old oil painting. She was on her way to dying, and she hadn't thoroughly lived.

All right. Take a lover, she told herself. But how about some nice man? Why do you have to make yourself a pariah as well as an adultress? Packs of dogs will snap at your heels. Gangs of small children will throw large stones. Why are you doing this?

Because I want to, came the answer.

But you'll ruin your safe neat orderly life.

Fuck it, came the reply.

She took Matt to the Museum of Natural History. On the way to his old friends, the dinosaurs, they passed her old friends in their glass cases—models of the ape men and early humans, Neanderthal Man, Java Man, Peking Man. She reflected that this, after all, was what sex used to be about—keeping the race going. Natural selection had ensured that a situation least likely to be enjoyable would prevail: Those strains survived in which males were able to pump the maximum amount of sperm into females. This occurred when males ejaculated quickly without bringing the female to orgasm. Perpetually turned on, she would demand unending ejaculations.

Obviously the race didn't need assistance in reproducing itself these days. But Scarsdale Man was stuck with this inherited physiology. Justin and she had it calculated to the thrust: the kind and amount of foreplay, the precise speed and angle that triggered orgasm for each. It had become a hygienic routine, like brushing teeth to remove plaque.

As she watched Matt studying the huge carcasses, she recalled that Justin and she hadn't always been so efficient. Sometimes in the winter they'd borrow a cabin in the Adirondacks and spend several days rolling around naked under bearskins by a fire. Many weekends they'd been in bed all day long discovering new ways to please each other. Rather than studying piles of old bones in museums. Their lovemaking had become efficient when they'd had to fit it in around naps and feedings and babysitters. This was nobody's fault. Routines and responsibilities were what parenthood was about. But they left little space for passion. Like a genie being released from the bottle of domestic duty, her attraction to Maria was taking on a life of its own.

After Matt was asleep, she put on a nightgown and robe and set a stack of records on the stereo. She sat on the couch reading a manuscript, with a pack of cigarettes and a bottle of wine. At some point she realized she'd smoked half the cigarettes and drunk most of the wine, and was only on page fourteen.

Someone was singing "Shenando." She listened and was soon weeping.

"*. . . oh Shenando, I long to see you. / Far away, you rolling waters . . .*"

She kept thinking she'd escaped from the goddam place, but at the least excuse, longing for it would flare up like residual malaria in her bloodstream. Continuity, Stability, Loyalty, the values that growing up in that lush green valley had bred into her—these were important over the long haul. Maria and that bunch, they were butterflies. They darted from place to place, cause to cause, person to person, leaving in their wakes unfulfilled commitments. They weren't serious people. Maria would make love with her, and the next day she'd be off. So what was the point in shaking up Justin and Matt (and herself)?

On the other hand, why not do something just for fun, or just out of curiosity? Who'd be harmed? Probably Justin wouldn't care. He might even be relieved. And how could it harm Matt if his mother were having fun?

Another record fell. Tammy Wynette's voice filled the room: "*Stand by your man. / Give him two arms to cling to, / And something warm to come to / When nights are cold and lonely . . .*"

She lit another cigarette, guzzled some wine and listened—about the brave wife waiting for the return of her carousing husband. Was Justin carousing at his meditation center? Did one carouse at a meditation center? What if he were? Justin had caroused from time to time, but he always came back to the Great Ear in the end. That was how men were. And how were women? A Real Woman waited with Patience and Loyalty. This was her role. And by God, she'd fulfill it! These were the values she'd been raised with, and they were admirable!

She smashed out her cigarette and marched into Matt's room. He slept so soundly, his hair damp and rumpled, his fists clenched. When she kissed his flushed cheek, he grunted, flung out an arm and turned over. Emily vowed she'd never do anything that might threaten his home life.

She hollowed out a nest among her blankets and pillows. As she lay with her head swimming from the wine, her hand sought her clitoris, and she moaned, trying to pretend it was Justin's hand rather than Maria's.

In the morning, hung over, she walked with Matt through Riverside Park. White, water-inflated prophylactics from midnight matings in the bushes quivered in the murky Hudson.

"What are those?" Matt demanded, as they leaned on the railing.

"Let's not go into it."

"But what are they, Mom?"

"Dead fish or something. Hell, I don't know. Leave me alone."

"Fish," Matt decided. "Look at those funny fish," he ordered the man next to him.

"Oh, do come on!" Emily dragged him away, aware of her missed opportunity to advance his sexual education. The less anyone knew about any of it, the better.

After lunch she read Matt a book about a family of anthropomorphic frogs who lived in a pond in Central Park. Then Matt went to play in his room, and Emily put on some records and gazed at the *Times*. Why they had to make the damn thing so thick was beyond her. People in other parts of the globe got through Sundays without four-inch-thick bundles of newsprint. She squinted through her hangover at the headlines of the latest atrocities. She suddenly reflected that you become an adult once you stop assigning human characteristics to animals à la Walt Disney and begin assigning animal characteristics to humans. The paper dropped into her lap as she tried to figure out what had come over her yesterday. All that yearning and renunciation. What nonsense.

The record changed, and a woman began singing the slow song Maria and she had danced to. She recalled abruptly what yesterday's seizure had been about. "*. . . I've been waiting so long for another song. / I've been thinking that I was the only one . . .*"

The phone rang. It was Maria inviting her to supper.

"I don't know if I can. Justin's away."

"Oh yeah, I forgot. Well, bring Matt along."

"He's got to get up early for the day-care thing. I'll see if I can find a sitter and call you back."

"Hey, are you OK?"

"Yeah, I'm fine. Why?"

"I don't know. You sound a little weird."

"I'm just hung over."

"While the cat's away, and like that?"

"Yeah, I guess so."

Emily sat down on the couch. She could call back and say she couldn't find a sitter. On the other hand, Maria was a close friend, and Emily couldn't avoid her indefinitely.

No, the whole notion was ridiculous. She'd been high on wine the night she'd danced with Maria, and again last night. She was lonely with Justin gone, and that was all. The loneliness was perching wherever it could, like a vulture on a tree branch. She wasn't reared to make love with women, and she wasn't reared to be unfaithful to her husband—it simply wasn't her. It was out of the question.

A Honey Sweet record came on, and she found herself listening intently.

"*A woman needs a man to hold, / Who'll protect her from the cold, / Who'll keep her safe from harm her whole life long . . .*"

Garbage! Wasn't this what she'd left Newland to get away from? Sally trapped in that little wooden box in the mill village, poaching onions, with Pampers in her pockets, and teething rings through her buttonholes. Yet was Emily's life different except in external detail? She too spent all her time doing only what other people wanted, never consulting herself to find out what *she* might want. She marched to the phone and called the sitter.

It was a long supper that included two bottles of wine. They discussed the headlines, did a postmortem of the party, and avoided looking each other in the eye. Emily knew the first move, if there was to be one, was hers. It was a point of pride with Maria not to seduce her straight friends. What if she'd misunderstood and Maria wasn't interested? Maria would reject her, she'd be humiliated, her sex life would be set back decades. Or Maria would accept, but be surprised and detached. For the first time Emily understood some of the agonies of men. Why hadn't she stayed home with a good book?

"Well!" said Emily. ". . . guess I'd better be going . . . baby sitter . . . beauty sleep . . . work tomorrow . . ."

"Oh. Yes. Right. Fine. Let me get your coat."

As Maria got up, Emily put her hand, trembling, on Maria's knee. They both looked at it as though it were a dying fish.

"Hmmm." Maria sat back down.

"Damn it, I don't know how to do this."

"You're doing just fine." Maria picked up Emily's hand in both hers. "But this is the last thing in the world I want."

Emily's heart collided with her stomach. She withdrew her hand, unable to look at Maria. "You're not . . . attracted to me?"

Maria retrieved her hand. "I'm very attracted to you. But I'm terrified."

"*You* terrified?"

"Well, it looks as though your plate's pretty full."

Emily removed her hand. "It feels empty to me."

Maria reclaimed the hand. "It's just that the cook's on vacation. But he'll be back, and I don't want to be responsible for shaking up your life."

"You flatter yourself." Maria laughed. "I promise I wouldn't fall in love with you, Maria, and get all mushy. I know you'd hate that."

"Emily, everyone starts out thinking she's fallen for someone who just 'happens' to be a woman. Or that she'll just have a piece of female flesh on the side, and that it's no big deal. But it usually becomes a big deal. It's not something to go into lightly. It involves a lot more than the sex of the people you sleep with."

"Jesus, you make it sound like Saul on the road to Damascus." Emily removed her hand. "Ah, shit, Maria, you're right. I know that much about myself. I can't keep things casual. When you grow up in a small town, you try to turn each encounter into a unique interpersonal experience."

"That isn't exactly what I meant. What happens is, you turn yourself into an outsider. You're no longer playing by society's rules, so how you perceive those rules and the people who abide by them starts shifting. It can be very heavy."

"But I've been an outsider all my life."

They sat in silence.

"Why is this stuff always so awkward?" inquired Maria.

"Is it? I wouldn't know."

She nodded.

"I don't know, it sounds as though this isn't fated to happen, Maria. But you should know how appealing I find you." Emily stood up, relieved.

"And me you, darling." Maria stood up, also looking relieved. They embraced. They kissed. The kiss went on and on. Emily found her hand of its own accord touching Maria's breast. A breast filling her shameless hand, the stiffening nipple nuzzling her palm . . .

Harold walked into her office and informed her he was switching companies. His projects here were being dropped. Emily stared at him. When editors left, they usually asked their secretaries to go with them. Emily noticed he was avoiding such an invitation. He muttered something about asking around to see if anyone here was looking for a "girl" and walked out. She tried to tell herself maybe he wasn't allowed a secretary at the new place, or one was already there.

She followed him into his office. "What about Maggie's book?"

"What about it?"

"Is it being dropped?"

He shrugged. "Don't know. Guess you'd be glad?"

"It's the jacket I hate, not the book."

"Lots of luck. Maybe she'll find another editor who won't be so crass." He began dialing the phone.

She understood she'd been trying to have it both ways—expecting Harold to part the corporate waters so she could skip dry shod into some editorial position. And at the same time, insisting on asserting contradictory opinions, when all he wanted was agreement. If it was patronage Emily was after, she had to fulfill her end. If she wanted to play in the big leagues, though, she had to take her chances just as he did. She'd been dumb enough to hitch her wagon to his star, but like everyone else up here, he was a comet—just passing through.

At supper she said to Matt, "Guess what happened to Mommy today? She got fired."

He blinked. "Like with matches and stuff?"

"No. The man I work for doesn't want me anymore."

"Oh goody, Mom! So you don't have to go to the office anymore. And you and me can stay home together all day?"

"I guess I'll have to find another job, honey."

Maria came over after Matt was asleep, and Emily told her about Harold and her new sympathy for the pressures men were under.

"The stupid fucker," Maria growled.

"No, he's not, Maria. He's actually a nice man. Come to think of it, it's so weird you don't know him. There are the people I know at work. The people I live with. The people I socialize with. And none of you know each other."

"What's weird about that?"

"Well, in Newland everybody knows everybody else. You could talk about your boss to friends, and they'd know him and his family and have opinions on whatever he'd done. It's like having a live-in backup band."

"Sounds horrible. You'd never have any privacy."

"Well, I guess that's one way of looking at it."

"Jesus, how many years have you been away from that fucking place? And it still occupies your every waking moment."

"Not all of them," Emily said.

"Yeah, right. We were going to discuss Friendship tonight, weren't we? And whether or not sex messes it up."

Emily described the ways in which sexual expectation had distorted her friendship with Raymond. Maria recounted a series of experiences, good and bad, involving sexual interludes with friends.

"What do you want out of this, Emily? Homosexual Experience?" Maria stood up. "You're an important friend. I don't want us to use each other."

They laughed nervously and kissed at the door. Maria drew Emily's tongue into her mouth and Emily's stomach dropped through the floor. As a friend, as an enemy, she wanted Maria in her bed right away. Instead she closed the door after Maria and locked the three locks.

Harold informed her later that week that the only opening was in the accounting department, but he offered to fire her so she could get unemployment. She was horrified. Her moral code reserved government assistance for the less privileged—the undereducated or handicapped or disabled or over-fecund. Emily was healthy, well-educated. Harold reminded her she was a taxpayer and that she'd been paying unemployment insurance. As she thought about it, it occurred to her that she was in fact handicapped: She had no penis. Freud was wrong, though. It wasn't a penis she wanted, but rather the prerogatives that mysteriously accrued to those who had them. The right to play on athletic teams in high school. The right to have a draft card to burn. Cut loose from Harold's noblesse oblige, cut loose from Justin's and her father's earning power, what were her prospects? She'd earn half as much as a man doing the same job. Just enough to get by on for Matt and her. Her situation was only marginally better than that of the people she'd helped get on welfare in Cincinnati. Newland said if you couldn't manage on your own, you weren't trying hard enough. Newland was sometimes full of shit.

Maria and she went to an old Katharine Hepburn movie at the Thalia and held hands, then they went to a Chinese restaurant on Broadway.

"Maria, I've been thinking about friendship."

"Me too," Maria said, her mouth full.

"What have you decided?"

"I've decided you're doing your passive Southern best to manipulate me into deciding for us."

Emily smiled. "A lot's been going on for me. With my job collapsing and all. And with Justin gone."

"If you say so."

"But I have decided what I want."

Maria waited for her to summon her courage, their chopsticks poised like the claws of grappling lobsters.

"Our friendship is real important to me . . ."

"I think we've been over this several times already."

". . . but if we have to choose between sex and friendship, let's take sex."

Maria collapsed onto her plate. "Outasight," she said, summoning the check.

Through Maria's skylight, past hanging baskets of plants, Emily could see the full moon. Her mind was vaguely cataloguing differences. No beard, as Maria's face grazed her breasts and stomach. No hair on the chest . . .

"God," Emily whispered eventually, rubbing her face with her hand.

Maria gave her several tiny kisses, like reassuring pats. "Was it OK?"

"God."

"You said that already."

"God."

"It was all right?"

"I'm going to miss you when you're gone, Maria."

"But I just got here." Maria laughed. "Don't start worrying about the crops in the field. Just this once, allow yourself to gaze directly into the sun."

Justin returned armored with otherworldliness and ready to plunge into corporate corruption. He'd met a holistic stockbroker at the meditation center who had really turned his head around, and taught him how to be into subordinated debentures but not of them. While he sat on the living room floor demonstrating meditation postures, Emily said in a low voice, "Justin, I think I'm bisexual. I made love with Maria while you were gone. I hope you don't mind."

He looked at her, trying to endow his face with the tolerant expression his intellect believed appropriate. But there was panic in his eyes. "That's cool. Why should I mind?"

"I was afraid you might feel rejected or something."

Life became one long orgasm, as eroticism drove her to Maria, as guilt drove her back to Justin. Each professed an absence of jealousy, and affection for the other. But Emily, devoted to keeping everyone happy, felt like a Ping-Pong ball in a championship match.

Sometimes Maria and she bit and scratched and moaned. Other times they lay like lizards on a rock. Emily was amazed by the variety of emotions that fitted under the label "sex."

She'd return comatose from a session with Maria, and Justin would grab her. Usually she feigned enthusiasm out of loyalty. As he tried exotic new holistic sex aids, Emily ground her teeth with irritation—that it had taken a third party to inspire them to experimentation, that Justin had forced her to be the heavy who blew the factory

ORIGINAL SINS

whistle on their routinized love life, that the notion she'd just been with a woman seemed to titillate him.

Once he gasped grimly as he thrust, "Women-got-nothing-I-don't-have.-And-I-got-plenty-they-don't!" He came on the second "don't."

Emily didn't say so, but he was wrong. Maria was able to sense the swelling and receding of Emily's desire and respond to it instinctively. It was the difference between a musical score and improvisation.

But one day Maria appeared to stop worrying about Emily and let herself go. She shouted and wept. Her body shuddered, twisted, and heaved until Emily collapsed in exhaustion and revulsion. The insatiability. The lack of decorum and self-control. Emily lay in prim silence.

"Hell, I've scared you, haven't I?" Maria murmured.

Emily couldn't think what to say. That great throbbing, slurping maw. Ugh.

Maria took Emily's chin in her hand and turned her face toward her own. "Ah shit, I blew it."

"It's all right." In Newland people parceled out emotions. If you were going to spend a lifetime with the same people, you couldn't afford intensity. But in Maria's world people came and went, like bouts of indigestion.

"What is it that scares you?"

"I'm afraid we'll burn ourselves out and have nothing left for the long haul."

Maria smiled. "But we're not talking about long hauls. It will last as long as it lasts. Let it be whatever it's going to be."

"But I don't want it to end."

"I don't either. But either it will, or it won't."

"I know lots of couples in Newland who've been together for years."

"Are we talking grand passion, or are we talking marriage?"

"Can't you have both?"

"Can you? You'd know better than I."

Emily said nothing.

"Marriage has its pleasures—mutual comfort, security, routine.

But passion isn't among them. And I thought you'd had your fill of domesticity for a while?"

"Well, I guess passion is OK. But can you base a life on it?"

"But you've got a life already, Emily. A husband, a child, work, friends. What you and I have is the frosting, not the cake."

Emily nodded numbly. It was beginning to feel like cake to her. And she knew that cake, once it went stale, crumbled.

At Sammie's apartment that night Sammie passed out some *Playboys* and *Harper's Bazaars*. The women's group studied the models, then took off their clothes and stood up one by one, reciting height, weight, and measurements. Most giggled or tried to shield parts of their anatomies with hands and arms.

Tall, short, thin, fat, big breasts or small, thin waists or thick, bulbous hips or flat, each had an attractive, healthy body. Yet each had gone through a lifetime of dieting, exercising, and worrying, frantic attempts to conform.

Afterward, they were angry or depressed. Finally, Gail said weakly, "Yes, but it's our problem. We fell for it. We didn't *have* to try to conform."

Maria growled, "Just one more example of that male totalitarian mind set. Monotheism. Monogamy. Monarchy. Monopoly capitalism."

"Same thing with skin color," grunted Lou. "White is right."

"When I *think* of the somersaults I've turned trying to convince men it doesn't matter what size their wretched penises are . . . ," Susannah mused.

"God, I just remembered something," Emily gasped. "In high school when the girls would walk into the cafeteria, the jocks would hold up cards with numbers on them, rating us like Olympic divers on our figures." Her smile crumpled.

"Jesus, that's so *bad*," Lou muttered.

Later, as Emily removed her clothes under Maria's skylight, she ran her hands down her sides. This waist she'd always thought was too thick (which Justin had agreed with), maybe it was OK after all?

Maria came up behind her and slid her own hands down the path Emily's had taken.

Emily turned to face her, and her eyes ran down Maria's body. "We're both gorgeous."

After making love, Emily lay with her mouth against an artery in Maria's neck, feeling with her lips as Maria's racing pulse slackened. Raindrops rolled down the skylight. Emily was swept with wave after wave of an aching tenderness.

"What was that?" Emily whispered.

"What?"

"I don't know. Tenderness?"

"You're really getting into this."

"I'm feeling things I didn't know were possible."

"Shrink types say it's pre-verbal sensations. Everyone's earliest experience of security and physical pleasure is associated with the female body, and contact with one in adulthood can trigger those sensations. Most women never get a chance because, unless you're sexually immature like us, you're supposed to switch your allegiance to male bodies."

"Well, that certainly killed that," Emily said, sitting up and lighting a cigarette.

"I'm sorry, darling. I didn't mean to get clinical."

With her unemployment checks and with Justin working, Emily didn't need a job right away, but she started looking anyway because she missed working. Finding a job in publishing was a word-of-mouth process. She was passed from person to person. But she was like a walking wound: If a potential male employer looked at her wrong, she'd stalk out, leaving him bewildered. Later she herself would be bewildered, and unable to explain to Maria precisely how the man had offended her. It was like trying to find a job for a land mine—you stepped on her by mistake and she exploded, demolishing herself in the process.

One Saturday as Justin and she came out of a movie, he said, just as he always had, "Well, what do you think?"

Emily told him. Just as always, he said, "No, you've missed the point, Emily. Do you remember when that guy said, 'Yes, and I'll show . . .'"

"Fuck it, man! I have eyes! I know what I saw!"

Passers-by stopped and stared. Justin looked at her, his mouth hanging open.

"I'm sorry," he mumbled, as they stalked back to the apartment.

"It's OK." Emily fought her need to apologize.

In bed that night her body responded to Justin in some of the ways it had learned with Maria. He was appalled, but then he got smug, taking credit.

Emily lay awake in a rage. And at 2 a.m. she saw the light! The institution of marriage was a penal institution. Set up and maintained by men, to domesticate the passion she now knew existed in women. The ominous feeling she'd had first making love with Earl, that he was trying to tame her like one of his mares—that's exactly what had been going on. Those passions unleashed, what would they do to the orderly male world of getting and spending and hoarding and defending? And willing it all at death to sons they were sure were their own. They filled their factories with machines. They filled their homes with machines. They preferred it if their wives were merely appliances: Plug them in, and they dispensed sympathy and meals and clean socks. Plug into them, and they got your rocks off. She got up and stalked to the bathroom.

She watched the sky across the Hudson turn from black to grey. When Justin awoke, she announced she couldn't make love with him anymore.

He listened, nodded, and turned away. She had imagined shouting and weeping. Silence unnerved her. Didn't he care?

"But I love you, Justin. I think there are other kinds of love, maybe more important kinds."

He wouldn't acknowledge he'd heard her.

She tried a joke: "Justin, you know I'll always have a vacancy for you in the motel of my mind?" He didn't smile. She spent the morning trying to placate him by cooking a big breakfast, by not scrambling the order of the sections in the *Times*.

She understood on her way to Maria's that she now wanted to do what she wanted, but that she wanted everyone else to be pleased with it. That was progress, considering the years the Great Ear had spent wanting to do only what everyone else wanted.

As Maria and she strolled through Riverside Park, she told Maria what she'd done. Maria tried to say something sympathetic about how painful it must be for them both. But delight showed in her eyes. She grabbed Emily's huge pocketbook, and searched for the diaphragm Emily kept there "just in case."

"What are you doing?"

She jumped up and with a flick of her wrist sent the diaphragm skimming above the condoms that quivered in the murky Hudson.

"What are you doing?"

"You won't be needing it anymore."

"How do you know, damn it?"

"If you do, then you deserve whatever happens."

As they walked to Maria's apartment, Emily realized she was delighted to have her diaphragm floating down the Hudson to the sea. She'd swallowed the Pill until she hemorrhaged, shot up with foam until an allergic reaction set in, worn an IUD until its string like a wick carried an infection into her uterus.

"God, it's a wonder they can get any women at all to sleep with them," Emily mused.

"Who?"

"Men."

"What do you mean?"

"All that contraceptive garbage."

"I know. I remember. It could put you off sex forever."

"Did you ever get your diaphragm all jellied up and bent for insertion, and have it slip and go flying across the room? You're good for me, Maria: one hundred percent effective, and no side effects."

"That's what you think."

Emily had hoped the Ping-Pong match was over. Instead, she ceased to be the ball and became a player in two simultaneous games, a paddle in each hand. After recovering from his sulk, Justin became friendly and forbearing.

"The thing is," he explained, "I'm jealous."

"Jealous?"

"Yeah, I wish I were a lesbian."

Emily laughed. "How come?"

"Because I love women, and so many of the neatest ones are gay."

"Can you blame them?"

"Anyhow, the women's movement is where it's all happening right now politically."

"I suppose it's not too pleasant to go from being the champion of the oppressed to being the oppressor?"

"No, it's not. It's like when whites got kicked out of the civil rights movement by the arrival of Black Power. Only then, we had Vietnam to move on to. I miss that sense of community we used to have. Do you remember? The feeling we were all working together on something really important."

Justin told the men's group, one of whom told Maria, that he was waiting for her and Emily's relationship to "burn itself out." Emily was going through a phase. He had learned at the meditation center the only way to hold on to something was with an open hand.

Emily began phoning Maria every morning around nine, after Matt and Justin had gone and before going out job hunting. She told Maria she liked knowing where Maria would be each day and what she'd be doing, so Emily could visualize her in situ. Maria seemed touched.

Since they were all old friends and sophisticated about sexual liaisons, Emily invited Maria to the apartment to dinner one night. As she brought out an eggplant casserole, Justin said, "You've got a good cook on your hands, Maria."

Maria glanced at him, her fork halfway to her mouth. "Yeah, this is great."

"Makes up for the way she cleans." He laughed.

Maria glanced at Emily. Apparently it was a joke. Emily smiled. Then frowned.

"She's good at what she likes. But she doesn't have much staying power."

"Uh, well . . . ," said Maria, "I don't think I see what you're saying."

"All I mean is that there's a certain brilliance about her. But there isn't much beneath that surface sparkle. Wouldn't you say?"

"Well . . ."

Emily was crawling with anxiety. She glanced from one to the other.

"I mean, I've known Emily for so many years now, and have seen her grow and change in so many ways. And sometimes I wonder if she has a core . . ."

Maria asked pleasantly, "Would you like this glass of wine in your face, Justin?"

He laughed amiably.

"Who wants coffee or tea?" Emily asked, Amy Vanderbilt racing out to avert catastrophe.

Maria made excuses and left.

Justin said, with a paternalistic twinkle, "Well, I'm glad you've got somebody who'll watch out for your interests, Emily." He patted her on the shoulder.

During their next phone call neither Maria nor she referred to the dinner. As they were about to hang up, Emily said, "When shall we get together?"

"Oh, I don't know. Give me a call soon. Or I will you."

"I've been wondering. How about if we set a couple of times each week to get together—say Tuesday afternoons and Friday nights or something."

"Huh?"

"Well, then we'd be able to plan our other stuff around those times."

"Well, I don't know . . . Sure, why not?"

Justin's work was going well, and he had rented loft space in Soho. He said, "You know, I've been thinking, Emily. Maybe we should move to the Village."

Emily stared at him. Who was this "we"? She thought that had been settled. Maria was ten blocks away here. "I don't really want to leave this area, Justin."

"Yeah, but it would save me over an hour a day commuting."

Emily said nothing.

"Plus subway fare. And I could come home for lunch."

"*Justin*. . . ," she began irritably.

"I mean, I don't like to pull rank, but I am the one who's paying the rent now. And maybe we need to alter our living arrangement to make things easier for me."

"Maybe we should think about living separately then," she snapped.

"Well, I suppose that's a possibility. But wouldn't you miss Matt?"

"What?"

"Well, I'm sure as hell not leaving my son alone with a bunch of man-haters."

"I don't hate men," Emily protested with hatred.

"Well, let's both think this over."

In bed with Maria, Emily said, "Justin's thinking about moving to the Village."

"What? By himself?"

"Actually he's thinking about 'our' moving to the Village."

Maria said nothing.

"Maybe we should live together, Maria."

"You can't afford to stay where you are on your unemployment?"

"Of course I can. Don't be so unromantic, silly. I was thinking how nice it would be to wake up next to you every morning. And to sit around in the evening and watch the news. Matt and Cleo could be like brother and sister."

She frowned. "Yeah, but I don't want to live with anybody, Emily. I've done that trip. I need my privacy . . ."

Emily shrugged.

As Emily walked back into the apartment, the men's group was meeting. As she washed the supper dishes, she heard them arguing about who had behaved worst to women and who was now the most full of remorse. After they left, Emily walked into the living room and began emptying ashtrays.

Justin looked up from his newspaper and nodded.

"Hi, Justin." She tried not to get too close because she hadn't washed and reeked of sex.

"Did you know Matt has a cold?" he asked.

"Yeah. I noticed. Poor kid."

"Yeah, I guess he's under a lot of strain."

She looked at him for a while before saying "Why?"

"Well, a kid must sense when his home life is weird."

"Is it?"

"Well, it sure isn't what most kids have."

"Oh, I don't know." She described the domestic arrangements of the women in her group, most of which were "different," to put it mildly. Then she realized she was sounding defensive.

"Why so respectable all of a sudden, Justin?"

"Well, I just want my son to have what any child needs from parents." He went into the bedroom.

Emily, chewing her nails, tried to visualize the hideous things that would happen to Matt because his mother had a woman lover. He would be ostracized on the playground. He would sprout breasts. He would need wall posters of Gertrude Stein to get off in adulthood. Jesus, what was she doing to her baby?

She raced into his room and stood over him as he slept. He *looked* OK, apart from a stuffy nose . . .

In bed Justin and she rolled over and hugged each other. It had seemed so natural for so many years. Now his body felt taut and bony. An erection prodded her stomach. Why not? It would be simple and friendly just to let him slip it in, as he'd done for eight years.

The thought repulsed her. "No."

"Christ, who *wants* you anyway?" He turned away. She was swept with anxiety. The Great Ear needed Justin to want her in order to be sure he would stick around. In order to be sure she wouldn't be left all alone far from home surrounded by strangers. Her pride wouldn't allow her to pursue him to his edge of the bed. She took her need to Maria the next morning, knocking on her door unannounced. Maria invited her in for coffee, looking simultaneously pleased and irritated. She handed Emily a mug and sat down. Under the guise of getting milk from the refrigerator, Emily stood behind her and massaged her breasts.

"Actually," said Maria, "I've got a deadline on an article. So I'm afraid I'll have to kick you out in a minute."

It entered Emily's head that Maria was lying: Kate was arriving for a morning in bed . . .

"I see."

"Come on, lady," she said, pulling Emily's mouth down to hers. "Don't use that tone of voice. You know I have to earn a living. We aren't all lucky enough to be on unemployment." She grinned, and Emily felt better.

"When will you be finished?"

"By two, I hope. Or I've had it."

"Can we get together then?"

"I'm afraid I'm tied up."

"Who with?"

Maria looked at her. "I have to hand-deliver the article and talk it over with the editor."

"Can I see you tonight then?"

"Is something wrong?"

"No, I just miss you, Maria."

"Tonight's the women's meeting."

"How about afterward?"

"I'm afraid I'm tied up."

"Who with?"

"I'm not sure it's any of your business, but I'll tell you anyway: Kate."

"Is she spending the night?"

Maria sighed. "You're doing a number. You know that? Listen, let's have lunch tomorrow. OK? And cool it, sweetheart. You know I'm crazy about you."

Emily spent the morning with her datebook and calculated that she'd phoned Maria almost twice as much as Maria had phoned her. She also reviewed the last several times they'd made love and realized that, almost without exception, she'd brought Maria to orgasm first. Presumably Maria then made love to her because she felt obligated.

Who was Maria *really* seeing this afternoon?

Emily disguised herself in a scarf and sunglasses and an old trench coat of Justin's and walked up to Maria's apartment building. She rang Maria's bell, but the buzzer didn't buzz for her to come up. Maria had already left for her assignation. Emily waited in the doorway across the street to see who Maria would bring home. She arrived at 3:05 with her daughter, Cleo.

When Maria left that evening's meeting with Kate, tears filled Emily's eyes. She got home to find Justin asleep. She sat on the sofa and imagined what Maria and Kate were doing at that moment.

Emily raced to the phone and dialed Maria's number. It rang half a dozen times. She pictured them pausing in their lovemaking long enough to decide not to answer. It rang six more times. By now Maria would be worried. It had to be important if someone was letting it ring so long.

Another five times. Their concentration would be broken. Maria would be sighing and searching for the phone with her hand.

On ring number nineteen she answered in a sleepy voice.

Emily hung up, triumphant that she'd stopped them!

At lunch the next day she said, "Maria, there's something I have to tell you."

"*What*, for Christ's sake?" Maria asked with a laugh.

"I think I'm falling in love with you."

"Oh God, don't do that."

"I thought you'd be pleased."

"If you mean what I think you mean by 'in love,' then I don't want any part of it. This manic-depressive trip where you give me the power to make you jubilant or miserable? Honestly, Emily, it's an illness to be recovered from, not a state to be cultivated. Don't succumb to it, sweetheart, please. We've got such a good thing. Don't wreck it."

"Well, what is it we've got, if it's not love?"

"If it's nice, which it is, why do you care?"

"Well, I think I have a right to know."

"Love, in love, friendship, marriage, divorce, separation, lust . . . We're presented with these categories. None fit our experience, but we all try to shoehorn ourselves into them. Don't label it. Just let it happen."

"But how do we know what we're doing then?"

"We don't. But I'm willing to try almost anything, because I know for a fact that the old categories don't work for me."

Justin took up with a new woman named Shelby. According to the men's group, she gazed at him entranced as he spoke and solicited his advice and opinions. She wore Oxford cloth button-down collar blouses, and sweaters tied by their arms around her neck. She was secretary to the chairman of the board of the paper company for whom Justin had done the public service campaign. She described everything as "terrific," through clenched teeth, moving only her lips. She had a son Matt's age named Joshua, which she also pronounced by moving only her lips. They began taking Joshua and Matt to the zoo in Central Park, to F A O Schwarz's, to Rumpelmayer's for ice cream sundaes, on boat trips around Manhattan, all the places Justin had never dreamed of taking Matt in his first five years of life. Reportedly, Shelby thought Justin was a "terrific dad." Matt talked about Shelby all the time: She baked cookies and made hot chocolate, played Monopoly.

Emily's parents arrived from Newland. They stayed at the Plaza, but Emily cleaned the apartment, served them carefully prepared meals, and took them to the Cloisters and on the boat trip around Manhattan. Justin behaved admirably, coming home at night rather than staying with Shelby, and discussing business with Mr. Prince, who looked relieved to be no longer under attack from his revolutionary son-in-law. Even Matt cooperated, watching his table manners, cleaning up his language, and not mentioning Maria or Shelby. Mr. Prince led them around the city on fruitless missions in search of bars and restaurants he remembered from his journeys in from Princeton.

After several days they decided to take a break from each other so that Emily could set up some job interviews. Justin and Matt went to Shelby's for the night. Late that afternoon Maria stopped by, and she and Emily ended up in bed. After making love, they fell asleep. Emily was awakened by her door buzzer. Groggily she got up and threw on a bathrobe and called through the door, "Who is it?"

"Your parents, dear."

It was too late to pretend she wasn't there. Like a doe blinded by approaching headlights, she opened the door.

"Are we disturbing you?"

"Uh, no. I was going to take a bath."

"We were over at Grant's Tomb and thought we'd stop by for some tea."

"Uh, great. Come in."

They sat in the living room. Emily was in a state of near collapse. At any moment the bedroom door would open and Maria would stumble out to the bathroom, naked.

"You're sure we're not interrupting you?"

"Oh no." She was sending brain waves to Maria to keep sleeping.

"We were thinking it might be fun," said her father, "to take you all to the Top of the Sixes when Matt and Justin get home."

Emily was speechless.

"We could go pick up Matt if you'll tell us where the day-care place is," offered her mother.

"He's going home with a friend tonight."

"Well, when does Justin get home?" inquired her father.

"Uh, he's staying in the Village for his Personal Growth Workshop tonight."

Her parents looked blank. She viewed her life through their eyes. In context it made a certain amount of sense. In the context of Newland, however, it was sordid and irresponsible. Oh dear God, please keep Maria sleeping. She looked at her parents' wrinkles and greying hair. They were good people. All they wanted was a peaceful old age. Quiet deaths. And here they had her for a daughter.

"Tea!" exclaimed Emily. "Let me fix you some. But first let me put on some clothes."

She raced into the bedroom and shook Maria awake. "My *parents* are in the fucking living room!"

Maria opened her eyes, then started laughing.

"Shut up, they'll hear you! Come on, you've got to hide in the closet."

Maria frowned. "Sorry, but I'm not going into a closet again for anybody."

"*Please,*" grunted Emily, dragging her from the bed.

"This is so childish," protested Maria as Emily shoved her into the corner of the closet and stacked blankets on top of her. "You're a grown woman. Who you sleep with is nobody's business but your own."

"In New York maybe. Not in Newland."

Back in the living room she poured them bourbon instead of tea, and rapidly tossed some down herself.

"Is something the matter?" her mother asked.

"Oh, no!"

By the time they left, Emily was passing out on the couch.

Maria emerged. "I resent being treated like a runaway slave, Emily. Jesus Christ, I'm your goddam *lover*. Couldn't you have introduced us? Couldn't we all have sat down and had a drink together like grown-ups? Wouldn't they want to know how happy I'm making their daughter?"

No doubt Kate had taken Maria home to meet the folks. Emily panicked. Why were things everybody else found so easy such a trial for her? Constantly torn between two ridiculous cultures, each sure its ways were right. Weeping, she wailed, "Give me a break, Maria."

Maria took her in her arms. "All right, never mind, darling."

Maria and Emily sat in a restaurant eating hamburgers. Every time the waitress whisked by, Maria's eyes followed her. Emily had just about decided to ask Maria to choose between her and her various other women. Emily was pretty sure Maria would pick her, which was why she was giving her the choice. Emily couldn't take her own seizures of jealousy anymore. She was turning into a nutcase.

Maria was reaching into her jeans pocket. Emily studied her green eyes and greying hair and tanned face. She loved this woman. She didn't want to share her. Maria handed her a ring with three keys on it.

Emily studied them blankly.

"To my apartment," Maria said.

Emily realized this was supposed to be a heavy moment. She remembered when Justin had given her the keys to his apartment. It was equivalent to a KT's giving you his lavalier. In a big city anyone who had your keys could rob you blind, rape you in the night, read your diary while you were away, interrupt your assignations. The giving of keys implied an extreme degree of trust. But Emily was from Newland, where doors were never locked, so the emotional impact eluded her. Nevertheless she grinned and said, "Thanks, sweetheart. I'll get copies of mine for you."

They ate on in a silence that was presumably fraught with significance for Maria. Emily tried to get into the spirit of the thing by slipping her foot out of her clog and rubbing it up and down Maria's calf. Emily felt waves of desire and tenderness. So intense that she knew this woman was the love of her life.

Maria kept eating her hamburger and following the buxom waitress with her eyes. How *could* she when they were sitting there with these great rushes of electricity passing back and forth between Emily's foot and Maria's leg? Emily sat back and glanced under the table. Her foot had been caressing the wooden table leg.

She sat in silence.

Maria smiled. "What are you looking so perplexed about?"

Emily said nothing. What did it mean if a table leg could trigger these sensations she'd been labeling "love"? Finally she replied, "I was just thinking you're the nicest gift I've ever given myself."

Maria thought it over, her eyes on the bustling waitress. "That sounds very sweet. But I'm afraid I don't much care for it."

"How come?"

"The implication that I'm an object you can own."

"You know that isn't what I mean." Someone once said the unexamined life wasn't worth living. What about the overexamined life?

"I'm not so sure. You've been acting pretty weird ever since you stopped sleeping with Justin."

"Have I?" She knew she had.

"You know you have."

Emily nodded.

"I think you've got this slot in your head you fit people into—Raymond, then what's-his-name . . . Earl. Then Justin. Now you're trying to do it to me. But, see, I can't handle your undiluted devotion, Emily. We've got good things to give each other, but they're not everything."

"Which is why you need Kate? And the others? Because I can't meet your needs?"

"What's Kate got to do with it?"

"What's Kate got to do with it? God, how can you compartmentalize your life like that? Whatever you do has ramifications on the whole. And I think your continued involvement with Kate is damaging us."

"Honey, Kate was here before you."

"Yeah, all right, fine. So why did you move on to me if things weren't over between you?"

Maria grimaced.

"What do you think this is, Maria—Malibu Beach or something?"

Maria looked at her plate for a long time. When she raised her head, she said, "Look, you're not working. And Justin and you are doing some weird trip. And you want me to make everything all right. But it's not within my power, Emily, as dearly as I love you. You don't need a man like that. You don't need a woman like that. Women have defined themselves through their relationships with men for so long that the temptation for lesbians is to continue to define ourselves through our relationships. I suppose to break out of this, we have to define ourselves through our work, or our politics, or our furniture or something."

The Great Ear couldn't believe her ears. A woman insisting there were limits to what she could do for others?

Finally she said, "I feel patronized. I raise an issue regarding you and me, and you give me some theoretical rap. It's what you Yankees always do—duck behind your political analyses."

"Oh, Christ, I'm in trouble now, I've just become a 'Yankee.' "

"Damn right," Emily snarled. "So what about Kate?"

"What about her?"

"Which is it going to be—her or me?"

"This is so childish."

"*Childish?* You're the one who's childish. Like a kid in a candy store. You have to take a bite of everything, don't you? The way you've been devouring that poor waitress with your eyes."

"I love women. I love their bodies. I love to watch them move. What's wrong with that? She's gorgeous."

"Jesus!" Emily stared at her. "Is that what women's liberation means then? We're free to behave as exploitatively as men traditionally have? Free to turn other women into sex objects? Wonderful."

"I'm not exploiting her, I'm admiring her. And if we met and enjoyed each other, we might go to bed. And it might be fun, or it might not. And we might continue for a week, or a month, or for years. All these rules in your head . . ."

"You people are sick."

"Which people?"

"You Yankees."

"Oh, Christ . . ."

"You treat each other like boxes of cereal. And when you go stale, or when you fail to find a prize at the bottom, you toss each other into the garbage."

"I think the Southern Baptist in you is overreacting, Emily."

"Fuck you!"

"I mean, sex isn't that important. It can be just another dimension to a friendship, a way to break down barriers and get closer . . ."

"General Foods ought to package it. Instant Intimacy! They'd make a fortune. What's wrong with you people that you can't get close without sex? It's pathetic."

"What's wrong with *you* people that you think you have to marry for life anyone whose genitals you touch? When are you going to grow up and stop behaving like a romantic adolescent?"

Emily glared. "When are *you* going to grow up and realize that just because you have the power to seduce someone doesn't mean you have to exercise it? I became a lesbian in the first place because I love women. If I wanted to be with someone who behaved like a man, I'd be with a man."

"Bullshit!" Maria hissed, bringing her fist down on the table. Silverware clattered to the floor. Heads turned. "Just because men have used sex as a weapon to dominate and degrade women doesn't mean we have to lock it away. Women can transform it into something sweet and sensual and pleasure-giving and life-affirming. And talk about male attitudes: this exclusivity of yours, regarding another person as a possession and trying to control her behavior. I don't want anything to do with it."

"And I don't want anything to do with your compulsive womanizing."

"So where does that leave us?"

Emily shoved the keys across the table.

"So you're determined to get on your high horse and ride off into the sunset?" Maria asked.

"I have no choice."

"You're making one. Own it."

"What? You can change, or I can change. But why should we?"

"No reason. Unless we care enough to want to stay together."

They gazed at each other. Emily reached across the table for Maria's hands. Necks craned throughout the restaurant.

"Let's think it over," Maria suggested.

Justin announced he was moving in with Shelby in the Village, would be filing for divorce, and wanted custody of Matt.

"Well?" he said. "Say something."

"All right. I'm upset. And what upsets me most is the discovery that if I won't let you instruct me, or sleep with me, or ramble on about your problems, you don't want to be involved with me. If I'm not doing something for you, you 'have no use' for me. How do you think that makes me feel?"

"But I *do* want a relationship with you, Emily. I've been knocking myself out trying to establish one. I simply don't know how to act with you anymore. If I'm nice, I'm patronizing. If I'm in pain about you and Maria, I'm guilt-tripping you. If I'm firm, I'm a bully. You women are out of your gourds."

"Your key word, Justin, is 'act.' That's all it is with you. You've been trying to find ways to lure or cajole or scare me back into the same old mold. You've got this slot in your head that has to be filled by a woman who'll service you sexually and domestically. I'd ceased to do this, so some woman who would had to be found. You aren't interested in what I'm really like, or think about, or might want to do."

"Crap," he said, walking toward the door.

"Can I have your new phone number? Matt might want to call you."

"Yeah." He pulled out an address book. She handed him pen and paper. The number was listed under "U" for "us."

"Thanks. Terrific," Emily said, her teeth clenched.

"Bitterness doesn't become you, Emily."

"Who's bitter?" she asked, laughing bitterly.

In the following weeks things deteriorated between her and Matt. All the characteristics he'd inherited and copied from Justin stood out in sharp relief and drove her crazy. The way his crew socks drooped. The way he sniffed when he woke up. Once when she asked him to pick up his room, he snapped, "You pick it up. You're the mommy."

She slapped him hard. He stared at her as a large red handprint appeared on his cheek.

She swept him into her arms, apologizing frantically.

Sammie's daughter, Angela, came over to play one Saturday. They were in Matt's room preparing to operate on one of his dolls. Emily had given up sleeping and eating by this time, in favor of pacing the living room floor smoking.

She overheard Matt say, "You can't be the doctor."

"Can too," Angela announced.

"Cannot."

"Can too."

"You have to be the nurse. Nurse, get the patient ready for the operation."

"I'm the doctor, Matt."

"Are not."

"Are too."

"Girls can't be doctors. Girls don't have penises."

Emily raced into Matt's room and spanked him hard several times, saying through gritted teeth, "I don't ever want to hear you say that again, Matthew Lawson!"

Both children stared at her, terrified. She stopped in midspank. Matt began howling. Angela joined him.

Emily closed her eyes. "I'm sorry, honey," she finally mumbled. "Angela is your guest. If she wants to be doctor, let her. Or take turns."

Matt's makeup was half Justin. He was linked to Justin in a way Emily could never be. And what did it mean if she despised Justin? It meant she was despising half of poor Matt. To earn her approval, he would come to despise half of himself. Maybe she should give him up to Justin without a fight. So that he could grow up despising instead the half of himself he got from her . . .

When Sammie came to pick up Angela, she said, "We're missing you at meetings, girl. When you coming back?"

"Ah, God, Sammie, I'm having a bad time."

"Why don't you let us help, child?"

"I don't think anyone can help. It's just a major personality difference between Maria and me."

"That's what I hear."

"What's she been saying?" Maria was probably lining up the entire women's group on her side.

"We've spent the last couple of meetings arguing over whether or not you got the right to privatize your emotional life like you been doing."

"What's the verdict?"

"Most says not. But I reckon it's cause we all miss you, girl, and want you to get your ass back to those meetings."

"I'll be back. Soon as I can bear to see Maria again."

"You love her a lot, don't you?"

"Yeah."

"I can tell she loves you too. In her way."

"But her way isn't my way."

"And your way ain't her way, child."

Sammie took Matt for the rest of the weekend. Emily stood smoking in the dark living room, watching the lights twinkle across the Hudson at Palisades Amusement Park. Tammy Wynette was singing "Stand by Your Man" on the stereo. Jesus, if only she had. Maria was right: What had started out as a succulent side order of female flesh had become a dinner-sized roast.

She drew on her cigarette, seeing her life laid out before her like a tarot deck. Justin with Shelby. Matt grown up and off on his own. Maria settled down in polygamous bliss, poaching her brain in some Malibu hot tub. Her parents dead. And Emily here alone in the night. All night, every night. Year after year. Watching the lights at Palisades Amusement Park. Sometimes she'd go visit them. They'd be kind, as though she were a maiden aunt, and impatient for her to leave so they could get on with their lives.

No one to bring you broth when you were sick. No one to eat Christmas dinner with. No one to file joint tax returns with.

She hadn't even spoken on the phone to Maria since their fight. She wasn't sure she could make the changes necessary to be involved with her—even if she wanted to. Maria: There was nothing she needed Emily for. She was earning her own living. She had other lovers. She could cook and clean as well as Emily. She had a full, complete life without Emily. Apparently she simply liked to be with her. Or used to. The Great Ear couldn't cope with this. The Great Ear was being loved for herself alone, and not for any services she could render?

If Maria didn't need her services, Emily had no hold over her. Maria was free to stay, or to leave as she chose. Emily couldn't bear it. If only she could cripple Maria and maintain custody of her crutches. If Maria were in an iron lung, she'd need Emily to feed her. She wanted Maria inert, inescapably dependent, unquestionably hers. So that Emily could begin to tire of having responsibility for her, and eventually start feeling contempt for her inability to care for herself. So that Emily's love could transmute into resentment, then hatred. So that Emily could finally free herself of this awful need to have Maria need her.

Emily put on her black leather jacket and went down to the Village. Next week she'd find a job. And tonight she'd get laid. She loved Maria. She wanted to be with her. She wanted not to be alone. She would try to play by Maria's rules.

Emily picked up an attractive young woman with curly red hair, who wore a blue and white football jersey. They danced, increasingly closely, and Emily bought her some drinks. Eventually, they secured a table. Emily gazed into the young woman's eyes, and pressed her knee with her own, and touched the woman's forearm with her fingertips as they talked.

By the end of the evening, the Great Ear had lent her twenty dollars and was giving her advice about how to deal with her difficult mother.

The Great Ear went home to bed alone. She couldn't fuck the youth of America—she had to take care of them. Emily realized what a talent Maria possessed—being able to assume that other people could take care of themselves and didn't need her to do it for them. She envied Maria her humility.

Emily devoted the next week to Meeting People. She searched underground newspapers for notices of meetings with compatible women. There was something for almost everyone—Bondage Support Group, Bisexual Biracials. But alas, no Cuckolds Anonymous. Gail phoned to urge her to go on the retreat the women's group was staging at her parents' vacation house in upstate New York. By now she was so lonely that she would have joined Hitler in his bunker.

When Emily arrived at the retreat, Maria came over and kissed her. She felt the old desire unhinging her joints one by one. "How's it going?" asked Maria.

"Fine."

They sat down by the pond, which shimmered in the heat. The others already lay naked in the sun, keeping their distance. Emily cleared her throat. "Look, I'm sorry I accused you of being a sultan in drag, Maria. I tried to join Cuckolds Anonymous this week, but I couldn't find one."

Maria laughed. "If you do, we'll all have to join." She added, "But that's a male concept. Why don't you drop that term from your vocabulary?"

"Why?"

"If you drop the word, maybe you'll drop the emotions that go with it."

"But presumably the word was invented to account for emotions that already existed."

"But not every culture has an equivalent word. Look, maybe you and Kate and I should do a threesome tonight."

"Huh?"

"To help you get over this jealousy trip."

Emily said nothing.

"What, you've never done a threesome before?"

Emily nodded no. Apparently there was no end to the adaptations she'd have to make to stay with Maria.

"Well, think it over," suggested Maria.

Emily watched her dive into the water, swim to the dock, and haul herself out. She stood there glistening in the sun, streaming with water. Why had she tried to tame Maria? Emily had resented it so much when Earl tried to do it to her.

As she and Kate and Maria walked toward the woods carrying sleeping bags, a lantern, a couple of bottles of wine, Emily felt not unlike Marie Antoinette on her way to the guillotine. But if this was what it would take to shed her feelings of possessiveness toward Maria—so that Maria would then want to be with her, and might even consider giving up Kate—by God, she'd do it.

They spread the sleeping bags on a floor of leaves and took off their clothes. Lying on the bags, they passed the wine, chatted, and touched each other. Kate and Emily, shy and wary. She'd just had a letter from Sally telling about a crafts course she was taking at the high school at night. What would she think about how her older sister spent her spare time? Being unfaithful to Justin would be bad enough in Sally's eyes. Making love with a woman would be unthinkable. But *two* women? What would her *parents* say? Nothing. They'd be speechless. At least no one could accuse her of thoughtlessly conforming to her conditioning.

Emily was in the middle, and Kate and Maria began stroking her and sucking her nipples. Emily lost track of who was doing what to whom. Although she was making love with Kate and Maria, she was locked into a private fantasy. It was more lonely than being alone. She watched Kate going down on Maria, waiting to be swamped with jealousy. But she felt nothing.

Once they had all experienced equal orgasms, they lay smoking cigarettes in the dark. Emily felt just as she had after being initiated into Ingenue. She walked back to the house alone. Once again the Great Ear had betrayed her into doing things to please other people. Shit.

The next morning as she lay by the pond in the sun, Emily contemplated her solitary old age, with no one to sit in the adjoining rocker on the porch of the old age home. At breakfast Maria had asked, "How do you feel about last night?"

Emily replied, "Well, it worked. I'm not jealous anymore." Emily hadn't gone on to add she'd probably never make love again, not with Maria, not with anybody.

The others lay nearby tanning. Maria and Kate were discussing the shape of things to come. In place of isolated couples would be tribes of strong women living on the land, in possession of all the skills necessary for survival apart from the hostile patriarchal world. They'd be family for each other, but extended family voluntarily chosen. They'd guarantee each other's bank loans, pierce each other's ears, buy tampons in bulk.

Emily listened as she lay in the grip of revulsion against all flesh. Including or excluding people on the basis of whether or not they had some bizarre flap of tissue hanging between their legs was about as absurd as including or excluding them on the basis of skin color. The Ingenues had excluded Ina Sue Bascombe because she didn't shave her legs, for God's sake.

The next women's meeting was at Emily's. When Susannah came in, she had two black eyes and a stitched-up cut stretching out from the corner of her mouth.

"God, you look terrible. What happened?" Emily demanded.

Susannah smiled as much as her wound would let her. "I was raped this week."

The room fell silent. Susannah sat on the sofa and told about walking down the street in early afternoon on her way to the Roosevelt in her nurse's uniform. A van pulled up, and two young black men hopped out, opened the back doors, and dragged her inside. Passers-by continued to pass by. As she struggled, one pointed to her thyroidectomy scar, flicked the blade of his knife on his thumb, and said, "Mama, you don't lie still you gon be one great *big* scar."

They unloaded her at the foot of a condemned high rise and dragged her upstairs to a room with broken windows. On a moldy mattress they took turns.

Her voice was matter-of-fact: "All I remember is their eyes. Bloodshot and dilated. Must have been on drugs. They kept up this patter: 'Hey, hey, big mama, les you and me play.' The one with the knife kept flashing it around saying, 'Gon carve me a big ole piece of this white man's meat.' And their cocks coming at me from every direction.

"I thought about you all, what you would have done." She laughed. "I said I was a lesbian and please not to put me through any more. They giggled, and one said, 'Hey mama, if you more of a man than us, les see your tool.' They pranced around comparing erections. 'Poor ole Mama, she ain't got no tool, so how she gon fuck pussy?'

"Then I told them I was pregnant. They screamed with laughter: 'You just said you was a mother-fucking bull dagger. Now you say you pregnant. We may be black, baby, but we ain't no *fools*.' Then one took off my shirt and started handling my tits and saying, 'All *right*, this here is one *big* mama.'

"I said, 'Look, yes, you've been fucked over. You can't get jobs or money. But it's the white *man* who's running this show. White women are as much victims as you. We should be allies. Take it out on those fuckers, not on us.' 'What she talking bout, man?' one asked another."

Gail cried quietly. Kate clenched and unclenched her fists. Maria had a knuckle between her teeth. Emily made periodic attempts to relax her grinding molars.

"Honey, what happened to your mouth?" asked Sammie.

Susannah breathed deeply. "Well, they'd each had me a couple of times, front and back. I screamed a lot, but after a while I decided it was pointless. Anyway, they seemed to enjoy it. Then they decided I should blow them. I clamped my mouth shut, so they cut it open. Then they started knocking me around and I passed out. They dumped me in a vacant lot. When I came to, these two white teenagers were poking me with their tennis shoes. I said, 'Help me please.' They looked at each other and grinned and unzipped their jeans and took their turns. After they'd left, some little kids saw me and went for the cops."

The group sat silent for several minutes.

"You seem pretty together," Lou finally said. "I'd be angry as hell."

Susannah laughed. "Together? I'm just on Valium. When I pass a man in the street now, I start shaking so hard I have to sit down. I know only a tiny percentage of men have ever raped. But I can't even sleep in the same bed as John now."

"You getting any help?" Kate asked.

"Yeah, my shrink has me exploring the body language I used to encourage them to pick me out of a whole streetful. When he found out about this group, he said I probably wanted to be raped in order to confirm my low opinion of men."

"Crap!" "Bullshit!" "That fucker!" they snarled.

Sammie gave them a nasty look. "I mean, Susannah child, I feel bad for you. But you got to look at it like this: You can't let yourself take it personal because those cats was driven to it. . . ."

"I'm sick of all this liberal shit!" Emily found herself yelling.

"Yeah, you'd like to get out the bloodhounds, wouldn't you?" snapped Sammie.

"It's society's fault, it's the fault of Susannah's unconscious. Marx says this, Freud says that. Fuck it! It's the fault of five motherfucking dope heads with Swiss cheese for brains, who ought to be strung up!"

"Scratch any Southern white and you'll find a cracker," drawled Lou.

"Fine," growled Emily. "You all go right ahead and donate to charity. Give your cast-off clothes to the Salvation Army. Write your senator about job training programs."

"Beats the hell out of a lynching," suggested Lou.

"I'm not talking about lynchings. I'm talking about individual accountability. What about the men who grow up subjected to poverty and injustice and humiliation who *don't* rape? Are they just weak or cowardly or insensitive or what?"

"They don't need to rape," explained Maria. "They got these cats keeping women down for them. Just like the Germans had their storm troopers, and the plantation owners had their overseers."

Susannah sat silent. Suddenly they all felt ashamed, having shifted into theory so as to stave off their rage and grief. "I was victim number fourteen of those men in the van," Susannah continued, "and the police actually caught one while they were picking up number fifteen. Shot him through the head while the other two drove off. John took me to the morgue to identify him. They rolled him out, and I looked at his face and the bullet hole in his forehead, and I . . ."—she began heaving and hiccoughing with sobs—". . . and I was glad. *I was just so goddam glad!*"

All the sweet sad brave women of Emily's youth—the church was packed with them. Beaten and abused and silenced and exploited their whole lives long. That night, listening to Susannah, the scales had fallen from Emily's eyes. In every country, throughout history: Breasts sliced off, clitorises torn out, spears shoved up vaginas. By men. By the hirelings of the motherfuckers sitting in these pews looking smug and devout. Raymond in his overalls and suit coat, immersed in the idiocies of rural life. His smug "self-made" father, with his slicked-down hair and long sideburns and stiff-looking suit. Her own father and grandfather down the pew from her. She kept trying to make exceptions for "her" men. But Maria was right: There could be no exceptions. They all profited from each act performed by other men that kept women afraid and in their service. And what about Matt sitting next to her, looking confused and troubled? Could she prevent his turning out exactly like them? Probably not, but she'd sure as hell try.

The moment everyone had been waiting for had arrived: Sally was gazing through her veil into the coffin at Jed, looking unable to make up her mind whether to weep softly like a Methodist, wail loudly like a Baptist, or bear it in dignified silence like an Episcopalian. Every eye was on her, savoring her widowly grief. She dabbed at her eyes with her handkerchief and her shoulders began shuddering.

Jesus, what a time it had been. Sally and her kids in pieces, the Tatros hysterical, Newland in an uproar, newspaper headlines. As everyone around them became more and more frantic, her own parents had become increasingly calm, grimly making all the arrangements. Emily had tried to follow their example, taking Matt and Joey and Laura to movies and drive-in restaurants. They even went on a scenic tour of the parking spots of Emily's adolescence, while she reviewed all the back seat grapplings and fumblings with Raymond and Earl.

She'd also done her best to give poor Sally some support, though she doubted she'd helped much, feeling as she did about Jed in particular, and about men in general. She'd finally managed to come out to Sally, who seemed shocked at first, then pleased that Emily had shared this with her. They'd been more or less estranged ever since the days in the Castle Tree. It felt good to Emily to be able to use this sad time as a way to get back in touch. After all, they were both women, shared a common plight.

She pictured The Five in the Castle Tree, Jed shirtless, ribs showing like a xylophone, grinning and sticking out his tongue at Sally, who giggled through her light brown braids, which she'd tied into a knot in front of her mouth. The world seemed so simple and benign back then, created solely to delight and entertain The Five . . .

Emily realized that the only thing she'd failed to cope with these last few days was her own grief at the brevity and difficulty of life, grief that was now surging around inside her like a caged tiger. She longed to get back to New York and to Maria, who would hold her, touch her, and gently stroke life back into her numb body. And to the women's group, who would hear her out, taking on her sorrow as their own, restoring to her the strength and the will to continue the struggle on behalf of all the downtrodden women of the world, so that none of their daughters would have to go through what Sally was now enduring.

The gospel quartet was singing, ". . . *proceed to that gate called Calvary. / Reservations secured from the Savior / For your one-way flight to Glory Land . . .*"

Emily heard Mrs. Webb behind her whisper to her sister, "Who does that Raymond Tatro think he is—Snuffy Smith? You'd think he could at least wear a suit to his own brother's funeral."

"Heard him talk lately? Sounds like he oughta be on 'Hee-Haw.'"

"Ain't he been up North? He making fun of us, do you reckon?"

# Chapter Two

## Raymond

His father took his mother's arm to hold her up, so Raymond took Sally's. According to the Bible, he should have been taking Jed's place in the marriage bed by now. He grinned, thinking that fucking Sally would be like fucking a chicken carcass. You'd come away full of bones. Then he realized it wasn't the most tactful thing in the world to be grinning as you walked away from viewing your brother's corpse.

Emily was sitting there watching him, wearing a suit and tie. Out front waiting to process, he'd heard Mrs. Webb whisper to her sister, "Why, honey, don't you know Emily's mama and daddy just hate it that they sent her up North to college?" His first true love a dyke. Well, that was the story of his life. He'd learned one thing from living in Tatro Cove for the past year and a half: Everybody betrayed you in the end and had been deceiving you all along. You couldn't count on nobody but yourself.

Staggering up the aisle and wailing, the relatives from Tatro Cove had already viewed Jed. Mr. and Mrs. Prince had looked shocked at this unseemly display as they peered into the coffin with dutiful tight-ass ruling-class dignity.

Sally stumbled and Raymond found himself practically carrying her. You always knew when there was a funeral on in Pine Woods because people holding fans from the Ready Funeral Home, decorated with Martin Luther King's picture, would be prancing around the sidewalks rejoicing that the Lord had seen fit to release the dear departed from this earthly prison. The folks from Tatro Cove didn't feel any such optimism, though. The corpse rotted in its grave and got eaten by worms was how they saw it.

They sat down in the front pew beside his parents and Joey and Laura. His mother's face was bright red and puffy. She hadn't stopped crying since she heard about the accident. She wouldn't have a son as vice president at the mill now. Raymond wondered if she'd be crying like this if it was his corpse in that casket. He doubted it. He and his father had had a terrible fight just before leaving for the church over Raymond's attire. But he didn't own a suit, much less a black one, and had no money to buy one, and wouldn't have bought one even if he had. Newland would just have to take him like he was. He wished his presence could be a comfort to his parents, though, instead of a trial. But it was a little too late to worry about that.

Mr. Marsh up front was enumerating all Jed's sterling qualities: football hero, foreman, husband, father, church usher. Sally shook with sobs. She put her hands to her face. Raymond felt real bad for her, and awkwardly put his arm around her shoulders. Jed couldn't have made it much more humiliating for her if he'd tried. Maybe he had. Totaled by a semi on the Chattanooga highway with his best friend's wife, after an evening at the Lazy Daze Motel. When he was supposed to be Joey's manager at Peewee Boxing at the Robert Prince Sr. Shopping Mall. It was the stuff great mountain ballads used to be made of. Old Jed always seemed like such a goodie, too. The town even swallowed the story about his secret marriage to Sally. But there wasn't no way he could deceive his way out of this one. Maybe that was partly why everyone was so upset. Virtue Unmasked: The Double Life of Big Jed Tatro, Public Goodie and Closet Kink.

Raymond wondered if now people would believe him about Jed's blowing up the Confederate statue during the strike. "Why, Jed Tatro would never do nothing like that," they insisted, down to the day he got himself smeared across the highway with Betty Osborne. Raymond realized that his bitterness was left over from childhood. He'd had to tote the burden of rebellion single-handedly, breaking the trail so that Jed could float right along it. Everything—riding a bicycle in the street, staying out after dark, crossing the highway to the drugstore, going out with girls, driving the family car—Raymond had had to lock horns with their parents over. By the time Jed came along, nothing was a big deal for them. But Jed never once thanked him. Or even allowed that he was aware of the situation. In fact, he grabbed every chance he could to side with their parents against Raymond. And during the strike he spread it all over town that Raymond was a Red, a faggot, a nigger-lover, a hippie, and God knows what. It had been so strange going overnight from Justin's calling him a cracker to Jed's calling him a Commie.

At his last FORWARD meeting when he'd announced he was returning to Newland, they'd just looked at him. Maria finally said, "You're kidding."

"No."

"Why, for God's sake?" asked Justin.

"My people need me."

"*Your* people?" sneered Morris.

"The working people of the South who're being enslaved by the Yankee capitalists."

"I think you've been reading too much Marx," murmured Maria.

At first it was like walking on egg shells. During his years in New York he forgot all the things you weren't supposed to say in Newland. When his mother asked him what he thought of her new winter coat, he said it was the wrong color for her. She burst into tears. He was baffled. Why had she asked him if she didn't want to know what he really thought? He'd forgotten those all-purpose Southern phrases, "That looks real nice" and "I'm just fine, thank you."

It irritated him when he walked down the street and some woman would rush up and squeal, "Why Raymond Tatro Junior! I heard you was back in town. What you wanna go up at New York City for anyhow? How's that nice mama of yours? Now, you tell her Velma says hidy." Perfect strangers would smile and say, "Purty day, ain't it?" Why couldn't they mind their own goddam business? In a matter of weeks he moved to a remote hill farm off the Kentucky highway.

He was sure it was just a question of describing to his fellow workers at the mill their exploitation by the capitalists. But when he tried, some would smile pleasantly without comprehension. Some would shrug and walk away. Others would ask what a capitalist was. Still others would try to initiate a discussion about the virtues of Fords over Chevys.

Thinking about it on his porch one night, he realized that a trait of Southern working people was the tendency to personalize situations. He had to adapt his tactics to the peculiarities of his constituency. Since his own field of perception had shifted so drastically during his last days in New York, he had no difficulty portraying Mr. Prince as a greedy slave driver. "Look at him setting in that big yaller house on the hill! You think he gives a shit bout yall down here in the village?" But they insisted on seeing Prince as the Messiah. Some scurried away when Raymond talked like that. Others tried to punch him out or called him a goddam Commie.

He was baffled. It was all so elementary. How could they fail to see it? Bunch of ignorant hillbillies who couldn't follow a rational argument if you marked it with skunk scent. He'd come home, milk the cow, collect the eggs, cook some supper, sit on the porch, and listen to the night sounds. From time to time he felt a gnawing in his stomach that he eventually recognized as loneliness. Nobody down here understood him. He began yearning for FORWARD meetings. Maybe they disagreed with him, but at least they knew what he was talking about.

On the highway was a truck stop with an attached motel, and a small store where he shopped. When the gnawing became too awful, he went down there for a meal. As he ate, he watched Thelma, the waitress, cope with leers and lewd remarks from truck drivers. He admired her calm refusal to take their shit. One night she asked him if he lived nearby. They began chatting, and before long he was going there every evening for supper. Thelma lived a few miles down the highway, was married to a man who'd been paralyzed from the neck down in Vietnam. She began fixing special treats for Raymond's dinners. Sometimes he sat there all evening drinking coffee and talking with her when she was free. He tried to explain what he was up to at the mill. With her simple native shrewdness she seemed to understand. Unlike Maria, Thelma didn't have theories, or quotes, or big words, but she actually *lived* what Raymond was talking about. Hard work for pitiful wages. A husband almost destroyed defending the interests of the capitalists in a place they had no business being in. Salt of the earth, Thelma. An honest hard-working woman. He especially admired her devotion to her disabled husband, her refusal to give the time of day to all those horny truck drivers.

"Jim, he got him no regrets," she insisted when Raymond tried to explain Vietnam to her. "He loves his country. Feels like that no sacrifice was too much to ask."

"Do you agree?"

"Honey, I got my regrets," she said. "You better believe it."

"That he was incapacitated defending interests not his own?"

"Naw, honey." She blushed. "That he can't put it to me no more like he used to could."

"Ah." Raymond had hardly thought about sex since he'd recovered from Maria. She'd inoculated him against "falling in love." Nobody would ever again be in a position to hurt him that much. Jerking off a few times a month was all he really needed. "So what do you do instead?" He liked his kid brother role with women. It beat the hell out of playing Lothario.

"Eat," she said, grabbing a fork and finishing his piece of chocolate cake. "And I complain a lot to whoever'll listen."

"I'll listen all you want, Thelma. After all, you listen to me."

"I been thinking, Raymond."

"Yeah?"

"You could do a lot more than listen, honey." She lowered her eyes.

He choked on his coffee.

"Think about it," she requested, moving away, her large buttocks swaying under her white uniform dress. He gazed at her back, wounded. What about Jim? Were there no trustworthy women in the world anymore?

"You don't let nobody near you, do you, honey?" she inquired the following week as she lay in his arms in a bed in a motel unit out back during her break.

"Not if I can help it," he murmured, swept with waves of gratitude. He hadn't fucked anyone since Maria, hadn't even been sure he could as Thelma led him from the restaurant. But she was delighted with him. He felt like a regular stud with her pitching, heaving, and moaning beneath him. And she didn't have any trouble having an orgasm. All these goddam castrating Yankee intellectual bitches.

"That's why you and me'll be good to each other, honey. I won't intrude on you, and you won't ask me to desert Jim."

"God, I'm going to be so good to you, Thelma." He gathered one of her large breasts in both hands and nibbled on the nipple as it stiffened.

By the grapevine he heard an ATW organizer was coming to town. Together they mapped out a strategy and persuaded a few of the more intelligent workers like Mrs. Pritchard and Hank and Betty Osborne to join an organizing committee. After winning the election and defeating Mackay's challenge that the votes hadn't been properly counted, they negotiated a pretty good contract. Even the workers who'd fought against the ATW seemed pretty pleased with the benefits package. Except his father and brother, of course, who'd go to their graves still tools for the bosses. Almost everywhere he went, Raymond was respected and admired. At union meetings when someone questioned something he said, someone else would say, "This boy's been up North. Better listen to him. Knows what he's talking about."

Raymond would reply irritably, "Look, down here we know everything they know up there, and then some." Sometimes he wondered if these people understood what he was telling them. He reminded himself to be patient, to remember that they'd been in thralldom for so long that they needed reeducation. Eventually he'd organize classes to teach them about their proud Southern working-class heritage—the strikes and union wars, Harlan and Evarts and Gastonia, Barney Graham and Mother Jones and John L. Lewis.

Then a new machine was brought into the card room, and Mackay announced he was hiring a new woman to run it, instead of giving it to Mrs. Pritchard, who'd been reinstated and had seniority. Raymond, as shop steward, went to Mackay, who said, "Mr. Tatro, you can't teach an old dog new tricks."

Raymond squared his shoulders. Who did this Mackay think he was anyhow, trifling with Southern working people? "Let me tell you this, Mr. Mackay: You put somebody new on that machine, and we'll all walk right out of this place."

He turned red. "Mr. Tatro, if you walk out, you'll walk back in over my dead body."

At the rally at the high school gym after the walkout the ATW district representative said he was impressed with the local's solidarity, but that they'd broken their contract, and that they'd better get their asses back into that plant and follow the grievance procedures. Raymond leaped up and yelled that if they went back in with that new machine still there, they'd never get it out again. He urged people to stay out until the machine was removed. The room erupted in cheers and angry shouts of agreement.

"People!" Raymond yelled. "We got right on our side! The Lord will lead us through this wilderness, friends, and succor us with manna!" Adrenaline pumped through his body.

Sitting on his porch that night, he was exhausted. Fired up by his speech, the local had voted to stay out. But here in the dark he felt silly. Who'd he think he was—a goddam preacher? All that Promised Land shit. His feelings of foolishness faded, and fear engulfed him. They were looking to him now as Moses. During the meeting he'd felt up to this role, but now he was just tired and worried. What if the strike failed and they all lost their jobs?

He stood up from his rocker, got in his Jeep and roared down to the highway. As she lay in his arms listening to his version of the meeting, Thelma murmured, "Raymond honey, I declare, I do believe you're just about the smartest man I ever did see. And I *know* you're the sexiest," she added, caressing his cock until it stood straight up, and rolling on top of him and impaling herself on it with a shuddering gasp.

As Raymond drove back to his house, he felt brave, strong and ready for anything management might come up with.

The next morning Raymond stood with the other strikers and watched the cars roll through the gates. He knew the scabs inside were just regular working people like himself, misled by capitalists. But damn it, they were stealing their brothers' jobs! Instead of salt of the earth, he saw thick-lipped black faces with slanty foreheads, fluffy blonde bouffants and bright red mouths, hillbillies full of hookworms. He wanted to murder the ignorant fuckers with his bare hands. Cunts, jigs, and trash, too dumb to see what the strikers were trying to accomplish. As the cars exited that afternoon, the strikers scattered tacks across the access road. They yelled insults, threw eggs and tomatoes, and waved signs saying "SCABS, DON'T COVER UP OUR WOUNDS!"

Prince and Mackay and several supervisors whisked across the line every morning in Mackay's big Buick, Mackay staring straight ahead. But Prince and the others who'd been there a long time looked upset. To Raymond they had become simply the Bosses, fattening themselves on his people's labor. He'd spit when Mr. Prince caught his eye. Jed and his father arrived every morning in Jed's Chevy. Jed would rev his engine and fly through the pickets with disdain for their safety. This infuriated Raymond, who gave Jed the finger. Once he shouted at them that they were traitors to the working class. His father rolled down the window and yelled, "Where was you when I was on Guam, you damned Commie?" Raymond didn't see his father's point, but it did wound him. His own father didn't understand what he was doing or why.

The union refused the strikers benefits, so they had to use their savings. Raymond knew it wasn't so bad for him because he didn't have a family. Plus which he had a big garden and some animals. But some of the others were really hurting. A few tried to find other work, but nobody would hire "Commie agitators." Some were starting to look worried. Raymond assured them management couldn't hold out much longer. He devoted himself to keeping morale up, getting the pickets to singing, "*Oh when them scabs / Go marching in . . .*" Townspeople stopped by with casseroles. Sometimes they donated money and told the pickets they were one hundred percent behind them, which cheered things up.

But then the Confederate statue was blown up and blamed on the strikers. Management got a restraining order so only two could picket each gate. Townspeople stopped coming by. If they did, they shouted that they wished they could be on vacation all year round too.

"You blew that thing up, didn't you?" he asked Jed at Sunday dinner.

Jed grinned. "Why would I do something like that?"

"So it'd get blamed on me. You done things like that all your life."

"Ah, you're crazy, Raymond."

But Raymond had to hand it to his kid brother: He was a lot smarter than he looked.

Strikers started drifting back in. Raymond ordered them, begged them, to stay out. But they looked at him sourly and explained that, unlike him, they had families, mortgages, and car payments. They'd sold off their belongings and gone into debt following his vision. Downtown they crossed to the other side of the street if they saw him coming. Some had to move away from Newland. The following year employees voted the ATW out. Pretty soon after, Arnold got a contract from the Defense Department to make zipper material for body bags for Vietnam. At the end of the year they declared a five percent stock dividend.

Raymond sat around his house. In a matter of months he'd gone from nobody to hero and back to nobody again. Worse than nobody, the whole town despised him. They'd be bound to, since they'd all sold out and he hadn't. He was ahead of his time, was all. In a hundred years what he was trying to do would be appreciated. Hell, in twenty years maybe. But what good did that do him now?

"What you wanna go being a hero for anyhow?" Thelma asked. "Look at poor old Jim in his wheelchair. There's a hero for you. You a hero to *me*, honey. Ain't that enough?"

He tried to convince himself that it *was* enough. He pumped diesel fuel at the truck stop, ate Thelma's dinners in the evening, went home and did chores and slept. It was an honest, hard-working life, full of integrity. It was how working people all over the world lived. Why then did he stalk the hills around his house missing FORWARD meetings, missing strike rallies? His analysis had been right. Where had things gone wrong? Some nights he'd listen to Thelma agreeing with every word he said and telling him how wonderful he was, and would miss Maria fiercely. If only Thelma would argue with him, put him down sometimes, challenge him. As long as he fucked her, everything was fine with her. But Maria had cared about his political analysis, spoke his language. Thelma didn't have a clue what he was talking about.

One night he gave her a copy of *Das Kapital* saying, "Thelma, there's more to life than slinging hash and having orgasms."

"Yeah, they's Saturday night TV and emptying your husband's bags."

"There's growing and changing. I try to help you, Thelma. If you'd just open your mind, you might learn something."

"Honey, if you'd just shut your mouth, *you* might learn something."

"What?"

"Look, Raymond, I'm nobody special. Just a regular waitress at a dinky old truck stop, with a paralyzed husband."

"But that's the whole point. That's not ordinary. Jim isn't in that wheelchair by accident."

"Honey, once you in a wheelchair, *why* don't matter."

"But it should. Why aren't you and Jim angry? Why aren't you planning an action around it?"

"Raymond honey, I don't know who it is you want me to be, but I ain't her. Now if you want me like I am, you come on back here as often as you like. If you don't, just keep your distance. Cause I like myself and I don't need you dumping on me."

"I'm trying to *help* you, Thelma, not dump on you. Sometimes I think you misunderstand me on purpose. But being misunderstood is nothing new to me."

"Look to me, honey, like you got you a *need* to be misunderstood."

"All I've ever wanted is to be in a setting where the people around me understand me and agree with me."

"Tell me about it."

As he roared back to his house, Raymond realized he was alone again. Thelma was deserting him right when he needed her most. That was just about what he'd come to expect from women.

Raymond went to Tatro Cove for his grandfather's funeral. After a service at the house they all "walked that last mile" with Grandpa Tatro, weeping up the hill behind his house to the family burying plot. Eight grandsons, including Jed and Raymond, toted the coffin. Grandma Tatro led everyone in her husband's favorite hymn in a wavering voice: "*Oh ye young, ye gay, ye proud, / You must die and wear the shroud. / Time will rob you of your bloom. / Death will drag you to your tomb."*

Those still living in the cove knew the hymn. Those who'd left could only join in on the chorus, which boomed out over the mountains: *"Then you'll cry, 'I want to be / Happy in eternity!'"*

As a kid, Raymond had been drilled like a Catholic learning the rosary on who lay beneath each headstone. The first Tatro of Tatro Cove was Corliss, a long hunter originally from the valley of Virginia, one of the over-mountain men who fought so fiercely at King's Mountain. The story went that if someone admired one of his possessions, he'd insist they take it: "I don't want nobody envying me on account of a lot of useless junk." He also used to say, "Tatros work to live, they don't live to work."

As the grandsons took turns with the shovels, Raymond looked past the stand of grey headstones down through the poplars to the cove. His grandpa's house sat on the site of Corliss's original log cabin. And down the cove toward the highway were the houses now inhabited by his cousins and aunts and uncles and nieces and nephews. Near each were barns, sheds, gardens, and pastures. Tatros had been breeding and loving and dying in this cove since 1760. Over 200 years, close to ten generations. A way of life had evolved here based on good manners, hospitality, self-reliance, leisure, and responsibility for neighbors and kin. Rather than production, consumption, competition, and confrontation. All his agitating at the mill was to get workers a few hundred more dollars a year, with which to buy a lot of "useless junk." The company, the union—two halves of the same plague. Why, he'd been nothing but a pawn!

He handed his shovel to Jed and stepped back. His grandma, Uncle Corliss IV, and Aunt Verbena stood in the front row. Next came his father and mother, Sally and her children, and his uncle Phil, a schoolteacher in Cincinnati. Then M.G.'s family. M.G. owned the Cadillac-Olds dealership in town and had a new brick ranch house on the highway. Then Lem's and Lyle's families. Lem worked at Associated Coal's #26 mine and was in the UMW. Lyle owned his own Mack truck with "The Flying Goose" painted on its cab and hauled coal to the tipples from small truck mines. In the last row was

Royal's family. Royal did some lumbering, some farmwork. Sometimes he worked for a day-labor pool in Cincinnati. He used to work in the mines, but had the beginnings of black lung and had refused to go back. During the War on Poverty he'd been a Happy Pappy, planting locust seedlings and learning how to fill in applications for nonexistent jobs.

They still honored age in his family, but otherwise it appeared to Raymond that they'd adopted the values of the capitalists, basing family status on accumulation of junk. This fall from grace, he realized in a moment of searing illumination that made the cove tremble before his eyes, occurred when the first Tatro sold his labor and used his earnings to buy necessities—rather than laboring directly to produce necessities. At that point he became dependent on outside forces. The solution, therefore, was to produce what you needed with your own hands from your own land, to decline the junk capitalists offered for sale, to pare your life down to essentials and see how much you could do without, rather than how much you could accumulate.

Back at the house, Raymond, still shaken by his hilltop vision, stood studying the color photo of his grandpa in his coffin. Next to it hung those of each family member who'd died since the invention of color photography. There was a sameness to Tatro corpses. Some year a photo of his own corpse would be hanging here. And what would he have accomplished? How would he be remembered? Would his descendants speak of him with respect, as the current Tatros did of old Corliss, the long hunter, the over-mountain man, the veteran of King's Mountain? Would anyone name his sons after Raymond? The best gas pumper in East Tennessee . . .

He overheard Lem in the corner of the room asking Jed what work Raymond did. Jed said, "Oh, I reckon he's some kind of professional bum or something." They laughed.

Raymond felt humiliated. Jed thought being married to Mr. Prince's daughter, being foreman at the mill, made him something special. He was too ignorant to realize that other people didn't necessarily share his values. But he preferred Jed's contempt to his pity, which he had bestowed upon Raymond in great quantities ever since the strike had flopped.

His grandma was saying, "Now, let's see, was that the year Lyle's baby died of the whooping cough?"

Aunt Verbena replied, "No, honey. Remember? It was right after Royal's boy rolled his Chevy offen Raven Ridge."

His grandma began talking vaguely of moving down the cove to Aunt Verbena's. Verbena, her sister, was married to Corliss IV, who was actually Verbena's second cousin. Everyone called him Cor Four. Verbena was a family name introduced in the 1800's by Corliss Three, an herbal doctor. Cousin Royal's full name was Pennyroyal.

"But law, I don't know. I don't reckon I ought to leave this place empty."

"I'll live here, Grandma," Raymond announced. He realized that his relatives in Tatro Cove were the Saving Remnant. That it was up to him to guide them back to their original mission, which they'd fallen away from.

When he moved in, the ground was still squishy from winter rains. He holed up with a stack of seed catalogs and emerged when things had dried out to dig up the garden and spread rotted manure and plant crops. He ordered fruit trees, vines, and asparagus roots by mail. He brought his chickens and cow up from Newland, and bought a couple of hives of bees and two unshorn sheep. He planted feed corn in his kinfolks' deserted patches and taught himself to make cottage cheese, cream cheese, hard cheese, butter. He figured out how to shear his sheep, and put the wool in bags till next winter when he'd have time to figure out what to do with it. He felled trees for winter fuel.

He decided it was like being crippled and learning to walk upright again. He watched Cor Four and asked questions, feeling sheepish that he had so resolutely turned his back on his family when he left for New York. Because it had now become clear to him that they were the Chosen People who'd preserved the ancient skills and traditions. His assignment was to render those skills and traditions operative again, to make his kinfolk aware of the value of the way of life they were now taking for granted. Capitalism was in its last days. And as the industrial valley in which Newland sat fell into ruins, here in the mountains would reside a race of people who could point the way to a more just and humane post-imperialist world. Meanwhile, during the period of decline, those in the valley who understood what was happening faster than their brethren would find refuge and inspiration here in Tatro Cove.

Although his house was wired for electricity, Raymond didn't use it. He got water in a bucket from the creek and stored dairy products in the old springhouse. He cooked on a wood stove and crapped in a smelly old two-holer out back. The summer days were long, and he was usually ready to sleep when it got dark. For entertainment he discovered which woods to walk in to see trillium, which rocks were covered with wild columbine. He began recognizing and naming individual chickens and watching their complicated social life. He became aware of the play of sunlight on the hill across from his house over the course of each day. At night he sat on the porch in the dark, watching the fireflies, listening to the animals settle down for the night, and trying to teach himself to play his grandpa's banjo.

He took delight in each item he discovered he could do without, lining them up one by one on a table in the living room. He decided two blankets on his bed instead of three were plenty. If he shivered a little at night, the shivers were pleasurable because he knew he was reducing his reliance on products of the capitalist system. Then he realized that if he had a down-filled sleeping bag, he could give up blankets altogether, plus not having to stoke the stove at night, thus reducing his need for gasoline for his chain saw. So he ordered an arctic sleeping bag by mail from L. L. Bean, from whom Justin had always ordered his chamois shirts. At the last minute he added a chamois shirt, a down vest, and a wool lumberjack shirt to his order, knowing they would be among his last purchases from the consumer society. Warm clothes meant he needed less firewood and less food. He also realized that he could cut down on store purchases if he did some serious hunting and fishing, so he added several hundred dollars' worth of equipment to the order.

But his two major indulgences from the industrial state were a chain saw and his Jeep. Both he would, of course, do without eventually, but first he had to learn to use an axe. He had a power take-off installed on the back of the Jeep, figuring he'd need it in the fields since he was going to be farming alone. Once refugees arrived from the valley, however, once he persuaded his kinsmen to leave their mines and their businesses in town, he'd have all the manpower he needed.

His cousin Ben, M.G.'s son, started coming up the cove to help with chores. The first time Raymond ever saw him, on a visit with his parents, Ben was a scrawny howling baby in his mother's arms. Raymond had gone up North, not seeing him again until their grandpa's funeral. Ben almost took his breath away that afternoon, standing there in the parlor looking awkward in a dark suit, with his dark blonde hair parted and plastered down. He was everything Raymond had been at sixteen—earnest, idealistic, confused. Plus everything Raymond hadn't been—good-looking, patient and polite, a basketball player, a good student. Behind a puppyish friendliness and playfulness was wariness: Once he took someone on, it was for life. In Tatro Cove there was no getting away from anyone.

He asked Raymond for advice. M.G. wanted him to go somewhere out of the mountains to college. He wasn't sure, had a girlfriend named Cheryl, thought maybe he was in love, would she wait, etc. Raymond was flattered. His real kid brother had never wanted Raymond's opinions on anything. Apparently Ben saw him as a man of the world. Raymond supposed he was, in a way. He saw other reasons why Ben should stay in the mountains, though: The kids bound for college never came back. But Tatro Cove needed them. Raymond needed them, to help him piece together their proud tradition, from the remnants that littered the area. Raymond had the knowledge, the experience, the vision. But he needed a mouthpiece, someone who'd grown up in Tatro Cove and spoke their language as Raymond never could.

"But sometimes I get to wondering what it's like out there," Ben would murmur.

"Ain't nothing worth bothering about."

"You know that because you been out there all your life. But maybe I got to find out for myself."

"How come you can't just take my word for it?" Raymond asked. If Ben had to retrace Raymond's exact steps, what was the point of anything? Raymond would teach him everything he needed to know about the outside—and about the strengths of Tatro Cove, the role its denizens would be playing in the future of mankind.

One afternoon he and Ben took a beehive apart in search of queen cells to cut out. Raymond explained that if any were allowed to develop, the reigning queen would waste energy that should have gone into egg-laying on hunting down and stinging to death her rivals. As alarmed bees swirled around and dive-bombed their veils, Raymond explained how this behavior resembled management's at the mill, or in any capitalist enterprise. Queens, drones, workers who gathered nectar, workers who tended the hive. Families, churches, schools, sports teams, the army—a pyramid with some authority figure at the top. Things were set up this way on purpose, Raymond told Ben, to prepare young people like himself to move into the hierarchy of some factory at the bottom.

"What's hierarchy?" asked Ben.

"Uh, rank, sort of like. Generals and lieutenants. You know."

"Like chickens?"

Raymond looked at him. He wasn't supposed to interrupt. "How do you mean?"

"You know how they peck at the red one until she don't have no tail feathers?"

"Yeah, like that."

"And up to Cor Four's milking parlor. The cows line up the same way ever day."

Raymond was supposed to be drawing these analogies. When Justin used to explain things to him, he never interrupted. "Now this is how things operate in nature," he continued, making the best of the interruptions. You couldn't blame Ben, he was just a kid, didn't even know what a political analysis was. "But the difference between us and animals is that we got brains and can see other ways."

"Like what?"

Raymond hadn't exactly worked this out yet. "When you're ready to hear it, I'll explain. You got to absorb things little by little or they don't take."

At dusk Raymond strolled down the cove. The creek gurgled, and bullfrogs hurled themselves into it with small splashes. As he walked past Aunt Verbena's, his grandma called from the porch, "How's it going, Junior?"

"Just fine, Granny. When you going to come down and see?"

"Law, child, I can't hardly get down them porch steps, never mind to the foot of this holler."

TVs rumbled as he passed Royal's and Lyle's. He was swept with irritation. Barn dancing, clogging, ballad singing, banjo strumming, dulcimer picking. Corn huskings, quilting bees, house raisings. But *television*, all day every day, and night after night? He climbed the steps and walked into Lyle's living room. Lyle, still in his yellow hard hat and green work clothes, lay on the sofa. His two children sat on the floor. All three gazed at Big Bird, who was shrieking at Oscar in his garbage can while some children played hopscotch on the sidewalk. Numbers began flashing on the screen while a chorus shouted out their names: "ONE! TWO! . . ."

Lyle glanced up. "Hey there, Raymond! How you doing, boy?"

"All right. How you doing, Lyle?" Actually he was annoyed. What did all this urban freneticism on the TV have to do with the children of Tatro Cove?

"Have a seat?"

"No, thanks. Just popped in to say hi." As he walked back to the door, he saw on the wall a framed picture of a baby cut from a magazine. He stopped and studied it. Under the glass in one corner was a lock of hair. A tiny bracelet from the hospital, with beads spelling "Tatro," was attached to the frame by a ribbon.

"Who's this, Lyle?"

"The wife done that. For our baby that died of the whooping cough. Seen one like it in a magazine."

"Nice." Never had he seen such a tacky item. The taste of his kin had been debased at some very elemental level. Women up here in their spare time used to make witch hazel brooms, coverlets, corn husk dolls. It was pathetic.

He crossed the highway to M.G.'s ranch house, which had puny little columns holding up the front porch roof. "For the dog to pee against!" M.G. had explained, chortling, slapping Raymond's back, and tapping the column with his white patent leather loafer.

Ben's face lit up when he saw Raymond. They walked down the highway to McCray's Grocery, which was roofed and sided with brown asphalt shingles. A couple of men lay on the porch. Raymond and Ben joined them, propping up their heads and necks against the wall. They were discussing who the ugliest man in the county was.

"Now you think about that nose on Lester. All mashed in like that. They say his mama dropped him when he was a baby."

"Naw, Lester can't hold a candle to you, Wash, in the Ugly Department. What you think, Ben? Don't you b'lieve Wash is just about the homeliest creature you ever did see, with them close-set eyes of hisn? You know, he can't hardly see off to one side. If Noah was to be standing over there on that hillside filling up the Ark, Wash'd walk right past him."

Ben had been doing this his whole life. As he launched into a teasing discussion of his neighbors and kin, Raymond took mental notes. He'd learned during voter registration, during union organizing, that you had to speak to people in their own language. And to do this, you had to study how they operated. Ben spoke this language instinctively, but it was up to Raymond to make him conscious of the strong tradition for which he would be the spokesman. The men on the porch floor always discussed who had the worst problems, the most boring job. A parody of hierarchy, Raymond decided, a negative ranking system. A peaceful ritual for draining off aggression . . .

They lay on the porch like snakes in the sun. Raymond realized that he lay like a board—rigid, poised to leap into activity. And his brain—the wheels wouldn't stop spinning. He tried to relax, tried to imagine himself as a dead groundhog hung on a fence post. He shrugged his shoulders to loosen them up, rolled his head on his neck.

"Yall right, Raymond?" Ben inquired. Raymond realized the conversation had stopped.

"Oh. Yeah. Sorry."

"You itching to get back home?"

"No. Yall carry on." He knew that his presence made them uneasy. Conversations often ceased in midsentence when he appeared. He wondered if he gave off an aura of urgency. They'd rather push away the cup he held out to them without drinking from it. But throughout history this had been the case. People didn't like being asked to disrupt their orderly little lives for the sake of the greater good. Prophets were always despised in their own countries. Raymond was getting used to it.

"Now Zeke there . . . You talk about ugly. That man's so ugly his own mama can't hardly look him in the face. . . ."

A large Mercury pulled up. They sat up. The driver pushed a button, and the window rolled down. The man asked in a New Jersey accent, "Can you tell me where I can find some typical hillbillies?"

They looked at each other. Finally Raymond replied, "Yeah. Go down this road across from us. Take your first right. Go one mile and take a right down Branch Holler Road. When you hit a hardtop road, turn right and go one mile."

"Thank you so much," he said, handing Raymond a quarter.

They lay on the porch and waited. Ten minutes later the man in the Mercury ended up where he'd started from, looking at them. The window rolled down, and the man laughed. "That was a pretty good joke, boys."

They faked laughs.

"How long have your people been in these parts," he asked Raymond.

"Going on two hunnert years."

"How did they get here?"

"They walked."

After he drove away, they all chuckled, and Raymond was pleased with himself. It was probably just a question of time until they accepted him without hesitation. If he could get Zeke and Wash up off this porch floor and back to tilling their fields and fishing their streams, they'd be among his staunchest lieutenants.

"You know, really I admire the way yall are together," he told them.

"Huh?" said Zeke.

"You don't realize how lucky you are up here. Under capitalism people don't have friendships, they have functions or possessions or skills that other people need."

The three turned their heads to look at him.

"But here in Tatro Cove it's just Wash or Ben—complicated individuals you can't categorize like that, because there's nothing of a material nature you need each other *for*. You can just sit back and watch each other's characters open, one petal at a time, like a sun-flower in the sun."

He looked at them, awaiting agreement. They smiled uncertainly.

"Uh, what's capitalism?" asked Wash.

"Those are good men," Raymond said as he and Ben walked back down the highway.

"Well, I think they like you, too. But you use some pretty fancy words sometimes, Raymond."

"That's where I need you to help me, Ben."

"Me?"

"Yeah, I need you to tell me which words are too fancy. They're all the same to me. Can I count on you for that?"

"Well, sure, Raymond." He seemed pleased at the notion that he might have something to offer Raymond. Raymond had to make him see that this very humility was a valuable part of the legacy of Tatro Cove.

Back at Ben's, M.G. insisted Raymond come see his new bath-room. "We just had it redid, Junior. I want you to be the first to see it!"

Raymond walked into a brightly lit, tiled cubicle. Fluffy green carpet covered the floor and the squat toilet like creeping mildew. A square sunken bathtub ordered from Lexington. Double sinks in a fake-marble Formica counter. Mirrors all over the place. M.G. flushed the toilet. "Listen, Junior! It don't make a sound."

"Well, it's really something, M.G."

"You're not just whistling 'Dixie,' son! I reckon it's the finest bath-room in these parts. What you think?"

"I wouldn't be surprised."

"Why, I bet you ain't even seen many bathrooms this grand up North!"

"No sir, I sure ain't." Raymond's lack of enthusiasm was driving M.G. in search of greater hyperbole.

"I do believe this is just about the most luxurious room I ever did see!"

"Oh Pa, come off it," Ben muttered in the doorway.

M.G. said in a huffy voice, "Why, I get the impression, Junior, you don't much care for it, to tell you the truth."

Raymond sighed. "M.G., I ain't got nothing against flush toilets. I just don't necessarily believe that owning one makes you a better person than you was when you had you an outhouse down the holler."

Early the next morning Raymond went to Cor Four's barn to help him milk. Cor Four never said much, and when he did, it was in a self-conscious drawl. As he sponged udders and attached suction cups to nipples, he spoke not at all. Working alongside him, Raymond honored this silence. Probably Cor Four was communing with his cows, keeping them content and productive, like a queen bee with her workers.

At one point Cor Four chuckled.

"What's so funny?"

"Hee hee, just thinking about old Cor Three."

"What about him?" This was wonderful stuff. Ancestors were living presences in Tatro Cove, formed part of the fabric of daily life.

"Used to hunt squirrels all the time and bile them up. Give the broth to you, no matter what ailed you. Verbena was down with the ammonia one winter, and he turns up in her room with a bowl of that stuff. She looks up at him and says, 'Uncle Cor, if hit was to take squirrel broth to bring me back, I'd just as soon go on home.'" He chuckled. Raymond didn't. He'd been reading up on it. There was lots to these folk remedies. Mockery of them was a tactic of the drug industry and the AMA.

"There's lots to be said for folk remedies."

"I reckon. But give me a shot of penicillin over squirrel broth any day, boy."

The problems here were graver than Raymond had recognized. Apparently even the older generation had fallen prey to the modern world. His work was cut out for him. But on behalf of the younger generation, he asked Cor Four what toys he'd played with as a kid.

"Toys?"

"Yeah, you know, wooden toys that your father and uncles probably carved for you from pieces of wood."

Cor Four took a bite of Red Man tobacco and sat chewing on a milk can outside the milking parlor. "Yeah, I recollect one or two. Something we called a gee haw flimmy diddle that you made out of laurel twigs. And this thing you whirled around your head on a rawhide cord. A bull roarer. This old Cherokee Indian who lived up the next holler used to make them for us." He laughed.

"Can you show me how to make them?"

He studied Raymond. "What you wanting old-timey junk like that for anyhow?"

"For Lyla and the other little kids in the cove."

"They got em the television now. Don't need no bull roarers."

But that evening Raymond handed Lyla a bull roarer, a slice from a hickory limb with a cord attached. She shifted her eyes from Big Bird long enough to look at it.

"Uncle Cor made it for you," Raymond explained. "You twirl it around your head and it makes a sound like rushing wind. The Cherokee Indians used to think they'd bring on storm clouds in a drought."

Lyla shrugged and returned her eyes to Big Bird.

"Mind your manners," Lyle growled from the couch. "Say 'Thank you, Cousin Raymond.'"

"Thank you, Cousin Raymond." She grinned, revealing several missing baby teeth, then looked back at the television.

"Well, see you," said Raymond, heading for the door. He didn't know how to act around kids. Hadn't been around them much. Nobody in FORWARD had any. In Newland he saw Joey and Laura some. They were brats—interrupted and talked back, showed off and threw tantrums, confident their parents would be enthralled, which they generally appeared to be. Capitalism bred brats: Only the new was worthy of respect in a consumer society.

"You got nice kids," he said to Lyle, who was seeing him out.

"You don't have to live with them." He laughed.

"They seem to do what you tell them."

"When they don't, I beat the shit out of them."

Raymond chuckled. He was sure Lyle was being modest, putting down his virtues as people so often did in Tatro Cove.

The sun woke Raymond, shining on his bed as it cleared the hill across the creek. He went outside, took a leak, then picked up the bucket and went to the creek. He sniffed the air and looked at the sky, the way his cousins used to when they were kids. You tried to figure out what kind of day it was so you knew what jobs to plan. It was still such a kick planning his days, after years of having them planned for him by employers.

He pulled on his overalls and chamois shirt and built a fire in the stove to scramble some eggs. The corn needed hoeing. The fence around the graveyard needed mending. When Ben arrived, he stripped some corn for the chickens and fought with the rooster over the eggs, while Raymond milked the cow and put the milk in the springhouse. As they chopped weeds in the corn patch, Raymond glanced at Ben from time to time. The sun shone off his blonde hair like a halo. Raymond thought about him all the time now—his guile-lessness, his native intelligence, his integrity, his uncomplicated en-thusiasm and curiosity. Ben touched him deeply. The responsibility frightened him every now and then. The opportunity to create the spokesman he needed was staring him in the face. But what if Ray-mond couldn't do it right?

He chopped at the purslane and began lecturing to Ben about the myth of progress: "Under capitalism Progress actually means profits for shareholders. Progress toward some infinitely desirable but never specified and always receding goal. The term is an anesthetic that keeps workers punching that time clock ever morning. But corn just grows, it doesn't progress." He liked the sound of that last phrase. Corn just grows, it doesn't progress. He saw himself feeding this analysis into Ben, and Ben passing it on to Zeke and Wash, and its spreading throughout the area. He himself would be like a radio transmitter.

"Uh huh," murmured Ben, avoiding Raymond's eyes.

Back at the house they smeared some butter and honey on bread Raymond had baked the day before, and set off up the stream with Raymond's L. L. Bean fishing equipment.

"Did you ever think," Raymond asked, "how many times Cor One must have waded up this creek with his fishing gear?"

"Naw, never did."

"Just imagine: This whole area empty of people except a Cherokee hunting party or two. Fish jumping out of the creek at you. Every-thing you needed you could make or hunt. Those guys were really something."

"I reckon."

Failing to catch trout, they ate their bread for lunch. As they sat licking honey off their mouths, Ben said, "Junior, did you ever, you know"—he blushed—"do it to a girl?"

"You mean make love?"

Ben ducked his head, mortified.

"Sure. Every now and then."

"Who with?"

"A couple of different women."

"Do you have a girl now?"

He thought about Thelma, whether she qualified. "Yes, I guess. She lives near Newland. I've been . . . involved with her for about a year. But we're not getting along too good right now." He'd been down to see her a few times to try to talk her into moving with Jim to Tatro Cove. He described the ever wider gap yawning between rich and poor, the fouling of the valley's air and water with wastes from the factories, the poisoning of its inhabitants, the eventual collapse of Newland, the deserted mills and factories inhabited only by hoot owls and black widow spiders.

"My goodness," said Thelma.

"This scene down here can't last much longer, Thelma. You need to learn how to supply your essentials with your own hands."

"Yeah, Jim'd be real good at that."

"In a place like Tatro Cove you'd get some help with Jim. Everyone would pitch in."

"I bet."

"They would," he insisted.

"Honey, I've lived in these parts all my life. I know how people flee when times get hard."

The last time he'd gone down there, she'd given him a TV set. "I think you're lonely up there in the woods all alone," she explained.

He tried to act pleased, but had to face up to the fact that she hadn't understood a word he'd been saying.

Ben grinned. "So *that's* where you go when you roar off in your Jeep like you're running shine!"

"You been wondering?"

"Shoot, we all been wondering. Sitting around discussing it for months. Most decided you was going to see your parents."

"Sometimes I do."

"You going to marry her?"

"Not if I can help it."

He looked shocked, so Raymond added, "She's a nice girl, but she's already married." This made it worse. "Her husband's in a wheelchair." Ben gasped.

"Don't look at me like that, please, Ben. I mean, life is pretty complicated."

"Doesn't it upset her husband?"

"He doesn't know." Things were getting more sordid in Ben's eyes. "Look, she needed sex, I needed sex, so we gave it to each other. He was hurt less than if she'd left him. Probably less than if she'd told him."

"But I mean, it's the most beautiful thing a man and a woman can do together. How can you just do it and then drive away?"

"Sometimes it's beautiful. Sometimes it ain't. It depends on the other person, your mood, the circumstances. Sometimes it's awful." He felt as though he were raping a virgin. He remembered his shock on that church rooftop when Maria let him in on the secret that it wasn't necessarily always and forever just because you sated your hungers on each other a few times.

"I would never do that," Ben murmured.

"Good. I hope you don't."

"When I make love, it will be the real thing."

"Yes, but . . ."

"Cheryl wants us to, but I'm not sure I want to marry her. Then I couldn't go away to college. But I'm not sure I want to go away to college."

Raymond looked at him. "Does she want you to marry her?"

"She says not. But once we'd done it, I'd have to, wouldn't I?"

Raymond frowned, trying to remember adolescent logic.

"And what if she got pregnant?"

"You know about rubbers, don't you? You can buy them in the men's room at that Mobile station in town."

"Yeah, but sometimes they don't work. It happened to a guy at school last month."

"That's true. But I guess that's a chance you have to take if you want her bad enough."

"I'm not sure I do."

As Ben strained to sort out the ethics of premarital sex, Raymond recalled his initiation with Wayne over the stamp album. It'd been kind and uncomplicated. Especially compared to the thing with Maria. It would be useful if Ben could get this sex business out of the way, so that he could move on to really important matters concerning the perpetuation of Tatro Cove. Raymond realized he only had to turn to Ben, put his hand on the spot on Ben's thigh where the sunlight now played . . .

The last time he'd seen Thelma, he'd driven her to her trailer because her car was in the shop. Jim sat in his wheelchair watching "The Newlywed Game" on TV. He was a pleasant good-looking man with a flat top and sideburns. Raymond felt a little guilty about fucking his wife, though it had turned out that there'd been another man before him. He and Jim got to talking, and Raymond sat down and drank a beer with them. Jim told about his accident. Training in Louisiana for jungle combat, his sergeant had yelled, "If it moves, fuck it or kill it!"

"I tried to fuck it when I should have killed it," Jim explained with a grim laugh. A Vietnamese woman had lured him into a hut, and someone had bashed him with a shovel as he climbed on top of her.

Raymond glanced at Ben, who talked on and on about this Cheryl creature, how far they'd gotten with necking and petting, and wondered if he had any idea how flirtatious he was being. Probably not. Ben was an innocent.

He recalled Injun Al's telling The Five a Cherokee recipe for predicting the sex of a white baby. Put the pregnant woman in the middle of a flock of wrens. The baby would be a boy if they flew away in terror, because white boys stalked and tortured and killed them. If it would be a girl, they'd cluster around singing, because girls ground grain and scattered some for the wrens. He thought about his father's story, of Grandpa Tatro driving the cow down Tatro Cove at dusk, chattering away to the baby on his hip.

He stood up. "Let's go home." Justin, Maria, and those people, it seemed to him, didn't really enjoy the physical sensations of sex. They used sex as a means to power. If they could lure someone into submitting sexually, they had attained power over them. Raymond had no wish to be like this.

Ben looked up, startled. "What's wrong, Junior?"

"Nothing."

"Did I say something dumb?"

"Naw. Come on."

On the way home he explained to Ben, " 'If it moves, fuck it or kill it.' This is the trip an imperialist culture imposes on people. You must dominate every living thing. Creatures are of value only insofar as they are of use to you."

"So you think I shouldn't do it with Cheryl, Junior?"

"How the hell should I know? Go fuck some little halfwit backwoods fruitcake. Get it over with! You got more important things to be worrying about."

"Basketball season, you mean?"

Raymond looked at him.

"I'm sorry, Junior. What'd I do?"

"Oh, never mind."

As it grew dark, Raymond sat on his porch listening to the frogs croak and felt more lonely than he could ever remember being. Thelma's response to his vision had been a TV set. Ben was interested only in fucking and playing basketball. Lyla didn't play with her bull roarer. M.G. insisted on giving guided tours of his new bathroom. Nobody understood what Raymond was talking about. The last days were upon them, and they all wanted life to go on as usual. As always, everyone around him was prepared to sell out in return for their creature comforts.

He watched the moon come up over the hill across the creek, the headstones in the graveyard up top silhouettes on the yellow backdrop. How many Tatros had sat in this spot watching that same moon? Corlisses I, II, III, and IV, his grandfather and grandmother, his own father. Now Raymond himself. Most now lay under those headstones. As Raymond himself would in a few decades. But he was leaving no children to take his place here on this porch. He was leaving no one to remember him, nothing to be remembered by. The gnawing started in his stomach, as though he'd swallowed a live rat that was frantic to get out.

He jumped up and raced into the house and lit a lantern. Taking out the charts on the corporate executives he'd drawn up in New York, he studied them. Plundering the world. Dirty capitalist fuckers. But once they'd done their worst, Tatro Cove would remain. The gnawing in his stomach subsided. Raymond's people would have preserved all the skills and traditions necessary to fashion a new world from the capitalist wreckage.

He'd lost the faith out there on the porch. Thelma, Ben, the others, they required patience. Tomatoes didn't ripen overnight. Bread took three hours to rise. Soup stock had to simmer all day long. What was "time" anyway? Capitalists tried to save it, as though it were money in the bank. It was place that was sacred in Tatro Cove. The passage of less than a decade was scarcely noticed. He'd come away from voter registration and union organizing thinking people were something to be manipulated. Well, they weren't. You had to let them evolve at their own tedious pace. The disconnected pieces of his life fell into place: Through non-example, it had all been preparing him for his mission here in Tatro Cove. He'd seen how the rest of the world was run, had rejected it, and could now get on with formulating a positive alternative.

He put the charts away and turned on the TV. He'd watch just one program. In order to see what kind of crap his kinsmen's heads were being filled with. You had to know what you were up against.

Toward the end of summer all Raymond's vegetables began ripening at once. He read up on food preservation and dried some things over the stove. There was a root cellar under the house for the squash and pumpkins. The potatoes and carrots and beets he left in the ground to dig up as needed. Ben and he picked gallons of wild blackberries and raspberries up the hillsides where former pastureland was returning to scrub. They went to Verbena's and asked their grandmother to teach them to can.

She looked up from her rocking chair on the porch. "Law, honey, canning is women's work!"

"But we ain't got us no women," Raymond replied. "So I reckon we got to do it ourselves."

She taught them reluctantly, and the whole family stopped by to watch. As Raymond boiled and stirred, he tried to look content. But the truth was, it bored the hell out of him. He didn't exactly see what all these hours over a hot stove had to do with the post-industrial society. If Ben hadn't been there, he'd have dumped the whole mess on the compost pile. As it was, he kept stirring, steam condensing on his glasses.

In the fall Ben and he went to an abandoned orchard on the hillside and picked bushels of wormy apples, which they cored and sliced and strung up over the stove. If Ben hadn't been there, he'd have watched "Bonanza" on the TV while he sliced, as research into contemporary culture.

Raymond's money nearly ran out, which meant he couldn't buy gas to go see Thelma. He noticed that after a couple of weeks away from her large welcoming body, he became tense and irritable. She was a soothing, softening influence, which he needed to offset the rigors of his demanding life. He had to get him some gas money.

He went out one afternoon with Royal, who showed him how to dig "sang" and cut galax, which Mr. McCray would buy and resell to brokers from New York, who shipped the ginseng to the Orient and sold the galax to florists.

"How come you ain't never married?" Royal asked, glancing out from under his battered felt hat.

"Guess I never met me the right woman."

"Pray the Lord you never do," he muttered.

"I'd like to," Raymond lied. "Sometimes it gets pretty lonely."

"Better lonely than nagged to death."

"Aw, Annie, she don't nag you much. You got you a good wife, Royal, and a nice bunch of kids." The family unit, eroded by capitalism, was the backbone of Tatro Cove. It had to be encouraged and preserved.

"Yeah, but you hate it when it's all you can do to keep food on the table."

"You do all right."

"I do all right, but I can't never buy them all that stuff they see on the TV." He hitched up his overalls, which were so old they were almost white.

"They don't need it."

"Tell them that. Most everbody else around here gets pretty much what they wants. I just can't figure out how they do it. Guess you might say I ain't never found myself."

"Or lost yourself, one."

"I reckon I'm just a quare turn or something."

"What's that?"

"A quare turn?" From Royal's lengthy explanation Raymond decided a quare turn was someone who wasn't content just to live life, but who insisted on trying to understand it too. A stance that incapacitated you in the ordinary world of getting and spending. Every now and then the Tatro family produced one. "Core Three, now there was a quare turn," Royal mused. "Always wandering through the woods, stooping down and touching plants. Not picking them or nothing, just touching them like he was talking to them or something."

Raymond felt as though he'd been handed the template to his personality. All along everyone had thought he was a weirdo. In Newland people avoided him because of his rayon shirts and reindeer sweater vests. In New York, where everyone had prefaced remarks with "My therapist says . . . ," there was some agreed-upon state known as Normality toward which everyone worked, as though on cars with engine knock. They "managed" their relationships as though dealing with a herd of cows. They advised him on what clothes to wear, what books to read in order to fit in. But actually he was a quare turn. He never fit in because it wasn't his nature to fit in! It was his nature to see what others couldn't, to blaze a trail for them into the post-industrial wilderness, just as Cor One had prepared a way into Tatro Cove for the more timid and "normal" settlers from the valley.

As Raymond wandered the hills searching for ginseng and galax, he squatted and touched plants. Sometimes he collected their seeds or leaves. These hikes were practically the only time he'd left the cove in six months, apart from his trips to Thelma. Late one afternoon under a threatening grey sky, he raised his head from his digging on a high hilltop and looked out over the entire area. The cove and its houses, the highway and McCray's store. Farther up the highway was the little town with its main shopping street, a couple of churches and a red brick courthouse. A few roads, trucks loaded with coal barreling down them. Railroad tracks with freight cars mounded high, like shiny black caskets. A couple of tipples, alighted like mosquitoes, sucking coal from the mountainsides.

In all directions as far as Raymond could see stretched forested ridges, valleys, creeks flashing silver under the glowering sky. And writhing across many ridges were contorted dark yellow scars. Several small mountains had had their tops shaved to form flat mesas, like in cowboy movies. Dirt and boulders and tree trunks cascaded down these mountainsides.

He picked up his sack and shovel and walked across the field and down through the woods back to the cove, where he forgot about what he'd seen as quickly as he could.

One weekend his parents drove up from the valley. Raymond cooked them supper Saturday night—fruits and vegetables he'd canned, dried, and stored, some ham Cor Four had given him for helping with haying.

They sat around the stove afterward. "What do you do for fun without no TV?" his father asked uneasily. Raymond had hidden his under the bed.

"Walk up the cove and visit somebody. Go lay on the porch floor at McCray's."

"Shoot, that's what I done all them years ago. Can you play that thing?" He pointed to Raymond's grandfather's banjo. "You oughta of heard Pa make that thang ring. Before he lost his arm. Used to play for barn dances, hour after hour."

"I'm teaching myself. But it's hard with no one to learn from. They don't have dances no more. All this stuff. It's like having to rediscover it from scratch."

"Now, what you looking at me like that for, boy?"

Raymond sighed. "You saw to it that I learned to read and write.

But you didn't never teach me how to take care of myself. How to garden, and chop wood, and all like that."

"Well sir, I didn't hardly expect a son of mine to come back to Tatro Cove, to tell you the truth. I thought reading and writing was what was important. Still do."

"You sold us all out for a bowl of potage, Pa. Like what's-his-name in the Bible."

"Cain," his mother murmured.

"That's easy enough for someone to say who ain't never been cold nor hungry."

"So now you're warm and fed, and dependent on those fuckers at the mill. And so is Jed. But me, I ain't dependent on nobody."

His mother was having a heart attack at his language.

"You let a flood come, like the spring of '28, and wash all your crops out, and then you'll see who you're dependent on. Or you lose an arm like your grandpa. You can live like this cause you got you a dozen relatives you could call on for cash if you was ever in bad trouble."

"Sure I could get washed out. But Arnold could switch all your contracts to Taiwan, and then where would you be? Crawling down this cove on your knees, begging for a meal." Raymond enjoyed picturing Jed and Sally and his parents arriving humbled on his doorstep, needing food and shelter, awaiting his guidance.

His mother interrupted, "That's why we been telling you all these years, Junior, to look to your Lord. Floods, depressions, what can you count on except the mercy of Jesus Christ our Saviour?"

Raymond looked at her.

She went on, "Oh Junior, I just wonder if you're ever going to make anything of yourself. Here you are a grown man, and you don't even have running water."

"But Ma, can't you understand I don't *want* running water? I'd have to get money to buy me a pump, and pay the electric bill, and repair it. I use less time getting me a bucketful from the creek every morning."

"But Junior, this is what your father and I have worked so hard to get away from. We wanted our boys not to have to spend all their time and energy just providing the necessities."

"So we'd have lots of time to sit around watching TV?"

"You just watch your tongue, Junior Tatro," his father snapped.

"So that you'd have time to contemplate the Lord and all His works."

"But I do, Mama. With every chore, I think about how well this world was set up. And what a mess the capitalists are making of it."

"Who're they?" asked his mother.

"I think we was meant to work to live, not live to work," continued Raymond.

"If you don't mind being common," replied his mother.

"You're living in a dream, son," insisted his father. "This ain't real. It's a game."

"It's more real what you do down there in the valley? Walking around watching people work, and sometimes going in and kissing Mackay's ass?"

Mr. Tatro gripped the arms of his chair. Mrs. Tatro gasped, "Why, Raymond Tatro Junior!"

"If this is a dream, I don't never want to wake up."

"It ain't in the nature of a dream to last a lifetime. So, buddy, you better get yourself ready for one rude awakening."

Winter came and with it rains that swelled the creek to overflowing. The road down the cove became a bog, the woods dripped incessantly. Raymond didn't go out much except to tend the animals.

Ben came by on weekends and in the evening after basketball practice. They took the beeswax they'd separated from the honey that fall, melted it in a deep pot on the stove, and dipped wicks time after time to make candles, which were a creamy golden color and smelled of honey. They got out the bags of wool. Searching through barns and attics and sheds up and down the cove, they assembled their own hand-operated yarn factory. In Tatro Cove nothing ever got thrown away—that included old refrigerators and automobile carcasses, but also looms and spinning wheels. They washed the wool, hand-carded it, oiled it, drew it out into rovings, and then spun it into yarn on a wheel pedaled by foot. They figured out how to make dyes from onion skins and leaves and barks.

Verbena almost collapsed when they asked her to teach them to knit. She'd forgotten how, but Grandma Tatro showed them. They also set up an old loom from Verbena's barn and began weaving a coverlet.

Raymond explained to Ben how their forebears had sold them out for an illusion of security. Now, in the mill and the mines, they didn't own the huge machines, the cloth or coal. All they owned was their labor, which they'd sold to management for cash with which to buy food and shelter. Management had purchased them, the way plantation owners used to purchase slaves. Ben and he, though, were resuscitating the family craft. They owned their equipment, their labor, and the end product, which they could either use or sell. They'd destroyed the worker-capitalist relationship at its source.

Ben blushed to the roots of his blonde hair. "Are you some kind of Communist or something, Junior?"

Raymond smiled. "Capitalism, Communism. Both concerned with the production and distribution of junk. Cor One got along with as little junk as possible—what could be produced by his own hands."

"What are you then—a Democrat or something?"

"I'm a Tatro, Ben. Of Tatro Cove. And so are you."

He frowned. "What does that mean?"

Raymond felt he was answering this question through illustration, not through abstract theoretical discussion, which was as foreign to Tatro Cove as Big Bird and M.G.'s white patent leather loafers.

Late one night he sat by the stove knitting and watching Johnny Carson, picturing himself being interviewed by Johnny. You'd want to simplify your terminology, intersperse it with little jokes, appear on this show rather than on some news analysis program on public broadcasting, so that you could really bring your message to the people. . . .

There was a knock on the door. Raymond started, poking himself with one of his needles. People hardly ever came down to the end of the cove, never that late, and not through that sea of mud called a road. He jumped up, turned off the TV, and slid it under the bed.

He opened the door on a tall, well-built man with a full red beard and thinning hair, who he figured was the guy from Philadelphia

Ben had been telling about. Ben was always enthusiastic about new people. But Raymond had really not been looking forward to this. Dred Allen, he said his name was. Raymond recognized it immediately. He'd done political work with Justin and Morris and those guys. Raymond decided not to mention mutual acquaintances. That was all behind him now. He was ashamed of his days as a missionary for Yankee imperialism.

"Just thought I'd stop by, introduce myself."

"Come in."

"Am I interrupting?"

Raymond laughed. "Hell, no. What's there to interrupt?"

"Yeah, this place is a drag, all right." He sat down and pulled out some cigarette papers. "You mind if I, like, smoke?"

"Not if you don't mind if I knit."

"Your cousin Ben said we should check each other out. That we, like, have a lot in common."

"Do we?"

"Well, he said you, like, lived in New York?"

"Yeah."

"What are you doing down here, man?"

"My family came from here. I grew up in the valley and decided to come back."

"Why?"

"I like it. It's quiet." This was probably the last person he'd describe his mission to. He'd learned you had to be sly around unbelievers.

"Jesus, you can say that again."

"Why are you here?"

"My old lady and me, we were organizing in Philly. She got offered this job to, like, set up this pre-school thing for the county Human Resources Agency."

"How bout you?"

"Me? Oh, I'm playing free-lance provocateur."

This was the fanciest name Raymond had heard yet for unemployment. "Where you living at?"

"We rented a house two hollows down."

"So how's it going?" Raymond had dropped a stitch and had to unravel a couple of rows.

Dred drew deeply on his joint. "Shit, man, I can't communicate with these cats, know what I mean?"

Raymond looked at him. He knew what it was like to be new kid on the block. Besides, Hospitality was part of the Tatro code. "Well, they're pretty stand-offish until they get to know you."

"Stand-offish? Man, I'd be glad if they were! I'm just afraid I'm going to get punched out, know what I mean?"

"Oh well, if you're at that point, you're fine. What you got to watch out for is silence, when they won't even bother to disagree with you."

"I was jogging up my road one day past this shack with a bunch of wrecked cars in the yard. This old guy was sitting on his porch. I ran up and introduced myself. Then I said maybe I could get someone to come haul away the cars. He said, 'What's wrong with them where they is?' " He laughed. "But I guess you got to figure that anybody with any get-up-and-go has already got up and gone!" He laughed. Raymond gazed at him, unamused.

Dred left behind an invitation for Ben and Raymond for supper the next week. "He's an outasight kid, your cousin. Can you help me persuade him to get the hell out of Tatro Cove?"

"Why?"

"Well, I mean, like, hell, man, this is one bright kid. And what's there for him in this disaster area. Know what I mean?"

"What's there for him out there?"

Their eyes met.

Raymond was just finishing kneading some dough the next night when Ben arrived, his hair slicked down from his shower after ball practice, and mud from the road almost to his knees. He dropped into a chair by the stove.

"Dred says he came by."

"Yeah."

"Isn't he neat, Junior?"

"Yes." He'd decided the best way to handle Ben's enthusiasm was to humor it. Dred was so awful that even Ben couldn't fail to perceive it

in time. Patience. Like the patience required to knead dough, let it
rise. He shaped the dough into loaves and slipped them into buttered
pans.

He sat down and handed Ben a dulcimer they'd found while ran-
sacking Verbena's barn. Raymond picked up Grandpa Tatro's banjo.
They strummed and plucked for a while, trying to figure out how to
play the damn things together.

"Let's face it," Ben suggested. "We're awful."

"At least we're not sitting staring at TV."

"What you got against TV? I bet you'd like 'The Waltons,' Junior."

Raymond realized he hadn't explained the difference between popular culture and mass culture. He'd reviewed his methods carefully
and had decided that verbal explanation had to accompany, and provide a framework for, practical illustration: "The ballads Tatros used
to sing until the arrival of the radio—they came from Scotland and
England. Something would happen—a murder or something. Someone would write a song about it. Other people would forget the words
or tune and add new ones. It'd be passed on from generation to
generation, getting polished like a stone in a creek. It expressed the
common experience of the entire community."

"How do you know what used to go on up here, Junior?"

Raymond paused with his mouth open, trying to decide if this
question was intended to be as impertinent as it sounded. Ben sometimes just didn't seem to grasp his role as disciple. Raymond decided
it was a genuine question, but that it deserved to be ignored, so Ben
would learn to absorb things at the pace at which Raymond fed them
to him. "You take television. Its messages are passed down from a
few capitalists in glass office buildings in New York City. The ads
make viewers want to buy a lot of useless junk. And the way different
groups are presented or not presented in programs reinforces the
pecking order that keeps those fuckers on top."

"What about 'Hawaii Five-O'? That's a real good show."

Raymond sighed, then reminded himself about rising dough.

"You think I shouldn't watch TV anymore, Junior?"

"Shit, how the hell should I know?"

Sitting in silence as rain splattered against the windows, Raymond
felt discouraged. It was a shock to realize how little Ben understood.

Did the kid have to go out there and get as fucked over as Raymond had been? What was the point of missing "The Price Is Right" if Raymond wasn't getting his point across?

"There's something I been wanting to tell you." Ben blushed.

Raymond looked up.

"We finally done it, Cheryl and me. We loved it. Been doing it all the time."

"I thought you hadn't been around much lately." Raymond felt a pang of jealousy. It wasn't a sensation he approved of, implying ownership of another person. But maybe it was inevitable in a society that treated people like things that could be bought and sold. The feeling began to fade as he performed his political analysis on it. All these reflexes from your upbringing lingered on. You had to examine them, then dismiss them.

"I want to bring her down to meet you, Junior. Is that OK?"

"Sure. Bring her by." He wanted to meet this chick almost as much as he wanted to meet Little Lulu.

Raymond had thought Dred looked like the type who'd serve whole wheat spaghetti, and he did. During supper Dred talked endlessly about starting a food co-op. "We could get staples a lot cheaper. Also items you can't find around here—mung beans and natural peanut butter and stuff. We could like borrow a truck and make runs to Lexington or Knoxville."

"I don't think you'll find much demand here for mung beans," Raymond said.

"Hostess cupcakes and Nehis maybe." Ben grinned.

"Shit, man, I can't get anyone interested in anything around this hell-hole."

Dred's son Humus specialized in spontaneity. At that moment he stood up on his chair and lisped "Solidarity Forever," thrusting his clenched fist into the air.

Ben, having known only mealtimes at which women stood behind the men, and children gazed at their plates and said nothing unless questioned, looked stunned. Dred and his old lady Cindy and Raymond, however, listened and smiled at Humus and applauded when he finished.

Dred resumed, "I tried to get the JayCees to buy that baseball field from Cletus Jones. Everyone said, 'Aw shucks, Cletus, he lets us use it when we want to.'"

"He does," Ben confirmed.

"But it's under water all winter."

"But nobody plays softball in winter," Raymond explained.

"Fuck it, man. I mean, like, I never saw such a lazy, backward, uncooperative bunch of people in my life. Know what I mean?"

Raymond glanced at Ben. But he appeared to accept every word the bastard uttered. "Maybe we like things the way they are," Raymond suggested. "When you call someone lazy, you might just be defining yourself as puritanically hyperactive." Cindy and Dred did strike him as frenetic, constantly jumping up to fetch food, tend the fire, or pace the floor for emphasis. He remembered these people liked nothing better than a good argument, and realized he was about to be lured into their stockade.

"No, man, it's not contentment. It's resignation. You can read it in the faces."

"That's really true," insisted Cindy. "I can find only four mothers who're willing to give their children a preschool experience."

"Maybe they like having them around."

"Yes, but think of the poor child. Plopped in first grade with no preparation."

"What about the poor child who gets plopped in a preschool experience with no preparation?"

"I want to talk now!" announced Humus.

"Shut up," Dred growled.

Humus picked up a broccoli spear and began beating Dred on his balding head, calling him a "fucking fascist bastard." Mock hollandaise sauce flew around the room. Ben's eyes got wider.

Ben took it upon himself to persuade his cousins to enroll their children in Cindy's preschool experience.

"What'd they say?" Raymond asked. This infatuation of Ben's was bound to burn itself out. And when it did, Raymond would be waiting patiently to continue Ben's instruction.

"Muriel said she'd have to give Clem up soon enough as it was, and she wanted him with her as long as she could keep him. And

Annie said little children belonged at home with their mothers. And Bertha said Cindy and Dred wasn't nothing but Communists, trying to break up the American family."

"And what did you say?"

"I told them they was being backward and old-fashioned."

"But Ben, they have a point. It's one way of looking at it."

"But Dred, he said . . ."

"Fuck Dred!"

Ben looked at him, alarmed.

Ben brought Cheryl down one afternoon. Raymond could tell at a glance that she was a silly little twit, but he realized she might be useful for chores like canning and knitting, which were boring Raymond to death. She fluttered in, with Ben beaming behind. She started chattering about what a pleasure it was to meet Raymond, how much she'd heard about him, modeling herself on Scarlett O'Hara. Ben acted like a turd, feeding her questions that were supposed to display her at her best. If this was her best, Raymond shuddered to contemplate her worst.

She looked around Raymond's kitchen. "No electric range?"

"I got me a wood stove."

"Why, I don't believe I could manage without a range. You're just a wonder, Junior. And no refrigerator?"

Who was this? Betty Furness? "I use a springhouse."

"Ben honey, I know how much you admire Junior. But when we get married, honey, I just got to have me my Gold Medallion kitchen."

Raymond decided Ben ought to fuck her in the mouth. At least it might shut her up.

"But you like to can, don't you, Cheryl?" Ben urged.

"Not if I can help it." She laughed. "How long you been here?" she asked Raymond.

"Close to a year."

"How long you staying?"

"My whole life, I hope."

"Really? Gosh, I can't wait to get away."

"How come?"

She laughed. "Whenever my sisters come home from Atlanta, they say Tatro Cove looks like a hurricane's been through."

"I think it's right pretty myself." Raymond's heart was breaking.

"Down here it's not so bad. But out on the main road it's a mess from all the stripping."

Raymond watched them walk back down the hollow. Ben put his arm around her. She snuggled up against him. They cut up through the woods. Probably they'd fuck on the leaves at the top of the cliff. Raymond went outside and began digging in his garden.

The next day he ran into Lyla as he walked past her house. "How you liking your new school, Lyla?"

She giggled, looked around, then whispered, "She crazy, that Mrs. Cindy lady."

"How come?"

Lyla put on an adult voice: " 'Lyla, no juice and cracker until you call me Cindy.' "

Raymond decided to go to the parish hall and see what was being done to his little cousins by this emissary of Yankee capitalism. The children sat coloring. Occasionally they sneaked glances at each other and giggled. Whenever Cindy spoke, they were polite, calling her Mrs. Cindy. Except for Humus, who called her Mom, and sometimes "stupid bitch woman." She wore a long dress and combat boots.

"How's it going?" Raymond asked, determined to be pleasant.

"Awful," she sighed. "All they do is sit there and obey me. I wish one would kick me or throw a tantrum."

"You do?"

"Well, they're just so repressed. From their authoritarian home lives. It shows in everything they do. Look at these pictures." She pointed to the wall at drawings of their houses. "So stark. No decoration or anything."

"But that's how their houses are. People don't have many extras around here."

"Material poverty I can handle. It's the emotional paucity, the paucity of the imagination I'm talking about, Raymond. For instance, this morning I tried to get them to imitate bacon frying. I even got down on the floor and demonstrated. They looked at me as though I were nuts or something."

Raymond suppressed a guffaw.

"The kids in the Philly Free School loved it," she said in a hurt voice. "They'd lose themselves in it, until you thought they really *were* bacon frying."

Raymond suggested this was a pretty sophisticated assignment for mountain children, but that she should try again, letting him explain. After his explanation and another demonstration, some appeared to understand. They flung themselves down and began writhing, cooperative strips of bacon. But Raymond couldn't figure out the babbling noises coming from their mouths. Sound effects? The snapping and crackling of fat? Eventually one little boy jumped up, went over to a girl who was just watching, put his hands on her head with a firm downward pressure, and barked in a gruff little voice, "Heal, sister! In the name of Jesus Christ our Lord, throw off your illness and be whole!"

Cindy's face assumed an expression of horror. She called a halt to the home revival and sent them out to play.

Raymond couldn't stop smiling as he and Cindy stood in the yard watching Humus. "You be the capitalist pig, and I'll be the revolutionary worker!" he ordered Clem. Clem looked at him, frowned, and joined the others under a tulip poplar. They sat watching the shifting pattern of leafy shadows on the grass.

"See what I mean?" Cindy demanded. "So sluggish. Sometimes I wonder if the poor little things aren't full of worms."

She marched over and said something. They got up and followed her to a dirt pile. She explained and gestured. Humus scrambled up the pile and stood on top with his hands on his hips. A couple of boys followed, and he pushed them down the pile.

They picked themselves up and stood blinking, looking at Humus with bewilderment as he shouted, "Ha, ha! *I'm* king on the mountain!"

A few others made attempts to climb the pile.

"I don't know," sighed Cindy upon her return. "They're all bottled up. No intensity to anything they do. They've been so harshly disciplined in their families that their aggression has been stalled."

Raymond felt his aggression about to be unstalled. He snapped, "They got very little aggression to start with. Why should they? Their world is warm and placid and friendly and accepting and noncompetitive. They know who they are and what's expected of them."

"Exactly! And with no conflict, they're failing to develop personalities with elasticity, resilience, and complexity. Conflict shouldn't be feared, but rather its absence, and the resulting inability to deal with it. I worry so for them."

"But if you don't have conflict, you don't need to deal with it."

"There's conflict everywhere. The alternative is death."

"I disagree."

"So disagree!" They glared at each other. She was delighted. She felt right at home. He tried to avoid noticing that he did too.

Half a dozen boys had just pushed Humus off the hill. He was howling, "No fair! You can't gang up!" Once in possession of the hill, the boys held out their hands and helped up the little girls.

"Cindy, Tatro Cove is different from Philadelphia. Not better, but no worse. People aren't machine parts—we don't have to be uniform and standardized. We can enrich each other's lives with our differences."

Humus charged back up the hill and pushed children off. Several kids, their faces red with rage but otherwise impassive, began beating the shit out of him.

"How's that for unstalled aggression?" Raymond called as Cindy raced to rescue Humus.

Ben's team won the regional play-offs and went to Louisville for the state championship.

"Wow, it was neat, Junior!" he reported upon his return. "Kentucky Fried Chicken, McDonald's, Burger King, Dunkin' Donuts, Howard Johnson's—all in a row, one right after another. Shopping malls. Everthing."

They were on their way up to the graveyard to mend fences. Ben said he had to do a project for Civics class and might do it on franchises, how you set them up and how they worked. "It might could be a way for me to stay in the Cove and still make a living. Dad might help me start up a Kentucky Fried Chicken place."

Raymond stared at him.

"What do you think, Junior?"

Raymond started pointing out the different headstones and talking about the men who lay beneath them: Purvis Tatro, a great-uncle who was shot during a union drive at his mine in the thirties. Arlen Tatro, mashed into eternity by a tree he cut for Remington to make rifle stocks with during World War II. Billy Jack Tatro, killed at Okinawa. Lucian Tatro, killed in Korea. Horten Tatro, killed at Dak To. Grandpa Tatro, minus his right arm, which lay smashed thin as a snakeskin under tons of slate in the middle of a nearby mountain.

Raymond explained how they were all casualties of Yankee capitalism, which made wars inevitable through the pursuit of raw materials, and of markets to consume the overproduction of junk. How capitalist profits peaked during and immediately after wars. How wars were fought by hillbillies and blacks and Puerto Ricans, how most men he knew up North managed to sidestep the draft.

"Don't hardly seem fair," mused Ben as he hammered.

"It ain't. Don't let yourself be deceived, Ben. The Kentucky Colonel is a Yankee capitalist front man, and Kentucky Fried Chicken ain't got nothing to do with Tatro Cove, Kentucky."

Raymond suggested he do a questionnaire for his project to send home with his classmates, to see if their grandparents could recall any of the old mountain ballads. Ben looked at Raymond skeptically. "She wants a paper. You know, double-spaced, with footnotes and all."

"You could write up your results."

"Well, Dred, he thought the franchise project was a good idea. Said Tatro Cove was the seam of the poverty pocket. Needed to bring in new jobs."

"Dred? What does Dred know about Tatro Cove? What does Dred know about what's best for you?"

"It's just that sometimes *he* thinks I have good ideas."

Raymond didn't know what to say.

"I like you a lot, Raymond. I just wish you could like me how I am."

"But I *do!*"

"No, you don't, Raymond. Not really. You want me to be somebody else."

Raymond thought this over as they walked down the hill. Maybe it was true. But only in the sense that Raymond could see in Ben undeveloped capacities, foresaw what was going to happen down in the valley, and understood the role Ben could play after the collapse. It was lonely seeing more than those around you saw. You were doomed to misunderstanding and isolation. People were constantly betraying you and betraying their potential, without even knowing it. He felt the familiar gnawing in his stomach. But then he thought about the long line of Tatro quare turns—Cor One alone in the Kentucky wilderness, Cor Three with only his herbs to communicate with. Looked at from a temporal point of view, yes, Raymond was alone. But when he retreated into inner solitude, he knew he was in good company. In the *best* company, the most recent in a race of giants. And Ben could join him if only he'd let in what Raymond had to teach him.

The county came to blacktop the road up the cove. Tatros had been trying to get this done for fifteen years.

"I feel like they're overdoing it, don't you, Granny?" Raymond asked one afternoon as he strolled past Verbena's porch. "All we asked for was some rock and gravel."

"Ain't you heard, Junior? They fixing to strip the backside of yonder hill."

Raymond stared at her. "They can't do that."

"How come not?"

"Belongs to us."

"What's up top does. But Cor Three sold off what's underneath back in '05."

"To who?"

She shrugged.

"We got to stop it."

She smiled and rocked. "Can't."

Large trucks loaded with logs moved down the cove to the highway for several weeks. Then flatbed trucks hauling yellow bulldozers and loaders rolled slowly up the road in the other direction.

"They got the right to earn them a living. Same as everbody else," said Lem as he sat on his porch, his face still black from work. "Same as *most* everbody else," he added, looking at Raymond.

"I'm earning me a living, Lem," Raymond said, hurt. Hell, it was a more permanent living than the mines could provide, not that Lem had the brains to understand why.

"Yeah. I reckon."

"I'm keeping food on my table and clothes on my back. I don't have a new Olds from M.G. like you do because I don't *want* one."

"All right, Junior. Don't get all touchy. You do what you want. But let other people do what they want."

"Even if it means wrecking what I'm doing?"

"They ain't hurting you none."

"Like fuck they ain't. The whole house shakes when they go by. My seedlings is coated with the dust they throw up."

"Just relax, Junior. You be all right."

Raymond decided Lem was right. He had things to reveal to Tatro Cove, but every now and then there were a few things they could teach him. He was upset now because factors beyond his control were entering his life. The whole point was to accept your lack of control and go with the flow, as Tatro Cove had always done. He had to be alert, scour from his character the scum deposited by all those years spent on the outside.

The blasting started. A rock the size of a basketball landed in his garden, leaving a crater several feet deep among the cauliflower.

"That could've been Lyla's head that thing landed on!" Raymond yelled at Lyle, who leaned out the window of the Flying Goose.

"But it weren't," he pointed out, chewing a piece of grass.

"Next time it might be. We got to stop this."

"Look around you, Junior. Half the men in this county got a missing leg, or a smashed back, or the black lung. Any miner'll tell you hit's safer stripping than crawling into the middle of a mountain."

Raymond clamped his mouth shut and made no reply. Lyle thought he was impractical. What could be more practical than learning to supply all your material needs from your own land with your own hands? Maybe Lyle couldn't see this now, but he would in time, once the system that was keeping him fed and clothed collapsed. Then he'd be looking at Raymond with respect rather than tolerant scorn. It was just lucky for this world that here and there were a few quare turns who didn't allow themselves to be deceived into believing that how things were wasn't necessarily how they'd always be. Probably Karl Marx himself was a quare turn.

All day long as Raymond weeded his garden, he could hear the roar of bulldozers shoving landslides down the backside of the hill on which the graveyard sat. There was another round of blasting. He could feel each explosion coming. The ground trembled as though an earthquake were under way. Then a deafening concussion. A cloud of orange smoke billowing silently into the summer sky, while boulders sailed upward, arched, then floated out of sight behind the hills. His living room wall cracked along one corner. Huge trucks, Lyle's Flying Goose among them, rolled past his house leaving a trail of gleaming black chunks down the cove.

As he walked along the blacktop back from McCray's, with trucks thundering past, he came upon Lyla sitting in her yard behind a card table that held a glass pitcher. Her sign read, "Kool Aid, 5¢ a glass." She was taking a trucker's nickel and handing him a Dixie cup.

As he roared off in a cloud of exhaust, Raymond asked her what she thought she was doing.

"Earning me some money," she said, gazing at him as though he were retarded.

"Does your mama know?"

"She hepped me."

"I don't think it's right, Lyla. You ought to be wading in a creek or something. Go play with your bull roarer. It's dangerous with all these big trucks."

"Mrs. Cindy, she say why don't I do it."

Raymond climbed up to the graveyard. Looking down the backside of the hill, he saw it had been scalped of its vegetation and topsoil, which now lay in jumbled heaps farther down. He watched down below as an auger six feet in diameter forced its way into what was left of the vein. It spewed out behind itself, into waiting trucks, ejaculations of shiny black coal. Withdrawing slowly, it shifted down the seam, then plunged in again, ripping and tearing out a new hole.

Endurance, he reminded himself. Fortitude. Stoicism. Disasters came and went in Tatro Cove. Wild animals, Indian raids, guerrilla bushwhacking, feuds, revenuers, floods, union wars, coal busts, accidents, disease, starvation, and VISTA workers. But Tatros remained. He felt like a man with his hands bound behind his back, watching his lover being ravished. He couldn't hurl himself against earth-moving equipment two stories high. It wasn't a question of over-powering or outwitting, just outlasting. If he could keep from going crazy, the strippers would be gone soon.

By autumn they were, leaving behind a road so rutted that cars could barely get down it. Ben hadn't been around much ever since their talk at the graveyard. Probably banging his brains out in the woods. Raymond concluded that endurance was the only answer. Patience like Job's. Ben would get tired of fucking and fed up with Dred's arrogance. He'd recognized that Raymond had his true best interests at heart, and he'd come back. Raymond just had to keep his distance so that Ben wouldn't feel pressured, and then make it easy for him to return once he recognized his mistake.

One day as Royal and Raymond walked the hills cutting galax, Royal said, "Looks like I won't have to cut this stuff no more, without I want to."

"You come into an inheritance, Royal?"

"Sort of like. Dred there, he hepped me to get onto the welfare."

Raymond straightened up and looked at him.

"He's starting him up this group. Needs my hep," he added proudly.

"To do what?"

"To go out and get folks onto the rolls."

"But Royal, once you're living off welfare, the Yankee capitalists have got you right where they want you—dependent on them. Not likely to make a fuss."

"I ain't never made no fuss nohow. Been too tired trying to keep food on the table."

"But Royal . . ."

"Son, don't you Royal me. The day you got six hungry kids is the day I'll be innerested in what you got to say about how I keep them fed."

"But Royal, you could keep them fed with a market garden. Sell the surplus for cash. I'll help you set it up."

"Naw, I'm sick, son. I need me the welfare."

"What's wrong with you?"

He clasped his chest and started wheezing. "My lungs. Done gone plumb punky on me. Some days I can't hardly breathe. Looky here, why don't you join our group, Raymond. You might could get on the welfare yourself. Then you wouldn't have to dig this shit no more."

Raymond looked out across the hills and down into the cove. If he did, he'd have more time to pursue his mission. . . . "Get thee behind me, Satan!" he snarled.

"Huh?"

These capitalists were brilliant, Raymond reflected, maneuvering men into engineering their own impotence. But it wouldn't last. Just as you had to sit out the stripping of your family graveyard, so you had to sit out all the wrenching death throes of capitalism.

One evening a red Mustang arrived in Raymond's front yard. Cheryl was sitting shotgun. Ben hopped out, grinning. "You like it, Junior?"

Raymond's heart leaped at the sight of his blonde head and open cheerful face. Ben was back! Just as Raymond had foreseen. "Like what?"

"My birthday present." He gestured to the car.

Raymond said nothing.

"Daddy got it as a trade-in on a El Dorado. Give it to me."

Raymond stared at it.

"Well?" he demanded.

"Very nice."

"Come go for a ride."

"No, thanks."

"Ah, come on, Junior. Let's go get us a hamburger at that new place in town."

"What new place?"

"Ain't you been to Hillbilly Heaven yet?"

Raymond nodded no.

"Come on, buddy. Get up off your ass and let's go!"

Reluctantly, Raymond climbed in.

The specialty at Hillbilly Heaven was the Hillbilly Burger, "barbe-cued with our own special sauce, laced with just a hint of home-brewed white lightning." The clientele were mostly film crews and journalists from the national networks doing specials on the destruction of the Southern mountains.

Dred sauntered in. Ben said, "We got a big surprise for you, Junior."

Dred held out a cardboard box on which was printed "Uncle Corliss Tatro's Old Timey Gee Haw Flimmy Diddle." There was a picture of Cor Four sitting whittling in his hat and baggy overalls. The copy read, "Tatros settled in Tatro Cove before the American Revolution, and they're still there, living much as their ancestors did. The Tatro children still play with handmade wooden toys such as this . . ."

Dred and Ben were setting up Old Timey Toys, Inc.—with a factory in Tatro Cove which Ben would run. Dred already had orders from a couple of stores on Fifth Avenue that carried other Appalachian products, as well as from craft shops in Cambridge, Massachusetts, and Woodstock, Vermont.

"Great, huh, Junior?" Ben demanded. "It's why you haven't been seeing much of me lately."

Raymond couldn't speak.

"I realize now," confessed Dred, stroking his red beard, "that I came to Tatro Cove thinking I had all the answers. Well, I know now these people have plenty to teach me. I want to help them preserve their culture and transmit its strengths to the American mainstream."

"What's wrong, Junior?" Ben asked in a worried voice.

"Don't worry about him." Dred gave Raymond a look of contempt. "He's just jealous he didn't think of it first."

That night the skies opened. Rain gushed down like fluid from a uterus at the onset of labor. Raymond sat on his porch and watched in the lightning as the topsoil from his garden washed into the creek. He felt nothing. Ben had betrayed him for a handful of silver. Well, he would just have to revise his plans. How, he had no idea. He'd just have to wait until new means were revealed to him.

The rains kept up for several days. When they stopped, the creek was choked with silt from the soil bank left by the strippers. Water rose over the creek bank and began flooding his yard. With a shovel he dug a new channel. The next rain brought down more silt and filled in the channel. Every few days Royal and Lem and Lyle and Cor Four and Raymond were all out in the creek in front of their houses with shovels.

Raymond climbed the hill to get some idea how much more silt would descend. He discovered the graveyard had sunk, the ground having collapsed into auger holes. Looking down the backside, he saw that a mud slide off the soil bank had dammed the valley through which the creek ran. Murky reddish water was building up behind it.

At Thanksgiving dinner, M.G. said, "Lord, we got so much to be thankful for here in Tatro Cove." Raymond reflected that M.G. sure did. He'd branched out into helicopters, was selling dozens to strippers. "We known hard times, which makes our present good fortune that much sweeter to partake of."

After everybody amened, while the women served, Raymond told about the mud slide, about his concern that the wall would break and flood the cove, about the need to get together and do something about it.

"If it breaks, it breaks," said Lem, shoveling mashed potatoes into his mouth.

"Son, you can't stop progress!" announced M.G., folding his hands over his stomach, which bulged out over the white patent leather belt that matched his loafers.

Royal said, "I figure it's worth the worry so them folks in the valley can run their factories."

Raymond felt the gnawing start up in his stomach. Here he was, telling them something essential for their immediate physical survival, and they wouldn't listen. How could he have expected them to grasp something as subtle as their mission? He'd been living among them for over a year, and they still hadn't recognized his function, still avoided, ignored, or patronized him. There was a limit to how long you could sustain patience in the face of unremitting ignorance. Just as everyone had always done, it appeared the people of Tatro Cove were bound to betray him. He looked around at the flushed smiling Tatro faces with their similar features. All these people were interested in was shoveling the maximum amount of poor-quality food into their babbling mouths.

After dinner M.G. ushered his relatives into the living room to inspect his new 23-inch Motorola color TV console. They all sat and watched "Hee Haw." Two men in straw hats were dancing and playing banjos and making faces:

"This old hillbilly, he watched this nurse get into this elevator. The Doc, he come up and says, 'Clem, why, what's wrong with you, son?' 'Doc,' he says, 'that girl, she climbed in that there box. The doors shet. And when they opened again, she'd plumb vanished!'"

Canned laughter roared. So did the room full of Tatros. Raymond tried to calm his stomach, reminding himself of the brutalization his relatives had endured—their land, their culture, their very bodies exploited, maimed, and destroyed to produce profits. It wasn't his kinfolks' fault that they were incapable of accepting the message Raymond was offering. He noticed Ben across the room, staring at him, perplexed. The others could have another chance, but it was too late for Ben.

A commercial came on. An earnest engineer in a construction helmet and work clothes knelt with a pine seedling in his callused hand and explained with a sincere blue gaze about how the multinational oil company he worked for was restoring the hillsides it had stripped until they were more attractive and more hospitable to wildlife than when God Himself first fashioned them.

Two men in overalls lay in the yard of a tarpaper shack, a coon dog sleeping beside them.

"You reckon we outta mend that roof one day, Pa?" one drawled, his eyes closed and his hand reaching for a brown jug.

"Why, son, I declare, I . . ."

Raymond's hand grabbed a heavy glass ashtray. He hurled it as hard as he could at the TV screen, which shattered, throwing glass around the room.

Everyone stared at him.

"Don't yall see what the capitalists are doing? Portraying us as stupid and lazy. Not human. Just like they do blacks. So they don't have to feel guilty about destroying our land and our people and our culture for their own goddam profit!" He was screaming.

M.G. said in a quiet voice, "Son, you just wrecked my brand-new

Motorola 23-inch color TV. You some kind of Communist nut or something?"

Raymond knelt by his stove in front of Ben, who'd hurt his knee in ball practice that afternoon. Raymond had persuaded him to let him rub some homemade salve on it. Ben was sitting in his underwear, while Raymond rubbed the swollen knee.

"I reckon M.G. is pretty annoyed with me?" He felt grateful to Ben for coming to see him. Everyone else was avoiding him.

"To tell you the truth, Junior, he ain't real happy."

"I reckon I ought to find some way to get his set fixed."

"It might help."

"I feel bad about it. I lost my head."

They heard a car pull into the yard. Red lights flashed through the window. Two state troopers and M.G. rushed through the door. They sniffed around the room like dogs looking for a spot to pee in.

M.G. said, "It's just like I thought. All right now, I want to know, Junior, what you doing to my son. Teaching a seventeen-year-old boy to knit. It's downright un-American!"

Raymond sat back in his chair and rubbed the salve from his palms onto his jeans.

"It ain't normal for no man your age to live all alone like this. How come you ain't got you no wife?"

Raymond looked at him.

"Come on, Ben. I'm taking you right now to Doc Dalton for a check-up."

"What for, Pa?"

"You know what for, son."

Ben looked at Raymond, who was starting to get sick to his stomach.

"You're wrong, M.G.," Raymond said.

"What?" asked Ben.

"Come on, son. And don't think I ain't gon have you locked up, Junior. We may share a last name, but a Commie faggot like you ain't no kin of mine."

"You're making a bad mistake, M.G." Raymond was unable to move from his chair.

"We'll see what Doc Dalton has to say about that."

"What, Pa?"

Lyla arrived on Raymond's doorstep the next afternoon and handed him a note.

"Thanks, Lyla. That's real sweet of you."

Lyla held out her grubby little palm.

"What, honey?"

"Tip please."

"Would you settle for a slice of whole wheat bread with some fresh butter and honey?"

"Cash only."

The note, from Ben, read: "Pa says I can't come down there no more. It ain't true, is it, Junior, what they're saying you wanted from me?"

That night Raymond set a fire in the woods below a new strip site in the next hollow. While the watchman was checking it out, he broke into the shed and stole some dynamite. The next day in town he bought some batteries and a couple of wind-up alarm clocks. That afternoon he heard about Jed's death and went down to Newland.

He walked to the front of the church with Lem, Lyle, Ben, Royal, M.G., and several others. Dodging the wreaths and bouquets, they shouldered the casket, looking at each other and nodding to coordinate the effort. Apparently death was the only thing Tatros could agree on. Brought them all together like a nest of rats. Well then, when he got back to the cove, maybe he'd just put his bombs under the mud dam so the inhabitants of Tatro Cove, clinging to the coffins of their forebears, would be flushed into the Big Sandy River. The only solution appeared to be to clear away all that human debris and start from scratch, like Noah.

They proceeded slowly up the aisle, while the organist played a dirge. Various people in the congregation wept and sniffled and eyed Raymond's overalls with disapproval.

Suddenly it occurred to Raymond that he bore his brother's dead body on his shoulder. Anguish swept through him like a brush fire, and he staggered, the coffin sliding off his shoulder and continuing up the aisle on other shoulders. As he caught up, tears dribbled from his eyes. Skinny little Jed, using every ounce of his strength to haul himself to the top of the Castle Tree. Raymond had loved him and hated him, but in both cases had spent a lot of his time preoccupied with him. And now he was gone. And there was a void in Raymond's life where a pain-in-the-ass kid brother, a hulking idiot of a jock, a bigoted loudmouth redneck used to be. A sob shook Raymond. Everyone in town was watching. He didn't know which was worse—to have them think he was fabricating this grief because it was appropriate to the moment, or to have them know it was genuine.

They slid the casket into the hearse like a shell casing into a gun. Raymond climbed into a black limousine from Creech's Funeral Home, which was being driven by Billy Creech. Billy gave him a somber nod, which he returned. Raymond had known Billy in high school. He wore big round glasses, and they'd called him Creech Owl. He used to sign everyone's annual on the page his old man had taken out for an ad, penciling in the slogan, "Let us be the last to let you down."

# Chapter Three

## Donny

It felt real strange being back in Pine Woods after such a long time. But probably stranger for Pine Woods than for him, Donny realized. His grandmaw looked at him in his black leather jacket and Afro like he was from Mars. "Now, what you spoze to be, nigger?"

"I ain't *spoze* to be nothing. I *am* a black man."

"Honey, you done been one of them your whole entire life, without growing no bush out of your head."

"No, I ain't. I ain't been neither in my own mind. But now I'm both. And proud of it."

"Humph," she said. "You reckon you too proud to run up the hill to the Princes' and fetch me my Christmas tree?"

Donny didn't want nothing to do with no Princes. The reason it took him so long in the first place to understand what was coming down was because he hung out in that motherfucking tree with those honkies all those years. Put it in his head they was all one big happy family. But he did want to help out his grandmaw. She looked so pitiful setting over her kerosene heater, all bony and bundled in a raggy old quilt. Used to tell him all the time he had to learn to be "clever." Where had all her cleverness got *her* to?

"How come you got to go fetch it? Ain't they always brung it down?"

"Ain't you heard? That poor little old Jed went and got hisself killed in a car wreck."

Donny stared at her. "Where at?"

"Out on the Chattanooga highway. Run over by a big old truck."

What was that cracker to him, man? Why should he care? "Yeah, I'll go fetch the tree."

He put the kids in the back seat of his mother's car, which he'd borrowed to drive Rochelle and them down here in. They drove down the highway, under the railroad bridge, past the red brick mill. Shit, had he changed since he used to push a broom through that place, grinning at all those white motherfuckers. Man, he didn't know what he thought he was doing back in those days. It was like he was in some kind of a trance or something. Prince wanted him to be grateful for the chance to mop his floors, so he was grateful while he mopped the floors. Rochelle wanted him to buy her a ranch house, so he felt bad cause he couldn't. His mother wanted him to Make Something of Himself, so he worked until he was so tired at night that he couldn't hardly hold his head up to watch the TV. His grandmaw wanted him to love the Lord, so he loved the Lord, not knowing nothing about the cat. But now didn't nobody tell Donny Tatro what to do.

Of course he went up North in the first place to try to get Rochelle her ranch house. Felt like he owed her that much after busting her up so bad. Plus which he now had all those doctor bills to pay, on top of everything else. They both appeared around Pine Woods with their faces all stitched together like softballs. One of her front teeth was broken. A few days later she miscarried. Nobody had been able to believe that Mr. Junior Church Usher could of done that to his own wife. He couldn't believe it himself. He'd become a different person for a few minutes there. He lived with his grandmaw for a while, all upset and confused. One week he'd be at church on Wednesday night and twice on Sunday. The next week he'd hang out in front of Dupree's every afternoon after work, and so late in the pool hall on Saturday night that he'd sleep through church. At church they'd tell him to shoulder his yoke. In front of Dupree's they'd tell him to split. All he knew was that he wanted Rochelle back, but that she'd look the other way when he passed her in the street. Eventually she let him move back in, but she wouldn't have nothing to do with him. "I feel sorry for your grandmaw having you around all the time, is all," she growled. She slept on the couch with Sue and Billy, while he slept in the bed with Nicole and Isaac.

Anyhow, he figured people who went up North usually came back with a bunch of money, and if they could, he could. Just a question of working hard and living right. If you didn't make it, you just weren't trying hard enough. He applied for a job at the Ford plant in Metuchen, New Jersey, and they put him on a wait list. Down here you couldn't join no union, up there you *had* to. He didn't much like neither situation. He just wanted a job that would earn him some bread, so he could buy Rochelle her ranch house, so she'd want to get next to him again. Sometimes being around her was like one of those fairy tales his mama used to read The Five—where you had to go through all these impossible trials to win the hand of the princess.

When he told his grandmaw he was leaving, she looked at him and said, "Lord, Lord."

"But I'll be back to visit you, Grandmaw."

"You'll come back, honey, but you won't be my Donny no more."

He laughed. "Course I will. Who else I gon be?"

She shook her head and spat tobacco juice across the room.

They'd taken him on a tour of that auto plant. He watched the men, some colored, running those big machines. If only he could run one that put in the rivets to hold the chassis together, he'd be stone living. The notion they'd *pay* him to do this was almost more than he could handle.

While he waited to be summoned by Ford, he hiked cars in an eight-floor underground garage near the United Nations. One day a white woman in a chinchilla coat drove in in a chocolate-colored Mercedes-Benz. She smiled at him as he slid behind the wheel. He drove off slow, to show her how careful he was. Two levels down he turned on the radio loud and floored it. On the fourth level he swung into a space between a Coupe de Ville and a Buick Riviera, spinning the wheel with one hand. Slamming on the brakes, he stopped the front fender an inch from the concrete pillar. He ran his hand over the brown leather seat and wiped the wooden dashboard with his shirt sleeve. He could smell that woman's perfume. Made him want Rochelle real bad.

He walked to the stairway whistling. He'd parked that mother perfect on his first try. Sometimes he had to stop and back up to pull in at the right angle. Monty, who mostly sat in the office collecting money and picking his nose, called Donny "Cowboy." He kept warning Donny that one day he was going to bash in one of those big cars, and then where would he be? (On the line at the Metuchen Ford plant, he hoped.)

Sometimes when Monty went out for coffee, Donny would climb into a Rolls or a Continental Mark IV, back it up, then pull it in. He'd do this several times, thinking about driving out the exit for a spin. But he was chicken shit.

What he'd buy next, after Rochelle's ranch house in New Jersey, was a Chrysler Imperial. Man, whenever he parked one of those mothers, he felt like he was in heaven. Every now and then colored men would drive in in big cars. And Leon had him an El Dorado. Up here anything was possible. It was up to Donny to make it happen, and, baby, he would. He kept meaning to borrow his mother's camera and get Monty to take his picture behind the wheel of an Imperial to send down to Rochelle. Maybe she'd get the idea he was on the right track. He hadn't sent her much cash yet, but if he got on at the Ford plant, they'd be minting it. Before long, he'd bring her and the kids up. They'd have their own place in a development near the Ford plant, with a yard all their own that the children next door couldn't trample. He'd buy him a self-propelled lawn mower like the Princes' and mow the grass every week. It'd be a pleasure once it was your own grass.

He grabbed a straight chair and carted it up the inclined driveway to the sidewalk. Leaning it back on two legs against the brick wall of an apartment building, he sat down with his feet on the rungs and his arms folded across his stomach. The spring sun felt good. It was so weak, though, filtering through the exhaust fumes and dodging all those huge buildings. He told Monty people up here didn't know what sunlight was all about. Monty told him sunlight was about the onliest thing niggers from down South knew anything about. Donny told him he also knew how to stop big mouths from talking jive insults. It tickled him when Monty actually shut up. Nobody up here knew Donny as Good Boy Tatro or Mr. Junior Church Usher. They didn't know *what* he might do. If Donny wanted to be somebody else altogether, wasn't nobody else's opinions to stop him. The exhilaration inspired by this thought rapidly faded into uneasiness. Nobody could box him in, but nobody knew the good stuff either—about him being a big basketball hero in high school, or being Ruby Prince's grandson, or being the first colored man on at Benson Mill. Even if he told them, wouldn't nobody care.

He began watching people go in and out of the hotel across the street. Foreigners. Worked at the United Nations. The getups they walked around in was something else—these turban jobs, sometimes these white nightgowns with suit coats. All kinda stuff. Pretty funny-looking. He tried to tell Rochelle about it when he wrote, but he wasn't no writer. Maybe he'd snap some pictures of them, too.

Two people he'd seen several times walked out the revolving door. They were colored people, but not like any he'd ever laid eyes on. Jet black. And the man wore this loose orange and red and black shirt job. The woman wore a long robe, same colors, and gold jewelry. Her hair kinked a foot out from her head, like she wasn't ashamed of it or nothing. The sun shining through it made it look like the Burning Bush. Rochelle had spent most of her life with her hair on big rollers, doused in this evil-smelling junk, trying to get it straight. He had to write her about this foreign chick.

They glided along like being pulled on roller skates—with their backs straight as boards and their heads high. The man had scars all over his cheeks. Monty claimed his tribe over at Africa would of did this to him on purpose. Donny ran his fingertips from the corner of his right eye to his jawbone, where Rochelle gouged him with the church key. They didn't have nothing over at Africa that wasn't right here in the U.S. of A. Wasn't never no lack of people who wouldn't just as soon cut you as look at you, claiming all along how much they loved you. He reckoned Rochelle had to do something to stop him that night, but did she have to be so energetic? She'd laid open the whole side of his face. He'd come out of the emergency room with seventeen stitches. Just lucky she'd missed his eye. Now the scar looked like a permanent stream of tears. People was always thinking he was sad when he wasn't.

His mother and Arthur were living in an apartment in a row house in Harlem. They'd gotten hitched, so that made Donny Arthur's stepson—although Arthur treated him like he was a cockroach. He stayed with them for a while, waiting to get a place of his own until he knew whether or not he'd get the Ford job. He hadn't wanted to tell his mother about the fight, wanted to tell her the scar was from a machine at the mill or something. But he knew she'd find out anyway. You couldn't have no secrets in Pine Woods. So he told her the truth. She shook her head and said, "Well, it's about time you got yourself out of there. Too bad that's what it took."

Every evening when Donny came home from the garage, Arthur would lift his bushy grey head from the newspaper, nod sharply, and look Donny up and down in his greasy work clothes. Arthur thought he was something extra special cause he always wore a white shirt and a loosened tie. Shoot, the cat was still a nigger. The first evening, Donny went over to sit on the couch, and Arthur said, "I trust you're not planning to sit on my brand-new Design Research couch in that outfit?" He always spoke real careful, like he was giving a sermon. Donny had been, but pretended the thought never crossed his mind.

One night after he'd gone to bed, Donny heard Arthur say to his mother in the living room, "Well, when's he going to get himself a place of his own, Kathryn?"

"Just as soon as he knows where to get one at."

"And when will that be?"

"Whenever that Ford plant lets him know whether he can work there or not."

"It's not right for a grown man to be living with his mother."

"I assure you, Arthur, he doesn't like the situation any better than you do." She was even starting to talk fancy like him. Even though the white nurse's dress she ran around in all the time wasn't no different from the maiding uniforms almost every woman in Pine Woods wore. This New York City went to people's heads. He vowed to make sure it didn't go to his. He was Donny Tatro from Pine Woods, Tennessee, and he didn't aim to forget it.

But what she said wasn't true. Donny loved coming back to this apartment in the evening and having his mother serve him up a home-cooked meal. He had missed out on several years of this back home and felt like that he was making up for lost meals. What he didn't like was Arthur around all the time, eyeing him like he was a steaming turd. The only time Arthur had treated him halfway decent was once when Donny was sitting watching TV. Arthur walked over, squatted down, and studied his scar.

"White doctor do this?"

Donny nodded yes.

"Figures. Kathryn, come over here and look at this. Looks like he thought he was sewing up a rip in the knee of a pair of old blue jeans."

As Arthur knelt before him, talking to his mother and touching Donny's cheek with his fingertips, Donny felt a warm rush of affection. But it hadn't lasted long.

The first time Leon turned up at the apartment, in a chartreuse suit with his hair all wavy and piled up high on his head, Arthur looked at him the same way he always looked at Donny. Seemed like Arthur believed owning a Design Research couch made you the cat's ass. He'd of liked to tell Arthur that Leon owned *him* an El Dorado Cadillac car. But instead he and Leon got out of there quick as they could. "That cat's bad news," muttered Leon. They went to a pool hall and played some games of Eight Ball for old time's sake, then ate some ribs and slaw at the Chicken Coop, and ended up in a bar called Clyde's drinking Four Roses. Leon introduced him to people as "the farmer."

"So what's coming down with you and Rochelle, farmer?" Leon, his elbows on the table, was turning his glass round and round.

Donny sat back and crossed his legs. "Ah, she kicked my ass out."

"Kicked your ass out?" He laughed. "Out of your own place? That you was paying the rent on? Where does that bitch get off?"

"Well, she didn't exactly kick me out. We had us a bad fight. She cut me all up." He traced his scar with his fingertips.

"With a knife?"

"Naw, with a can opener."

Leon guffawed. "A can opener? Jesus Christ, farmer, you some kind of faggot, getting beat up by a woman?"

"Well, I messed her up pretty good too. But it ain't something I'm proud of."

"Ah hell, man, you got to knock them around some. Show em who's boss."

"Yeah, well, we know who's boss around our place. Her."

"Ah shit, that's the whole trouble, baby. All our lives they been bossing us around. 'Leon, you go out and earn you some wages, boy.'

'Now don't be ugly to the white folks, Leon. Do like they wants.' Should of taught us how to stand up for ourselves. But at least you still had balls enough to get out, man."

"Yeah, but I want to bring her and the kids up soon as I got us a place to live at."

Leon looked at him like he was mental.

Donny shrugged. "I love her, man."

"Love ain't got nothing to do with nothing, farmer. It don't put clothes on your back. It don't put you behind the wheel of no El Dorado car. It don't even keep a woman in your bed. Cause they want that stuff too. Love is cheap, farmer. Fur coats ain't."

"Well, that's why I'm up here—to get me some cash."

"Yeah well, you ain't gon cop no long green getting bored to death on no auto line. When you gon smarten up, farmer?"

"When are you, Leon? I like you, man. But I'm not like you, if you see what I'm saying. Never have been."

"Too bad for you, baby."

They got into his white El Dorado. Now and then he'd pull over to the curb, get out, and talk to some woman in a doorway. One he slapped several times. As Donny watched, he felt his guilt toward Rochelle let up a little. Another woman Leon patted on the ass and laughed with.

As they drove across 125th Street, Donny realized he really *wasn't* like Leon. It made him mad that Leon kept calling him farmer, but Leon was right. This street was jammed with dudes doing their hustle. Pimping and pushing and running numbers and fencing. They were mostly farmers too, or sons of farmers. They'd left the South, or got run out. Too mean or too itchy to stay put. The ones that stayed, like his grandmaw, were the "clever" ones who could of waited out an Ice Age. The ones who left thought niggers like his grandmaw were just plain backward. Well, Donny didn't want to do anything wrong or bad up here. He still loved the Lord and meant to do His works. He just wanted a job where they'd pay him enough to save up for a down payment on Rochelle's ranch house. The bunch in front of Dupree's congratulated themselves when he said he was leaving. But it wasn't like they thought. He was leaving so he could make it all up to Rochelle, not to get away from her. He loved that woman.

Monty put his hand over the phone. "Cowboy, you want to deliver Mrs. Marvin's Mercedes?"

"Who she?"

"That old girl in the dog fur coat."

"Where at?"

"Fifty-third and Third."

Donny thought it over.

"You might could get you a big tip come Christmas."

Donny didn't like to say he wouldn't be around at Christmas if he could get the Ford job. "I don't mind."

He pulled up in front of a large apartment building. Mrs. Marvin stood outside the glass doors talking to a doorman in a green uniform. As Donny handed her the keys, she slipped him a dollar.

After that, Mrs. Marvin would sometimes be upstairs. The doorman would take the keys and buzz her apartment. On those days Donny didn't get a tip, but other days she tipped double.

One afternoon the doorman called down the sidewalk after him, "She wants you to bring the keys up, boy."

Donny walked through the carpeted lobby, which had a fountain, and these chandelier jobs like in the houses on Tsali Street. The elevator was made out of polished wood. He walked down the carpeted hall to her door and rang the bell.

She opened it, took the keys, and handed him a ten dollar bill. He stared at it. He couldn't wait to tell Rochelle. This was more than he used to earn for a whole afternoon mowing lawns and clipping hedges for the Princes. All for driving a Mercedes car five blocks. Which he would of done for free. Or even paid to do.

"I owe you for the last several times," Mrs. Marvin explained in a deep voice.

"Thank you, ma'am."

"You're welcome, sir," she said with a mocking smile. "You want a Coke or a cup of coffee or something?"

His glance darted like a snake's tongue up and down the hall, and past her into a room with thick drapes and low sofas. "Thank you, ma'am, but I got to get back to the garage."

The keys fell. She and he looked down. He bent over, picked them up and laid them on her outstretched palm.

"Seems a shame to rush off."

"Yes, ma'am." He began backing down the hall.

"Wait a minute. I'll get you a Coke to take with you."

That night at Clyde's Leon said, "It sounds like you could of had you some white pussy this afternoon, farmer."

A long shiver went through Donny.

"Next time go for it, baby."

Donny shrugged.

"But you know, sometimes with a white woman it's like sliding into a hunk of ice."

"Uh huh." Donny looked down at his hands, unable to confess that he hadn't been in but one woman his whole life.

Leon laughed abruptly. "Ah shit, farmer, you don't know, do you?"

"Maybe I do." Donny glared.

"Honest to God, farmer, I swear I don't know why I stay up-tight with you. You so dumb you think Fucking is a city in China! Guess I must like to recall my origins."

"Yes, I guess you must." Donny's head was in an uproar. He kept picturing that dying oak tree in the school yard back home and feeling sick. One time some boys from Cherokee Shoals sneaked into the school yard with a doll they'd doused in brown liquid shoe polish. They put a noose around its neck and hanged it in the old oak, for the colored kids to find when they came out for recess. He reminded himself that New York City wasn't Pine Woods, Tennessee. People didn't do each other that way up here. But he was still Donny Tatro, and wasn't studying to go sleeping with no strange women of any color whatsoever, when he was trying to get back into his own wife's good graces. And into her hot wet pussy.

He felt alarmed. That was how Leon and the men in front of Dupree's talked about women. Donny never had. And certainly not about Rochelle. He'd better watch himself up here without his grandmaw and the congregation of Mount Zion to keep him in line. No telling what he might find himself doing.

That night he had to lie and listen to Arthur and his mother's bedsprings creaking and clattering through the wall like the assembly line at the Ford plant. He wrapped his pillow around his ears, but could still hear them. Finally he jerked off in time to the creaking, wondering if some cat was putting it to Rochelle under the willows by the river. There was Tadpole in his Green Beret disguise, with all his medals and shit, his wallet full of bills. And that whole gang in front of Dupree's in their fancy clothes, drinking all day. Donny had to get him some money, so he could get Rochelle up here and keep his eye on her. So he could get her her ranch house and make her glad again to be his woman. After all his years of trying to do right, he just didn't believe she'd hold his one slip-up against him forever.

When he told her he was leaving, he was glad to see a look of alarm in her eyes. She hid it right quick and shrugged like she didn't give a shit, but he'd seen it.

"I'll get me a good job and find us a ranch house to live in. Then you and Isaac and Nicole can come up, too." He felt bold telling her this instead of asking. But he could have sworn she was glad. Even though all she said was, "We just see."

When he got on the bus, she pressed her hips against his like she hadn't in a long long time.

"I don't want you running off with Tadpole, now," he tried to joke.

"I ain't running nowhere with nobody, Donny."

Late one night the chocolate Mercedes pulled into the garage. Donny was there with Hitler, Monty's German shepherd, who carried on something fierce. Out stepped this chubby white man in a coat with a little black velvet collar, and a shiny scarf with fringe. He opened the other door and out came Dog Fur, with these pearls around her neck and hanging from her ears. She smiled and said, "How are you tonight, Donny?"

"Just fine, thank you, ma'am." He was grinning and wondering how come she knew his name.

They walked up the driveway. Chubby put his arm around her shoulders. Donny got in the car. It smelled like Dog Fur. He'd dress Rochelle up like that once he was on at the Ford plant. A fur coat, and jewels in her ears. Fancy perfume. She could stay home all day fixing up the ranch house if she wanted to. He'd turn into their driveway in the evening in his Chrysler Imperial. The children would leave their color TV to climb up his legs and search his pockets for candy, like Rochelle's mother's kids used to before him and Rochelle got married, before he got too wore out to do anything but drag himself from one job to the next. But Rochelle would shoo them away and lead him into their own private bedroom and *lock the door.* . . .

On his next afternoon off, he went with Leon to see Leon's favorite woman, Flo. Flo had auburn hair done up in a bouffant. She wore a silver lamé mini-skirt and high red boots. As Flo and Leon went into her bedroom, Leon said to Flo's friend Sylvia, "Educate this farmer for me, Sylvia honey."

Sylvia's long legs were crossed, and she swung the top leg back and forth rapidly, her spike heel moving like a piston.

"I think you and me is spoze to be getting acquainted here," she announced in a husky voice.

Donny laughed. "All right, mama. Let's do it." He knew what to say. He just didn't know what to do. He stared at the new alligator shoes Leon had made him buy with some tip money he'd been fixing to send Rochelle. Knobs, Leon called them. Donny heard giggling in the bedroom.

"Where you from?" Donny asked.

Sylvia grimaced. Donny didn't see why. It was the most natural thing in the world to ask someone you didn't know. "I'm from up the street, sugar." She studied her long red fingernails.

"I'm from Tennessee."

"Well, I wouldn't brag about it if I was you."

Donny hadn't known he was bragging. He was just trying to get acquainted. How did people do that up here anyhow?

She got up abruptly and looked out the window, her hands on her hips. "Look, you want you some pussy or not?"

Donny's mouth fell open.

"Cause if you don't, honey, I got better things to do with my afternoon than setting around watching some farmer trying to get up his nerve."

"But I . . ."

She plopped down and began undoing his belt, murmuring, "I just know you got you a candy cane in there, farmer. And it's getting all hard and sticky."

She didn't give him a chance to say no. Which he assured Rochelle and the Lord that he would of done. But you couldn't insult a woman by rejecting her advances. And he didn't want Leon making any more fun of him than he already had. And yes, all right, after all those months of wanting Rochelle and getting turned down, it felt good pushing himself into a woman again. And feeling the long slow grind of her hips against his as she slid up and down on him murmuring things about her wet pussy sucking on his big hard candy cane. He'd never experienced anything like it. He and Rochelle used to have a pretty good time every now and then. But this was so *dirty*. He tried to deny to the congregation of Mount Zion, who inhabited his head, that he loved it. But shoot, if Rochelle didn't want him, looked like others did.

Afterward Leon and Donny sauntered down the street past a storefront that had been turned into an office. There was a poster in the window of this cat in a beret sitting with a rifle between his knees. Out front was a bunch of mean-looking motherfuckers with their hair kinking out like dandelions gone to seed.

"Man, ain't that nigger gorgeous with all that slick hair?" one cooed, nodding at Leon.

"Yeah, he outasight. I believe he almost as purty as George Wallace."

"Later for these dudes," Leon murmured, looking straight ahead.

"Who they?" Donny asked.

"Bunch of thugs off the block. Think they're badder than anybody else. I gon show them who's bad."

Down at the corner were some good-looking chicks. Leon started talking to one. Said in his line of work you never had no time off, you was always on the lookout for new merchandise. While Leon ran down all his virtues to this one chick, Donny stood around smiling, getting ignored, and feeling guilty toward Rochelle for having had such a good time with Sylvia, for having set up a date with her a couple of nights later.

The chick said in a loud voice, "Listen here, brother, I don't give nobody nothing who don't know the Ten-Point Platform. If you want to get next to me, you got to get hip to the revolutionary ideology."

"What you on about, woman?" Leon muttered, glancing uneasily up the street at those dudes, who were watching.

"What I'm saying, brother, is you don't get this in your bed, and you don't use it on the street. You talk about all the nice things you gon do for me. You want to do something nice, you do you some revolutionary work so our people can be free. Fascist pigs is murdering us every day, and you standing here blowing about smack and coke and pussy and Cadillac cars."

"Right on time, sister. Run it down," the woman next to Donny snarled.

Leon started backing down the street. "Well, you just suit yourself now."

"That's just exactly what I always do!" Her eyes flashed.

"Honey, I got women waiting in line . . ."

"Too bad for them."

Leon muttered as they walked away, trying their best to swagger, "Jive bitches. Putting out for them cats with the kinky hair."

Donny was starting to really supplement his income taking the Mercedes over to Dog Fur. Seemed like she couldn't hardly live without that car. She was on the phone asking for it all the time, day and night. Or else showing up at the garage with the fat husband. Donny took a real dislike to Old Chubby. All the time smiling and sucking on these unlit cigars. He'd flip half dollars, and Donny would have to run around catching them or picking them up. At least Dog Fur sometimes blushed when he did this. Donny didn't mind chasing after money, though. He needed it for taking Sylvia places. He and she, Leon and Flo, were spending a lot of time together at Clyde's and the Chicken Coop. Every now and then they went out to a fancy restaurant or club, but Leon knew Donny couldn't afford it and was tactful about not suggesting it often, and picking up the bill when he did. Donny felt guilty not sending his tips home, but he was sending a big chunk of his salary. He figured tips were extra. You earned them by being cheerful and quick, and being with Sylvia kept him that way. So he guessed it was right to spend them on her. Even if it wasn't right to be with her in the first place.

One evening Chubby called and asked Donny to bring over the car. As Donny drove on to the street, something evil came over him. He roared downtown a dozen blocks, shot over to Park Avenue, then crawled slowly back up to Fifty-third with the radio blaring. Chubby and Dog Fur were standing outside looking impatient. Donny switched off the radio right quick. As he climbed out, Chubby flipped him a half dollar. "Here, boy. Thanks. We're in a rush." Donny pocketed the coin, feeling good. He might drive that mother all over town, and old Chubby wouldn't never even know it. He chuckled.

In bed that night he felt ashamed. He'd always done what he was supposed to. And when he hadn't—like when he sneaked down to Dupree's, or when he beat up Rochelle, or now with Sylvia—at least he'd had the decency to feel bad about it. But he hadn't felt bad about driving Chubby's Mercedes downtown. He felt wonderful. What was happening to him up here in New York City? Was he becoming one of the godless Reverend Stump was always preaching about, who'd arrive in Pine Woods from the cities in big cars and fancy clothes, with no morals or decency left in them? He wondered, horrified at himself, if maybe being among the godless wasn't worth it.

Leon and Flo started having bad times. When the four of them went out together, they'd snap and bicker about dumb things. And Leon wasn't around much otherwise. He didn't say where he was spending his time, and Donny got the message not to ask. Donny supposed he had him a new woman, that he'd talk about her when he was ready.

In recent letters and phone calls Rochelle seemed to be warming up a little. She even started talking about missing Donny and wanting to move up there to be with him. Donny decided the thing with Sylvia had to stop. He couldn't keep track of his feelings for both of them. And if he saved his tips, he and Rochelle could be together that much sooner. He knew this decision was cruel. Sylvia had been good *to* him and *for* him. He hated to hurt her. But he had to. What he'd been doing was a sin, and once you knew that through and through, you had no choice but to repent and atone.

"I got a confession to make," he told her one night at Flo's apartment. "I'm a married man, Sylvia. Got me a wife and two children back in Tennessee."

She shrugged. "Sugar, we all married. Or have been."

"We are?"

"Shoot yeah, I got me three children."

"You do? Where at?"

"My grandmaw in South Carolina's raising them." Donny looked at her, feeling contempt stirring. What kind of a woman gave away her own children to somebody else to raise? His own mother, he realized. Still, this made it easier for him to say that he had to move on. It was Rochelle, struggling to raise their children, who deserved his support and devotion. Sylvia didn't need it.

She shrugged. "Well, bye bye, sugar."

He'd expected anger, tears, reproaches. "You don't mind?"

"Hell, no, honey. I was just doing Flo a favor for Leon. Now that Leon ain't around, it don't make no difference to either of us."

Donny stood up. What kind of a place was this New York City? These people were monsters.

"You gon give me one last gallop on that long black hobby horse, sugar?"

His penis sprang to attention, caressed by her filthy talk, which he delighted in. "I got to go."

She laughed. "Suit yourself, farmer."

He hobbled toward the door, then turned around, threw off his trousers and leaped on her, ashamed as she laughed and writhed underneath him.

The next time Leon stopped by Donny's mother's apartment, he'd quit conking his hair and was wearing a black leather jacket.

"Leon! What's happened to you, man?"

"Let's go get us some dinner and I'll tell you."

They walked down the steps. Donny looked around. "Where's your car at?"

"Sold it."

"You *sold* it?"

"Most of the brothers and sisters got to hoof it, so why not me?"

"What you mean? Your brother Jesse, he got him a '65 Fairlane. Ain't you seen it the last time you was home?"

"I don't mean Jesse, man. Brothers and sisters—that mean like all our people."

When someone in Pine Woods said "my people," he meant his relations. But seemed like Leon meant even people he wasn't kin to.

"See, man, all my fancy living, I was playing right into the hands of the man."

"Which man?"

"The white man, farmer."

"Which white man?"

"Whole motherfucking bunch." Leon looked irritated.

Donny couldn't believe his ears. He wondered if Leon knew about that good-looking cat on the TV a while back who called them "white devils" and got himself shot dead.

"Whitey had me where he wanted me. Course where he wanted me most was in a hole in the ground. But failing that, he had me committing slow suicide with my horse. Had me waging chemical warfare on my own people selling them the stuff. Had me hustling all the time for cash for my clothes and cars. But I don't need nothing he got no more, man. This is one slave that's set hisself free."

Donny couldn't figure out what he was blowing about. Colored people hadn't been slaves for a hundred years. This New York City definitely did weird things to people. Suddenly the light dawned. "That chick you was after, you get you a piece?"

"Brother, that chick laid some righteous facts on me. How pimping the sister on the block wasn't no different from slavery times, only it was the black brothers collecting the cash instead of Whitey."

"You get you a piece?"

"Shit, that ain't the point, farmer."

Donny wondered how come people was all the time preaching at him?

When Donny got home, Arthur looked up from his medical journal. "Have you heard yet about that Ford job, Donald?"

"Naw, I ain't."

"When do you suppose you will?"

"Dunno."

"Perhaps you should phone, or go out there and inquire."

"Say they get in touch."

"You can't just sit back and rely on other people's largess, Donald. You have to make your own way in this world."

"I reckon."

"I *know.* Do you think I'd be where I am today if I'd just sat back and waited for someone to send me to medical school? They wanted me to stay an orderly. *I had to make things happen.*"

"Yes sir." Donny just wished the cat could like him like he was. He was doing the best he could.

Arthur sighed and returned to his journal. Donny turned on "Sanford and Son."

Leon had started spending most of his time with the dandelion heads. Donny missed him and was glad one evening when Leon invited him to go along. When they walked into the office, the chicks were all typing and running off this newssheet on the mimeo machine. These three cats and Leon did a complicated Patty Cake routine Leon said later was the solidarity salute. Donny couldn't get the hang of it.

The men started putting on these bandoliers full of shotgun shells like the Cisco Kid used to wear on TV.

"I'm coming too," announced the chick Leon had been after, name of Lucille.

"Naw, you ain't," said a man named James, who wore horn-rimmed glasses.

Lucille picked up a rifle and headed for the door.

"I said stay here and get that motherfucking newspaper out!"

She stopped in midstep.

"Goddam, woman, I'm captain here!"

"You can call yourself captain, James honey. You can call yourself Donald Duck for all I care."

"*You ain't going!*"

"Now, be cool, baby," said a man in a beret, leading James to the door. "Ain't no need in you yelling at her."

A man named Phil with red hair and lots of freckles, who looked white to Donny, was standing around outside looking nervous. He moved over to the old Chrysler with the rest of them. James snarled, "What you all the time hanging round here for, white boy?"

"I told you, man. My maternal grandfather was black."

"Gwan. Get out of here."

"I just want to help."

"You was raised white. To the world you is white. The biggest help you can give us is to go back where you come from. Work with your own people, man. They our whole problem."

"Ah, come on, man. Give me a break."

The man in the beret said, "Hey, I'm driving."

"No, you ain't," insisted James. "I'm captain."

"Fuck it, man. It's my car."

They all got in, and the others set their rifles upright between their knees. As they rode around following patrol cars, Leon explained to Donny that they were keeping an eye on the police in case they got into any brutality on the block.

James was saying, "That Lucille, she just counterrevolutionary, what she is."

"You tried to get next to her, man, and she didn't dig you," said Beret, "so now you call her counterrevolutionary."

"She all the time telling everybody what to do. But shit, I'm the captain, man."

"Yeah, but she sharp, that Lucille. She smart."

"Hell, I ain't listening to no woman, don't care how smart."

They pulled up next to a cop car at a light. James muttered out the window, looking straight ahead and scarcely moving his lips, "Rotten fascist swine, low-life scurvy redneck bastards, bigoted racist sons of sharecroppers . . ."

The eyes of the cop who was driving narrowed and the muscles in his jaw twitched.

"Hey, don't do that, man," Donny whispered. Leon like to impaled him on his elbow.

As the car wove in and out of the blocks, they started comparing .357 Magnums and M-1's and shotguns with double O buckshot and 30.06's and 9mm pistols. Donny didn't have no opinions on the subject. The only thing he'd ever shot was mistletoe out of oak trees with The Five. For a minute he wondered what the others were up to. Rochelle heard from Sally that Raymond had gone to Kentucky. Emily was supposed to be up here somewheres. What part of town did she live in? Maybe somewhere near the parking garage.

James was saying, "Plastic's best, man. One and one-half inches will stop a 220-grain slug from a .45 submachine gun."

Beret, who'd been over at Nam, explained, "Yeah, you take a

brother with a flamethrower in an armored van. Another cat with an M-60 machine gun, and one with an antitank rocket launcher . . ."

Seemed like they'd gone plumb hysterical. Donny just couldn't see it. All that brother and sister and our people shit. Seemed like they most of them grew up here and didn't have the real thing, so they had to go out and fake it. But Donny had just come from Pine Woods, where he really was related to everybody. Or at least knew everything there was to know about them. Didn't feel no need to play these games. All that hate-whitey shit he didn't have no use for neither. He couldn't say he was crazy about most of them, but he couldn't see wasting his time hating them. Seemed like that these cats used the hate to get up tight with each other. The more they said Them, the easier it got to say Us.

Besides, a few white people had been pretty good to him. Like Dog Fur, who'd asked him to start calling her Deirdre and stop saying "ma'am." Like Mr. Prince at the mill. Like The Five in the Castle Tree.

After that, when Leon invited him to go down to the office, he usually had reasons why he couldn't. If that was what he had to put up with to be with Leon, he'd rather be alone. Leon started calling him Mr. Junior Church Usher again.

One night walking back to his mother's from the subway, he passed an alley. An old blind wino he'd seen stumbling around the streets with his white cane was sprawled in it. When Donny was halfway down the block, he looked back and saw a patrol car pull up. Two cops hopped out and walked into the alley. He heard some grunts and thumps. Crossing the street, Donny walked back toward the alley. Those laws had that wino on his feet and was throwing hands at him like he was a punching bag.

Donny wondered what that old guy had done. Looked to him like he'd been out cold, but he must not of been to provoke them like that. He felt bad for the old man, but it wasn't his business. The cops dropped him against the wall, kicked him a few times, and walked out of the alley and down the street, twirling their nightsticks.

When Donny wasn't working, he didn't have a lot to do, what with Leon playing army and Arthur wanting him out of the house. He'd shoot some pool, or go to Clyde's for a drink, and a few cats Leon had introduced him to might nod and say, "What's happening, farmer?" But he realized right away they didn't really want to hear. He had to admit he was lonely. He wasn't used to passing somebody on the street and not knowing them, not stopping to talk. In Pine Woods he was Donny Tatro, star forward class of '63, grandson of Ruby Tatro, first colored man on at Benson Mill, youngest deacon at Mount Zion, husband of Rochelle and father of Isaac and Nicole. Up here he wasn't nobody.

Seemed like Arthur and his mother took pity on him, for once: One Saturday night they invited him to go with them to a Ray Charles concert at the Apollo. Big shiny cars pulled up out front, and out stepped people dressed like he'd never seen colored people dressed before—except maybe the Supremes on television or something. Furs and jewels and slithery gowns, tuxedos and lacy shirts. Just like Chubby and Dog Fur. His own mother wore a fox stole with tiny shining eyes and paws. When he got on at the Ford plant, him and Rochelle would dress up like this and come in from New Jersey every now and then.

Ray was led to his piano in his tuxedo. His backup band in their glittering gold tuxes stood up as sections, threw back their heads, and blared out their parts. The Rayettes in long sequined gowns and straight-hair wigs danced complicated but perfectly coordinated routines, while singing the backup in close harmony.

As Ray began singing "Georgia on My Mind," the huge room became quiet. ". . . *Just an old sweet song keeps Georgia on my mind. / Other arms reach out for me, other lips smile temptingly. / Here in this peaceful dream I see her face come back to me . . .*"

"Yeah, sing it!" a man called.

Several people moaned as though in pain.

Donny started thinking about Pine Woods—the sun in the willows down by the river, bare feet slapping on sticky red clay. Donny felt like moaning himself, but managed not to. For Arthur's sake. Arthur wouldn't want no funky nigger of a stepson moaning in public.

But he hadn't been able to earn a living down there. A white doctor had stitched his cheek up all wrong. Jed Tatro and his friends drove through Pine Woods throwing bottles. Why was everybody moaning with homesickness, or wanting to? Damned if he could figure out why he felt tonight like a Hebrew in Egypt, driving cars around that pyramid downtown.

"Shit, how come we left, Mama?" he asked as they drove home.

"Pine Woods?"

"Yeah. Big old ugly place up here, full of hateful strangers."

"Honey, I know why I left. And I reckon you got your reasons, too. You just a little homesick right now. But you'll get over it."

The next morning he wandered around the streets trying to think what to do with himself. In Pine Woods Sunday had never been a problem—church in the morning, a big dinner, an afternoon of visiting, church in the evening. As he watched his alligator shoes moving along the grey pavement, he thought about how many hundreds of miles of sidewalk he'd covered up here, rarely the same section more than a few times. That sidewalk down the middle of Pine Woods, his feet knew it as well as his hands knew Rochelle's body—each dip and bump and crack. Every point at which your roller skate wheels switched from a humming rumble to a clatter. The new sections, decade after decade, which contained the initials of almost every child in town—many now middle-aged, like his own mother. You had to tame a sidewalk like a bronco, make it your own. Up here the only spot he really knew was the one in front of his chair at the parking garage, and he didn't know that very well. But it wasn't something you could just up and do. Took years of traveling down it and lounging around it, in every season, on every conveyance you could think of.

He passed a Baptist church. Arthur and his mother said they didn't want nothing to do with no church, that it'd been used to keep colored people—"black" people, they said—down for 300 years. But they weren't him, man, and he thought maybe he'd just go in, sing a few hymns, maybe not feel so bad.

A nice-looking man standing out front in a dark suit handed him a handbill that invited all "black Christians" to some temple that afternoon to hear about a "program for the Black Man which does not require you to love those who do not love you." Well, this got him curious to find out who this was. He went into the church and sang

"I'll Fly Away" and felt better thinking about his grandmaw and everybody probably singing the same thing right then in Mount Zion back home, fanning themselves with their programs.

From there he went to this temple, which was actually just an old empty store. In the vestibule these two huge cats in suits with little red buttons on their lapels frisked him, turned his pockets inside out. He wondered if he had the right place. Seemed more like jail than church. One ushered him into the packed room, which was ringed with more big men in dark suits.

A little old man with grey hair and glasses walked in, and the congregation whispered and shifted in their seats. He said something foreign-sounding, and they said something foreign back. Then he started in to preaching. Sometimes somebody yelled, "That's right!" But there wasn't any clapping or foot-stomping or singing or testifying. Every now and then dudes in dark suits marched up front and traded places with the ones already there. And these big brown grocery bags kept passing up and down the rows, getting fuller and fuller of money.

The preacher was scribbling on this blackboard and kept pointing to the mess he'd made like it was a sentence or something. But Donny couldn't read his writing. Maybe he was some kind of foreigner or something who didn't know how to write in English. The actual truth was, Donny couldn't figure out what was coming down here at this store they called a temple.

"Black princes were wearing silk robes and plotting the stars in Asia and Africa while white men, huddled in caves in Europe in animal skins, were ripping apart raw meat with their bare hands. You people know none of this because the white man has censored what you've been taught. You need to relearn history."

History was history, and the less Donny had to do with that shit, the better he liked it. The only C he ever got in high school was in World History.

"The slavemaster controls the economy and sees to it that the Black Man has difficulty finding a job. And when he finds one, it usually pays less than his wife can earn. The wife is lured into despising her husband and admiring the slavemaster, who sends her back home to her humiliated husband with blue-eyed babies."

Naw. Naw, he couldn't see it. Blaming your problems on someone else. If you worked hard and lived right, you'd get your reward. At least, *he* aimed to. He walked out while the women on one side and the men on the other embraced each other, exchanging greetings. Slavemaster. These people up here was crazy.

One evening in the Chicken Coop, he ran into Leon, sitting reading a newspaper over a plate of bones picked clean. Donny wouldn't of thought Leon could read, but up here in New York City surprises never ceased.

Leon stood up and tried to Patty Cake Donny. "Hey, farmer. What's happening, baby?"

Donny ordered him some chicken. Leon pointed to a picture on the front of the paper. "Man, that is one bad black beautiful nigger."

The cat was behind some bars. There was a chain around his waist, attached to handcuffs. He was glaring into the camera with one clenched fist raised as high as the chain would allow.

Leon sighed. "That dude is ten motherfuckers."

Donny chewed his chicken. "I don't see what's so beautiful about being in prison."

"That cat had the courage to put himself on the line, man."

"My daddy died in prison."

"All our fathers and brothers are dying in prisons all over this country."

"No other kin of *mine*, just my daddy."

Leon looked at him, irritated.

"Yall up here all the time talking slavery. Ain't provoking people into tossing you into jail just like selling yourself down the river?"

"You ain't got to provoke nobody, farmer. You got you a dark skin, they as soon toss you in jail as look at you. Rather would."

"If you live right and treats people good, they going to treat you good."

"Oh Jesus Christ, farmer, you just pathetic, is all." Leon stood up, shrugged on his black leather jacket, and walked out.

Donny ate his chicken wing, but felt like crying. To be up tight with Leon, seemed like he'd have to buy him a costume and learn a new bunch of words and talk a lot of junk. He wished there was somebody around could like him just the way he was.

He decided he'd go to bed early, maybe jerk off. But when he walked in the door, his mother shoved the want ads from the newspaper in his face.

"But I got me a job, Mama."

"It's a dead-end job, Donny. You got to get moving, child, if you gon make something of yourself up here."

"Mama," he said menacingly, "I'm waiting to hear on that Ford job."

She sat down, looking upset. "Honey, maybe you ought to start looking around for a place of your own, think about bringing up Rochelle and the children?"

First she runs off and leaves me, he thought. Now she runs me out. How bout that for a mother? It was that motherfucking Arthur.

The phone rang. It was Rochelle. She said her and the kids missed him, all like that. "When you gon send me some more money, sugar?"

"I'm sending you all I can, Rochelle."

"Honey, we supporting four children. Got us loans to pay off. I just ain't making it on my maiding money, Donny. Thought with you up there things might ease up some."

"Doing the best I can," he mumbled. "Still waiting on that Ford job."

"You reckon you'll get it?"

"Let you know. Who you seen lately?"

"Well, saw Charlene at the laundromat today. She's having her another baby. Uh, Tadpole's home on leave."

Donny's stomach clenched. "He all right?"

"He just fine." A long pause.

"Well, it's nice hearing your voice."

"Yeah, you too, honey."

As Donny stood at Deirdre's door handing her the Mercedes keys, she studied the scar down his cheek with concern. "Were you in a knife fight, Donny?"

Donny realized he didn't *have* to tell her he had a wife who'd cut him with a can opener. He could tell her anything and she'd never know the difference. Besides, seemed like she *wanted* him to have been in a knife fight.

"Tangled with some thugs on the block. Bunch of mean mother-fuckers."

As she winced, he glanced past her into the carpeted living room. She handed him a twenty dollar bill, which he looked at with surprise. "Use it for something special for yourself," she said in a husky voice.

As he walked back to the garage, he whistled. Deirdre didn't give a damn what his take-home was. Looked like she just liked him for himself. For a moment, he tried to imagine what it would be like to take her on her thick wall-to-wall carpet, hard fast jabs with her heaving like a bucking horse and clawing at his back with her long red nails. Then he felt bad. The woman was just being friendly, and here he was having evil ideas.

The next night, Chubby left off the Mercedes, flipping him a half dollar. Donny watched it arch in the air and fall on the concrete with a clunk. He let it lie there while Chubby glanced at him, surprised. He didn't need no half dollar from Chubby when Chubby's wife was slipping him twenty.

As Chubby walked up the driveway, Donny wondered if his rod stuck out far enough under that big belly to get it into Deirdre. She sure didn't seem like no hunk of ice. Then he was seized with remorse. It was sinful to think like that about her. More important, he was wronging Rochelle. Whether or not she was running around on him with Tadpole. But there couldn't be nothing wrong with being Deirdre's friend, stopping by to see her when he felt lonely, like she'd started urging him to do. He liked the idea of her as his friend, like Emily was when he was a kid.

The Ford plant called to say they weren't hiring at the moment. His mother got all hysterical and started telling him to do this, do that and the other.

"Just shut up, woman!"

Both were surprised when she did.

"All the time bossing me around. This is *my* life and I'll live it like I want."

"Not in my place that Arthur and I pay the rent on, you won't."

"You know what you can do with your place."

Her eyes opened wide. Was this her baby boy?

"I'm moving out quick as I can. Like living in a motherfucking prison."

His mother cocked her head. "First you tell me I deserted you and didn't give you enough guidance. Now you accuse me of giving too much. Now, which is it, baby boy? Make up your mind."

Donny stomped out, slamming the door.

When he came back for his stuff, Rochelle called, asking when they could buy the ranch house.

"Ain't gon be no motherfucking ranch house."

A long silence.

"I decide where we gon live. And when I tell you to come up here, woman, that's when you come."

She hung up right quick.

Donny ran into Leon at Clyde's. They got to drinking, and he told Leon about starting to get up tight with Deirdre.

Leon snorted. "Up tight, my ass, farmer. She wants her some black cock, is all."

"That ain't true."

"It's an insult, what it is. To Rochelle and your mama and your grandmaw, and to all the beautiful black sisters."

"Fuck it, man. Them bitches never done nothing but nag me to death."

Leon shook his bereted head. "I know where you coming from, farmer. But you got to do you a political analysis. Now, how come the sisters has nagged us to death? Whitey done put them up to it. . . ."

"Fuck it, man. I don't *have* to do nothing. You niggers up here is all nuts. Everybody white out to get you just because your skin is dark."

"You just wait, man."

One night when Chubby was out of town Donny went up to Deirdre's and drank a cup of coffee with her. She seemed nervous and plucked a couple of times at his shirt sleeve as he told her about wanting on at the Ford plant and all. When he said he had to go, she said, "So soon?"

As Donny walked through the lobby, the doorman gave him a look. The other day he'd tried to send Donny to the service entrance. He probably thought Donny was putting it to Deirdre and couldn't stand it. How come people was all the time thinking sex, sex, sex, up here?

He was walking down the sidewalk to the subway when a cop car pulled up. Two cops jumped out. Donny kept on walking.

"Hold it, son. It's you we're looking for."

Donny stopped and turned and stared at them.

"Me?"

"Now, don't act so surprised, boy."

"What can I do for you, sir?" He remembered his grandmaw saying good manners was the best life insurance a nigger could own.

"A woman was just raped two blocks over."

"Yes sir?"

"So what are you doing in this neighborhood?"

"I work here. In the parking garage at Second Avenue."

"Sure you do, buddy."

He looked at them for a minute. "I do, sir."

"Yeah, that's why you're racing along this street at one in the morning. Shift changes sure happen at funny times in parking garages, don't they, Al?"

"I got done at eleven. Then I visited with a friend."

They laughed. "What's a black boy doing with friends in this neighborhood?"

It occurred to Donny that he was in trouble. His eyes shifted all over the place. "Go over to the garage, sir. They'll tell you I works there."

"You telling me how to do my job, boy?"

"No sir." Donny wondered which would get him in worse trouble —not having an alibi, or having one that involved a white woman whose husband was out of town. The slow shiver crept up his spine.

"Let's see some identification."

He felt for his wallet. Wasn't there. "Guess I left it at the garage."

"Come on, son. Hop in the car here. We're going to the station."

"But man, I ain't done nothing." Donny was scared. He didn't want to go down to no jive police station.

"That's what you say. We'll see what the woman you raped has to say."

"I don't know nothing bout no rape." He looked up and down the deserted street.

"Are you getting in, or do we have to throw you in?" asked the cop, holding open the door. Donny eyed the guns on their hips and climbed in.

On the way downtown he tried to decide what he should have done. What would Leon have done? Run? Would they have shot him? Fight? Insist they go to Deirdre's so she could tell them he'd been with her?

What did he do now? On TV people got to call Perry Mason. He'd demand to call his mother. She'd get him a lawyer. Christ, how could he pay a lawyer? This was dumb. He hadn't done nothing to pay no lawyer for.

They locked him in a cell. "Sir, do I get to make me a phone call?" They walked away. "Hey, I know I get to make me a phone call!"

"Man, ain't no point in you yelling." A black man sat in the shadows on a cot at the rear of the cell.

"I get to make a phone call. I know my rights."

"Just stay cool. You be all right."

Later they came back and moved him to another cell. "May I please use the bathroom?" he called after a while.

No one came.

"Hey, I gon piss all over this motherfucking floor!"

A large man with a wart on his chin the size of a bullet came and unlocked the door. "You want to use the toilet?"

"Yes sir, I do. And then I want to make my phone call."

Donny started walking down the hall. The man planted a fist in his stomach. Donny doubled over. The man brought his locked fists down on the back of Donny's neck. He lay on the concrete.

"I don't like being ordered around, understand?" said the large shadow looming between Donny and the bulb hanging from the ceiling. The guard dragged Donny back to the cell and locked the door. Donny lay on the floor and found he'd wet his trousers.

For what must have been a day or two guards came and led Donny to a room with bright lights where men in shirt-sleeves asked questions, the same ones time after time.

"Why'd you do it?"

"I didn't do nothing."

"Where you from?"

"Tennessee."

"How long you been here?"

"A few months."

"Why'd you rape that woman? Answer me, boy."

"I didn't."

"How come you're not in the army?"

"I'm married with kids."

"Why'd you do it?"

"I didn't do nothing."

One time a Negro guard took him back to his cell, muttering, "Sick of all you down-home jive-ass niggers flocking up here and getting in trouble and giving the rest of us a bad name."

Back in his cell Donny told himself that his mother would find him when he didn't come home. Then he remembered he had his own place now. Well, Monty would miss him, call his mother. But the day after he got picked up was his day off. What a way to spend a day off.

Well, but he hadn't done nothing wrong. He didn't have to worry.

Bright lights. No sleep. Pukey food he couldn't eat. Shivering and sick to his stomach. Why'd you do it, boy? Before long, he couldn't remember what he had and hadn't done. Started to seem like they was asking him about Deirdre. Yes, I did it. I fucked that white woman. Or had he? Perry Mason. Oak trees. Naw sir, I don't know what you're talking about. Yes sir. No sir. Yes sir.

He was in a line-up just like on "Dragnet," blinded by bright lights. And the next thing he knew, he was standing on a street, blinking in bright sunshine, with no idea where he was. He wandered up the sidewalk looking for a street sign.

Donny was working late one night when the phone rang. Dog Fur said in her deep voice, "Hello there, Donny."

"Hello."

A long pause. "I was wondering if you'd bring my car by after you get off tonight."

He said nothing. He guessed he owed her some kind of explanation. But he didn't want to get close enough to give her one. Besides, Rochelle and the children were arriving in a few days and he was busy renting and fixing up an apartment.

"Why haven't you stopped by lately?"

"Been tied up."

"Well, why don't you stop by after you get off tonight?"

These white women didn't have no pride when it came to trying to get their pussies stuffed. "Yeah. See you later, Deirdre."

As he walked toward Deirdre's, he saw a white woman at the far end of the otherwise empty street. As she approached, he could see her giving him quick glances. When he got close enough, he could see terror all over her face. Suddenly she dashed across the street and ran down the opposite sidewalk. Donny felt an urge to chase her, tackle her, hurt her. If she thought she could escape if he really wanted to get her, she was dead wrong. Then he felt irritated. They saw a black face and they panicked. But he also felt pleasure. He had power over that white woman. She was terrified of him—not from anything he'd done to her, but from what she imagined he might do, based on the fact that his face was dark. His mere existence could impel her to switch sides of the street and race for home, not even venture out in the first place. Stupid fuckers, not to recognize Mr. Junior Church Usher.

"Oh, I *like* this jacket," Deirdre said, touching the black leather.

"Get away from me, woman," he snarled. He felt consumed with disgust looking at her eager ugly painted pink face, with her tiny little close-set piglet eyes.

She looked startled.

"I've missed seeing you, Donny."

"Yeah, I bet you have."

"But I *have*."

"How could you miss me, you white bitch, when you don't even know me?"

"I've been trying to get to know you, Donny," she insisted in an injured voice.

"Naw, you haven't, Deirdre. You don't know that I couldn't get it up for several months a while back. You don't know that my TV set got repossessed down in Tennessee. You don't know that I used to be a basketball star and a church deacon. All you know is that I got a long black cock between my legs. You honkies is sick. You see a black man and all you can think of is a good hard fuck. Well, they's a lot more to me than that!"

"But that's not true," Deirdre gasped as he stomped toward the door. "How can you say that?"

He made no reply.

"If that's what you think I've wanted from you, Donny, then you don't know me either!"

He slammed the door behind him.

Donny got up early to supervise at the breakfast program for the children before going to work. He'd started out a buck private in James's group but was now a corporal. As the little children ate their cornflakes in the store that had been turned into a community center, they glanced up at him and Lucille real shy-like. Like they was heroes or something. He felt proud to be doing his part toward raising up the children of the black community to be strong and courageous warriors.

He recalled the morning when he realized it was time to get his own family up here. Nicole and Isaac were down in Pine Woods looking up with respect at that old Tom, Reverend Stump. And at his "clever" grandmaw. They were good people, meant well and all, but was just plain backward. You didn't get nowhere with these white motherfuckers by asking politely year after year. They took good manners to mean you was weak, and could be exploited that much easier. He wanted Isaac looking up to Leon and to James, and to himself as he was now. He wanted Nicole copying Lucille.

He looked over at Lucille. That woman was something else. Hair kinking a foot out from her head, like those Africans he was all the time seeing in front of the parking garage, on their way to the United Nations to run their countries. Had a mouth on her like a machine gun. Didn't take no shit from nobody. But she could be tender, too, sitting in a child's chair telling those little children stories about Harriet Tubman and Nat Turner, Sojourner Truth and Brother Malcolm. Urging them to eat a good breakfast and do good at school so they could help in their people's struggle to be free. Leon was right. Lucille was a woman who left you no choice but to respect her. Made you look at all women different. He knew he had to get Rochelle up here right quick, expose her to Lucille and the other sisters, let them turn her head around, get her over this diddly thing she had about living in some motherfucking ranch house.

He had phoned Rochelle and told her to get ready, he'd send bus fare. She seemed thrilled and scared to death, both at once. He worried a little about bossing her around like that, but she seemed to like it when he did it over leaving Pine Woods himself. And she seemed to like it this time. Maybe it made her feel secure to know that he was in charge now.

"Where we gon live at?"

"I'm gon find us a place right quick."

"A house?"

"Can't afford no house."

"Well, make it a big place, Donny."

"Woman, you just get your ass up here. I'm the man. I'm running this show."

"Well, I declare," she laughed.

He met them at the Port Authority. She grabbed him and spun him around, while Isaac and Nicole tried to climb up his legs. He splurged on a taxi to take them uptown with all their junk.

Rochelle glanced around the small fifth-floor apartment doubtfully. "You fixed it up real nice, honey."

"It'll do. Where you live at ain't important."

"To who?"

He looked at her. "Rochelle, just shove it. Don't start in on me, woman. Ever again."

Stunned, she said nothing. That night in their new bed with the children asleep in the next room, they made love with the old fervor that Donny had thought was gone for good. They both cried a little, laughing in between the tears. Seemed like the pieces of his life was starting to fall into place.

But Rochelle didn't want to model herself on Lucille. She just wouldn't quit trying to straighten her hair. And when he asked her to go to meetings with him, she'd say, "Can't. Too tired."

"But I need you beside of me, Rochelle. To support me in the struggle."

"Honey, you gon have to struggle by yourself this evening cause I'm plumb wore out."

She called the group his "gang" and spent her spare time, when she wasn't clerking at Woolworth's or looking after the apartment, with his mama and Arthur. Seemed like her and his mama was thick as thieves now. Donny reckoned Rochelle spent a lot of time complaining about him because his mama was always lecturing him on letting other people do like they wanted. After she'd spent half her life telling *him* what to do.

Every morning it was a big deal to get Nicole and Isaac out the door to the breakfast program. "Wanna eat with Mama," Isaac would wail, while Rochelle watched ironically.

"Come on, you little bastard."

On the way to the center, a child holding each hand, he gave them instruction. "See those men?" He pointed down an alley to some ragged winos. "They're drunk. Do you know why they drink so much?"

Isaac was staring straight ahead, sucking two fingers. "Do you know why, Isaac?" Donny jerked at his hand. His grandmaw and his mama were hopeless. Even most people his own age were hopeless, like he was starting to think Rochelle was. They'd been raised up under oppression and took it for granted. But it'd be different with the children of the community. He was determined they'd grow up with a head start on understanding the plight of their brothers and sisters. Rather than in some fairy tale land where everybody but the witches was full of goodwill and justice. His children would face the realities of life for black people in this country, rather than scrambling around in some dumb tree with a bunch of spooks thinking you was something extra special.

He removed Isaac's fingers from his mouth. "Want to eat breakfast with Mama," he whined.

"Do you know why, Nicole?"

"Because the white man won't give them good jobs or money. So they're sad."

"That's right."

Pitiful Phil with his red hair and freckles and black grandfather was still hanging around the office, wanting to be useful. Brothers flicked switchblades in his face and called him a honky until they were blue in the face. He wouldn't be budged. They called him a leprous white pig and a blue-eyed devil and the son of a motherfucking slavemaster. He smiled and begged for errands.

Donny thought up a job for him. He invited Phil to his apartment. Phil was thrilled. Donny brought out Isaac. He pointed to Phil and said, "White man." He pinched a piece of Phil's forearm. "White."

"White," Isaac repeated, looking in Donny's eyes for approval. Tentatively Isaac touched Phil's arm. "White, Daddy."

"White man, Isaac." Donny jabbed his index finger at Phil's chest. "White man."

Donny nodded to Phil.

"You sure this is a good idea, man?" Phil asked, picking up the child.

"You all the time asking how can you help. I done told you. Now do it."

Phil held Isaac at arm's length and smiled at him. Isaac smiled back. Phil bounced him playfully. Isaac grinned. Phil tossed him gently in the air and caught him. Isaac giggled.

"White man," Donny repeated.

"White man!"

Phil suddenly tossed Isaac almost to the ceiling, letting his arms fall to his sides. Isaac crashed to the floor and began screaming.

"White man, Isaac!"

They stood over him while he shrieked. "Watch this, Isaac." He kept wailing. "Isaac, watch me, son." He looked up, hiccoughing with sobs. Donny drove his fist into Phil's mouth. He hadn't told Phil about this part of the deal.

"What you doing to that child?" Rochelle called. She raced in from the other room and swept Isaac into her arms, glaring at Donny.

"What you gone and done to him now, nigger?"

"I'm the man here, woman. I'm in charge of raising him up to be a warrior."

"You in charge of turning him into a crippled nutcase, is what you is, Donny Tatro. You ought to be shamed."

"Just keep talking, woman."

"Don't you threaten *me*, sugar. Everbody else may be scared of big bad Donny Tatro, but I know you from way back when. And don't you forget it."

"Seem like you don't know when to shut that hole in your face, woman."

"Honey, I don't know what's got into you. You getting uglier than any honky that ever was."

"Well, ain't that what the white folks wants from us? And, mama, you *know* I aims to serve em."

Donny pulled up in front of the Princes' yellow palace. Walking up the sidewalk were two white men—one in a suit, the other in overalls and a suit coat and work shoes—and three children. He got out and walked toward them, a child holding either hand.

This definitely wasn't his favorite thing to be doing. As he got closer, he realized the one in the suit wasn't no man. It was Emily Prince. Now, what was she supposed to be? And that was Raymond there in the overalls, looking like a farmer. Some kinda costume party going on here. The children—must of been Emily's and Raymond's—dressed up all fancy.

"Daddy, looky there at that big old house," Nicole whispered.

"Yeah." Donny was remembering crawling through the shoes in an upstairs closet playing Hide-and-Go-Seek on rainy afternoons, and thinking he'd never seen so many shoes in one place before in his whole life, except in a shoe store. Hiding in the pantry and eating everything in sight while he waited to be found. Hanging blankets over card tables in the den to make houses. Jed and Sally in one house, Raymond and Emily in another, and him in a third. They were going to get married so their children could be double-first cousins. And he was going to be like the uncle who came to visit.

And now Jed was dead? Didn't seem possible so much time had gone by. He felt a stab of pain.

He shook himself. Pack of ignorant kids with their self-deceiving games. Wouldn't never happen to his children. He hoped he could pick up that Christmas tree right quick and get on back to Pine Woods without having to talk a lot of "how are you" junk. Really he wished Rochelle hadn't been so dead set on coming down here for Christmas. He would of rather stayed in New York and gone to dinner with James and Leon and Lucille and them.

He realized he'd timed it bad. Maybe they was just back from church or the funeral parlor or somewheres. But would you go to a funeral looking like that? Hell, wasn't no telling what honkies might do.

# Chapter Four

═══════════

# Sally

Sally watched Creech Owl and his brothers lower Jed's coffin into the ground with cloth straps. Her and Jed's families and neighbors surrounded her. She imagined how she must look: so young and beautiful to be all alone with two children to raise. And where was the man she'd pledged herself to for life? Where was the father of her babies? Dead on the highway with another woman, with his best friend's wife.

She began weeping noisily. Raymond put one hand under her elbow, and the other arm around her shoulders. He was about as comforting as Li'l Abner, showing up at his own brother's funeral in dirty overalls. Mrs. Tatro joined her, sobbing against her husband's chest. Sally's parents clenched the muscles in their jaws and looked embarrassed. The whole Tatro clan took up the refrain, wailing vigorously.

Sally wasn't sure she'd ever speak to Mother Tatro again. When the Tatros arrived at her house after receiving the news, Mother Tatro hissed, "If you'd been giving my son what he needed, he wouldn't of been roaming the highways in the middle of the night!"

"Now Mother, just stop that!" barked Mr. Tatro.

Sally had begun sobbing. "I gave him my life. What more could I give him?"

Was there any truth to this horrible accusation, Sally wondered as his relatives wailed. Hadn't she devoted herself to Jed and their home and children?

As she regained control of herself, the Tatros began to quiet down, too. She discovered she could lead them in weeping for Jed just as she used to lead the crowds in cheering for him on the football field. So young and beautiful, and all alone. Where was her sweet Jed? She began weeping again, and so did they.

Emily was watching her with a look of irony. Now, whatever was that supposed to mean? Emily was a man-hater. You couldn't expect her to understand how it felt to lose the man you love. Emily thought all week she was being so helpful, but she always said the wrong thing, like agreeing when Sally moaned that Jed was nothing but a low-down bastard. Emily assumed they had all these bonds just because they were sisters. The truth was, they'd hardly seen each other in years. Sally didn't *want* to hear that Emily had separated from Justin and was now sleeping with several different women. What a time to pick to tell her something so disgusting. And then she'd acted as though Sally should be pleased she'd told her, saying, "I'm so glad we can finally be up front with each other after all these years, Sally." Sally had nodded vaguely, wondering what "up front" meant. It had something to do with telling people revolting things about yourself that they didn't want to know.

Mr. Marsh dumped a shovelful of dirt into the grave, talking about dust to dust. She remembered Jed asking her in high school when she wouldn't go all the way, "Who're you saving it for, Sally? The worms?" And now here he was, his huge muscled body he'd spent so much time building already beginning to decay. She couldn't believe the door wouldn't open tomorrow night, and in would clomp Jed, grumbling about who had done what horrible thing at the mill and opening the refrigerator for a beer. Couldn't imagine not having to mop up the bathroom floor after he left for work. Couldn't imagine reaching out in bed and being unable to wrap her arms around that big furry chest. She stopped crying and became still, as the reality of the situation began to seep through the hysteria she'd concocted in order not to face it.

Standing across the grave from her was Hank, looking white and haggard. Betty's funeral was tomorrow. Sally wasn't sure if she should go or not. Probably not. Hank was Jed's friend, but she wasn't Betty's. Hank had said to her at the funeral home, "When this is over with, let's you and me get together and talk it out." She'd agreed.

Maybe together they could figure out why their spouses had done this. But she doubted if knowing that would bring much solace.

She looked at Joey and Laura, who held Emily's hands. They looked baffled, kept asking, "When's Daddy coming home?"

The limousine dropped off Jed's parents at their house. Mr. Tatro said, "We be up at Tsali Street directly." Sally decided she was just about all cried out. Her father was patting her hand. He'd been wonderful, making all the arrangements, sorting out Jed's messy finances. But there wasn't much else he could do to comfort her. Jed and she had been dead to each other for such a long time that lowering him into the ground was just a formality.

She felt bad thinking that way. Just because they were washed up as a couple was no reason for him not to have gone on with a life of his own. He was probably right when he used to insist that she was stuck on herself. But he was pretty stuck on himself too. Really, it was about the only thing they'd had in common.

He'd been a big man during Raymond's strike, running around with his rifle. Almost happy, she'd of said. Especially compared to how he became later. But then Coach Clancy was found dead in the Whirlpool at the high school with his hands bound behind his back and a plastic bag tied over his head. For a long time they called it suicide. Then the Newland *News* did an exposé claiming he'd been rigging ball games for his entire career and had been murdered for failing to throw the state basketball championship that year. Jed took it hard, harder than you would have thought normal for a grown man. Started .frowning like a clenched fist all the time, till his forehead turned dark red with white frown lines.

"Coach Clancy couldn't of thrown games without you knowing it, could he, darling?" she'd asked one night at supper.

"Sure he could of. You call the wrong play, substitute the wrong player, call a time-out and break up your momentum. Hell, I remember times when I wondered what he was doing. But I thought he knew best, and was watching out for us all." He rubbed his jaw with his hand, which was trembling badly.

"But you played the best you knew how, honey."

"That ain't the point. You work hard, play fair, you try to do what's right. And you're nothing but a sucker. Other people is just using you for their own gain."

She tried to comfort him, but he wasn't finding her real comforting at that point because the whole town was laughing about her and Hank under the Chevy. Seemed like Jed was the only one who failed to see the humor. Said it would undermine his authority on the job. Maybe it would get back to her father and keep him from making Jed foreman. It wasn't right—his wife, the mother of his children, running around acting like Betty French in high school.

But Sally had stopped caring how he thought she should act. That afternoon in the empty stadium had been a turning point. She'd realized she had to get herself out of that house and develop some interests of her own before she started sneaking gin like Elvira on "Love for Life." She'd been trying to get from Jed as much attention as she'd gotten in high school from the whole town. It wasn't fair to him. But it wasn't fair to *her* to expect that she cease to exist just because she'd gone and gotten married too young.

So on registration night for adult education classes she went down to the high school to sign up for almost anything. At a table sat a large jolly woman who said her name was Bonnie. A row of dolls stood in front of her—all kinds of dolls, sea captains, Mexicans, cowboys, old ladies. Sally discovered their heads were made of apples, peeled and carved and dried to a leathery consistency. On a whim Sally wrote her name on that sheet. Now it seemed like Fate must have guided her hand. Bonnie looked so friendly, and apple carving was something Sally could do at home without having to use Jed's money on special equipment or supplies. She could make dolls for Laura and not have to feel guilty about taking time away from the kids. It would give her something to do while they played and she watched soap operas.

She also joined the Ladies' Auxiliary at the hospital as a Senior Candy Striper. She wore a pink and white striped jumper, white shirt, and white oxfords. Each week she got to pick a job in a new area. If she found something she especially liked, she could specialize. So far, she'd tried wheeling patients down to get X-rayed, being receptionist at the front desk, carrying meal trays in to patients, reading stories in the children's ward. She especially liked delivering flowers. Always made the patients so happy. She was close to earning her thirty-hour pin. In a few years she could be a Pink Lady and wear a pink smock and do even harder jobs like admitting patients at the emergency room, or comforting their families.

She started taking Joey and Laura to her or Jed's mother on her afternoon at the hospital. And Jed babysat on Tuesday nights when her applehead class met. "It ain't right, Sally," he'd mutter. "A mother ought to be with her children."

"Darling, I'm with them all day long."

"Except when you dump them on our mothers."

"They're the kids' *grandmothers*, honey. They're glad to have them."

"Then how come mine called while you was at that class last night and asked how come you couldn't take care of your own children yourself?"

"She *didn't?*" Her own personal opinion was that Jed was itching for trouble. The gossip about Coach Clancy, and about her and Hank, had died down. The statue of the Confederate soldier had been blown up and brought the strike to a halt. A reporter from the Newland *News* came by one night and informed Jed that Al Grimes claimed to have spotted him near the statue shortly before the explosion. Jed denied it.

"Why would Mr. Grimes have told them that?" Sally mused afterward.

"Don't know," said Jed, grinning.

But that gossip had died down, too. Jed had been promoted to foreman. The union was voted out. Raymond moved to Kentucky. Things got quiet and peaceful. Sally figured this was why Jed had to go arguing about babysitters. When she refused to argue back, though, he dropped it and started looking around at new-model cars. He haunted the auto lots. Every week he came home with a new deal—bigger trade-in on the Chevy, accessories thrown in free, no freight charge. He had huge stacks of racing magazines and consumer guides and manufacturers' literature by his Naugahyde La-Z-Boy Lounger in the living room. In the end he bought him a rose-colored T-Bird, just as he had wanted to ever since high school. He got a license plate that read "STUD," which embarrassed Sally to death whenever she rode with him, or had to think about him roaring through town to the mill. But he just laughed and said the reputation he had to maintain was partly her doing, what with the business with Hank under the Chevy. He began buying a new wardrobe to go with the car—colored and striped and checked shirts and bright ties to wear under his coveralls.

She meanwhile was just beginning to identify the possibilities all around her. Looking back, she realized that in the stadium that afternoon she'd recognized who she was, and she'd accepted it: She was no longer a teenage beauty queen, she was a wife and mother, a homemaker. The real challenge was to take this reality and do something useful and interesting with it. The house and children defined her and confined her only insofar as she allowed them to. She could use them instead as a framework around which to build a satisfying new identity all her own.

Her bottled-up creativity was now just pouring out. Instead of singing the boring old lullabies everybody knew to Joey and Laura, she began composing her own. As she sang, she'd imagine she was holding a microphone. One night she was belting out, *"Hush, hush my little larvae, / Cause dreamland can't be far be- / hind those tired little eyelids . . ."*

Laura rubbed her fists in her eyes and wailed, "Can't sleep. Mommy sings too loud."

"Hush, darling, Mommy's composing." She was trying to decide what picture she wanted on the album cover of "Mother Sally Tatro's Bedtime Ballads."

As she was carving the head of a geisha girl doll from a Red Delicious apple for her term project, she grasped the fact that the course was almost over. It would leave a big void. She could go on carving apples on her own, true. But she'd miss the contact with Bonnie and the other women. Jed just wouldn't give her any support for her appleheads. When he found the heads for her Cherokee Indian tribe hanging to dry from pipe cleaners over the furnace in the cellar, he threw them out. She cried for a week. "Shit, woman," he muttered. "Just a bunch of moldy old rotten apples." He had no idea how much time had gone into carving and pinching them into shape. Three of the four weeks required for them to dry had been up. He wouldn't even try to understand why his throwing them out made her so upset.

Bonnie had talked about setting up an Advanced Applehead-Carving course, but the Adult Education people felt that one applehead course was enough. Sally could take the beginning course over again, but that would be just marking time when she should really be moving on to more complicated techniques. She didn't know what to do. She popped the piece of apple she'd just cut to form the temple and cheek into her mouth.

Jed walked in as she was coring the geisha girl's head and packing the hole with salt. "Ah shit, Sally, I reckon supper's gonna be late again tonight?"

Sally looked up as she brushed the applehead with lemon juice and salt. "I'm sorry, honey. This is real important. It's my term project."

He stomped into the bedroom and began throwing his clothes around the room. Then he turned on the TV and lay back in his La-Z-Boy Lounger.

As Sally stood over the sink cutting up peaches and cantaloupe for a fruit salad, she thought some more about what to do once the course ended. The girls in the class had become very friendly with each other and with Bonnie. Seemed a shame never to see them again, never to exchange ideas on common problems, such as what kind of paring knife to use so as not to discolor your appleheads. As she pondered this, holding a half-peeled peach and a knife over the sink, her eyes fixed on the seeds and pits that lay in the Dispose-All hole. Seemed such a waste just to wash them into the sewer. All of a sudden, wind seemed to rush around her ears. A bright light blinded her. In a flash she realized those pits and seeds were as potentially valuable as Red Delicious apples. Why couldn't you clean and shellac and string the peach pits to make bead curtains for windows and doorways? Why not turn the cantaloupe seeds into bracelets and necklaces and earrings? She glanced frantically around the kitchen. Possibilities were being revealed to her at such a pace that she only hoped she could remember them all when she returned to her normal everyday self. Aluminum foil. It could be crumpled and pinched into silver roses.

"Jed honey," she announced at supper, "I just realized you could cut up one of those plastic trays you buy meat in to look like a peacock. Make a tail with those cups from an egg carton. Glue it all to a piece of black velvet."

"Huh?"

She sighed. "It'd be *beautiful*, honey. Don't you think?"

Jed kept chewing.

She looked at him. "You just don't care, do you, Jed?"

"About what?"

"As long as your meals are on the table."

"Care about what?"

"As long as there are clean socks in your drawer."

Jed shrugged.

"There. See?" She imitated his shrug. "I could be murdering babies, and you'd never know or care as long as there's enough beer in the refrigerator when you get home."

"Damn it, Sally, what are you talking about?"

"Oh, just never mind." She knew what she had to do. Jed might regard her as nothing more than a convenience, a household appliance, but she knew she had other potential.

At her next class she told the girls about her vision at the sink. "Every day we homemakers are just surrounded by raw materials, if only we could train ourselves to view familiar things creatively." She proposed that the class meet in each other's homes after the term ended, to share ideas on applehead carving, but also to branch out into other materials. Everyone agreed enthusiastically.

Jed was disgusted. "I don't want my wife setting around stringing no seeds."

"But if it's fun for me, why should you mind?"

"It's dumb, is why."

"It's *not* dumb, Jed. It's creative." She began crying. "*Please*, honey. It's real important to me."

"Ah hell, stop crying, Sally. Shit, go ahead and string some goddam seeds then. But don't come telling me about it."

"That's why I need this group, honey." Privately she thought that if Jed couldn't meet her needs, she'd just have to look elsewhere.

"Shit, you don't *need* to string no seeds, Sally."

"Jed, I need something besides you and the children."

"Why? What's wrong with us?" He jutted out his chin.

"Nothing, darling. But I got to have something all my own."

"Shit, your underwear pants is all your own. You got plenty that's all your own."

Each week was more exciting than the last, as one of the girls came in with some object they'd always tossed thoughtlessly into the garbage transformed into something else. Tin cans turned into doll house furniture. Eggshells turned into miniature bird feeders. Things Sally had always taken for granted leaped out at her, shimmering with new meanings.

She walked in the kitchen door one night following a meeting at Bonnie's house where Loretta had shown them how to make brooches from diaper pins. She knew her face must be glowing with excitement. Jed sat in his La-Z-Boy Lounger, the rug around it stacked with empty Budweiser cans. He looked up. "What're you so fucking happy about?"

She slipped back her coat to show him the brooch. "Made from diaper pins," she announced with a triumphant smile.

"Looks like it."

She looked at it. "You don't like it?"

"I don't give a shit about it one way or the other. But I *do* give a shit about getting stuck babysitting all the time."

"One night a week?" Apparently he didn't have enough arguments to keep him occupied at work.

"Do I ever ask you to sit here all alone at night?"

"Sometimes. Like during the strike."

"That's different. That was important."

"But so is this."

"Making junk from diaper pins is as important as keeping the Free World safe from Communism?"

"Listen, honey, maybe we should each have one night a week out. You could join a bowling league or something."

"Don't wanna join no goddam bowling league. Wanna come home to my wife and kids after working all day to keep them fed and clothed."

As he grumbled, she was looking absently at the beer cans by his lounger. Suddenly they took on a new life. Jed was feeling left out by her projects. Well, she'd include him then, make him a gift from his empty six-pack for his upcoming birthday! Jed joined a bowling league that met every Thursday night. The next Thursday he rushed through supper, then ran out the door to his T-Bird, glaring at her. "Just remember: This is what *you* wanted, Sally."

She waited until the T-Bird turned the corner before bringing out his birthday present to work on—a hat made of flattened beer cans, crocheted together with yarn through a row of holes along their edges. She knew once he opened it, he'd feel all right about her meetings. He hadn't yet been able to see how her projects could enrich his life, but he would.

The phone kept ringing. The Scheduling Chairman for the Candy Stripers was on vacation, and Sally was filling in. She'd recently earned her silver 100-hour pin and was now working toward her first gold 500-hour star. She kept having to put down her crochet hook to write down the hours and jobs the girls were requesting. As she wrote, she looked at Joey and Laura sitting two feet from the TV eating potato chips and watching "Charlie's Angels." It was past their bedtime, and that wasn't a good program for children, according to the PTA list. Some nights lately they hadn't had baths or a story. As guilt threatened to engulf her, she told herself that it was better for children to have an active happy neglectful mother than a bored depressed attentive one. If she turned all her energy onto them, they'd be suffocated. She'd supervise each detail of both their lives so ferociously that they'd be swamped. She remembered watching Joey get on that big yellow bus to kindergarten. She'd been seized with panic. How would he find the boys' room without her? He wouldn't. He'd wet his pants. The other children would make fun of him and exclude him.

In fact, he'd gotten along just fine that day and every day since. And Laura was getting along fine too at her nursery school two mornings a week. As Sally now saw it, the only good nest was an empty nest. Surely this was progress for her?

When Jed marched back into the house that night, he stumbled over Joey's howitzer. He looked around the living room. "Jesus, Sally, this place is turning into a junk heap."

She said nothing. He must have bowled poorly.

"I mean, hell, I don't mind you having no hobby. But I can't see getting so busy at it that the whole house goes to pot."

"Ever since Rochelle went to New York, I've had a hard time keeping up."

"I just don't understand why it's so tough to keep a house this small clean."

"You were the one who insisted that Rochelle come in the first place."

"Yeah, but for the hard stuff, like washing windows."

Sally thought this over. It was true that things were getting a little sloppy. Often she failed to curl her hair or put on her face before Jed got home. Sometimes the kids wore unironed clothes to school. Toys were scattered all over the house. "I guess you're right, honey. But I am trying to find me another girl to come clean."

"I don't see why I have to pay out good money to some no-count nigger when my own wife is here all day long with nothing to do. Why, the kids are even in school now." He paused. "Am I right?"

She didn't reply.

"Am I right?"

"I guess."

"Damn right I am."

As she opened her legs in bed so he could push himself into her, she realized she had to earn some money. If she had money, she could hire twenty cleaning ladies and half a dozen babysitters—so she could work on her projects as much as she wanted. Her father would probably give her the money he'd put away for her if she asked him. But that would humiliate Jed. Besides, if her projects earned money, Jed would have to regard them with more respect. There had to be some way to do this.

As Jed jabbed harder, she moaned and breathed heavily, as he'd decided he liked her to do—and thought about egg cartons. The girls had already figured out how to cut them into lilies and dahlias, and Sally thought carnations should be possible too. So far they'd confined themselves to the white cartons, but you could get pink ones too, and turquoise and yellow. She considered different angles for cutting the egg cups. As Jed jerked and came, she visualized a way she was pretty sure would work. With impatience she waited for Jed to roll off her and fall asleep so she could sneak into the kitchen and try it out.

"Was that OK for you?" he asked.

"Just fantastic, honey. You're such a wonderful lover."

He grunted and turned his back.

As she stood at the kitchen table in her nightgown snipping egg cups into a perfect carnation, she decided all these skills should be written down in one place, like the recipe collections church guilds were always doing. That way more girls could share the skills, and the skills wouldn't be forgotten. Each girl in the group could write up her own ideas. They could get the collection printed up and maybe sell a few copies to people around town, split up any profits toward babysitting expenses and supplies. This might impress Jed, both the money and also her name on a real book.

The girls elected Sally Book Chairman. Each wrote up her ideas and did rough sketches. Sally typed them up and asked her father if she could have some of the money he'd put away to hire an artist to render the sketches, and to have the volume printed up in a spiral binding. After some hesitation he agreed, saying, "Well, if you're sure this is how you want to spend your inheritance, Sally." They spent several meetings discussing the title. *From Trash to Triumph. Your Triumphant Trash. Your Glorious Garbage. From Garbage to Glory.* They settled on *Turn Your Trash into Treasures.* And for the cover one of their husbands took a picture of them all sitting around a table carving appleheads. They placed copies in local bookstores and hobby shops. Sally had the inspiration of mailing review copies to radio and TV stations, to magazines and newspapers in the region. To their delight, a few reviews drifted in. The local radio station interviewed Bonnie about her applehead-carving course.

And then one day came a letter from a magazine in Nashville that had a book-publishing branch. Would they consider licensing a mass market paperback edition to be distributed throughout the region? There would be an advance of $3,000 and a royalty of 7 percent on a cover price of $1.95. After Sally read them the letter, they sat in stunned silence. "Ladies," Bonnie announced, "I think we're on to something big."

Jed was getting more and more difficult. For his birthday he asked for tight leather driving gloves. When he opened the beer can hat, he stared at it. "Don't look like no driving gloves to me."

"I made it, honey."

"I can see that."

Sally wondered whether to burst into tears. Then, for the first time ever, she thought, Well, just pooh on him. Other people loved the beer can hats. She was getting comments from people around town who'd read the collection, made the hats and were just thrilled to death. If Jed didn't like it, that was just too bad, wasn't it?

Jed announced he was going to buy himself a boat for his birthday.

"But honey, I don't much like boats."

"Well, I don't like dolls made out of no apples neither. Ain't no reason we have to do everthing together all the time. Said so yourself. So on weekends sometimes I'll go out in the boat, and you can just set at home and carve your goddam apples."

"But apples don't cost a lot of money, darling."

"Hell, it's *my* money, ain't it?"

Sally looked at him. Always in the past Jed's earnings had been "their" money. They'd decided together how to spend it. "Then maybe I'll just spend my book royalties on a trip to the Bahamas."

He laughed. "Your money from that book ain't gonna get you to Knoxville and back."

She said nothing. She'd show him!

A woman who ran a talk show on the local TV station phoned Sally and invited someone from the group to appear on the show. Sally thought about having the group elect someone. But after all, she was the chairman. And Bonnie had already been interviewed on the radio. So she accepted for herself. She spent the rest of the week deciding to wear her lime green polyester pants suit, and a choker of shellacked cantaloupe seeds. At the last minute she pinned an egg carton carnation in her hair.

On the show the hostess said, "We're just so pleased to have here with us this afternoon as our Guest Artist a local girl who's making quite a name for herself in the craft field—Newland's own Sally

Tatro. And here to discuss her art with Sally is Associate Professor Dorothy Anderson, who teaches courses in art and women's studies at Volunteer State University. Sally, to get things started, could you please say a few words about how you came to be involved in the craft field?"

Sally told about the applehead-carving class, and about realizing that a wealth of materials lay unrecognized under her very own nose. As she talked, her fear left her. Words seemed just to flow from her mouth, as they had during the question-and-answer portion of the Miss Newland contest. She told about her group and the torrent of ideas generated by it, about the compiling of the book.

The professor talked about the rich tradition to which Sally and her group were heirs: "Throughout history women have taken their household equipment and turned them into works of beauty. We think of the pottery and basketry down through the ages, wooden bowls and implements. Women were never content to produce them simply for utility. And when you have something designed for grace and beauty, as well as for function, you have Art."

Sally had never before thought of what she was doing as Art, or of herself as an Artist. But as she left the studio that afternoon she thought to herself, Well, why not?

She was such a success that Mr. Hitchcock, the station manager, a tall dark man with sad eyes like a basset hound's, asked her to do a half-hour program one morning a week. She asked members of the group to appear as Guest Artists to talk about and demonstrate their ideas.

Meanwhile, the paperback had been published. Sally began getting several letters each week: "Dear Sally, You look like such a nice woman on the TV and on the cover of your book. I've always meant to write a book myself, but *I've* never had the time. I just found out my husband is having an affair with the paperboy. What should I do? I raise white rats for laboratories and would like to send you one in appreciation for all the pleasure knowing you has given me." Sally took her responsibilities to her readers very seriously. She knew what it was like to feel trapped by your life and helpless to change it. But she herself was a living example that it was possible to prevail over your circumstances. She'd write back, "Dear Mona, Thank you so much for your nice letter. I'm glad you enjoy my book and show. About your husband, why not cancel your newspaper subscription? Please do not send me a white rat, as I have no place to keep one."

Every now and then there was a nasty letter from some sickie saying he wanted to lick her pussy, or carve up her pretty face like an applehead, but she always threw those away and forgot about them quick as she could.

Soon answering her fan mail was taking up a lot of time, so she had a skeleton letter printed up, on which she could fill in the blanks and cross out inapplicable words:

Dear _____,
    Thank you so much for your _____. I'm glad/sorry you _____ my show/book, and I really appreciate your letting me know. Please do not send a _____.

These were printed on her own letterhead, with SALLY TATRO in bright green letters an inch high. She also enclosed an autographed copy of the photo from the book jacket.

She'd been made Scheduling Chairman of the Candy Stripers by now. The demands on her time were so great she thought about quitting, but she decided it was important to *make* time for Candy Striping because it was volunteer work for the community and shouldn't be sacrificed just because her other activities were bringing in money. Besides, she liked it to be known that Sally Tatro was still just a plain old ordinary person, in spite of all her achievements. She'd whisk into a patient's room carrying a floral arrangement, and the patient's mouth would fall open: "Ain't I seen you on the TV this morning? *Naw*, you ain't Sally Tatro? Shoot, wait'll I tell Opal!" She liked bringing such pleasure into diseased lives. Sometimes she'd autograph their casts.

Her Nashville publisher had told her to call him collect when she needed to. Whenever she gave her name to the operator, the operator would say, "Sally Tatro? The Authoress?"

Sally would laugh modestly. "Yup, that's me, all right."

A broker phoned her from downtown to try to sell her shares in an offshore oil rig in the Gulf of Mexico. "Why, someone with the money Sally Tatro must be raking in needs her a good tax shelter. Why don't you talk to your husband about it?" Sally was so flattered to have it widely known that she was making money that she said she would, although she knew Jed knew nothing more about tax shelters then she did.

At Kroger's now when she wrote a check, the check-out girl would stammer, "I declare, *the* Sally Tatro?"

Sally would give a self-effacing laugh. "No, honey, the other one!" And as she walked out the door beside the bag boy, she could hear the check-out girls whispering and feel their eyes on her back. She liked it to be known that it hadn't gone to her head, all her fame. That she still did all her own shopping. Except when she was overwhelmed with work and Jed had to do it.

In fact she finally became so overwhelmed that she had to hire a full-time babysitter who also cooked suppers, and a cleaning lady. The little house was getting so crowded that one night she suggested to Jed they start looking for a new ranch house in one of the developments across the river, maybe one with white columns out front.

"But we ain't paid this one off yet," Jed protested. "I got to make payments on the T-Bird and the inboard. Can't afford no bigger mortgage."

"I can," she pointed out. The book contract was in her name, so she was earning all the royalties plus the fee from the TV show every week. Once or twice she wondered if she shouldn't split up the money with Bonnie and the other girls, but the initial idea had been hers, and the money to get the collection printed up had been her daddy's. So it looked to her like she deserved the profits.

"Well, why don't *you* go live across the river then?"

Why was he looking at her like that? She could have sworn there was malice in his eyes.

A reporter from the Newland *News* came to interview her for a piece on "Sally Tatro at Home." She'd given her babysitter and cleaning lady the day off, was wearing an apron made from country ham bags and was peeling Laura a banana when he and a photographer arrived.

"That's perfect," said the photographer, bending his trunk at a right angle to his legs and snapping several pictures of Sally smilingly handing Laura the banana.

"I don't *want* a nana!" shrieked Laura, shoving it in Sally's face. Sally had to pat Laura on the head to stop herself from clobbering the kid for messing up her makeup. Laughing weakly, she dabbed at the mashed banana on her face with a sponge.

In response to the reporter's questions, Sally gave a tour of her kitchen, describing her realization that untapped treasures lay hidden in her garbage can. She told about how she used to feel victimized by her appliances, as though their glass doors were eyes that mocked her for her lack of accomplishment. But that she had learned to make friends with her appliances once she realized they could be her accomplices. For instance, appleheads required four weeks to dry over the furnace in the cellar, but just thirty hours in her Amana self-cleaning oven.

They sat down in the living room. The reporter asked her what she thought of the sewage bond issue.

"Well . . ." Sally hadn't actually known there was such a thing. But the reporter was gazing at her with such respect. Clearly, she *should* know about such things. And her opinion, after all, was as valid as the next person's. That was what democracy was all about. More valid maybe, because she'd been around a lot, was on TV every week, had written a book that was being read all around the area. ". . . yes, I think sewers are a real good idea."

She dropped Laura at her mother's and raced to the TV station to tape that week's show. Bonnie, the Guest Artist, showed how to make a measuring tape dispenser from a walnut shell. Afterward Bonnie said, "We been missing you at meetings, Sally."

"Oh Bonnie, I've just been *frantic!*"

"I've noticed," drawled Bonnie. "Made anything lately?"

Sally wouldn't say so, but she had much more interesting fish to fry now. "Haven't had time to make a thing in months."

"You don't think you're throwing the baby out with the bathwater?"

"What?" Bonnie walked away. Now, whatever was that supposed to mean? All Sally could think of was that Bonnie was jealous. The others had been acting funny too whenever she saw them around town. She guessed she'd better get herself to a meeting pretty soon and find out what was going on.

Mr. Hitchcock came up. "Just wanted you to know, Sally, that I think you're doing a real fine job. I'm getting lots of mail from viewers saying how much they like your show."

"Why, thank you, sir!" She beamed. She liked Mr. Hitchcock. It was important that he like the show. He could cancel it at any moment.

"Might write you a fan letter myself one of these days." His basset hound eyes gazed into hers for a few seconds too many, and Sally felt a little tingle shoot through her body. Now, just what did the naughty man mean by that?

As she sat under the dryer at the beauty shop later that afternoon, she read an article in *Cosmopolitan* called "How to Sleep Around Without Feeling Promiscuous." The idea of cheating on Jed had never seriously occurred to her until this afternoon. Mr. Hitchcock was so exciting running that TV station and deciding on all the programming. She really liked the idea of him needing something from her. She pictured him kneeling naked over her with a big old erection, and her trying to decide whether or not he could put it in her. While he begged and pleaded and offered her a daily show for life. And Jed . . . well, poor old Jed was just such a sad sack these days. Always moaning about her not having time for him and the kids anymore. And the more he moaned, the farther away from him she wanted to be.

The article said, ". . . a healthy self-respect for one's needs is essential to the sound functioning of the total personality." Well, she needed someone who appreciated what she was doing. And let's face it, Jed didn't now, and never had. Mr. Hitchcock, on the other hand . . .

She glanced up at the Castle Tree as she drove home. Seemed to her like she was the only one of The Five who'd actually gone right ahead and fulfilled the dreams they'd all had for themselves in its branches. Raymond was running around barefoot in Kentucky. Emily had gotten herself to New York City, but, big deal, that was about all she could say for herself. An ordinary job, an ordinary child, a repulsive husband. Donny was parking cars up there. And Jed—well, just poor old Jed, was all she could say.

As she drove up to the house, Jed and the kids and half a dozen women in suits and flowered hats stood outside. A Torino sat by the curb. Jed was wearing his beer can hat for the first time ever. He and the kids had apparently just returned from a boat ride.

". . . now are *you* Sally Tatro's husband?" a woman was demanding. Another was snapping his picture. The cat stalked across the yard. A woman shrieked, "Look! There's her cat!" They all grabbed their cameras and began snapping. The cat froze, then bolted into the shrubbery.

Sally parked the Dodge in the driveway and got out. A woman screamed, "There she is! It's Sally Tatro!" Sally chatted with them while Jed and the kids went in the house. They'd driven up from Chattanooga in hopes of catching a glimpse of her. They asked for her autograph, but had left their copies of her book at the motel, so she autographed their forearms.

Jed lay in his La-Z-Boy Lounger with his eyes closed. Sally had forgotten she'd given the babysitter the day off, so there was no supper. As she pulled TV dinners from the freezer, she heard Jed on the phone: "Yeah, well, just be on the alert, in case you get a call, OK?"

"Who was that, honey?"

"The cops."

"The *cops*?"

"Yeah, I don't want a bunch of nuts hanging around my house, see?"

"Those weren't nuts, Jed. They were fans."

"Nuts, fans, who can tell the difference?"

"I don't want any police harassing my fans."

"Today they were fans. Tomorrow it might be some lunatic wanting to kill you."

"Why would anyone want to kill me?"

"Don't be a jerk, Sally. Lunatics always want to kill stars. I told the neighbors to call the cops if they see anyone prowling around the house."

"Don't you think you're being a little melodramatic? It's not like I'm Bobby Kennedy or something." She was annoyed at being called a jerk. Thousands of people around the area thought otherwise.

"It ain't right, Sally. It's getting all out of hand."

"Nonsense! It's just beginning."

"All I wanted was a wife, not some goddam celebrity."

"I thought it was *me* you wanted," she snapped.

"You like you was. Not you like you is."

"When you take someone on, you take your chances." She was through apologizing for being herself. To her amazement, he said nothing else. He gave up so easily these days. If she was different, well, so was he.

That night in bed it occurred to her that she didn't have to open her legs to him if she didn't want to, which she didn't. "I'm too tired," she announced.

"You *what?*"

"Tired. I'm tired." She felt panic. If she didn't do exactly as he wished, what would happen? She held her breath.

Nothing happened. He turned over, wrapped his arms around himself and fell asleep.

The headline in the women's section of the *News* was "Sally Tatro, Authoress, Artist, and TV Star, Favors Sewage Bond." Jed glanced at it and threw it in the garbage. After he left and after she retrieved the *News*, she found a copy of *Modern Wife* lying on the dinner table open to an article called "100 Ways to Lose Your Man." Someone, Jed presumably, had underlined and starred various sentences. "Let your house turn into a wasteland. . . . Give him the cold shoulder in bed. . . . Serve TV dinners when he comes home from work. . . . Put your own interests ahead of him. . . . Leave him to babysit the kids while you go out. . . . If you earn more money than he does, flaunt it."

She tossed the magazine into the trash. After a few minutes she retrieved it. Maybe this was Jed's way of trying to tell her something?

Lately, the girls in the group had started declining her invitations to be on the show. Sally couldn't figure out why. She went to the next meeting to find out what was the matter. When she walked into Bonnie's house, the whole group fell silent. She felt them studying her with critical eyes from where they sat around a table holding scissors and paint brushes.

"Well, long time no see!" said Loretta.

"Hi!" said Sally, smiling brightly.

No one responded. Sally sat down and picked up an egg carton and handled it with unfamiliarity. She looked at what they were working on—a large American flag made from egg cartons, each star a cup, rows of painted cups as stripes. "Why, that's a real nice idea. We'll have to use it on the show!"

"We?" inquired someone.

"OK, Sally," said Bonnie. "We'll give it to you straight: We feel you've used us."

"Used you?"

"Used us and our ideas to become a star and make a lot of money."

Sally was stunned. "But I've had each of you on the show as Guest Artists, and paid you for it."

"Yeah. Twenty-five dollars each. While you was making ten times that."

"And what about paperback royalties?"

"And all them interviews?"

A barrage of complaints assaulted her. It was like being the subject of an Ingenue Lemon Squeeze, only nobody said anything nice. Sally thought about crying, but instead sat in stony silence. Finally she stood up and announced, "I don't have to put up with this."

"Let's face it, honey," said Bonnie. "It's all gone to your head. And if your friends don't tell you, who will?"

Sally flounced out. After all she was Sally Tatro, and they were just a bunch of dinky old homemakers sitting around a kitchen table with paring knives. The nerve! She'd used her concepts and her daddy's money to try to give them all an outlet from the tedium of their dreary housebound lives, and now they were turning on her.

In the upcoming weeks they refused to appear on the show. And since Sally herself had been too busy giving interviews and answering fan mail to come up with any new ideas, she had to repeat some of her old ones, like the necklace of dried beans and pumpkin seeds. When viewers wrote in complaining about the lack of new material, she realized she had no choice but to offer the group whatever it would take to gain their cooperation. This turned out to be equal shares in the royalties and fees. Sally was horrified. There was just no justice left in this world.

"And we want to take turns being hostess on the show," Bonnie insisted relentlessly.

"But it's called 'The Sally Tatro Kitchen Craft Show'!"

"Well, we'll just have to think of a new name, won't we?"

Sally saw her life collapsing around her like a house of cards. No longer would she be able to afford the babysitter and cleaning lady— or a new ranch house to put them in. Or the weekly hairdos at the beauty parlor. But she wouldn't need any of these any longer either because she wouldn't be a star. The flow of fan letters would dry up, reporters would no longer besiege the house. Check-out girls and telephone operators would cease to recognize her name. It was too awful. But she had no choice. She'd run out of material.

Jed was already in bed when she got home. She began weeping. He held her with reluctance. "It's all over, Jed," she wailed. "I'm finished."

A look of suspicious hope came into his eyes. "Whadaya mean?"

"I've given up the show, Jed. For you and the children. I know I haven't been doing right by you. But I'll make it all up to you, honey."

"No kidding?" He rolled on top of her and pumped her full of semen, while she renounced all thoughts of Mr. Hitchcock, station manager.

She sat in her tiny living room watching on TV as Bonnie showed how to make mock cattails from corncobs. Mr. Hitchcock had reluctantly agreed to the new plan, once he grasped that the alternative was no kitchen craft show at all. Sally would be hostess a week every other month, but in between—nothing. She felt like the character in the kids' fairy tale when the genie arrived and removed all the riches he'd previously bestowed. But over the long painful weeks she'd come to see that this was how it had to be. It *had* gone to her head. She'd betrayed the group. She'd neglected Jed, Joey, and Laura. The star she'd followed had turned to cinders. There was more to life than money and fame. She wasn't sure what.

She meant to make it all up to everybody. The house was now neat and clean, her meals were exciting again, the children's clothes were ironed. Every day she did her hair and changed her clothes and put on makeup before Jed got home. Christmas was three months away, but she'd already finished her shopping and wrapping. And as penance for her folly, she was making a nativity scene. The stable was a large plastic Clorox bottle with one side cut out, and straw pasted all over it. The animals were made of corncobs and painted rocks. The manger was cups from an egg carton, and the baby Jesus was peanut shells wired together. Mary and Joseph and the wise men and shepherds were to be applehead dolls.

But she had to confess that there was a hollowness to her life now, after those months of glamour. She looked around for her reflection larger than life in the eyes of others and found—nothing. Already they'd forgotten her. Once again she was just Jed's wife. Laura's and Joey's mother. She'd tried so hard and come so far, and here she was right back where she'd started from.

She sighed and carved on the apple that was to be Mary's head. She'd never done a halo before and was managing to find some challenge in that. It could maybe be the topic of her next show.

After Bonnie signed off, there was an announcement on the Homemakers' News that nominations were being taken for the Mrs. Tennessee contest, which the General Appliance Housewares Division was sponsoring. Sally gathered it was similar to the Miss Tennessee contest but was for homemakers. The notice said that General Appliance, Inc., wanted to give recognition to the values of home and family, which had made America great and which were now under assault from within this great nation as well as from without. Sally had to admit that she herself had been a little lax about upholding these values in recent months. But she'd realized it and was reforming. Surely that counted for something?

". . . volunteer work, motherhood, hobbies, hostessing . . . If you have a neighbor of outstanding ability in these fields, who you think should be considered for our contest, please write for information on how to nominate her. . . ."

Sally memorized the box number, then jumped up and wrote it down. After thinking it over, she wrote off for the information.

Jed and the kids seemed to be flourishing under her efforts to atone for her neglect. Jed talked about maybe joining the Elks Club, and was speculating on the likelihood of being supervisor at the mill in a few years. At supper that night he was describing the machinations of his rivals. Joey and Laura explained their struggles on the playground. Sally listened to this with half an ear, the rest of her brain busy with the Mrs. Tennessee contest. If she was already functioning as an outstanding wife and mother and citizen, why not get recognition for these things? The trouble was, she hadn't been able to think of how to go about asking someone to nominate her.

For several days only a few fan letters straggled in. "Dear Sally, My son sleeps under an electric blanket. As he wets the bed, I'm scared to death he'll electrocute himself. Any suggestions?" She threw them away without responding. She had to wean herself from the life of a celebrity. Sally Tatro was just an ordinary old homemaker again.

Finally the brochure arrived. Mrs. Tennessee contestants competed in six categories: hostess, homemaker, church member, mother, community volunteer, and hobbyist. Sally decided she was weakest in the church member category. She went every week, but to Jed's church, the Methodist one in the mill village. She'd never felt real involved. But she'd join the choir right away. The winner would go to the Mrs. America contest in Sioux Falls, South Dakota. There was a picture of last year's Mrs. America, Brenda Gill of Des Moines, Iowa. Smiling tightly, she looked as though she had no upper lip and unusually long teeth. She said winning the contest had changed her life. She didn't say how.

That settled it. Sally took up a pen and filled in the nomination form for herself, signing it Dolores Lee Whittaker, a name that just popped into her head. She gave her parents' address and warned her mother that any mail arriving for Dolores Lee Whittaker should be directed to her. Her mother was confused. "It has to do with a surprise for Jed. For Christmas," Sally improvised. Dolores received a letter asking her to write an essay on why Sally Tatro should be Mrs. Tennessee, with reference to the six categories. Dolores wrote about Sally's creative approach to homemaking, her devotion to her husband and children, her self-sacrifice on behalf of her community as

Scheduling Chairman for the Candy Stripers, her original use of her free time in making a nativity scene from materials found around the house.

A few days later Sally received a letter informing her of her nomination by "an admiring neighbor" for the Mrs. Tennessee contest. Showing it to Jed, she asked, "Why, who do you think it could be, honey?"

"Nobody in this town, that's for sure."

Her chin quavered. Couldn't he tell how hard she was trying to do right? He thought she was a lousy homemaker? Well, it was just possible that people all across America might disagree with him before long.

The Committee wrote saying they'd like to spend an evening observing her around her home. On the basis of these visits they'd pick a certain number of homemakers from each region to come stay at the Grand Ole Opry Hotel in Nashville and compete in the Grand Ole Opry itself for the title of Mrs. Tennessee. The day they mentioned was only a week away, and Sally was swept with excitement and terror. She was almost ready—except for enlisting Jed's cooperation. She decided he had to be out of the house that night. If he wasn't, he'd insist on demonstrating how he could crumple a beer can with one hand. He'd belch at dinner and eat with his forearms resting on the table edge. He'd get into an argument with the Committee, or belittle Sally in front of them. If he wasn't there, though, she could apologize for his absence, saying he was out of town on business, or had to work late, counting on her to keep the home fires burning, for him to return to when he could. She started right away trying to persuade him to work a double shift that evening.

"I'm a foreman now. Don't do that no more."

He and Hank had the hood up on the T-Bird under the floodlight out back. They hung suspended over the engine like surgeons over an open heart. Sally tripped out and said, "Don't you boys want to go on a fishing trip or something?"

They looked up at her. Jed said in a bemused voice, "It's the middle of October."

Later, in bed, he asked, "Hey, what's going on anyhow?"

"Why don't you go bowling straight from work next Thursday,

darling? It'd save you a trip back here. It's OK. We can get along without you for supper one night."

"What're you up to, woman?"

"Oh, all right, I'll tell you! The Mrs. Tennessee Committee is going to be here all evening next Thursday. I know you don't care much for all that stuff, and I was just trying to help you avoid it."

"Are you lying to me, Sally?"

She looked at him with surprise.

"Why do you *really* want me out of this house?"

"I just told you, honey."

"And I'm supposed to *believe* that?"

"Well, yes. Because it's the truth."

"Shit, have your fucking meeting then. Don't worry about me. I don't need to come home after being on my feet all day. I can go wander the streets half the night."

"Never mind, Jed. Come home, honey. But *please* behave."

"Behave? *Behave?* Let's face it, Sally, you're ashamed of me. Always have been. I'm not good enough for you, am I? I've known it since high school, but I've tried to pretend it wasn't so."

"It's not that, Jed."

"Well, what is it then?"

"To tell you the truth, I don't think you much want me to be Mrs. Tennessee."

"Ah shit, *be* fucking Mrs. Tennessee, Sally. I don't give a good goddam. Don't worry about it. I'll stay away next Thursday evening."

"Thanks, hon. I'd do the same for you, you know."

"Hell, I don't wanna be no Mrs. Tennessee."

The Contest Committee consisted of three wives of vice presidents in suits and heels and stockings. Sally showed them around the house and yard, wishing it was the ranch house in the development with the white pillars. She showed them her new method for rolling socks. She brought out her Candy Striper uniform and explained the rows of pins and bars and stars. She showed them her nativity scene in the bleach bottle, which was still under construction, and assured them it would be completed in time for the contest. She showed them her peach-pit window curtains. She told them how flattered she was that

Dolores had nominated her, what an honor it was even to think about being the one chosen to uphold the standards that had made America great.

Joey and Laura were being very good. Sally had told them she'd cut off their allowances and not let them watch "Charlie's Angels" for an entire month if they uttered any sound other than "yes, ma'am" or "no, ma'am." She put them to bed early, and the Committee watched as she sat on their bedsides and sang one of the lullabies she'd composed:

"*Hush, Mommy's little larvae, / Slumberland is so marve- / lous for good little children . . .*"

She felt really pleased when she heard one woman whisper, "I declare, what a cunning little song."

But if anything would get her to the Grand Ole Opry Hotel, she knew it was her dinner. It just so happened that her dishwasher was a General Appliance brand. She wrapped a mackerel in a square of aluminum foil. As the Committee watched in amazement, she placed the packet in the dishwasher and turned it on. As the machine ran through its cycle, she described how she began homemaking feeling intimidated by her appliances, as though she was nothing but an appendage made of flesh. But how over the years she made friends with her machines and even came to regard them as accomplices in this business of homemaking. By the time she finished, so had the dishwasher. She took out the packet and served them perfectly poached mackerel; pickled green beans and zucchini bread from Jed's mother, which they thought Sally had made, an impression Sally didn't correct; and lemon Jell-O and grapefruit segments molded in scooped-out grapefruit rinds whose edges she'd scalloped.

Afterward they sat drinking coffee and admiring her candle holders made from the top halves of bleach bottles. One bottom half she'd turned into a basket and filled with dahlias, carnations, and lilies made from pink, yellow, blue, and white egg cartons. The Committee also commented admiringly on her meat-tray peacock plaque hanging on the wall above the table.

The Committee started talking about having to go back to their motel to rest up for their visit to the next candidate the next day. "Now, we'll be talking to some folks around town who've worked with you, Sally. The head of the Candy Stripers, people like that. You won't mind, will you?"

Sally hurriedly tried to recall what names she'd given them. Not Bonnie's, she hoped.

". . . and of course we'd like to meet that nice Dolores Whittaker, who was kind enough to put us on to you . . ."

"She's out of town," Sally assured them.

"What a shame."

"Went to the Virgin Islands last week."

". . . and of course we're just so sorry to miss that nice husband of yours. But we'll have a chance to meet him in Nashville, won't we?"

Sally beamed. So she'd be going to Nashville?

Just then a siren sounded at the end of the street. It stopped in front of her house, the red light flashing through the window.

"My goodness!" gasped the Committee.

They heard shouts and running feet. Sally rushed to the door. Out by the curb two policemen held a man in a hammerlock. He wore a battered beer can hat low over his face.

"But I live here," he was insisting. "This is my house."

"Sure it is, buddy."

Another cop was walking up to the back door. He said to Sally, "Your neighbor saw this guy looking through your window. Called us. We'll take him in. Don't worry about a thing, ma'am."

"Sally, tell them it's me," Jed called faintly.

Sally glanced behind her at the Committee seated around the table. She murmured, "Thank you so much, officer."

One of the women exclaimed, "Why, it's just horrible what goes on these days. That's why our contest is so important. We have to re-affirm decency in this nation once again, before all our values get eroded."

After the Committee left, Sally locked the doors. But when Jed got home from the police station, he kicked in the back door.

"I'm just so sorry, honey," she cooed. "We were right smack in the middle of our meal."

"Not half as sorry as you're gonna be." He clenched his fists.

"But what were you doing sneaking around like a peeping Tom in the first place?"

"Wanted to see who he was."

She studied her fingernails. "And did you, silly?"

"Didn't get a chance before them cops jumped me."

"Well, it wasn't a man, darling. It was the Mrs. Tennessee Committee. Just like I told you." Poor Jed. Just a great big baby. She went over and put her arms around him.

"Sure it was."

"It *was*, honey." She was starting to get alarmed. She'd never seen him like this.

He shoved her across the room. She fell on the La-Z-Boy Lounger, fear on her face. "Please be quiet, darling. You'll wake the children."

"It's *you* I want to wake up, Sally. Don't you see what you're doing to me? Doing to *us*?"

"But I'm not doing anything, honey."

"I thought it'd be different once you quit that goddam show."

"But it *is* different, Jed. Can't you tell?"

"Naw, it ain't. You're still pushing me and the kids away."

"But I'm not, honey. I'm devoting myself to you. Didn't I get nominated for Mrs. Tennessee?"

He kicked her in the ribs and began punching her.

Sally coated her black eyes and bruises with pancake makeup. How would she explain her appearance to the Committee if they reappeared? She suspected one of her ribs was broken, but couldn't risk publicity by going to the hospital while the Committee was still in town. Last night Jed had stormed out, leaving her in a whimpering heap on the floor. He hadn't returned. She guessed she deserved this for neglecting him all those months. But she'd paid her dues. Once was enough. Now that she'd reformed, if he did this again, she'd have no choice but to leave. She wouldn't be able to live with a man who thought so little of her as to beat her up on a regular basis for nothing. But she had no income, had saved nothing from the book or show. She had spent part of what her daddy had put away for her on the book. She couldn't ask him for more. He'd probably fire poor Jed or something. No, to be ready to leave Jed, she'd have to earn some more money on her own. If she were Mrs. Tennessee, there'd be product endorsements, like Anita Bryant and citrus fruits. There'd be personal appearances. If she were Mrs. America, General Appliance would pay her to travel around the country for a year, talking about the pleasures of being at home; then maybe they'd give her some kind of public relations job. But to become Mrs. America she had to make up with Jed for long enough to become Mrs. Tennessee.

A few days later she had a letter from the Committee thanking her for a charming evening and inviting her and her lovely family to Nashville for the Mrs. Tennessee finals. The only problem, as usual, was Jed. He finally came home, sullen and uninterested in making up. He even turned down her offer to blow him, mumbling something about her "treacherous mouth that had been sucking cock all over town." She assured him this was untrue, that she'd never sucked any cock except his, and never would as far as she knew.

"Why should I believe that?"

"Because it's *true*, honey."

He shrugged her off. She was confused: He'd beaten her up, and now she was the guilty one, for things she hadn't done.

He began staying out all night a couple of times a week, sometimes saying, "You can fuck your little fanny off in our bed tonight, Sally, cause I won't be home."

"But Jed, I don't want to, honey," she insisted as he stomped out.

He didn't say where he stayed on these nights. She didn't care too much if it would help him get over this. He hadn't wanted to make love with her for a long time, and men had their needs. She didn't mind just as long as the Committee didn't hear about it. There was no such thing as a Mrs. Tennessee with an adulterous husband. She had to glue this marriage back together again somehow.

The next time he failed to come home after work, she hired a babysitter and went out in the Dodge to look for him. She toured all the motels but didn't see the T-Bird. She went to the Mill House, which she'd heard him mention ever since high school, and there was the car. She pulled into the shadows and waited. Eventually he came out alone.

She just barely managed to keep up with the speeding T-Bird by telling herself that her chance to be Mrs. Tennessee depended on winning him back, which meant she had to know who her competition was.

He stopped up ahead, so she did too, and watched him attach a chain to the trailer hitch on the T-Bird. He twirled the chain around his head like a lasso and wrapped it around the post on which sat someone's mailbox. Then he revved up the T-Bird and roared forward, ripping the post out of the ground. He did this three more times, Sally watching in puzzlement. She'd thought it was another woman who was keeping him out all night.

He stopped the T-Bird under the flashing red lights in front of some train tracks that crossed the highway. The engine swept up to the intersection, its headlights bathing the T-Bird in light. With a great roar the T-Bird seemed to leap across the tracks, the engine missing it by a few feet. The whistle blasted indignantly as the train clattered across the highway.

Sally returned home. Jed seemed angry or something. The following day she received in the mail a photo of the T-Bird, with the license plate that read "STUD," parked in front of a house trailer with a sign on it that read "TENDER TOUCH MASSAGE PARLOR." It was a Newland postmark. Her address on the envelope had been typed, and there was no return address. She wondered if Jed was responsible for this. Trying to make her jealous or something. Or maybe one of the other Mrs. Tennessee contestants in the area? Well, it was just a horrible spiteful thing to do, was all.

Two days later Jed was supposed to be managing Joey in Peewee Boxing at the new mall. But he didn't come home for supper. Joey cried. Sally couldn't understand it. It wasn't like Jed to disappoint the children. Toward midnight the highway patrol phoned to tell her Jed was dead in a car wreck with Betty Osborne in front of the Lazy Daze Motel.

The Creech's Funeral Home limousine pulled up to the curb in front of her parents' house. Her father had to ride downtown with them to pick up his own car, but they were letting her off so she could rest up before neighbors and relatives started arriving to comfort her.

But it was no use. There was no such thing as a widowed Mrs. Tennessee.

She climbed out of the car and arranged her veil. On the sidewalk she saw the kids, and Raymond in his overalls. And Emily in her suit. And a tall mean-looking Negro man with wild frizzy hair and a black leather jacket, a child holding each hand. Sally saw herself through their eyes: Jed had left behind only a totaled T-Bird and an inboard he still owed money on. Here she'd quit her career for him, and where was he? Where was the only man she'd ever loved? Where was her best friend since childhood? Dead on the highway with another woman. While his own wife waited patiently and lovingly for him to come home. Every night she'd crawl into that big cold empty bed by herself.

As she walked toward the group on the sidewalk, she sniffed and dabbed at her eyes with her handkerchief. She comforted herself with the thought that in a few weeks she'd call the reporter at the *News* who'd written "Sally Tatro at Home" and offer him an exclusive interview. He could call it something like "Portrait of a Bereaved Widow."

# Part

# Five

---

# The

# Castle

# Tree

Emily and Raymond, Matt and Joey and Laura were standing on the Princes' sidewalk as a car pulled up to the curb. A black man in a short leather jacket with a lot of flaps and zippers and snaps got out, along with two children.

"I'm sorry," he murmured as he approached. "I come for Grandmaw's tree and all. But I reckon I timed it bad."

"Hi, Donny," said Emily. "How are things?"

Emily, then Raymond, extended hands to Donny, who shook them quickly.

"Didn't hardly recognize you," Donny murmured to Emily. He turned to Raymond. "Heard about Jed. I'm real sorry."

"Yeah, it's a big shock. These two is his kids."

"Used to know your daddy," he said to the children. "He was a real fine man." Joey and Laura stared at his bushy head with wonder.

"How's Ruby?" asked Emily.

"She just fine."

Another limousine arrived at the curb. Sally stepped out, dabbed at her eyes with a handkerchief, and arranged her veil. As she walked up to them, she said in a wan voice, "Oh, how nice to see you, Donny. I didn't recognize you at first."

"Real sorry about Jed."

"Thank you." She sighed. "Me too, Donny. Me too."

As they discussed Christmas, the weather, each other's families in the quiet polite manner they'd been trained in and had never quite managed to shed, they eyed each other. The children clung to their parents' hands and stared at each other, half-hidden by coat sleeves. Eventually Joey stuck out his tongue at Matt. Then Nicole offered Laura a stick of Beech-Nut.

Suddenly Joey yelled, "Last one to the top of that tree's an old rotten egg! Everyone included!" He shot across the yard, the others chasing after him, Isaac bringing up the rear.

The adults watched the straggly line of five stumbling children weave across the frost-stiffened grass of the neighboring yard toward the Castle Tree. A new ranch house sat behind the bare tree, in what had been Mr. Fulton's side field. The children's shrieks of laughter filled the still winter afternoon. Their frosty breath puffed up like Indian smoke signals. The small bodies, dark splotches against the overcast sky, began their ascent of the skeletal branches.

"Be careful!" Emily called. "Don't climb too fast, or you'll fall!"

"Nicole, watch out for Isaac!" yelled Donny.

No one in the tree listened, as they dragged themselves from branch to branch.

Finally assembled like crows in the branches, the children began cawing down at the adults, "Ha, ha! Yall four is rotten eggs! Rotten eggs! Rotten eggs!"

The adults glanced at each other with faint smiles. Emily said to Donny, "Can you come in?"

"Naw, I got to get on back home. Grandmaw's waiting on us. But thanks."

"I'll get Ruby's stuff." She went into the house.

Sally asked Raymond, "Do you think it's all right for them to be doing that at a time like this?"

Raymond shrugged. "They're just kids. Don't have no idea what's going on. Let them have some fun if they can."

"But what'll the neighbors think?"

"Fuck the neighbors."

Donny gave a startled guffaw.

Emily emerged, completely hidden behind a small cedar tree on a stand and a grocery bag of gifts. She set down the tree, handed Donny the bag, and reached in her suit coat for an envelope. Handing him the envelope, she blushed and laughed. "What can I say?"

Donny smiled. "Ain't nothin *to* say."

"About what?" inquired Sally.

The children lost interest in tormenting their parents and began gazing around them through the bare twisted branches at the town, spread out below them like a toy village.

"Yonder's my house," pointed Joey.

"There's Grandmaw's," said Nicole.

"Probably New York is over there," announced Matt, gesturing to the mountain ranges that heaved and rippled off into North Carolina. "New York's better than here."

"Ain't neither," snarled Joey.

"Is so."

"Ain't."

"Is so."

"What's a-b-s-c-e-s-s mean?" asked Laura, who was studying the word carved into the limb beside her.

"Let me see," commanded Joey, scrambling on to the Throne and studying the footrest of the Couch. He ran his fingers over the swollen cuts in the bark. "Says absent," he announced. "Like when you stay home from school." The others nodded.

"Look at them," said Matt, nodding disdainfully at the landbound adults. "Couldn't climb up here to save their lives."

"Big old clumsy things," agreed Nicole.

"Yeah," said Joey, "we could sit up here all week, and they couldn't do nothing about it!"

They shouted with laughter.

The adults looked up. "What's so funny?" Raymond called.

"Yall look like toy soldiers!" yelled Joey.

"Can't catch us, Daddy!" taunted Isaac.

Abruptly the sun broke through the racing clouds. Shafts of sunlight pierced the bare tree. Whispers and giggles floated down from the topmost branches.

Raymond murmured, "It's a hell of a way to run a world, ain't it?"

"Gon be different for them," announced Donny, nodding his bushy head toward the tree.

"Damn right," snarled Emily.

"Lots of luck," muttered Raymond.

"What is?" asked Sally.

A gust of wind swirled across the yard. The long twisted branches of the tree swayed and beckoned like fingers on the outstretched hand of a wise old witch.

# Acknowledgments

## A Note on the Type

THIS BOOK IS SET IN ELECTRA, A LINOTYPE FACE
DESIGNED BY W. A. DWIGGINS. THIS FACE CANNOT
BE CLASSIFIED AS EITHER MODERN OR OLD-STYLE.
IT IS NOT BASED ON ANY HISTORICAL MODEL,
NOR DOES IT ECHO ANY PARTICULAR PERIOD OR
STYLE. IT AVOIDS THE EXTREME CONTRASTS
BETWEEN THICK AND THIN ELEMENTS THAT
MARK MOST MODERN FACES AND ATTEMPTS TO
GIVE A FEELING OF FLUIDITY, POWER, AND
SPEED.

COMPOSED BY THE MARYLAND LINOTYPE
COMPOSITION COMPANY, INC., BALTIMORE,
MARYLAND. PRINTED AND BOUND BY THE HADDON
CRAFTSMEN, INC., SCRANTON, PENNSYLVANIA.
BOOK DESIGN BY
MARGARET M. WAGNER